Praise for Rick Campbell

ICE STATION NAUTILUS

"Not many writers have the knowledge and experience to write authentic submarine military adventures. Rick Campbell does have the chops, and he proves it in *Ice Station Nautilus.*"
—The Big Thrill

"Exciting and intense! I realized when I finished that I had been holding my breath for way too long!"
—BookLikes

"Fans of Clancy-style techno-thrillers won't be disappointed!"
—Open Letters Monthly

THE TRIDENT DECEPTION

"A terrific thriller. Campbell does an amazing job, balancing character interaction with high-octane action, all the while keeping the technical jargon to a level understandable by nonmilitary readers. This is the best novel about a submarine since Tom Clancy's classic *The Hunt For Red October.*"
—*Booklist* (starred review)

"Fans of submarine thrillers who are saddened by the demise of Tom Clancy will welcome Campbell."
—*Publishers Weekly*

"No one puts the reader inside a submarine like Rick Campbell does in *The Trident Deception.* I couldn't put it down. Compelling and thrilling, this novel is a must read." —Jack Coughlin, *New York Times* bestselling author of *Shooter* and *Time to Kill*

ALSO BY RICK CAMPBELL

The Trident Deception
Empire Rising
Ice Station Nautilus

BLACKMAIL

RICK CAMPBELL

St. Martin's Paperbacks

To Brett—your journey through life has been incredibly difficult, but you've managed to do so with a smile on your face. You bring joy to those around you and an appreciation for everything we would otherwise take for granted.

BLACKMAIL

Copyright © 2017 by Rick Campbell.

Maps by Rhys Davies.

For information address St. Martin's Press, 175 Fifth Avenue, New York, NY 10010.

ISBN: 978-1-250-16039-3

Our books may be purchased in bulk for promotional, educational, or business use. Please contact your local bookseller or the Macmillan Corporate and Premium Sales Department at 1-800-221-7945, extension 5442, or by email at MacmillanSpecialMarkets@macmillan.com.

Printed in the United States of America

St. Martin's Press hardcover edition / June 2017
St. Martin's Paperbacks edition / April 2018

St. Martin's Paperbacks are published by St. Martin's Press, 175 Fifth Avenue, New York, NY 10010.

10 9 8 7 6 5 4 3 2 1

ACKNOWLEDGMENTS

Many thanks are due to those who helped me write and publish this novel:

First and foremost, to my editor, Keith Kahla, for his exceptional insight and recommendations to make *Blackmail* better. To others at St. Martin's Press—Justin Velella and Martin Quinn—who assisted in many ways as *Blackmail* progressed toward publication. And finally, thanks again to Sally Richardson and George Witte for making this book possible.

While writing each book, I've relied on subject matter experts to ensure I get the details correct. While I can handle the submarine part, other areas require assistance. For *Blackmail,* I needed help of an altogether different type than information on weapon system employment, tactics, and operational protocols, and so I thank LynDee Walker, Kris Herndon, Sara Walsh, and Ramsey Hootman for their insight and assistance. Additionally, to those who have helped my writing career get off to a great start—there are too many to thank individually here, but I really appreciate your help getting the word out. You've done a fantastic job.

To Captain William (Bill) Kennington USN Retired,

former commanding officer of USS *Sand Lance* (SSN 660), who passed away last year, and to the thousands of others who have gone before us in the armed services, protecting our country. You deserve a debt of gratitude. My heart and thoughts will always be with you.

I hope you enjoy *Blackmail*!

MAIN CHARACTERS
COMPLETE CAST OF CHARACTERS
IS PROVIDED IN ADDENDUM

UNITED STATES ADMINISTRATION
KEVIN HARDISON, chief of staff
BOB MCVEIGH, secretary of defense
DAWN CABRAL, secretary of state
CHRISTINE O'CONNOR, national security advisor
BILL DUBOSE (Colonel), senior military aide

USS *MICHIGAN* (OHIO CLASS GUIDED MISSILE SUBMARINE)
MURRAY WILSON (Captain), Commanding Officer
JAKE HARRISON (Lieutenant), SEAL Platoon Officer-in-Charge

USS *HARRY S. TRUMAN* (NIMITZ CLASS AIRCRAFT CARRIER)
DAVID RANDLE (Captain), Commanding Officer
BILL HOUSTON / call sign Samurai (Lieutenant Commander), F/A-18E pilot

RUSSIAN ADMINISTRATION / MILITARY
YURI KALININ, president
BORIS CHERNOV, defense minister
ANDREI LAVROV, foreign minister
SEMYON GOREV, director of the Foreign Intelligence Service (SVR)

Sergei Andropov (General), chief of the general staff
Oleg Lipovsky (Admiral), Commander-in-Chief,
  Navy

OTHER CHARACTERS

Alexander Lukashenko, president of Belarus
Xiang Chenglei, president of China
Deepak Madan, president of India

1
WESTERN PACIFIC

USS *THEODORE ROOSEVELT*

Night was falling over the Western Pacific as USS *Theodore Roosevelt* surged through dark green waters, headed into a brisk wind. Seated in the Captain's chair on the Bridge of his Nimitz class aircraft carrier, Captain Rich Tilghman observed two F/A-18E Super Hornets locked into the bow catapults, their engines glowing reddish orange in the twilight. In a few seconds, both aircraft would head out to relieve fighters in *Roosevelt*'s combat air patrol, as the carrier strike group cruised several hundred miles off the coast of China, just beyond range of China's DF-21 missile, nicknamed *carrier-killer.* A few months ago, that's exactly what the Chinese missiles had done.

The war between China and the United States was short, but devastating. There had been no declaration of war by either country or a formal cease-fire; the combat had halted once the outcome became clear. Although America prevailed, the cost was high. Four heavily damaged aircraft carriers were in shipyards being repaired, while a fifth rested on the bottom of the Pacific Ocean, leaving USS *Ronald Reagan* as the sole operational Pacific Fleet carrier. Submarine losses had been heavy, with the opposing sides virtually wiping each other out, and U.S. surface ship losses had been high as well.

What remained of the U.S. Pacific Fleet had been augmented with Atlantic Fleet units shifted to the Pacific, joining USS *Ronald Reagan*. Not far to the south, the *Reagan* strike group was also on deployment, with the United States keeping two carrier strike groups off China's coast at all times.

Captain Tilghman's attention returned to the two Super Hornets as the bow catapults fired. The aircraft streaked across the Flight Deck, then rocketed upward, their paths marked by the white-hot glow of their afterburners against the darkening sky. Not long thereafter, the first of the returning aircraft landed, announced by the squeal of tires hitting the deck and the hydraulic hum of arresting wire motors as the Super Hornet's tailhook snagged number three wire. The F/A-18 was soon headed to the nearest elevator for a trip to the Hangar Deck, while a second aircraft landed.

Tilghman pushed himself to his feet and left the Bridge for a short tour of his ship before calling it a night. So far this deployment, it had been all quiet on the western front.

K-456 *VILYUCHINSK*

Captain First Rank Dmitri Pavlov stood at the back of the Central Command Post aboard his Antey class guided missile submarine, called Oscar II by NATO, surveying his men at their watch stations as they shadowed an American carrier strike group to the west. The crew's orders and reports were calm and professional, reflecting the proficiency a crew gains after several months at sea. *Vilyuchinsk*'s Watch Officer, Captain Lieutenant Dolinski, monitored the submarine's depth, steady at seventy meters, occasionally checking the status of their communications, verifying they were copying the broadcast on the floating wire antenna trailing several hundred meters behind the submarine.

The Communications Post was downloading the latest round of naval messages, and nothing seemed out of the ordinary until the speakers near Pavlov energized.

"Command Post, Communications. Have received a Commanding Officer Only message."

Pavlov acknowledged and entered the Communications Post, stopping by the two printers.

"Ready."

The radioman hit the print button and a message slid from the left printer. Pavlov read the directive, then read it again.

He took the message to the Central Command Post, addressing one of the two Messengers. "Request the First Officer's presence in the Command Post."

The senior seaman acknowledged and departed in search of the submarine's second-in-command, and a moment later Captain Second Rank Mikhail Evanoff arrived. Pavlov motioned Evanoff to join him by the navigation table, also requesting the Watch Officer's presence. When the two men approached, Pavlov slid the message across the table.

"Read."

Pavlov waited while the two men read the directive, then, like him, read it again. Confused and then concerned expressions worked across their faces, and the two men exchanged glances before Pavlov's First Officer spoke.

"This cannot be correct," he said. "We have been directed to fire upon the American strike group, targeting their aircraft carrier. Surely there has been a mistake. An errant message from a training scenario, perhaps."

Pavlov's Watch Officer studied the message as the

First Officer spoke, searching for formatting irregularities. But the message was properly formatted, with the required weapon release authorization. Dolinski looked up.

"We should request verification. We aren't at war with the United States, but this might start one. We must be certain this directive is properly authorized."

Pavlov answered, "It's authentic. And expected. I met with Fleet Admiral Lipovsky before our deployment. He informed me that we might receive this message."

"Why would we be directed to fire upon the Americans?" his First Officer asked.

"He did not elaborate," Pavlov answered. After a slight pause, he said, "Do you have any additional questions or reservations?"

When neither man replied, Pavlov ordered his crew to full readiness.

"Man Combat Stations. Proceed to periscope depth."

USS *THEODORE ROOSEVELT*

Three levels below the Flight Deck, in the aircraft carrier's Combat Direction Center, Captain Dolores Gonzalez settled into her watch routine as the CDC Operations Officer. She examined the Video Wall, a collection of two eight-by-ten-foot displays mounted beside each other, with a half-dozen smaller monitors on each side. After failing to note anything unusual, she shifted her thoughts to the combat air patrol to the west. They were keeping eight Super Hornets airborne at all times, along with an E-2C Hawkeye at twenty-five thousand feet, its radar searching the skies for hostile aircraft and missiles. Two of the F/A-18 fighters were approaching bingo fuel and would return to the carrier shortly. Her eyes shifted to the Flight Deck display; two more Super Hornets were moving toward the bow catapults and would be on their way out to relieve the returning fighters in a few minutes.

That was the daily routine, with days turning into weeks, then months. Across the Combat Direction Center from Gonzalez, the strike controllers were idle, as was the Tactical Action Officer who supervised them, with no inbound targets to engage and no outbound strike sorties.

The bow catapults fired, launching the Super Hornets, and it wouldn't be long before the two fighters approaching bingo fuel returned. Gonzalez settled in for what would be a long but hopefully boring night on watch.

K-456 *VILYUCHINSK*

Vilyuchinsk tilted upward, rising toward periscope depth. The submarine's Watch Officer kept his face pressed to the attack periscope, the aft of the submarine's two scopes. Despite the crowded Central Command Post, now at full manning, it was quiet while the submarine rose from the deep.

Dolinski announced, "Periscope clear," and started turning the scope swiftly, completing several sweeps in search of nearby contacts. *Vilyuchinsk* settled out at periscope depth and Dolinski declared, "No close contacts!"

Conversation resumed now that there was no threat of collision or detection by surface contacts, and Dolinski completed a more detailed scan of the ocean and sky, searching for distant ships or aircraft. "Hold no contacts."

Pavlov ordered, "Raise primary communication antenna."

One of *Vilyuchinsk*'s antennas, able to communicate with satellites, slid upward. Although Pavlov knew the

American carrier strike group was to the west, he needed a detailed tactical picture to ensure he was targeting the correct ship. *Vilyuchinsk* was beyond visual range and couldn't use its radar either, as that would give away the submarine's presence. Instead, Pavlov would rely on the tactical summary from the broadcast, containing all warships and merchants at sea and updated every five minutes.

The Communication Party leader's voice came across the speakers. "Command Post, Communications. In sync with the broadcast."

A moment later, the two fire control displays updated with the current tactical picture, and Pavlov and his First Officer, along with *Vilyuchinsk*'s Missile Officer, gathered behind the men at their consoles. As Pavlov studied the display, he realized the tactical situation couldn't have been better. The American carrier strike group was arranged with every surface ship escort except one positioned between the aircraft carrier and China, leaving only one destroyer on the back side between *Vilyuchinsk* and its target. It was a loose formation, which meant there would be little chance their missiles would lock on to the incorrect target. The only question was—how many of *Vilyuchinsk*'s missiles would make it past the destroyer and the aircraft carrier's defense systems.

Pavlov announced, "Set contact eight-five-one as the target of interest. Prepare to fire, full missile salvo."

The Missile Officer acknowledged and prepared to launch all twenty-four of *Vilyuchinsk*'s P-700 Granit surface attack missiles, each one armed with a warhead weighing almost one ton.

"All missiles are energized," reported a watchstander seated at one of the fire control consoles. A moment later, he said, "All missiles have accepted target coordinates."

Captain Lieutenant Dolinski initiated the next step. "Open all missile hatches."

The hatches lining the submarine's port and starboard sides retracted.

"All missile hatches are open," the Missile Officer reported. "Ready to fire, full missile salvo."

Pavlov surveyed the tactical situation and the readiness of his submarine one final time, then gave the order.

"Fire."

USS *THEODORE ROOSEVELT*

Inside *Roosevelt*'s Combat Direction Center, a wave of yellow symbols appeared on Captain Gonzalez's display. Surprisingly, they were to the east of the carrier strike group instead of the west. A few seconds later, each yellow icon switched to a red symbol with a sharp point, representing hostile surface-to-surface missiles. Gonzalez picked up the handset and punched the Bridge button on the communications panel.

"Bridge, CDC. Have twenty-four inbound bogies from the east, classified surface attack missiles. Request permission to set General Quarters."

"Set General Quarters."

Gonzalez gave the order, and the *gong-gong-gong* of the ship's General Alarm reverberated in CDC, followed by the announcement, *General Quarters, General Quarters. All hands man your Battle Stations. Move up and forward on the starboard side, down and aft on port.*

As the announcement faded, Gonzalez focused on shooting down the incoming missiles. *Roosevelt*'s defense would fall primarily on the shoulders of USS *Stockdale*, an Arleigh Burke class guided missile destroyer, outfitted with the Aegis Warfare System and SM-2 Standard missiles. However, air defense of the carrier strike group rested with the Air Warfare Commander, stationed aboard the Ticonderoga class cruiser, USS *Port Royal*. His voice came across the speakers in CDC.

"All units, this is Alpha Whiskey. Shift Aegis Warfare Systems to auto. You are Weapons Free."

Gonzalez watched as the computer aboard USS *Stockdale* began "hooking" contacts, assigning them to missiles in the ship's vertical launchers. A few seconds later, missiles streaked skyward from the destroyer. On her display, a stream of blue icons headed out toward the red ones. The incoming missiles had been fired at close range; there would be insufficient time to launch a second round if *Stockdale*'s SM-2 missiles didn't destroy the inbound bogies. Gonzalez watched the display as first one, then another SM-2 intercepted their targets.

But not all. Six missiles continued inbound, targeting *Roosevelt*. It was time for the self-defense phase. Gonzalez turned to her Tactical Action Officer.

"Shift SSDS to auto."

The TAO acknowledged, then shifted *Roosevelt*'s SSDS—Ship Self Defense System—to automatic.

He called out, "Missiles inbound. All hands brace for shock!"

Gonzalez reached up and grabbed on to an I-beam, watching as the SSDS targeted the inbound bogies. Sea Sparrow and Rolling Airframe missiles were launched in succession, taking out three inbound missiles, and the CIWS engaged next, taking out another.

Two missiles made it through and Gonzalez felt the deck shudder as the missiles detonated. On the aircraft carrier's damage control status board, red symbols illuminated the Hangar Deck and the carrier's Island superstructure, where the Bridge was located. *Roosevelt*'s deck trembled again, more violently, and a loud explosion rumbled through CDC. On the damage control status board, red symbols radiated outward from the middle hangar bay. Some of the ordnance staged in the bay had detonated.

Assessing the damage, Gonzalez surveyed the Video Wall. The destruction was more severe than expected. The Island superstructure was a mangled mess of twisted metal, while orange flames leapt skyward from a massive hole in the Flight Deck, the edges peeled upward from the explosion in the hangar bay below. Gonzalez studied the red symbols on the status board, her eyes shifting uneasily toward amidships, where the nearest ammunition magazine was located. If the fires reached the magazine, it'd be all over.

Damage reports flooded into CDC, and it wasn't long before Gonzalez realized *Roosevelt* was incapable of continuing flight operations.

Turning to her Tactical Action Officer, Gonzalez ordered, "Bingo all airborne aircraft to *Reagan*."

The two missiles had inflicted significant damage, but *Roosevelt* had survived. As damage control parties fought the fires, focused on preventing them from spreading toward the ship's ammunition magazines, Gonzalez's thoughts shifted to whatever had launched the missiles. There were no air or surface contacts to the east, which meant the missiles were submarine launched.

It was time to deal with that.

K-456 *VILYUCHINSK*

Minutes earlier, Captain First Rank Dmitri Pavlov had ordered the missile hatches shut and his submarine down from periscope depth. The Americans would identify the launch point and it wouldn't be long before *Vilyuchinsk* had company, and not the friendly kind. However, when the Americans arrived at the launch datum, Pavlov intended to be long gone. Once clear of the area and their safety assured, he would return to periscope depth and download the latest tactical information, plus satellite photographs for a visual assessment of their mission.

In the meantime, he would order his submarine deeper and faster. "Watch Officer. Increase depth to two hundred meters. Ahead full. Set Ultra-Quiet mode."

Captain Lieutenant Dolinski acknowledged and gave the requisite orders. *Vilyuchinsk* tilted downward, increasing speed. It was time to decide on a course. With American strike groups to the west and south, that left east or north. Heading farther east offered the possibility that any pursuing American submarine would reach the edge of its operating area. The area could be adjusted, of course, but that would take time and a trip to periscope depth to send the request and receive the authorization.

To the east it was.

"Watch Officer. Come to course zero-nine-zero."

Dolinski acknowledged and relayed the order to the Steersman.

As his submarine turned east and settled out at two hundred meters, Pavlov reviewed what his crew had done. A plan had been put in motion, and he hoped it wouldn't be long before he understood its goal and the part *Vilyuchinsk* would play in the future. Assuming, of course, *Vilyuchinsk* slipped away from the Americans.

Pavlov listened as the Watch Officer ordered, "Hydroacoustic, Command Post. Report all contacts."

USS *THEODORE ROOSEVELT*

Captain Dolores Gonzalez monitored the damage reports streaming into Damage Control Central. The fires amidships, initially spreading out from the Hangar Deck, had been contained, but casualties in the Island superstructure were high, with the ship's Captain wounded. To what extent Dolores didn't know, until Captain Rich Tilghman arrived in CDC, his arm in a sling and his face covered in soot. Dolores saw the rage on his face, even though it was covered in grime and tinted blue from the CDC displays. Tilghman's first order had been to hunt down whatever had launched the missiles.

Gonzalez had vectored two Super Hornets to the east for a visual, just in case there was a surface contact they weren't detecting for some reason, but the report was negative. The TAO was conferring with the SUBOPAUTH—the Submarine Operating Authority—aboard *Roosevelt*. There were two fast attack submarines assigned to the *Roosevelt* strike group, USS *California* to the west and USS *Mississippi* to the east. The missile launch datum placed the location of the enemy submarine inside *California*'s assigned waterspace, which meant the carrier strike group was Weapons Tight; they could not attack a submerged contact in that operating area for fear of sinking their own submarine. Hunting down the enemy submarine would instead be *Mississippi*'s responsibility.

The TAO announced, "Request a bell-ringer for *Mississippi*. I have a flash outgoing message."

USS *MISSISSIPPI*

Twenty miles from the *Roosevelt* strike group, USS *Mississippi* was already headed east at ahead full. Moments earlier, they had detected missile launch transients bearing zero-eight-two, and were proceeding to investigate. The submarine's Commanding Officer, Commander Brad Waller, was seated in the Captain's chair in front of the navigation table, assessing the tactical situation while his crew manned Battle Stations. The launch transient was faint, which meant it was distant, but exactly how far was unknown. The only datum they had was the bearing. They needed more information, which meant they would proceed to periscope depth when Battle Stations were manned.

The submarine's Officer of the Deck, Lieutenant George Skeens, sat at the tactical workstation near the front of the Control Room, shifting his attention between the left monitor, selected to the narrowband sonar display, and the right screen, showing the geographic display. The Navy's Common Operational Picture reported the positions of the *Roosevelt* strike group to the west, although their locations were several hours old. There were no contacts to the east, in the direction of the launch transient. But there was definitely something there. Perhaps a contact would appear when their Common Operational Picture was updated during their next trip to periscope depth.

Seated in front of Lieutenant Skeens, the Co-Pilot reported, "Officer of the Deck, Battle Stations are manned."

Skeens acknowledged and passed the report to Commander Waller, who announced, "This is the Captain. I have the Conn. Lieutenant Skeens retains the Deck," which meant Waller would manage the tactical situation and control the submarine's movements, while Lieutenant Skeens would monitor the navigation picture and handle routine ship evolutions.

"Pilot. Ahead two-thirds," Waller ordered. "Make your depth two hundred feet. All stations, make preparations to proceed to periscope depth."

Mississippi tilted upward, leveling off at two hundred feet while the sonar technicians scoured the surrounding water for surfaced and submerged contacts. Skeens was cycling through the various sonar displays on the left screen of his workstation when the Sonar Supervisor, standing only a few feet away behind the Broadband Operator, spoke into his headset.

"Conn, Sonar. Receiving a bell-ringer."

Waller acknowledged the report. The small explosive charges dropped into the water nearby directed *Mississippi* to establish communications with the *Roosevelt* carrier strike group. Since they were already preparing for a trip to periscope depth, there was nothing else to do.

After giving the sonar technicians a few minutes to complete their search, Waller ordered, "Sonar, Conn. Report all contacts."

"Conn, Sonar," the Sonar Supervisor replied. "Hold no contacts."

"Pilot, come to course one-eight-zero." Waller

ordered a turn in case there were contacts hidden in the submarine's baffles behind them.

The Pilot tapped the ordered course on the Ship Control Station display, and *Mississippi*'s computer adjusted the rudder to the optimal angle, turning the submarine to starboard. After steadying on the new course and waiting a few minutes for the towed array to stabilize, Waller ordered, "Sonar, Conn. Report all contacts."

The Sonar Supervisor again reported no contacts, which wasn't surprising this far off China's coast and far from the shipping lanes. However, it also meant they hadn't closed the gap on their adversary.

Waller ordered, "Co-Pilot, raise Number Two Photonics Mast. Pilot, ahead one-third. Make your depth six-two feet."

Mississippi tilted upward, beginning its ascent.

The fast attack submarine leveled off with the top of its sail four feet below the ocean surface, and the receiver mounted atop the photonics mast downloaded the latest round of naval messages and tactical updates. Waller watched the geographic display on the Officer of the Deck's workstation update with the current positions of the *Roosevelt* strike group, accompanied by a white, scalloped symbol ten miles east of *Mississippi*. The launch datum.

As Waller studied the geographic display, the Quartermaster reported a GPS navigation fix had been received, then Radio followed.

"Conn, Radio. In receipt of a flash message."

Waller replied, "Radio, Conn. Bring the message to Control."

A radioman arrived a moment later, message clipboard in hand. Waller read the directive. A missile salvo had been fired at USS *Roosevelt*, with two missiles making it through, damaging the aircraft carrier and terminating flight operations. *Mississippi* had been directed to track down and sink whatever launched the missiles. They were Weapons Free.

Waller handed the clipboard back to the radioman, then ordered, "Pilot, make your depth four hundred feet, increase speed to ahead full." Turning to the Quartermaster, he said, "Report bearing to launch datum."

"Bearing zero-nine-three," the Quartermaster announced.

"Pilot, come to course zero-nine-three."

The Pilot entered the new course, and *Mississippi* turned back to the east, surging toward the launch datum.

Thirty minutes later, with *Mississippi* closing on the launch point, Commander Waller ordered *Mississippi* to slow to ahead two-thirds, reducing the flow of turbulent water across the bow, flank, and towed array hydrophones, extending the range of the submarine's acoustic sensors. It had been an hour since they detected the launch transient, and whatever created it surely hadn't loitered in the area. Assuming a transit speed of twenty knots, the evading submarine would be twenty nautical miles away by now, beyond the range of *Mississippi*'s sensors, assuming it was a quiet fourth-generation submarine.

Waller waited for the report nonetheless, which the Sonar Supervisor delivered moments later. "Conn, Sonar. Hold no contacts."

It was a guessing game now, attempting to determine which direction the target had headed. *Mississippi* was near the eastern edge of its operating area and would have to request additional water if Waller decided to head east. The *Reagan* strike group was to the south, which meant it was unlikely the target had headed that way. The north seemed most probable, skirting around the top of the *Roosevelt* strike group, headed home to China.

Assuming, of course, the submarine was Chinese. Waller was sure the Office of Naval Intelligence was already working on it, evaluating the flight parameters of the missiles, as well as having *Roosevelt*'s crew scavenge the carrier for missile pieces. Hopefully, enough would be gleaned to determine the perpetrator, which would lead to the next question. Why?

Someone else would answer that question. Waller had been tasked with sinking their adversary. But he had to find it first.

"Pilot, come to course north. Ahead full."

Mississippi swung to port, increasing speed.

WASHINGTON, D.C.

Christine O'Connor, the president's national security advisor, leaned back into the leather upholstery of the black Lincoln Town Car as it pulled away from the Pentagon's mall entrance, returning her to the White House after her weekly visit to the Pentagon. Seated beside her was Secretary of Defense Bob McVeigh, carrying an orange Top Secret folder in the locked courier pouch on his lap. Christine could tell his mind was churning, reviewing the information the Office of Naval Intelligence had gleaned from the attack on USS *Roosevelt*, as well as the implications.

It was only a day ago when SecDef McVeigh called the president, informing him of the missile attack. Inside the folder in his courier pouch was the information collected over the last twenty-four hours, which he'd shared with Christine this afternoon. The evidence left little doubt in her mind as to who was responsible. Just when she'd reached the verge of pushing the Russians from her thoughts, they'd been thrust to the forefront again.

As the Town Car traveled across the Arlington Memorial Bridge into Washington, D.C., sliding past bumper-to-bumper traffic headed out of the District, not even the clear blue sky and warm spring weather could pull her thoughts from the wintry landscape atop the polar ice cap. Despite her best efforts, the memories were constantly there, crowding her thoughts during the day and haunting her dreams at night. Each time she looked at her hands, she couldn't escape the memory of what she'd done to Captain Steve Brackman, the president's former senior military aide. *Former*, as in deceased.

Christine felt emotion gathering in her chest, so she peered out the sedan window. She studied the pedestrians traversing the sidewalks, the construction along Constitution Avenue, the federal building facades. Anything to distract her. She brushed a lock of hair away from her face, and ice-cold fingers touched her skin. The events above and below the polar ice had left a chill in her body that wouldn't thaw. It was only a matter of time, she told herself, before the memories faded, the pain eased. Until then, stay busy, stay focused.

Upon her return from Ice Station Nautilus, she'd thrown herself into her work, spending sixteen-hour days in the West Wing, seven days a week, stopping only to eat, sleep, and work out at the Pentagon gym. Thankfully, her acquaintances at the gym didn't bring it up. Didn't ask why she had killed her good friend. As she returned to the White House, she was grateful McVeigh was accompanying her and would sit in the Oval Office chair Brackman would normally have occupied while discussing military issues with the president. The empty chair during her meetings with the president the last few weeks had been a painful reminder of what she had done.

The only silver lining in the ordeal was the reaction of the president's chief of staff, Kevin Hardison, her White House nemesis. Their relationship had become poisoned by opposing viewpoints and personal animosity, but upon her return to the White House, he'd refrained from his usual aggressive behavior. How long this reprieve would last she didn't know, but was thankful nonetheless.

The Town Car stopped under the West Wing's north portico and Christine and McVeigh stepped from the sedan, passing between two marines in dress blues guarding the formal entrance to the West Wing. After a short walk down the seventy-foot-long hallway, they reached the open door to the Oval Office. Hardison was already seated in one of the three chairs facing the president's desk, and after the president waved them inside, Christine and McVeigh settled into the empty chairs.

Christine waited for McVeigh to begin. Although she was involved on the periphery, the attack on U.S. military forces was in the SecDef's domain. He wasted no time getting started.

"I wish I had better news, Mr. President. *Roosevelt* will be out of commission for several months. She suffered extensive damage to her Flight Deck and Island superstructure. The Navy estimates she'll be in the shipyard for five to six months." McVeigh waited before continuing, letting the president absorb the loss of yet another aircraft carrier. "That leaves us with four operational carriers, which means we're going to have to drop to two carrier strike groups on deployment. The Navy is assessing whether to pull a strike group from Fifth Fleet in the Persian Gulf, or drop our presence off China to one strike group."

The president asked, "How long before one of the carriers damaged in the war with China returns to service?"

"Another year at the earliest," McVeigh answered. "As extensive as *Roosevelt*'s damage is, she'll be the first back in service."

"Is there any way we can speed up the repairs?"

McVeigh shook his head. "Every yard is already in

twenty-four-seven shiftwork, and we'll be delaying the repairs of other carriers, refocusing our efforts on *Roosevelt* as soon as she arrives at Pearl Harbor."

The president nodded. "Have you determined who attacked *Roosevelt*?"

"We have," McVeigh answered as he unlocked the courier pouch and retrieved the orange Top Secret folder. "There are several critical pieces of information. The first is that *Roosevelt* was attacked by a twenty-four-missile barrage." He pulled a printout from one of the Aegis Warfare System displays, showing twenty-four inbound missiles, placing it on the president's desk.

"The second piece of information," McVeigh said as he placed another printout on the desk, "is that the missiles were launched from a submarine. As you can see," he said, pointing to the second printout, "there were no surface or air contacts in the launch area."

McVeigh pulled a report from the folder, laying it beside the printouts. "Next is ONI's analysis of the missile flight trajectory—speed, altitude, and evasive maneuvers prior to impact—which identifies the missiles as SS-N-19 Shipwreck missiles. SS-N-19s are Russian-made P-700 Granit missiles, and only Russia has this weapon in its inventory.

"Finally," McVeigh said, "the only submarine capable of firing a twenty-four-missile salvo of Shipwreck missiles is an Oscar II. There is no doubt, Mr. President. *Roosevelt* was attacked by a Russian guided missile submarine."

The president leaned back in his chair, a surprised expression on his face. Until this moment, the obvious perpetrator was China.

The president asked, "Do we have any intel that explains why Russia would attack us?"

"No, Mr. President. We have no answers at this point."

The president asked no further questions as he assessed the complicated situation: the reason for Russia's aggression, how to broach it with the Russians, what to release to the American public, and last, but most important, the United States' response.

Finally, the president spoke. "This doesn't make any sense. Russian fingerprints are all over this attack. They can't deny it."

"They can always deny it," Hardison replied. "And I wouldn't put it past them."

"What do you recommend?" the president asked, surveying the three members of his staff and cabinet.

Christine answered, "You could call President Kalinin directly. But rather than confront him, I recommend you just lay out the facts and let him explain. As you pointed out, the evidence seems irrefutable. See what he has to say, and you can take it from there."

The president turned to Hardison, who agreed, then McVeigh, who said, "I think that's a good start. Hopefully, there's a reasonable explanation for what happened. The last thing we need right now is a conflict with Russia, right on the heels of our war with China."

After a moment of reflection, the president nodded his agreement. Looking at the documents on his desk, he said to McVeigh, "Make copies I can give to the Russians, redacting whatever is appropriate."

To Hardison, he said, "Get the Russian ambassador over here. Today."

WASHINGTON, D.C.

Dusk was settling over the city skyline as Ambassador Andrei Tupolev emerged from the rear entrance of the Russian embassy, slipping into the back seat of his limousine, its door held open by his driver. The door closed with a thud and a moment later, his car pulled into traffic on Wisconsin Avenue for the short drive to the White House. The driver said nothing during the transit and Tupolev's thoughts turned to his pending meeting with the U.S. president, reviewing the information hastily provided by the Kremlin.

Ambassador Mushroom. That should be his official title tonight. Like a mushroom, he was being kept in the dark and fed manure. Which, in turn, he would feed to the Americans. Tupolev had been a diplomat for forty years and knew when he was being lied to. He had a suspicion as to what was really going on, and if he was correct, the American president's reaction would determine Russia's next step.

The American capital glided past him during the transit, and his car ground to a halt in front of black steel bars blocking the entrance to the White House. After the gate guards checked the ambassador's identification and completed a security sweep of his vehicle, checking for explosives inside and underneath his car, the gate slid aside and Tupolev's sedan pulled forward, coasting to a halt beneath the curved overhang of the West Wing portico.

One of the two marines stationed by the entrance saluted as Tupolev stepped from the car, and the ambassador nodded his appreciation as he made his way up the marble steps toward the White House. Standing at the entrance was Kevin Hardison, the president's chief of staff, who greeted Tupolev, then led the way down the blue-carpeted hallway. Instead of heading into the Oval Office, Hardison turned left into a conference room. It took Tupolev a moment to realize what room they had entered and the irony therein. *The Roosevelt Room.*

Hardison guided Tupolev to the center of five chairs on one side of the table, then departed, returning a moment later with another man and two women, followed by the president. Tupolev stood as the president entered the room.

The obligatory greetings were exchanged, and Tupolev noticed the forced smiles on the American faces.

"Be seated, Ambassador," the president said. He took a chair opposite him, instead of at the head of the table as expected. As he pulled his chair in, Tupolev noticed the portrait of Theodore Roosevelt on the far wall, literally framing the American president. The selection of the Roosevelt Room and the president's place at the table didn't go unnoticed. The Americans were making a subtle statement of their displeasure.

Tupolev settled into his chair as the other four Americans did the same, flanking the president. On the president's left sat SecDef McVeigh and Secretary of State Dawn Cabral, while to his right was the president's chief of staff and national security advisor. Tupolev's eyes settled on Christine O'Connor, meeting her tonight for the first time. The rumors were true. Although she was half Russian and half Irish, her Russian genetics dominated; she could pass for a beautiful Russian woman anywhere in his country. Tupolev wondered if she had any idea whom she resembled. Under different circumstances, he would have taken a moment to enlighten her. Instead, Tupolev returned his attention to the American president, who placed a folder on the table.

"I hope you don't mind if I get directly to the point."

"Not at all, Mr. President. I don't want to take up any more of your time than necessary."

"I'm sure you're aware by now," the president said, "of what occurred off the coast of China yesterday."

"Yes, I am aware."

When Tupolev offered no other information, the president slid the folder across the table. "I'd like you to explain this."

Tupolev opened the folder and examined the documents. After reviewing the evidence of Russia's transgression, he closed the folder and looked up.

"On behalf of President Kalinin, I offer a sincere apology for this accident. President Kalinin learned a few hours ago that one of our guided missile submarines accidentally launched a missile salvo at your aircraft carrier."

Tupolev slid the folder back to the president.

"You expect us to believe," the president replied, "that one of your submarines *accidentally* launched not one, but twenty-four missiles at our carrier?" The anger in the president's voice was palpable.

"Yes, Mr. President, because that is exactly what happened. The submarine crew was engaged in a training evolution, simulating a missile launch against a high-value target—your aircraft carrier in this case—and there was a malfunction in the fire control system. The launch command should not have been sent. Clearly, something went horribly wrong and I assure you we'll investigate thoroughly and put additional safeguards in place to ensure this does not happen again.

"In the meantime, President Kalinin has agreed to pay reparations to any crew member injured in the accident and the families of those killed, and we will also cover the cost of the aircraft carrier's repair. The details will need to be worked out, but Russia takes full responsibility for what happened and we offer our sincerest apology. President Kalinin would normally have called you by now, but he is aware of our meeting and is working to determine how this happened. I'm sure he'll call in the morning, offering an apology of his own."

Tupolev maintained a sincere expression when he finished, contrasting with the surprised looks from the Americans. No doubt, they had expected him to deny Russia's involvement. Admitting culpability was a bold but savvy move.

"I have little else to offer tonight," Tupolev said, "but I will brief you or your designated representative whenever we learn more."

Tupolev leaned back slightly, waiting for a response. The president's jaw muscles flexed as he digested Russia's confession, most likely attempting to decide whether he was being lied to. Tupolev was telling the truth, of course. Someone in Moscow was doing the lying.

Finally, the president replied, "I appreciate your candid response, accepting responsibility for what happened. I hope you determine what went wrong quickly, so it doesn't happen again. Please keep Secretary of State Cabral advised of what you learn."

The president stood, extending his hand. "Thank you for joining us tonight."

Tupolev shook the president's hand as he stood, surveying the other four Americans. Not a smile in the room. "Thank you for your understanding," Tupolev said. "We will work aggressively to ensure this tragedy is not repeated."

The president nodded toward Hardison, who escorted the Russian ambassador to the West Wing exit. Tupolev descended the steps toward his awaiting car without a farewell from the American chief of staff.

He climbed into his sedan and the door closed with a solid thud again. After his driver slid into the front seat, he looked in the rearview mirror. "The embassy, Ambassador?"

Tupolev nodded and the car eased from the West Wing portico, reversing course toward the White House gate. Tupolev let out a deep breath. That had gone much better than expected.

WASHINGTON, D.C.

"He's lying," Hardison said as he joined the president and the other three members of his staff and cabinet, still seated in the Roosevelt Room.

"We've already come to that conclusion," the president replied. "The question is—why did they attack us?"

"Maybe a more specific question should be asked," Christine said, then amplified. "Why did they attack *Roosevelt*?"

"Good point," the president said. "This wasn't a random attack against one of our ships. They wanted to take out one of our carriers."

"Maybe not," McVeigh joined in. "Even a couple of Shipwreck missiles wouldn't normally knock an aircraft carrier out of commission. They got lucky, detonating ordnance staged on the Hangar Deck and hitting the aircraft carrier's Island superstructure."

Turning to his secretary of state, the president asked, "What's going on in Russia that might explain their attack?"

Dawn Cabral replied, "Internally, Russia's economy is on the brink of recession due to the world oil glut. Oil and natural gas exports provide fifty percent of the Russian government's revenue, and the low prices are hitting them hard. The ruble has dropped to twenty-five percent of its value from only two years ago, causing disaffection within the Russian population. President Kalinin's popularity is plummeting ahead of next year's election, which is causing consternation within his administration. You never know what straws desperate politicians will grab at to shore up their popularity.

"Regarding external events, Russia is still upset over the addition of the Baltic countries to NATO and has taken a hardline stance against the addition of Finland. Within the Russian administration, the most commonly used phrase translates to 'Over my dead body.' Elsewhere, you've got Russia's annexation of Crimea and their support of separatist factions in eastern Ukraine. Then there's Russia's involvement in Syria, with their level of commitment vacillating every few weeks."

Dawn finished up with, "Finally, there's the issue of Ice Station Nautilus. There are three Russian submarines on the bottom of the Barents Sea. Although Russia's official demeanor since the incident has been conciliatory, the attack on *Roosevelt* could be payback."

The president contemplated the potential reasons for Russia's aggression, then said, "We're not going to solve this tonight. Start working the problem. What we know is that this was Russia's opening move. We need to figure out what their endgame is, so we can respond appropriately. Without knowing where this is headed, we'd be flailing about in the dark."

Turning to McVeigh, he said, "Coordinate with the intelligence agencies and see what they can glean from human sources and electronic means. What kind of ability do we have regarding access to Russian classified information?"

McVeigh replied, "Most of their military and political communication protocols are secure, although we can break some of their encryptions. I'll get with Cyber Command and see what we can hack into."

The president nodded his agreement, then shifted his gaze to Christine as she spoke.

"One more thing, Mr. President. I'm scheduled to head to Moscow on Monday for the next round of negotiations for the follow-on to New START."

The president leaned back in his chair, assessing the situation before replying. "Let's go with business as usual. Give them the impression we accepted their explanation at face value. At this point, there's no reason to derail our negotiations with Russia over a mere . . . *accident*."

Turning his attention to the entire group, the president said, "Put a full-court press on this. Russia's up to something, and we need to figure out what that is."

WASHINGTON, D.C. • MOSCOW

WASHINGTON, D.C.

Seated at his desk in the Russian embassy, Ambassador Tupolev loosened his tie as he relaxed in his leather chair, watching the minutes on the clock tick upward. It was almost 11 p.m. in Washington, D.C., which meant it was approaching 6 a.m. in Moscow. That he'd been directed to report the result of his meeting with the American president tonight, rather than in the morning when it was a more reasonable time in Moscow, was telling.

When it was only a minute before 11 p.m., Tupolev retrieved a security card from his desk drawer and slid it into the slot in the secure phone on his desk. After he entered his access code, the display on the phone reported the expected message.

Secure.

Tupolev punched the numbers into the phone. When the clock struck 11 p.m., there was a click on the other end, and a man's digitized voice emanated from the speaker.

MOSCOW

Russian Defense Minister Boris Chernov spoke into the telephone, selected to speakerphone so the other seven individuals in the conference room could overhear the conversation. Seated at the head of the table this morning was Russian President Yuri Kalinin, and to his right sat Semyon Gorev, director of the Foreign Intelligence Service—the successor to the First Chief Directorate of the KGB—referred to as the SVR due to its Russian spelling, Sluzhba Vneshney Razvedki.

Defense Minister Chernov was next in line, followed by Russia's foreign minister, Andrei Lavrov. On the other side of the table sat four military officers: Kalinin's senior military advisor—Chief of the General Staff Sergei Andropov, and the commanders of the Russian Ground Forces, Aerospace Forces, and Navy.

"Good evening, Ambassador Tupolev," Chernov said. "I'm here with President Kalinin." Chernov glanced at the other six men, who would not speak during the teleconference. "How did your meeting with the Americans go?"

"They were upset, understandably, but accepted our apology." Tupolev provided the details, with Chernov exchanging glances with the other men around the table as they digested the American response. Tupolev ended with, "The American president has requested we keep them abreast of our investigation of the mishap, providing them with updates as we learn more."

"Of course," Chernov replied. "An investigation is already under way, and we will forward to you what we learn. We will contact you again soon."

Chernov looked to President Kalinin, who leaned toward the phone. "Ambassador Tupolev. Thank you for your service today."

"It was not a problem, Mr. President."

Chernov terminated the call, his thoughts turning to this morning's meeting. The plan they would hopefully put in motion was his, carefully crafted over the last three years. Following America's war with China, a window of opportunity had opened where its success was virtually assured. However, the decision to proceed would be made by President Kalinin, who still had reservations. Chernov had assembled the three military chiefs and his chief of the general staff, along with the head of the SVR, in the conference room this morning with the hope of persuading the Russian president.

Yuri Kalinin was approaching the end of his third year in office, having succeeded Vladimir Putin as president of the Russian Federation. Although Kalinin had a similar background as Putin, with time spent in the KGB during the waning years of the Cold War, he was far less disposed to using military force to achieve Russia's objectives. Had Putin still been in office, Chernov lamented, he would not have had to go through such extraordinary measures to convince the Russian president of the wisdom of his plan.

As all eyes turned to him, Chernov launched into his prepared oratory. "Our attack on the American aircraft carrier provided the proof we needed. We bloodied America's nose and they do nothing. They have no stomach for another conflict following their war with China. What remains of their Navy is stretched too thin, and their Marine Corps is still replacing its losses. The Americans will avoid another war at any cost, even if they have to bury their heads in the sand, accepting our preposterous explanation for the attack on their aircraft carrier."

There were nods of agreement from the military staff, but no sign from Kalinin. Chernov continued, directing his words at the Russian president. "Our plan will succeed. You've reviewed the military forces at NATO's disposal compared to ours. NATO has never been weaker, while Russia has not been stronger since the dissolution of the Soviet Union. NATO is a paper tiger without the United States, and with America restrained, NATO will have neither the will nor ability to respond.

"Now is the time," Chernov said with conviction. "The American Navy is down to four aircraft carriers and less than fifty percent of their surface warships and submarines. The window on this opportunity will close in a year when their Navy begins exiting the repair yards, quickly returning to near full strength."

Kalinin turned to his chief of the general staff. "What is your assessment?"

General Andropov replied, "From a military standpoint, we will succeed. NATO has insufficient forces to mount an adequate response. However, I can attest only to the military aspect of NATO's capability. There are other ways the West can respond."

"That's what I'm worried about," Kalinin said. "The economic sanctions imposed could exacerbate the situation we are in, overriding the gains made by the military."

Chernov replied quickly, "With the additional insurance we added to the plan, there will be no economic sanctions. The West will have no choice but to acquiesce to our demands."

"Perhaps," Kalinin said. "Predicting how the United States will respond is not as simple as you make it out to be."

Chernov said, "It's the right decision for Russia. It's the right decision for *you*." He didn't need to elaborate. He'd had many discussions with Kalinin, attempting to influence his decision by capitalizing on Russia's flagging economy and the growing unrest among the population. Unless something changed, Kalinin would be defeated soundly during the presidential election next year. Russia—and Kalinin—required a bold stroke to rectify their deteriorating situations.

"And the justification?" Kalinin asked.

"The Russian people don't need ironclad justification," Chernov answered. "They long for the days when Russia was a superpower, and resent the second-tier status our once great country has been relegated to since the fall of the Soviet Union. As long as there are no negative consequences to the people, they will support your use of force. Any reasonable justification will suffice."

President Kalinin surveyed the men around the table before replying. "Each of you plays an important role in this plan. I will not approve unless you agree it is in Russia's best interest to proceed and that in your assessment, we will succeed."

Kalinin's eyes fell first on Admiral Oleg Lipovsky, Commander-in-Chief of the Russian Navy and the most junior military officer at the table. His forces had the most difficult assignment, and Chernov knew he was the least enamored with the plan.

After hesitating a moment, Lipovsky replied, "It is in Russia's best interest, and the Navy will not fail."

One by one, the three generals beside Lipovsky concurred with the plan and its success, leaving only the head of the SVR. Semyon Gorev smiled and placed his hand on Kalinin's shoulder.

"I'll do whatever you ask, Yuri."

"That isn't my question," Kalinin replied. "Will you succeed?"

Gorev pulled back slightly, as if offended by the question. "Of course the SVR will succeed. Our part is relatively easy."

Silence descended on the conference room as Kalinin moved toward his decision. Finally, he announced, "I approve the operation, but only the preparations." Turning to Chernov, he said, "Proceed with the plan and brief me when you are ready to execute."

Chernov replied, "We will commence preparations today."

VLADIVOSTOK •
SEVEROMORSK

VLADIVOSTOK, RUSSIA

Vladivostok, with jagged snow-capped mountains rising in the background, is the largest Russian port on the Pacific Ocean. Off-limits to foreigners for thirty-five years during the Soviet era, the city is often envisioned by Westerners as an ice-coated military outpost in the Russian Far East. The reality is contrary, with harbor cranes rising skyward along the shores, titanic merchant vessels anchored in the emerald-blue water, and sleek white yachts rocking gently at their moorings. Vladivostok, which translates to "Ruler of the East," is also home to the Russian Pacific Fleet.

This morning, with the green knolls to the west shrouded in a light morning mist seeping down toward the coast, Admiral Pavel Klokov, commander of the Pacific Fleet, was seated at the head of a conference table on the second floor of Pacific Command headquarters, flanked by members of his staff as they delivered the morning briefing. The only noteworthy news, Klokov thought, was that the *Truman* carrier strike group was departing the Sea of Oman and headed east, ostensibly to replace the *Roosevelt* strike group, which was headed to the Pearl Harbor Naval Shipyard for repairs.

On the matter of repairs, K-295 *Samara*, the newest

Akula II in the Pacific Fleet, had just completed its sea trials after a midlife overhaul and modernization. *Samara*, along with seventeen other guided missile and attack submarines in the Russian Pacific Fleet, was fully operational. Although the United States had shifted the bulk of its Atlantic Fleet submarines to the Pacific after the devastating losses during its war with China, there were only fifteen operational American submarines in the Pacific. Russian submarines outnumbered the Americans'.

Klokov's morning briefing was interrupted by his Operations Officer, entering the conference room with a message clipboard. Klokov read the message. The Pacific Fleet warships were being sortied to sea. However, the destination coordinates were unusual. What would the Pacific Fleet's task be, so far from home?

SEVEROMORSK, RUSSIA

It was still dark along the shore of the Murmansk Fjord when Admiral Leonid Shimko entered the headquarters of Russia's Northern Fleet. Awakened by a phone call from the duty officer an hour ago, Shimko was informed that a rare Priority One message had been received. A car had been dispatched to his residence, and during the short drive to his headquarters, Admiral Shimko mentally reviewed the status of Russia's most formidable fleet. Scattered among a half-dozen bases on the Kola Peninsula were twenty-five submarines, numerous surface ship combatants, and Russia's only aircraft carrier.

The aircraft carrier *Admiral Flota Sovetskovo Soyuza Kuznetsov*, commonly referred to as *Admiral Kuznetsov*, was the flagship of the Russian Navy. Although described as an aircraft carrier by the West, the Russian classification of *heavy aircraft–carrying missile cruiser* was wordier but more accurate. Carrying Su-33 and

MiG-29K air-superiority fighters and Ka-27 helicopters for anti-submarine warfare, *Kuznetsov* was also capable of offensive operations on its own, carrying a dozen P-700 Granit Shipwreck missiles, 192 surface-to-air missiles, and sixty RBU-12000 rockets with various payloads for anti-submarine warfare.

When Admiral Shimko arrived at his office, the lights were already on and coffee was brewing in the Admiral's mess. Not long after he took his seat, a steaming cup was delivered to his desk, along with the message he'd come in early to read. He read the directive as he sipped his coffee, then put the cup down. Every Northern Fleet warship was being sortied to sea. Although the destination wasn't surprising, the application of so much force was.

Shimko lifted the message up, reading another Priority One message, this one directed to the Pacific Fleet, copy to Admiral Shimko. Russia's two most powerful fleets were setting sail.

KURSK, RUSSIA

Major General Vitaly Vasiliev, head of the 448th Missile Brigade of the 20th Guards Army, relaxed in the back of his sedan as it sped toward his headquarters. Peering through the side window, he spotted the early morning sun rising above the twenty-four-meter-tall Kursk Triumphal Arch. Not far from the monument, atop a pedestal stood the resemblance of Marshal Georgy Zhukov, the co-mastermind of the Stalingrad counteroffensive in 1942, which surrounded Germany's 6th Army and signaled the end of the Wehrmacht's expansion across Russia. As the triumphal arch and Marshal Zhukov's statue faded in the distance, Vasiliev's thoughts turned to a battle much closer, and perhaps even more influential.

In the spring of 1943, after the surrender of the German 6th Army in Stalingrad, the Wehrmacht counterattacked, delivering a crushing defeat to Soviet forces, retaking Kharkov and Belgorod. A bulge of Russian forces around Kursk remained, and with Hitler bent on revenge for Stalingrad, Operation Citadel was launched with the goal of encircling the opposing Soviet forces. The Battle of the Kursk Salient ensued, and with German Panzer formations breaking through the Soviet defenses, the Soviets directed the 5th Guards Tank Army to stop the II SS-Panzer Corps at Prokhorovka.

The Battle of Prokhorovka on July 12, 1943, was the largest tank battle in history, involving over one thousand tanks. The armored battle was considered a tactical success for Germany due to the high number of Soviet tanks destroyed, but a strategic victory for the Soviet Union because it prevented a German breakthrough. As Operation Citadel ground to a close, the initiative on the Eastern Front swung permanently over to the Red Army.

The glorious days of the Soviet Red Army, Vasiliev thought, crushing the German aggressors. Although the Red Army had been devastated by the breakup of the Soviet Union, the Ground Forces of the Russian Federation had slowly regained strength in both men and equipment, finally able to flex its muscles again. Part of that power resided in Vasiliev's missile brigade, fielding the Iskander ballistic missile, capable of delivering conventional or nuclear warheads out to five hundred kilometers.

Vasiliev's sedan pulled to a halt in front of his headquarters building, and it wasn't long before he was at his desk reading the morning radio messages. His Intelligence Colonel hovered nearby; there was an important message on the boards, on top, as expected. What wasn't expected, however, was the directive. His unit was being deployed.

Curiously, although the readiness of all units in the Western Military District was being increased one notch, only two other units had received orders: the 53rd Anti-Aircraft Rocket Brigade with the potent S-400 air defense system, and the 2nd Guards Motor Rifle Division. Vasiliev raised an eyebrow. The 2nd Guards was the only division-strength motor rifle unit in the Army, with all other motor rifle divisions being downsized to the brigade level. Comprising a motor rifle brigade and tank brigade, the 2nd Guards Motor Rifle Division was one of the most formidable units in the Russian Federation Army. Vasiliev read further, identifying the destination of all three units—Kaliningrad Oblast.

Most in the West were unaware of Kaliningrad Oblast, a region of Russia separated from the rest of the country. Home to Russia's Baltic Fleet, Kaliningrad Oblast is surrounded by Lithuania to the north and Poland to the south. Ground transit to and from the oblast is controlled by Lithuania and Poland, with visa-free travel to the rest of Russia possible only by air or sea. As Vasiliev prepared to mobilize his missile battalion, he knew Lithuania and Poland might attempt to prevent the transfer of so much firepower into Kaliningrad Oblast.

It was infuriating, being forced to obtain the permission of foreign governments for travel between two autonomous regions of Russia. It was Russia's sovereign right to station whatever troops and military equipment it desired in Kaliningrad Oblast without the approval of another country. But years earlier, when Russia announced its intentions to send advanced surface attack and air defense systems to the oblast, the Baltic States and NATO had objected. Now, Russia had a much stronger military and could press the issue.

Vasiliev smiled. *NATO will not be pleased.*

9
MINSK, BELARUS

Defense Minister Boris Chernov gripped the leather satchel in his lap as his limousine wound through the Belarusian capital, moving along sweeping boulevards flanked by imposing Soviet bloc–style buildings, a reminder of the city's rebirth following World War II. During Minsk's liberation from Nazi occupiers, eighty percent of the city was razed to the ground, then rebuilt in the 1950s to Joseph Stalin's liking. Chernov's sedan passed the House of Government, a monumental example of Stalin-era architecture, comprising symmetrical boxy buildings of varying heights, with the wings of the complex wrapping around an expansive front courtyard. A twenty-three-foot-tall statue of Vladimir Lenin, a tribute to the country's past and indicative of its current alliances, rose in the center of the courtyard, greeting those entering the National Assembly of Belarus.

The Republic of Belarus, situated to the west of Russia, beneath the Baltic countries and above Ukraine, was Russia's most steadfast ally. Since the establishment of the country in 1991 following the dissolution of the Soviet Union, there had been only one president, Alexander Lukashenko, and his five-term presidency along with accusations of voter fraud resulted in some Western journalists labeling Belarus as "Europe's last dictatorship." Lukashenko's firm grip on power would be a key factor in fulfilling his end of Belarus's pact with Russia.

Chernov's car pulled to a halt in front of the Residence of the President, where Chernov was greeted by his Belarusian counterpart, who led the way to President Lukashenko's office. The Belarusian minister of defense glanced at the satchel in Chernov's hand before retreating, leaving the two men alone.

Chernov settled into a chair beside Lukashenko's desk. After the standard greetings and diplomatic exchange, he broached the sensitive reason for their meeting.

"Have you made a decision yet?" Chernov asked.

"You request much," Lukashenko said, "and my support will place me in a precarious position during the next general election. If this does not turn out well . . ."

Chernov listened as Lukashenko highlighted the risks to himself and his country; it was clear he was preparing to request more from Russia than had been offered. At the end of his soliloquy, Lukashenko made his demand.

"Your offer of a twenty percent reduction in natural gas and oil prices is insufficient. A fifty percent reduction is required, for a term of twenty years."

Chernov replied, "Your current prices are the cheapest in Europe, only forty percent of what other countries pay. You already receive a steep discount, which should be factored in."

"Let us be clear," Lukashenko said. "Your low prices benefit Russia, keeping Belarus on the teat of the sow, dependent on your . . . *generosity*."

Chernov hadn't expected Lukashenko to address their delicate relationship so directly. Although Belarus was a staunch Russian ally, its loyalty was due in part to its energy dependence on Russia, receiving all of its oil and natural gas from its eastern neighbor, and the Russian monopoly of Gazprom controlled the entire natural gas infrastructure of Belarus. Beneath the offer of reduced prices lay Russia's threat. There would be consequences should Lukashenko refuse Russia's request.

Chernov conceded Lukashenko's point. "Russia benefits from your dependence on our natural resources, but Belarus benefits more. Your economy thrives due to the low prices, and your country will benefit even more as we reduce the costs further. We are willing to offer an additional twenty-five percent discount, guaranteed for five years."

"That is insufficient. I cannot commit for less than a forty percent reduction for fifteen years."

"Thirty percent, ten years."

Lukashenko studied the Russian defense minister for a moment, then said, "Make it thirty-five percent for ten years, and we have a deal."

"Agreed," Chernov said, pulling a folder from his satchel, withdrawing a thick document. He flipped to the last page and signed it, then slid the agreement to Lukashenko.

The Belarusian president skimmed the document, searching for the terms of the agreement. Looking up, he said, "This agreement is already filled out with the terms—a thirty-five percent reduction for ten years."

Chernov smiled. "We knew you would drive a hard bargain."

"I'll have to review this agreement in more detail before signing."

"That's understandable," Chernov said. "However, we'd like a commitment within forty-eight hours."

"That won't be a problem."

ZAPORIZHIA, UKRAINE

From across the crowded street, Randy Guimond watched a dark gray sedan grind to a halt along Lenin Avenue, stopping in front of Korchma, a quaint restaurant specializing in traditional Ukrainian food. From the sedan stepped a middle-aged man, who, after a quick glance in both directions, entered the small restaurant. The man had a lot to learn about surveillance, Guimond thought, although his own knowledge of the profession would have been a surprise to his co-workers at Metinvest, an international Ukrainian mining and steel holding company; Guimond's public identity and employment with Metinvest was a front. His real employer was the SVR, better known as the successor to the KGB.

Guimond waited a moment, then returned the carved wooden jewelry box he'd been examining to a disappointed shopkeeper and headed across the street. Upon entering the restaurant, he paused briefly, taking everything in: staff dressed in authentic Ukrainian clothing, four couples to the right, a family of six to the left. The interior of the restaurant was decorated with trinkets and heirlooms reminiscent of a rural Ukrainian village, but what interested Guimond most was a small room in the back, closed off from the rest of the restaurant. He nodded to the hostess as he made his way to the door, knocked, then entered.

Although the windowless room could seat twenty guests, only Alex Rudenko was present, sitting at a table with a menu in his hands. Guimond took a seat opposite him as a waiter entered, then departed after both men placed their order. When the door shut, Guimond turned to business.

"We've been given authorization to proceed," he said.

Rudenko, a Ukrainian of Russian descent, shot an uneasy look toward the door, then focused on Guimond. "I cannot agree without assurance."

"You won't be killed," Guimond replied, failing to divulge the most important detail. "However, the others on the podium . . ." He trailed off before continuing, "There will be several deaths. This we cannot avoid. I suggest you carefully consider who will accompany you."

Rudenko nodded. "I have already decided."

"Good, then," Guimond said, pushing forward even though Rudenko hadn't formally agreed. He was part of the conspiracy now. "We need the event scheduled quickly. Well publicized; a major announcement forthcoming, perhaps."

"Yes, yes," Rudenko replied. "I have a plan. Covered by all the media outlets." Rudenko fell silent as the door opened and the waiter entered, depositing their drinks before exiting.

"The second event?" Guimond inquired.

"Not yet planned," Rudenko said, "but it won't be a problem. It'll be a large gathering, well attended by the media again."

"Excellent," Guimond said.

Rudenko asked, "How do I inform you once the events are scheduled?"

"It won't be necessary. We'll be following your activity. It would be best if there was no further contact between us." Guimond withdrew his wallet, tossing one hundred hryvnia onto the table as he stood. "This should cover my meal."

Rudenko grabbed Guimond's wrist. "My reward? Has the Kremlin agreed?"

"Yes, Alex. The Kremlin has agreed to your request."

A smile creased Rudenko's face as he released his acquaintance's wrist.

Guimond returned a warm smile as he slid his wallet into his pocket. The required events had been arranged. Whether Rudenko fully understood what would transpire wasn't his concern.

11

WASHINGTON, D.C.

In her West Wing corner office, National Security Advisor Christine O'Connor scanned the documents on her desk, paying no attention to the rain droplets splattering against her triple-paned, bombproof windows. It had been an unusually harsh winter, but the snow had finally melted, giving way to a wet spring. The heavy rain and overcast skies darkened her mood this morning, but she did her best to remain focused on her task—preparing for her trip to Russia.

She was headed to Moscow for the next round of negotiations for the follow-on to New START, the treaty governing the two countries' nuclear weapons. Russia made several concessions following the events at Ice Station Nautilus, but everything to this point was verbal. Christine was intent on ensuring the agreements became codified in the new treaty. Her eyes shifted between the printed document on her desk—the most recent draft of the new agreement—and handwritten comments in her notepad, recording the issues resolved since their last meeting.

There was a knock on her open door, and Christine looked up to find the president's chief of staff, Kevin

Hardison, in the doorway. "The president wants to see us."

Grabbing her notepad, she joined Hardison for the short journey to the Oval Office, finding SecDef McVeigh seated on one of the two couches. As the president pushed back from his desk to join them, Hardison said, "SecState will be here soon."

"Be seated," the president said, and Hardison settled onto the couch beside McVeigh while Christine took a seat opposite them.

The president approached the three members of his staff and cabinet, taking a chair at one end of the two sofas. As they waited for SecState Dawn Cabral's arrival, the president noted Christine's position opposing the two men, and his thoughts turned to her unique situation, the only member of the opposite political party on his staff.

Three years ago, on a recommendation from Kevin Hardison, he had interviewed Christine for his national security advisor. She had the requisite background, serving as a congressional staffer specializing in weapons procurement, followed by a stint as assistant secretary of defense for special operations and low-intensity conflict, along with several years as the director of nuclear defense policy. During her interview, he'd been surprised: Christine pulled no punches, explaining how his proposed policies would be disastrous for the United States. After being surrounded by staffers eager to please and agree with the president-elect, he found Christine's candor a breath of fresh air. He hadn't made the phone call until the next morning, but he'd made his decision before the interview was over.

Hardison no doubt regretted his recommendation; Christine was far more forceful now than when they worked together twenty years ago, when she was an impressionable young staffer. Now, Christine was quick to engage Hardison and the president whenever she disagreed with their proposals, which was exactly the way the president liked it. Although he didn't always agree with Christine, her opinions and recommendations often distilled clarity into cloudy, contentious issues.

However, since her return from Ice Station Nautilus, she'd been uncharacteristically withdrawn, saying what needed to be said and nothing more, working long hours into the evening and on weekends. It wasn't hard to realize what she was doing. She was staying busy to keep her mind off of what she'd done. Even Hardison had backed off, toning down his interactions with Christine. He'd become aware of the role she played in Captain Brackman's death, and it was easy to discern the guilt she felt, deserved or not.

SecState Cabral's knock on the Oval Office door pulled the president's thoughts back to the pending meeting, and as Dawn settled onto the couch beside Christine, the president turned to McVeigh. "Go ahead, Bob."

McVeigh replied, "We've detected some disconcerting Russian military activity over the last twenty-four hours. Their two largest fleets, the Northern and Pacific Fleets, have sortied to sea, taking every combatant including their aircraft carrier *Kuznetsov*. Russia's Baltic and Black Sea Fleets haven't deployed, but their level of readiness has been increased, as has that of Russia's ground and air forces.

"In addition to the deployment of Russia's two largest fleets, there have been several troop movements. Most are probably related to Russia's upcoming Victory Day celebration in Moscow, commemorating the end of World War Two in Europe. The parade through Red Square typically features ten to twenty thousand troops and the latest Russian military hardware. However, three Russian units are heading northwest, toward

Kaliningrad Oblast. Russia has previously threatened to move more troops and advanced missile systems into the oblast, and appears to be following through. A mechanized infantry division is en route, along with two missile brigades."

After McVeigh fell silent, the president said, "Let's talk about the Russian fleet deployments first. What are they up to?"

"Our best guess," McVeigh replied, "is that their Northern Fleet is headed into the Mediterranean to provide additional firepower off the coast of Syria, although it's curious as to why they would use their Navy instead of additional land-based missile batteries. As to where their Pacific Fleet is headed, we don't have a clue yet. All we know right now is that they're headed south, skirting around the *Reagan* strike group. We'll learn more over the next few days."

"Let's think out of the box," the president said. "Syria is one option. What else could Russia be up to?"

"Ukraine could be a focal point," Christine answered, "although the Northern Fleet would have to transit into the Black Sea. They'd be in an excellent position, on Ukraine's southern border. Russia could be coordinating its ground and naval forces, bringing as much firepower as possible to bear on the Donbass region of Ukraine."

"How are things going in Donbass?" the president asked SecState Cabral, referring to the civil war between the Ukrainian government and separatist forces in the Donetsk and Luhansk Oblasts, collectively referred to as the Donbass region.

Dawn answered, "The conflict is currently at a stalemate, with separatist forces controlling most of Donbass. Although an official cease-fire is in effect, sporadic fighting continues along the line of engagement, and tensions remain high. Additionally, a separatist movement has gained momentum in Moldova, on Ukraine's western border, with ethnic Russians requesting support from the Russian Federation. With unrest in Ukraine's eastern provinces and now to the west, things are getting dicey for Ukraine."

The president nodded. "What else could Russia's Northern Fleet be up to?"

After no additional ideas were offered, the president said, "What about the Pacific?"

Christine answered, "Most of the conflict in the Pacific concerns ownership of natural resources, but I'm not aware of any claims Russia would try to enforce with their Pacific Fleet, unless they intend to join the fray in the South China Sea. But I don't see that happening."

Both SecDef and SecState agreed, and after no further ideas were presented regarding the purpose of Russia's Pacific Fleet deployment, the president said to McVeigh, "Keep working the problem and let me know what you come up with. What about Russia's ground unit movements?"

McVeigh answered, "It looks like they're deploying the Second Guards Motor Rifle Division and two missile brigades into the Kaliningrad Oblast. One of the missile brigades is an offensive weapon system, employing the Iskander short-range ballistic missile, which can carry nuclear or conventional warheads. The second missile brigade employs the S-400 Triumf air defense system, which is Russia's most advanced version, able to engage targets out to two hundred and forty miles. They're deploying twenty-four battalions, which translates to over one thousand missiles. And that's just what's being added. Kaliningrad Oblast already has a significant air defense capability.

"By adding a Guards mechanized infantry division and the two missile brigades, Russia is turning Kaliningrad into a fortress from which they can neutralize NATO airpower in northeastern Europe, undermining a central pillar of NATO war planning. Additionally, their 448th Missile Brigade gives them a significant surface attack capability. The Baltic States are concerned, to put it mildly. It's possible Lithuania and Poland will refuse to allow the additional Russian troops across their border into Kaliningrad Oblast, and if so, Russia will be incensed. We're not sure how they'd respond."

The president contemplated the information laid before him, then said, "As far as the Russian Navy goes, let's keep an eye on both fleets, with forces close enough to engage quickly if necessary. What are our options?"

McVeigh answered, "Most of the Atlantic Fleet has been transferred to the Pacific, but we have five submarines we can send across the Atlantic to shadow Russia's Northern Fleet. We also have a guided missile submarine near the Persian Gulf that we can send into the Mediterranean via the Suez Canal, where she can await the Northern Fleet's arrival. As for Russia's Pacific Fleet, we can have the *Reagan* strike group shadow it as it heads south, or assign that task to the *Truman* strike group, which is in transit from the Indian Ocean to replace *Roosevelt* off China's coast."

The president replied, "Let's leave the *Reagan* strike group where it is. I don't want to go from two strike groups off China's coast to zero. Have the *Truman* strike group rendezvous with the Russian Pacific Fleet as soon as possible, but keep them at a reasonable distance. Between Russia and China, tension in the Western Pacific is high, and I don't want any interactions that could escalate out of control.

"Regarding the Russian ground force redeployments,"

the president said, "keep me informed as the situation develops."

As the meeting drew to a close, the president said to Christine, "You're heading to Russia on Monday, right?"

"Yes, Mr. President."

After a moment of reflection, the president said, "Proceed with the trip."

WASHINGTON, D.C.

Christine returned to her office and had resumed reviewing the draft nuclear arms treaty for only a few minutes when there was a knock on her door. She looked up to see a Marine Corps Colonel standing in her doorway along with Sheree Hinton, one of Hardison's interns.

"Miss O'Connor," she said, "I'd like you to meet Colonel Bill DuBose, the president's new senior military aide."

At the mention of Captain Brackman's replacement, Christine's stomach tightened. She rose from her desk and strode across the office, forcing a smile onto her face as she extended her hand. "It's a pleasure to meet you, Colonel."

The Colonel's handshake was firm, matching his muscular physique. "If you'll excuse me," Sheree said, "I have to run an errand for the chief of staff. I'll let you two get acquainted and be back in a minute."

That was the last thing Christine wanted to hear. At the sight of the president's new senior military aide, the memory of what she'd done to Brackman resurfaced; she was aboard the sunken submarine again, the cold metal handwheel in her hands, turning it shut, sealing Brackman in the flooded compartment. Through the portal in the door, she watched Brackman drown, sucking in a lungful of cold seawater with his last breath, staring at her until his eyes glazed over and he drifted into the darkness.

The memory of what she'd done had slowly faded over the last few weeks, but the arrival of Brackman's replacement ripped the wound open anew.

"I'm looking forward to working with you, Miss O'Connor," he said.

"I, as well," Christine replied, before retreating to her desk. As she slipped into her chair, she said, "I apologize for being abrupt, but I'm pressed for time. I leave for Moscow on Monday and have a lot to review."

She looked down at the documents and picked up a yellow highlighter, trying to focus and push Brackman from her thoughts. The Colonel remained in her doorway, waiting for Sheree to return and continue his introductions to the White House staff.

"How did you end up on the president's staff," DuBose asked, "being from the other party, I mean?"

"I interviewed for the job," Christine answered without looking up.

"Will I have routine meetings with you and the president, or only when required?"

"When required," Christine said quickly, attempting to conceal her irritation; could he not decipher she wasn't in a talkative mood?

"Sheree told me that you and Captain Brackman worked closely together. I hope we can do the same."

Christine replied without thinking, "I won't make that mistake with you." She clamped her mouth shut, but it was too late.

There was a long silence before Colonel DuBose said, "Is there something about me or marines that you don't like?"

"My father was a marine," Christine replied, her eyes still glued to the document in front of her.

There was an awkward pause before DuBose asked, "Was he a good father?"

"He was never a father."

Another long silence, then DuBose said, "I'm sorry."

"Don't be."

It seemed DuBose finally got the message, because he asked no further questions before Sheree returned. As she prepared to continue with his West Wing introductions, Colonel DuBose said, "It was a pleasure meeting you, Miss O'Connor."

Christine knew she should say something gracious, but all she could manage was, "Please close my door."

The door closed with a solid click. Christine put the highlighter down and pushed back from her desk. Visions of her trip to Ice Station Nautilus—Brackman drifting off into the murky water, of the Russian's hand around her throat as she jammed an ice pick through his, of her tumbling through the darkness into the icy water—swirled through her mind. She didn't know how long she'd been sitting there, trying to stuff those thoughts back where they belonged, when there was another knock on her door. She pulled up to her desk and retrieved the highlighter, then acknowledged the knock.

The door opened to reveal Kevin Hardison.

"Do you have a minute?" he asked.

"Not really," Christine replied. "I'm preparing for my trip to Moscow." She dropped her eyes to the document on her desk.

Hardison closed the door and settled into a chair in front of Christine's desk. "Sheree introduced the president's new senior military aide, and the Colonel and I had a nice chat. The typical introductory stuff, until he asked if you were always this . . . *cold*."

"It *is* a bit chilly in my office," Christine said without looking up. "Perhaps you could take care of that."

Hardison replied, "I lied and told him you were normally quite nice, but that you had a lot on your mind and were pressed for time."

Christine highlighted a section of the draft treaty that needed to be modified, and when she didn't respond, Hardison asked, "Do you remember when we first met, twenty years ago on Congressman Johnson's staff?"

Christine replied, "You mean, when you weren't an ass?"

Hardison glared at her for a moment, then continued. "I admired you then. Smart, driven, easy to get along with. With the experience you've gained over the last twenty years, I thought you'd make a great national security advisor. The president interviewed you based on my recommendation, which you've never thanked me for, by the way."

"Thank you, Kevin." Christine's highlighter kept moving, her eyes shifting between her notes and the draft treaty.

"But that's beside the point," Hardison said.

"What *is* your point?" Christine asked, her eyes still downward. "It's hard to talk to you and concentrate on what I'm doing."

Hardison reached over and grabbed the highlighter from Christine's hand. She looked up, an exasperated expression on her face. "What do you want?"

"What I want," Hardison answered, "is for you to stop blaming yourself for Brackman's death."

"I don't have time for this," Christine replied, reaching for the highlighter.

He pulled it back out of her reach. "You're going to make time for it, because this conversation is overdue." Christine leveled an icy stare at him as he continued,

"It was Brackman's decision, not yours." His words seemed to have no effect, so he added, "Yes, I know. You spun the handwheel, sealing him inside the flooded compartment. But you had no choice."

"Everyone has a choice." Christine's voice quavered as she spoke; her facade was beginning to crumble.

"Not in this case," Hardison said. "You need to accept that. You are not responsible for Brackman's death."

Christine pushed back from her desk and folded her arms tightly across her chest, attempting to maintain control of her emotions, forcing her breathing to remain steady.

"I want you to take some time off," Hardison said.

"I don't work for you," Christine replied.

"It's Friday morning. Take the rest of today off."

"I have too much to do." Christine pulled her chair back to her desk, reaching for the highlighter in Hardison's hand again.

He kept it beyond her reach. "I don't want to see you here over the weekend either. I'm going to leave an order for the marines at the entrance to not let you in."

"They don't work for you, either."

"They don't, but they work for the president, and I'm sure he'll give the order if I ask. I'm not the only one who's noticed your demeanor since you returned from Ice Station Nautilus."

Hardison added, "Do something to take your mind off of things. Have a few drinks with a friend. You do have one, right? Someone who can tolerate your presence?"

Christine reached for the highlighter again, this time keeping her arm extended. "Give me the highlighter."

Hardison brought the highlighter almost to within reach. "Only if you take the rest of today and the weekend off."

Christine dropped her hand. "Keep the damn highlighter." She opened her desk drawer, rummaging through its contents for another one.

Hardison slammed his hand on her desk. "Christine!"

She paused, then slowly closed the drawer and folded her arms across her chest again, staring at the documents on her desk. Hardison was right. She needed time away. From all of it.

"Fine," she said. "I'll take the rest of today and the weekend off."

Hardison placed the highlighter on her desk. "I'm not leaving your office until you do."

Christine closed her notepad and slid the draft treaty back into its folder, placing both in her leather briefcase along with the highlighter and several other documents she'd need on her trip. After grabbing her briefcase and umbrella, she left without a word.

ARLINGTON, VIRGINIA

In the Pentagon gym locker room, Christine dried her hair with a white towel, then tossed it onto a nearby bench. After leaving the White House, she had mulled over what to do the rest of the dreary, rainy day and decided to start with a good, hard workout. It was still morning and she had plenty of pent-up energy, so hitting the gym was a perfect way to start her weekend.

Upon leaving the Pentagon, Christine headed toward her town house in Clarendon. During her journey, the rain slowed to a drizzle, then ended. After a moment of indecision, she stopped at a grocery store and selected two flower bouquets. After placing them on the passenger seat of her car, she opened the glove compartment and retrieved two yellow envelopes, one new and one worn. She pulled the documents from the new envelope, which included a car pass, placing it on the dashboard.

Christine grasped the steering wheel and steeled herself for the encounter. She didn't know how long she sat in the parking lot, but her hands began to hurt and she noticed they had turned white from gripping the steering wheel so hard. She relaxed her hands, letting the blood flow back into them for a moment, then shifted the car into drive. A few minutes later, she was heading down Memorial Avenue, then turned left onto Eisenhower Drive, where a sentry examined the pass on her dashboard and waved her into Arlington National Cemetery.

Established on the grounds of Arlington House, a mansion owned by Robert E. Lee's wife, Mary Anna, and seized by the federal government during the Civil War, Arlington National Cemetery spans 624 acres, containing almost three hundred thousand headstones. As Christine headed down Eisenhower Drive, up the gently sloping hill to her right was the Tomb of the Unknowns, commonly referred to as the Tomb of the Unknown Soldier. She'd stopped by there many times as she left the cemetery, watching the Tomb Guards, soldiers from the 3rd Infantry Regiment, The Old Guard. She had memorized the words inscribed on the western panel of the tomb:

HERE RESTS IN
HONORED GLORY
AN AMERICAN
SOLDIER
KNOWN BUT TO GOD

The graves she would visit today weren't unknown, and after entering the cemetery, her car coasted to a halt. She didn't need to read the headstone number on the document on her passenger seat; the grave was easy to identify. The dirt was freshly turned. After taking a deep breath, she selected one of the flower bouquets and stepped from the car, looking up into the gray, overcast sky. It had stopped raining, but it looked as though the clouds could open up again at any moment. After a short traverse across wet grass, Christine reached Captain Steve Brackman's grave.

She stood at the foot of his grave, reliving the last few

minutes of Brackman's life. As the ocean poured into
the submarine, they couldn't shut the watertight door,
their feet slipping on the wet, sloping deck as water
surged through the opening. They'd had a short but
heated argument. Brackman was convinced there were
only two options: either he died or they both died. As
he pulled himself into the adjacent compartment, where
he could put his back and legs into the effort to shut the
door, she could have refused to help, sentencing them
both to death. Instead, she pushed the watertight door
closed, then spun the handwheel, sealing him on the
wrong side.

Brackman had sacrificed himself for her, and unfortunately, there was no way for Christine to repay the
debt. She knelt and placed the flowers against his headstone, then stood and thanked him. She said a short
prayer for Brackman and the family he left behind, then
returned to her car. After one final glance at Brackman's
grave, she put the car in drive and pulled slowly away.

After a right turn onto Patton Drive, Christine pulled
to a halt in front of section 70. With the other flower
bouquet in hand, she headed across the thick grass, stopping in front of headstone 1851. There were two names
on the marker: Daniel O'Connor on the front and Tatyana O'Connor on the back. Christine placed the flowers atop the gravesite, and although the grass was wet
and she was wearing a business suit, she sat in front of
the headstone.

Daniel O'Connor died when he was only twenty-two,
having never seen his daughter. Serving as a marine
during the Vietnam War, he was killed during the waning days of the conflict, and Tatyana gave birth a few
weeks later. As Christine told Colonel DuBose, Daniel
O'Connor had never been a father.

Christine was raised by her mother, a first-generation
Russian immigrant who arrived in the United States as

a teenager. Tatyana never remarried, dying from cancer when Christine was in her early twenties. In accordance with policy at Arlington National Cemetery, she was buried atop Daniel in the same grave, her name inscribed on the back of the headstone.

As she sat on the wet grass, Christine wondered if her parents would have been proud of her. Professionally, yes. But she'd made a mess of her personal life. She was in her forties now, divorced with no kids, and her ex-husband had ended up dead on her kitchen floor while the man she truly loved had married another.

Jake Harrison had proposed twice, the first time during their senior year in high school. However, she was headed to Penn State on a gymnastics scholarship and had no time for marriage, much less motherhood. Although she accepted the night he proposed, she returned the ring the next morning. Jake proposed again when she graduated from college, but she'd been swept into a life of Washington politics and wasn't ready to settle down. She'd be ready in a few years, she'd told Jake. Apparently, eleven was too many, and by the time she was ready, he'd proposed to another woman.

Christine's thoughts returned to her mom and dad. She said good-bye to her parents, then pushed herself to her feet and returned to her car. After sliding into the front seat, she pulled her cell phone from her purse. Hardison had recommended she get together with a friend this weekend, and Christine decided a girls' night out was exactly what she needed. She tapped in a number and her best friend, Joan, answered.

"Hey, girl," Joan said. "Long time no hear. Where are you?"

Christine looked around the cemetery. "Arlington."

Christine spent a few minutes catching up with Joan, who had been on Penn State's gymnastics team with Christine and a political science major as well, also ending up in Washington, D.C. Unlike Christine, however, Joan was married with three teenagers, and their different social circles and busy schedules made it difficult to get together.

"I was wondering if you're available this weekend," Christine said. "I'd love to go out for dinner and drinks."

"Oh, this is a bad weekend," Joan said, "I have plans with John tonight, Jonathon has a soccer tournament on Saturday, and Anna has a play recital on Sunday. What about next week?"

"I'm headed to Russia on Monday, and I'm not sure when I'll be back. Depends on how things go."

There must have been something in Christine's voice, because Joan picked up on it. "Are you okay?"

"I'm fine," Christine said. "I could use some company, though."

After a short pause, Joan said, "How about tonight? Say . . . seven o'clock."

"I don't want you to break your date with John."

"Don't worry," Joan said. "He owes me. Make a reservation wherever you'd like. I'll pick you up."

"Sounds great," Christine said. "See you tonight."

As Christine returned her cell phone to her purse, her thoughts turned to Jake Harrison again, and she decided to give him a call. She had no idea if he was on deployment or not, but figured it was worth a try. She found his number and hit call.

To Christine's surprise, a woman answered. "Hello. This is Laura."

Christine was taken aback for a moment, then remembered Laura was Jake's wife. "Hi, Laura, this is Christine O'Connor. I'm calling for Jake. I must have the wrong number."

Laura answered, a coolness in her voice. "You've got the right number. Jake forwards his calls home when he's on deployment, in case one of his *buddies* tries to contact him." Laura's emphasis on the male term didn't go unnoticed.

"I'm sorry to bother you," Christine said. "Please say hi to Jake when he returns."

"No problem," Laura replied, although Christine was certain there was. Without another word, Laura hung up.

As Christine slid the phone into her purse, she wondered where Jake Harrison was.

14
USS *MICHIGAN*

On the Conn of the Ohio class guided missile submarine, Lieutenant Jayne Stucker surveyed the watchstanders on duty in the Control Room, pausing to examine the navigation parameters:

Course: 040
Speed: 10 knots
Depth: 180 feet

Her eyes shifted to the red digital clock. It was 9:40 p.m., and with the Captain's night orders directing a trip to periscope depth at 10:00 p.m., it was time to begin preparations.

"Quartermaster, rig Control for gray."

The bright Control Room lights were extinguished, leaving only a few low-level lights. Lieutenant Stucker reached up, activating the microphone on the Conn.

"All stations, Conn. Make preparations to proceed to periscope depth."

Sonar, Radio, and the Quartermaster acknowledged, and the Electronic Surveillance Measures watch was manned. While Stucker waited for Sonar to complete a detailed search of the surrounding water, she examined the electronic chart on the navigation table. *Michigan* was approaching the Strait of Hormuz outbound, repositioning from the Persian Gulf into the Gulf of Oman, now that the latter had been vacated by the *Truman* carrier strike group.

There were few places more hazardous for ships than the Strait of Hormuz. The opening to the Persian Gulf is only thirty-five miles wide at its narrowest point, and the shipping lanes in the center are even narrower—only two miles wide—separated by a two-mile buffer zone. Thankfully, *Michigan* was to the southeast, outside the busy traffic lanes, but there were still many ships transiting through the strait in the shallower water where *Michigan* lurked.

After waiting several minutes, giving Sonar time to adjust their equipment lineup and complete a detailed search, Stucker announced, "Sonar, Conn. Report all contacts."

Sonar acknowledged and reported several contacts. But the ship's spherical array sonar, mounted in the bow, was blind in the aft sector, or baffles, blocked by the submarine's metal structure. With *Michigan*'s towed array stowed due to the shallow water, Stucker had no idea if there were contacts closing on *Michigan* from behind. She had to turn the ship to find out.

"Helm, left full rudder, steady course two-nine-zero. Sonar, Conn. Commencing baffle clear to port." Stucker followed up, "Rig Control for black."

Sonar acknowledged as the lights in Control were extinguished, leaving only the faint multicolor indications on the submarine's control panels and the red digital navigation repeaters glowing in the darkness. Stucker adjusted the sonar display on the Conn, reducing its brightness to the minimum. *Michigan* steadied up, headed west, but couldn't remain on that course for long, as they were headed toward the shipping lanes.

After waiting a few minutes for Sonar to complete its search of the previously hidden area, Stucker examined the traces on her sonar display, then called out, "Sonar, Conn. Report all contacts."

"Conn, Sonar. Hold twelve contacts, all are far-range except for Sierra three-two, bearing two-six-zero, classified merchant, and Sierra three-three, bearing two-four-zero, also classified merchant. Both contacts are outside ten thousand yards."

Stucker acknowledged Sonar, then ordered, "Helm, right full rudder, steady course zero-four-zero," returning *Michigan* to base course for the trip to periscope depth.

Reaching up, she pulled the microphone from its holder and punched the button for the Captain's stateroom. "Captain, Officer of the Deck."

Murray Wilson answered, "Captain."

Stucker delivered the required report, to which Wilson replied, "I'll be right there."

Captain Murray Wilson entered the Control Room and joined Lieutenant Stucker on the Conn, settling into the Captain's chair on the starboard side. After reviewing the sonar display and the submarine's parameters, Wilson said, "Proceed to periscope depth."

Stucker acknowledged the Captain's order, then reached up in the darkness and twisted the port periscope locking ring. The barrel slid silently up through the submarine's sail, and Stucker folded the periscope handles down as the scope emerged from its well, then placed her right eye against the eyepiece.

"Helm, ahead one-third. Dive, make your depth eight-zero feet. All stations, Conn. Proceeding to periscope depth."

The Helm rang up ahead one-third on the Engine Order Telegraph as the Dive directed his planesmen, "Ten up. Full rise, fairwater planes."

As *Michigan* rose toward the surface, silence descended on Control, aside from the occasional depth reports from the Diving Officer.

"Passing one hundred feet."

The Dive reported the submarine's depth change in ten-foot increments until the periscope broke the ocean's surface. Stucker began circling, completing a revolution every eight seconds, scanning the darkness for nearby ships. She spotted two distant white lights to the west, correlating with Sierra three-two and three-three.

"No close contacts!"

Conversation in Control resumed, now that *Michigan* was safely at periscope depth, and after a quick aerial search detected no air contacts, Stucker slowed her rotation, periodically shifting the scope to high power for long-range scans.

The Quartermaster announced, "Conn, Nav. GPS fix obtained."

A moment later, Radio followed up. "Conn, Radio. Download complete."

Stucker announced, "All stations, Conn. Going deep. Helm, ahead two-thirds. Dive, make your depth one-eight-zero feet."

The Helm and Dive acknowledged and *Michigan* tilted downward. The periscope optics slid beneath the ocean waves, and Stucker lowered the scope back into its well.

"Rig Control for gray," she announced, and the low-level lights flicked on.

A few minutes later, as Lieutenant Stucker ordered the Control Room rigged for white, a radioman entered with a message clipboard in hand. Captain Wilson flipped through the messages: all routine traffic except for one. *Michigan* wouldn't stop after entering the Gulf of Oman. Their journey had become longer and perhaps more hazardous—they would enter the Mediterranean Sea, passing through the Suez Canal.

Wilson stepped from the Conn and entered *Michigan*'s Battle Management Center, located behind the Control Room, where his crew did Tomahawk mission planning and managed SEAL operations. *Michigan* had been converted into a guided missile submarine, carrying Tomahawk cruise missiles in twenty-two of its twenty-four missile tubes, with the remaining two tubes providing access to two Dry Deck Shelters attached to the submarine's missile deck. Within one shelter rested a SEAL Delivery Vehicle—a mini-sub able to transport Navy SEALs miles underwater for clandestine operations, while the other shelter contained two Rigid Hull Inflatable Boats.

Aboard *Michigan* tonight were two platoons of Navy SEALs, ready should their services be required, along with sixty tons of munitions stored in two of *Michigan*'s missile tubes: small arms, grenade launchers, limpet mines . . . anything a SEAL team might need.

Inside the Battle Management Center, Commander John McNeil, in charge of the SEAL unit aboard *Michigan*, was meeting with his two platoon Officers-in-Charge, Lieutenants Jake Harrison and Lorie Allen, reviewing the potential operations they might be tasked with now that they were repositioning into the Gulf of Oman. Lieutenant Allen was in his twenties, while Harrison was much older; the prior enlisted SEAL had reached the rank of chief before receiving his commission as an officer. If there was ever a poster child for the prototypical SEAL, Harrison was it: tall, lean, and muscular, with a chiseled jawline and deep blue eyes.

"Change in plans," Wilson announced, handing the message board to McNeil. The senior SEAL read the message, handing it to Harrison as he asked, "Do you know what's up?"

"Not yet. This is just the waterspace message. We should receive an operational order soon, but right now all we know is—we're headed into the Med."

MOSCOW

Seated at his desk in his office, Yuri Kalinin listened intently as his chief of the general staff, General Sergei Andropov, delivered the daily update on Russia's progress. So far, things were proceeding well, but all that had been authorized were the preparations. Despite his outward confidence and decisiveness, Kalinin hadn't committed. The time was rapidly approaching, however, when a final decision would be required, and if he approved, Russia would step onto a precipice from which it could not retreat. In the meantime, he monitored the progress.

"Everything required to achieve the primary objectives has been arranged," Andropov said. "The initial military units are en route, agreements have been made in Ukraine, and President Lukashenko has agreed to his part. Our oil and natural gas price discounts to Belarus had to be significantly increased, but came in as projected.

"We are now focused on the insurance aspects you requested be added to the plan. Defense Minister Chernov has already met with Iran and is meeting with India and China this weekend. Of the three countries, the commitment from Iran is the most crucial and they have agreed. China and India's participation isn't essential, but would place the United States in an untenable position, eliminating their ability to intervene."

Kalinin nodded his understanding. "Keep me apprised of our progress."

BEIJING, CHINA

Defense Minister Boris Chernov peered out the side window of his sedan, its armored frame riding low to the ground, as it wound through the center of Beijing. Joining Chernov in the back of the car was the Russian ambassador to China, Danil Sokolov, who would translate during this morning's meeting with Xiang Chenglei, China's president and general secretary of the Party. The sedan came to a halt in front of the Great Hall of the People, where President Xiang's executive assistant greeted the two Russians as they stepped from their car. Sokolov translated as the men spoke.

"Welcome to Beijing, Minister Chernov. I am Xie Hai, the president's executive assistant."

Chernov shook Xie's hand. "Thank you for arranging this meeting."

Xie smiled. "It was my pleasure."

Xie escorted the two Russians up the steps toward the building entrance, framed by massive gray marble colonnades. As Chernov entered the Great Hall of the People, his thoughts turned to Belarus. The request Chernov would make today would be similar, but the dynamics were different. Although Russia's share of oil and natural gas imports to China was rising, it was still a small fraction due to China's insistence, wisely so, on multiple sources. Still, the deal could be sweetened other ways.

Whether China was willing to enter another conflict so soon was unknown. Russia and China's relationship over the last several centuries had been contentious, but there was much common ground, particularly when it came to the United States. Chernov was a firm believer in the proverb *The enemy of my enemy is my friend*. The Soviet Union had employed the construct during World War II, working with the West despite their inherent distrust. Now, Russia would strive for an allegiance with the East.

The meeting didn't take long. As Chernov and his translator exited the Great Hall of the People and slid into their waiting sedan, Chernov reflected on his discussions with the Chinese president and the head of the People's Liberation Army. Neither man asked many questions, and when they did, Chernov had difficulty gauging their level of interest. The Chinese language was complex, with many nuances lost in translation. Still, the proposal had been made, and President Xiang was mulling the offer over.

As Chernov's sedan headed toward the airport, he pulled a folder from his leather briefcase and reviewed the document inside, preparing for his next meeting.

NEW DELHI, INDIA

Under a clear blue sky with the heat shimmering along the brick path before them, Chernov walked beside Indian President Deepak Madan as they strolled through the gardens behind Rashtrapati Bhavan, the presidential mansion atop Raisina Hill. Among the verdant trees and colorful flowers in Mughal Gardens, two channels of water ran north to south and another two east to west, dividing the garden into a large central court surrounded by a smaller grid of squares on the periphery. The air was still today and the water tranquil, its surface reflecting the imposing presidential residence, a four-story, 340-room mansion located within the sprawling 320-acre estate.

As the two men walked among lush vegetation, the sun beating down on them, Chernov was convinced Madan had left the air-conditioned spaces of his presidential palace not for privacy reasons, but to subject the Russian defense minister to the intense Indian heat. Perspiration dotted Chernov's forehead and he resisted the urge to loosen his tie; it was only mid-spring, but the heat was suffocating, the temperature already cresting toward one hundred degrees Fahrenheit. Additionally, they had left their interpreters behind, with Madan insisting they continue their conversation in English, as if to point out the ubiquity of America's influence.

Thankfully, Madan led the way to a shaded gazebo, where the temperature dropped considerably. After he took his seat at a marble picnic table, Chernov sat opposite him, preparing to deliver his pitch, which he'd rehearsed in his mind many times during the flight to New Delhi. Chernov had already explained the basic plan. The challenge was convincing President Madan that an alliance with Russia was in India's best interest.

"America is in decline," Chernov began, "while Russia is rising, reestablishing itself as a superpower. In the twenty-first century, you can align with the United States, Russia, or China. The American sphere of influence is shrinking each year, and it won't be long before the United States becomes inconsequential in the Western Pacific. That leaves China or Russia, and your interests are much better served by an alliance with Russia."

"This is not debatable," Madan agreed. "However, I noticed that you met with China's president yesterday. As you point out, China is our primary economic and military competitor, and I am curious as to what was requested of them, and what was promised."

Chernov took a few minutes to lay out China's role—most of the details, that is—finishing with, "China hasn't committed yet, which makes India's role more critical, and also more lucrative. Your participation will be greatly rewarded."

"You ask much," Madan replied. "Although I concur with your assessment—America is in decline—the United States is still a formidable economic and military force, with much influence around the world."

Chernov pressed the issue. "The United States has become weak, both politically and militarily. They lost half of their Fleet in the war with China, and they have no stomach for additional conflict. We attacked one of their aircraft carriers—a blatant assault—knocking it out of commission and killing scores of Americans, and they did nothing. With the proper alliances, America will again look the other way and do nothing. And if they do not"—Chernov paused for effect—"we will make them pay dearly. All that remains is India's commitment."

Madan answered, "What you propose is within my authority as president. However, I will not commit unilaterally. This must be discussed among my National Security Council."

"I understand," Chernov said. "There are many issues to be considered."

"When do you need an answer?" Madan asked.

"May ninth."

Madan raised an eyebrow. "Victory Day?"

Chernov smiled. "There is no better day."

18
MOSCOW

Christine O'Connor peered out the window of the C-32 executive transport, the military version of Boeing's 757 and designated Air Force One when the president was aboard, or Air Force Two when the vice president was being flown. As the aircraft descended, it broke through the heavy gray clouds, revealing a sprawling metropolis—the capital of the Russian Federation and home to twelve million. In the distance, she spotted the Kremlin, where the next round of negotiations for the successor to New START would occur.

Today, Christine would meet with the Russians for the second time. The first round hadn't gone well, with Russia refusing to allow inspections of their new Bulava missile or the Borei class submarines that carried them. However, following the Russian assault on Ice Station Nautilus and the American president's threat to go public with what Russia had done, President Kalinin acquiesced, agreeing to allow inspections of their new missiles and submarines. However, the concession was only verbal up to this point, and Christine was bent on ensuring the agreement became documented in the next draft of the treaty.

The C-32 touched down at Moscow's Vnukovo

Airport, and after descending the staircase onto the tarmac, Christine was met by her Russian counterpart, National Security Advisor Sergei Ivanov. This was her first time meeting Ivanov, who'd been out of town during her last visit. Although Christine was handling the negotiations from the American side, Russia had defaulted to the Ministry of Foreign Affairs, which negotiated New START. As they shook hands, Ivanov gave her an odd look, reacting the same way many within the Russian administration did upon meeting her for the first time.

Standing beside Ivanov was Mark Johnson, Christine's interpreter for the negotiations, supplied by the American embassy in Moscow. Christine and Johnson joined Ivanov in the back of his limousine, which sped from the airport toward the Kremlin. Along the way, Ivanov described the Russian landmarks they passed, and it wasn't long before Red Square appeared through the car windows.

Preparations were under way for Russia's Victory Day celebration, commemorating the surrender of Nazi Germany to the Soviet Union at the end of World War II, referred to within Russia as the Great Patriotic War. Huge banners draped the facades of buildings along the perimeter of Red Square, and the roar of jet engines pulled Christine's eyes skyward as a dozen jets streaked overhead; a squadron of Sukhoi Su-35s, Ivanov explained, practicing for the Victory Day parade, which would include a flyover by 150 military aircraft.

The limousine passed within the five-hundred-year-old Kremlin walls, pulling to a halt in front of the triangular-shaped Kremlin Senate, the Russian version of the White House, with its distinctive green dome. Ivanov escorted Christine to the third floor of the building, entering a twenty-by-sixty-foot conference room containing a polished ebony table capable of seating thirty persons. As before, on one side of the table sat Maksim Posniak, director of security and disarmament in Russia's Ministry of Foreign Affairs, along with his interpreter, although neither side had needed one for the initial discussions. Posniak's accent was thick but his English understandable.

Waiting in the conference room along with Posniak was Russia's minister of defense, Boris Chernov. The three men at the table rose as Christine and Ivanov entered the room.

"Welcome back to Moscow, Christine," Chernov said. "It's good to see you again."

Christine noticed Chernov's use of her first name, instead of addressing her as Miss O'Connor as was customary. "It's good to see you again, too, Boris."

Chernov smiled. "You should find Russia's recent concessions incorporated into the new document Maksim has for you, but if not, please don't hesitate to contact me. As for the details, I leave that for you two to work out."

He checked his watch. "I cannot stay, but before I leave, I must inquire. Will you be attending the ball tomorrow night?" Chernov's eyes wandered as he spoke, examining her body; he seemed unaware she could follow his eyes.

"Yes," Christine answered. "I received the itinerary for my visit and packed the necessary attire. If I may ask, what is the occasion?"

"It's a Victory Day gala."

"I thought Victory Day was on the ninth."

"We have managed to turn the entire month into a celebration," Chernov replied. "Several foreign leaders have already arrived, and we plan to keep them entertained." He added, "If you'll excuse me, I'll stop by to see how things are going tomorrow, and of course, I'll see you tomorrow night."

"I'm looking forward to it."

Chernov and Ivanov departed the conference room, leaving Christine with Posniak and the two interpreters.

Christine turned to Posniak as she eased into her chair. "Let's get started, shall we?"

19

ARISH, EGYPT

The Sinai Peninsula in the northeast corner of Egypt, with the Mediterranean Sea to the north and Red Sea to the south, serves as a land bridge between Africa and Asia. Given Egypt's arid climate and vast desert terrain, it's counterintuitive that almost half of the peninsula's northern coastline is a swampy lagoon: three hundred square miles of brackish water and marshland separated from the Mediterranean Sea by a narrow limestone ridge.

As a result, Arish is the only major city along the Sinai coast. Serving as an outpost during the Egyptian dynasties and fortified during the Roman and Ptolemaic eras, Arish is a city with a great deal of history and very little to show for it: a litter-strewn beach giving way to a sprawling city of low-rise cement-block buildings. Even so, Arish is one of the country's better holiday destinations—less than two hundred miles from Cairo—and as close as many will come to the clear blue waters and pristine sands of the Menorca coast or French Riviera.

Not far from the palm-fringed coastline, Anton Belikov worked quickly in the dark, attempting to gain access to a small building. The temperature south of

Arish had dropped significantly after sunset, and for that, Belikov was thankful. Although the temperatures in the Arctic, where Belikov and his team had worked less than forty-eight hours ago, were frigid, he preferred the colder climate. That was expected, however, since Belikov was from Norilsk, Russia, located above the Arctic Circle and encased in snow up to nine months each year.

The door unlocked and Belikov pushed it slowly open. There was no one inside, only automated equipment. Belikov activated the pale blue light strapped to his forehead, providing just enough illumination for him to tend to his task. Moving swiftly toward the massive machinery, Belikov slid a black duffel bag from his shoulder, laying it carefully on the ground. As he worked in the faint blue glow inside the building, the other members of his platoon were working at various points farther inland.

It didn't take long and everything was soon in place, with one last item remaining. It had been disconcerting at each previous location—with the equipment controlled remotely—and this time it was no different as he entered the required sequence of numbers. The panel activated, confirming proper operation. Belikov wrote down the GPS coordinates and, after collecting his empty duffel bag, headed to the exit. After securing the light on his forehead, he stepped into the cool night.

20

USS *MICHIGAN*

Captain Murray Wilson climbed the metal ladder through the Bridge trunk, pulling himself through the hatch into the darkness at the top of the submarine's sail. Stepping into the Bridge Cockpit, faintly illuminated by a full moon hovering in a cloudless sky, he stood between the Officer of the Deck and the Lookout, the latter with binoculars to his eyes, scouring the barely discernible horizon for contacts. Wilson breathed in the fresh air, and after verifying there were no contacts nearby, he shifted his gaze to the navigation repeater, examining the submarine's position. Hours earlier, *Michigan* had reached the northern end of the Red Sea, surfacing before entering the shallow Gulf of Suez. Behind Wilson and atop the submarine's sail, the American flag fluttered in the brisk wind as *Michigan* headed northwest at ahead standard, and it wouldn't be long before they began their journey through the Suez Canal.

The 120-mile-long Suez Canal, enabling travel from the Pacific into the Mediterranean Sea without transiting around Africa, would cut *Michigan*'s transit from weeks to mere days, but the transit wasn't without risk. Less than a year ago, during America's war with China, mercenaries sank three oil tankers with shoulder-fired missiles, temporarily blocking the canal, forcing America's Atlantic Fleet to take the long route around Africa into the Pacific. During the Arab-Israeli Six-Day War in 1967, both ends of the canal were blocked by scuttled ships, trapping fifteen merchants in the canal for eight years.

With the risk of direct and indirect attack weighing on Wilson's thoughts, he focused on the pending transit. The canal was a single-lane waterway with passing locations in the Ballah Bypass and the Great Bitter Lake. As a result, ships transited the canal in convoys, with a northbound convoy departing from Suez at 4 a.m., synchronized with a southbound convoy from Port Said. *Michigan* would be the first ship in the northern convoy this morning. Wilson checked the time on the navigation repeater. It was 3 a.m.: time to station the Maneuvering Watch. He gave the order, and the Officer of the Deck passed the word over the shipwide 1-MC announcing circuit.

An hour later, *Michigan* approached the southern entrance to the Suez Canal, passing several dozen merchants at anchor awaiting their designated transit time. Loitering near the entrance was *Michigan*'s security detail, two patrol boats armed with .50-caliber machine guns. The real danger was ashore, however, and the patrol crafts' machine guns would be of little use against shoulder-fired rockets or missiles.

A shoulder-fired rocket would likely hit the submarine's sail, and it wouldn't take much to put the submarine out of commission. Destroy the submarine's periscopes and antennas, and *Michigan* would be on the way home for repairs. Not to mention the loss of life; most, if not all, of the personnel atop the sail would be killed.

Assuming *Michigan*'s transit through the Suez Canal was uneventful, things could get interesting once the guided missile submarine entered the Mediterranean Sea. According to the last intelligence update, the Russian Northern Fleet had also entered the Mediterranean, steaming east. The best estimate was that the Northern Fleet was headed to Latakia, Syria. Satellite reconnaissance had detected the buildup of replenishment stores along the wharves at the Syrian seaport. If things went as planned, *Michigan* would intercept the Russian fleet not far from Latakia.

As they approached the entrance to the Suez Canal, Wilson requested a handheld radio, which the Officer of the Deck passed to him. After selecting the proper channel, he brought it to his mouth.

"Canal Operations, this is inbound United States warship. Request permission to enter the canal at time zero-four-hundred."

After a short squawk, the radio emitted the expected response. "United States warship, this is Canal Operations. You have permission to enter the canal at time zero-four-hundred."

Wilson checked the navigation repeater. His Officer of the Deck, plus his Navigator stationed in the Control Room below, had done a superb job, timing *Michigan*'s approach perfectly. The submarine's security detail took their positions, one boat in front and one behind the submarine, with each machine gun manned and ready. Rather than stand during the 120-mile journey, Wilson pulled himself to a sitting position atop the sail, with his feet dangling in the Bridge Cockpit, settling in for the tense fifteen-hour transit.

21

FORT MEADE, MARYLAND

In a windowless cinder-block building off Taylor Avenue, Tim Johns leaned back in his chair at his computer workstation, waiting for the algorithm to begin sending data. Johns, a Cryptologic Technician Networks Petty Officer Second Class, was assigned to the U.S. Cyber Warfare Command, which was responsible for centralized control of all military cyberspace operations. Comprising 133 teams with varying assignments, Cyber Warfare Command employed over six thousand cyber warriors.

Johns was a member of a combat mission team, a cyber unit loosely modeled after special operation forces. During offensive operations, Johns's unit would plant cyber bombs in target networks, but the current assignment was less ambitious, simply hacking into encrypted Russian diplomatic and military networks. After identifying another vulnerable node, he had planted a new *spider*, an algorithm capable of decrypting all messages transiting the router, searching for keywords.

The new spider started sending data, scrolling down his screen, which would be reviewed by the intelligence analysts. So far, the spiders had detected thousands of hits using the supplied keywords, but most were meaningless sentences and phrases. His eyes shifted to the top of the display as a new keyword appeared: *Блок TM85.1051*. As it moved down the screen, he read the sentence, translating it into English in his mind: *Unit TM85.1051 reports the order was executed flawlessly*. Not particularly interesting, Johns thought. But at least it was something new for the analysts to chew on.

22

WASHINGTON, D.C.

It was midafternoon in the Oval Office, with SecDef McVeigh seated between Kevin Hardison and Colonel DuBose, across from the president's desk. There had been a breakthrough in the investigation into Russia's attack on USS *Roosevelt*, and a blue folder resting on McVeigh's lap contained the critical snippet of information, along with the Pentagon's assessment.

"What have you got?" the president asked.

McVeigh answered, "Cyber Command has been scouring Russian military and diplomatic message traffic—emails and official messages. We have the ability to decrypt the lowest level of Russian classified messages—those corresponding to our Confidential level—and we detected an important keyword in a weekly summary provided from the Russian Navy to its minister of defense."

McVeigh opened the folder on his lap and read the pertinent sentence: "Unit TM85.1051 reports the order was executed flawlessly." He looked up and added, "The unit designation TM85.1051 cross-references to an Oscar II submarine in the Russian Pacific Fleet, K-456 *Vilyuchinsk*." McVeigh refreshed everyone's memory about the significance of the Russian unit. "*Vilyuchinsk* was the submarine that launched twenty-four missiles at *Roosevelt*."

The president replied, "You're saying the attack on *Roosevelt* was intentional?"

"Yes, Mr. President. The date in the report coincides with the Russian attack. This is what we've suspected all along, and this evidence is enough to convince everyone in the Pentagon that the attack was deliberate."

"I have to agree," the president said, "which puts us in a difficult situation. We have to either ignore the attack despite what we know, or respond. Your thoughts, gentlemen?" The president turned first to his chief of staff.

"There has to be payback," Hardison answered. "A quid pro quo."

The president turned to Colonel DuBose, giving his new senior military aide the opportunity to weigh in on the first significant issue during his White House assignment.

DuBose replied, "A response is required, but we need to ensure it doesn't spiral out of control, either in a tit for tat that ratchets up, or a response that escalates into a broader conflict."

When the president turned his attention to McVeigh, the SecDef said, "I agree with Kevin and Colonel DuBose. A response is required, although I'm not sure we can prevent an increasing tit for tat. That decision will rest with Kalinin. However, as Colonel DuBose recommends, our response should be narrow, minimizing the possibility this blows up into a wider conflict."

"What do you recommend?" the president asked.

"One option," McVeigh offered, "is to damage a major Russian warship. The Russian Northern Fleet has entered the Mediterranean Sea, and most of their surface combatants have docked in the Syrian port of Latakia, loading food and fuel. Their aircraft carrier, *Admiral Kuznetsov*, remains at sea with Russia's other nuclear-powered combatants. This gives us a number of targets and options.

"*Admiral Kuznetsov* is the most appropriate choice as quid pro quo for *Roosevelt*. However, it also has the highest potential for escalating, depending on how we engage and the response from her escorts. A better target, perhaps, is *Marshal Ustinov*, a Slava class cruiser docked in Latakia. She's the most formidable Russian warship in port, and the third most powerful in Russia's Northern Fleet after *Admiral Kuznetsov* and the battle cruiser *Pyotr Velikiy*, both of which are nuclear powered and remain at sea."

"How would we execute the attack?"

"You could order an air attack, hitting *Marshal Ustinov* with enough missiles to send her back to Russia for repairs. However, she's tied up along the waterfront with several merchants nearby, and there's the possibility of collateral damage if any missiles lock on to the wrong target. We could go with a torpedo. *Michigan* will enter the Mediterranean Sea soon, only a short distance from Latakia, but you've got the same problem: their torpedo could lock on to the wrong target with so many ships nearby.

"Another alternative," McVeigh said, "is the SEAL detachment aboard *Michigan*. They're trained to sink enemy combatants in port, which is the scenario we're looking at, plus they can ensure we get the right target."

"Is that too aggressive," Hardison asked, "sinking one of their ships in return for damaging one of ours?"

McVeigh replied, "*Marshal Ustinov* won't be a permanent loss. Sunk alongside the pier, the Russians will raise her, like we did for most of the ships sunk during Japan's attack on Pearl Harbor and the ships we lost in the Taiwan Strait last year. But we can put her out of commission for six months to a year, which is a reasonable response for what was done to *Roosevelt*."

"Assuming we sink the Russian cruiser," the president said, "what do we tell Russia when they imply our involvement?"

McVeigh suggested, "You could tell President Kalinin the same thing the Russian ambassador told you. That SEALs from *Michigan* were on a training mission, and *accidentally* attached real ordnance to the bottom of their cruiser." McVeigh smiled.

After a moment of deliberation, the president replied, "Send the order to *Michigan*. Sink *Marshal Ustinov*."

MOSCOW

It was 8 p.m. when the sedan carrying Christine O'Connor and her interpreter, Mark Johnson, pulled to a halt not far from the Kremlin Senate, stopping behind a procession of cars depositing their guests for the evening's event. As the men and women, dressed in tuxedos and formal evening gowns, stepped from their cars onto a red carpet, they were welcomed by Kremlin officials who escorted them into the green-domed building. For this evening's gala, Christine had selected a blue dress that hugged her curves. Her hair was up, pulled back to reveal the sleek lines of her neck, accenting her high cheekbones and slate-blue eyes. Diamond earrings, matching pendant, and blue Valentino heels completed the look.

Christine and Johnson's car inched forward, eventually reaching the red carpet. Stepping from the sedan, they were greeted by Russian Foreign Minister Andrei Lavrov. After passing through the security screening, Christine and her interpreter were escorted by a young man to the building's third floor, entering an expansive ballroom with crystal chandeliers illuminating a glossy parquet floor. The room was faced with white marble, with one wall decorated by a painting depicting Moscow, and the other wall, St. Petersburg, symbolizing the centuries-long rivalry between the historic and "northern" capitals of Russia.

Christine and Johnson mingled as waiters carried silver platters of drinks and hors d'oeuvres throughout the crowd, and Christine selected a glass of champagne as a tray passed by. Several Russian dignitaries introduced themselves, with most needing the help of her interpreter. But others kept their distance, shooting quick looks her way. Christine was used to turning heads when she entered a room, but these glances were more furtive, not the typical wide-eyed, admiring stares. She observed the scene more closely, seeing heads bent in whispered conversations as she passed by, and felt sure they were talking about her.

Spotting the American ambassador to Russia not far away, Christine decided to inquire about the strange looks. As she moved toward her, Defense Minister Boris Chernov appeared, stopping Christine halfway to the ambassador.

"Good evening, Miss O'Connor," he said. "It's a pleasure to see you again."

Christine offered a smile as Chernov's gaze swept her from head to toe.

They talked briefly, then Chernov excused himself to mingle with other diplomats. Christine scanned the crowd for the American ambassador again, spotting her in line to greet Russian President Yuri Kalinin, who was talking with the new Chinese chairman of the Central Military Commission—the head of China's armed forces—and a female companion. Given what occurred during Christine's last visit to China, when she'd been detained during China's war with the United States, she decided it'd be best to wait until the two Chinese moved on before joining the ambassador.

Assisted by her interpreter, Christine chatted with

several Russian dignitaries while she kept an eye on President Kalinin. After the Chinese bade farewell, Christine excused herself and headed in the president's direction. However, she didn't get far before a voice stopped her.

"Miss O'Connor."

Christine turned as Semyon Gorev, head of Russia's counterpart to the CIA, approached.

"It's nice to finally meet you," he said as he shook her hand. "I have heard much about you."

Christine had heard much about Semyon Gorev as well; the authoritarian director of Russia's Foreign Intelligence Service had earned a reputation for ruthlessness and a thirst for revenge during his time as a field agent.

"Only good things, I hope," Christine said, keeping her tone deliberately light.

"But of course," Gorev replied.

He offered a friendly smile, but Christine registered tension behind his expression. She wondered if he'd read her file. She'd killed two Russians at Ice Station Nautilus, but considering Russia lost almost one hundred men in the conflict, her role had been small.

Their discussion remained cordial, however, and Christine glanced occasionally in Kalinin's direction, watching the American ambassador work her way up the line. Confident and poised, President Kalinin greeted his guests with ease. During one of her glances, she noticed Kalinin looking her way and their eyes locked for a few seconds. When Christine returned her attention to Gorev, there was a scowl on the director's face, replaced quickly with a forced smile.

When the American ambassador was next in line, Christine prepared to disengage from Gorev and join the ambassador. But then the ballroom lights dimmed momentarily. The ballroom floor cleared as guests moved to the perimeter, and a Russian dance company took the floor. Christine deposited her empty champagne glass on a tray as a waiter passed by, then turned back to Gorev. But the Russian was gone.

The evening's entertainment began with an exhibition by the dance company, performing two Russian folk dances. Christine recognized the first as a khorovod, a circular dance where the participants hold hands and sing, with additional dancers in the middle of the circle. The khorovod was followed by a plyaska, a dance that told a story, like a play. This particular plyaska told the tale of two men's quest for a woman's love and her struggle making a choice.

After the two folk dances, the floor opened up for the guests, with the first dance being a waltz. Christine declined the request of a young Russian, choosing to observe first, quickly determining the waltz was ballroom style as opposed to Viennese, with an international left-right-left step, rather than the American right-left-right. During the dance, her gaze occasionally drifted to President Kalinin, who was deep in conversation with SVR Director Gorev. But while Gorev's eyes were fixed on the president, Kalinin's were pointed straight across the ballroom—at her—and she could feel the intensity of his stare from forty feet away.

She'd been on the business end of that kind of look a few times in her life—always from a man who wanted her either in the ground or in his bed. Christine cast another glance in Kalinin's direction. He was still staring at her, and she wasn't sure which scenario Kalinin was contemplating. Was Gorev, with his reputation for revenge, discussing her role at Ice Station Nautilus? Christine shivered involuntarily, then refocused on the waltz.

From across the crowded ballroom, Yuri Kalinin watched the American woman intently. Gorev followed his eyes to the attractive woman.

Gorev said, "Please tell me you are not seriously considering this."

"She could be Natasha's twin," Kalinin replied.

"Her likeness is remarkable," Gorev agreed, "but you cannot have a relationship with her."

"Why not?"

Gorev replied with an exasperated edge to his words, having to explain the obvious. "She's American."

"She's half Russian," Kalinin countered.

"She cannot be trusted," Gorev said with a tone of finality.

"I appreciate your concern," Kalinin said, "but I don't think dinner with her would jeopardize national security."

Gorev turned to the Russian president, placing his hand gently on his shoulder. "I know how close you and Natasha were, and how difficult those last few months were. Forget about this American. I will find you a suitable Russian woman."

A smile broke across Kalinin's face. "A bride selected by the SVR? I think my secrets would be safer if I married the American."

Gorev grinned. "You are a wise man, Yuri. Still, the president of Russia cannot have a relationship with America's national security advisor. Do not let her likeness to Natasha influence you."

Kalinin replied, "I've already given the matter much thought."

The first waltz wound to a close, and confident she could perform the international version, Christine prepared to accept the next request. She wasn't prepared, however, when the invitation came from Defense Minister Chernov.

She accepted, and standing in front of him, Christine embraced Chernov in the semi-closed position, keeping her body a safe distance from his. The music started and Christine focused on following the left-right-left sequence. After a minute with no mishaps, she settled into the rhythm of the dance, her motions becoming more fluid, and she noted that Chernov was an excellent dancer.

When the waltz ended, Christine released her embrace as she commented on Chernov's ability. "You also are a superb dancer," Chernov replied. "If you don't mind, I would love the next dance as well."

Christine was about to reply when a man tapped Chernov on the shoulder. The defense minister turned aside, revealing Russia's president.

"May I have the next dance?" he asked.

Christine glanced at Chernov, who stepped back with disappointment on his face.

She turned to President Kalinin, fixing a smile in place that she hoped covered her nerves, and accepted. The Russian president caught the attention of the bandleader, requesting another waltz. Christine embraced Kalinin, choosing the semi-closed position again, resting her fingers lightly on Kalinin's right shoulder as their lead hands joined. The music began, and having worked out the kinks in her dance with Chernov, Christine fell immediately into rhythm.

To her surprise, Kalinin was an even better dancer than Chernov. He was also much better looking, with a trim, muscular physique, and only a few years older than her. As they glided through the turns, changes, and whisks, he kept the same intense gaze he'd had earlier trained on her. However, Yuri Kalinin didn't seem the type to waltz with an enemy. If he was attracted to her . . . *well*. That opened up a number of interesting possibilities.

During the dance, the sensation she was being watched

grew stronger. Letting her eyes slide away from Kalinin's, she scanned the room; the stares from Russians in attendance were even more obvious than before. That was to be expected, as she was dancing with their president, but she couldn't shake the feeling that there was something more.

When the dance ended, with her fingers still on his shoulder and their lead hands joined, Christine said, "President Kalinin, I have to ask. Why do I get such strange looks from everyone?"

Kalinin offered her a piercing gaze, then released her. "Come with me."

Christine followed Kalinin from the ballroom, spotting Semyon Gorev along the perimeter, monitoring their departure. They passed two Presidential Security Service agents, the Russian version of America's Secret Service, before walking silently down a long hallway. After a left turn, Kalinin unlocked and opened a mahogany-stained door, flicking the lights on as they entered what Christine surmised was his office. Stopping in the foyer, Kalinin pointed to a picture on the wall.

"My wife, Natasha," he said.

Christine might as well have been looking into a mirror. She knew her Russian genetics dominated her looks, but was surprised at how closely she resembled Natasha. The facial structure and even her hair and eye color were the same. It was then that Christine recalled Kalinin was a widower, his wife succumbing to cancer soon after he was elected president.

"I'm very sorry for your loss," she said.

Kalinin nodded, the pain of his wife's death evident on his face. His normally impassive mask slipped further, and Christine watched indecision play across his face as his eyes shifted from Natasha's picture to her. It became clear that Kalinin was contemplating the controversial prospect of a relationship with America's national security advisor.

On one hand, it wasn't that far-fetched. Christine knew she'd make one hell of a politician's wife if the idea ever appealed to her: beautiful, intelligent, and comfortable dealing with powerful men. The main obstacle in a relationship with Kalinin, however, was obvious. She lacked the loyalty he required. Not only to him, but to Russia.

Just as Christine decided a relationship with Kalinin was far too complicated and doomed to fail, the president of Russia asked her out.

"On future trips to Moscow," Kalinin said, "if you'd like to spend time together, maybe for dinner, let me know. This is a busy month, but once Victory Day preparations are over and a few other issues are resolved, I will have more time. On your next trip, perhaps?"

The *I'm not sure that's a good idea* stuck in Christine's throat. Instead, she replied, "Perhaps." She wondered if he heard the reservation in her voice, but if he did, he gave no sign.

"Wonderful," Kalinin said. Checking his watch, he added, "We should return to the party before any unseemly rumors begin."

While Christine contemplated whether Kalinin was concerned about her reputation or his, there was a knock on the open door. Semyon Gorev and Boris Chernov were in the doorway.

"See," Kalinin said. "They are already getting suspicious."

Gorev cast a glance at Christine before saying, "Boris has a matter he needs to discuss with you in private. It won't take long. I'll escort Miss O'Connor back to the ballroom."

"Please do," Kalinin said. Turning to Christine, he

said, "It was a pleasure dancing with you, and I hope you enjoy the rest of your stay in Moscow."

The door closed, and as Gorev escorted Christine down the hallway, he asked, "What did you and President Kalinin discuss?"

Christine's first thought was to tell Gorev it was none of his business. She bit her tongue instead, then answered, "Yuri explained why I've been getting such strange looks. He showed me a picture of Natasha."

Gorev replied, "On a first-name basis with President Kalinin after one dance? You move quickly."

Christine stopped, irritated by the accusation. "For your information, I have no romantic interest in President Kalinin."

"I overheard the end of your conversation. You said you'd consider his proposal to spend time together. That doesn't sound like a lack of interest."

Christine's anger smoldered as she met Gorev's accusatory stare. "I don't need to explain myself to you." She started moving down the hallway again.

Gorev planted his hand against the wall, barring her path. She stopped abruptly, almost running into his arm. He said, "I don't know what's going on in that pretty little head of yours, but let me make one thing clear. You are not interested in President Kalinin."

Christine bit down on her anger. "I didn't realize that as director of the SVR, your duties included matchmaker."

"I have many responsibilities, Miss O'Connor. I do the . . ." Gorev paused, his eyes narrowing as he searched for better words. "I do what is best for Russia and for Yuri. He doesn't always appreciate what I do, but I assure you, my actions are in his and our country's best interest.

"As far as your best interest goes," Gorev said, "I suggest you maintain your relationship with Yuri completely professional. Your likeness to Natasha is a distraction, one he does not need."

Christine said, "I'll take your recommendation under consideration."

"It is not a request."

There was something about Gorev that reminded Christine of Kevin Hardison: a domineering man who tried to force his will on others. But like Hardison, Gorev had no authority over her. As she stood in the hallway in front of the two-hundred-pound man barring her path, she could have walked around him; the hallway was wide enough. However, she would not be intimidated, not even by the head of the SVR.

She placed a hand on Gorev's shoulder. "You're in incredible shape," she said as she felt the muscles beneath his suit jacket. "You must work out." Gorev stared at her as she continued. "I was a gymnast for seventeen years. A national champion on the beam."

"And your point?" Gorev asked.

"My point," Christine said as she ran her hand slowly down his arm, "is that elite gymnasts require three essential elements. Most people think flexibility is key, and it is, but strength is just as important. There are some moves many gymnasts can't do because they aren't strong enough. The third element is alignment," Christine said as she stopped with her hand resting on Gorev's wrist.

"If you begin a move even a degree or two out of alignment, it can spell disaster, especially when performing on a four-inch-wide beam. Alignment is also key for strength. If your muscles aren't properly aligned, you won't have the strength to power yourself through some of the moves."

Christine clamped her hand around Gorev's wrist.

"For example, if I were to rotate your hand ninety degrees"—she twisted firmly, rotating Gorev's hand inward—"a small woman like myself could overpower a strong man."

A grin creased Gorev's face. "Care to try?"

"If I succeed," Christine asked, "will you keep your nose out of my business?"

"If you succeed," Gorev replied, "you'll have the satisfaction of winning this little game of yours. Nothing more."

"Fair enough," Christine said.

She pushed down on Gorev's wrist and he resisted. She pushed even harder, and his hand inched down the wall. He strained against her, halting the downward movement.

Gorev's grin widened. "Is that all you've got?"

Christine pushed down suddenly with all her strength and Gorev reacted, countering her move with an upward thrust. Christine released his wrist and Gorev's arm swung upward. Twisting to the side, she slipped past him before he could recover and bar her path again.

She turned around, facing him. "I was wrong. You're too strong for me."

The muscles in Gorev's jaw flexed as Christine walked backward down the hallway, still facing him. Gorev replied, "We shall play another game soon, yes?"

"Perhaps," Christine said in a much chillier tone than she'd used with Kalinin. "In the meantime"—she blew Gorev a kiss—"give my love to Yuri."

Gorev gritted his teeth.

Christine turned and headed down the hallway, passing the two Security Service agents as she entered the ballroom. Gorev followed closely behind, then monitored her from the ballroom's perimeter as she mingled among the crowd. It wasn't long before President Kalinin returned from his meeting with Chernov. Undeterred by Gorev's surveillance, Christine approached Kalinin as the band prepared to play another waltz.

"Care to dance?" she asked.

"It would be my pleasure," he replied, then escorted her onto the dance floor.

With Gorev glaring in her direction, Christine embraced Kalinin in a closed instead of semi-closed position, pulling him close so he could feel the curves of her body during the changes and turns. The music began, and during a spin turn, she caught fury on Gorev's face.

Christine smiled and pulled Kalinin even closer.

24

USS *MICHIGAN*

Lieutenant Chris Shroyer kept his eye pressed to the periscope as Israel's coast slid by to starboard, searching for surface ships on the horizon or for approaching air contacts. Shroyer, as well as Murray Wilson, who was seated in the Captain's chair on the Conn, listened intently to the speaker connected to the sensor atop the periscope as it emitted a constant buzz of activity, the beeps and chirps reporting a plethora of radar transmissions. Fortunately, none had threat parameters; all were navigation radars from merchant ships transiting the Eastern Mediterranean Sea.

Yesterday afternoon, *Michigan* completed an uneventful journey through the Suez Canal and headed toward the northeast corner of the Mediterranean, submerging as soon as the water was deep enough. Before submerging, the last intelligence message they'd received reported that several Russian surface combatants and diesel submarines had pulled into Latakia, Syria, to replenish food and fuel, while the battle cruiser *Pyotr Velikiy* and the Northern Fleet's nuclear-powered submarines remained at sea with their aircraft carrier, *Admiral Kuznetsov*. The Russian carrier and battle cruiser were to the west of *Michigan*'s assigned waterspace, although there was no telling where the Russian submarines were.

A satellite navigation position for *Michigan*'s inertial navigators had already been received, and the radioman's report indicated their objectives at periscope depth had been achieved.

"Conn, Radio. Download complete."

Lieutenant Shroyer acknowledged and after the requisite orders, *Michigan* tilted downward. As the submarine leveled off at two hundred feet, a radioman delivered the message board to the submarine's Captain. Wilson flipped through the messages, reading the latest intel report on the Russian Northern Fleet, followed by a new operational order for *Michigan*. As he read through the OPORD, he noted the unusual nature of the mission, as well as the target: *Marshal Ustinov*, the newest cruiser in the Russian Northern Fleet.

Wilson called the Messenger. "Have Commander McNeil and the XO report to Control."

The Messenger departed and a moment later, *Michigan*'s Executive Officer, Lieutenant Commander Dave Beasley, arrived. Wilson handed Beasley the message board, with the OPORD on top. After he read the message, Beasley looked up. "*Marshal Ustinov?* In port?"

Wilson nodded and was about to expound when Commander John McNeil, head of the SEAL detachment aboard, arrived. Beasley handed him the message, which McNeil quickly read.

"When can you be in position?" McNeil asked. "We'll need to be in range of our SDV."

Wilson evaluated the time required to transit within range of the SEALs' mini-sub. "We'll arrive shortly after midnight. When will you be ready to brief?"

McNeil replied, "It's a pretty standard mission. Give me two hours to have the plan tweaked for this scenario and personnel selected for the mission."

"Let's brief at zero-nine-hundred," Wilson said, "in the Battle Management Center."

Turning to his XO, he directed, "Have one of the officers prepare a pro report on *Marshal Ustinov*."

25

USS *MICHIGAN*

Two hours later, Wilson entered *Michigan*'s Battle Management Center, located aft of the Control Room. The former Navigation Center had been transformed during *Michigan*'s conversion from ballistic to guided missile submarine, and was now crammed with twenty-five consoles, each with two color displays, one atop the other. Thirteen consoles were on the port side of the ship, running fore to aft with an aisle between them, while the other twelve consoles were on the starboard side, arranged in four rows facing aft. Mounted on the aft bulkhead were two sixty-inch plasma screens, with a third sixty-inch display on the forward bulkhead.

Six Michigan crew members and five SEALs were already present, occupying consoles on the starboard side: *Michigan*'s Executive Officer, four department heads, and Lieutenant Jayne Stucker, along with Commander McNeil and four other SEALs. At the front of the Battle Management Center, Lieutenant Jake Harrison stood beside one of the sixty-inch plasma displays hanging on the bulkhead. Wilson settled into the lone vacant console, beside McNeil, and the senior SEAL nodded in Harrison's direction.

Lieutenant Harrison kicked off the mission brief, be-

ginning with a summary of the information provided
in *Michigan*'s message.

"As you're aware, *Michigan* has been tasked with
sinking the Russian cruiser *Marshal Ustinov*, which is
docked in Latakia. The Navigator will brief the submarine's transit to within range of our SDV, Lieutenant
Stucker will brief us on the target, and I'll add the pertinent mission details."

First up was the submarine's Navigator, Lieutenant
Charlie Eaton, with Lieutenant Stucker controlling the
bulkhead display from her console. A nautical chart of
the Eastern Mediterranean appeared, zooming in on
Latakia. Lieutenant Eaton's brief was short and uneventful: Latakia jutted slightly into the Mediterranean Sea,
with no geographic issues posing a problem during the
submarine's transit to within launch range of the SDV.
Eaton shifted to a satellite image of Latakia, showing
the arrangement of the piers and wharves at the seaport,
as well as the location of *Marshal Ustinov*.

Next up was Lieutenant Jayne Stucker, who had been
assigned the pro report on *Marshal Ustinov*. A sche-
matic of the Russian ship appeared on the bulkhead
display beside her.

"The target is *Marshal Ustinov*, a Slava class cruiser.
Three have been completed, with one assigned to each
Russian fleet except the Baltic. She's heavily armed,
carrying sixteen surface-to-surface and one hundred
four surface-to-air missiles, along with six close-in
weapon systems like our Navy's Phalanx Gatling gun.
The cruiser also has significant anti-submarine warfare
capabilities, with one hundred ninety-two depth charges,
an anti-submarine helicopter, and ten torpedo tubes
capable of launching Type 53 torpedoes.

"*Marshal Ustinov* should be easy to distinguish underwater. She's six hundred eleven feet long at the waterline, with a twin shaft/single rudder design, and the

bulbous sonar dome on the bow will easily distinguish it as a combatant as opposed to a merchant ship. Additionally, she'll have her hull number painted on the side.

"Any questions, sir?" Stucker aimed her question at Captain Wilson and Commander McNeil. None were forthcoming, and Stucker took her seat while Lieutenant Harrison continued the brief.

"*Michigan* is configured differently for this deployment, carrying only one SDV. However, one SDV is sufficient for this mission. Once within launch range, Petty Officer Maydwell and I will transport a limpet mine in the back seat of the SDV, then attach it to the hull of *Marshal Ustinov* behind the sonar array. The explosion should damage the sonar dome and flood the forward compartments."

After a few questions and a short discussion, the mission brief concluded.

McNeil asked, "When will *Michigan* be in position?"

Wilson turned to the Nav, who replied, "We'll be in launch range by zero-two-hundred."

26

MEDITERRANEAN SEA

Lieutenant Jake Harrison, outfitted in a dive suit and accompanied by Petty Officer First Class Rob Maydwell, stepped through the circular hatch in the side of Missile Tube One. Maydwell shut the hatch with a faint clank and spun the handle, engaging the hatch lugs, sealing the two men inside the seven-foot-diameter missile tube. Harrison climbed a steel ladder up two levels as Maydwell followed, entering the Dry Deck Shelter, bathed in diffuse red light.

The Dry Deck Shelter was a conglomeration of three separate chambers: a spherical hyperbaric chamber at the forward end to treat injured divers, a spherical transfer trunk in the middle, which Harrison and Maydwell had entered, and a long cylindrical hangar section containing the SEAL Delivery Vehicle, a black mini-sub resembling a fat torpedo—twenty-two feet long by six feet in diameter. The hangar was divided into two sections by a Plexiglas shield dropping halfway down from the top of the hangar, with the SDV on one side and controls for operating the hangar on the other side.

Harrison stepped into the hangar, which was manned by five Navy divers: one on the forward side of the Plexiglas shield to operate the controls, and the other four

divers in scuba gear on the other side. Maydwell sealed
the hatch behind him, then the two SEALs ducked
under the Plexiglas shield, stopping at the forward end
of the SDV, which was loaded nose first into the Dry
Deck Shelter. The SDV had two seating areas, one in
front of the other, each capable of carrying two persons,
with the back seat containing a limpet mine.

Lieutenant Harrison helped Maydwell into a re-
breather, a closed-circuit breathing apparatus that produced no bubbles, reducing the probability their
presence in the Syrian port would be detected, and Maydwell returned the favor. After donning their fins, the
two men climbed into the front seat of the SDV. Harrison manipulated the controls and a contour of the
Syrian coast appeared on the navigation display. They
were ten miles from shore.

Harrison put his face mask on, as did Maydwell, then
rendered the *okay* hand signal to the diver on the other
side of the Plexiglas shield. Water surged into the hangar, gushing up from vents beneath them. The DDS was
soon flooded except for a pocket of air on the other side
of the Plexiglas shield, where the Navy diver operated
the Dry Deck Shelter. There was a faint rumbling as the
circular hatch at the end of the shelter opened, and two
divers on each side of the SDV glided toward the chamber opening with a kick of their fins.

The divers pulled rails out onto the submarine's
missile deck, and the SDV was extracted from the hangar. Harrison manipulated the controls and the SDV's
propeller started spinning. The submersible rose slowly,
then moved forward, passing above the Dry Deck Shelter
and along the starboard side of Michigan's sail, cruising over the submarine's bow into the dark water ahead.

An hour later, Harrison eased back on the throttles and
the mini-sub slowed. In the distance, faint white lights

appeared, wavering on the water's surface. As the SDV continued onward, the ghostly images of barnacle-encrusted ship hulls drifted toward them.

Harrison angled the SDV to the right, reaching the end of the wharves at Latakia, then turned left and traveled slowly past each ship, searching for the target of interest. *Marshal Ustinov* should be the thirteenth ship along the wharf. Per Stucker's pro report, Harrison kept an eye out for a ship with a twin shaft/single rudder design and a sonar dome on the bow.

The thirteenth ship fit the description as expected, but Harrison required one additional piece of information. He adjusted the SDV controls and the mini-sub descended toward the seafloor, coming to rest on the sandy bottom. After pulling himself from the SDV, he surged upward, heading toward the ship's bow. Upon reaching the surface, he read the hull number painted on the side of the ship.

Marshal Ustinov.

Harrison descended to the SDV, where he helped Petty Officer Maydwell lift the limpet mine from the back seat. The explosive device was designed with buoyancy chambers so it was only slightly negatively buoyant, but they had selected the largest limpet mine for this mission, which was awkward to carry alone. The two men swam toward the bow of *Marshal Ustinov*, slowing as they approached the cruiser's sonar dome. The SEALs placed the mine gently against the hull, where its magnetic base attached suddenly with a faint clank.

Maydwell set the fuse timer for two hours, allowing enough time for the two SEALs to return to *Michigan*. Harrison checked his watch, then activated the timer, and the two men returned to their mini-sub on the seafloor. A minute later, the SDV was headed away from the Syrian seaport. Behind them, the shadowy hull of *Marshal Ustinov* faded into the murky water.

An hour later, as Harrison headed toward the rendezvous coordinates, *Michigan* materialized from the darkness. Harrison slowed the SDV and adjusted its course to approach from astern, coasting toward the two Dry Deck Shelters. The SDV slowed to a hover behind the starboard chamber, sinking until it came to rest with a gentle bump on the rails extended onto the missile deck. Two divers appeared on each side of the submersible, latching it to the rails as Harrison and Maydwell pulled themselves from the vehicle. A minute later, with the SDV retracted inside the Dry Deck Shelter, the chamber door shut with a gentle thud.

It wasn't long before the water was drained into one of *Michigan*'s variable ballast tanks and the two SEALs exited the Dry Deck Shelter, descending into Missile Tube One. After stripping their gear and warming up under the hot showers inside the tube, they dressed and headed to the submarine's Battle Management Center, where Harrison debriefed Commander McNeil. Everything had gone according to plan.

Lieutenant Harrison stepped into the Control Room, which was rigged for black. The submarine was at periscope depth at night, with Control illuminated only by the faint indications on the Ballast and Ship Control Panels. Lieutenant Chris Shroyer was the Officer of the Deck again, circling on the periscope, his face pressed to the eyepiece. On the Perivis display, Harrison watched as the scope turned; there was nothing but darkness except for a few tiny white lights in the distance moving from right to left as the periscope rotated.

Harrison had reported the time the limpet mine fuse had been activated, which was relayed to Captain Wilson, who had decided to remain at periscope depth. As the time approached, he heard the Captain's voice, and

Harrison spotted Wilson's faint outline in the Captain's chair.

"Officer of the Deck, expose nine feet of scope."

Lieutenant Shroyer acknowledged and gave the requisite order, and the Diving Officer of the Watch made the necessary adjustments. *Michigan* rose slowly upward, pushing the top of its sail to within a few feet of the water's surface.

Harrison sensed an individual in Control moving toward him, and it took only a few seconds to realize the five-foot-five-inch-tall officer stopping beside him was Lieutenant Jayne Stucker, observing in the Control Room, as was Harrison. He leaned in her direction.

"Why nine feet of scope?" he asked quietly.

Stucker replied softly, "The earth is round, you know." A smile flashed across her face in the semidarkness as she poked fun at the stereotypical Special Forces image: all brawn and no brain. Harrison returned the smile. Although the young Lieutenant was barely half Christine O'Connor's age, there was something about Stucker that reminded him of his former fiancée.

As he wondered what Christine was up to, Stucker elaborated. "Due to the curvature of the earth, how far you can see is determined by your height of eye. Captain Wilson ordered *Michigan* as close to the surface as possible, raising the scope optics. Depending on what type of fireworks your limpet mine produces, we might see something."

"Got it," Harrison said. His eyes shifted to the red digital clock in the Control Room. Five more minutes.

The minutes passed slowly, and as the clock approached the designated time, Lieutenant Shroyer paused his circular rotations and steadied the periscope on the bearing to Latakia. Harrison's eyes shifted back to the Perivis display.

The time counted down, reaching the two-hour point,

but there was no visible indication the mine had detonated. Harrison sensed the tension in the Control Room as the Captain and his crew tried to assess whether their mission was a success.

A report over the speakers broke the silence in Control. "Conn, Sonar. Detect explosion on the spherical array, bearing zero-nine-five. Correlates to Latakia."

Harrison felt the tension dissipate. The limpet mine had probably just blown a hole in the bottom of the ship and hadn't detonated any munitions aboard. They'd have to wait until morning, when satellite reconnaissance was received, combined with local HUMINT—human intelligence—to fully assess mission success.

Captain Wilson ordered his Officer of the Deck, "Come down to two hundred feet, course two-zero-zero, speed standard."

It was time to vacate the area.

27

MOSCOW

Defense Minister Boris Chernov eased into a chair in the small conference room in the Kremlin Senate, wondering if the unexpected news he'd deliver would help or hurt his attempt to persuade President Kalinin. Gathered around the conference table this morning were the same men who had been present during the initial briefing. Kalinin was seated at the head of the table, and to his right sat SVR Director Gorev, Chernov, and Foreign Minister Lavrov. On the other side of the table were four military officers: Chief of the General Staff General Sergei Andropov and the commanders of the Russian Ground Forces, Aerospace Forces, and Navy.

Chernov delivered the awaited update. "All essential elements have been arranged, Mr. President. The preliminary ground units are en route to Kaliningrad Oblast, an agreement has been forged with President Lukashenko in Belarus, and arrangements have been made in Ukraine. We are confident we'll achieve the primary objectives."

"And the insurance?" Kalinin asked.

Chernov answered, "Iran has agreed to their part, which is the one essential agreement we required. India hasn't replied, although we expect a response by Victory

Day. China also has not yet committed, and we don't have a timeline on their decision. We feel good about India, but less certain about China."

Kalinin replied, "I will not proceed based on good feelings."

"India and China aren't required," Chernov reminded Kalinin. "If either one commits, however, our position will be ironclad. America will be paralyzed."

"And if neither commits"—Kalinin's eyes swept the military officers at the conference table—"can we keep the United States from interfering?"

General Andropov answered, "Without India and China, we cannot prevent the United States from intervening. However, if they do, we will defeat them."

Kalinin shifted his gaze to Admiral Lipovsky, Commander-in-Chief of the Russian Navy, who would shoulder the burden of their insurance plan. "Admiral?"

Lipovsky replied, "The Northern and Pacific Fleets are underway and will reach their objectives at the prescribed time. However . . ." Lipovsky glanced at Defense Minister Chernov. "An issue has arisen."

Kalinin turned to Chernov, who provided the details. "A few hours ago, there was an explosion aboard *Marshal Ustinov*. Her forward compartments are flooded, sonar is out of commission, and there is significant damage to her tactical systems."

"What was the cause of the explosion?"

"We don't know yet. The explosion didn't originate from ordnance aboard the cruiser, so we are unsure what detonated. It's possible a mine was attached to the ship's hull, but there are very few entities with that ability, and even fewer with the inclination."

"What's the impact?" Kalinin directed his question at Admiral Lipovsky.

"It's a significant blow," Lipovsky answered, "but not fatal. *Marshal Ustinov* is the third most potent combatant in the Northern Fleet, and will be out of action for several months. However, her loss can be compensated for with additional land-based missile batteries."

Kalinin turned to Colonel General Viktor Glukov, Commander-in-Chief of the Russian Ground Forces.

"We have the assets," he said.

There was a knock on the conference room door, and the conversation paused as Kalinin responded, "Enter."

The door opened, revealing Kalinin's executive assistant. "I apologize for interrupting, Mr. President, but I thought you'd want to take this call."

"Who is it?"

"The American president."

Kalinin raised an eyebrow as he said, "Put him on speaker."

The assistant tapped the necessary buttons on the conference room phone, then said, "Mr. President, can you hear me?"

"Loud and clear," was the response.

The assistant left the conference room, and as the door shut, Kalinin said, "This is President Kalinin."

After the requisite pleasantries were exchanged, the American president broached the reason for the call. "I have bad news to share with you, Yuri. It turns out we've had a mishap similar to your submarine that accidentally attacked *Roosevelt*. We were executing a training mission with one of our SEAL teams in the Mediterranean, and they accidentally attached real ordnance, instead of a dummy mine, to the hull of *Marshal Ustinov*. You have my sincerest apology for this mishap, and we're launching an investigation immediately. Once we determine the root cause, we'll put additional safeguards in place to ensure this doesn't happen again."

There was silence in the conference room as all eyes turned to Kalinin, waiting for his response. Chernov noted the heat rising in Kalinin's face as he processed what the United States had done. Finally, Kalinin spoke, his words failing to match the anger on his face.

"Thank you for the call. It is unfortunate, but these things happen. I hope both countries get to the root cause of each incident to ensure future mishaps do not occur."

"I agree wholeheartedly, Yuri. We'll keep you apprised of what we learn."

After the call ended, Kalinin turned toward Chernov. "It turns out the Americans aren't as spineless as you predicted."

Chernov shifted uncomfortably in his seat before replying, "I admit their response is unexpected, but my overall assessment is unchanged. Attaching a mine to a ship is one thing. Committing their entire military to a conflict is another. Once everything has been arranged, they will not engage."

There was silence again as Kalinin evaluated whether to proceed with the plan. Chernov sensed Kalinin wasn't convinced their plan was ultimately in their country's best interest, and the Russian president's next words confirmed his assessment.

"Initiate the SVR operation in Ukraine and mobilize all required military units. However, do not proceed further until I approve."

28

USS *MICHIGAN*

Lieutenant Jayne Stucker turned slowly on the periscope as the guided missile submarine cruised just beneath the surface of the Mediterranean Sea. It was late afternoon and her watch as Officer of the Deck was drawing to a close. Stucker couldn't have been more thankful, after going round and round on the periscope for almost six hours straight, aside from an occasional break by a fire control technician.

After departing the vicinity of Latakia the previous night, *Michigan* had taken station in the Eastern Mediterranean in the gap between Syria and Cyprus, awaiting further orders. Those orders arrived this morning, and *Michigan* had crept closer to Latakia, where they would await the departure of the Russian warships, then shadow them as they rejoined the Russian combatants at sea.

When Stucker shifted to a high-power scan of the quadrant in Latakia's direction, a new object appeared on the horizon—the distinctive superstructure of a modern warship: gray steel bedecked with a plethora of navigation and tactical radar antennas. The entire ship wasn't yet visible, as it was still *hull-down*, the hull of the ship blocked from view due to the curvature of the earth, but there was no doubt as to the contact type.

Stucker called out to the microphone in the overhead as she circled on the periscope. "Sonar, Conn. Hold a new contact, designated Victor five-seven, classified warship, outbound from Latakia on a bearing of zero-four-five. Report any contact on that bearing."

"Conn, Sonar. Aye, wait," was the response from the Sonar Supervisor. Not long thereafter, he reported, "Conn, Sonar. Hold a new contact, designated Sierra three-two, bearing zero-four-five, classified warship with twin four-bladed screws."

"Conn, Sonar. Aye," Stucker replied. "All stations, Conn. Correlate Victor five-seven and Sierra three-two as Master one. Track Master one."

With her eye still to the periscope, Stucker pressed the button on the communication panel for the Captain's stateroom and retrieved the microphone, then informed *Michigan*'s Commanding Officer of the new contact. Wilson entered the Control Room a moment later, his arrival announced by the Quartermaster: "Captain in Control."

Wilson stepped onto the Conn. "Let me take a look."

Stucker swiveled the periscope to a bearing of zero-four-five, then stepped back as Wilson placed his face against the eyepiece. After examining Master one, he handed the periscope back to Stucker, who continued her circular sweeps.

"Take an observation of Master one," Wilson ordered.

Stucker repeated back the order, then hesitated. Determining a contact's bearing was easy, but range was another matter. To determine the range, she needed to know the contact's masthead height. To determine that, she needed to classify the contact. Submarine officers memorized surface ship silhouettes—their superstructure design, antenna placement, and weapon launcher arrangement—but it was sometimes difficult to distinguish between the various classes. Sonar would often help, classifying surface ships based on their screw configuration, but the Russian ubiquitous twin four-bladed screws on this contact provided little insight. Wilson had most likely classified the Russian warship during his brief look, but Stucker wasn't sure.

Her hesitation conveyed her uncertainty, and Wilson gave her a clue. "If I told you Master one carries eight Sunburn missiles and two Shtil missile systems, what ship class would you be looking at?"

Stucker stopped on the contact during her next revolution, shifted to high power, and activated the doubler. Based on the ship configuration and armed with Wilson's critical data, she now knew what she was looking at.

"It's a Sovremenny class destroyer."

"Correct," Wilson replied.

Stucker called out, "Prepare for observation, Master one, Number Two scope. Use a masthead height of one-two-zero feet."

The Fire Control Technician of the Watch (FTOW), seated at one of the combat control consoles, reconfigured his displays, then replied, "Ready."

Stucker tweaked the periscope to the left, centering the crosshairs on the target, then pressed the red button on the periscope handle, sending the bearing to combat control. "Bearing, mark."

"Bearing zero-four-five," the FTOW called out as an image of the contact appeared on his console. Using the dual trackballs, he outlined the length and height of the contact, then reported, "Range, one-two-thousand yards."

Stucker called out, "Angle on the bow, starboard thirty."

The FTOW called out, "Matches," indicating Stucker's estimate of the contact's course matched what fire control had calculated. They now knew its range and course, and with another observation in a few minutes, they'd nail down the contact's speed.

Wilson settled into the Captain's chair on the Conn, and as Stucker waited a few minutes for another observation of Master one, another gray superstructure appeared on the horizon, and a moment later a third. As Wilson monitored the situation on the Perivis display, it didn't take long to conclude what was occurring. The Russian warships were sortieing from Latakia. However, they were headed in an unexpected direction.

Captain Wilson had positioned USS *Michigan* west of Latakia, planning to fall in behind the departing Russian warships as they headed northwest, around Cyprus, rejoining the rest of the Russian Northern Fleet as it headed toward the Black Sea. Instead, they were headed southwest.

Turning to Stucker, Wilson ordered, "Station the Fire Control Tracking Party. Rig ship for Ultra-Quiet."

Stucker relayed the orders to the Chief of the Watch, and the announcements went over the shipwide 1-MC announcing system. Personnel streamed into the Control Room, and several minutes later, every console was manned and a new Officer of the Deck, Lieutenant Charlie Eaton—the ship's Navigator and the Battle Stations Torpedo Officer of the Deck—was on the Conn.

"I am ready to relieve you," Eaton announced.

As the two officers completed their relief, Stucker's thoughts went to the Russian warships headed southwest. *Where the heck are they going?*

29

ZAPORIZHIA, UKRAINE

From across the crowded cobblestone plaza, Randy Guimond peered through the open window of the darkened fifth-story apartment, studying the temporary four-foot-tall wooden platform, its sides draped in white-, blue-, and red-striped bunting that matched the colors of the Russian Federation flag. Although the crowd had thickened in anticipation of tonight's speeches, the platform, with a podium placed near the front, remained empty. Guimond checked his watch; another five minutes before Alex Rudenko and his associates took the stage.

It was only a few days ago when Guimond met with Rudenko in the private room at the back of the Ukrainian-cuisine restaurant Korchma. Rudenko was a leading member of Ukraine's Opposition Bloc, an amalgamation of six political parties opposing Ukraine's attempt to join NATO, preferring a pro-Russian, or at least neutral, stance. Their position had strong support here in the Zaporizhia Oblast, where twenty-five percent of the residents were ethnic Russians and seventy percent of the population spoke Russian.

During Ukraine's recent Euromaidan revolution, President Viktor Yanukovych's Russian-leaning administration had been replaced with a pro-Western government. Public sentiment had been sharply divided, with the Donbass—the oblasts of Donetsk and Luhansk—declaring their independence from Ukraine. A full-fledged civil war erupted between the separatists and the Ukrainian government, with the Donbass separatists supported discreetly by Russian troops and equipment.

Many in Zaporizhia also favored independence from Ukraine or outright assimilation into Russia, but the oblast remained part of Ukraine. With Donbass to the north and Crimea, already annexed by Russia, to the south, Zaporizhia would be the next domino to fall. All it needed was a nudge. As Rudenko and his associates climbed onto the stage, Guimond raised his rifle to his shoulder and placed his eye to the scope.

Guimond had chosen the apartment carefully, five stories up to provide a clear view of the participants on the platform, along with a short trek down a nearby stairwell to a car behind the building. Also carefully selected was the Ukrainian-made Zbroyar Z-008 Tactical Pro sniper rifle in his hands, outfitted with a scope and five-round box magazine. Five rounds weren't many, but would be sufficient for tonight's festivities. Guimond was wearing gloves, so his fingerprints wouldn't be added to those of the Ukrainian national who had unwittingly sold the rifle to an SVR agent.

Rudenko moved forward to the podium, flanked by two men on one side and a man and woman on the other. The five men and women joined hands and raised them in unity, drawing cheers from the crowd. After releasing hands, Rudenko greeted the gathering throng, his voice booming from speakers beside the podium. Guimond listened as Rudenko's speech progressed through the expected tenets, keeping the scope's crosshairs centered on Rudenko's head.

As Rudenko reached the climax of his speech, advocating for Zaporizhia's succession from Ukraine, Guimond adjusted his aim, down and to the right, stopping on Rudenko's left shoulder. He had told Rudenko he wouldn't be killed, but failed to mention he'd be shot.

Guimond pulled the trigger, moving to his next target as Rudenko lurched backward. Two quick squeezes and the men to the right dropped onto the podium. Guimond swung left, where the third man and the woman were scrambling toward the podium steps. Another squeeze and a round hit the woman in the side of her head, sending her tumbling down the steps. The final man dove off the side of the podium onto the cobblestone plaza, but not before Guimond put a bullet into his thigh.

As the crowd scattered in every direction, Guimond examined the carnage through his scope: three dead and two wounded politicians. No one would be suspicious of Rudenko. Guimond pushed away from the window and headed toward the door, leaving the rifle and its fingerprints behind.

30

ZAPORIZHIA, UKRAINE

Randy Guimond pulled the curtain back from the window of his room in Hotel Intourist, not far from the apartment he had occupied the previous day. His eyes scanned the crowd gathering in Central Square, site of the murder of three pro-Russian politicians last night. As expected, the crowd was largely ethnic Russian, demanding the government hunt down the assassin and protect the Russian minority from pro-Western radicals. The platform erected for last night's event still stood at one end of the square, its wood floor stained with the blood of the fallen.

A half-dozen men and women had taken possession of the stage, taking turns with the microphone, preaching to the growing crowd, while off to the sides of the square, all the major news organizations were covering the event, their cameras rolling. Antigovernment demonstrations and murder, Guimond mused, made for excellent television ratings.

Guimond leaned forward, obtaining a better view of the square and the regional administration building across Sobornyi Avenue from the square. A few years earlier, Central Square had been the site of Euromaidan protests, leading to the occupation of the government building by four thousand pro-Western demonstrators. However, the shoe was on the other foot this time, with the protesters being predominately pro-Russian. Last night's attack on Russian sympathizers in Zaporizhia hadn't been the first, but this time the pro-Western sympathizers had gone too far. The pending arrest of the radical tied to the rifle's fingerprints would only add fuel to the fire. For now, however, Guimond added fuel of his own.

Guimond watched several dozen men work their way through the crowd. They were *titushky*, mercenary agents who supported the Ukrainian police during President Yanukovych's administration, who were now in desperate need of a paycheck, one Guimond had arranged. However, their goal for this outing had been reversed: rather than intimidate and disperse demonstrators opposing the government, their task today was to reinforce and agitate the crowd.

In response to the growing mass of people in Central Square, city officials were taking measures to ensure the regional administration building wasn't overrun again. Zaporizhia's police force, its members wearing riot gear and holding clear full-body shields, assembled in front of the government building, forming two solid lines. With the help of the *titushky*, however, this only served to agitate the crowd, drawing their attention to the government building, providing a focus for their frustration.

Off to the side, the crowd parted as a man, his left arm in a sling, worked his way to the platform. Guimond cracked open the window as Alex Rudenko, one of the two survivors of last night's savage attack, stepped onto the stage. Taking the microphone in his good hand, he addressed the crowd, and not long into his speech, he pointed out how the occupation of the administration building during Euromaidan had helped pro-Western demonstrators force the government of Zaporizhia to side with western Ukraine instead of its neighboring oblasts to the north. They should seize the building and not leave until Zaporizhia declared its independence. The crowd began moving toward the building, spilling across Sobornyi Avenue.

An additional squad of Ukrainian police, similarly dressed in riot gear, joined the formation, reinforcing the two lines against the burgeoning crowd of protesters already pushing against the wall of police. What the men and women below didn't know, however, was that the new squad of police were also *titushky*, hired for a much different purpose from that of those in the crowd.

Rudenko's voice boomed across the square, working the crowd into a frenzy, and the mass of demonstrators surged against the long blue line, attempting to break through to the government building.

A shot rang out and a protester in front of the police fell to the ground. The crowd simultaneously broke in two directions, some fleeing from the police while others charged the line. Additional shots were fired and another dozen protesters collapsed onto the ground. There was pandemonium in the street as the spectators scattered, with Ukrainian police continuing to gun down the protesters. All captured on camera.

Guimond released the curtain, letting it drift across the window.

31

MOSCOW

It was 5 p.m. when Christine O'Connor's limousine pulled up to the century-old Hotel National, only a stone's throw away from the Kremlin, with her hotel room offering a stunning view of the five palaces and four cathedrals enclosed within the Kremlin walls. After a hard day's work negotiating the finer details of the follow-on treaty to New START, Christine stepped from the limo, bidding farewell to her translator. As she entered the hotel lobby, she noticed crowds gathered around the television monitors. She stopped and watched a video of protesters being gunned down in a city square, followed by interviews of injured and bloodied victims. Christine stopped by the hotel concierge, asking him what was going on.

The concierge explained what had occurred in the Zaporizhia Oblast of Ukraine, situated just below the Donbass. Tensions in the oblast had run high since Euromaidan, with the population split between pro-Western and pro-Russian sympathizers, and public demonstrations had sometimes turned violent. However, nothing like this had occurred before—government forces gunning down pro-Russian protesters.

Christine thanked the concierge and was about to

head to her hotel room when Russian President Yuri Kalinin appeared on the TV screens. He was giving a press conference, camera bulbs flashing, as he stood behind a podium emblazoned with the Russian Federation seal. Christine leaned toward the concierge, asking him to translate as Kalinin spoke.

President Kalinin was furious, the concierge explained, due to yet another case of ethnic Russians being persecuted by the new Ukrainian government. Russia had a responsibility, Kalinin proclaimed, to ensure the safety of all Russians, even those beyond its borders, and he would evaluate options on how to respond to Ukraine's aggression. When a reporter asked if the options included the use of military force, Kalinin stated all options were on the table, and he'd already given the order to mobilize military units in western Russia.

Kalinin stepped away from the podium, and the TV shifted to talking heads in news studios, speculating on what Russia's response might be.

Christine thanked the concierge for the translation, her mind churning as she headed toward her room. Kalinin was rattling his saber, but whether he intended to use it, she couldn't predict, nor could she predict NATO's and the United States' response. Ukraine wasn't a member of NATO, and as such, the United States had no obligation to respond if Russia invaded. However, all of Western Europe, as well as the United States, would have to decide whether to come to Ukraine's assistance.

With the prospect of Russia going to war with Ukraine, her thoughts shifted to her last trip to China, when she'd been detained in the Great Hall of the People at the start of China's war with the United States. After the unpleasant experience, the last thing she wanted was to get stuck in Russia during a conflict that might draw in the United States.

Christine decided she would end the second round of

nuclear weapons negotiations, coming up with an excuse to cut her trip short, then continue discussions once things settled down. She pulled her phone from her purse and dialed the U.S. embassy in Moscow, informing them of her change in plans. She'd be departing Russia as soon as transport was arranged.

32

KAMENNYI LOG, BELARUS

Major General Vitaly Vasiliev, head of the 448th Missile Brigade, peered through the passenger-side window of his green GAZ Tigr all-terrain infantry vehicle at the passing Belarusian countryside. Behind him, stretched out on highway E28, was a convoy of Iskander missile batteries headed toward Russia's Kaliningrad Oblast on the Baltic Sea. As Vasiliev's missile brigade headed toward Lithuania, through which they would transit to reach Kaliningrad, he reviewed the capabilities of his unit, wondering if it would soon be called into service.

The hypersonic Iskander missile, traveling at Mach 6 speed, could target weapon batteries, command posts, and communication nodes, and was accurate enough to engage individual tanks using a variety of targeting methods: satellite, aircraft, or even by scanning a photograph with GPS coordinates of the target. If the target moved, Iskander could be retargeted during flight. The Iskander was a lethal missile indeed, Vasiliev thought, with the ability to target frontline units as well as reinforcements traveling along the region's highways.

Vasiliev was jarred from his thoughts as his vehicle ground to a halt. Stretching out before him on the road to the border checkpoint were the units of the 53rd Anti-

Aircraft Rocket Brigade with its potent S-400 air defense system, and in front of them, on the road curving toward the west, were the rear elements of the 2nd Guards Motor Rifle Division, all stopped.

It wasn't long before Vasiliev's adjutant arrived, his Tigr pulling up alongside Vasiliev on the shoulder of the road. He stepped from the vehicle, saluting as he approached.

"I have bad news, General," he said. "Lithuania is refusing to let Russian military units transit through their country."

Vasiliev asked, "How much of a delay will there be?"

"No timeline has been provided. Only—*No transit allowed.*"

"What about Poland?" Vasiliev asked. They could retrace their steps a few kilometers, then head southwest into Poland, then north into Kaliningrad Oblast.

"Second Guards has already inquired. Poland is also refusing to allow transit."

Vasiliev nodded. Lithuania and Poland, acting in concert, were preventing the transfer of additional Russian forces into Kaliningrad. It was infuriating, although not completely unexpected. Vasiliev's eyes shifted to the 2nd Guards Motor Rifle Division ahead of them. It could easily force passage for the three Russian units through the border crossing, reaching Kaliningrad before Lithuanian forces could respond. Whether the mechanized division would soon be given orders to that effect, Vasiliev didn't know.

He tried to contain his anger. Russia was again subject to the decisions of others when it came to simple transit between two regions of its country. During the days of the Soviet Red Army, Lithuania and Poland wouldn't have dared prevent transit. After the dissolution of the Soviet Union and the weakening of Russia's military, the two countries had become emboldened.

With Russia's military on the resurgence, it was finally time, Vasiliev thought, to *adjust* Lithuania's and Poland's thought processes. In the meantime, however, he would await new orders.

33

WASHINGTON, D.C.

In the basement of the West Wing, the president of the United States entered the Situation Room and took his seat at the head of the rectangular table, his eyes sweeping over the four individuals already seated: Hardison and Colonel DuBose to his right, and SecDef McVeigh and SecState Cabral to his left. On the far wall, the video screen was energized, displaying a map of Europe.

The president turned to McVeigh. "What's the status?"

"Things are heating up," McVeigh answered. After describing President Kalinin's remarks, McVeigh followed up with an update on Russian military activities. He nodded toward the video display on the far wall, where Russia was divided into four colored regions.

"All units in three out of four Russian military districts have been ordered to full readiness. The Western and Southern Districts, which border Ukraine, along with the Central District, are mobilizing. However, no units have begun moving, except for a motorized rifle division and two missile brigades headed toward Russia's Kaliningrad Oblast. They've stopped at the Lithuanian border, with both Lithuania and Poland refusing to allow additional Russian military units into Kaliningrad

Oblast. Russian air assets haven't been redeployed, although it wouldn't take long to move them.

"On the naval front, the Black Sea Fleet, which has been dormant up to now, is getting under way, and Russia's Northern Fleet has begun moving again, with its ships departing Syria and rejoining the units at sea. However, the surprising news is that the Northern Fleet is headed to the Suez Canal, and not toward the Black Sea and Ukraine as expected."

The president raised an eyebrow. "Into the Pacific?"

"Yes, Mr. President. The Northern Fleet has requested priority passage through the canal when its ships arrive."

"So they're rendezvousing with their Pacific Fleet?"

"We believe so. Based on the transit speeds of both fleets, we expect them to join forces somewhere in the Indian Ocean."

"How do we plan to respond?"

"Regarding Ukraine," McVeigh answered, "the situation is muddy. Ukraine isn't a NATO member, and if Russia invades, we'll have a dilemma on our hands. NATO and the United States have no formal obligation to intervene on Ukraine's behalf, but it will be difficult to do nothing and let Russia invade a sovereign nation. All NATO units are being mobilized, although obtaining authorization to respond will be contentious; you're talking about a war between Russia and over twenty Western European nations. The conflict could expand across the continent.

"Regarding our Navy's response, Pacific Command plans to pull the *Reagan* strike group from China's coast and route them south at maximum speed to join the *Truman* strike group. With the Northern Fleet submarines joining those of Russia's Pacific, we'll need to strengthen our anti-submarine warfare screen, with both strike groups working together as a task force. Additionally, the two carrier strike groups on the West Coast are preparing to deploy, and will join the *Truman* and *Reagan* strike groups as soon as possible.

"The five fast attack submarines entering the Mediterranean have been given orders to follow the Northern Fleet into the Pacific, leaving *Michigan* as the sole submarine in the Med. Due to her arsenal of Tomahawk land attack missiles, she'll be routed into the Black Sea to assist if Russia invades Ukraine. However, we have one mission for her first."

McVeigh pointed the remote control at the video screen, and the image of Europe was replaced with a map of Egypt.

"Once we noted the Northern Fleet's transit toward the Suez Canal, we reviewed all Russian activity along the route and we detected a Russian Spetsnaz unit deploying inside Egypt a few days ago, some of them near the Suez Canal."

McVeigh pressed the remote again, and a dozen locations appeared throughout Egypt where the Russian Special Forces unit had been detected.

"We have no idea what they were up to; there's nothing of significance at these locations, mostly just vast stretches of sand. However, before we send five fast attacks through the canal, we're going to check things out. *Michigan* will send a SEAL team ashore to examine the nearest location, not far from the coast."

The president reflected for a moment, then ordered, "Keep the *Reagan* and *Truman* strike groups a safe distance from the Russian fleet. Things haven't blown up yet, and I don't want incidental contact to spark a conflict. Regarding Ukraine, mobilize all Army, Marine Corps, and Air Force assets."

"Yes, sir," McVeigh replied.

"Hopefully, this is just a false alarm," the president said. "Russia rattling its sword to obtain concessions from Ukraine."

As the president examined the four individuals around the table again, he was met with uncertainty in their eyes.

34

MOSCOW

VICTORY DAY

As the sun climbed into a cloudless sky, President Yuri Kalinin sat in the front row of a grandstand in Red Square, looking on in silence as troops in crisp formations, interspersed with Russia's most advanced military hardware, passed by. Flanking Kalinin were the leaders of thirty countries, joining Russia's celebration of the Soviet Union's victory over Germany in World War II. Behind Kalinin and occupying a prominent place in the grandstand were the surviving Red Army officers who had defeated the Wehrmacht.

Seventy-five years ago, the Soviet Union had bled for the West, and it was Russia, and not the United States, that had defeated Germany. In June 1944, as the Allies invaded Normandy, the German Army defended its Western Front with 66 divisions. At the same time, Germany deployed 150 divisions along the Eastern Front, opposing the Red Army's advance. Had Germany been able to transfer another 150 divisions to Normandy, or even a third of those, the Wehrmacht would have annihilated the Allied invaders.

Even with Germany opposing the Red Army with three-fourths of its military, it was the Soviet Union that pushed Germany back to its capital, taking Berlin and

Hitler's bunker, where the dictator committed suicide in the final hours of the conflict. The Soviet Union had bled for the West, its contribution to defeating Nazi Germany minimized by American historians.

The West's memory, in addition to being inaccurate, was short; they no longer held commemorations of their role during World War II. In the West, World War II was a distant memory, the sacrifices of its people nothing more now than a footnote in history books. In contrast, Russia held annual Victory Day parades and remembrance marches, keeping the memory of its sacrifices alive.

Russia would not forget.

As the last light of day faded on the horizon, Yuri Kalinin stood on a third-floor balcony of the Kremlin Senate, his hands on the cold granite railing. As his eyes moved over the city, they came to rest on Red Square, where the crowds were dwindling after the day's activities. It was there that he'd begun and ended the day's celebrations, beginning with the Victory Day parade and ending with the March of the Immortal Regiment, where Kalinin led the annual citizens' remembrance march through the city, leading a procession of over one million relatives and descendants of those who lost their lives in the Great Patriotic War.

The painful memories of the conflict weighed heavily on the Russian psyche, something the West seemed incapable of understanding. The United States, for example, extolled its Greatest Generation—those who fought in World War II—along with their enormous sacrifice: over four hundred thousand dead. A sacrifice that paled in comparison with the Soviet Union's: seven million military personnel killed, along with twenty million civilians as the German Army exterminated ethnic groups during their occupation and razed entire cities to the ground as they retreated.

Twenty-seven million.

And these were the casualties from just the last invasion by a Western European power. First the Poles in the seventeenth century, followed by Napoleon's army in the nineteenth century, with both armies sacking Moscow. The French Army had occupied the Kremlin Senate; Napoleon had stood on this very same balcony and watched Moscow burn.

Never again.

Russia would never again endure the genocide of its people or the destruction of its cities. Following World War II, the Soviet Union established a buffer zone of Eastern European governments friendly to the Soviet Union. The next time the West invaded Russia, there would be advance warning as troops moved through the Eastern European countries on Russia's border, and next time, the war would be fought on another country's soil. Unfortunately, the buffer zones to the west had eroded since the fall of the Soviet Union. The Baltic States had joined NATO, and now Ukraine, Russia's longtime ally, was turning to the West. It was time Russia rectified the situation, re-forming a buffer zone of friendly provinces to the west, even if that meant employing its military.

Kalinin looked to the side as Boris Chernov joined him on the balcony. Chernov stood beside him in silence for a moment before speaking.

"All preparations are complete," he said. "You must decide, Yuri."

Kalinin's eyes swept across Russia's capital again before coming to rest on Red Square, where the March of the Immortal Regiment ended.

Twenty-seven million dead.

Never again.

Kalinin turned to Chernov. "You may proceed."

35

WASHINGTON, D.C.

It was almost 10 p.m. when the president called it a day and ascended to the second floor of the White House, entering the presidential bedroom suite. The first lady was already in bed, with a book in her hands and her back propped up with three pillows. As she looked up to greet her husband, the phone on the nightstand rang, accompanied by the vibration of the cell phone in the president's suit jacket. Pulling the phone from its pocket, he examined the caller: SecDef McVeigh.

"Yes, Bob. What is it?"

"Russia has invaded Ukraine and Lithuania. Troops started pouring across the borders a few minutes ago."

The president absorbed the information and its implications, then replied, "Meet me in the Situation Room with the Joint Chiefs as soon as possible."

"How about midnight?" McVeigh asked.

"See you then."

As the president slid his cell phone back into his suit jacket, he met the concerned eyes of the first lady, who had placed her book on her lap. "What is it?" she asked.

As the clock struck midnight, the president entered the Situation Room in the basement of the West Wing, taking his seat at the head of the rectangular table. Members of his staff and cabinet were seated to his right and the Joint Chiefs to his left, with the Situation Room walls lined with additional military and civilian personnel. SecDef McVeigh, seated on the president's right, began the brief.

"We're still analyzing the data, Mr. President, bringing more satellites into play and querying local sources on the ground, but here's what we know. At four thirty a.m. local time, a Russian mechanized infantry division invaded Lithuania, and six mechanized infantry brigades invaded Ukraine. Another twenty-four brigades from Russia's Western, Southern, and Central Military Districts are racing toward Lithuania and Ukraine—six toward Lithuania and eighteen toward Ukraine.

"I'll discuss Lithuania first, because Russia's objective seems clearer. Satellite recon shows the Second Guards Motor Rifle Division taking defensive positions on the Polish border and along a parallel line fifty miles to the north."

"They're establishing a corridor into Kaliningrad Oblast?" the president asked. "What for?"

"Our best guess is that the Russians plan to permanently annex this region of Lithuania, removing the thorn in their side—having to request permission from a NATO country anytime they want to move military personnel or equipment between Kaliningrad Oblast and the rest of Russia. They'll still have to go through Belarus, but Belarus is a staunch Russian ally.

"Ukraine, on the other hand, is murkier. Russia is launching a broad assault across the entire length of Ukraine's eastern border. Whether the Russians intend to annex a portion of Ukraine or control the entire country is unclear. Once all twenty-four brigades reach Ukraine and Russia begins its push farther into the country, we'll get a better idea of their intentions.

"Which gets me to an important and perhaps critical flaw in Russia's plan. The invasion was sudden, without the usual buildup at the border before an invasion, which helps and hurts us. It hurts us because Russia got a head start on Ukraine and NATO. However, by not massing troops at the border ahead of time, their invasion is piecemeal, with only six brigades currently inside Ukraine. The lead units have seized the key transportation hubs just across the border and appear to be waiting for the remaining Russian units before beginning a coordinated push westward. This gives Ukraine a fighting chance; not to defeat Russia, but to hold out long enough for NATO to intercede should it choose to do so.

"This brings me to the crux of the issue," McVeigh said. "Lithuania and Ukraine cannot repel Russia without NATO assistance. Lithuania has only a few thousand combat troops, barely more than a brigade, compared to eight Russian brigades they'll be facing. Ukraine is in a much better position with twenty-two brigades, but their training and equipment is significantly inferior to Russia's. Still, there's hope they can hold off Russia long enough for NATO to provide assistance."

"What do we have at our disposal?" the president asked.

McVeigh answered, "For immediate response, there's NATO's Very High Readiness Joint Task Force, deployable within twenty-four hours. However, it's a single brigade of only five thousand troops. It's a component of the NATO Response Force, with another thirty-five thousand troops, deployable in five to seven days. But even if NATO agrees to assist Ukraine, forty thousand troops won't be enough. They'll buy time, but forcing Russia from Ukraine will require the mobilization of additional NATO troops; it could take weeks or even months before the troops and equipment arrive in Ukraine."

The president replied, "Let's cross each bridge when we get there. The priority right now is to obtain NATO authorization to assist Lithuania and Ukraine. If NATO doesn't agree to assist Ukraine, we'll build a coalition of our own."

"I take it your mind is already made up?" McVeigh asked. "We're going to help Ukraine, with or without NATO?"

"Damn right," the president replied. "There's no way we can stand by and do nothing. We took the Neville Chamberlain approach when Russia annexed Crimea, choosing appeasement rather than war, and it emboldened Russia. We have to draw the line somewhere, and this is it."

Turning to Dawn, the president asked his secretary of state, "How soon can we expect a NATO decision?"

Dawn replied, "An emergency meeting of the North Atlantic Council will occur within the hour, but there is zero chance the council representatives will have authorization to commit NATO to a full-blown war with Russia. That's going to take a meeting with the heads of state from all twenty-eight nations. The best we can hope for is that the council will order the mobilization of all NATO assets today, and the heads of state will meet tomorrow. I'll keep you informed as I learn more, but you should plan to travel to Brussels later today."

The president nodded his understanding, then wrapped up the meeting. "We've got a lot of work ahead of us, on both the diplomatic and military fronts. We'll sort out the details of our military response once the political landscape becomes clear."

36

CASTEAU, BELGIUM

Five levels underground in a hardened bunker, General Andy Wheeler stood at the back of the NATO command center, examining the video screens mounted on the front wall. Located just north of Mons, SHAPE—Supreme Headquarters Allied Powers Europe—was the headquarters of NATO's Allied Command Operations. As the commander of NATO's military force, General Wheeler was referred to as SACEUR, Supreme Allied Commander Europe.

The lighting in the command center was dim so personnel could more readily study the video screens, each displaying a different section of Europe. The maps were annotated with symbols of varying colors and designs, each representing a NATO, Ukrainian, or Russian combat unit—armor, mechanized infantry, artillery, and air defense, to name a few.

As the first day of Russia's invasions of Lithuania and Ukraine drew to a close, the fighting thus far had been sporadic. Lithuania was quiet, with the country's government wisely deciding it was futile to send its four thousand combat-ready troops against forty thousand Russians who had taken position along the fifty-mile-wide corridor on the country's southern border.

In Ukraine, fighting had been limited to Ukrainian units engaging the lead Russian brigades, which seemed content with consolidating their early gains into the country while they awaited additional Russian units. As night fell across the continent, Russia thus far had amassed fourteen brigades inside Ukraine, controlling the key transportation hubs along the eastern border. Another ten units were still en route, bringing Russian forces invading Ukraine to twenty-four brigades: five tank and nineteen mechanized infantry units. Ukrainian units were likewise rushing to the front, with all twenty-two brigades already across the Dnieper River and into the eastern third of Ukraine. The war thus far had been mostly a race to the start line.

By daybreak, the battle lines would be clearly formed and Wheeler was certain Russia's main offensive would begin. Whether Ukraine would withstand the assault long enough for NATO or a U.S.-led coalition to assist was unknown. A meeting of the North Atlantic Council, with all heads of state attending, had been scheduled for 8 a.m. the next morning, with most of the NATO heads of state already in Brussels and the last few on the way. If NATO was going to assist Ukraine, they needed to commit in the morning.

Wheeler examined a video screen at the front of the command center, displaying a map of Eastern Europe, studying the red symbols representing Russian combat units amassing in Lithuania and eastern Ukraine. He found it odd that Russia's two premier forces were missing from the map. Russia had several brigades of Spetsnaz scattered throughout their military and intelligence organizations, along with numerous airborne units, the most well-trained and -equipped units in the

Russian military aside from Spetsnaz. Airborne and Spetsnaz had been the first to be employed in recent Russian conflicts, including the wars in Chechnya and Georgia, but they were absent thus far from the current conflict.

Where the hell were they?

37

NOVAJA HUTA, BELARUS

As day transitioned to night, an orange-purple glow on the horizon greeted Belarusian Army Colonel Edward Aymar as he stood in the hatch of his T-72 main battle tank, idling at the edge of the forest only a kilometer from the Ukrainian border. He pulled the binoculars to his eyes and surveyed the countryside, the dense trees giving way in the dusk to rolling meadows blanketed by a layer of light evening fog. In the still air, his company of tanks produced a low rumble in the otherwise quiet forest.

Behind him, in the trees east of highway E95, were the other tanks and infantry fighting vehicles of the 120th Guards Mechanized Brigade, and behind them, also hidden in the dense forest, were another three brigades. To the southwest, the 6th Guards Mechanized Brigade would lead four brigades into Ukraine near Pustynky, while the 11th Guards Mechanized Brigade would lead another four brigades south from Rayffayzen.

Thirty hours ago, Aymar received orders from the Belarusian Northwestern Operational Command, sending his unit south toward the Ukrainian border. It didn't take much to discern the purpose of his deployment, nor was he surprised they had repositioned during the night under the cover of darkness, pulling off the highway into the forest just north of the Ukrainian border before daybreak. He was surprised, however, when the Belarusian units were augmented with six Russian Spetsnaz brigades, transiting into Belarus before their journey south. Russia wanted a quick and decisive victory.

As Colonel Aymar prepared to begin his unit's assault into Ukraine, he knew his men wouldn't get much sleep over the next few days. The encouragement he offered them at times like this echoed in his mind.

You'll sleep when you're dead.

As the last light of day faded to darkness, Aymar called down to his tank driver, ordering the 120th Guards Mechanized Brigade into motion. His tank pulled forward, followed by the others, emerging from the trees. Their objectives were far, making speed essential.

38

KIEV, UKRAINE

In the tail of the Ilyushin IL-76 jet aircraft, Sergeant First Class Roman Savvin sat in his webbed seat along the transport bulkhead, the last soldier in the 125-man detachment. Wearing full combat gear and two parachutes—a main on his back and a reserve strapped to his stomach—he waited patiently, taking comfort in the familiar vibration from the aircraft's four turbofan engines. Tonight, Savvin's aircraft was one of over one hundred IL-76s and a slew of other transports carrying Russia's VDV—Vozdushno-Desantnye Voyska—airborne troops and their equipment.

They had initially headed west over Belarus, with some aircraft carrying only troops, while others carried a small cadre of soldiers and the airborne units' armored vehicles. Unlike its Western airborne counterparts, which were essentially light infantry, the VDV was a fully mechanized infantry fighting force with significant firepower. Each unit was outfitted with a plethora of air-dropped armored vehicles: Typhoon armored personnel carriers, BMD infantry fighting vehicles, and self-propelled mortars, howitzers, anti-tank guns, and air defense missile systems. Compared to Western airborne troops, the Russian VDV was a heavily armed force.

The IL-76 banked to the left, beginning its journey south behind the Ukrainian front line. As the aircraft steadied on its new course, the Russian airborne motto echoed in Savvin's mind:

Nobody but us.

For the objective assigned to his unit tonight, the motto was apropos. A few minutes after turning south, Savvin felt the aircraft descending, and he knew it wouldn't be much longer. The light at the front of the aircraft fuselage still glowed red, and as he waited for it to turn yellow, his thoughts drifted to his joint training with American airborne troops several years earlier.

After the Cold War ended and during the brief period Russia and America embraced each other as friends, Savvin had trained for a short time with his American counterparts at Fort Benning, Georgia. He had memorized the American airborne cadences during their training, and although there were many variations of the C-130 cadence, one in particular tumbled through his mind as he prepared for tonight's jump:

Stand up, hook up, shuffle to the door.
Jump right out and count to four.
If my main don't open wide,
I've got a reserve by my side.
If that one should fail me too,
Look out below, 'cause I'm coming through. . . .

He remembered stopping by a training session at Fort Benning, where the instructor was explaining the aircraft exit procedure, which included the requirement to count to four—one thousand, two thousand . . . By the time you reached four, you should feel a tug on your harness as your main parachute deployed.

A trainee raised his hand. "What do you do if you reach four and don't feel a tug?"

The instructor replied with a scowl on his face, "Count to six, stupid."

The trainee raised his hand again, timidly, and asked, "What do you do if you reach six and don't feel a tug?"

He had apparently asked a sensible question this time, because the instructor answered, "Look up and check your main, 'cause you got a problem."

The Jump light at the front of the aircraft fuselage shifted from red to yellow. Savvin and the other men in his unit stood, hooked their parachute static lines to a cable in the overhead running the length of the fuselage, then turned aft, watching the aircrew open the cabin door. Less than a minute later, the light turned green and all 125 paratroopers moved toward the open door in unison, exiting at one-second intervals.

Upon reaching the end of the fuselage, Savvin turned toward the opening and, in one fluid motion, placed a hand on each side of the opening and launched himself from the aircraft. In a reflex action practiced hundreds of times, he tucked his chin against his chest, pressed his elbows against his sides, and snapped his legs together, bending at the waist into a pike position just before his body was buffeted by the aircraft's slipstream. As Savvin tumbled through the darkness, he began his count.

One thousand, two thousand . . .

39

AIR FORCE ONE

Air Force One cruised thirty-six thousand feet above the Atlantic Ocean, headed east toward Brussels, escorted by a pair of F-22 Raptors periodically refueled in flight. Secretary of State Dawn Cabral and National Security Advisor Christine O'Connor entered the president's office on the main deck of the aircraft and took their seats in a brown leather sofa opposite the president's desk. Two days ago, Christine had watched events unfold on the televisions in her hotel, only a few hundred yards from the Kremlin. Her decision to depart Moscow early had proven wise, given Russia's invasion of Lithuania and Ukraine not long thereafter.

Thus far, however, the Russians had made no attempts to detain American diplomats. On the contrary, it was business as usual in Moscow, with Russia downplaying its dual invasions, labeling its *incursion* into Ukraine a temporary security measure to ensure the safety of ethnic Russians until the time, determined by President Kalinin, the Ukrainian government instituted adequate safeguards. Lithuania was also billed as a limited military deployment protecting the rights of Russia and its citizens, responding to the hostility of NATO countries—Poland and Lithuania—abusing their power by preventing the transit of Russian citizens and military units between Russia proper and Kaliningrad Oblast.

The president had invited Dawn and Christine to his office on Air Force One to discuss Russia's transgressions and the pending NATO meeting in Brussels, and he directed his first question to Dawn. "Help me understand Kalinin's thought process. What does he want that's worth risking war with NATO and international sanctions that could cripple Russia's economy?"

"In my assessment," Dawn began, "if Russia were a person, he or she would be diagnosed with post-traumatic stress disorder. They've been invaded by Western European countries three times, and Nazi Germany's occupation was horrific, resulting in the death of twenty-seven million men and women and the destruction of hundreds of cities. In simple terms, Russians are paranoid, justly or not, and their paranoia increases each time one of their former allies joins NATO. They simply don't trust the West, and many Russians believe it's only a matter of time before NATO finds a reason to invade.

"Ukraine's turn toward the West was pivotal in Russia's approach to this issue. Not only did they feel betrayed by one of their closest allies, but most of Russia's Black Sea Fleet is homeported in Crimea. The annexation of Crimea was essential to ensure they retained access to their main Black Sea port, and their support of separatists in Donbass is an attempt to reestablish a buffer zone between Russia and the West, should Ukraine eventually become a NATO member."

The president digested Dawn's assessment, then turned the conversation to the impending NATO meeting. "Russia invaded Ukraine previously, annexing Crimea, and no one came to Ukraine's assistance. How do we shape a different outcome this time?"

Dawn replied, "Russia's annexation of Crimea was a

unique situation. Its population is two-thirds ethnic Russian and the province was part of Russia for two hundred years before it was gifted to Ukraine by Nikita Khrushchev in 1954. From a Russian perspective, they simply took back what was rightfully theirs. Additionally, although Ukraine protested, they ceded the region without conflict. There was no war for NATO or the United States to intervene in.

"This time, however, there's no historical justification for Russia's invasion of Ukraine or Lithuania. The Russians will argue they were provoked and had no alternative, but we all know the excuses are a sham. The obvious reason is that Kalinin wants to reestablish buffer states between Russia and Western Europe. Additionally, this time Russia invaded a NATO country and the Alliance will have to respond."

Turning to Christine, the president asked, "Do you have anything to add?"

Christine answered, "I concur with Dawn's assessment of Kalinin's motives. However, I'd like to expound on NATO's obligation. Lithuania isn't as cut-and-dried as it appears. Article Five of the North Atlantic Treaty states that an armed attack on one or more members shall be considered an attack on all, and that all members will assist, taking actions deemed necessary. However, the treaty doesn't spell out what *assist* means, nor the *actions deemed necessary*. The wording keeps NATO's options open, with the possible responses ranging from nuclear war to a stern protest sent via postcard. Even though Lithuania has been invaded, there is no obligation to engage Russia militarily.

"We'll also have to deal with NATO's unique decision-making process. On its surface, NATO's principle of requiring consensus on each resolution might seem a hindrance, in that one nation can torpedo a proposal. However, consensus doesn't mean unanimous approval. All twenty-eight countries don't have to vote *yes* in order for a resolution to be adopted. Instead, as long as no country votes *no*, consensus is achieved. Additionally, each country doesn't have to vote; they can abstain if they want. The ability to abstain from a vote, called the *silence procedure*, allows governments to tacitly approve a NATO resolution without officially doing so, thereby not putting their vote on the record, which could be used against them by political opponents back home.

"Another issue to consider is that even if NATO authorizes the use of military force, member states aren't bound to provide assets. So you really have two diplomatic battles to win, Mr. President. You have to convince the other twenty-seven members to either vote *yes* or abstain, then you'll need to persuade as many members as possible to contribute forces."

The president nodded his understanding, then turned back to Dawn. "How do you think this is going to shake out?"

Dawn answered, "If NATO authorizes the use of military force and Russia doesn't back down, we're talking about a full-scale continental war. Even if a country abstains from the vote and initially refuses to provide forces, if NATO begins to lose, they'll be drawn into the conflict. It's not likely NATO would lose given our combined forces, but the potential is one many countries fear. And if Russia gains the upper hand, they might not stop at Lithuania and Ukraine. Armed conflict with Russia is a can of worms many NATO members won't want to open."

"I understand their concern," the president said. As he prepared to ask another question, there was a knock on his door. After the president acknowledged, McVeigh entered with a somber look on his face, taking a seat on the leather sofa beside the two women.

"I have bad news, Mr. President. Belarus has invaded Ukraine, launching an assault against the Ukrainian Army's north flank, while Russia has begun a major assault from the south. Additionally, Russia's airborne troops are being deployed along the Dnieper River, which runs north–south through the entire country, seizing the bridges. The initial invasion was bait, drawing Ukrainian forces toward its eastern border. It won't be long before the entire Ukrainian Army is surrounded.

"The outcome in Ukraine was never in doubt. Without outside assistance, Russia will prevail. We were hoping Ukraine could hold out long enough for NATO or the United States to assist. That's not going to happen. This war will be over in the next few days, and expelling Russia from Ukraine just became significantly harder. Instead of assisting Ukraine in a fluid battle, Russian units will be dug in along the Dnieper River."

After absorbing the news, the president replied, "This at least provides clarity to the way forward, eliminating the urgency in committing NATO's rapid response forces. Driving Russia from Lithuania and Ukraine is going to take a concerted, well-planned effort. It won't be easy, but at least we'll have time to build consensus and deploy the required forces to Europe.

"However, it's imperative we not go it alone. We need a NATO resolution authorizing the use of military force against Russia, and we need as many NATO members as possible to contribute forces." The president finished with, "We have our work cut out for us. Engage your counterparts in Brussels and do what you can to influence the outcome."

The members of his staff and cabinet departed his office, and as the door closed, the president's thoughts went to the conversations earlier that day, when he'd contacted most of NATO's leadership. The prime minister of the United Kingdom was on board, as were the leaders of the Baltic States and Poland. Most of the remaining leaders were noncommittal, except for France, Italy, and Germany, who were leaning against military action. As the last few hours of the flight to Belgium drew to a close, the president knew he'd have a difficult task come morning.

40

USS *MICHIGAN*

In *Michigan*'s Battle Management Center, Lieutenant Harrison stood beside a plasma screen displaying a map of Egypt, briefing *Michigan*'s next mission. Seated in the Battle Management Center were Captain Wilson, his Executive Officer, and four department heads, plus Commander McNeil and the three other SEALs assigned to the mission.

Following Russia's invasion of Ukraine, *Michigan* had received new orders, routing the submarine into the Black Sea. However, before heading north, *Michigan* had to complete another mission; Harrison and three other SEALs would be sent ashore into Egypt. The Navigator had already briefed *Michigan*'s approach to Arish, located on the coast of the Sinai Peninsula, which presented no challenges, and it was Harrison's turn to brief. A single fire team of four SEALs would be sent ashore.

"Once *Michigan* is in position off Egypt's coast, the fire team will debark using one of the two RHIBs in the port Dry Deck Shelter," Harrison said, referring to the Rigid Hull Inflatable Boats SEALs sometimes used for missions ashore. "Accompanying me will be Maydwell, Mendelson, and Brown."

Harrison nodded and one of the SEALs advanced the slide on the display, which shifted to a satellite view of Arish. There was nothing noteworthy in the vicinity as far as Harrison could tell, no government or military facilities, just a single building.

"Our mission is to recon the area. Find out why Russia was interested enough to send Special Forces personnel to this building, and what, if anything, they did while they were there. Any questions?"

There were none, and Harrison wrapped up the briefing.

An hour later, with *Michigan* at periscope depth off the coast of the Sinai Peninsula, Lieutenant Harrison led his fire team into Missile Tube Two and into the port Dry Deck Shelter. Stowed in the shelter were two RHIBs, one of which would be used for tonight's mission. Unlike SDV operations, there were no Navy divers in the shelter to assist aside from the diver on the other side of the Plexiglas shield, operating the hangar controls.

The four SEALs donned scuba gear and the shelter was flooded down, then the hangar door moved slowly open to the latched position. Harrison and the other SEALs hauled one of the RHIBs from the shelter onto the submarine's missile deck and connected a tether line from the RHIB to one of the SDV rails, then activated the first compressed air cartridge.

As the RHIB expanded, Rob Maydwell and Richard Mendelson swam aft along the missile deck and opened the hatch to a locker in the submarine's superstructure. The two SEALs retrieved an outboard motor and attached it to the RHIB, then actuated the second air cartridge. The RHIB fully inflated, rising toward the water's surface. Maydwell and Mendelson followed the RHIB upward, and a few moments later, Mendelson returned, rendering the *okay* hand signal. Harrison informed the

Navy diver inside the Dry Deck Shelter that the RHIB was operational and they were proceeding on their mission, then disconnected the tether line from the shelter and headed toward the surface with Mendelson and Brown.

Harrison and the other two SEALs hauled themselves and the tether line into the RHIB, joining Maydwell. The outboard engine was running, but barely audible as expected. Maydwell shifted the outboard into gear, and as their position updated on his handheld GPS display, he pointed the RHIB toward their insertion point on the Egyptian coast.

41

ARISH, EGYPT

As they approached the coast, Maydwell eased back on the throttle, reducing the engine noise to a low purr, inaudible above the waves breaking upon the shore. The SEALs had shed their scuba gear, and their diver face masks had been replaced with night-vision goggles and headsets. Under the faint moonlight filtering down between scattered clouds, Maydwell spotted their destination and angled the RHIB toward a rock outcropping, shifting the engine to neutral.

The RHIB coasted to a halt as it reached the rocks. Mendelson slid into the water, tether in hand. After securing the RHIB, he returned to retrieve his Heckler & Koch MP7 submachine gun, and Harrison led the team ashore onto the rock-strewn beach.

An hour later, they approached the specified latitude and longitude coordinates on the outskirts of Arish, spotting a windowless, single-story building. As they closed on their destination, Harrison noted a three-foot-diameter pipe exiting the building, turning down into the sand a few feet later. They stopped beside the building; there was no indication anyone was inside—the only audible activity was the steady hum of machinery. Moving along the perimeter, Harrison identified an entrance on the south side, along with another three-foot-diameter pipe exiting the building.

Harrison stood beside the door while their breacher—a demolitions expert—Petty Officer Maydwell, examined the door. Inside his backpack was the material required to gain entrance: C-4 explosives, initiators, and detonators, but he examined the lock first. It was nothing fancy, just a normal door lock. Maydwell pulled a set of universal keys from his backpack, and on the third try, the door unlocked.

The other three SEALs raised their MP7s to the firing position, and Maydwell shoved the door open. Harrison surged inside, stepping to the left as Mendelson followed, moving to the right to make room for Brown, who entered next, stopping in the middle of the three SEALs.

Harrison scanned the room. The two sections of pipe passed through opposite walls and were connected to machinery inside, which occupied almost the entire interior of the building. The wall to the left was lined with control consoles, with indicators of various colors glowing in the darkness. Maydwell entered and the four SEALs spread out, searching the facility for personnel. After scouring the building and finding no one, the four men gathered in front of the control panels.

Harrison directed his men, "Figure out what this equipment does and why Russian Spetsnaz would be sent here."

The three other SEALs fanned out again as Harrison studied the panels against the wall. The nomenclature on the controls was Arabic, which Harrison couldn't translate, but there were numerous pressure gauges on each panel, which indicated the machinery were pumps. Given the pipeline passing through the building, Harrison concluded the facility was a pumping station for either oil or natural gas. Harrison retrieved a camera from his backpack and took photographs of each panel and the machinery behind him. As he returned the camera to his backpack, he heard Mendelson's voice in his headset.

"I found something. North side of the building."

Harrison joined Mendelson and the two other SEALs, who were standing near the pipe entering the building, where it connected to the first piece of equipment. Mendelson pointed to a crevice in the machinery, where something had been placed. Harrison and the other SEALs lifted their night-vision goggles to get a better look as Mendelson activated a flashlight, examining a small one-foot-by-one-foot object. It was an explosive charge, with enough C-4 to blow the building sky-high. The detonator, however, was of an unusual design, one Harrison hadn't seen before: no wires to cut, just an electronic module pressed into the C-4.

Maydwell moved forward and examined it, then stepped back.

"Russian design," he said. "Their newest and most sophisticated. There's no way to remove or disarm it." As Harrison gave him an inquisitive look—there was always a way to disarm a detonator—Maydwell expounded. "It has built-in motion sensors, so if you try to remove it, it goes off. It's detonated via a satellite signal, and if you jam it for too long, it goes off. This charge is coming off only one way—in a million pieces, along with the rest of this building."

Harrison took photographs of the explosive charge and its detonator, and as he returned his camera to his backpack, he reflected on the intel provided for this mission: Russian Spetsnaz had been dispatched to various points throughout Egypt. If their missions had been the same as this one, the entire Egyptian oil and natural gas pipeline infrastructure had been wired with explosives.

42

BRUSSELS, BELGIUM

Seven hours after departing Joint Base Andrews, with the early morning sun hidden behind overcast skies, Air Force One landed at Zaventem Airport, a few miles northeast of Brussels. The president was met on the tarmac by the U.S. ambassadors to Belgium and NATO, along with senior NATO staff and Belgian government representatives. After the requisite greetings, the president slipped into the back of the presidential car, nicknamed Cadillac One. A hybrid Cadillac built upon a truck frame and extensively modified with armored plating and bulletproof windows, Cadillac One had been transported to Brussels during the night with the rest of the president's motorcade and backup vehicles.

Christine, Dawn, and McVeigh were escorted to their sedan, several cars behind the president's, and the motorcade headed into Brussels. After penetrating the northeast perimeter of the city and turning down Boulevard Leopold III, the presidential motorcade arrived at a mammoth new complex, in front of which stood a twenty-three-foot-tall oxidized steel star, symbol of the North Atlantic Treaty Organization.

The entourage was led to a lobby outside the Alliance's main conference room, where the leaders of NATO's other twenty-seven countries were already gathered. Another round of introductions ensued, accompanied with a maddening amount of protocol dictating who greeted whom first and what order followed.

The clock struck the appointed hour and the conference room doors opened. The twenty-eight NATO leaders took their seats at a large round table with twenty-nine chairs: one for the leader of each NATO country, with the final chair for the secretary-general. The president inserted a wireless earpiece into his ear, listening to the English translator as the secretary-general, Johan Van der Bie, a well-respected diplomat from the Netherlands, gave a short introductory speech. An update on Russia's dual invasions followed, with the information displayed on a dozen video screens mounted along the circumference of the conference room.

It was quiet in Lithuania, with Russia's 2nd Guards Motor Rifle Division and six additional motor rifle brigades, totaling forty thousand combat troops, digging in along the corridor they had occupied. The Russians seemed content with the sliver of Lithuania, while their goal in Ukraine was more ambitious. Ukraine's Army of twenty-two ground combat units were engaged to the east by twenty-four Russian brigades, and early last night, Russia had launched two offensives on the Ukrainian Army's flanks. Ten Russian brigades had broken through from the south, while twelve more brigades— six Belarusian mechanized infantry and six Russian Spetsnaz units—had penetrated Ukraine's northern flank. Within the hour, Russian and Belarusian units would complete the encirclement of the Ukrainian Army.

Additionally, four Russian airborne divisions and another five independent brigades—forty-five thousand paratroopers—had been dropped along the Dnieper River. Russia had gained control of every bridge across the river, separating the eastern one-third of the country from the rest. The Ukrainian Army was cut off with no means of resupply and would surrender before NATO rapid response forces could assist.

Not that NATO could make a difference, with only forty thousand rapid responders opposed by 265,000 Russian and Belarusian troops. Russia would achieve a quick and decisive victory, occupying the eastern one-third of Ukraine. Whether Russia would stop at the Dnieper River or continue its assault into the rest of Ukraine was unclear.

Following the secretary-general's update, there was a somber silence in the conference room until he recognized Lithuania's president, ceding the floor to her. Dalia Grybauskaitė, the country's first female president, shook off the bad news concerning Ukraine and began her prepared speech. Dalia's plea for NATO intervention was passionate, ending with a reminder of NATO's obligation under Article 5 of the North Atlantic Treaty. At the conclusion of her speech, she announced Lithuania had submitted a resolution authorizing the use of Alliance military force to expel Russia from Lithuania.

Following Dalia's speech, the American president requested to speak. The secretary-general turned the floor over to the president, who pulled the microphone in front of him closer.

"Thank you, Mr. Secretary-General. Ladies and gentlemen, I'll keep my remarks short. Russia's invasion of Lithuania and Ukraine is only the beginning. Russia is using the blueprint created from their annexation of Crimea, expanding it to encompass eastern Ukraine. Annex part of a country, sow civil unrest within the adjacent provinces, then invade those countries to protect ethnic Russians. If NATO doesn't take a stand, the three Baltic States will be next, and Poland will follow. Russia won't stop until it has re-created a buffer zone of puppet states on its western border. War with Russia is inevitable. We can act now, or when the situation is more dire."

The president glanced around the conference table before continuing. "The United States proposes a resolution authorizing military intervention to remove Russian forces from Ukraine."

After the president finished his speech, French President François Loubet was the first to be recognized by the secretary-general. "Assisting Ukraine is out of the question," Loubet said. "Ukraine is not a NATO member, and it is not our responsibility to come to its aid."

"Then whose responsibility is it?" the American president asked. "As Russia occupies Ukraine, are we supposed to turn a blind eye because Ukraine isn't a member of our club?"

"It's the responsibility of the international community, not NATO's. Each country must evaluate the situation and decide. But that should be done outside the framework of NATO."

"Is not NATO a subset of the international community?"

"Yes, but intervening on Ukraine's behalf isn't our responsibility."

The president said, "You stated it was the responsibility of the international community to decide, and also agreed NATO is a member of that community. I think we are in agreement. As a member of the international community, NATO *can* intercede on Ukraine's behalf. The decision to be made is—*will* we?"

Loubet replied, "If we engage Russia militarily, the outcome is unclear. We aren't talking about Kosovo or Iraq. We're talking about Russia, with well-trained troops and sophisticated air defense systems in quantities that will neutralize NATO air superiority. Assaulting fortified Russian positions in Lithuania and Ukraine without air superiority will result in drastic casualties, if not outright defeat. We should avoid war and implement economic sanctions instead, crippling Russia until it vacates the occupied territories."

Lithuania's president interjected, "We imposed sanctions after Russia annexed Crimea. What has that achieved? Nothing. Which is exactly what new sanctions will accomplish."

Dalia's features hardened. "We wouldn't have joined NATO, infuriating Moscow and placing a target on our back, were it not for NATO's assurance that you would come to our assistance if required."

The German chancellor, Emma Schmidt, joined the conversation. Ignoring Dalia's remarks, she directed her question to the other country leaders. "Is NATO willing to go to war over an eighty-kilometer-wide strip of land?"

If the president of Lithuania was upset, the president of Latvia was apoplectic. "You are content to look the other way because you aren't next on the menu. Once Russia's war in Ukraine is over and they take note of NATO's weakness—our unwillingness to intervene in a blatant invasion of a NATO country—they'll be emboldened and take the rest of the Baltic States. Poland will be next, completing their effort to eliminate NATO from their flank and reestablish buffer states between Russia and Western Europe."

Chancellor Schmidt responded, "Ceding a few square kilometers is vastly different than the occupation of an entire country. The borders of my country have been redrawn dozens of times, often under threat of occupation. How is the situation in Lithuania different?"

Lithuania's president replied, "Your borders have been redrawn primarily because of your own failed aggression."

The German chancellor's face turned red, and as the

council debate threatened to degenerate, the American president interjected, "Let's get back to the issues. Russia has invaded Lithuania and Ukraine. The question we must answer is—Are we going to look the other way or assist?"

The Italian prime minister joined the discussion. "Russian troop deployment in Lithuania already equals NATO's rapid response force. We'll have to mobilize additional forces for this effort, both across the continent and from North America. This will take time, during which Russia will consolidate its position in Ukraine and redeploy additional troops to Lithuania. Considering the number of Russian troops we'll be facing and Russia's formidable air defense and land attack missile systems, the cost will be extremely high. We must ask ourselves, is war with Russia, which could escalate into the use of tactical nuclear weapons, worth a few square kilometers of sparsely populated countryside?"

The British prime minister interjected, "We are discussing a policy of appeasement, which will fail just as it did before World War Two. Have we not learned from our mistakes? In the words of George Santayana, 'Those who cannot remember the past are condemned to repeat it.'" He pulled a sheet of paper from his suit pocket, which he unfolded on the table. "Let me read to you the words of Winston Churchill:

> When the situation was manageable it was neglected, and now that it is thoroughly out of hand we apply too late the remedies which then might have effected a cure. . . . Unwillingness to act when action would be simple and effective, lack of clear thinking, confusion of counsel until the emergency comes, until self-preservation strikes its jarring gong—these are the features which constitute the endless repetition of history."

Looking up, the prime minister said, "I agree with the American president. War with Russia is inevitable. We can either act now, when we can control the time and location of the conflict, or wait and let Russia dictate those terms."

Upon the conclusion of the prime minister's comments, the discussions around the conference room table degraded into individual debates. After a few moments, an aide approached the secretary-general, whispering in his ear. When the aide finished speaking, Johan Van der Bie pounded his gavel on the strike plate.

The conversations faded and Van der Bie announced, "President Kalinin wishes to address our Alliance. If no one objects, I'll put him on-screen."

After no objections were voiced, the secretary-general nodded to his aide.

The displays lining the circumference of the conference room energized and President Kalinin appeared, sitting behind his desk with the Russian Federation flag displayed behind him. The president of the United States listened to the English translation from his earpiece as Kalinin began.

"Thank you for the opportunity to address your Alliance. I understand your apprehension over recent actions by my government, and I want to assuage your concerns. I will address Lithuania first, then Ukraine.

"Our desire in Lithuania is modest: a small strip of land only eighty kilometers wide, which will be incorporated into Kaliningrad Oblast. I regret using force to obtain this land, but Russia will no longer tolerate the constraints of foreign governments, preventing the transit of Russian citizens and military units between two regions of my country. Our annexation of this land is non-negotiable. However, I realize we cannot take this land without suitable compensation. We will begin formal discussions with Lithuania and craft a proposal acceptable to both countries.

"Ukraine might appear to be a more serious issue, but I assure you it is not. Once the safety of ethnic Russians can be ensured by local governments, all Russian troops will be withdrawn. The only contentious issue, perhaps, is that while the overbearing hand of the Ukrainian government is removed from eastern Ukraine, each oblast will be given the opportunity to choose its future. Referendums will be held, allowing each oblast to choose to remain part of Ukraine, become independent, or join Russia. My country will abide by the results, and you have my assurance that all Russian troops will then be withdrawn.

"I want to express, in the clearest terms, that Russia does not desire war with NATO. However, if you are entertaining the thought of intervening, I offer you this to consider. If attacked, Russia will terminate the delivery of all oil and natural gas to NATO members. Additionally, over the last week, Russian Spetsnaz units have attached explosives to every major oil and natural gas pipeline supplying Western Europe and the United States. Finally, as I speak, the Russian Northern and Pacific Fleets are taking station at the entrance to the Persian Gulf. If any NATO country attacks Russia or imposes economic sanctions, I will give the order to destroy these critical pipelines and sink all oil and natural gas tankers supplying Western Europe or the United States. Eighty percent of Western Europe's natural resources will be cut off, and your economies will crumble.

"These are only precautionary measures, however. I wish no harm to your countries. I simply request you not interfere with the security actions I have taken in Lithuania and Ukraine." The Russian president finished with, "Thank you for your time."

Silence gripped the room as Kalinin's image faded from the displays. After a long, tense moment, the meeting descended into chaos as country leaders discussed Kalinin's remarks, with some of the conversations becoming heated.

The secretary-general gaveled the meeting to order, pounding the wooden strike plate repeatedly until silence returned. "I can see we won't be ready to vote today," he said. "Considering the new information President Kalinin provided, additional evaluation will be required. A time frame for consensus will be established for the proposals authorizing military force to liberate Lithuania and Ukraine from Russian forces. I am invoking the silence procedure. Any country that objects to either proposal must do so in writing by the stipulated date."

With another thud of his gavel, Secretary-General Van der Bie adjourned the meeting.

As the president of the United States pushed back from the table, there were two things he was convinced of. The first was that under the given circumstances, NATO would not come to the assistance of Lithuania or Ukraine. The second was that the United States needed to *modify* the given circumstances, removing Russia's energy choke hold on the West.

Striding into the lobby, he was joined by McVeigh, Dawn, and Christine. He turned to his subordinates. "Determine exactly what Russia has done, and devise a plan to destroy Kalinin's choke hold."

WASHINGTON, D.C.

Less than a day after departing Brussels, Christine was seated at the Situation Room conference table between Hardison and Colonel DuBose, with McVeigh and Dawn opposite them. The president, sitting at the head of the table, listened as McVeigh delivered an update.

"Russia's Northern and Pacific Fleets are stationed in the Gulf of Oman, where they can block the entrance to the Persian Gulf if desired. However, two Russian fleets aren't as formidable as it sounds, at least when it comes to surface combatants. Russia has only nineteen in the gulf: one aircraft carrier, three cruisers, thirteen destroyers, and two corvettes. Not exactly quake-in-your-boots forces, considering we should be able to muster four carrier strike groups comprising four aircraft carriers and forty cruisers and destroyers in opposition. We have two problems, however.

"The first is that Russia has apparently struck a deal with the Iranians, allowing the deployment of Russian military units inside their country. Over a hundred Russian missile batteries are being positioned along the north shore of the Gulf of Oman, which will eliminate our surface combatant advantage and threaten our aircraft once launched. Additionally, several Russian tactical fighter squadrons, totaling over four hundred aircraft, have been deployed to Iranian air bases. With the additional missile batteries and fighter aircraft, they've leveled the playing field against four carrier strike groups.

"An even bigger problem is the subsurface picture. After our war with China, we have only twenty-four operational fast attack submarines, with twenty in the Pacific. Russia, on the other hand, has combined the submarines from its four fleets and has forty-eight attack and guided missile submarines in the Gulf of Oman. We're significantly outnumbered, which places our carriers at risk when they engage the Russian surface combatants.

"At the end of the day, to ensure free passage of oil and natural gas tankers in the Persian Gulf area, we'll have to eliminate all Russian surface combatants and submarines in the gulf, along with the missile batteries and air squadrons in Iran. We're working on the details and when we're further along, we'll provide a formal operations brief."

"Thanks, Bob," the president said. "Anything else?"

McVeigh answered, "Dawn has some worrisome news."

Turning to SecState Cabral, the president asked, "What have you got?"

Dawn answered, "It's obvious that Russia made arrangements with Belarus and Iran, and we wondered who else might be involved. We reviewed the itineraries of high-level Russian officials and identified meetings between Russia's minister of defense and the presidents of Belarus and Iran. Additionally, the defense minister met with the Indian prime minister and the president of China in the following two days."

The president's eyes narrowed as he turned back to McVeigh.

"This is bad news," McVeigh said. "India and China have the most powerful navies in the Pacific besides ours and Russia's. India has two carrier strike groups, with a new carrier undergoing sea trials, and although we wiped out China's submarines, their surface Navy is still intact. If Russia builds a coalition of the three largest navies besides our own, we won't be able to engage at our current strength. It'll be two years before all five aircraft carriers in the shipyards return to service, along with the cruisers and destroyers under repair."

The president asked, "What if only one country joins Russia?"

"If either country joins Russia, the outcome would tip in Russia's favor."

"We know China's no friend," the president said. "Where do we stand with India?"

Dawn answered, "India plays on both sides of the fence. Historically, they've had strong ties with Russia, although they've been warming up to the United States lately, increasing their procurements of our military hardware. For example, India bought ten Kilo class submarines and is leasing an Akula II nuclear attack submarine from Russia, but procures anti-submarine hardware—the P-8A aircraft and the torpedoes they drop—from us. They seem unwilling to commit to a relationship with the West or with Russia, keeping their options open."

The president said, "Arrange meetings with India and China. If possible, find out what deal Russia offered them and if there's anything we can do to influence their decision. Don't bother with Iran. They've already committed, and we can't trust a damn thing they say anyway."

Dawn replied, "Meeting with the Indians shouldn't be a problem. However, China is still giving us the silent treatment on all diplomatic overtures. They haven't responded to a single request to meet at any level since the war ended."

"Keep trying," the president said, then turned to Christine and Hardison, who had been working on Kalinin's natural resource threat. "How bad is this oil and natural gas pipeline issue?"

Christine answered, "It doesn't look good, sir. We've verified Kalinin's claim. *Michigan*'s SEALs discovered explosives attached to a natural gas pipeline pumping station, which if detonated, would take out the Arish-Aqaba section of the Arab Gas Pipeline. Additionally, Russia provided several coordinates so we could verify Kalinin's claim. Our Special Forces have checked, and in each case, explosives are wired to oil and natural gas pipelines or pumping stations."

"Can we remove or disarm the explosives?"

"No, Mr. President. The detonator attached to each explosive charge has motion sensors to detect if it's being removed. Each detonator is activated remotely via satellite signal, and it cannot be jammed. If the detonator loses the satellite signal for too long, it'll activate."

"How long are we talking about?" the president asked.

"Probably about a minute."

"What's the impact if Russia destroys these pipelines?"

Kevin Hardison, who had pulled the requisite data, replied, "Every major oil and natural gas pipeline in the Middle East and Western Europe has been wired with explosives. Russia has also wired our Trans-Alaska Pipeline System, mostly on principle rather than for impact, since taking out the Alaskan oil pipeline would cut off only fifteen percent of our oil supply. It'd put a dent in our flow of natural resources, but it wouldn't be catastrophic.

"Western Europe, on the other hand, is in a different

situation. Overall, Europe gets thirty-three percent of its oil and almost forty percent of its natural gas from Russia, and many countries are critically dependent. Four countries receive one hundred percent of their natural gas from Russia: Lithuania, Latvia, Estonia, and Finland; Bulgaria and Hungary receive eighty to ninety percent; and Austria, Poland, Turkey, the Czech Republic, and Greece are sixty percent dependent. Germany receives forty percent, and Italy—thirty percent. And that's just what Russia can turn off.

"If Russia destroys the oil and natural gas pipelines and blockades the Persian Gulf, Western Europe will receive almost no oil or natural gas. Kalinin didn't deliver an empty threat; the Western European economies would crumble, and do so much faster than we could harm Russia with economic sanctions."

The president absorbed the somber information, then asked, "What if we prevent a Persian Gulf blockade, but Kalinin destroys the pipelines?"

Hardison answered, "We can't withstand either one."

"Got it," the president said. "McVeigh is working the Persian Gulf issue. What are our options regarding the pipelines?"

"We have none at the moment," Hardison answered. "There's no way to override these detonators."

"Every explosive device has a built-in safety," the president replied. "There *must* be a way to deactivate these detonators. Any ideas?" he asked, canvassing the four men and women at the table.

"Ask the designer," Christine replied.

"What?" Hardison said. "Just knock on his door and ask him for the master override code?"

"Something like that." Christine smiled.

"That . . . ," the president said, "isn't a bad idea." To McVeigh he said, "Find out who designed these detonators, and arrange a—*conversation*."

In the Operations Center three levels beneath the Moscow Senate, five rows of military personnel, seated at their consoles, snapped to attention as Russia's president entered. Minister of Defense Chernov and Foreign Minister Lavrov followed Kalinin into a conference room in the back, where General Andropov and his aides rose to their feet and waited as Kalinin took his seat at the head of the table. After everyone settled into their chairs, one of Andropov's aides manipulated a remote control, and the opaque panoramic window on the wall opposite President Kalinin turned transparent, enabling a clear view of the Operations Center displays.

General Andropov began the brief. "All military objectives have been achieved, Mr. President. The corridor connecting Kaliningrad Oblast to Belarus has been secured, and all units are preparing defensive positions. In Ukraine, the operation could not have been more successful. Our airborne units hold all bridges across the Dnieper River, cutting off eastern Ukraine from NATO reinforcements. All Ukrainian ground combat units are encircled, and we have halted offensive operations for the time being, negotiating a surrender of all Ukrainian units.

"Regarding the Navy's objective, the Northern and Pacific Fleets, along with all attack submarines from the Baltic and Black Sea Fleets, have taken station in the Gulf of Oman, ready to implement a blockade of the Persian Gulf if directed. As far as NATO's response goes, an American carrier strike group has moved into the Indian Ocean, shadowing the arrival of our Pacific Fleet, and a second strike group is being sent to the gulf, pulled from China's coast. The remaining two operational American carriers have departed the West Coast of the United States. Aside from America's carrier strike groups, NATO appears paralyzed. Although all NATO military units in Europe and North America are mobilizing, none have been deployed."

"Thank you, General," Kalinin said. Turning to Foreign Minister Lavrov, he asked, "Where do we stand politically?"

"As expected, Lithuania submitted a proposal authorizing the use of NATO military force to expel Russian troops from Lithuania. Additionally, the United States submitted a proposal to assist Ukraine. A vote on both proposals was postponed after your videoconference with NATO, as the member countries digest the economic disaster they'll endure if they respond either militarily or with sanctions."

"The United States has four carrier strike groups under way," Kalinin said. "What if they challenge our Persian Gulf blockade? Where do we stand with India and China?"

"Neither country has formally responded," Lavrov replied. "It appears both countries are keeping their options open, and won't accept or decline unless the situation forces them to."

"I understand," Kalinin said. He asked Defense Minister Chernov, "How do things look regarding the oil and natural gas pipelines?"

"The United States checked the locations we provided them, so we are certain they understand we aren't bluffing. We have been monitoring via satellite, and there has been no further activity at those or any of the other locations we've attached explosives."

Chernov finished with, "Everything is proceeding according to plan."

45

WASHINGTON, D.C.

Two days after their last meeting in the Situation Room, the president was joined again by Christine, Hardison, and Colonel DuBose, along with McVeigh and Dawn. This time they were accompanied by CIA Director Jessica Cherry, whose services had been called upon to locate the engineer who had designed the Russian detonators. During the previous forty-eight hours, the news from Europe and the Western Pacific had been universally bad, and McVeigh was bringing the president up to speed.

The Ukrainian units in eastern Ukraine, which essentially amounted to Ukraine's entire ground forces, had surrendered. Regarding Russia's potential blockade, the Pentagon was developing an engagement plan for the Russian Navy in the Gulf of Oman, but the two-to-one submarine disadvantage was proving to be a difficult nut to crack. At the conclusion of McVeigh's brief, the president turned to Dawn, who delivered her update.

"On the diplomatic front, we've engaged India and China, requesting a meeting with each country's foreign minister. India has agreed, and I have a meeting in New Delhi tomorrow, but China continues to give us the silent treatment. Russia has also been busy in the diplomatic arena, inviting Lithuanian representatives to Moscow to negotiate new territorial boundaries. However, President Grybauskaitė is giving Kalinin the Heisman for the time being."

The president smiled at Dawn's use of the football metaphor—comparing Grybauskaitė's response to the Heisman football trophy pose—a stiff arm to the face.

Dawn continued, "Russia also invited Ukraine to Moscow to discuss their *security operation*. Moscow is doing its best to portray their dual invasions as just another day at the office; no big deal. They're incredibly brash—they've even proposed a continental security summit with all NATO countries, no doubt to solidify their gains in Lithuania and Ukraine, and permanently put to bed the prospect of military or economic responses."

The president replied, "This could work in our favor. Keep the lines of communication with Moscow open. Give the indication that we're open to a diplomatic solution, that we've concluded our hands are tied. Also, delay the NATO vote on the Lithuania and Ukraine resolutions. We need time to eliminate Russia's stranglehold on Europe's natural resources. Speaking of that, where do we stand with the pipeline sabotage?"

CIA Director Jessica Cherry answered, "We've identified the detonator designer. He's Anton Fedorov, one of Russia's top explosive engineers, working at a facility in Velikiy Novgorod, west of Moscow. He lives in a villa on the outskirts of town, where he's picked up each morning and driven to the facility, then returned home each night. We've collected limited intel thus far, but we were able to review the last thirty days of satellite images. He appears to be a homebody; he hasn't ventured outside his villa in the last month. Not that it matters, because that's where we're going to visit him.

"Regarding that visit, we're preparing a joint CIA-military operation, utilizing a Delta Force unit specializing in hostage rescue. The operation isn't particularly challenging, aside from transporting the Delta Force unit inside Russia. Fortunately, Velikiy Novgorod isn't far from the Latvian border, which will enable a quick insertion and extraction. We've also arranged a suitable location for Fedorov's interrogation. With your permission, Mr. President, we'll proceed with the operation."

"You may proceed."

The meeting was about to wrap up when an aide to SecState Cabral entered the Situation Room, delivering her a handwritten message. After reading it, she looked up sharply.

"Mr. President. I have an update on our outreach to China. They've agreed to a meeting, but there are two unusual terms. The first is that the meeting will be with the president of China and not his foreign minister."

There was a favorable response from everyone around the Situation Room table. There was no smile from Dawn, however, which was explained when she conveyed China's additional condition. "The second stipulation is that the meeting will occur only if Christine O'Connor is the American representative."

There was silence in the room as all eyes turned to Christine, whose face paled at the news.

"Absolutely not," Hardison said. "The last time Christine was in China, she held a gun to President Xiang's head, forcing him to guarantee her safe passage from China. That was a onetime deal, not a permanent travel visa."

"China is critical," McVeigh replied. "They have the second-largest surface navy. If they join forces with Russia, it's over for us. We can't defeat both at our current strength."

"What if we pull India to our side?" Dawn asked. "Could that offset China?"

"I'll go," Christine said.

The discussions continued in the Situation Room, with Christine's response unheard.

"I'll go."

Conversation ceased as all eyes shifted to Christine again.

The president replied, "I'm not sure that's a wise decision. As Hardison pointed out, President Xiang promised you one safe trip out of the country, not two."

"We need to engage China. If this is the only way they'll meet with us, I'm willing to go."

Dawn turned to her. "It's obvious why they requested you. It's too risky."

"It's my decision," Christine replied. Turning to the president to request his approval, she said, "It should be my decision."

The president leaned back in his chair, contemplating Christine's assertion. After what happened in China, Christine had been skittish when things deteriorated in Moscow. Now, she was willing to walk into the lion's den. A private discussion with her would be necessary, but for now, he needed to address her assertion. He replied, "You're correct. It's your decision."

He turned to Hardison. "Replace Christine's Diplomatic Security Service protection with Secret Service for this trip. We'll lose control once Christine enters the Great Hall of the People, but I at least want my best people with her."

To Dawn, the president said, "Set up the meeting with President Xiang."

46

NEW DELHI, INDIA

Secretary of State Dawn Cabral's sedan pulled to a halt in front of Rashtrapati Bhavan, India's presidential mansion and the largest residence for a head of state in the world. Stepping from the cool sedan into the blistering Indian heat, already surpassing one hundred degrees Fahrenheit, she paused to examine the grandeur of the four-story palace, constructed at the beginning of the twentieth century for the British viceroy of India. From a distance, the 180-foot-tall copper dome in the center of the palace, inspired by the Pantheon of Rome, seemed to float above the haze of the New Delhi summer heat.

Dawn was greeted by an Indian external affairs aide, who escorted her up the broad, alabaster steps into Durbar Hall. In the center of the hall, surrounded by columns of yellow marble supporting the dome's perimeter, India's minister of external affairs, Rahul Gupta, was conversing with several men and women, wisely awaiting Dawn's arrival within the cool confines of the residential palace. Gupta moved across the marble floor to greet his American counterpart, then escorted her to a conference room in the northeast corner of the hall.

The doors to the conference room closed, sealing

Dawn and Gupta inside for the private meeting she'd requested. No interpreters would be required; Gupta was fluent in English.

"Please be seated," Gupta said, motioning to a chair at the corner of the twenty-person conference room table. Dawn placed a thin leather satchel on the table as she took her seat, and Gupta slid into a chair at the head of the table. Gupta waited for Dawn to begin.

"Thank you for your time, Minister. I suppose you've deduced the reason for this meeting?"

"We have an idea or two," Gupta replied, failing to elaborate.

"We know your president met with Russia's defense minister and that Russia asked you to join forces with them in the Indian Ocean." The last part was a lie—she didn't know what had been discussed, but she was confident her assertion was correct. She continued, "I offer you a counterproposal. Join forces with the United States and help us defeat the Russian Navy."

Gupta remained silent.

"We can provide attractive incentives: price discounts on American military hardware, and we'll relax the restrictions on our most sensitive equipment. You'll benefit greatly from our alliance; your military will become more formidable."

"Only if we choose the winning side, and there is something left of our Navy."

Dawn tucked away Gupta's response; he admitted Russia had made a similar proposal. Dawn pulled a document from her briefcase and slid it across the table. "These are the benefits you will receive in return for your assistance."

Gupta flipped through the document, skimming its contents. He looked up and said, "We will consider your proposal."

"There's a right and wrong side of this conflict,"

Dawn added. "Russia invaded two sovereign countries and is threatening to impede international maritime traffic."

"History is littered with the bodies of the righteous."

"Join us," Dawn replied, "and we will defeat the Russian Navy."

"I will bring your request to President Madan. Of course, he'll need to discuss this with his National Security Council."

"Do you have a rough time frame?"

"I cannot say. That will be up to President Madan."

"I understand," Dawn said. "Thank you for your consideration."

Not long after the American secretary of state departed, Indian Minister of Defense Ankur Kumar joined Gupta in the conference room. "What did she want?" he asked.

After Gupta explained, Kumar asked, "What did you tell her?"

"I was noncommittal, as directed by President Madan."

"If America engages the Russian Navy, our hand will be forced. A side must be chosen."

"Not necessarily," Gupta replied. "We can remain neutral."

"We can remain neutral and alienate both Russia and the United States, not to mention leaving their incentives on the table. Or we can choose a side and gain a strong ally."

"We must choose wisely," Gupta said.

Kumar nodded his agreement.

47

BEIJING, CHINA

It was almost dark by the time the C-32 descended toward Beijing Nanyuan Airport. Like Secretary Cabral, Christine carried a thin leather briefcase containing the details of America's proposal. As the C-32 banked to the left, providing a view of Beijing stretching into the distance, she wondered how Dawn had fared in India. Dawn's task was somewhat easier, though, as there was no threat to her life.

Before Christine departed Washington, D.C., the president had pulled her into the Oval Office for a private conversation, questioning her reasoning for agreeing to China's request. It had taken her a moment to open up, but she had explained how she'd been running away from what she'd done in Beijing and Ice Station Nautilus. Sooner or later, she would have to face her demons, and now was as good a time as any. Her answer seemed to satisfy the president, and she would soon face President Xiang.

The C-32 touched down and after coasting to a halt, Christine and the four Secret Service agents detailed to her exited the aircraft. On the tarmac, members of the Secret Service advance party were waiting, along with Katrina Wetzel, America's ambassador to China.

As Christine descended the staircase, she spotted Ambassador Wetzel standing near a black sedan. Two additional black sedans served as bookends to the three-car motorcade that would take her to the Great Hall of the People. There, her security would become seriously diminished; her Secret Service escort would have to leave their weapons behind at the security checkpoint before entering the Politburo section of the Great Hall.

Ambassador Wetzel greeted Christine as she stepped onto the tarmac. "Welcome to China, Miss O'Connor." Before Christine could reply, Wetzel added, "There's been a change of plans. You're not going to the Great Hall of the People." She nodded toward a helicopter not far away, in front of which stood three men in black suits, who Christine figured were Cadre Department bodyguards—the Chinese equivalent of the Secret Service.

"Where is the meeting?"

"They won't say."

Ambassador Wetzel led Christine and the four Secret Service agents toward the helicopter. When they reached the Cadre Department bodyguards, one stepped forward.

"Only Miss O'Connor," he said.

"I'm supposed to accompany her," Wetzel said, "and serve as her interpreter."

"That won't be necessary," the bodyguard replied. "President Xiang's English will be sufficient."

Wetzel glanced at Christine, who nodded. Xiang's accent had been thick during their previous meetings, but his English was understandable.

Christine was wanded with a handheld metal detector and her leather briefcase searched. Satisfied that she carried no weapons, the lead bodyguard gestured toward the helicopter. Christine slid into the back of the four-passenger aircraft, where she was joined by the three Cadre Department bodyguards.

After a command from the lead bodyguard to the pilot, the helicopter lifted from the tarmac, tilting forward as it accelerated upward. As they headed north, the multicolor illumination from the city below faded to a few sporadic yellow lights, then disappeared altogether, leaving only a full moon in a cloudless sky and the pinpricks of distant stars. Christine tightened her grip on her leather briefcase as the helicopter continued on in the darkness.

A change in the beat of the helicopter's rotors announced the end of their journey was approaching. The helicopter descended, coming to rest in the countryside with a soft landing. As Christine stepped onto damp grass, the sound of waves crashing ashore greeted her ears. The three bodyguards exited the helicopter with Christine, and the lead man pointed toward a narrow trail, faintly illuminated by the full moon, winding up a steep mountain slope.

After determining the three men had nothing to say, she began the trek up the winding trail. At the end of a six-hundred-foot climb, Christine emerged onto a grassy plateau containing another helicopter and a circular stone building flanked by a curving thicket of magnolia trees. In front of the building, a Cadre Department bodyguard stood on each side of a dark entrance. Upon reaching the building, she climbed a half-dozen cracked stone steps, stopping in front of the two men. Neither man spoke, but one pointed to the opening. After taking a deep breath, she passed between the two men.

Christine entered a temple illuminated by flickering torches, bathing a stone goddess in dancing hues of amber and burnt orange. Sitting upon a throne with a tablet in one hand and a staff in the other, the goddess was accompanied by two dragon guardians coiled at her feet, one on each side. Kneeling on the granite floor in front of the statues was President Xiang, his back to Christine and his hands clasped in front of him.

Xiang made no indication he heard Christine enter, and she hovered near the entrance before spotting a stone bench along one side of the temple. She sat quietly on the cold granite, waiting while Xiang finished his prayer.

After a few minutes, Xiang placed his hands on the floor, and Christine could see he was having difficulty standing. Xiang glanced at her and extended his hand, and Christine moved forward, offering hers in return. Xiang leaned heavily on Christine as the seventy-year-old president pulled himself to his feet, straightening to his full six-foot height, his gaze settling on her. She waited for him to speak first, but he remained silent as the flickering torches cast shifting shadows of stone dragons on the wall behind him.

Xiang finally spoke. "I am surprised you came."

"Why did you request me?"

Xiang studied her a moment before replying. "I wanted to know how important this was to America. What they were willing to risk. What *you* were willing to risk."

Christine refrained from asking the question that had hovered at the forefront of her mind since China's request. Would she be allowed to leave after the meeting?

Xiang motioned to the stone bench. "Sit with me."

Christine settled onto the bench again, her back against the cold stone wall, with the president of China beside her, his hands on his knees.

"What is this place?" Christine asked.

"It is the temple of my forefathers," Xiang replied. "Mazu"—he gestured toward the stone goddess—"is the patron saint of fishermen and sailors. I was raised in the small fishing village at the base of this plateau, and I came here often with my mother when I was a child. I knelt beside her each time, praying for the safe return of my father. My mother, on the other hand, prayed for much more. She prayed for revenge."

"Revenge for what?"

"My mother was a Japanese comfort woman during the Sino-Japanese War. I assume you are aware of the horror my mother endured?"

Christine nodded, recalling the Japanese Imperial Army had created comfort houses throughout its occupied territories during World War II, forcing young women to satiate the sexual desires of up to thirty men a day.

"Did your mother get her revenge?"

"She did not," Xiang replied. "But my mother's blood flows strongly in my veins." He cast a stern glance at Christine.

Christine suppressed a rising wave of fear. "Is that why you chose to meet me here? To obtain revenge in the temple of your forefathers?"

"Yes and no," Xiang answered. "This place brings clarity of thought. I come here whenever I face a difficult decision."

Christine didn't ask what that decision entailed and Xiang did not elaborate. Instead, he shifted the conversation to the reason for Christine's trip. "What does the United States want?"

After Christine explained, Xiang said, "The shoe is on the other foot. Russia is doing to you what you did to my country—placing a stranglehold on vital natural resources. For that reason alone, I should side with Russia."

"We can make amends," Christine offered. Pulling the document from her briefcase, she said, "These are the concessions we'll make if you join us in our battle against Russia."

Xiang waved the document away. "Assisting the United States is out of the question. With the memory of our war so fresh, there would be stiff resistance within the Politburo. However, with the proper incentives, China could remain neutral."

Xiang laid out his demands.

With the proper price and guaranteed supply of natural resources, along with the elimination of all economic sanctions against his country, China would remain neutral.

Christine replied, "The United States can drop only the sanctions we imposed unilaterally. However, we can intervene on your behalf concerning the international sanctions."

"That will be sufficient," Xiang said. "I will convey the desired concessions formally to the American embassy. There will be no need for you to relay my request."

Xiang's comment about her services no longer being needed did not go unnoticed.

After a long pause, Xiang said, "Which brings us to the second topic of our meeting tonight." The flickering torches in the distance seemed to dim.

"You murdered the chairman of the Central Military Commission. You put a bullet into the head of a defenseless man who knelt at your feet."

"He deserved it," Christine said. "He was responsible for Prime Minister Bai's death."

"It was not your duty to dispense justice."

Christine evaluated Xiang's words. He was correct. Besides, that wasn't the real reason she killed him. "I'm impulsive," she said, making her best attempt at an apology. "I needed to convince you I was serious. That I would kill you if necessary."

"You succeeded," Xiang said.

He said nothing more, and there was a strained silence between them. Christine's thoughts went to Xiang's order to imprison her in the bowels of the Great Hall of the People during her last visit to China. Finally, she asked, "What are you going to do with me?"

"Until tonight," Xiang replied, "I had not decided."

There was another long silence, his dark eyes probing hers. Finally, he said, "The question I had to answer was—*should I be as ruthless as you.*"

Xiang pushed himself to his feet. Looking down at her, he said, "The helicopter at the base of the plateau will take you back to the airport."

48

VELIKIY NOVGOROD, RUSSIA

The faint beat of a helicopter's four-bladed rotor dissipated in the darkness as an MH-60M Black Hawk skimmed fast and low over the thick forest canopy. Although it could carry nine combat-equipped troops, there were only four men aboard the helicopter piloted by a Night Stalker, a member of the U.S. Army's 160th Special Operations Aviation Regiment, a special operations force providing helicopter support. Unseen but not far behind, a second Black Hawk, also transporting four men, followed an identical flight path east.

In the lead helicopter, Army Captain Joe Martin checked his equipment one last time. Like the three men beside him and the four in the other Black Hawk, Martin was a member of the 1st Special Forces Operational Detachment-Delta, commonly referred to as Delta Force, an elite U.S. Army unit trained for hostage rescue, counterterrorism, and missions against high-value targets.

With no security forces to deal with, this mission was as straightforward as they came. Break in, kidnap the scientist, and the Delta Force unit and Russian egghead would be on their way in only a few minutes. Although this mission posed little danger, they weren't taking the operation lightly. The area surrounding the villa on the outskirts of Velikiy Novgorod had been extensively surveyed via satellite, and an eight-man team had been assigned. In case they encountered mechanical difficulties, two Black Hawks were being used, with one helicopter capable of transporting the full contingent of Delta Force personnel and the Russian to safety.

The only item of concern was the cameras mounted atop the security fence surrounding the villa. However, with no one inside the villa besides the Russian scientist, analysts had concluded they were part of a home security system, which at best would be monitored remotely. With the nearest civilization fifteen minutes away, Martin and the rest of his Delta Force team would be long gone before anyone arrived.

The Night Stalker's voice came across Martin's headset, announcing they were approaching their destination. Martin and the other three men pulled their night-vision goggles over their eyes and retrieved their weapons. The Night Hawk airframe shuddered as the pilot pulled back on the cyclic and adjusted the collective, and the helicopter dropped toward the trees and into a clearing with startling speed. The wheels bounced once, then the Black Hawk settled into the grass. The second Night Hawk touched down nearby and Martin led his team from the clearing into the woods, stopping to examine the GPS display on his wrist.

They were two hundred yards west of the single-story villa. Martin moved forward, stopping at the edge of the trees. After increasing the magnification of his night-vision goggles, he examined the villa. It was surrounded by a security fence, with an automatic car gate and a manual pedestrian gate. The villa was dark, and at 2 a.m. local, the Russian scientist would likely be asleep in bed. The internal arrangement of the villa was unknown, but it wouldn't take long for Martin's team to complete its search.

Martin examined the security cameras, mounted at intervals atop the fence. It was difficult to tell which direction they were pointed, but they appeared fixed, rather than sweeping back and forth. Martin signaled to his two four-man teams; one team would enter the villa and extract the Russian scientist, while the other took positions outside along the villa's perimeter, should unexpected guests arrive or the occupant attempt to escape.

Martin gave the signal and the two teams sprinted across the open expanse, with Martin's team heading toward the pedestrian gate while the other team fanned out along the villa's perimeter. Upon reaching the gate, the operator beside him, Patrick Terrill, pulled out a set of universal keys, and fifteen seconds later, the four men passed through the open gate and moved up the sidewalk. When they reached the front door, Martin spotted a security panel beside it. After a close examination, he determined it was wireless rather than hardwired.

Child's play.

Terrill pulled a jammer from his backpack and selected the appropriate frequencies. Not only would they jam the signal between the sensors and the control panel, but they would jam the system's anti-jam feature—a signal sent to the monitoring station if it detected it was being jammed.

Terrill activated the jammer and used a universal key to unlock the door. He pushed the door open and the four operators surged into the dark foyer. There was no one present, and Martin closed the door softly behind him. As the door closed, Martin's sixth sense kicked in. Something was wrong. He couldn't put his finger on it, but his gut instincts had never misled him. With a sense of urgency, Martin led his team through the villa, weapons raised.

They entered the living room—unoccupied.

Dining room—unoccupied and immaculate.

Family room—empty and neat.

Kitchen and breakfast nook—several plates and glasses in the sink.

Martin spotted a narrow hallway leading farther back into the villa. He led his team into the corridor, stopping by the first door. He turned the handle slowly and pushed the door open. A study with a built-in computer desk and bookcase. No one present. Martin moved to the next room and opened the door. A queen bed—empty and made up. That left the room at the end of the hallway.

Martin stopped at the door, placing his hand on the doorknob. With this being the last room in the villa, there was no more need for stealth. Martin turned the knob slowly, then burst into the bedroom, followed by the rest of his team.

There was a man asleep in bed. He jolted to a sitting position, and a quick look at his face told Martin he was their target. The man's mouth dropped open after seeing four men with weapons pointed at him, then he clamped his mouth shut. Two operators moved forward and the Russian's hands were quickly bound and a black hood shoved over his head. Martin led his team, with the Russian in the middle, to the villa's exit. Upon reaching the front door, he twisted the doorknob, but it didn't rotate.

He tried again, but it wouldn't move. He searched for a security panel nearby, but there was none to be found. Upon examining the doorknob more closely, he understood the reason for his nagging feeling when he'd entered the villa: there was no keyhole or lock mechanism, just a plain, inoperable doorknob. They were locked inside. Peering out the nearest window, Martin examined the cameras atop the security gate. They were pointed inward.

Martin yanked the hood off the scientist. "What the hell is this?" he asked in Russian.

"Welcome to my humble abode," he replied with a grin.

Martin shoved the hood back onto the Russian's head and forced him to the ground while the other three operators took up defensive positions in the foyer. There was no indication of anyone else in the villa or nearby, however. After evaluating whether to blow the door or bust out through a window, Martin spoke to the second team outside, explaining the situation. A few seconds later, one of the team members moved swiftly up the sidewalk. Upon reaching the front door, he twisted the knob and the door opened.

Martin led the way from the villa, recalling the other team as they approached the tree line. It wasn't much longer before Martin's men and the Russian were aboard their Black Hawk, which lifted off swiftly at a tilt, barely clearing the treetops as it raced west toward the Russian border. Not far behind, the second Black Hawk followed. As Martin removed his gloves, he glanced at the Russian, lying on his side, still bound and wearing the black hood.

Why was he a prisoner in his own home?

49

JASLYK, UZBEKISTAN

Jaslyk Prison, a penal colony in northwest Uzbekistan, is notorious for having the harshest prison conditions in the country. While it is well-known as "the concentration camp of death," little is known concerning who is incarcerated and how the prisoners are treated; but this hasn't deterred Western journalists from circulating reports of beatings, sexual assault, and torture. Some experts even claimed that several prisoners who died at Jaslyk were boiled alive. These allegations, of course, were all true.

CIA interrogator John Kaufmann sat at a scarred wooden table inside a small concrete-block room. With only a cot, a table, and one chair, the musty-smelling cell was the most hospitable room in the facility. As he skimmed through a folder, he stopped when he reached the most recent entry, containing new information discovered after their *guest*, for lack of a better term, had been extracted from his villa west of Moscow. After reviewing Anton Fedorov's dossier, Kaufmann closed the folder and tapped his index finger on the table as he sorted through the data. He couldn't connect the dots. Something critical was missing.

Kaufmann took the folder with him as he left the

room, along with a pack of cigarettes and a lighter. After traversing a dingy, concrete corridor illuminated by bare bulbs hanging from the ceiling, he reached a guarded cell door. A burly, uniformed man unlocked and opened the door as Kaufmann approached, closing it after he entered the cell.

Seated on one of two metal chairs in the otherwise bare room was Anton Fedorov, naked except for boxer shorts, his hands tied behind his back and to his chair. Kaufmann settled into a chair across from Fedorov, who seemed none the worse for wear aside from a few bruises on his face. Kaufmann commenced the interrogation, speaking in Russian.

"I see you've met your Uzbekistani caretakers."

Fedorov replied, "Let's dispense with the pleasantries. What do you want?"

Kaufmann offered the Russian a cigarette.

Fedorov shook his head. "You intend to kill me slowly, with lung cancer?"

Kaufmann slid the cigarette pack into his shirt pocket, then pulled a photograph of a detonator from the folder, showing it to Fedorov. "Do you recognize this?"

"Of course," Fedorov replied. "I designed it."

"We have an issue," Kaufmann said, "that requires your assistance. Your detonators have been attached to explosives, and we need to remove or disarm them. A simple problem, yes?"

"Not exactly." Fedorov grinned, a wide, toothy smile.

Under normal circumstances, the Russian would have started bleeding profusely from his mouth and nose right now, courtesy of Kaufmann's fist. However, Fedorov wasn't your average terrorist, and Kaufmann had already decided to take a more civil approach.

Kaufmann asked, "Can you elaborate?"

"They are the most sophisticated detonators ever

designed," Fedorov said. "They cannot be removed or jammed. They are truly tamper-proof."

"It turns out," Kaufmann said, "that our experts agree. You have done a masterful job." Kaufmann waited a moment while Fedorov basked in the praise. "However, they also believe these detonators can be disarmed by sending an override code. All you have to do is give me the code, and after we verify it works, you will be released."

"If I give you the code," Fedorov said, "I'm a dead man."

Kaufmann filed away the first important detail from his interrogation—there was indeed a master override code.

"I don't know about that," Kaufmann said. "But I do know that if you *don't* give me the code, you're a dead man." He paused, waiting for his words to sink in. "However, if you give us the code, we'll release you and guarantee your safety."

"You cannot protect me," Fedorov replied with disdain on his face. "The Russian government does not look kindly on traitors. They will find me."

Kaufmann evaluated Fedorov's claim; whether it was true or not was immaterial. That he believed he would be killed was what mattered. Kaufmann shifted gears.

"Why were you a prisoner in your own villa?"

Fedorov didn't answer.

Kaufmann decided to become more aggressive. Perhaps there was something the Russian would be willing to trade his life for. He pulled a second picture from his folder.

"Do you recognize this woman?"

Fedorov examined the photograph for a split second before rage flashed in his eyes. He surged toward Kaufmann, lifting his chair, bound to his hands behind his body, off the floor. Kaufmann lifted his right foot and planted a boot in Fedorov's chest as the Russian tried to reach him. The muscles in Fedorov's neck strained and his face turned red as he struggled against his bonds, but he uttered no words.

Unstable, Kaufmann noted. The picture was becoming clearer.

Fedorov's rage subsided and he dropped his chair onto the ground, then slumped into it. Kaufmann left his boot on Fedorov's chest but said nothing, waiting for the dam to break. Finally, Fedorov began talking.

"She meant everything to me. My only child. The bastard murdered her." Fedorov surged forward in his chair as rage overtook him again, but it subsided more quickly this time. When the anger faded, Fedorov's head sagged onto his chest, and he started weeping.

Definitely unstable, Kaufmann thought, noting the irony. An unstable engineer working with explosives. He dropped his foot to the ground and waited for Fedorov to regain his composure. When the tears ended, the Russian sat up in his chair.

Kaufmann pulled a third photograph from the folder, showing it to Fedorov. "Is this the man responsible?"

Fedorov spit on the picture.

I'll take that as a yes.

Kaufmann was making progress, but a key piece of the puzzle was missing.

"There's something I don't understand. Your daughter is discovered strangled and her body dumped in a back alley, you think her boyfriend is responsible, and you end up a prisoner in a villa on the outskirts of Velikiy Novgorod. What am I missing?"

"I tried to kill him," Fedorov replied.

Suddenly, the missing puzzle piece was in Kaufmann's hand. But it still didn't fit.

"There's no evidence you tried to kill him. No arrest,

not even a news article about the incident. An attempt on this man's life would have been splattered across every newspaper in the country. But it was swept under the rug?"

Fedorov nodded. "He's a powerful man, and the government didn't want the issue to go public. So they gave me a pass and put me under surveillance so I couldn't get near him again. But that didn't stop me."

"How's that?"

"I hired the Russian mafia. They had him in their sights. One more second . . . ," Fedorov said, his voice trailing off. "After that attempt, they transferred me to the research facility at Velikiy Novgorod, where I was given a plush villa prison cell with no outside communication. I can't get near him, nor hire anyone to do the job."

Kaufmann mulled the new information over. Under normal circumstances, Fedorov would be in a wooden box six feet underground after two assassination attempts, but he happened to be a brilliant engineer developing stuff the Russian government really wanted. So they kept him alive and put him to work at a remote location, transporting him between the research facility and his villa prison each day.

"I *know* he's responsible," Fedorov said. "My daughter and I were close, and she confided in me before her death. Their relationship was deteriorating and she knew too much."

"I see," Kaufmann said. Now that the picture was clear, he realized an *arrangement* might be possible. He returned the photograph to the folder and tossed it onto the floor.

"Let's assume you're correct, and if you give me the override code, you're a dead man. Let's also assume you're dead if you *don't* give me the code. You're in a pickle, as we say in baseball." Fedorov gave him a blank stare. "I offer you a deal," Kaufmann said. "Give me the code and we'll take care of this matter for you."

"You'll kill him?"

Kaufmann nodded.

"I want him dead *before* I give you the code."

Kaufmann hesitated. He knew time was critical. However, it was clear Fedorov wasn't going to budge on his demand. "Agreed," he said.

"I want proof," Fedorov said. "I want to see his dead carcass."

"We'll provide a picture of his body."

The Russian's eyes bored into Kaufmann for a moment, then he said, "I have a better idea. I want to watch him die. And before he takes his last breath, I want him to see my face and know who is responsible."

"You cannot leave this facility before you give us the code. You cannot be there to watch him die."

"A video link will be sufficient," Fedorov replied, "between two cell phones. After I watch him die, I'll give you the code."

"We'll make the necessary arrangements," Kaufmann said.

Fedorov leaned back in his chair, a look of satisfaction on his face.

Kaufmann was about to leave when a thought struck him. "Anton," he said, "can we get our hands on some of your detonators?"

"Of course," Fedorov replied. "What do you have in mind?"

Seated at her desk in her West Wing corner office, Christine rested her fingers on her computer keyboard as she stared at her display, replaying President Xiang's words in her mind for the thousandth time.

Should I be as ruthless as you?

His question at the end of their meeting had stung. She wasn't ruthless by any stretch of the imagination, yet Xiang implied she was more ruthless than him. How was that possible? By ordering the invasion of Taiwan, Xiang was responsible for the death of over one hundred thousand men and women. Yet by killing one defenseless man, she was more ruthless? She wondered if something had been lost in translation.

There was a knock on Christine's door, and after she acknowledged, Colonel DuBose entered. "Good afternoon, Miss O'Connor. Just a reminder, the briefing begins in five minutes."

"Thanks, Colonel." She'd lost track of time. Grabbing a notepad from her desk, she joined the marine, then headed down one level into the Situation Room, where they joined Hardison, McVeigh, Dawn, and CIA Director Jessica Cherry.

It wasn't long before the president arrived, taking his

seat at the head of the table. He wasted no time, turning to Dawn. "Bring me up to speed on the diplomatic
front."

"I'll start with Lithuania and Ukraine. NATO leadership is still debating the use of military force and it
looks like several countries are preparing to submit a *no*
vote to the secretary-general. Russia is taking advantage
of the indecision within NATO, continuing to push for
a continental security summit, and a few NATO countries are considering Kalinin's offer. The Alliance is
unstable, and could capitulate to Kalinin's demands at
any moment.

"In the Pacific, there's been no word from India, but
thanks to Christine, President Xiang has agreed to remain neutral, and our embassy in Beijing has received
the list of concessions he's requesting. We're negotiating a few things, but when the dust settles, we'll have a
deal."

The president replied, "Do you think we can trust
China?"

There was silence in the Situation Room as the president's eyes canvased the men and women at the table.
His question was rhetorical. No one knew the answer.

Turning to McVeigh, the president asked, "Where do
we stand militarily?"

McVeigh answered, "The *Eisenhower* and *Bush*
strike groups are on their way across the Pacific. However, positioning four strike groups in the Indian Ocean
will telegraph our intention and we'll lose the element
of surprise. To cover our tracks, we'll jam Russian and
Indian satellites, and those of any other country that
might be inclined to pass intel to Russia."

"Won't jamming the satellites alert Russia that we're
up to something?"

"Jamming isn't the best term," McVeigh replied.
"We have the ability to upload modified satellite images,

like a closed-circuit camera being fed prerecorded tape. It'll look like the two carrier strike groups leaving the West Coast are headed to China, to replace the two we've sent into the Indian Ocean."

"Got it," the president said.

"Although we're moving naval assets into position," McVeigh said, "we're having difficulty with Air Force units. Every country in the region except Afghanistan is refusing to let us base military assets in their territory, fearing Russia will blow their pipelines in retaliation. That means we can't get tactical missile batteries close enough to the Gulf of Oman, and Afghanistan is too far away for significant tactical air support. The best we can do is provide air support using long-range strategic assets, which will play a role at the beginning of the conflict but quickly lose relevance once the battle begins. Given those constraints, however, we've developed a plan.

"It'll be a phased approach," McVeigh said, "taking out the Russian air bases in Iran before attacking Russia's surface combatants. We'll then concentrate on the mobile land-based missile batteries once they engage and give away their positions, hoping they don't do too much damage before we take them out. Once we begin the offensive above the water, we expect Russia will attack with their submarines, and their two-to-one advantage poses a significant challenge. The plan is to hold off the Russian submarine assault long enough to eliminate Russia's surface combatants and missile batteries, which will allow the carrier strike groups to focus their efforts on the subsurface battle or vacate the area if things get out of hand."

"What about NATO naval assistance?" the president asked.

McVeigh answered, "As Dawn explained, NATO countries are currently paralyzed, refusing to commit military assets to the conflict. It's not much of a loss, though. Compared to our Navy, other NATO maritime assets are marginal."

"Thanks, Bob," the president said. "Where do we stand on the pipeline sabotage? We can't move forward in the Persian Gulf unless we've disarmed the explosives."

McVeigh turned to CIA Director Jessica Cherry.

"I have mostly good news," Cherry said. "We've extracted the Russian who designed the detonators, and there is indeed a code that will disarm them. He's agreed to give us the code, but on one condition."

Cherry went on to explain what happened to the Russian's daughter and the deal they had made. "Unfortunately, this is going to be a difficult operation for two reasons. The first is the target itself." She paused, as if to heighten the tension, then explained. "The man who supposedly murdered our friend's daughter is Russian Defense Minister Boris Chernov."

Christine sucked in a sharp breath. Chernov had wandering eyes, but she had never suspected anything sinister. "You're sure?" she asked.

"We're not," Cherry replied. "But our Russian friend believes it and that's what matters. We kill Chernov and we get the code. However, there's another complication. We need to establish a video link between the killer and our Russian friend just before Chernov is axed, so our friend can watch him die and Chernov can see his face before he takes his last breath. That means we can't kill him from afar, with a sniper, for example, by wiring his car with explosives, or by destroying his house with a missile. It has to be an up-close-and-personal affair.

"This wouldn't be difficult if the target was an ordinary citizen, but we're talking about a high-ranking government official, who happens to be well guarded due to two attempts on his life, courtesy of our Russian scientist." Cherry let everyone absorb the challenges they were facing, then continued, "We're working on a plan, leveraging Chernov's reputation as a ladies' man, hoping to get him alone with the right beautiful woman. We've already selected the agent." Cherry opened a folder in front of her and passed out several copies of a portfolio.

"Elena Krayev," she said. "An ethnic Russian working at the U.S. embassy in Moscow as a translator. She's also a highly trained field agent, who runs *errands* for us on occasion."

Christine received a copy of Elena's portfolio and turned to the first page, containing a head shot and full-body picture. She was stunningly beautiful.

"The last element of the plan we're working on is how they meet. It needs to be innocuous, in a way that doesn't raise Chernov's suspicion, nor that of his security detail. We're thinking about some sort of official government reception in the evening, because he rarely leaves without a beautiful woman on his arm. Unfortunately, Russia's invasion of Lithuania and war with Ukraine have put a damper on these types of activities. I understand time is critical, but we're currently at a loss on this aspect of the plan."

Christine suggested, "Kalinin's continental security summit. Would that work?"

Cherry pondered Christine's suggestion, then replied, "Yes, that would work. Elena can be assigned as a translator for the American representatives." Cherry looked to the president, who turned to Dawn.

"Agree to the summit," he ordered, "and get it scheduled ASAP. Try to get as many NATO countries as possible to attend, but time is critical, so give them a twenty-four-hour deadline to decide, then move forward with whoever has agreed. While you're at it, let the Alliance leaders know we don't intend to capitulate to Kalinin's demands; we're working on something. But don't mention Elena. We can't afford to let our plan leak out."

Turning to Christine, he said, "You're familiar with the players and have experience negotiating with the Russians. Accompany Dawn to Moscow for the meeting, and you can introduce Elena to Chernov."

After Dawn and Christine acknowledged the president's order, McVeigh said, "Mr. President, it's going to take time to get our naval assets into position. With your permission, we'll begin uploading fake images into the appropriate satellites."

The president gave his concurrence, and after reflecting for a moment on the day's briefing, he said to McVeigh, "I want . . . a plan B."

"Plan B?" McVeigh said.

The president spent the next few minutes explaining his idea while McVeigh took notes. When the president finished, he asked, "Can we do this?"

"Yes, Mr. President, it's doable. We'll have to begin mobilizing assets and redeploying others, but I don't foresee any obstacles."

"Good," the president said. "Get started."

USS *HARRY S. TRUMAN*

In the southern Arabian Sea, just west of the Maldives, USS *Harry S. Truman* headed into the wind as an F/A-18E Super Hornet moved forward on the Flight Deck, locking into the starboard bow catapult. Seated in his chair on the Bridge, Captain David Randle watched as the jet blast deflector behind the fighter tilted up, shielding the F/A-18F behind from the aircraft's twin-engine exhaust. A moment later, the Super Hornet raced forward, angling up and to the right after clearing the bow, headed out to relieve one of the fighters in *Truman*'s combat air patrol.

The next Super Hornet also launched successfully, completing this launch cycle. In another thirty minutes, the returning fighters would land aboard *Truman*. In the meantime, Randle's eyes scanned the video screens mounted below the Bridge windows. The *Reagan* strike group was a hundred miles to the west, with both strike groups staying a safe distance from the Russian Northern and Pacific Fleets camped out at the mouth of the Persian Gulf. However, if events unfolded as expected, it wouldn't be long before *Truman* headed northwest, with *Reagan* and two new strike groups alongside. The *Eisenhower* and *Bush* strike groups were fresh out of maintenance periods, as were their air wings, but that wasn't the case for *Truman*.

USS *Harry S. Truman* had been at sea for eight months, and the grind was beginning to wear on personnel and equipment. Aircraft carriers had tremendous repair departments, well stocked with spares and well-trained technicians, and *Truman* was no exception. However, the higher than normal flight tempo had taken its toll and the failures requiring depot-level repair were mounting. With combat looming on the horizon, Randle had been pushing hard to ensure every aircraft aboard was fully operational.

The ship's Communicator approached, handing Randle the message board. He read the OPORD, then reflected on his new operational orders. The basic battle plan had been laid out, although the start time was TBD. There was still time to prepare, and his repair department needed to fix all inoperable aircraft, while Randle crossed his fingers and hoped no more broke in the meantime.

Five miles east of *Truman*, Lieutenant Commander Bill Houston aimed his single-seat Super Hornet toward the moving gray postage stamp in the Indian Ocean. It'd been a long five hours on combat air patrol and he was approaching bingo fuel. He was glad to be heading back to the floating bird farm, his home on the water for the last eight months. Real home, with his wife and three kids, would have to wait. Houston's eyes went to a small, worn photo of his family wedged against the rim of his instrumentation panel. He had his arm around Nell, with the kids in front, his hand on John's shoulder while Nell pulled Kate and Jackson close.

As he returned his eyes to his instrumentation, he caught the reflection of a Japanese Imperial Navy ensign—the Rising Sun flag—in the canopy. Bill Hous-

ton, half Japanese and half English Channel mix, had
been awarded the call sign Samurai by his fellow pilots
in flight school. The top of every pilot's helmet had to
be covered in reflective paint or tape in case they ejected
into the ocean and required retrieval, and with a call
sign of Samurai, Houston had decorated his helmet
with the red sun near the front, and red and white stripes
radiating over the top.

As Houston closed on *Truman*, he heard Approach
in his headset. "Bravo-one-five, Air Ops. Mode one
landing."

Houston acknowledged and turned control of his aircraft over to *Truman*'s SPN-46 automatic carrier landing system, which would adjust engine speed and flaps
to land the fighter at a designated point on the Flight
Deck. He wasn't a fan of delegating control of his aircraft to a computer, but orders were orders and Houston
prepared for the hands-off landing.

Not long after enabling the automated landing, Houston heard *Bitching Betty* in his headset—the female
voice of the F/A-18 audio warning system, with its distinctive southern drawl—proclaiming a warning he'd
heard only in the simulator.

"Engine right! Engine right!"

Houston's Super Hornet slowed and yawed to the
right, and a glance at his instrumentation revealed a
flameout in his starboard engine. He went to afterburner
on the port engine and half flaps, straightening his flight
trajectory.

Into his headset, he said, "Approach, bravo-one-five
is single-engine at four miles."

Approach acknowledged, and while they passed word
to the Flight Deck to prepare for an emergency landing,
Houston noticed the engine fuel display ticking rapidly
toward empty. He'd developed a fuel leak, which explained the reason for the starboard engine flameout.

Houston disengaged the automated carrier landing system, taking manual control. After evaluating whether to ditch the aircraft into the ocean or risk a landing with one engine and a fuel leak, he decided.

"Approach, bravo-one-five. I'm bringing it in."

Captain Randle stood on the port side of the Bridge, looking aft. The damaged Super Hornet appeared in the distance, a small gray speck growing slowly larger, wobbling as it was buffeted by strong winds. Randle's attention shifted from the jet to the Landing Signals Officer, standing on the Flight Deck. The LSO held a radio handset in one hand, advising the pilot on engine power and glide path. In his other hand, he held the *pickle* switch controlling the Optical Landing System, containing red *wave-off* and green *cut* lights, which directed the pilot to either abort the landing or make adjustments during his approach.

The Super Hornet angled down toward the deck, its tailhook extended. The pilot's control of his aircraft was impaired with the engine flameout, and if he landed late and his tailhook missed the arresting cables, he would have to bolter, pushing his remaining engine to full throttle to regain sufficient speed before he ran out of carrier deck. A bolter was always an exciting event, and with only one engine, a hazardous one.

Randle watched the green *cut* lights flash periodically during the jet's descent, sending last-second guidance to the pilot. He followed the Super Hornet in, its wings wobbling one last time before the wheels hit the Flight Deck. The jet's tailhook snagged the number two arresting wire and the aircraft screeched to a halt. Randle let out a deep breath, relieved the pilot had landed safely. However, that was one more jet down, adding to the repair department's workload.

52

USS *MICHIGAN*

With his submarine at periscope depth, Wilson sat in the Captain's chair in the darkness listening intently to the Conn speaker, which was broadcasting intercepts from the submarine's Electronic Support Measures sensor. This evening's trip to periscope depth had been uneventful, with the only required tasks being a radio broadcast download and a position fix for the inertial navigators. After the tense forays to the surface during the past week, in proximity to Russian combatants, tonight's trip to periscope depth had been leisurely and stress free.

The bleeps and buzzes emanating from the ESM speaker were a foreign language to the untrained, but Wilson's experienced ear told him there were no surface combatants nearby. Confirming his assessment, the ESM Watch called out, "Conn, ESM. Hold no threat radars."

The Officer of the Deck acknowledged the report, and as Lieutenant Jayne Stucker rotated slowly on the periscope beside him, Wilson reflected on how the U.S. Submarine Force had changed in his almost forty years of service.

Wilson was a *mustang*—a prior-enlisted officer,

having joined the Navy fresh out of high school. After ten years as a nuclear electronics technician, he received his commission as an officer and worked his way up the ranks, eventually becoming Captain of the nuclear-powered fast attack submarine USS *Buffalo*. Following command, he was assigned as the senior instructor for newly assigned submarine commanding officers, overseeing their training during tense at-sea tactical engagements as they completed final preparations for command.

When his instructor tour ended, Wilson accepted command of *Michigan* instead of a submarine squadron, choosing to end his career at sea instead of behind a desk. With commands of fast attack and guided missile submarines under his belt, along with several years training future commanding officers, Murray Wilson was the most experienced submarine commanding officer in the Fleet.

Michigan tilted downward as Lieutenant Stucker ordered the submarine back to the safety of deep water, and the low-level lights flicked on. Wilson read *Michigan*'s latest OPORD, containing the details concerning his next mission. With transit through the Suez Canal on the surface deemed too risky under current conditions and *Michigan*'s Tomahawk missiles no longer needed in Ukraine at the moment, Navy leadership had identified an alternate use for the guided missile submarine. *Michigan*'s tactical systems were being called into service.

Although *Michigan* was built as a ballistic missile submarine, it was a far different ship today from when it was launched three decades ago. With the implementation of the Strategic Offensive Reductions Treaty, the Navy reconfigured the four oldest Ohio class submarines as special warfare platforms. In addition to carrying Dry Deck Shelters with SEAL mini-subs inside, *Michigan* had been reconfigured with seven-pack Tomahawk launchers in twenty-two of the submarine's twenty-four missile tubes.

During the conversion from SSBN to SSGN, *Michigan* and her three sister ships received a slew of tactical system upgrades. The combat control consoles were now the most modern in the submarine fleet, as were *Michigan*'s new sonar, electronic surveillance, and radio suites. The torpedoes aboard Wilson's submarine were also the newest in the U.S. Navy's arsenal; *Michigan* was fully loaded with MK 48 Mod 7 torpedoes, the most advanced heavyweight torpedo in the world.

Wilson approached the Quartermaster, seated at the navigation table. "Hand me the waterspace advisories."

Petty Officer Pat Leenstra handed the folder to Wilson, who perused the messages, which detailed the routes of all fast attack submarines transiting across the Atlantic Ocean, so the ballistic missile subs on patrol could stay out of the transit lanes. There were two fast attack submarines, one from Groton and one from Norfolk, fresh out of maintenance periods, late to the party and hightailing it across the Atlantic toward the Mediterranean.

Wilson estimated they'd be a few hours behind, and *Michigan* would lead the way.

53

MOSCOW

Darkness had enveloped the Russian capital by the time three black sedans pulled up to Hotel National, not far from the Kremlin. Christine O'Connor and Dawn Cabral, weary from the long flight from Washington, D.C., stepped from the center car while Diplomatic Security Service agents emerged from the other two vehicles. Christine was looking forward to a good night's sleep; the Russian morning would come soon enough, followed by the first day of the continental security summit. Without much prodding, Russia had arranged a reception the first evening, where the summit participants could socialize while discussing less contentious topics. It was there that their translator, Elena Krayev, would attempt to snare Boris Chernov.

While the bellhops collected their luggage, Christine and Dawn entered the hotel lobby, where they were met by Barry Graham, an aide to the U.S. ambassador to the Russian Federation. After introductions, he handed the two women their door cards, informing them their rooms were on the tenth floor. As Christine and Dawn prepared to call it a night, Graham informed them that their translator for the summit was on her way over and would arrive shortly.

It wasn't long before Elena Krayev entered the hotel lobby, wearing a form-fitting skirt and tailored blouse accentuating her figure, draping a garment bag over a shoulder while pulling a carry-on suitcase behind her. Elena was even more stunning in person than on paper. Heads turned, both male and female, following her as she walked through the lobby.

Elena spotted Christine and Dawn and headed their way. Upon reaching the Americans, she greeted them with a firm, confident handshake. She was given a hotel room on the same floor as Dawn and Christine, purportedly in case the negotiations went later than expected, so she wouldn't have to endure the long trek to her home on the outskirts of the city. In reality, she'd been given a hotel room nearby with the hope she could entice Chernov to *her place* instead of his tomorrow night. In case things didn't go as planned and she needed assistance, a CIA extraction team was only a few doors down the hall. If they went to Chernov's place, an emergency extraction would be much more complicated.

The three women headed to the tenth floor, where they gathered in Christine's room. Elena explained the one detail of her assignment pertinent to the other two women. One of them would introduce her to Chernov, and she would take it from there.

After Elena left, Christine prepared for bed, donning a silk nightgown before slipping under the sheets. Although she was tired from the long trip, her body told her it was only midafternoon due to the jet lag. She tossed and turned for a while, her thoughts shifting frequently to Elena's assignment to assassinate Chernov, before she eventually drifted off to sleep.

The morning arrived quicker than Christine had hoped. After a shower and a cup of strong coffee, brought to her by one of the Diplomatic Security Service agents, she was ready to begin the day. Elena was waiting in the hallway, wearing a business suit and leaning against the wall, a black attaché case in one hand. Christine knocked on Dawn's door and she answered, and they headed to the lobby.

After their car pulled to a halt in front of the Kremlin Senate, they were greeted by an aide to Foreign Minister Lavrov, who escorted them to a conference room on the third floor, one Christine knew well. The first two rounds of follow-on nuclear arms reduction talks had been held here. The thirty-seat conference table was already half-full, and Christine spotted the three seats reserved for them, with placards on the table in front of each chair.

Foreign Minister Lavrov approached Christine and her two companions. "Miss O'Connor," he said, "it is a pleasure to see you again. I'm glad you were able to join us."

"It's good to see you again as well, Minister Lavrov." Turning to Dawn and Elena, she introduced America's secretary of state and their interpreter.

Russia's foreign minister engaged them in conversation, containing nothing of substance, until the meeting was called to order. Before Christine headed to her seat, she searched the conference room for Defense Minister Chernov. He was nowhere to be found.

She turned to Lavrov. "Will Defense Minister Chernov attend the summit?"

"He is disposed otherwise," Lavrov replied.

Christine's stomach knotted. Their plan hinged on Elena meeting Chernov.

"But he plans to join us tonight at the reception."

The tension eased from Christine's body. Their plan was still on track.

The summit progressed slowly at first, then picked up speed once the participants settled on the objective for the meeting. Without full NATO participation, no agreement could be reached. However, it was decided that the summit would develop a framework for formal negotiations, and that plan suited both sides. The Russians were pleased because things were progressing toward a peaceful and favorable solution, and the United States and its NATO allies were satisfied since the plan stalled substantive discussions; the United States had no intention of negotiating away part of Lithuania or the eastern one-third of Ukraine. Although the participants were prepared to work through the weekend, it soon became clear that a suitable framework would be developed by the end of the day.

54

WASHINGTON, D.C.

Seated at his desk in the Oval Office, the president hung up the phone, then turned sideways in his chair, looking across the south lawn as the early morning sun illuminated the rose garden's red, pink, and white flowers. Deep in thought, he smoothed his blue tie against his white shirt, failing to notice that his tie, a gift from the first lady, matched the color of the drapes and the presidential seal on the rug.

The president's telephone discussion with CIA Director Cherry had been short and nondescript, the details of their conversation deliberately vague. The continental security summit in Moscow had wrapped up and the *operation* was on track. In a few hours, if everything went as planned, the detonator disarm code would be obtained and the president would give the order, placing thousands of men and women in the military in harm's way. There would be a significant loss of life, SecDef McVeigh had explained: hundreds, if not thousands, of Americans dead. It was a decision the president did not take lightly, but one he had already made. The United States could not sit by and let Russia annex portions of two sovereign countries.

The president pressed the intercom button on his

phone, directing his executive assistant to get Prime Minister Susan Gates on the line. With the assistance of the British prime minister, the stalling tactics had worked, pushing off the votes on the resolutions authorizing the use of NATO force to expel Russia from Ukraine and Lithuania.

"Mr. President." The voice of his executive assistant emanated from the phone's speaker. "I've got Prime Minister Gates on the line."

The president picked up the phone, and after thanking Sue for her assistance within NATO, he broached the sensitive subject, informing her that the United States would go it alone, attacking Russian forces within a few hours if things went as planned. Once the order was given and the attack imminent, the United States' permanent representative to NATO would inform the remaining NATO countries of the U.S. military response.

As the president prepared to conclude his conversation with Minister Gates, he considered revealing plan B, the second phase of the campaign. However, it was a delicate operation, its success dependent even more on secrecy. He decided to leave that part out.

The president hung up, then checked his watch. Evening was approaching in Moscow, and with it, the reception where Elena Krayev would meet Boris Chernov, and the one obstacle standing between them and the detonator disarm code would be overcome.

It was 6 p.m. by the time the summit ended, and after a quick dinner in the hotel restaurant with Dawn and Elena, Christine returned to her room and changed into a formal dress for the evening's reception. After touching up her makeup, she stepped from her room and knocked on Elena's door. It was slightly ajar and Christine pushed it slowly open, calling Elena's name. She was sitting on the edge of her bed, wearing an elegant, form-fitting Russian Federation–red evening gown with her hands folded in her lap, staring at the wall. She turned her head slowly when Christine opened the door, then stood without a word. After grabbing a small purse from her desk, she joined Christine in the hallway as Dawn emerged from her room.

They descended to the lobby and headed to the hotel entrance, where a black limousine, situated between two sedans containing Diplomatic Security Service agents, was waiting to take the three women to the Kremlin Senate. During the short drive, Elena was silent, staring out the side window at the buildings along Mokhovaya Street. As they approached the southwest corner of the Kremlin, her attention was drawn to the five-century-old Borovitskaya Tower, with its green decorative spire rising to a ruby-red five-pointed star, symbol of the Soviet Union. After passing through Borovitskaya Gate, their car pulled to a halt in front of the Kremlin Senate.

They were escorted by a Kremlin aide to a ballroom on the third floor—the same one the Victory Day gala had been held in: a white marble–clad room with exquisite crystal chandeliers, their sparkling lights illuminating a glossy but crowded parquet floor. Waiters dressed in tuxedos made their way through the crowd, carrying silver platters filled with hors d'oeuvres and glasses of wine and champagne, offering the contents to the guests.

Upon entering the ballroom, Elena transitioned from the quiet, reserved woman in the car to an outgoing, enchanting personality. Christine watched in fascination as Elena turned on the charm, gathering a small crowd around her. The intended victim of her charm—Defense Minister Chernov—was nowhere to be found, however.

The three women engaged various diplomats, with Elena translating on occasion. Christine kept an eye out for Chernov, eventually spotting him enter the ballroom, stopping to chat with a representative from France. Elena also noticed Chernov's entrance, and the two women broke from their conversation with several Italian and Russian diplomats.

As they headed toward Chernov, Christine whispered, "Are you ready?"

Elena replied, "I'll have him eating out of my hand in no time."

Boris Chernov turned his attention to the two women as they approached, commenting to the French diplomat as Christine and Elena joined them, "Are there two more beautiful women here tonight?" He eyed Christine briefly before turning his attention to Elena. "And you are?"

Christine answered, "I'd like to introduce Elena Krayev, our translator for the summit."

Elena extended her arm, her hand bent at the wrist as she greeted Chernov in Russian. Chernov's eyes took in Elena's body as he bent slightly forward and kissed the back of her hand.

He turned to Christine. "An ethnic Russian translator. I commend you on the upgrade." He said something to Elena in Russian and she laughed.

Stepping closer to Chernov, Elena placed her hand on his arm as she said to Christine, "You never told me what a good sense of humor Minister Chernov has."

As Elena turned back to Chernov, Christine glanced over his shoulder and spotted Semyon Gorev, head of Russia's SVR, standing along the ballroom perimeter, intently watching Christine and Elena's interaction with Russia's defense minister.

"If you'll excuse us," Elena said, then she wrapped her arm around Chernov's and pulled him away for a private conversation. When Chernov and Elena drifted off, Gorev headed in Christine's direction. As the SVR director approached, the French diplomat excused himself.

"Welcome back to Moscow," Gorev said. "What game are we playing tonight?"

Christine's pulse quickened. Had Gorev deciphered their plan?

"I'd like to redeem myself," he added.

Christine's concern subsided when she realized Gorev was referring to their encounter during her last trip to Moscow, when he barred her path in the hallway outside Kalinin's office and she tricked her way past him.

"No game tonight," Christine replied. She knew she shouldn't antagonize the head of the SVR, but couldn't resist. "I don't want to embarrass you again."

Gorev smiled. A tight, malevolent smile. "Well then,"

he said, "perhaps we could play a game of my choosing." He glanced around the crowded ballroom. "When there are fewer witnesses."

Christine had already decided she should probably avoid Gorev during this visit. Now, she was certain.

"If you'll excuse me," she said, then turned and left him standing alone on the parquet floor.

Ambassador Natasha Graham wasn't far away, and Christine joined her, Dawn, and several Russian diplomats who had homed in on America's ambassador and secretary of state. The conversation was quite cordial; from the moment Christine arrived at the Kremlin Senate that morning, the Russians had done everything possible to create a business-as-usual atmosphere, as if they were here to discuss a minor dustup at a border crossing.

She glanced periodically in Gorev's direction; he engaged various dignitaries, both Russian and foreign, and every once in a while she caught him looking at her. As the evening wore on and she lost Gorev in the crowd, Christine decided she could use some time alone. She had introduced Elena to Chernov and figured her job was done. She retreated from the ballroom onto a balcony overlooking the city, stopping at the stone railing. Her eyes swept across the venerable city, surveying the historic buildings in the distance and the sparkling lights blending into the horizon.

Christine broke from her thoughts when Elena passed through the doorway onto the balcony, her cool facade replaced with a frustrated look. She stopped beside Christine.

"It's not working," Elena said. "The bastard doesn't seem interested."

Elena's news was unexpected. With Chernov's reputation, it hadn't crossed her mind that he'd turn down the advances of a woman as beautiful as Elena.

"What do we do now?" Christine asked.

"I keep trying," Elena said. "I need to be careful I don't raise suspicions by coming on too strong, but I have no choice but to dial up the charm." She looked down and adjusted her dress, exposing more cleavage. "Wish me luck," she said, then headed into the ballroom before Christine could reply.

Christine contemplated returning to the ballroom as well, but wasn't in the mood for more frivolous banter with Russian and NATO diplomats. She turned and looked out over the city again, letting her eyes fall on Red Square. The Victory Day banners that had draped the buildings had been taken down and the bleachers disassembled, leaving redbrick facades framing a gray cobblestone square. On the north end of the square, the iconic multicolored bulbous domes of Saint Basil's Cathedral rose skyward.

Her thoughts were interrupted when a man stopped beside her, offering a glass of champagne. She turned and was surprised to see President Kalinin. She glanced toward the ballroom; through the entrance, Gorev was watching, as were two Presidential Security Service agents.

"Welcome back to Moscow," Kalinin said.

"Thank you," Christine said as she took the champagne glass.

She took a sip, and there was an uneasy silence between them until Kalinin said, "Considering I ordered the invasion of two countries, you must think despicable things about me."

"Pretty much," Christine replied.

Kalinin smiled. "You certainly do speak your mind." After a short pause, he added, "Is there anything I can do to make amends?"

"You can withdraw your troops from Lithuania and Ukraine."

"Is there anything *reasonable* I can do to make amends?"

"That's reasonable."

"Not from my perspective."

"Has anyone pointed out your perspective is warped?"

"Not lately," Kalinin replied.

Christine debated whether to continue the conversation. It was pointless; a discussion on a Kremlin balcony wasn't going to convince Kalinin to withdraw his troops. However, Kalinin was the president of Russia, and she couldn't abruptly terminate the conversation as she'd done with Gorev. If nothing more, continuing the dialogue gave her the opportunity to deliver a few barbs to the man who had invaded two countries. He seemed not to mind so far, remaining in a good mood. Then again, he controlled southern Lithuania and eastern Ukraine, and it looked as though NATO was on the verge of capitulating. He had good reason to maintain a cheery disposition.

She took another sip of champagne. "So what's next? What countries do you have your sights set on?"

"None at the moment."

"At the moment?"

"One cannot predict the future. The world is a dangerous place, and I will do what is necessary to protect my country."

"You're right," Christine replied. "The world *is* a dangerous place. Primarily because of you."

"Has anyone pointed out how warped your perspective is?" Kalinin asked.

"Not lately." Christine smiled.

"Look around the world," Kalinin said. "Terrorists streaming across borders, religious fanatics inciting genocide. These are the threats of the twenty-first century. You don't need to worry about Russia."

"Care to ask a few residents of Lithuania and Ukraine about that?"

"Those citizens may be disgruntled, but they won't be killed or oppressed. They will wake up, go to work each day, and enjoy the fruits of their labor and the liberties of a democratic society. Does it really matter whether their government is Ukrainian, Russian, or independent? When you consider the true evils in the world, my actions amount to minor sins."

Christine agreed there were significant issues facing Western societies. Whether Russia was at the top of the list, however, depended on Russia's endgame.

She replied, "The problem is, we don't know where you're going to stop. How many countries you'll gobble up before you feel safe."

Kalinin replied, "You bring up an excellent point. Russia and the West are in conflict because we don't trust each other, and there is no trust because we don't understand one another. Get to know my country. Get to know me, and you will understand Russia poses no threat to the West."

As Christine pondered Kalinin's assertion, he said, "The offer I made during your last trip still stands. Any time you visit Moscow, it would be my pleasure if you joined me for dinner or even a weekend getaway."

Christine couldn't foresee a situation where she would take him up on his offer, but didn't want to turn him down outright, so she just nodded.

When she didn't reply, Kalinin asked, "Do you have any encouraging words to offer?"

"Not at the moment."

Kalinin turned toward the balcony, placing his hands on the stone railing. "I see."

Christine joined him, looking out over the city. "Now isn't a good time for this discussion," she said.

"I understand," Kalinin replied. "My offer remains open."

He turned abruptly and left.

Her eyes followed Kalinin into the ballroom, and Gorev and the two Security Service agents moved away with the president. Alone on the balcony, she took a deep breath and let it out slowly. She had managed to piss off the two most powerful men in Russia, in less than an hour. Not the smartest moves.

She just didn't have the patience anymore, not that she had a lot to begin with. The last few years in the administration had worn her too thin. She had signed up to be a paper pusher, with confrontations limited to those across a conference room table, not those that required a gun or a bloody ice pick. It was time to think about handing the president her resignation when the issue with Russia was resolved.

Christine was about to return to the ballroom when Boris Chernov stepped onto the balcony. Over his shoulder as he approached, Christine spotted Elena, wearing an unhappy expression. She shook her head slightly. She'd failed to snag Chernov.

"Hello again, Christine," Chernov said as he joined her at the railing.

"Good evening, Minister Chernov."

"Please, call me Boris."

"Boris," Christine said, then took a sip of her champagne.

"It looks like the summit wrapped up quicker than expected."

"It did," Christine agreed. "But we established a solid framework for future discussions."

"Which I hope," Chernov said, "will lead to a peaceful resolution of our differences."

"There is always hope."

"When do you head back to America?" Chernov asked, changing the subject.

"Not until Monday."

"Do you have plans for the weekend?"

A sick feeling grew in the pit of Christine's stomach. Chernov was making a move on her. She tried to deflect his interest onto Elena.

"I happened to notice that Elena is quite smitten with you."

Chernov replied, "Hens don't peck at pretty Russian faces." When Christine gave him a curious look, he explained, "It's a Russian idiom. An appropriate translation in English would be—*beautiful Russian women are a dime a dozen*. I prefer something more challenging." Sliding closer to Christine, he said, "I want what Yuri wants. And I want it first."

Christine resisted the urge to step back, creating ample space between them. Instead, she stayed close as she tried to figure out how to redirect his desire. America's attack in the Persian Gulf couldn't proceed unless the pipeline explosives were disarmed, and that wasn't going to happen unless Chernov and Elena were alone.

"I think you would enjoy Elena's company."

"Not as much as I'd enjoy yours."

"I don't know, Boris," Christine replied, searching for a solution. Finally, she latched on to an idea. If she agreed to his proposal, but gave him Elena's room number instead of hers, it might work. With Elena opening the door while properly attired—scantily clad, that is—it'd be hard for Chernov to say no when she pulled him into her room.

"How about tonight. An hour from now. Hotel National, room 1051."

Chernov shook his head. "Unfortunately, I have meetings tonight, which will run late. However, I leave for Sochi tomorrow morning. My first weekend off in months. I have a villa on the shore of the Black Sea and a yacht we could spend the day on. Much more pleasurable than dreary Moscow. I'll have a driver pick you up at your hotel at seven a.m."

Christine had painted herself into a corner, agreeing to a liaison with Chernov. Unfortunately, tomorrow in Sochi, with Elena in Moscow, wouldn't work. Her mouth felt dry as she worked through the implications. Their plan to kill Chernov had failed, and now she was stuck with him for the weekend.

MOSCOW

Standing beside Christine O'Connor, Elena Krayev waited impatiently as the elevator rose to the tenth floor of their hotel. The doors slid open and she headed briskly down the hallway, Christine at her side. When they reached Elena's room, she pulled Christine inside.

"We need a new plan," Elena said after the door closed.

"Agreed," Christine said with disappointment on her face. "You need to let your superiors know, so they can start working on it."

Elena shook her head. "It's unlikely we can gain access to Chernov at his villa, and once he returns to Moscow, an opportunity might not present itself soon enough."

She pulled Christine to the bed, and both women sat on the edge.

"You, on the other hand, will be with Chernov this weekend."

Christine stared at Elena for a moment, finally realizing what she was proposing.

"Not a chance," Christine said. "I'm not a field agent."

"You'll do fine," Elena said. "With the right equipment, you can kill Chernov quietly and no one will suspect. It will appear he died of natural causes. There is no danger to you."

The last sentence, of course, was a lie.

"I know you can do this," Elena said as she dumped the contents of her purse onto the bed: the usual assortment of cosmetics and feminine products, along with a cell phone.

"No," Christine said emphatically. "I'm a White House staffer, not a trained assassin."

"You have killed before."

"Only because I didn't have a choice. I have a choice this time, and I'm not doing it."

Elena paused, reevaluating the situation. Time was critical; the United States needed to disarm the pipeline explosives and break the threat of a Persian Gulf blockade before the NATO resolutions were scuttled. The odds of planning and executing a new operation within the next few days were slim. She shifted tactics, reviewing Christine's profile in her mind.

Prior to the mission, Elena had studied the dossier of her target as well as those working with her. A review of Christine's portfolio had raised a few red flags: she was impulsive and vindictive, traits that could turn into a liability to those working with her. Her role in this operation was marginal, though, and Elena hadn't been worried. However, the situation had changed dramatically, and Elena realized she could use Christine's traits to her advantage.

"There is something you need to know," Elena said. Christine stared at her pensively, and confident she had her full attention, Elena elaborated.

"After the incident at Ice Station Nautilus, President Kalinin fired Fleet Admiral Ivanov. After dedicating his life to serving Russia, Ivanov became disgruntled and we have established a relationship with him. We haven't gleaned much information yet, but we do know that the incident at Ice Station Nautilus wasn't his idea; he was following orders. The attack at the ice station, both above and below the ice, was ordered by Defense Minister Chernov."

Elena watched her words sink in slowly. Boris Chernov had given the order to torpedo the submarine Christine and Captain Brackman were aboard. Chernov was responsible for Brackman's death.

Christine's features hardened, then she glanced at the items on the bed. "Show me how these work."

Elena repressed a smile as she reached for one of the lipstick applicators. She pulled the cover off, revealing a reddish-purple lipstick. "Looks like a normal lipstick applicator." She replaced the cover and unscrewed the base, revealing a ring inside with a sharp metal point the size of a tack and covered by a transparent plastic sheath, rising where the gemstone would normally be mounted. Elena slid the ring onto her finger, then rotated it until the metal point faced in toward her palm. She held her hand up, showing Christine the back of her hand; it looked as if she were wearing a plain silver ring. She closed her hand into a fist and then opened it again, then turned her hand over, palm up, showing Christine the sharp point.

"The tip of this ring is coated with a poison that will paralyze Chernov in thirty seconds. All you have to do is remove the plastic sheath, then puncture the skin behind his neck. Do it above the hairline, to minimize the potential the puncture wound will be discovered during the autopsy. The tip is also coated with a numbing agent, so Chernov won't feel the puncture and suspect anything until it's too late."

Elena returned the ring to its compartment in the base of the lipstick applicator and screwed the bottom back on, then reached for the second applicator, pulling its cover off, revealing crimson lipstick. She unscrewed the base, revealing an identical ring. "This ring will kill Chernov, making it look like a heart attack. Again, puncture the skin behind his neck above the hairline."

Elena said, "Remember—purple paralyze, crimson kill," then repeated the phonetic mnemonic.

"After you paralyze him," Elena said as she screwed the base of the lipstick applicator back on, "you'll need to establish a video link with the Russian engineer who designed the detonators." She reached for the cell phone and showed Christine the power button on one side and the up/down volume tabs on the other.

"Press the power button and the up volume simultaneously," she said, "and you'll establish a video link with our Russian friend. If you get in trouble and need assistance, press the power button and the down volume tab. Right now it alerts a team in a room just down the hallway, but we'll move assets into place in Sochi to extract you if things go south.

"Remember, power up to upload the video link. Power down if things have gone south and you need help."

Christine nodded her head slowly. Her determination was fading as the shock of what she had agreed to do set in. Elena placed a hand on her shoulder.

"You will do fine."

57

SOCHI, RUSSIA

Sochi, located on the shore of the Black Sea, is part of the Caucasian Riviera, one of the few places in Russia with a subtropical climate. With the scenic Caucasus Mountains to the east and pebble-sand beaches to the west surrounding a vibrant city with a bustling nightlife, it's not surprising that Sochi is Russia's largest and most popular resort city.

Descending toward Sochi International Airport in a Dassault Falcon executive jet, Christine was seated beside Defense Minister Chernov. Configured to transport a dozen passengers, the jet carried only eight today. Behind Christine and Chernov were a Russian oligarch and his wife, both in their mid-sixties. Vagit Alekperov, the seventh-richest man in Russia, was president of LUKoil, one of the world's most powerful oil companies, with reserves second only to Exxon. Alekperov and his wife spoke only broken English, and Chernov translated when required.

Rounding out the passengers was a detachment of four Russian Federal Protective Service agents, each man dressed entirely in black, wearing a sport coat over a turtleneck. Christine, on the other hand, was wearing something more colorful: a blue blouse over tan capri pants.

Having checked the Sochi weather forecast and noting temperatures approaching eighty degrees, Christine realized most of her attire—business suits and slacks—would be inappropriate for the warm weekend. After rifling through her clothes, she put together two outfits suitable for Chernov's villa and yacht, along with two evening gowns in case they headed into the city for dinner or other festivities. Finally, her white silk nightgown would come in handy, as would the two lipstick vials and Elena's cell phone, which she had transferred to her purse.

The conversation during the journey south was light and enjoyable, and Christine learned that Chernov had done well in the new, democratic Russia, managing to gain significant holdings in various industries. His wealth paled in comparison with that of LUKoil's Alekperov, but Chernov had amassed enough of a fortune to afford a luxury beachside villa on the shore of the Black Sea as well as a small yacht.

The Falcon jet landed at Sochi International Airport and pulled to a halt near one of the private hangars. Chernov and his entourage descended onto the tarmac, where they were met by a black limousine and two sedans. Their luggage was transferred to the caravan and Chernov and his three guests slid into the center limousine, while Chernov's security detail took the lead and rear sedans. With the airport less than a mile from the coast, it wasn't long before they arrived at Chernov's villa. A heavy black metal gate, part of a twenty-foot-high security wall around the property, opened slowly, and the three cars pulled into a circular driveway.

Chernov's residence was a six-bedroom, single-story open-air villa with fans swirling slowly in each room. A maid, who greeted the group upon their arrival, showed Christine to her bedroom, the master suite she would be sharing with Chernov. After freshening up,

Christine left the bedroom in search of Chernov and his two guests, passing a living room with adjoining bar, where she was surprised to see two of Chernov's security detail pouring themselves a drink. Her presence didn't go unnoticed, with one of the agents eyeing her as she passed.

She continued down a long hallway, between an indoor pool on one side and outdoor pool on the other. Hearing voices ahead, Christine stepped onto a blue flagstone patio framed by a curved granite balcony overlooking the Black Sea. Chernov and his two Russian guests were standing beside the railing, and Christine joined them.

The view from Chernov's villa was breathtaking. Built on a rock outcropping dropping down to clear blue water thirty feet below, the villa overlooked a shoreline curving into a semicircular cove. On the right side of the shore, a pier jutted into the sea, with Chernov's yacht tied alongside, as well as a smaller motorboat. At the base of the pier was a large boathouse.

The maid stopped by, dropping off drinks for Chernov and his two Russian guests, and Chernov asked Christine what she'd like. More for irony than anything else, Christine asked if she could have a White Russian. After a bit of translation, the maid nodded and returned a few minutes later with the requested cocktail. When they finished their drinks, Chernov asked his visitors if they'd like to head out on his yacht, an eighty-foot tripledecker. Chernov seemed to apologize to Alekperov and his wife for the modest size of his boat.

Chernov led the way from the villa, down a curving brick walkway to the pier, accompanied by two men from his security detail. After boarding the sleek white ship, the Russian defense minister took the controls in the flying bridge. The lines were taken in and Chernov's yacht headed out into the Black Sea.

58

YASENEVO, RUSSIA

It was late afternoon when Semyon Gorev, seated at his desk in the Y-shaped headquarters of Russia's Foreign Intelligence Service, scrolled through the daily update on his computer. At the end of the intelligence summary, he reviewed the whereabouts of high-ranking foreign and domestic diplomats. Not only did the SVR keep tabs on foreign diplomats, they also kept track of their own, maintaining a record of their acquaintances and activities. One could never have enough information on Russian politicians; the hidden details of their lives had proven useful on countless occasions.

Gorev had a special interest in Christine O'Connor, and a quick check on her status produced a surprise result. She had left her hotel this morning, picked up by one of Chernov's Federal Protective Service agents. After reading further, he noted Christine and Chernov had departed for his villa in Sochi, accompanied by the president of LUKoil and his wife.

What was Chernov up to, gallivanting around with one of the richest men in the country? Vagit Alekperov would want something in return for his friendship. Also, what game was Christine O'Connor playing? She had turned down President Kalinin's offer for the weekend, only to accept one from Chernov? Kalinin was the clear winner on all fronts: more powerful, better looking, with a notably better personality. Choosing Chernov didn't add up.

As head of the SVR, Gorev received background summaries of the diplomats visiting Russia, including Christine. However, he decided to examine her entire file. He left his office and headed to the Operations Center, a dimly lit room with over one hundred men and women at their workstations, poring over data on their computer screens while supervisors studied the most pertinent information on a dozen six-foot-wide video screens mounted along the front wall. Gorev stopped at one of the supervisor workstations.

"Pull up Christine O'Connor's file."

The supervisor complied, and Gorev peered over his shoulder as he scrolled through the information.

"Stop," Gorev said when he noticed an entry about a meeting between Christine and Israel's intelligence minister, who died about the same time as their meeting.

"Pull up Barak Kogen's file," Gorev directed.

The requested information was displayed, and at the end of Kogen's file, Gorev found the information he was looking for. Barak Kogen's death was publicly reported as a heart attack, but the SVR's official assessment was that he was poisoned. Gorev examined the date. Kogen died the same day he had lunch with Christine O'Connor.

Gorev pulled his phone from his jacket, looking up Chernov's contact information. The Operations Center was shielded from radio transmissions, so he called Chernov on a landline.

No answer.

"Get me a number for Chernov's security detail."

The number was provided and one of Chernov's agents answered, explaining the defense minister was on his yacht in the Black Sea with Alekperov and his wife, along with O'Connor and two Federal Protective Service agents.

Gorev decided to pay Chernov and O'Connor a visit. "Give me two men," he told the Operations Center supervisor, "and air transportation to Sochi immediately."

59

SOCHI, RUSSIA

The afternoon aboard Chernov's yacht passed quickly as they cruised northwest along the Black Sea coast under a cloudless sky. From the flying bridge, Christine had a spectacular view of Sochi's pebble-sand beaches, transitioning to green hills ascending toward the Caucasus Mountains to the east and wooded uplands to the north. With no chef aboard to prepare a meal suitable for his guests, Chernov docked at the Sochi Yacht Club for lunch at a French brasserie-style restaurant on the waterfront. Lunch was delicious, and after returning to the yacht, they continued northwest along the Black Sea coast. As the sun slipped toward the horizon, Chernov turned the yacht around and increased speed.

It wasn't long before they cruised between steep cliffs framing the entrance to the cove beneath Chernov's villa, then coasted to a halt beside the pier. It was almost dinnertime, and the aroma of rosemary and garlic greeted Christine as she entered the open-air villa. She headed to Chernov's bedroom to change clothes, swapping her capri pants and blouse for a one-shoulder emerald-green chiffon dress.

The three Russians likewise changed attire, with Chernov and Alekperov donning sport coats over open-collar shirts, while Alekperov's wife changed into a stylish white satin evening gown. Drinks on the patio were followed by a delectable dinner, during which the wine flowed freely. Christine paced herself, limiting her consumption to two glasses. She would normally have stopped at one considering what she was about to do, but decided a second glass would help calm her nerves.

A Russian crème over fresh fruit for dessert completed the meal, and as darkness descended on the shore of the Black Sea, the conversations ebbed. Alekperov and his wife excused themselves for an early repose, leaving Christine and Chernov alone at the table. Chernov rose, extending his hand, assisting Christine to her feet, then led the way to his bedroom suite.

After they entered the room, Chernov pulled his cell phone from his coat pocket and turned it off, then closed the door behind them. As he locked the door, Christine's apprehension began to mount, and she began trembling. Chernov noticed and inquired, considering the temperature was in the mid-seventies. Christine played it off as the chills from too much sun on Chernov's yacht. Backing up her claim, her exposed skin had a pink tinge.

Chernov turned off the ceiling fan, then stopped in front of Christine, rubbing the sides of her shoulders to warm her up. As he looked down at her, Christine wrapped her arms around his neck and offered a kiss, which Chernov eagerly accepted. She let the kiss linger while Chernov's hands wandered, doing her best to simulate a passionate response. When the kiss ended, she pulled away.

"Let me change into something more appropriate."

Chernov grinned as Christine gathered her silk nightgown and her purse, then headed into the bathroom.

60

SOCHI, RUSSIA

It was dark by the time Semyon Gorev's Falcon executive jet landed at Sochi International Airport. During the flight, Gorev examined Christine O'Connor's file in more detail. She wasn't an undercover agent; there was no indication she had received field training or had ties to the CIA. It seemed Christine was one of the unluckiest women in the world, however, frequently ending up in the wrong place at the wrong time. An SVR field agent would've had to work hard to end up in the predicaments Christine found herself in during her stint as America's national security advisor.

After the aircraft coasted to a halt, Gorev and two SVR agents descended onto the tarmac, where they were met by a sedan. Gorev pulled his cell phone from his jacket and dialed Chernov, but the call went directly to voice mail. He contacted Gorev's security detail, who relayed that Chernov and O'Connor had retired for the night.

Chernov had survived lunch and dinner with Christine, and Gorev wondered if his concern was misplaced. With only suspicion and no proof, Gorev decided to allow Chernov a few moments alone with the beautiful

American. A more detailed *discussion* with Christine would be required, which he would conduct once he arrived at the villa. With the airport only a kilometer from the coast, he would be there in a few minutes.

61

SOCHI, RUSSIA

Once inside the bathroom, Christine exchanged her evening dress for her white silk nightgown, which went down only to the top of her thighs. Sexy enough, she concluded, before turning her attention to her purse. She placed Elena's cell phone on the counter, then withdrew the two lipstick applicators. Remembering Elena's mnemonic—*purple paralyze, crimson kill*—she removed the ring from the base of the wine-colored lipstick applicator. The silver band was made of a flexible material, which fit snugly to the ring finger of her right hand. After verifying the clear plastic sheath still covered the ring's sharp point, she closed her hand into a fist, verifying the tack didn't interfere with the movement. Not that it mattered; she planned to keep her hand open and palm toward her until the appropriate time.

She examined herself in the mirror. Her face had turned pasty white. She was trembling again and her blood pounded in her ears. She took a few deep breaths, exhaling slowly each time, but it didn't help; she was almost shaking. Attempting a different tactic, she turned her thoughts to Brackman—what she had been forced to do aboard the sunken submarine. She focused on the months of guilt and anguish she had endured due to

Chernov's order. The trembling slowly subsided, followed by a determination that settled low and cold in her gut. She turned and headed toward the door.

Christine emerged from the bathroom to find Chernov supine on the bed, feet crossed and his jacket and shoes removed, but fully clothed otherwise. With his head resting on a pillow, she had a problem; it would be difficult to puncture the skin behind his neck. Fortunately, Chernov stood as she approached.

"You look ravishing," he said when she stopped in front of him.

Christine wrapped her arms around his neck again, resting her forearms on his shoulders, leaving her hands free while she offered him another kiss. Chernov accepted, and as his hands slipped beneath her nightgown and explored her bare skin, Christine removed the plastic sheath from the ring.

She let the kiss linger, and when she sensed Chernov pulling away, she plunged the sharp point into the back of his neck, just above the hairline as instructed. There was no reaction from Chernov; the numbing agent performed as advertised.

Chernov reached down to the bottom of Christine's nightgown, pulling it upward. As Christine raised her arms above her head so he could slip it off, Chernov stopped halfway up. His face went slack and his muscles flaccid, and he collapsed onto the bed. His eyes darted around the room and his mouth moved slowly, as if trying to talk, but he appeared paralyzed otherwise.

Christine headed to the bathroom, replacing the plastic sheath on her ring, then exchanged it for the other one. She grabbed Elena's cell phone and simultaneously pressed the power and up volume button. The phone energized, displaying a man's face.

"What is the status?" he asked.

"Chernov is paralyzed," Christine replied.

"Excellent. Point the cell phone at him."

Christine returned to the bedroom, standing near the bed as she aimed the cell phone at Chernov. The video went to a split-screen mode, showing Chernov and whoever was on the other end. Another man appeared on-screen—an unshaven man whose eyes burned with a mix of hatred and glee.

The man spoke in Russian, and when Christine heard the defense minister's name, Chernov's eyes shot toward the cell phone. The man continued, the pitch and tempo of his words increasing, slowly approaching madman status; his face turned red and spittle flew from his mouth as he screamed at Chernov. Abruptly, his rage subsided and he smiled.

The first man she'd seen on the cell phone appeared again. "Kill Chernov now," he said.

Christine placed the cell phone on the bed and removed the plastic sheath from her ring. Unceremoniously, she grabbed Chernov's hair and lifted his head up. As she slipped her hand behind his neck and prepared to pierce his skin, there was a knock on the bedroom door and a query in Russian.

Christine hesitated. Chernov's death would look like a heart attack, but she needed time for the poison to take effect before she called for assistance. She had already paralyzed him, however, so there was no turning back. Another round of knocks emanated from the door, forcefully this time, accompanied by a second query in Russian with a more urgent tone.

Without further delay, Christine plunged the ring into the back of Chernov's neck, then picked up the cell phone, aiming it at his face. As the knocking on the door was replaced with a heavy pounding, Christine called out, "Just a minute."

The pounding subsided, and Christine watched as Chernov's breathing ceased. His skin turned a bluish tint and his eyes roamed around the room aimlessly until they stopped moving altogether, leaving Chernov staring at the ceiling with lifeless orbs.

The pounding on the door resumed and Christine answered, saying she'd be there in a minute. As she turned off the cell phone, the wooden door frame splintered and the door flew open. Two men with their pistols drawn surged into the room, their weapons pointed at Christine as Semyon Gorev stepped between them.

Christine hurried toward Gorev. "Something's wrong with Boris. I think he's had a heart attack."

Gorev glanced at Chernov, then a cold, hard look settled on his face as he turned toward Christine. He knocked the cell phone from her hand, sending it flying across the room. His eyes went to Christine's other hand, and after spotting the sharp tack protruding from her ring, he punched her in the face, knocking Christine backward, dropping her to one knee.

As blood trickled from her nose, she spotted a gap between the three men and the bedroom doorway, and she bolted toward the opening. Before she reached the doorway, one of the agents intercepted her and smashed the butt of his pistol into her head. By the time Christine's body thudded onto the floor, her world had gone black.

62

VALDEZ, ALASKA

Staff Sergeant Stu Nelson studied the display on his control console as he pushed forward on his joystick, directing the small dual-track robot toward its destination two hundred feet away—the terminus of the Trans-Alaska Pipeline System. Minutes earlier, the Commanding Officer of Nelson's explosive ordnance disposal unit had received the word: the disarm code had been transmitted.

The small robot closed the distance, stopping a foot away from the explosives attached to the pipeline. The initial indication was favorable. The detonator pressed into the claylike C-4 had gone dead; the red blinking light had been extinguished. Placing both hands into the control mitts, Nelson activated the robot's claws, reaching forward with one arm. After opening the claw, he slid it over one edge of the detonator, digging the claw's bottom finger gently into the C-4 explosive beneath. He slowly closed the claw until a firm grip on the detonator was obtained. Shifting to the other arm, Nelson repeated the process, ending with both claws clamped on to the detonator.

Nelson glanced at the unit's Commanding Officer, Captain John Brown.

"Remove the detonator," Brown said.

Nelson slowly pulled the robot's claws back, gradually extracting the detonator from the explosive. His eyes focused on the detonator panel, looking for a reaction. It remained dark. Once the detonating probe cleared the claylike C-4, Nelson put the robot in reverse, quickly opening the distance from the explosive.

Once the robot was safely away, Nelson let out a deep breath. It could not have gone smoother.

Captain Brown spoke into his handheld radio, sending orders to five other units of his explosive ordnance disposal company, which were deployed at other points along the pipeline where explosives had been discovered.

63

ARLINGTON, VIRGINIA

Forty feet underground in the Pentagon basement, the president strode down the hallway, bracketed by SecDef McVeigh and Colonel DuBose. Upon reaching the end of the corridor, McVeigh swiped his badge and punched in his pass code, and the door opened to the Current Action Center of the National Military Command Center. The CAC dropped down in increments, with workstations lining each tier, descending to a fifteen-by-thirty-foot electronic display on the far wall. Unlike the adjacent Operations Center, which focused only on nuclear weapons, the CAC handled all aspects of the country's defensive and offensive operations around the world.

McVeigh led the way to a conference room along the top tier, where the president stopped to examine the monitor on the far wall, displaying a map of the Indian Ocean. Blinking green circles in the Arabian Sea marked the planned starting positions of the four carrier strike groups, while blue circles tracked their present locations. Two strike groups were loitering in their starting positions, with two more rapidly approaching from the southeast, not far away.

The president entered the conference room and took

his seat at the head of the table. Joining him on one side were the Joint Chiefs of Staff—the heads of the Army, Navy, Air Force, Marine Corps, and National Guard, along with the chairman and vice chairman. On the other side of the table sat Vice President Bob Tomkins and members of the president's staff and cabinet—McVeigh, Dawn, Hardison, and Colonel DuBose. On the far end of the table was CIA Director Jessica Cherry.

McVeigh kicked off the brief, with each applicable service chief outlining his service's role in the operation. The Chief of Naval Operations, Admiral Brian Rettman, whose forces were by far the largest component of the operation, spoke at length, outlining the possible Russian responses and America's plan to counter each one.

The Admiral finished with, "It appears our fake upload into Russian and Indian satellites is working. There's no indication Russia has detected the two additional carrier strike groups entering the Indian Ocean. All available submarines in the Pacific are on station, and will coalesce around the four carrier strike groups when the operation begins."

When the brief concluded, the president asked McVeigh, "Where do we stand on disarming and removing the pipeline explosives?"

"The override code worked as advertised. We've successfully removed a half-dozen detonators from explosives attached to the Alaskan oil pipeline. We've also informed our NATO allies that they can remove the explosives from the pipelines and pumping stations in their territory, and will inform all other affected countries once military action against Russia commences; we don't want word that we've disarmed the detonators to leak out to Russia until after we engage.

"However," McVeigh added, "we have more details on the operation to assassinate Minister Chernov, which

I wasn't aware of until Director Cherry provided more information."

When the president looked in Cherry's direction, she said, "The plan to kill Chernov had to be modified. Chernov worked late after the summit reception, leaving no time for a liaison with Elena Krayev. Then he traveled to his villa in Sochi for the weekend, and unfortunately, he didn't take Elena with him."

"Then how was he killed?"

"He took Christine."

The president raised an eyebrow.

"She did an admirable job," Cherry said, "establishing the video link before she killed Chernov. However, there's a complication. Someone was attempting to enter Chernov's bedroom as Christine killed him, and we don't know if she was able to pass his death off as a heart attack or she was discovered."

"What's the plan?"

"She hasn't requested assistance, but we don't know if that's because she doesn't need help or doesn't have access to Elena's phone. If we bust in with an extraction team, the Russians will figure out what we've done, plus there's the possibility Christine will be killed in the process. We'll monitor the situation via satellite and communication intercepts from Chernov's villa. Until we know whether Christine is in danger, I recommend we sit tight."

After a moment of reflection, the president nodded his concurrence.

Silence settled over the conference room until McVeigh said, "Mr. President, all preparations are complete and we are ready to proceed."

The president didn't hesitate. "Engage Russia with all assigned units."

64

USS *HARRY S. TRUMAN*

"This could be a problem."

"Could be," Randle agreed.

Captain David Randle stood beside his Operations Officer in the aircraft carrier's Combat Direction Center, reviewing nearby friendly, hostile, and *currently* neutral forces. His eyes, along with those of his Operations Officer, Captain Brent Sites, were focused on the Video Wall displays. On one of the large screens, Sites had pulled up the Common Operational Picture, which displayed blue, red, and yellow icons of various designs, each symbol representing the location of a surface, air, or subsurface combatant.

The *Truman* strike group was loitering in the Indian Ocean, just south of the Arabian Sea. The *Ronald Reagan* strike group was twenty miles to the west, and the *Bush* and *Eisenhower* strike groups were closing fast from the southeast. Once assembled, the American task force would comprise four aircraft carriers, forty cruisers and destroyers, and twenty fast attack submarines—a formidable armada.

In contrast, the Russian Navy in the Arabian Sea fielded only one aircraft carrier and eighteen cruisers, destroyers, and corvettes. Although the Russian combatants were fewer in number, they were more heavily armed than their American counterparts. The aircraft carrier *Kuznetsov* was a good example. In addition to carrying up to thirty-two fixed wing aircraft and twenty-four helicopters, she was outfitted with a dozen Shipwreck surface attack and 192 Gauntlet anti-air missiles. The other surface ships were similarly outfitted; the Russians loaded weapon systems on their combatants like ornaments on a Christmas tree.

Although there were no hostile symbols ashore, Randle knew there were over a hundred surface-to-air missile batteries hidden on the Iranian coast, ready to engage. The Russians had also deployed four hundred tactical aircraft to Iranian bases, keeping one-fourth aloft at all times. After observing what China did to American air bases at the outbreak of their war, they were keeping a significant portion of their aircraft airborne, rotating them in six-hour shifts.

Even though the Russian Navy was augmented with missile batteries ashore and aircraft at Iranian bases, Randle was reasonably confident the United States would prevail in the air and surface engagement. Russia's real threat lurked beneath the water: thirty-seven attack and eleven guided missile submarines, with the latter carrying deadly surface attack missiles.

Captain Randle's assessment of the surrounding forces was interrupted by a flashing message on Captain Sites's console. Sites pulled up the message. A new OPORD. The four aircraft carriers were being combined into a single task force and had been directed to destroy all Russian units in the Indian Ocean theater of operations—all air, surface, and submerged combatants. More detailed orders would be forthcoming.

Randle picked up the 1-MC microphone and directed all department heads to meet him in the Wardroom. Before he left CDC, he examined the neutral forces in the area, which was the original source of his concern; it would be problematic if they joined the battle on the wrong side. India had two operational aircraft carriers and sixteen surface combatants, with the two carriers normally deployed on opposite sides of the country. However, both carrier strike groups were now operating off India's west coast, not far from *Truman* and *Reagan*. Compounding the matter, India's first indigenous aircraft carrier, undergoing sea trials, had joined them.

Randle repeated his Operations Officer's assessment. "This could be a problem."

65

USS *MICHIGAN*

Captain Murray Wilson turned slowly on the periscope in the darkness, monitoring the surface traffic. *Michigan* was in the Aegean Sea at the mouth of the Dardanelles, preparing for its journey through the Turkish Straits. It would be a long, tense transit, with the thirty-eight-mile-long Dardanelles narrowing to just over a thousand yards in some spots. Once into the Sea of Marmara, *Michigan* would complete its journey by transiting the Bosphorus, a seventeen-mile-long channel only half as wide as the Dardanelles.

When Wilson received his new orders a few days earlier, he hadn't been surprised. The Turkish Straits, connecting the Black Sea to the Mediterranean, have been of strategic importance for millennia, dating back to the Trojan War, fought near the Aegean entrance. During the twenty-first century, it served as a crucial international waterway for countries bordering the Black Sea.

Michigan's trip wouldn't be easy. Russian submarines transiting the straits did so on the surface, but that was a luxury *Michigan* couldn't afford. At the northern end of the Bosphorus, four Russian frigates patrolled. That meant *Michigan* would transit submerged. However, even at periscope depth, there were several spots along the way that were too shallow, and *Michigan* would have to alter course into the southbound channel while passing Kadıköy İnciburnu and Aşiyan Point.

Compounding the potential for discovery were the one-thousand-plus east–west crossings each day, transporting 1.5 million inhabitants across the Bosphorus on intercity ferries and shuttle boats. The nighttime transit up the straits would minimize the risk of discovery, but not eliminate it.

Wilson turned slowly on the periscope, looking for a merchant that would suit his needs. With so many waterborne contacts nearby, Sonar was overwhelmed sorting things out, and Wilson's eyeball was a better sensor at times like this. Finally, he spotted the desired contact: a two-hundred-thousand-ton Suezmax class tanker. *Michigan* would travel closely behind, its periscope hopefully obscured by the ship's wake.

"Helm, right twenty degrees rudder, ahead two-thirds."

Michigan turned slowly to the right, falling in behind the northbound tanker.

66

USS *HARRY S. TRUMAN*

Captain David Randle stood on the Bridge, one level beneath Primary Flight Control in the aircraft carrier's Island superstructure, as *Truman* surged northwest into the darkness. Fifty feet below, the first four F/A-18 Super Hornets, their engine exhausts glowing red, eased toward their catapults. Along the sides of the carrier, additional Super Hornets were being raised to the Flight Deck from the hangar bays. As the twenty aircraft in *Truman's* first cycle prepared for launch, Randle knew the *Reagan*, *Bush*, and *Eisenhower* air wings were doing the same.

Lieutenant Commander Bill Houston pulled back on the throttles, slowing his Super Hornet as it approached the starboard bow catapult. In the darkness, he followed the Shooter's directions, his yellow flashlights guiding Houston's jet forward. The Shooter raised his right arm, then dropped it suddenly. Houston responded by dropping the fighter's launch bar, which rolled into the CAT One shuttle hook as the aircraft lurched to a halt. The Shooter raised both hands in the air and Houston matched his motion, raising both hands to within view inside the cockpit, giving the Shooter assurance that Houston's hands were off all controls. The Shooter pointed his flashlight to a red-shirted Ordie—an Aviation Ordnanceman—who stepped beneath the Super Hornet, arming each missile.

A signal from the Shooter told Houston his weapons were armed and it was time to go to full power. He pushed the throttles forward until they hit the detent, spooling his twin General Electric turbofan engines up to full Military Power. He then exercised the aircraft's control surfaces, moving the control stick to all four corners as he alternately pressed both rudder pedals. Black-and-white-shirted Troubleshooters verified the Super Hornet's control surfaces were functioning properly and there were no oil or fuel leaks.

Satisfied his aircraft was functioning properly, Houston returned the thumbs-up and the Shooter lifted his arm skyward, then back down to a horizontal position, directing Houston to kick in the afterburners. Houston's Super Hornet was heavy tonight, with ordnance attached to every pylon; tonight's takeoff required extra thrust. Houston pushed the throttles past the détente to engage the afterburners, then turned toward the Shooter and saluted, the glow from his cockpit instruments illuminating his hand as it went to his helmet.

The Shooter returned the salute, then bent down and touched the Flight Deck, giving the signal to the operator in the Catapult Control Station. Houston pushed his head firmly against the headrest of his seat and took his hands off the controls, and a second later CAT One fired with the usual spine-jarring jolt. Houston felt his stomach lifting into his chest as the Super Hornet dropped when it left the carrier's deck, then he took control of his aircraft, accelerating upward. His seat pressed into him as he ascended to twelve thousand feet, where he settled into a holding pattern while *Truman* finished launching its first cycle.

67

FURY 21

High above southeastern Turkey, Air Force Major Mike Peck checked the map on the multifunction display of his B-1B Lancer long-range bomber, call sign Fury 21. Seated beside him in the four-person cockpit was his co-pilot, while behind them sat the DSO and OSO—Defensive Systems Operator and Offensive Systems Operator. Also behind Peck was a second B-1B from the U.S. Air Force's 9th Bomb Squadron, headed to the same target. Sixteen other Lancers had similar assignments, with their flight paths and speed coordinated such that all eighteen Lancers commenced their attacks simultaneously.

As his B-1B bomber approached the Iranian border, Peck adjusted his wings to full sweep, pulling them back to a fifteen-degree angle, then dropped in altitude and increased speed to just under Mach 1. As the ground rushed up to meet his aircraft, he engaged the ground-hugging, terrain-following mode of his AN/APQ-64 radar, and the B-1B leveled off, skimming across the landscape just above treetop height in an effort to avoid detection by Iranian radars and Russian anti-aircraft missile batteries.

Peck adjusted his flight path, running parallel to the

Zagros Mountains as they cut southeast across Iran, hugging the valleys of the multi-ridge mountain range. After an hour-long transit, the mountain peaks tapered off and Peck turned south, cutting between the Folded Zagros Mountains, not far from his target. As the second Lancer pulled alongside, Peck's OSO began final preparations to drop their payload of twenty-four GBU-31s: two-thousand-pound bombs, each outfitted with a JDAM—Joint Direct Attack Munition—a bolt-on guidance package with aerodynamic control surfaces and GPS capability, converting free-falling gravity bombs into precision-guided munitions.

The voice of Peck's OSO came across the speaker in his flight helmet. "One minute to release point."

Peck lifted a switch on his panel, opening the triple bomb bay doors. After a green light illuminated on his panel, he activated the microphone in his flight helmet. "OSO, you have permission to release."

The OSO acknowledged the order, and when the Lancer reached the release point, he dropped their ordnance. On Peck's left, the second B-1B did the same.

Peck banked to the right for a return trip home as twenty-four tons of ordnance streaked toward their targets.

68

BANDAR ABBAS, IRAN

Under the bright air base lights, Russian Air Force Major Vadim Aleyev guided his tactical fighter toward the left strip of the two-runway base. The Iranian Air Force had been kind enough to open its runways and facilities to Russian aircraft, and Bandar Abbas Air Base, occupying a strategic location on Iran's southern coast near the Strait of Hormuz, was now home to several squadrons of Russian tactical fighters.

Bandar Abbas's hot desert climate, with summer temperatures peaking near 120 degrees Fahrenheit, wasn't much different from Aleyev's last assignment. Having spent several months in Syria flying over one hundred missions in support of President Bashar al-Assad's regime, Aleyev was one of Russia's most experienced combat pilots. He now was preparing to relieve one of the fighters aloft in Russia's combat air patrol over their ships in the Gulf of Oman, ready to defend them if necessary.

Aleyev applied the brakes, coasting to a halt beside another Sukhoi Su-35S waiting on the adjacent runway, while ahead, another fighter completed final preparations for takeoff. Although Aleyev's Su-35S was one of Russia's most advanced multi-role fighters, designed to engage air, land, and sea targets, Aleyev's aircraft was

armed with ten R-77-1 active-radar homing missiles tonight. Like the jet beside him and the one in front, they
were configured for air-to-air combat, should the American carrier strike groups in the Arabian Sea attack.

The engines of the Su-35S in front of Aleyev flared,
and the aircraft accelerated down the runway. As the jet
beside Aleyev pulled forward, next in line for takeoff
in the alternating sequence, a bright flash at the end of
Aleyev's runway caught his attention. The Su-35S taking off disintegrated in an orange fireball, and chunks
of runway and aircraft rained down on the air base.

The Su-35S beside Aleyev began streaking down its
runway and Aleyev followed suit, engaging both afterburners as another explosion rocked the base. As his
fighter accelerated to takeoff speed, a crater opened up
just ahead of the fighter on the adjacent runway and the
jet disappeared into the roiling orange-and-black cloud,
with only bits and pieces of the aircraft emerging on the
other side.

Another explosion bathed Aleyev's cockpit in an
orange hue, leaving a crater in his runway only fifty
meters ahead. He was below takeoff speed but had no
choice; he pulled back on his stick when he reached the
crater. His wheels cleared the far edge with only a foot to
spare, and Aleyev climbed into the night sky as additional bombs hit the air base, the explosions illuminating
the landscape below in a pulsating orange glow.

As he rose into the darkness, Aleyev checked his instrumentation. Only eighteen aircraft from his cycle,
launching from various bases across Iran, had made it
airborne. There were another hundred above the Sea of
Oman, and although they'd be running low on fuel, there
were several tankers aloft. Aleyev turned southeast with
a grim determination. With the assistance of the missile batteries on the Iranian coast, they would teach the
Americans a lesson they would not soon forget.

69

ARABIAN SEA

Lieutenant Commander Bill Houston cruised at twelve thousand feet, headed northwest toward the Gulf of Oman, where the Russian surface combatants awaited. Houston and the other seventeen Super Hornets in *Truman*'s first cycle were divided into nine two-fighter packages, with each package assigned a different target. At this point in their approach, the eighteen fighters were strung out side by side at half-mile intervals, with an EA-18G Growler on each side of the formation, jamming incoming missiles and aircraft radars.

Three more waves of aircraft were headed northwest, one from each of the other carriers, forming a diamond formation with *Truman*'s cycle in the lead. The Russian surface combatants were arranged in a single task force resembling a two-carrier strike group, with the aircraft carrier *Kuznetsov* and the battle cruiser *Pyotr Velikiy* in the center.

Although the four waves of American fighters had been tasked with sinking the Russian surface ships, they would have to deal with the Russian combat air patrol first. The Super Hornets in his cycle were carrying a mixed load: air-to-surface missiles for the ships and air-to-air missiles for the tactical fighters. The Russian ships, aircraft, and missile batteries ashore would fire a bevy of missiles against the incoming American fighters, and defending against them would be challenging. Houston would have to rely on chaff, infrared decoys, and his organic jammers, as well as the more powerful electronic countermeasures aboard the accompanying Growlers.

Houston's Radar Warning Receiver activated, its audible warning pulling his attention to the display. E-2C Hawkeye early warning aircraft, operating high above and to the rear, were relaying their contacts to the inbound fighters. Missiles had appeared over the Iranian coast, headed Houston's way on an intercept course. Each missile was represented by a red 6, which indicated they were long-range 40N6 surface-to-air missiles fired by Russian mobile missile batteries. The 40N6 was designed to kill high-value targets, able to defeat EA-18G jamming.

There were four waves of outbound missiles, each wave headed toward a cycle of American fighters. In response to the incoming threat, the pilots from all four carriers did as they had been instructed to do. They banked hard left and dropped to the deck, skimming just above the ocean surface as they streaked away from the missiles.

In layman parlance, Houston and his fellow pilots turned and ran.

70

AIEA, HAWAII

In the fall of 1941, Takeo Yoshikawa stood in the grassy knolls of Aiea Heights overlooking Pearl Harbor and took notes. Assigned to the Japanese consulate in Honolulu, Yoshikawa left the consulate around 10 a.m. each day, returning to his office after lunch to review the product of his reconnaissance. In mid-November, he answered ninety-seven questions from Japan's Foreign Ministry, including:

> *On what day of the week would the most ships*
> *be in Pearl Harbor on normal occasions?*
> *Answer: Sunday.*

In the early morning hours of Sunday, December 7, 1941, his efforts culminated in a succinct message sent to Vice Admiral Chūichi Nagumo, which he read in the darkened Bridge of the Japanese heavy aircraft carrier *Akagi*:

> *Vessels moored in harbor: 9 battleships, 3 class*
> *B cruisers, 3 seaplane tenders, 17 destroyers.*

In the foothills of Aiea, not far from where Yoshikawa stood while surveying Pearl Harbor, is Camp H. M.

Smith, home to the United States Pacific Command. Within Camp Smith, accessing satellite surveillance is the Cruise Missile Support Activity, Pacific, providing precision targeting, route planning, and strike management for Tomahawk cruise missile missions. Today, in the early morning hours, the men and women at their workstations were busy reviewing the product of their reconnaissance.

Red icons had populated their displays, and each mission planner, assigned a small section of Iran's southern coast, was busy transmitting GPS coordinates. Thirty minutes earlier, three guided missile submarines, each loaded with a full complement of 154 Tomahawk missiles, had launched a fraction of their ordnance. However, the eighty missiles had been launched without destination coordinates. The missiles were circling just above the surface of the Arabian Sea, not far from the Iranian coast, waiting.

The Tomahawk missiles fired by the three guided missile submarines were Block IV Tactical Tomahawks, or TacToms, which could loiter after launch, doing doughnuts in the air while awaiting targeting information. Although Tomahawk missiles were extremely accurate, it took hours for launch orders to be generated, transmitted, and loaded aboard older variants prior to firing. During that time, enemy units could reposition, resulting in the Tomahawk destroying a vacant building or deserted patch of dirt. The TacTom missile overcame this deficit, already launched and loitering nearby while it waited for its final GPS coordinate, reducing the time between target identification and ordnance-on-target from hours to mere minutes.

The Tomahawk mission planners were busy sending coordinates of the Russian missile batteries that had fired on the incoming waves of F/A-18 fighters, which had been used as bait. They worked quickly, hoping each TacTom reached its target before the missile battery repositioned. For those that moved or hadn't opened fire yet, the mission planners had several hundred more TacToms at their disposal.

71

MOSCOW

President Yuri Kalinin, accompanied by General Sergei Andropov, his chief of the general staff and senior military advisor, traveled briskly down the corridor, entering the Operations Center in the Kremlin basement. There was an eerie silence within, as the men and women monitored the red and blue symbols on their screens, with blue ones appearing at a steady rate while red ones disappeared.

The Operations Officer on duty greeted President Kalinin, then briefed him on America's assault on Russian forces. The runways and hangars of every Iranian base housing Russian tactical aircraft had been destroyed, and they'd lost two-thirds of their mobile missile batteries on the Iranian coast.

He concluded with, "The United States prepared well for this attack and their intentions are clear. They aim to destroy our ability to blockade the Persian Gulf." He added, "The main battle is about to begin. The American air wings will engage our surface ships, and Admiral Shimko has ordered our submarines to sink the American carriers."

Kalinin could barely contain his fury, both at the United States and at his senior military aide. General

Andropov had assured him there would be no war between Russia and the United States. Their blackmail plan, placing a stranglehold on Western Europe's natural resources, would restrain them. His thoughts shifted to his discussion with Christine O'Connor on the Kremlin Senate balcony, where he'd explained that Americans didn't understand Russians. Now, it was painfully clear that Russians didn't understand Americans either. They were cutting the throats of their allies; Kalinin would destroy their oil and natural gas pipelines and their economies would sputter, throwing their countries into chaos.

Perhaps the Americans didn't believe him and were calling his bluff. He turned to his chief of the general staff.

"Destroy several pipelines and pumping stations, including America's Alaskan oil pipeline. That should get their attention."

72

GULF OF OMAN

Twenty minutes earlier, as a wave of Russian missiles surged from the Iranian coast, Houston and the other F/A-18 pilots had turned tail and run, increasing speed as they dropped close to the ocean waves. The tactic worked well. They had outrun the first barrage of missiles while the TacToms destroyed two-thirds of the Russian missile launchers. Another wave of Tactical Tomahawks was inbound, with mission planners in Hawaii assigning their targets as more Russian missile batteries revealed their locations.

With the majority of the shore-based missile batteries destroyed, Houston and the other pilots turned back toward the Russian surface ships. However, over one hundred Russian aircraft lay ahead, forming a protective ring just beyond the range of the F/A-18s' anti-ship missiles. This time, however, Houston and his fellow pilots weren't going to run.

Truman's first cycle of aircraft slowed and the other three cycles pulled alongside, forming a two-level front of seventy-two F/A-18s interspersed with eight electronic jamming Growlers. The Super Hornets needed to get close enough to the Russian surface combatants to launch their AGM-84 Harpoon anti-ship missiles. With only nineteen surface combatants to destroy, Houston's fighter was loaded with a single Harpoon, with the other ten hardpoints carrying anti-air missiles. Making it through the Russian fighters was the challenge.

When the Russian aircraft were within range of his radar-homing AMRAAM anti-air missiles, Houston and the other F/A-18 pilots fired a two-missile volley, knowing the Russian pilots were doing the same, like two armies of archers shooting guided arrows at each other. Houston watched his missiles close on the Russian jets while his Radar Warning Receiver alerted, displaying incoming air-to-air missiles. He fired a second volley, keeping two AMRAAMs and four Sidewinder infrared-seeking missiles in reserve.

The Russians also fired a second volley, and as the first wave of missiles closed on the F/A-18 formation, Houston focused on avoiding them. He was fortunate, flying beside one of the EA-18G Growlers. As the missiles approached, his Radar Warning Receiver indicated the missiles had failed to lock on to his aircraft. The Growler's electronic jamming worked well. Just in case, Houston broke left as other Super Hornets took evasive action. As the first wave of missiles passed by, pinpricks of light illuminated the darkness. After checking his radar display, Houston determined they'd lost six aircraft.

The next wave of missiles approached quickly, and Houston's Radar Warning Receiver told him the missiles had radar-seeking heads and that at least one had locked on to his aircraft. Right before the missile arrived, Houston dispensed a burst of chaff, then broke right. His jet veered out of the way as the missile headed toward the chaff, attracted by the cloud of aluminum-coated glass fibers.

After verifying the missile continued straight ahead instead of turning back toward his aircraft, Houston examined his display again. Another five aircraft lost. Still, there were sixty-one Super Hornets remaining, and a quick scan told Houston their AMRAAM missiles had performed well, destroying twenty-two Russian fighters. The odds were starting to even, but Houston and his fellow pilots were still outnumbered.

The two formations of aircraft closed on each other, and had it been daylight, they'd have been within visual range. Houston had several targets to choose from, and after identifying a gap he'd try to slip through, he targeted the two nearest fighters with his remaining AMRAAM missiles. Houston kicked in his afterburners, increasing speed.

73

USS *HARRY S. TRUMAN*

Inside the aircraft carrier's Combat Direction Center, the blue glow from the consoles illuminated Captain Brent Sites's face as he studied the displays on the Video Wall. The left monitor was zoomed out to a bird's-eye view of the Indian Ocean, displaying the Russian forces in the Gulf of Oman and American units in the Arabian Sea. Minutes earlier, blue inverted U's had appeared beside the aircraft carriers as they launched their air wings, and the first cycle of eighty aircraft had sped northwest toward the Russian battle group.

As the first cycle approached the Russian combat air patrol, Sites listened to the calm, monotone reports from the strike controllers as the casualties mounted.

"Loss of alpha-two-one."

"Loss of charlie-four-two."

The opposing waves of aircraft finally met and the display became a jumbled mosaic of shifting red and blue icons, the concentration of both colors growing gradually thinner.

The blue icons broke through the red barrier and continued toward the Russian surface combatants while the red icons regrouped, preparing for the assault of another blue wave; the second cycle of American aircraft was approaching. As the first wave closed on the Russian surface ships, surface-to-air missiles streaked from the combatants, with the missiles reaching the F/A-18s before their Harpoons were within range. The blood drained from Sites's face as two dozen blue icons disappeared from his display.

The surviving F/A-18s launched their Harpoons, then turned away, racing back to their carriers. Thankfully, the Russian tactical fighters were about to engage the next incoming wave of F/A-18s, and given that the outbound aircraft had expended most, if not all, of their weapons, they focused on the approaching, fully armed aircraft.

The second wave of eighty FA-18s and EA-18G Growlers penetrated the Russian combat air patrol with noticeably fewer losses, but they still paid their dues when the Russian surface combatants engaged. The longer-range Russian missiles inflicted heavy casualties, but several dozen Harpoons streaked toward the Russian battle group.

Captain Sites brought up satellite reconnaissance on the right screen of the Video Wall, displaying an infrared picture of the nighttime scene. Bright flares erupted as the second wave of Harpoons hit their mark, and when the flashes faded, Sites counted thirteen Russian combatants on fire. He couldn't tell if they were out of commission, but they had at least been damaged, hopefully impairing their ability to defend themselves against the next wave of aircraft. The American battle plan was pretty much a *wash-rinse-repeat* process, with each cycle of aircraft attacking the Russian surface ships, returning to their carriers to refuel and rearm, then attacking again.

As Sites studied the satellite image, the picture deteriorated into a haze of gray-and-black static. Sites selected another satellite feed and got the same result. The Russians were jamming the American reconnaissance satellites.

The first wave of fighters returned to their carriers and Captain Sites tallied the losses: thirty-three of the eighty aircraft had been shot down. The losses were heavy, but they could trade a few aircraft for each surface combatant sunk. Plus, the American losses would decrease with each successive attack, since the Russian combat air patrol, comprising mostly land-based fighters, now had nowhere to rearm due to the destruction of all nearby Iranian air bases. *Kuznetsov* was the only facility in the area that could refuel and rearm aircraft, which made her a priority for destruction.

Although thirteen Russian surface combatants had been hit, *Kuznetsov* and *Pyotr Velikiy* remained untouched. It was only a matter of time, however, before all of the Russian surface combatants were reduced to burning hulks.

Assuming, of course, the Russian submarines were kept at arm's length. Sites studied the display, searching for the forty-eight Russian attack and guided missile submarines. There were no red U-shaped icons, representing hostile submarines, on the display.

So far, so good.

74

USS *HARTFORD*

Commander Dave Thames, standing on the Conn between the two lowered periscopes, surveyed his men in the Control Room. They were at Battle Stations and every console was manned, with supervisors standing behind them. Free to roam the Control Room was Thames's Executive Officer, Lieutenant Commander Joe White, in charge of the Fire Control Tracking Party. The waterspace around *Hartford* had been quiet thus far, with Sonar reporting no submerged contacts.

USS *Hartford*, a Los Angeles class submarine, was in the middle of its ten-mile-wide by twenty-mile-long operating area, patrolling slowly side to side, giving *Hartford*'s towed array a clear view of the northern end of its operating area. With only twenty submarines to protect the four-carrier task force and ample ocean for the Russian submarines to do an end-around, the U.S. fast attacks were arranged in a single line of defense wrapping around both flanks of the task force formation, with *Hartford* assigned to one of the northern sectors. The battle had started an hour ago, and as Thames wondered how long it would take the Russian submarines to begin their assault, his thoughts were interrupted by a report from Sonar.

"Conn, Sonar. Hold a new contact on the towed array, designated Sierra five-seven, ambiguous bearings three-five-five and two-seven-five, classified submerged. Analyzing."

Hartford's towed array detected contacts at longer ranges than the submarine's other acoustic sensors. However, the array couldn't determine which side the sound arrived from, resulting in two potential bearings to the contact. With the American task force to the south and other U.S. submarines prohibited from entering *Hartford*'s waterspace, it was obvious which side of the array the submerged contact was on and that it was hostile.

The Sonar Supervisor's next report confirmed Thames's assessment. "Conn, Sonar. Sierra five-seven is classified Akula II."

"Attention in Control," Thames announced. "Designate Sierra five-seven as Master one. Track Master one."

Thames turned his attention to the four men seated at the submarine's combat control consoles. Three men were dedicated to determining the contact's solution— its course, speed, and range—and a fourth man sat at the Weapon Control Console, which would send the desired search presets to the MK 48 Mod 7 torpedoes in the submarine's four torpedo tubes. The weapons were powered up and in communication with combat control, and each torpedo tube was flooded with its muzzle door open.

After maintaining an eastern course for several minutes, watching the contact's bearing drift aft, Thames reversed course.

"Helm, right full rudder, steady course two-seven-zero."

Hartford steadied on its new course and as Thames evaluated Master one's new bearing drift, Sonar reported another contact.

"Conn, Sonar. Gained a new submerged contact on the towed array, designated Sierra five-eight, ambiguous bearings zero-two-zero and one-six-zero. Analyzing."

A second Russian submarine had entered the top right corner of *Hartford*'s operating area. As Thames turned his attention to the new contact, Sonar followed up. "Conn, Sonar. Gained a new submerged contact on the towed array, designated Sierra five-nine, ambiguous bearings three-two-zero and two-two-zero. Analyzing."

It looked as though the Russians were attempting to penetrate the American submarine screen at even intervals, resulting in three inbound Russian submarines in *Hartford*'s operating area.

Thames announced, "Designate Sierra five-eight as Master two and Sierra five-nine as Master three. The contact of interest is Master one." Master one was likely the closest of the three.

Lieutenant Commander White acknowledged and directed each of the three men developing contact solutions to track a different submarine, with *Hartford*'s most experienced fire control technician assigned to Master one.

White followed up, "Ambiguity has been resolved. All three contacts are to the north."

The XO's announcement didn't surprise Thames, but his next report did.

"Master one is operating at high speed. Best estimate—twenty knots."

Although twenty knots was less than two-thirds of an Akula II's maximum speed, it was excessive for submarine-versus-submarine engagements, where high speed amplified a submarine's radiated noise and dulled its acoustic sensors. However, with the Russian submarine approaching so rapidly, Thames would have to act soon, without a refined firing solution.

Thames figured Master one was functioning as a bird

dog, flushing *Hartford* from its hiding spot. Once
Thames fired a torpedo, all three Russian submarines
would know where *Hartford* was and would counterfire.
The scenario would degenerate into a free-for-all, with
all four submarines maneuvering aggressively, launching decoys and jammers and more torpedoes. On the
wrong end of a three-to-one scenario, *Hartford* would
not likely survive. Thames's only hope was to determine a solution for each Russian submarine and attack
all three at once. Sonar's next announcement threw a
wrench into that plan.

"Conn, Sonar. Gained Master one on the spherical
array."

The spherical array had a shorter detection range
than the towed array, so the detection told Thames that
Master one was getting dangerously close; the Russian
crew would detect *Hartford* at any moment.

Thames stopped by his XO. "I need a firing solution
on all three contacts, now."

He was pushing his Executive Officer for target solutions, but they didn't need to be exact. They needed
to place each torpedo close enough to detect the Russian submarine once the sonar in the torpedo's nose activated. It would take over from there and adjust course
to intercept the submarine.

Lieutenant Commander White studied the solutions
on the consoles, then after a moment of hesitation replied, "I have firing solutions, Master one, two, and
three."

Thames announced, "Firing Point Procedures, Master
one, two, and three. Normal submerged presets. Assign tube One to Master one, tube Two to Master two,
and tube Three to Master three. Tube One will be first
fired, then tube Two. Tube Four will be backup in case
we have a cold shot."

Although submarine weapon systems were very

reliable, they weren't perfect, and on occasion, a torpedo failed to launch. If the crew pulled the trigger and the torpedo didn't eject, it was deemed a cold shot, and the crew would quickly attempt to identify whether it was a tube problem, combat control issue, or bad torpedo.

The first report during Firing Point Procedures came from the XO, reporting the best solution for each contact had been selected and sent to Weapon Control.

"Solutions ready!"

Hartford's Weapons Officer, stationed as the Weapon Control Coordinator, announced, "Weapons ready!" reporting that all three torpedoes had accepted their weapon presets.

"Ship ready!" the Navigator announced, informing Thames that the submarine's torpedo countermeasures— their decoys and jammers—were ready to deploy.

"Shoot on generated bearings," Thames ordered.

The first four-thousand-pound weapon was ejected from its torpedo tube, accelerating from rest to thirty knots in less than a second. In rapid succession, tubes Two and Three were also fired. Inside Sonar, the sonar technicians monitored the status of their outgoing units, referring to each torpedo by the tube that launched it.

"Tube One is in the water, running normally."

"Fuel crossover achieved."

"Turning to preset gyro course."

"Shifting to medium speed."

Hartford's first-fired torpedo turned to the ordered course and began its search for Master one as *Hartford*'s second and third torpedoes raced toward the other two submarines.

Thames ordered, "Helm, left full rudder, steady course two-zero-zero. Ahead full."

In preparation for counterfire from the three Russian submarines, Thames maneuvered *Hartford* to an optimal torpedo evasion course, although optimal didn't mean good in this case. With Russian submarines about to counterfire from three different directions, there was no good course to turn to.

Master one responded immediately, firing a two-torpedo salvo before turning away.

Sonar's report, "Torpedo in the water, bearing three-five-zero!" was followed shortly by, "Second torpedo in the water, bearing three-five-two!"

Thames ordered, "Helm, ahead flank. Launch countermeasures."

The fast attack submarine increased speed to maximum, and the Officer of the Deck launched a torpedo decoy.

Hartford's first-fired torpedo locked on to Master one a moment later, its status reported via a thin copper wire trailing behind it, attached to the submarine's torpedo tube.

"Detect, tube One!" the Weapon Control Coordinator announced.

A few seconds later, after the torpedo verified the contact met the parameters of a submarine and not a decoy, it sent a follow-up message.

"Acquired!"

The torpedo calculated the evading target's course, speed, and range, then increased speed and adjusted its trajectory to intercept the Russian submarine.

"Tube One increasing speed to high-one."

Whether the evading Russian submarine would eject a torpedo decoy or jammer, or both, Thames didn't know, but it likely didn't matter. The MK 48 Mod 7 torpedoes carried by *Hartford* were the most advanced heavyweight torpedoes in the world, able to discriminate between submarines and decoys, and loaded with sophisticated algorithms to deal with jammers.

The next report sealed Master one's fate.

"Tube One is homing. Increasing speed to high-two."

All this happened quickly, within thirty seconds, and Thames turned his attention to the two incoming Russian torpedoes while *Hartford*'s other two sped outward, searching for the other Russian submarines. After assessing the bearing drift of the two-torpedo salvo, he determined the Russian crew had fired on a line-of-bearing solution: the spot where *Hartford* was when it fired, as opposed to an intercept solution based on *Hartford*'s course and speed. That was the good news. Bad news followed.

"Torpedo in the water, bearing zero-three-zero!" The submarine to the northeast had fired.

Another report from Sonar followed. "Torpedo in the water, bearing three-zero-zero!" The third submarine followed suit.

Thames evaluated the situation. The two-torpedo salvo was drawing behind *Hartford* as desired. Unfortunately, the third Russian torpedo was drawing up *Hartford*'s port side, while they were on a collision course with the fourth torpedo. Remaining on course wasn't an option, and maneuvering to the left would turn *Hartford* toward the torpedo on her port side. Thames reluctantly concluded his only option was a dangerous one.

"Helm, right ten degrees rudder, steady course three-five-five." There were no torpedoes in that direction, but unfortunately, there were three Russian submarines.

The sound of an explosion rumbled through the Control Room, and the Weapons Officer announced, "Loss of wire continuity, tube One."

Make that two Russian submarines.

Sonar reported, "Breaking up noises, bearing three-five-zero." Master one was going to the bottom, its compartments and internal tanks imploding.

As *Hartford* headed north, Thames adjusted course,

aiming for the one spot he knew there was no Russian submarine. "Helm, steady course three-five-zero."

There were two more Russian submarines out there, and Thames didn't know if his two outbound weapons would find their targets. Time to reload.

"Weapon Control, reload tube One." Tube Four was already loaded, and although tubes Two and Three were empty, the outgoing torpedoes were still attached to the tubes via their guidance wires, which would come in handy if Thames needed to insert a steer or send other instructions to the torpedoes.

Hartford was at ahead flank, which wasn't a great idea now that they were headed toward the two other Russian submarines. Sonar had lost contact on both due to the flow noise across the submarine's sensors and *Hartford* was putting a lot of noise into the water, making the submarine easy to track. If the other Russian submarines were at slow speed, *Hartford* would be burning into their sonar screens. *Hartford* needed to melt back into the ocean.

Thames ordered, "Helm, ahead two-thirds."

The Helm transmitted the new bell to the Throttleman in the Engine Room, who slowed *Hartford* to ten knots as a second explosion reverberated through the water.

"Loss of wire continuity, tube Two."

Hartford's second torpedo had found its target.

Thames turned his attention to the Russian torpedoes again; the first three had drawn down *Hartford*'s starboard side and were now outbound, no longer a threat unless a steer was sent to a torpedo. The bearings to the fourth torpedo, however, weren't changing. It was heading in from the west on an intercept course. It'd been steered.

As Thames determined a new evasion course, Sonar announced, "Gained broadband contact on the spherical array, bearing three-four-zero."

Before Thames responded, Sonar reported, "Launch transients, bearing three-four-one!"

The third Russian submarine had also turned toward the first explosion and had slowed earlier, gaining *Hartford* on its sensors. A detection on *Hartford*'s spherical array broadband told Thames the Russian submarine was close, as would be its incoming torpedo.

"Torpedo in the water, bearing three-four-two!"

"Torpedo evasion!" Thames announced.

Responding to the code word phrase, the Helm ordered ahead flank and the submarine's Officer of the Deck launched a torpedo countermeasure.

"Helm, hard right rudder, steady course one-three-five."

With two torpedoes headed *Hartford*'s way, one directly ahead and one on the submarine's port side, Thames's only hope was to turn southeast and run away from both torpedoes, hoping neither passed close enough to acquire.

Thames's turn away came too late.

"Conn, Sonar. Torpedo bearing two-seven-zero is range-gating."

The Russian torpedo to the west had acquired *Hartford* and was homing. If that weren't bad news enough, as *Hartford* swung to the southeast and picked up speed, Sonar reported, "Torpedo bearing three-three-five is range-gating."

The second torpedo had also acquired *Hartford*.

As Thames ordered another round of torpedo decoys and jammers into the water, he knew this wasn't going to turn out well.

ARABIAN SEA

The MH-60R Seahawk helicopter slowed to a hover and lowered its dipping sonar into the ocean again. Minutes earlier, the Sensor Operator in the cabin had detected two explosions in Alpha-eight, one of the submarine operating areas to the north, and Lieutenant Leo Falardeau, seated beside his Tactical Mission Officer, had repositioned his helicopter to the center of Bravo-eight. Unlike the Alpha operating areas, which were patrolled by submarines, the Bravo areas were monitored by MH-60R anti-submarine warfare helicopters. The MH-60Rs were the newest and most capable ASW helicopters in the American arsenal, equipped with an advanced sensor suite and three lightweight torpedoes. In Falardeau's case, three new MK 54s.

Lieutenant Falardeau was joined by another MH-60R, also patrolling Bravo-eight, dropping its dipping sonar into the ocean. As the sensor descended through the water, it approached the thermocline, a layer of water where the temperature changed rapidly and reacted with sound, like light reflecting off a window. Depending on the frequency and angle of the sound wave, some tonals couldn't make it through, bending back toward the bottom or up toward the surface. Ideally, the sensor would be placed on whatever side of the thermocline the enemy submarine was operating in. Falardeau's Sensor Operator let his dipping sonar pass through the thermocline, while the MH-60R beside them kept its sensor above.

Falardeau's dipping sonar was brought back on-line, and not long thereafter, the Sensor Operator reported a third explosion in the direction of Alpha-eight. Whether it was an American or Russian submarine being hit, he didn't know. However, with only one American submarine in the area and three explosions, he knew at least two Russian subs had gone to the bottom.

The MH-60R hovered sixty feet above the water as Falardeau's Sensor Operator searched Bravo-eight. As long as there were no detections in the Bravo areas, life was good. The American submarines were constrained to the Alpha areas and wouldn't venture into the Bravos, since the MH-60Rs were Weapons Free. Anything detected in the Bravo areas would be attacked.

The voice of Falardeau's Sensor Operator crackled in his headset. "Gained a new contact, designated Sierra one, bearing three-three-five."

They held only a bearing and no range, and as Falardeau hoped it was just a strong tonal from the American submarine in Alpha-eight, his Sensor Operator reported, "Sierra one is classified Akula II."

This was bad news, at least for the crew of the American submarine in Alpha-eight. The third explosion had sent it to the bottom, and now a Russian submarine had leaked into Bravo-eight. Where there was one, there would undoubtedly be more, but first things first.

The Sensor Operator retrieved the dipping sonar, and Falardeau repositioned his MH-60R so they could calculate the Russian submarine's position, course, and speed. It wasn't long before the sonar dipped beneath the thermocline again and the Sensor Operator reported, "I have a firing solution."

Falardeau ordered his Tactical Mission Officer to engage Sierra one. The TMO selected the proper presets on his panel: depth, search pattern, and other attributes, although almost any would do. All they had to do was place the lightweight torpedo reasonably close to the Russian submarine and the MK 54 would do the rest.

After retrieving the dipping sonar again, Falardeau repositioned his MH-60R just ahead of the Russian submarine, while his TMO sent presets to the middle MK 54 strapped beneath the helicopter. Satisfied that the torpedo was properly preset and they were close enough to the target, the TMO released the lightweight torpedo. As it fell toward the ocean, the torpedo's small parachute deployed, which slowed the weapon slightly and adjusted its angle as it fell, so that it slipped nose first into the water, where it disappeared from sight.

Unlike heavyweight torpedoes, lightweight torpedoes had no guidance wire attached, so the initial presets would have to do. The Sensor Operator monitored the engine tonals and the active transmissions from the sonar in the MK 54's nose. The engine lit off and the torpedo went active immediately, beginning its search. They had dropped the MK 54 almost directly on top of the Russian submarine, so it wasn't a surprise when the Sensor Operator reported the torpedo was homing less than twenty seconds after it hit the water. Engine speed increased, while the interval between pings decreased. With only a few hundred feet to travel, the torpedo exploded shortly thereafter.

Falardeau waited for the Sensor Operator to report breakup noises, verifying the submarine was headed to the bottom, although that likely wasn't the case. Most

Russian submarines, unlike American ones, were double-hulled, with the outer hull several meters from the inner pressure hull. Lightweight torpedoes had a difficult time punching through both hulls, and while one hit would likely result in a mission kill, one could never be certain.

The other MH-60R dropped a MK 54 into the water while Falardeau's Tactical Mission Officer readied another one from their helicopter. Both torpedoes slipped into the water and two more explosions followed. After the third explosion, Falardeau's Sensor Operator reported breakup noises. They'd punctured the pressure hull in at least two compartments, and the submarine was descending past Crush Depth.

76

USS *HARRY S. TRUMAN*

Captain Brent Sites viewed the icons on the Video Wall with concern. The air and surface battles continued, with each wave of American fighters inflicting and receiving damage. The Russian air defense systems were robust, and although every Russian surface combatant had been damaged by now, almost half were still operational, including *Kuznetsov* and *Pyotr Velikiy*.

In the process, however, the American carrier air wings had been reduced to half strength. This wasn't without consolation, as the Russian combat air patrol was almost nonexistent now, either having been shot down or vacating the area after running out of weapons. The few Russian fighters protecting their surface combatants were from *Kuznetsov*, and there were fewer than two dozen of those remaining.

While the Russian surface ships and aircraft had taken a pounding, not a single American surface ship had been damaged. Above the ocean's surface, the Americans were taking the fight to the Russians, and doing a good job of it. However, red submarine icons were starting to appear in the Bravo tier; they'd breached the Alpha ASW barrier in seven areas. So far, the MH-60Rs were performing admirably, and no Russian submarine had approached close enough to attack the American task force. Things were proceeding about as well as could be expected.

77

ARABIAN SEA

Major Vadim Aleyev kept his Sukhoi Su-35S close to the water, just above the ocean waves. Accompanying him in the darkness were seventeen other tactical fighters of various designs, each outfitted with air-to-air missiles. The eighteen aircraft were all that remained of the three hundred fighters at Iranian air bases, making it aloft as the runways and hangars were destroyed. Although originally assigned to relieve aircraft in Russia's combat air patrol, they had a new mission. As the Russian fighters streaked toward their targets, Aleyev looked forward to revenge.

They could have gone after the American aircraft carriers. But the Americans had a solid screen of destroyers and cruisers designed to shoot down incoming aircraft, plus the task force had retained thirty F/A-18s for combat air patrol above their carriers. Few, if any, of Aleyev's fighters would make it close enough to attack the carriers. Besides, Aleyev and the other Russian fighters were armed with air-to-air missiles, with no opportunity to change them out for air-to-surface ones. However, for their assigned targets, air-to-air missiles would suffice.

Aleyev looked down as the targets appeared on his

radar display. The Americans realized the real threat to their task force lurked beneath the ocean surface, and had established a three-layer Anti-Submarine Warfare defense: submarines, ASW helicopters, and surface combatants. To inflict major damage, Russian guided missile submarines had to penetrate only the first two layers. Aleyev and his fellow fighters couldn't do much regarding the American submarines, but they could address the next tier.

As Aleyev's Su-35S closed on the targets, his early warning receiver alarmed. He'd been spotted by American radars. Aleyev was beyond the range of the American surface ship air defense missiles, but a quick check of his display told him the combat air patrol above the carrier task force was racing toward him and the other inbound Russian aircraft. It wouldn't be long before the American fighters were within range, launching their missiles. However, the missiles would arrive too late.

Aleyev targeted the first twelve MH-60Rs, assigning one missile to each helicopter. Although the MH-60Rs had advanced self-defense systems, they were sitting ducks compared to tactical fixed-wing aircraft. They wouldn't fool many of Aleyev's missiles. Aleyev fired a volley, releasing all twelve missiles, then banked to the right and headed toward shore, staying close to the ocean in an attempt to evade the incoming American fighters. If he made it back to the coast, he wouldn't be able to refuel and rearm, but at least he could land and fight another day.

As his fighter streaked toward the Iranian shoreline, Aleyev watched the MH-60Rs disappear from his radar.

78

ARABIAN SEA

USS *HARRY S. TRUMAN*

Captain Sites watched in dismay as the blue icons representing the MH-60Rs vanished from his display. The attack was sudden, with the approaching Russian jets lost in the sea clutter as they kept close to the ocean waves. As the Russian fighters turned outbound, chased by eighteen F/A-18s, Sites listened to the speaker as the ASW Commander dealt with the carnage. Almost every airborne MH-60R had been shot down, with only a half-dozen lucky survivors having successfully jammed the incoming missiles. The only other MH-60Rs available were those refueling or rearming aboard the aircraft carriers and destroyers; not enough to cover each sector in the Bravo tier.

K-456 *VILYUCHINSK*

With his crew at Combat Stations, Captain First Rank Dmitri Pavlov stood in the Central Command Post of his guided missile submarine, surveying his men at their watch stations. Their orders and reports remained calm and professional, although they'd been unable to suppress the surge of pride and excitement when they sent the American fast attack submarine opposing them to the bottom less than thirty minutes ago.

As Pavlov's submarine crept into the next tier of America's ASW barrier, they'd been detected again, this time by ASW aircraft. Hydroacoustic reported rotary wing contacts headed their way—the helicopter rotor wash on the ocean surface was detectable as they approached. But then, suddenly, the contacts disappeared, accompanied by nearby splashes. Pavlov smiled. *Vilyuchinsk* was safe, at least for the time being.

Vilyuchinsk was at one hundred meters, proceeding at ten knots toward the third tier of the American task force's ASW screen. Unlike Russian attack submarines, *Vilyuchinsk* didn't need to penetrate the screen; his weapons had a far greater range than torpedoes. However, he'd need to get close enough to the American surface combatants to eliminate their ability to react, which would place his submarine dangerously close. Additionally, he wouldn't have the advantage of surprise he'd had several weeks ago, when he'd attacked the *Roosevelt* carrier strike group and damaged its aircraft carrier.

Pavlov had returned to port following the successful mission, for which ship and individual awards would be forthcoming. In the meantime, *Vilyuchinsk* had reloaded all twenty-four silos with replacement P-700 Granit missiles and was back at sea, ready to add to its recent glory. After checking the two fire control consoles, displaying the positions of the American ships they were approaching, Pavlov decided they were close enough.

He announced, "All stations, Command Post. Proceeding to periscope depth."

Vilyuchinsk tilted upward, rising toward the ocean's surface as Pavlov kept his face pressed to the attack periscope. Despite the crowded Central Command Post, it was quiet as the submarine rose from the deep toward periscope depth. Pavlov couldn't keep the periscope raised for long; *Vilyuchinsk* was close to the American destroyers and cruisers, and their periscope detection radars would identify a scope if it remained up for too long.

Pavlov announced, "Periscope clear," as *Vilyuchinsk* settled out at periscope depth at a speed of five knots to minimize the wake created by their periscope. After several sweeps to verify there were no combatants close enough to pose an immediate threat, Pavlov searched the horizon for his targets, pressing the red button on the periscope handle twice, sending the bearings to fire control.

Pavlov lowered the scope, announcing, "No close contacts."

Close was a relative term, as the American surface combatants were a few thousand meters to the southeast. In the distance, Pavlov had detected two gray specks on the horizon. Two of the American aircraft carriers. The other two carriers were farther back, undetectable visually at this range. However, two targets would suffice.

Pavlov checked the bearing to the two aircraft carriers, then announced, "Prepare to fire, full missile salvo, twelve missiles to each contact. Set arming range at ten thousand meters." Pavlov needed to ensure the Granit missiles enabled after they passed over the American cruisers and destroyers, not before.

The Missile Officer acknowledged and prepared to launch *Vilyuchinsk*'s surface attack missiles, each one armed with a warhead weighing almost one ton. It wouldn't take many hits to seriously damage the American aircraft carriers.

"All missiles are energized," reported a watchstander seated at one of the fire control consoles. A moment later, he added, "All missiles have accepted target bearing."

"Open all missile hatches," Pavlov ordered.

The hatches lining the submarine's port and starboard sides retracted.

The Missile Officer reported, "All missile hatches are open. Ready to fire, full missile salvo."

Pavlov surveyed the tactical situation and the readiness of his submarine one final time, then gave the order.

"Fire."

USS *HARRY S. TRUMAN*

Red icons appeared on Captain Sites's display, almost on top of the task force's cruiser and destroyer screen. As the red icons moved swiftly toward the center of the American task force, he realized there was insufficient time for the cruisers and destroyers to target and launch their SM-2 missiles and destroy the inbound weapons before they reached *Truman*. As the icons moved across the screen, they split into two groups, twelve missiles targeting *Reagan* and twelve heading toward *Truman*. Sites turned to his Tactical Action Officer.

"Shift SSDS to auto."

The TAO acknowledged, then shifted *Truman*'s SSDS—Ship Self Defense System—to automatic. The SSDS would assign contacts to their Sea Sparrow and Rolling Airframe missiles, then target any leakers with their CIWS Gatling guns. It was out of Sites's hands. All he could do was watch.

The TAO called out, "Inbound missiles. Brace for impact!"

Sites reached up and grabbed on to an I-beam, watching as the SSDS automatically targeted the inbound missiles. It all happened in a matter of seconds. Sea Sparrow and Rolling Airframe missiles were launched in succession, taking out six of the inbound missiles, and the CIWS system engaged next, taking out three more.

Three missiles made it through and Sites felt the ship shudder when the missiles hit. On the damage control status board, red symbols on the carrier's port side marked each missile impact and damage radius. Thankfully, the Hangar Deck hadn't been penetrated, nor was the carrier's Island superstructure damaged. Fires raged in three compartments, but *Truman* had survived the missile onslaught relatively unscathed.

Reagan, however, didn't fare as well. One of the screens on the Video Wall switched to a real-time feed from one of the F/A-18 tankers refueling the task force's combat air patrol. In the darkness, flames leapt skyward from USS *Ronald Reagan*, giving the water's surface an orange hue.

It wasn't long before the TAO announced, "*Reagan* has terminated flight ops."

Sites wasn't surprised. *Reagan*'s crew would have their hands full for a while, battling to get the fires under control. In the meantime, things would get busier aboard *Truman* and the other two carriers, with *Reagan*'s aircraft aloft looking for a new home.

Sites returned his attention to the Common Operational Picture on his display, fusing all sensor data. More red U-shaped icons, representing Russian submarines, had appeared in the Bravo ASW tier. If they were guided missile submarines, the remaining MH-60Rs would arrive too late to prevent them from launching. The situation was deteriorating rapidly.

The ASW Commander reached the same conclusion, and Sites listened to his orders over the speaker as he called in the cavalry.

79

PELICAN ZERO-EIGHT

The P-8A Poseidon aircraft, call sign Pelican zero-eight, cruised at twenty thousand feet, high above and well behind the American task force. Normally, anti-submarine warfare platforms wouldn't be so far from the action, but the VP-45 Pelican submarine-hunter aircraft was a modified Boeing 737-800ERX, the replacement for the venerable P-3C Orion. Cruising at a high altitude and distance from the enemy helped keep the new P-8As out of harm's way. Plus, with the new weapons they carried, they didn't need to descend to less than a thousand feet and be right on top of the target to drop their torpedo.

Seated in Pelican zero-eight's cabin with four other operators at their consoles, Lieutenant Commander John Martin, the crew's Tactical Coordinator, or TACCO, monitored the status of the five weapons in the aircraft's bomb bay. In each bomb stow was a HAAWC—High Altitude ASW Weapon Capability—a MK 54 torpedo with a wing kit. Once the torpedo was ejected, the HAAWC's wings would pop out and guide the torpedo, changing its descent angle and course as required, aiming for a GPS coordinate in the ocean.

Although the P-8A didn't have cabin windows, Martin knew that in the distance there were seven squadrons of the Navy's new Poseidon aircraft, each aircraft loaded with five HAAWCs. As Martin wondered whether their weapons would be called into service, launch orders were received by Martin's Communicator, seated beside him.

The aim point coordinates were transferred to Martin's console, and he spoke into his headset, informing the pilots and other operators of the pending launch.

"All stations, TACCO. Set Battle Condition One. Coordinates have been received for all five torpedoes."

Each member of the crew, from the pilots to the Sensor Operators, pulled out their weapon release checklists, methodically accomplishing each step. As a P-3C TACCO, Martin would have calculated the Release Points—the locations where the aircraft would drop its free-falling torpedo ordnance. However, that was no longer necessary, since HAAWCs could fly to their destination, as long as they had enough glide path.

After verifying that was the case for all five weapons, Martin reported, "All weapons are in the launch basket. We are Weapons Red and Free."

As Martin reviewed the weapon impact coordinates, he was surprised they were releasing all five HAAWCs at once with their aim points almost on top of each other. There couldn't possibly be that many submarines so close together, nor would you want to waste five torpedoes on a single target. Martin looked over at his Communicator's screen, spotting orders going to twenty of the P-8As aloft. Each had been ordered to drop their entire contingent of weapons. One hundred HAAWCs, all at once. Martin finally realized what they'd been ordered to do.

It was a torpedo version of carpet-bombing, saturating the operating areas with MK 54s.

"Flight, TACCO. Give me bomb bay open, Master Arm On."

The aircraft shuddered as the bomb bay doors swung open. Martin selected Bay One first, holding his hand over the Storage Release button.

An amber light illuminated on Martin's console.

"Flight, TACCO. I have a Kill Ready light. Standing by for weapon release."

"TACCO, Flight. You are authorized to release."

Martin pressed the Storage Release button for Bays One through Five.

Bombs away.

80

K-456 *VILYUCHINSK*

Captain First Rank Dmitri Pavlov stopped behind his men seated at the fire control consoles, examining the solutions for the American surface ships ahead. Having launched his twenty-four missiles against two American aircraft carriers, Pavlov had gone deep and ordered his submarine toward the American destroyers and cruisers. If he made it past them, he could bring his six torpedo tubes and twenty-eight torpedoes to bear on the wounded aircraft carriers.

As Pavlov's submarine approached the American surface combatants, the first indication *Vilyuchinsk* was in trouble was the report from Hydroacoustic.

"Command Post, Hydroacoustic. Splash detected on bow array, bearing zero-five-zero."

Before Pavlov could respond, Hydroacoustic reported three more.

"Additional splashes, bearing one-four-zero, two-two-zero, and three-one-zero."

With four splashes surrounding his submarine, Pavlov realized they'd been boxed in by whatever entered the water. He had a suspicion as to what they were, and Hydroacoustic's next report confirmed it.

"Torpedo in the water, bearing zero-five-zero!"

Pavlov's eyes went to the nearest fire control screen as the bearing to each splash appeared. They truly were boxed in; there was nowhere to turn.

"Ahead flank!" Pavlov announced. "Launch torpedo countermeasures."

Vilyuchinsk's Watch Officer launched a torpedo decoy, then a moment later a jammer to ensure the torpedoes behind them saw only the decoy and not *Vilyuchinsk* speeding away. However, there was no good option for the torpedoes in front of them. *Vilyuchinsk* would loom large and enticing on their sonar returns.

Pavlov decided to turn ninety degrees to starboard. "Steersman, right full rudder, steady course two-seven-zero." Turning to his Watch Officer, he ordered, "Launch decoy."

Vilyuchinsk steadied on course, and with the decoy behind him, Pavlov ordered another jammer into the water. Maybe, with the jammer partially obscuring *Vilyuchinsk* as it sped away, one of the torpedoes would suck up on the decoy.

The torpedo off *Vilyuchinsk*'s port bow wasn't fooled, however. It had a clear view of the submarine speeding to the west and altered course to intercept. Additionally, the torpedo off his port stern sniffed out the decoy and went around, locking on to *Vilyuchinsk* as the submarine attempted to slip away. Likewise, the two torpedoes off *Vilyuchinsk*'s starboard side correctly identified the small object in the water pretending to be a submarine as a decoy, and went around. One torpedo veered to the east and the other to the west, and the latter torpedo detected the Russian guided missile submarine.

With three torpedoes closing fast, one from each side and one from behind, there was nowhere for Pavlov to turn. *Vilyuchinsk* was at maximum speed and it was obvious more decoys would be ineffective, nor could his

submarine outrun the speedy torpedoes. That left one
option.

Ride it out.

The three torpedoes chasing him were lightweight
torpedoes, armed with one-sixth the explosive carried
by a heavyweight. *Vilyuchinsk* was a double-hulled submarine, with the outer hull 3.5 meters away from the
critical pressure hull in most areas, to handle situations
like this.

As the first torpedo homed on *Vilyuchinsk*, approaching from off its port bow, Pavlov braced for the explosion. It came seconds later, jolting the submarine, but
not as severely as he expected. The men in the Central
Command Post waited tensely for the report of flooding. But no report came. Pavlov breathed a sigh of relief. They'd weathered the first attack.

There was no doubt the torpedo had torn a gaping
hole in the outer hull, with twisted and mangled edges,
but that was a small price to pay. Pavlov turned his attention to the next torpedo, this one approaching from
starboard. The second jolt felt much like the first, and
after a few tense seconds awaiting an emergency report
that never came, Pavlov focused on the last torpedo. *Vilyuchinsk* had decreased speed by two knots; the jagged holes in the submarine's outer hull were slowing it
down. But that didn't matter. Two knots weren't going
to make a difference.

As the third torpedo approached, Pavlov realized the
scenario was different. The first two torpedoes had hit
Vilyuchinsk broadside, where the submarine had a full
3.5-meter separation between hulls. However, the third
torpedo was approaching from astern, where the outer
hull tapered in toward the pressure hull.

"Steersman, hard right rudder!"

Vilyuchinsk's bow swung toward the torpedo, but it

was too late. The third MK 54 detonated as it sensed
the magnetic field from the guided missile submarine,
and this time, the jolt was followed by an emergency
report.

"Flooding in Compartment Nine!"

A hole had been blown in *Vilyuchinsk*'s pressure hull,
and as water surged into the submarine, the lights flick-
ered, indicating the electrical power grid had been
shifted to the battery. They'd lost their electrical turbine
generators, which meant propulsion would go next. As
Pavlov's Watch Officer tried frantically to ascertain the
status of the Engine Room, *Vilyuchinsk* slowed, and the
stern tilted downward.

Pavlov turned to his Compensation Officer, who had
lined up the drain pump to the Engine Room and was
now blowing the submarine's variable ballast overboard,
increasing *Vilyuchinsk*'s buoyancy in an effort to offset
the water rushing into the submarine.

"Keep us level!" Pavlov ordered. If the submarine up-
ended, all would be lost.

The Compensation Officer opened the valves to Forward Ballast, flooding water back in. But the tank was
only so big, and water was surging into the Engine
Room faster than the drain pump pushed it back out.
Vilyuchinsk's stern continued sinking, and the submarine's angle steadily increased to thirty, then forty
degrees. At the same time, *Vilyuchinsk* was getting
heavier. They sank through three hundred meters, then
four hundred.

Pavlov was again caught in a scenario with no good
answer. Continue downward and the submarine would
implode. Emergency Blow to the surface, and the Americans would sink them. Still, going up was a better
prospect than down, and Pavlov gave the order.

"Emergency Blow all main ballast tanks!"

The Compensation Officer pulled the emergency levers, porting high-pressure air to the tanks.

Water surged from the grates beneath the hull as it was displaced by air, but Pavlov had waited too long. *Vilyuchinsk* was tilted up at forty-five degrees and the air in the ballast tanks surged toward the front of each tank, making the bow of the submarine more buoyant than the stern. *Vilyuchinsk* tilted upward more rapidly, and once a bubble formed in the top of each ballast tank, the excess air spilled out the grates, leaving too much water inside.

Pavlov and the men in the Central Command Post hung on to consoles and railings as the submarine tilted ninety degrees upward, and Pavlov knew they would not recover.

Slowly, stern first, *Vilyuchinsk* sank into the ocean depths.

81

MOSCOW

Foreign Minister Lavrov and the chief of the general staff, General Andropov, strode down the long Kremlin hallway toward the president's office. After a knock on the president's door and an acknowledgment from within, Andropov entered an office filled with the president's staff, all with notepads in their hands. It wasn't even 7 a.m., but it wasn't often that two of the world's major military powers went to war.

Kalinin ordered the room cleared, and Minister Lavrov and General Andropov eased into their chairs opposite the president. Andropov tried to assess the president's mood. Following the discovery of America's attack on their forces in the Arabian Sea and Iran, Kalinin had been furious. He was a seasoned and normally unemotional politician, but he'd been rattled by America's attack, and Andropov could not predict how he'd respond to the new information.

"I have unsettling news, Mr. President. The Americans have disarmed the pipeline detonators. We activated over a dozen, and none blew. When we tried to discuss the problem with the detonator's designer, we learned he was abducted from his villa a few days ago.

The Federal Security Service," Andropov said, referring to the domestic half of the former KGB, "was aware of this matter, but didn't think it necessary to elevate it to our attention until now."

Kalinin replied, "He gave the Americans the master code?"

"It appears so."

"Is there a way to override it?"

"Not that we're aware of."

Kalinin folded his hands across his waist and leaned back in his chair, deep in thought. The Americans had broken one-half of Russia's stranglehold on Western European energy and were trying to break the other.

"How is the battle going?"

"The outcome is still in doubt," Andropov answered. "There won't be much left of our surface combatants, but our submarines are having success. We've broken into the second tier of their anti-submarine screen and have damaged two of their aircraft carriers, knocking one out of commission. We've suffered a few submarine losses, but as best we can tell, we still have at least thirty-five submarines pressing the attack, while the American attack submarines have been reduced to around a dozen. We are going around the few that remain now; they cannot plug the holes."

Kalinin didn't respond, and Andropov sensed he was considering ending the battle.

"We cannot stop now," Andropov said. "With most of our surface combatants heavily damaged or sunk, compared to only two American aircraft carriers damaged, we will emerge in far worse shape. However, our submarines are making progress and it's still likely that we'll sink the four American carriers or force them to withdraw."

Kalinin turned to his foreign minister. "If we are

victorious and blockade the Persian Gulf, will that be enough to force the United States and NATO to capitulate in Ukraine and Lithuania?"

"It's possible. But I agree with General Andropov. It's the only path forward. If we withdraw, we lose all leverage."

"Speaking of leverage," Kalinin said, "where do we stand with India and China?"

Lavrov replied, "We just received China's answer, and we've been in discussions with India." Lavrov explained China's position, and after Kalinin provided his thoughts, Lavrov went on to say, "My opinion is the Indians are watching the battle unfold, waiting to commit to the side that pulls ahead."

Kalinin's irritation bled through his words. "Sweeten the deal; whatever they ask for. We'll sort out what we'll really concede later. But tell the Indians they have one hour to join us. After that, our offer is void."

"Yes, Mr. President."

As the meeting wound to a close, Kalinin asked, "Where is Minister Chernov? He should have returned from Sochi by now."

Andropov replied, "I was about to inform you." He paused, uncertain how to deliver the news. Finally, he said, "Chernov won't be returning."

"Why not?"

Andropov relayed the details of Chernov's death. When he finished, Kalinin stared at him for a long moment.

"Where is O'Connor?" he asked.

"Gorev has her in custody at Chernov's villa, awaiting your instructions."

Another long stare, then Kalinin nodded.

82

NEW DELHI, INDIA

On the ground floor of Rashtrapati Bhavan, Indian President Deepak Madan stood at the fifteen-foot-tall arched window in his study, looking out over Mughal Gardens. With water canals, sandstone fountains, and over seventy seasonal flowers, including 159 varieties of roses, the gardens are considered by many to be the soul of the presidential palace. Madan remembered the first time he set eyes on the beautiful grounds. He had hoped the future of his country would be as bright and vibrant as the flowers in Mughal Gardens.

In the last few days, however, a darkness had settled over Rashtrapati Bhavan and Mughal Gardens. The Russians, and now the Americans, were pressuring India to intervene in their conflict. A decision had to be made, and soon. Time was running out, like the proverbial sand in an hourglass, each grain representing the incentives offered by each country. He had discussed the matter with his National Security Council, and their advice was conflicting. Now, with the battle in the Indian Ocean reaching a climax, Madan knew he would be forced to decide.

There was a knock on the door and his ministers of defense and external affairs, along with his national security advisor, entered. Madan motioned the men into upholstered chairs resting atop a handwoven Kashmir carpet. When he joined them, his minister of external affairs, Rahul Gupta, brought Madan up-to-date.

"Russia has offered additional incentives and also given us an ultimatum. We have until eight a.m. to accept."

"And the Americans?"

"They are awaiting our answer without further discourse."

Madan spent the next few minutes discussing the new Russian incentives, along with the choice to be made: become a Russian ally in this war, aid the Americans, or remain neutral. Of course, China's response in the matter weighed heavily on his thoughts.

After considering the options carefully, Madan made his decision.

83

USS *HARRY S. TRUMAN*

"Brace for impact!"

Captain David Randle gripped his chair tightly as he peered through the Bridge windows toward the incoming missiles. The Russian P-700 Granits were called Shipwreck missiles for good reason. A single missile could wreck an entire destroyer or cruiser, and if it hit *Truman*'s Island superstructure, where Randle was located, there would be nothing left.

Through the open side windows of the Bridge, Randle heard his ship's defensive systems engage. Sea Sparrow and Rolling Airframe missiles streaked from their launchers, leaving trails of white smoke. A moment later, the three Phalanx CIWS Gatling guns engaged.

Four more missiles hit *Truman*, the ship shuddering with each blast, and four more spires of black smoke rose skyward from the carrier's port side, joining seven others.

This attack on *Truman* brought the total to five. Five Russian guided missile submarines had approached close enough to launch their missiles at the task force's carriers. Three of the four aircraft carriers had been hit, with only USS *Eisenhower* spared thus far. *Bush* was down hard, with fires raging inside the hangar bays.

Reagan, on the other hand, despite taking additional missile impacts, was inching closer to resuming flight ops.

That left two operable carriers, but two were sufficient for the remaining seventy Super Hornets. The task force had lost almost two-thirds of its fighter complement, but they had accomplished their mission. The Russian combat air patrol had been annihilated, and every Russian surface combatant had been sunk or heavily damaged. Only *Pyotr Velikiy* and *Kuznetsov* were putting up a fight now, and *Kuznetsov* could no longer support flight operations. The Russian surface Navy was in its death throes. Unfortunately, the Russian Submarine Force was not.

Randle examined the horizon; the hazy gray dawn had given way to a spectacular day—a cloudless blue sky with moderate winds, blowing the columns of black smoke rising from three American carriers northward. On the Flight Deck below, two Super Hornets glided toward the bow catapults, preparing for another assault on the two remaining Russian surface combatants. Now that the Russian combat air patrol was nonexistent, the F/A-18 weapon mix had been changed, trading their air-to-air missiles for more anti-surface weapons. It wouldn't be long before every Russian surface ship had a new, permanent berth on the bottom of the ocean.

"Bridge, CDC."

Randle answered, "Captain."

"Captain, OPSO. We're detecting activity from the Indian carriers."

Randle acknowledged the report, then switched one of the quad screens below the Bridge windows to the COP—Common Operational Picture. The three Indian aircraft carriers to the east, including their newest one allegedly on sea trials, had begun launching. Randle watched the yellow neutral icons accumulate on the screen as the

Indian air wings assembled above the carriers. India was preparing to join the battle, and given there had been no official coordination between the American task force and Indian Navy, the scenario did not bode well.

He shifted his radio to Strike, listening as the strike controllers in CDC vectored the combat air patrol to the east and launched all ready aircraft. On the Flight Deck, Aviation Ordnancemen hustled to the two F/A-18s on the bow catapults, swapping out their surface attack missiles with anti-air. It didn't take long, and the two F/A-18s streaked forward as the bow catapults fired. Randle watched the two fighters turn east to join the rest of the CAP.

As the three Indian fighter wings headed toward the American task force, Randle did the math. Seventy-two inbound tactical fighters opposed by thirty-two Super Hornets. The American aircraft were superior, but quality overcame only so much quantity. Additionally, although there were several cruisers and destroyers on the back side of the formation, the task force was lightly defended in that area compared to the front and flanks.

Randle listened as the strike controllers recalled all aircraft headed toward the Russian surface combatants, ordering them back to *Truman* and *Eisenhower* to swap out their air-to-surface weapons with air-to-air. That would take time, unfortunately, during which the task force's CAP of thirty-two fighters would have to suffice.

The battle unfolded quickly. The Indian aircraft closed within range of the task force's protective screen of cruisers and destroyers, and the bulk of the seventy-two inbound aircraft launched their missiles: over two hundred inbound bogies.

The Aegis Warfare Systems aboard the American ships performed admirably, but two dozen missiles made it through, striking the six destroyers and cruisers in that sector. Randle watched in dismay as three of the ships dropped off the grid, including the heavily armed cruiser *Vicksburg*. A review of the visual feed from that sector revealed black smoke billowing up from all six ships.

The Indian aircraft launched a second volley of missiles, this time bypassing the damaged ships, their missiles headed toward *Eisenhower*. Twenty made it through. Luckily, the aircraft air-to-surface missiles were much smaller than Russian Shipwrecks, and *Eisenhower* survived. Unfortunately, the damage was severe enough to halt flight operations.

Black smoke was now spiraling up from all four American carriers, with only *Truman* operable at the moment.

84

ARABIAN SEA

On USS *Truman*'s Flight Deck, Lieutenant Commander Bill Houston, call sign Samurai, waited in the cockpit of his F/A-18E Super Hornet. He'd lost count of how many times he'd returned to the carrier for rearming and refueling. To save time, *Truman*'s crew was *hot pumping*, refueling his jet with the engines still running, one at a time. Houston kept the port engine running while they refueled starboard, then they'd reverse the procedure for port. Meanwhile, Ordies were attaching more ordnance to his fighter, all air-to-air missiles this time, as he'd be heading out to engage the Indian air wings.

Wisps of smoke occasionally drifted across the Flight Deck, partially obscuring his vision. Although most of the black smoke was pouring from the aircraft carrier's port side, blowing away from the ship as it rose skyward, some leaked from the elevators on starboard as the crew battled the fires raging inside the ship. He had to give credit to *Truman*'s crew, keeping the aircraft carrier operational despite the extensive damage.

Truman's crew completed refueling and rearming Houston's aircraft, and the yellow-shirted Shooter guided him toward CAT One, the starboard bow catapult. Houston pulled up beside his new wingman, Lieutenant

Dave Hernandez, call sign TexMex, who had just dropped
his launch bar into CAT Two. It was an ill omen for the
Mexican from Texas. Houston had lost two wingmen
already, one during the night and another one this
morning. Perhaps the third time would be the charm.

Houston dropped his launch bar into CAT One's shuttle hook, and the Flight Deck crew verified his aircraft
was ready for launch. The Shooter then lifted his arm
skyward, then back down to a horizontal position, directing Houston to kick in the afterburners. Houston
pushed the throttles past the détente, then turned toward
the Shooter and saluted. The Shooter returned the
salute, then bent down and touched the deck, but not
before Houston caught the reflection of the Rising Sun
off the canopy of his aircraft.

Thus far, Houston hadn't needed the reflective tape
affixed to his helmet, having made it back to *Truman*
after each mission rather than splashing into the ocean.
He hoped it wasn't a premonition, catching the reflection just before takeoff. He didn't have much time to
dwell on the matter, however. The operator in the Catapult Control Station took his cue from the Shooter and
the starboard catapult fired; six hundred pounds of
steam sent Houston's aircraft streaking toward *Truman*'s
bow. As Houston climbed to ten thousand feet, TexMex
pulled up alongside and both jets headed east.

It wasn't long before Houston and Hernandez reached
the task force perimeter, joining what remained of the
combat air patrol. The original thirty-two F/A-18s had
engaged over twice that number of Indian fighters, and
Samurai and TexMex brought the total number of F/A-18s
aloft to twenty. Houston checked his AN/APG-79 radar
display, noting four more aircraft on their way out, including a pair from *Reagan*. The heavily damaged carrier was back in business. That was good news, as there

were another thirty-five Super Hornets returning from the assault on the Russian surface ships, and the Flight Deck crews could refuel and rearm them only so quickly.

Samurai and TexMex joined the northern end of the combat air patrol, which was strung out on a north-to-south line facing the three Indian strike groups. It was quiet for the time being, as the Indian aircraft returned to their carriers to refuel and rearm. The reprieve was welcomed, as the additional Super Hornets trickled in from *Truman* and *Reagan*. However, the reprieve drew to a close when the three Indian air wings assembled above their carriers, then headed west.

As the Indian aircraft approached, Houston counted them up. Forty-seven aircraft. They'd lost twenty-five on their last assault, compared to fourteen F/A-18s lost. The odds were still two to one, though, with the combat air patrol now up to twenty-four Super Hornets. The three Indian air wings combined again, and it took only a few minutes to close the distance.

Samurai and the other F/A-18s fired two volleys of AMRAAM missiles as the two air wings approached each other, then evaded a barrage of incoming missiles. Moments later, the thirty-eight remaining Indian aircraft slammed into the twenty remaining American fighters, and the sky was filled with a dizzying array of aircraft and missiles as pilots dispensed chaff and targeted enemy fighters while weaving past exploding aircraft and streaking missiles.

This time, however, the Indian fighters didn't continue in toward the American task force. They had learned their lesson the last time, taking a beating from the American combat air patrol despite their numerical superiority. For this assault, every Indian fighter was fully armed with air-to-air missiles and they remained engaged with the F/A-18s. Their objective became clear: they were going to wipe out the American CAP.

The sky began to thin and the hectic melee degenerated into individual dogfights. Houston did well, shooting down two Indian fighters, and as the second one splashed into the ocean, his wingman's voice broke across his headset.

"Samurai, tally two bandits on your six!"

Houston glanced at his APG-79 radar display, locating the two Indian fighters settling in behind him. "I see 'em," he replied.

TexMex said, "I can't help. I'm tied up with two of my own."

Samurai spotted his wingman headed south with two bandits in trail, then banked hard right to bring his Super Hornet around toward the two Indian aircraft behind him. He flicked a switch on his flight stick during the turn, selecting another AMRAAM. As his F/A-18 came around, he identified the two bandits as MiG-29Ks and targeted the closest one.

He fired the AMRAAM and its internal radar took over, locking on to the MiG-29. The Indian fighter dispensed chaff and banked hard left, but the AMRAAM detected the aircraft speeding away from the chaff and adjusted course. As the missile sped toward the evading aircraft, Samurai turned his attention to the second MiG-29. It had launched one of its missiles, which *Bitching Betty* dutifully notified him of—*"Missile inbound!"*—and Samurai's Radar Warning Receiver identified as a radar-homing Vympel R-77.

There was an explosion to Samurai's left. His AMRAAM had found its target, with the missile and MiG-29 morphing into a cloud of fire and shrapnel. There was no time to celebrate, as the R-77 was closing fast. Houston dispensed a burst of chaff, then banked right and inverted, turning his F/A-18 upside down. Pulling back on his flight stick, he streaked down toward the water, away from his chaff. The R-77 continued toward the reflective cloud of aluminum-coated fibers, passing through it. After verifying the missile lost track of his aircraft, Houston pulled back on his flight stick, leveling off at eight thousand feet, headed back toward the incoming MiG-29 as *Bitching Betty* alerted again.

"Missile inbound!"

The MiG-29 pilot had fired a second R-77 during Houston's maneuver, and the missile was already dangerously close. Houston selected another AMRAAM and fired at the Indian jet, then dispensed a second round of chaff and banked hard right again. The R-77 stayed locked on to Houston's F/A-18, veering toward his aircraft as it ignored the chaff. Houston dispensed another round and banked hard left, looking through his canopy to see if the chaff worked.

This time, the chaff deployment was a success; the missile stayed locked on to the reflective aluminum fibers. He was about to return his attention to the MiG-29 when *Bitching Betty* alerted a third time. Houston's APG-79 identified this missile as an infrared homing R-73. The MiG-29 had worked its way behind Houston, and after watching two radar-homing missiles fail, the pilot had shifted to a heat-seeker.

Samurai dispensed a round of infrared decoys, then banked hard right, but the missile stayed locked on, swiftly closing the last few hundred yards. Houston tried another burst of infrared decoys and a hard bank to the left, but the missile remained locked on to the larger heat signature of the F/A-18's twin engines.

Houston banked hard left again just as the missile reached his aircraft, and a bright flash was accompanied by the sound of shrapnel tearing through his aircraft. Samurai's F/A-18 began trailing orange flames and black smoke from its starboard engine as *Bitching Betty* informed him of the obvious.

"Engine right! Engine right!"

Another engine gone, Samurai thought. This time, however, he wouldn't make it back to the carrier. In addition to an engine on fire, Houston's flaps were damaged and he had difficulty maintaining a straight course. His F/A-18 was shuddering and losing altitude rapidly, despite pushing his left engine to maximum power.

Being half Japanese and with his aircraft going down, Houston entertained the thought, if only for a few seconds, of a kamikaze attack. However, there were no enemy surface ships nearby and better judgment prevailed anyway. He reached between his knees and pulled the ejection handle beneath his seat. The canopy's explosive bolts blew, sending the top of his cockpit spiraling away, and Houston was blasted into the air along with his seat.

After his parachute opened and he began drifting toward the ocean, Houston realized that the reflective tape on his helmet was going to come in handy.

85

USS *HARRY S. TRUMAN*

"Loss of bravo-two-one."

The strike controller's report aboard *Truman* was professional and monotone, his voice failing to match Captain Sites's mounting concern. Standing in the aircraft carrier's Combat Direction Center, Sites monitored the task force's engagement with the Indian Navy with rising trepidation, paying little attention to the thin layer of smoke hanging in the overhead. Even though the aircraft carrier's compartments had been sealed when setting General Quarters, smoke seeped inside CDC as *Truman*'s crew battled the fires. Air samples were being taken to ensure breathing protection was not required.

A second strike controller reported the loss of another F/A-18, and Sites assessed the tactical situation. *Bush* and *Eisenhower* were still down, but *Reagan* was back on-line. However, her ability to sustain flight operations was tenuous, easily knocked out again if the carrier was hit by another round of Shipwreck missiles. Russian guided missile submarines were continuing to penetrate close enough to launch their surface attack missiles, but the task force was making each submarine pay dearly, vectoring a round of HAAWCs into the surrounding water. Russian attack submarines were probing the third

ASW tier, but the destroyers and cruisers, along with the few MH-60Rs that remained, seemed to have kept the Russians at bay.

To the east, the task force's combat air patrol was losing aircraft faster than replacements arrived. As the Indian aircraft whittled away at what remained of the task force's combat air patrol, Sites spotted another wave of thirty aircraft inbound from the Indian carriers. He studied the red icons; the numbers didn't add up.

The task force's F/A-18s had splashed over thirty of India's seventy aircraft, yet the Common Operational Picture still showed seventy aloft. Sites finally realized what the Indians were doing. Although the American task force was beyond range of India's land-based tactical fighters, naval aircraft could land on the three Indian carriers and refuel. The Indians were ferrying additional aircraft aboard their carriers, replacing their losses, something the American aircraft carriers couldn't do in their current location. As American airpower attrited and Indian forces were replenished, the battle would tilt rapidly in favor of India.

It was time to vacate the area. The task force's first objective had been accomplished, destroying the Russian surface Navy. The carriers could retreat and conduct repairs, then reengage with additional ASW assets to deal with the Russian submarines. Sites examined the Common Operational Picture on his display, searching for an exit route. Russian submarines were pressing the task force's northern and western sectors, with the Indian Navy to the east. That left the south, although there was no guarantee the Indian Navy's submarines weren't closing in from that direction. However, there were several American submarines on the back side of the task force, guarding against a Russian or Indian end-around.

As Sites's eyes shifted to the narrow escape route to the south, yellow surface ship icons appeared on his display. Confusion worked across his face, and when the icons turned red, beads of cold sweat formed on his brow. A new enemy strike group had arrived, cutting off the retreat path for the American task force. As he wondered what ships they were, his Common Operational Picture tagged the contact in the center of the enemy formation as CNS *Liaoning*, the formidable Chinese aircraft carrier and sister ship of *Kuznetsov*, sold to China after the fall of the Soviet Union.

Son of a bitch!

Sites slammed his fist onto his console. He'd been told the Chinese had agreed to remain neutral. Now, with the outcome of the battle tilting away from the United States, China's entry into the conflict was the nail in the coffin.

Red icons appeared beside the Russian-built carrier as its fighters launched. Ten, twenty, thirty . . . *Liaoning*'s crew was proficient, rapidly launching its air wing. When there were thirty aircraft aloft, they began their journey, moving swiftly north toward the American task force.

Sites's shoulders sagged as he monitored the Chinese air wing's journey. As the aircraft approached the task force's air defense perimeter, provided by the cruisers and destroyers to the south, the Chinese fighters shifted their flight path, vectoring to the northeast. It looked as if the Chinese fighters were going to join the Indian aircraft and wipe out the remaining American combat air patrol, then penetrate the task force in the weakened sector to the east, where Indian aircraft had heavily damaged or knocked six of the surface combatants off-line.

Sites's eyes went to the blue icons representing the damaged surface combatants. The Ticonderoga cruiser *Vicksburg* was still down, and another destroyer had dropped off the air warfare grid. That left two damaged destroyers in the area. They'd be overwhelmed.

As the Chinese aircraft continued toward what remained of the task force's combat air patrol, four more F/A-18s—two from *Truman* and two from *Reagan*, were racing out to support.

Too little, too late.

When the thirty Chinese fighters closed to within missile range of the American and Indian melee, their icons switched from red to yellow. As Sites studied his display in confusion, their color changed to blue, as did the icons representing the Chinese ships to the south. The unit designation of the aircraft carrier also updated, and a wave of relief swept over Sites.

The aircraft carrier to the south wasn't *Liaoning*.

It was USS *Roosevelt*!

86

USS *THEODORE ROOSEVELT*

Captain Dolores Gonzalez monitored the Common Operational Picture on her console in CDC, wondering what her counterparts on the other four American carriers had endured. *Bush* and *Eisenhower* had been damaged severely enough to terminate flight operations, and it looked as if *Truman* and *Reagan* were limping along. The sky above the American task force was mostly clear, aside from the air battle to the east and several dozen Super Hornets circling above *Truman* and *Reagan*—about three squadrons—waiting to refuel and rearm.

Gonzalez knew the pilots aloft were exhausted by now, while *Roosevelt*'s were fresh, chomping at the bit since they'd left Pearl Harbor under the cover of darkness. Several weeks ago, with the aircraft carrier's Island superstructure reduced to twisted and molten metal by a Russian Shipwreck missile, *Roosevelt* had arrived at Pearl Harbor for repairs. The initial damage assessment estimated it would take six months to return the carrier to service, but Captain Debra Driza, commander of the Pearl Harbor Naval Shipyard, had challenged her workforce, invoking USS *Yorktown* as inspiration.

USS *Yorktown* (CV-5), operating in the Pacific in

May 1942, had participated in the Battle of the Coral Sea as the Allies tried to thwart Japan's expansion across the Pacific. During the hectic battle, as dusk settled over the Pacific, six Japanese pilots incredibly mistook *Yorktown* for one of their own carriers and attempted to land, their mistake pointed out by *Yorktown*'s anti-aircraft gunners. Other Japanese pilots properly identified *Yorktown*, and the carrier was hit with a bomb that penetrated the Flight Deck and exploded belowdecks, causing extensive damage that experts estimated would take three months to repair.

When Allied intelligence decoded a Japanese message a few days later, learning of a major operation aimed at gaining a foothold at the northwestern tip of the Hawaiian Island chain, Admiral Chester Nimitz gathered his comparatively meager naval forces, rushing them toward Midway Island. With four Japanese heavy aircraft carriers approaching and having only Task Force 16—USS *Enterprise* and USS *Hornet*—at his disposal, Nimitz directed *Yorktown* be made ready to sail alongside Task Force 16. Pearl Harbor Naval Shipyard workers labored around the clock, and three days later, *Yorktown* set sail with her sister carriers.

Captain Driza's challenge had been met, and USS *Roosevelt* set sail a day behind *Eisenhower* and *Bush* as they passed Hawaii, westbound for the Indian Ocean. *Roosevelt*'s Island superstructure was still a molten mass of steel and her hangar bays scorched black from the fires that had raged inside. But her flight systems—catapults, arresting wires, and elevators—were operational. Shipyard tiger teams had remained aboard *Roosevelt*, continuing repairs as the carrier sailed across the Pacific, with the ship navigated from Secondary Control, located beneath the Flight Deck, instead of the mangled Bridge.

Roosevelt, along with several destroyer escorts exiting the repair yards, had traveled across the Pacific under darkened ship and complete EMCON—Emissions Controls; no radar or communication emissions—staying beyond visual range of other ships during the transit. Additionally, as they approached the American task force and their Indian opponents, *Roosevelt* and her destroyer escorts had activated their electronic countermeasure suites, emitting the radar signature of Chinese ships while the outbound aircraft kept their Identification-Friend-or-Foe transponders secured.

Gonzalez turned her attention to Flight Deck operations as *Roosevelt* began launching another thirty aircraft from her bow and waist catapults. Navy leadership knew the carrier would arrive late to the battle and replacement aircraft would be sorely needed, so *Roosevelt* had been outfitted with six Super Hornet squadrons instead of the standard four, plus two squadrons of MH-60Rs. The first wave of thirty F/A-18s would engage the Indian fighters tangling with the task force's CAP, while the following wave of F/A-18s would attack the second wave of incoming Indian fighters.

Whatever survived those two battles would join forces with the three F/A-18 squadrons above *Truman* and *Reagan*, then deliver a warm welcome to the three Indian aircraft carriers.

87

PENTAGON

The president took a sip of lukewarm coffee, keeping his eyes fixed on the thirty-foot-diameter screen at the far end of the Current Action Center as red and blue symbols moved slowly across the display. The tension and silence of the first few hours had been replaced by the murmur of quiet conversations, loosened ties, and unbuttoned shirt collars as the men and women around the table monitored the battle's progress.

A few hours earlier, USS *Roosevelt*'s air wing, with the assistance of the task force's combat air patrol, had shot down all Indian aircraft aloft. After refueling and rearming her F/A-18s, *Roosevelt* had joined forces with the remaining task force aircraft, finishing off *Pyotr Velikiy* and *Kuznetsov*. Turning their attention back to the Indian Navy, a one-hundred-plus aircraft assault was en route toward the Indian aircraft carriers, which were retreating rapidly toward shore with their destroyer and frigate escorts. A single strike likely wouldn't sink the three carriers, but it would bloody their noses.

Now that the outcome of the battle was clear, the president turned to his advisors.

"What's the next step in the Indian Ocean?" he asked McVeigh.

"We'll pull the task force back temporarily while we continue repairs on all four carriers. Hopefully we can get *Eisenhower* and *Bush* back up without a shipyard visit. We've got shipyard tiger teams waiting in Diego Garcia, plus four replacement air wings, stripped from the aircraft carriers in the repair yards, on their way. Once all five carriers are operational and their air wings are at full strength again, we'll engage the remaining Russian submarines."

"What's the status of the two submarine forces?" the president asked.

McVeigh deferred to Admiral Brian Rettman, the Chief of Naval Operations, who answered, "It's difficult to say this early, as submarines don't communicate during battle. By doctrine, they stay at optimal search depth and speed until the conflict is over or have previous orders directing them to report in at a specific time." Admiral Rettman glanced at the clock. "In another two hours, whoever survived will report in, as long as there are no hostile contacts in their operating area.

"As far as the Russian submarines go, it's also difficult to say. We know how many lightweight and heavyweight torpedoes exploded, but we don't know which submarines were sunk—ours or theirs—or how many of the lightweight torpedoes were expended on the same target. There haven't been any subsurface missile attacks against our carriers in the last few hours, so it looks like we've sunk all eleven guided missile submarines, either before or after they launched.

"Russian attack submarines continue to probe our ASW defenses, so it looks like there's a fair number of those left. We have insufficient numbers of MH-60 Romeo helicopters to cover the Bravo sectors, but they're being augmented by P-8As monitoring via sonobuoy fields they've dropped. However, they're running low on sonobuoys."

When Admiral Rettman finished, McVeigh followed up. "As I mentioned, we'll pull the task force back and refit with additional ASW assets and supplies, then engage the remaining Russian attack submarines. Depending on how plan B goes."

"Are we ready?" the president asked.

"Yes, Mr. President. All we're waiting for is your authorization."

The president replied, "Proceed with the next phase."

88

USS *MICHIGAN*

Lieutenant Chris Shroyer turned slowly on the periscope as USS *Michigan* loitered in the Sea of Marmara, watching tankers and other merchant ships pass by in the distance. He was nearing the end of his watch, and after almost six hours going round and round, he had his left arm draped over the periscope handle like a seasoned World War II captain. He knew it was unprofessional, but the submarine's Executive Officer, Lieutenant Commander Dave Beasley, on watch in the Control Room with him, said nothing. He had more important things to worry about.

Beasley was stationed as the Command Duty Officer. While lurking in the Sea of Marmara, either the Executive Officer or Wilson would be in the Control Room, alternating in six-hour shifts. Earlier this morning, *Michigan* emerged into the Sea of Marmara after following a Suezmax tanker up the Dardanelles, and Captain Wilson and his crew waited patiently for orders. Via the radio receiver at the top of the periscope, *Michigan* was in continuous communication.

"Conn, Radio. In receipt of a new OPORD."

Lieutenant Shroyer acknowledged, then pulled the

microphone from its holder and pressed the button for the Captain's stateroom.

"Captain, Officer of the Deck. In receipt of new operational orders."

Wilson acknowledged and entered the Control Room as a watchstander emerged from the Radio Room, message board in hand.

The submarine's Captain read the new OPORD, then handed it to his Executive Officer. Lieutenant Shroyer, still going round and round with his face pressed against the periscope, waited for one of the two senior officers to enlighten him. Wilson did the honor, informing Shroyer they'd been ordered into the Black Sea. The last two fast attack submarines in the Atlantic Fleet weren't far behind, but *Michigan* would lead the way.

The journey up the Bosphorus was seventeen nautical miles long, which would take less than two hours, plus another tanker to follow. As with the trip up the Dardanelles, *Michigan* would transit submerged, close behind the largest tanker they could find, and this time, they'd do it without the periscope raised, since it'd be visible in the daylight.

It didn't take long for a suitable tanker to enter the Marmara Sea, headed north. Wilson took a look, then after verifying they held the contact on Sonar, lowered the periscope.

Wilson announced, "I have the Conn, Lieutenant Shroyer retains the Deck. Helm, ahead two-thirds, right twenty degrees rudder." As *Michigan* increased speed and swung around behind the tanker, Wilson ordered, "Steady as she goes."

As *Michigan* headed up the Bosphorus, the tension in the Control Room rose as the remaining miles counted down. Wilson and his crew were unsure what awaited them, relying on the latest intel report for the basic order of battle. If the report was correct, there were no Russian submarines remaining in the Black Sea. Five Kilo class attack submarines, along with a Slava class cruiser and Kashin class destroyer, had transited the Turkish Straits into the Mediterranean, where they joined the Northern Fleet as it headed toward the Suez Canal and into the Pacific. What remained in the Black Sea were four anti-submarine warfare frigates, patrolling near the northern end of the Bosphorus.

Wilson guided *Michigan* up the narrow channel while leaving the submarine's Deck in Lieutenant Shroyer's capable hands. The junior officer monitored the two inertial navigators, watching the two white dots on the electronic navigation chart creep up the Bosphorus, and when *Michigan* was one nautical mile from the channel's exit into the Black Sea, he informed the Captain as instructed.

Michigan's Commanding Officer announced, "Raising Number One scope," then twisted the orange periscope locking ring above his head, raising the attack periscope.

Wilson did a quick 360-degree sweep, returning to a forward view, sweeping back and forth as *Michigan* entered the Black Sea. As Shroyer wondered if there were Russian combatants in the area, Wilson's next order clarified the situation.

"Man Battle Stations Torpedo."

89

SIBERIA, RUSSIA

Delta Force operator Joe Martin, wearing a ram-air parachute system strapped to his body, sat quietly in the cargo hold of the MC-130H Combat Talon II, awaiting the end of his journey. After taking off from Dolon Air Base in Semey, Kazakhstan, and heading north, Martin and the other operators in his Delta Force unit were flying at thirty thousand feet, having entered Russian airspace moments earlier. Although the aircraft was outfitted with terrain-following radar that enabled operations as low as 250 feet, it wouldn't be needed today. The MC-130H Combat Talon, flying at the same altitude and flight path as commercial airliners traveling between Kazakhstan and Russia, would blend into the traffic.

Under normal circumstances, deploying against heavily defended installations, Martin and his team would have been dropped under the cover of darkness. This wasn't the case today, as it was approaching noon in the Siberian province. Martin wasn't worried, however. The facility would be lightly defended, if at all. Plus, the small size of the metal objects they carried meant they wouldn't be detected by radar during the jump, and the speed of their descent would give their opponents little time to respond even if they were.

As Martin's unit headed north, he knew that two dozen Delta Force and Navy SEAL units were aloft, heading toward their targets. Martin surveyed the other fifty-one men in the aircraft's cargo hold. Each was outfitted with a helmet, goggles, and oxygen mask, which wasn't surprising given their plan for a HALO—High Altitude Low Opening—insertion. Martin was breathing oxygen supplied by the Combat Talon to help clear the nitrogen from his bloodstream, and would shift to his own oxygen supply shortly before the jump.

Although Martin would breathe oxygen during his descent, there was always the risk of hypoxia, which could result in unconsciousness. As a safeguard, his parachute would deploy automatically at a designated altitude—four thousand feet in this case—and his team would assemble in the air and land together in the designated drop zone. Martin was also dressed warmly, with a layer of polypropylene knit undergarments, to guard against frostbite, since temperatures during HALO jumps could dip to minus fifty degrees Fahrenheit.

Additionally, today's jump would be a heavy one. Martin's rucksack weighed over one hundred pounds, filled with weapons, food, water, first-aid kit, and a special selection of armaments required for this mission. With a parachute system weighing forty pounds, his rucksack, plus ammunition and body armor, Martin would exit the aircraft today weighing almost four hundred pounds.

A burst of static from Martin's radio was followed by an order, and the fifty-two men in the cargo hold stood. Martin switched over to his own oxygen supply and disconnected from the aircraft's, and when the jump light switched from red to yellow, he checked his equipment one last time. The ramp at the rear of the MC-130H slowly lowered, and frigid air filled the cargo hold. Hand signals followed, and Martin led the way toward the back of the aircraft. When the jump light switched to green, he stepped off the ramp and plummeted toward earth.

During the free fall, Martin's team maneuvered to stay together, forming several tactical groups. Martin monitored his HALO altimeter during the descent, and his parachute opened as programmed at four thousand feet. As he approached the ground, Martin disconnected and dropped his rucksack, suspended by a lanyard, keeping the heavy bag away from his body in preparation for landing. As the landing zone rose up to greet him, Martin pulled on his parachute risers and angled toward his target.

90

USS *MICHIGAN*

"Bearing, mark!"

Captain Wilson pressed the red button on the periscope handle, sending the bearing to combat control, then flipped the handles up as he stepped back. "Angle on the bow, port twenty."

The Periscope Assistant reached up and rotated the locking ring, lowering the scope into its well. The entire periscope observation, from the time the scope broke the water's surface until it slipped beneath, took ten seconds.

Shortly after exiting the Bosphorus, Wilson had spotted four Russian frigates patrolling the entrance to the Black Sea. With each combatant armed with periscope detection radars, Wilson couldn't afford to leave the periscope up longer than a few seconds.

Wilson examined the nearest combat control console, which displayed a picture of the contact when he pressed the *pickle*—the red button. Using the two trackballs on his console, the fire control technician drew a box around the frigate, framing the waterline and top of the ship's superstructure, along with its stern and bow. Wilson had identified the frigate as a Burevestnik M, referred to as Krivak II by NATO forces.

"Matches," the petty officer reported. Wilson's angle on the bow matched the contact's calculated course, which put the frigate headed toward them, offset twenty degrees to port.

Wilson paused to assess the tactical situation. The nearest contact, Master one, was approaching at ten knots and would get dangerously close. *Michigan* couldn't move out of the way, with the submarine's speed limited to five knots to prevent a white wake behind the periscope while it was raised. However, Wilson didn't need to move out of the way. *Michigan* was Weapons Free.

Taking out the incoming frigate wouldn't be a problem. Steady on course and speed, he could have hit it with a straight-running World War II torpedo. The problem was, a torpedo exploding beneath its hull would inform the other three frigates of *Michigan*'s presence, and instead of patrolling the Black Sea in semi-boredom, the crews would go to General Quarters. As long as the frigates didn't realize *Michigan* was nearby, the advantage weighed heavily in Wilson's favor, an advantage he didn't want to give up.

"Attention in Control," he announced. "I intend to engage all four frigates simultaneously. I'll do a round of observations on the other three contacts, then proceed to Firing Point Procedures. Carry on."

Taking his position behind the attack periscope again, he ordered, "Prepare for observations, Master two, three, and four."

Lieutenant Commander Beasley assigned each of the three operators on the combat control consoles to a different contact, and each man called out, "Ready."

"Raise Number One scope," Wilson ordered.

The Periscope Assistant twisted the periscope locking ring above them, porting hydraulic fluid beneath the scope barrel, and the periscope slid silently upward.

Wilson snapped the handles down and pressed his face against the eyepiece as the periscope rose from its well. After lining up on Master two, he pressed the pickle and announced, "Master two. Bearing, mark," then shifted to Master three.

The next two observations were completed quickly, and Wilson flipped the handles up as the Periscope Assistant lowered the scope. The round of observations took thirty seconds. Not optimal with a frigate so close, but he needed the data.

The watchstanders manning the combat control consoles used the picture of each contact to calculate its course and range. Wilson called out the target angles from memory and each man reported, "Matches."

Beasley hovered behind the three men on the combat control consoles, examining the three solutions. After verifying they were in agreement with the periscope observations, he tapped each man on the shoulder.

"Promote to master solution."

The three men complied and Beasley announced, "I have a firing solution."

Wilson called out, "Firing Point Procedures, Master one through four, tubes One through Four, normal surface presets, all weapons."

Michigan's crew went through their weapon release checklists and the required reports soon followed.

"Solutions ready," Beasley announced.

"Weapons ready," the Weapons Officer reported.

"Ship ready." The Navigator completed the required reports.

Wilson examined the geographic display, updated with the four target solutions. Two of the frigates were ahead of *Michigan*—one near and one distant, with the other two frigates behind—also one close and one distant. Per protocol, Wilson would shoot the farthest target first, then time the release of his following weapons so all four torpedoes reached their targets simultaneously.

By cycling through the torpedo solutions on the Weapon Control Console, the submarine's Weapons Officer, Lieutenant Mike Lawson, could have calculated the precise interval between shots. But that would take time, during which the nearest frigate would get dangerously close or a ship could maneuver, invalidating its target solution. Wilson would have to guestimate instead.

Wilson announced, "Tube four, first fired. Match Sonar bearings and shoot."

The latest bearing to Master four was sent to Weapon Control, and Wilson heard the characteristic whir of the torpedo ejection pump as it pressurized and ported a slug of water behind the torpedo, ejecting it from its tube.

Sonar monitored the outgoing weapon, verifying it transitioned from solid to liquid fuel and turned onto an intercept course with Master four. The sonar technicians had their hands full monitoring their outgoing torpedo, because three more followed, with Wilson adjusting the interval between each shot as required.

After the Weapons Officer fired the last torpedo, Wilson moved behind the Weapon Control Console, monitoring the four outgoing weapons, speeding out on intercept courses with the four frigates. He'd done a decent job with the firing interval; it looked like the four torpedoes would go active at about the same time. The variable, however, was how good the target solutions were. A course, speed, or range error, even by a little on the distant frigates, could mean the difference between a hit and a miss.

As the four torpedoes approached their sonar enable points, Wilson returned to the Conn, stopping behind the attack periscope again.

"Prepare for observation."

The Periscope Assistant reached up, waiting for the Captain's order.

"Raise Number One scope."

The attack periscope broke the surface of the water as the Weapons Officer announced, "Tube One, enabled."

Reports for the other three torpedoes followed, reporting they had turned the sonars in their noses on, and Wilson watched for a reaction from the frigates.

Three of the four frigates seemed oblivious to the rapidly closing danger, but one maneuvered sharply away about thirty seconds after the torpedoes went active.

"Detect, tube One!" Lieutenant Lawson announced, followed shortly by, "Acquired, tube One!"

The torpedo from tube Three also detected and acquired, with both torpedoes increasing speed and adjusting course to intercept their targets. The Weapons Officer followed up, "Homing, tubes One and Three."

The torpedo from tube One closed the remaining distance, and as it passed under the frigate's keel, seven hundred pounds of explosive detonated. The shock wave from the expanding bubble ripped through the frigate's keel, and the upward water jet produced when the bubble collapsed tore through additional compartments, severing the ship in half.

The other two frigates reacted instantly, altering course and increasing speed, but not before a second torpedo detonated, producing a similar result. The halves of two Krivak II frigates bobbed in the water, drifting slowly apart as they filled with water.

Wilson focused on the two surviving ships, trying to calculate steers for the torpedoes chasing them. However, both frigates changed course at random intervals and in unpredictable directions. Wilson gave it a shot.

"Insert steers, tube Two, left one-eighty. Tube Four, right one-twenty."

Lieutenant Lawson acknowledged and passed the order to the fire control technician manning the console, who entered the steers. The torpedoes accepted the new commands and veered onto the new gyro courses, while Wilson ordered his submarine reloaded.

"Reload Tubes One and Three, and make ready in all respects."

Down in the Torpedo Room, the Torpedo Reload Party cut the flex hoses, letting the guidance wires snake out of both tubes, then shut the muzzle doors, drained the tubes, and opened the breech doors for reloading. Meanwhile, the two torpedoes chasing the evading frigates ran to fuel exhaustion and shut down. The two frigates immediately turned toward *Michigan*. The submarine's four torpedoes, traveling close to the surface at high speed, had left a green trail in the water, easily followed back toward its source.

Wilson called to his Weapons Officer, "How long until tubes One and Three are ready?"

Lawson queried the Torpedo Room on his sound-powered phone headset, then reported, "Five minutes."

Peering through the periscope at the frigates racing toward *Michigan*, Wilson realized he didn't have five minutes. He stepped back and ordered the periscope lowered.

"Helm, ahead full, hard left rudder. Dive, make your depth six hundred feet."

Michigan's main engines came alive and the submarine picked up speed as it turned away from the incoming frigates and angled toward the bottom of the Black Sea. The frigates' sonar systems went active, sending powerful pings echoing through *Michigan*'s hull, and the rhythmic churn from their screws grew louder as the frigates approached.

The first frigate passed overhead as *Michigan* leveled off at six hundred feet, and the Sonar Supervisor's report came across the speaker. "Receiving multiple splashes on spherical array broadband. Bearings unknown."

Wilson knew why Sonar couldn't determine the bearings—the splashes were directly overhead. "Brace for shock!" he ordered as he grabbed on to the nearest railing.

Wilson had identified both frigates as Admiral Grigorovich class, each outfitted with an RBU-600 rocket launcher capable of firing salvos of up to twelve depth charges, automatically reloading from a magazine carrying ninety-six projectiles. Thankfully, Russian depth charges had only fifty pounds of explosives, give or take a few pounds depending on the projectile type. However, even fifty pounds, detonated close enough to the hull, could breach it. Seconds later, *Michigan* jolted as the first depth charge exploded.

The equipment consoles shook as a deafening roar swept through the Control Room. Before Wilson could request a damage report from the Chief of the Watch, several more charges detonated, shaking the submarine each time. The explosions continued, growing more severe. After the twelfth detonation, it grew silent. But not for long as the second frigate sped overhead.

Sonar reported, "Receiving splashes on broadband," and Wilson gripped the Conn handrail firmly again.

This round of explosions was more violent, knocking unsecured items to the deck. Wilson requested a damage report, and the status of each compartment flowed in to the Chief of the Watch, who relayed the results from all spaces.

No damage.

However, the last pass of depth charges was too close for comfort, and as approaching twin screws and sonar pings announced the return of the first frigate, Wilson turned to the Quartermaster.

"Take a sounding."

The Quartermaster complied, activating the submarine's fathometer for one cycle. "Sixty fathoms beneath the keel."

Wilson acknowledged, then ordered the submarine deeper. "Dive, make your depth eight hundred feet."

The Dive complied, ordering a ten-degree down bubble and full dive on the fairwater planes, and *Michigan* tilted downward. As *Michigan* leveled off at eight hundred feet, the first frigate launched another salvo of depth charges, and their explosions were notably fainter than the first pass, with only minor tremors felt through the hull.

As the first frigate headed away and the second approached, announced by the increasing power of its sonar pulses, Wilson wondered if the frigate held *Michigan* on its active sonar, determining its depth. Splashes followed and Wilson's crew waited with upturned faces, as if they could see the depth charges sinking toward them.

The next round of depth charges began to detonate. Lighting fixtures shattered and Wilson struggled to maintain his feet as he held on to the Conn railing. Water started spraying from the port periscope barrel seal in the overhead and Wilson looked up to examine it, shielding his face from the spray. In the midst of the last few explosions, the submarine's flooding alarm sounded, followed by a report over the 4-MC emergency circuit.

"Flooding in the Engine Room!"

91

OMSK, RUSSIA

Omsk Oil Refinery is the largest in Russia and one of the biggest in the world, processing over twenty million tons of crude oil each year. On duty today in the refinery's main control station, filled with a dozen operators at their consoles, Bogdan Melikov sat at the supervisor's station on an elevated tier at the back of the control room, preparing to eat lunch. Although there was a cafeteria in the refinery, Melikov preferred homemade food prepared by his wife, even if it was a sandwich.

Russians weren't big on sandwiches; ask for a sandwich in Russia and you'd likely get a confused look and asked what kind of soup you wanted instead. However, Melikov was fond of Doktorskaya bologna, the love child of bologna and sausage, and his wife had prepared his favorite sandwich this morning: a few cuts of Doktorskaya between rye bread, a layer of garlic spread, and a slice of salo, which could be described as either raw pig fat or meat-free bacon, depending upon one's point of view.

Melikov opened his mouth wide and took a big bite, wiping a dab of garlic spread from the corner of his mouth with a napkin. From his peripheral vision, he thought he saw movement on one of the security monitors, displaying feeds from the cameras atop the perimeter fence. He stared at it for a moment as he chewed, and after convincing himself it was just an animal passing by in the wilderness, he focused again on his lunch.

He opened a can of mint-flavored kvass and took a swig. As he took another bite of his sandwich, security alarms went off in the control room. As he tried to ascertain the reason for the warning, searching the security monitors for a clue, the door to the control room blew open and a dozen armed men surged inside, weapons raised and pointed toward the control room personnel.

The men halted after taking positions offering a clear view of the control room staff, and one of the armed men stepped forward, lowering his weapon.

He spoke in Russian. "Who is in charge here?"

The dozen men and women at the consoles turned and pointed toward the man seated at the supervisor's station. Melikov still had a partially chewed bite of sandwich in his mouth. He swallowed hard.

92

USS *MICHIGAN*

As the Black Sea flooded into the submarine's Engine Room, *Michigan*'s stern tilted downward. During flooding, Wilson's crew was trained to automatically increase the submarine's speed. The hull served as a hydrofoil, like an airplane wing, with the amount of lift determined by the submarine's speed and angle. The faster the submarine traveled and the higher the angle, the more flooding it could endure without sinking into the ocean depths. However, there were two frigates patrolling above *Michigan*, trying to pinpoint her location. Increasing speed would put additional propulsion-related noise into the water, making it easier for the frigates to accomplish their mission. Wilson decided to remain at slow speed instead, unless the flooding was severe.

The Engine Room watchstanders responded as trained, with the Throttleman opening the ahead throttles and relaying his actions to Control. The Engine Order Telegraph shifted to ahead standard, whereupon Wilson overrode the automatic response.

"Helm, ahead two-thirds."

The Helm relayed the order back to the Engine Room, and the initial surge from *Michigan*'s main engines faded, with the submarine settling back out at ten knots. As the stern tilted downward, Wilson waited tensely while the Chief of the Watch lined up the drain pump to the Engine Room bilges, cross-connecting the trim pump as well. When the twin eight-foot-tall pumps kicked in, *Michigan*'s angle stabilized, then the stern slowly rose, returning the submarine to an even keel. The flooding wasn't catastrophic; the trim and drain pumps were keeping up.

Wilson turned his attention to the leak from the port periscope barrel seal, spraying into Control. *Michigan* wasn't in peril, however. The leak was minimal, more of an annoying shower. Two Auxiliary machinist mates stepped onto the Conn to address the seawater spraying from the overhead. They adjusted the packing around the port periscope, tightening the gland until the leak slowed to a trickle, then stopped. With the gland clamped tightly against the barrel, the port periscope was inoperable, but Wilson still had the starboard scope if needed.

A moment later, an update was received from the Engine Room.

"Conn, Maneuvering. The flooding is stopped."

Wilson picked up the 2-JV handset, conferring with the Engineering Officer of the Watch, in charge of the watchstanders in the Engine Room. The flooding was from the port Auxiliary Seawater system and had been stopped by shutting the hull isolation valves. Watchstanders were in the process of isolating the damaged section and cross-connecting the port and starboard sides of Auxiliary Seawater, with both sides supplied from the starboard intake.

Wilson's relief was short-lived, as one of the frigates approached for another pass and Sonar reported more splashes. As the depth charges drifted downward, he decided to maneuver; it looked like the two frigates had a pretty good bead on *Michigan*'s course and depth. He glanced at the combat control consoles: the operators were working on solutions for the two frigates using sonar bearings, and preliminary estimates indicated they were on east–west runs.

"Helm, hard right rudder, steady course zero-one-zero."

Michigan wasn't far from the bottom and Wilson couldn't go much deeper, so he turned north, where the Black Sea floor sloped quickly down to the Euxine abyssal plain, reaching a depth of seven thousand feet.

The next round of depth charges detonated, jarring *Michigan*. But the effects weren't as severe as the last round and no new reports of flooding were received. Wilson turned his attention to his weapons load; they should have reloaded tubes One and Three by now.

Tubes Two and Four could also be reloaded now that their torpedoes had run to fuel exhaustion and their guidance wires were no longer needed, but Wilson decided to wait. It was risky enough to have two torpedo tube breech doors open for loading while being depth charged. Opening all four was asking for trouble. If one of the muzzle door seals failed, it'd be all over; there'd be no way to shut the breech door and *Michigan* would go to the bottom.

Lieutenant Lawson announced, "Tubes One and Three are ready in all respects."

Wilson examined the frigate solutions on the combat control system consoles. It was clear the two ships held *Michigan* on their sonar systems; they had maneuvered to a north–south pattern, following *Michigan* into deeper water. It was only a matter of time, Wilson figured, before they got lucky; it would take only one depth charge close enough to the hull to breach it. The new solutions for the two frigates were shaky, but he didn't need refined solutions. Put the MK 48 torpedoes near the two contacts, and they'd take it from there.

"Firing Point Procedures," Wilson announced, "Master two and four, tubes One and Three, respectively. Use normal surface presets, both weapons."

The required reports followed, and Wilson studied the solutions to both targets on the geographic display. Not wanting to endure another depth charging, he decided to shoot the closest frigate first.

"Tube One, first fired. Shoot on generated bearings."

When Lawson received a *Ready* report from the torpedo, he ordered the tube fired. Sonar monitored the torpedo, verifying it performed properly and didn't shut down prematurely.

Sonar followed up with, "Tube One is merging onto the track for Master two."

The first torpedo was closing on the nearest frigate. However, firing torpedoes was a loud event due to using pressurized water to eject the torpedo, with that noise serving as a beacon for the two frigates.

"Helm, ahead flank. Right full rudder, steady course one-eight-zero."

Michigan turned south, and with the second frigate behind the submarine, Wilson ordered an over-the-shoulder shot.

"Shoot tube Three."

Lieutenant Lawson complied and *Michigan*'s second torpedo was ejected.

Both frigates began evasive maneuvering, but the closest ship wasn't far from Wilson's first torpedo. The weapon went active, identifying its target immediately.

"Detect, tube One!"

"Acquired!"

"Homing!"

The first torpedo increased speed and adjusted its trajectory to intercept the frigate, altering course each time the frigate maneuvered. Sonar reported jammers and decoys being ejected into the water, but the torpedo closed the remaining distance.

A loud rumble echoed through the Control Room after the first torpedo exploded.

Wilson turned his attention to the last frigate, examining the geographic plot. It had maneuvered early enough, and the torpedo failed to detect it as it passed by and continued outbound. However, it wasn't far away from the frigate and a quick steer might do the trick.

Wilson ordered, "Insert steer, tube Three, left one-hundred."

The Weapons Officer complied, and Wilson watched the display as the torpedo veered sharply left toward the red surface ship symbol. It wasn't long before Lieutenant Lawson made the report Wilson hoped for.

"Detect, tube Three!"

In quick succession, the torpedo reported it had acquired a valid contact, calculated the evading frigate's course and speed, and increased speed to close on its prey. A minute later, with the frigate maneuvering wildly and its crew ejecting numerous countermeasures into the water, a second explosion rumbled through *Michigan*'s Control Room.

It grew quiet in Control as Wilson examined the new target solutions. Based on sonar bearings, both ships were dead in the water, and their machinery noises were growing fainter. Wilson decided to take a look.

"Helm, ahead one-third. Dive, make your depth two hundred feet. All stations, make preparations to proceed to periscope depth."

The Dive, Quartermaster, Radio, and Sonar acknowledged, and it wasn't long before *Michigan* was at two hundred feet, then at periscope depth a few minutes later. Wilson spun on the scope as it broke the water's surface.

"No close contacts!"

Wilson steadied on the bearing to Master two, watching the two halves of the frigate fill with water, then upend and slip beneath the surface of the Black Sea. Master four soon followed. There were survivors in the water, floating on the surface in orange life vests. However, Wilson couldn't stop to pick them up. He had follow-on orders, plus there was plenty of debris in the water to cling to and they weren't far from shore.

Wilson announced, "All stations, Conn. Heading deep."

He swung the periscope to a forward-facing position, then lowered it into its well.

"Helm, ahead standard. Left full rudder, steady course zero-five-zero. Dive, make your depth four hundred feet."

Michigan increased speed as it angled downward and turned to the northeast.

93

OMSK, RUSSIA

Captain Martin placed his rucksack on the ground and, after sorting through its contents, retrieved the desired items. One was a material he was familiar with, having employed C-4 explosive many times. The other was an item he hadn't seen before, although it was easily identified as a detonator. A bit exotic, he thought, with an integrated design leaving no wires between the electronics and detonator. Also missing was a remote initiator, and after pondering its absence, he realized the detonator was activated via a remote cellular or satellite signal.

With the items laid out before him, Martin focused next on where they'd be used. The Omsk Oil Refinery was a massive installation: a maze of metal facilities, pipelines, and storage tanks. While researching his target, Martin learned that the Omsk Oil Refinery, in addition to being Russia's biggest, was one of its best, winning Industrial Product gold prizes for its Euro-98 Super Petrol and Euro Diesel for cold weather conditions.

Not for much longer.

The men in his unit carried twelve sets of detonators and C-4, and Martin selected several key locations: the catalytic cracking gasoline and diesel fuel hydrotreatment units, the AT-9 distillation unit, and the nine biggest storage tanks. He gathered his men around before they set out on their tasks, reminding them of the warning they'd been given. Once it's been activated, do *not* move the detonator.

94

MOSCOW

In the Operations Center conference room, deep in the bowels of the Kremlin, the air was cold and the tension thick. President Yuri Kalinin sat at the head of the table, flanked by his military and civilian advisors, absorbing the somber information. When General Andropov completed his update, Kalinin cast his eyes across the large video screen on the far wall, assessing the carnage.

Every one of Russia's surface combatants in the Pacific had been destroyed, most floating aimlessly on the surface—blackened hulks or red torches with spires of smoke rising into the sky—while others had gone to the ocean bottom after internal explosions ripped their hulls apart. In return, all four of America's aircraft carriers had been damaged, but none fatally, and only a few of the American cruisers or destroyers were disabled. Additionally, the United States had attacked what remained of Russia's Black Sea Fleet, sinking the four frigates patrolling the mouth of the Bosphorus. America's goal in the Black Sea wasn't clear, but Kalinin had an inkling.

One of General Andropov's aides, with a flustered look on his face, entered the conference room and delivered a folder to the General. It contained a single-page message, which Andropov reviewed, then slid to Kalinin without a word. As Kalinin read it, the heat rose in his face. He was about to ask Andropov what Russia's response should be, when the aide cleared his voice.

"Excuse me, Mr. President. I have an additional message."

Kalinin shifted his attention to the Army Colonel, who said, "The American president has requested a videoconference with you."

"When?" Kalinin asked.

"Now," the Colonel answered. "We can proceed if you desire."

Kalinin surveyed the men and women at the table, implicitly asking for their input. None came, with several of his advisors avoiding his gaze, their eyes staring at the table.

"Put the American president on-screen," Kalinin directed.

A moment later, the American president appeared on the display, with the video feed showing a situation not much different from Kalinin's: the president seated at a conference table, flanked by his advisors.

"Good morning, President Kalinin."

Kalinin checked the clock on the wall, annotated with Washington, D.C., which read 4 a.m.

"Good morning to you as well."

"I'll cut to the chase," the American president said. "I've considered the ultimatum you gave NATO and the United States. Although you have a few valid concerns regarding your borders, I've come to the conclusion that a Russian occupation of Lithuania and Ukraine isn't a good idea, so you'll have to leave. I also realize that isn't going to happen if I just say *please*, so I've been searching for a way to convey my request in a more convincing manner."

Kalinin didn't miss the flippancy in the president's words. He had the upper hand and was using it.

The American president continued, "Your attempt to blackmail the United States and NATO was both brilliant and inspirational, and it gave me an idea."

The right half of the screen morphed into a nine-grid, three-by-three display, showing video feeds from oil refineries and natural gas facilities, with the American president's image remaining on the left half of the screen.

"American forces have taken control of Russia's twenty-four largest oil and natural gas facilities," the president said, "wiring them with explosives."

The nine videos zoomed in, focusing on explosives attached to equipment, each with a sophisticated detonator pressed into the explosive material.

"Do these look familiar?"

The American president reached for a small electronic tablet and tapped in a ten-digit code. The detonators on-screen activated, and the videos zoomed back out.

"All of the explosives attached to your facilities have been armed, and I probably don't need to inform you, but if anyone tries to remove or jam them, they'll detonate. Also, in case you get any clever ideas, the master disarm code has been changed."

The American president added, "I've also moved several submarines into the Black Sea, which I'm sure you've noticed by the absence of a few Russian frigates. In two hours, unless ordered otherwise, they will commence sinking all merchant ships departing Russian ports on the Black Sea. At that time, you can also say good-bye to your twenty-four largest oil and natural gas facilities."

Kalinin realized the implications; the Black Sea

terminals loaded the vast majority of oil and natural gas destined for Asian and African markets, not to mention being the largest grain ports in the country. By destroying the twenty-four facilities and cutting off the flow through the Black Sea, America would cripple Russia's economy.

The American president interrupted Kalinin's thoughts. "Of course, none of this will occur if you withdraw your troops from Lithuania and Ukraine. You have two hours for us to detect your troops returning to Russia."

The American president let his demand sink in, then asked, "Any questions, Yuri?"

Although a few choice words came to mind, Kalinin had no questions. The American president's ultimatum, as well as Russia's response, was clear.

Kalinin replied, "We will begin withdrawing troops immediately."

"Excellent," the American president said. "As a show of goodwill, I'll disable the detonators at your oil refinery in Omsk, the largest and most modern in Russia, I believe."

The president tapped in a ten-digit code and pressed enter.

One of the nine video feeds blanked out in a blinding white flash, fading to reveal a dozen orange fireballs rising skyward from a mass of twisted metal engulfed in flames.

"Sorry, Yuri," the American president said. "I'm all thumbs."

The screen went black.

95

SOCHI, RUSSIA

Christine's eyes opened slowly, then fluttered back shut as her blurry vision was greeted by a throbbing headache. She opened her eyes again and lifted her head slowly, and her vision cleared. She was lying on her stomach on a wooden floor in a dimly lit room, with the only source of light being shafts of sunlight streaming through slots near the top of the room. There was a brackish smell in the air and the sound of waves lapping against pilings.

She was in the boathouse, inside a storage room.

Confirming her assessment, there were several piles of crates cluttering the room, along with a few old life preservers and vests.

Christine tried to push herself to her feet, then realized her hands were cuffed behind her back. She rolled onto her side and then to a sitting position. She was still in her nightgown and barefoot. Looking around, she examined her new accommodations more closely. She was in a twenty-by-twenty-foot room with no windows and a single door. The only openings to the outside were several six-inch-wide slots at the top of the wall to her left. Above, a few pipes ran the width of the room a few feet above her head.

She rocked forward onto her feet, and on the slim chance the door was unlocked, she pushed the lever down with one foot, then hooked her toes behind it and pulled. No luck. She heard a man's voice on the other side of the door, speaking in Russian. At first, she thought he was talking to her, but then there was a squelch of a handheld radio, and she realized the man was a guard posted outside, most likely informing Gorev she had regained consciousness.

The door unlocked and opened, and one of Chernov's Security Service agents, pistol drawn, appeared in the doorway. Christine froze where she was. The man studied her for a moment, then closed and locked the door again. After evaluating her predicament, she realized her options were limited. As in none. At least while her hands were cuffed behind her back.

However, she could fix that. Christine had been an elite gymnast in high school and college and was still both flexible and strong. She lay on her back, and supporting herself with her shoulders and feet, arched her back, curving it until her hands slipped past her hips. After pulling her legs through, she was on her feet again with her hands in front. They were still handcuffed, but at least she could use them now.

She examined the slots along the top of the wall again, and wondered if she could create a larger opening; the boathouse was made of wood. She searched through the crates, hoping to find something she could pry the planks apart with. After finding nothing useful, she decided to try with her bare hands. She stacked three crates against the wall, climbed up, and pulled on a board between two slots. As she pulled with all her strength, her hands slipped off and she lost her balance, the pile of crates tilting to the side as she fell. She twisted instinctively while in the air and landed on her feet. Being a former gymnast had its advantages.

The crates came crashing to the ground behind her, and the door opened a moment later. A single incandescent bulb hanging from the ceiling turned on, illuminating the room in weak yellow light. This time, Semyon Gorev and two SVR agents entered, along with Chernov's Security Service agent.

Gorev eyed Christine's hands, in front of her instead of behind her, and the crates against the wall. He spoke in Russian and Chernov's agent stepped forward, unlocking one side of her handcuffs. As Christine wondered if Gorev was going to release her, the agent raised her right arm and locked the handcuff to a pipe above her head. After pulling a second pair of handcuffs from his jacket, he connected Christine's left hand to the same pipe.

Gorev smiled as he unwrapped a peppermint candy and popped it into his mouth.

"A breath mint?" Christine asked. "Are you hoping for a kiss?"

"Not exactly," he replied as he pulled a pistol from inside his jacket. He left it down by his side.

A cold shiver ran down her spine, and she forced her eyes back up toward Gorev's face, searching for a clue to his intentions.

"You did an admirable job on Chernov," he said. "I'd like to tell you that you failed and he survived somehow, but unfortunately that is not the case. Unfortunately for *you*, there are ramifications."

He stepped closer. "What do you think is fair compensation for the life of Russia's defense minister?"

When Christine didn't answer, he said, "Putting a bullet into your head would be too easy and, frankly, boring. Instead, since you are so fond of games, we are going to play one now. It's called—*Seemon says*."

Christine replied, "It's pronounced *Simon says*, you moron."

Gorev stared at her with cold eyes, then cracked the mint between his teeth. "I know that, Christine. My first name is Semyon, but most Americans have trouble pronouncing it correctly, so I make it easy for them. Seemon. So the game we will play is called *Seemon says*. Understand?"

Christine nodded slowly.

Gorev pointed his pistol at her, pressing the barrel against her stomach. She felt the cool metal through the thin fabric of her nightgown, and a chill raked her flesh.

He slid the barrel slowly up Christine's stomach, then between her breasts. The pistol continued upward, the barrel caressing her neck, then Gorev tilted the gun up and pressed the barrel hard under her chin.

"It's a pity I have to kill such a beautiful woman."

His words filled her with a crippling wave of terror. But instead of pulling the trigger, Gorev smiled again, then rode the barrel over her chin, leveling the pistol when the barrel rested against Christine's lips.

"Seemon says, *Open your mouth*."

Christine clenched her jaw and turned her head away.

Gorev spoke in Russian, and Chernov's agent grabbed her head and forced it back toward Gorev until the barrel rested against her lips again.

"If you play the game," Gorev said, "the end will be painless. If not, I promise you the most excruciating pain you have ever experienced."

Christine kept her teeth clenched together, trying to keep the fear from showing in her eyes.

Gorev clamped a hand around her neck. "Open your mouth."

When Christine refused again, Gorev nodded to the two SVR agents. One pinched Christine's nose shut while the other tried to pry her mouth open. Christine kept her jaw clenched, but it wasn't long before she felt light-headed, and when she could hold her breath no longer, she gasped for air. When her mouth opened, Gorev jammed the pistol barrel into her mouth.

He let the barrel rest in her mouth a moment, and Christine tasted the ferrous tang of metal. Her pulse started racing, and her breathing turned rapid and shallow.

Gorev said, "As I reviewed your file again, I tried to find someone important to you. I would have let you live long enough to see them die. But you have no husband, no children, no siblings, no parents. Your lack of loved ones takes most of the fun out of things. But not all."

He leaned close, whispering in her ear, "Seemon says, *Time to die.*"

Christine's eyes shot to Gorev's index finger as he slowly squeezed the trigger, and she watched in horrified fascination as the color of his finger gradually changed from pink to white. A low moan began to build in her throat and her legs started to give way. With one last tremendous effort, she pushed the terror down and steadied herself.

The end of Gorev's finger turned white.

She closed her eyes as tightly as she could.

The pistol hammer fell.

Christine didn't hear the shot. Only a metal click.

The pistol didn't fire.

She heard Gorev laugh as he pulled the barrel from her mouth.

Christine opened her eyes as Gorev said, "It looks like I forgot to put the bullets in."

It took a moment for the terror to subside, to collect her thoughts.

"You sick bastard."

Gorev smacked her across the face with the back of his hand, and Christine felt a sting as metal sliced into her cheek.

"Now look at what you've done," Gorev said as he

wiped the blood away from an ornate gold ring that sparkled under the incandescent light. He lifted the hem of Christine's nightgown and dabbed away the blood on her cheek. "It's only a small cut. Do you think we should get stiches?" Gorev smiled.

Christine's eyes narrowed, doing her best to convey hatred.

Gorev grabbed her throat with one hand again, squeezing hard. "You're lucky Yuri has taken a fancy to your pretty face, or you would be fish food at the bottom of the Black Sea by now. Instead, you get to entertain me until I discuss the issue with him. He's busy at the moment, but once I explain what you've done, he will leave it to me to dispose of you."

He released her throat and slid his pistol into the harness under his jacket. "Until then," he said, "you can hang out here." His eyes went to Christine's handcuffs, her body hanging from the pipe. He laughed at his own joke, then left the room, as did the two SVR agents. The last man, Chernov's security agent, turned off the light, then closed and locked the door.

As the door shut, Christine's legs gave way. The handcuffs cut into her wrists from the weight, but the pain didn't register. The tears came first, then the sobs. The emotions that had built up over the last few years— the terror as her ex-husband drove a knife into her neck, the panic as her car plunged into the lagoon off the coast of China, and the guilt as she watched Brackman take his last breath and drift off into the murky water—were amplified by what Gorev had done, and she could no longer keep it all in. Hanging from the handcuffs in the semidarkness, she let it all out.

96

SOCHI, RUSSIA

Christine wasn't sure how much time passed, but her tears had dried and she was on her feet again, her hands on the pipe so the handcuffs no longer cut into her wrists. Her mind and body were numb, her muscles so drained that she barely had enough strength to hang on to the pipe. As the bright shafts of sunlight streaming through the boathouse openings faded, replaced with dirty-gray light filtering into her cell, her mind began to clear and her strength returned.

Night was setting in, and she knew it wouldn't be long before Gorev discussed her fate with Kalinin. Her thoughts returned to escape. She didn't have a plan yet, but it would start with freeing herself from the pipe. She examined the ends, which passed through flanges bolted to each wall. Hoping the pipe was just connected to the walls rather than running through them, Christine wondered if she could break one of the flanges free.

She gripped the piping and put her full weight on it, then yanked down as hard as she could. The piping didn't move. She tried several times more, hoping she could loosen one end, but the flanges didn't give. Undeterred, she slid her handcuffs sideways on the pipe, reaching one end to get a closer look at the flange. It was

securely bolted to the wall. She slid her handcuffs along
the pipe in the other direction, and an examination of
that flange produced the same result. There was nothing
she could do.

Her handcuffs sliding on the pipe produced a commotion, and she heard the door unlock. It opened to reveal one of Chernov's Security Service agents—the
one who had handcuffed her to the piping run. He turned
the light on and examined Christine, then barked something in Russian to her and closed the door with a thud,
locking it again. As the door closed, the single light
hanging from the ceiling swayed slightly, and Christine
got an idea. There was a metal shroud above the bulb,
casting a dark shadow across the top of the storage
room.

She was handcuffed to the piping only eight feet from
the door and just to the left. She looked up, disappointed
to see a clearance of only three feet between the pipe
and ceiling. Had there been a seven-foot clearance, she
could have used the pipe like an uneven bar, swinging
down at full extension. Still, with some creativity, the
pipe would suffice.

Christine gripped the pipe with both hands, then
pulled herself up with enough force to continue through
to a waist pull-up. She finished with her arms straight
down toward the pipe and her hips resting against it.
Her head was only a few inches from the ceiling, her
upper body in the shadows. Leaning forward, she bent
her knees slowly, pulling her legs into the darkness, and
placed her feet onto the pipe. It wasn't the most graceful
position, but she had to improvise. Now that she was
ready for the next move, she took a deep breath and
yelled for the security agent. There was no response and
she screamed again, as loud as she could.

The door unlocked and the security agent peered
inside.

Startled by Christine's disappearance, he stepped into the room to inspect more closely, pulling his pistol from its holster. As he moved toward where she'd been handcuffed to the pipe, Christine straightened her legs, pushing her hips up high, then released her feet from the bar, thrusting down as she pivoted toward the agent. Her feet connected solidly with his chest, slamming him back into the wall.

Christine had hoped to knock the guard out when his head hit the wall, and if he fell forward within range of her feet, her plan would've worked. But the guard was only stunned, dropping his pistol as he rebounded and staggered forward. Christine also rebounded after the impact, and she swung toward him again, this time clamping her thighs around his neck and scissoring her legs behind his head. She twisted sideways in the air, shifting her grip around his neck ninety degrees so she could cut off his airway. She pulled him toward her, hoping he'd trip in the process, giving her the opportunity to snap his neck, but he maintained his balance.

She squeezed her thighs tightly together, straining from the exertion as he clawed at her legs, trying to pry them apart. His face turned red and his eyes began to bulge. He dropped to his knees, his attempts to free himself becoming weaker. His lips turned purple and his body went slack, his arms dangling by his side.

Christine kept her legs clamped around his neck for another minute to make sure, then released him, letting him fall onto his face. After turning him over with her feet, she slipped a foot inside one of his jacket pockets, but found nothing. Inside the other pocket, however, she felt a metal key attached to a ring. Pinching the key between her toes, she pulled it slowly from his pocket. After firmly gripping the pipe, she piked at the waist into a V, bringing her feet up until the key was in her right hand.

She dropped to her feet and pulled her hands together, then unlocked the handcuffs. After retrieving the agent's pistol from the floor, she stopped by the door, then peered outside. There was no one in sight, so she crept along the wall until she reached the corner, where she had a view of the cove. The pier to her right ran out to Chernov's motorboat and yacht, both deserted, and the brick walkway to her left wound up to the villa. It was still dusk, but it wouldn't be much longer before it was dark. After debating whether to stay put until it was dark instead of exposing herself in the fading light, she decided to get moving.

Christine hurried down the pier, slipping into the motorboat. Crouching down, she examined the boat's ignition system. Like Chernov's yacht, it was a push-button start, but needed a key. She searched the motorboat but came up empty. Peering over the edge of the boat, she examined the shoreline, wondering if she could make it out on foot. But the cove terminated on both ends in jagged rocks transitioning to steep cliffs. The only way out was up toward the villa, but there was a twenty-foot-tall security wall between the villa and the road, which also merged into steep cliffs on each side. Chernov's villa had been built in a secure location indeed. As Christine dwelled on her predicament, she remembered Elena's cell phone was programmed to request assistance from an extraction team nearby, which was exactly what she needed. Gorev had knocked it from her hand in Chernov's bedroom.

She examined the rugged terrain rising toward the villa for a concealed path, but it looked like the only trail up was the winding brick walkway. Thankfully, the path was sheltered by lush vegetation on both sides, which would obscure her approach. She slipped from the motorboat onto the pier again, quickly reaching the winding path.

By the time she reached the end of the walkway, darkness had fallen, and Christine stopped at the edge of the vegetation only a few feet from the open-air villa. She heard the faint sound of voices and concluded it was either the television or two agents, but in either case, the sound was coming from the living room or farther away. She emerged from the path and stopped beside the villa wall, and after convincing herself there were no Russians nearby, she slipped into a hallway leading to the bedrooms.

She reached Chernov's bedroom and stopped at the door. It was slightly ajar, with Gorev's men having damaged the frame when they broke into the room. She pushed the door slowly open and slipped into the darkness. She gently closed the door, then turned on a bedside light. The bed was neatly made up, with no sign of Chernov.

Christine searched the room, including the closet, bathroom, and under the bed, failing to locate Elena's cell phone. Her heart sank at the failed discovery, but then she realized all of her belongings were missing: her clothes, purse, even her carry-on suitcase. She hoped Gorev's men had deposited everything into her luggage, and if she could find her suitcase, she would locate Elena's phone. She turned off the light and slipped back into the hallway.

She stopped outside each bedroom, and after verifying there was no light leaking from under the doors, slipped inside each room. There was no suitcase to be found, nor the belongings of Alekperov and his wife, who had apparently departed the villa. With no suitcase in the bedrooms, that left the formal living areas, and Christine moved forward, stopping at the edge of the kitchen. The lights were on and she heard water running and the clinking of pans. She pulled her pistol up, holding it with both hands, then peered around the corner. Chernov's maid was at the sink, her back to Christine.

Christine stepped quietly past the kitchen, pausing to peer into the lit dining room, where there were a few dirty dishes, but no suitcase. Next up was the living room, and as she approached, the sound of men's voices grew louder. She stopped at the entrance, pistol ready again, peering around the corner with one eye.

There were four men inside, one seated on a couch with his back to Christine, facing a wide-screen television on the far wall. At the adjoining bar were the two SVR agents and one of Chernov's Security Service agents, each seated on a bar stool with a glass of clear liquid in one hand. The TV was on, but the four men were talking. She spotted her suitcase, on the floor beside the couch, open with one of her dresses hanging over the side, then she pulled back around the corner.

It was feasible. The couch was close to the living room entrance, and if she dropped onto the ground, she could enter unseen by the men at the bar, their view blocked by the back of the couch. Likewise, the men couldn't see her suitcase, also blocked by the couch. She knelt into a crouch and peered around the corner again. She was still too high; the faces of the three men at the bar were still visible above the back of the couch. Christine lay prone, and after verifying she could no longer see the three men, she crawled slowly into the living room.

She reached the back of the couch, then made her way slowly toward the end. She looked up; the man had his arms spread out along the top of the couch, gesturing with his hands on occasion before returning them to their resting place. Christine pulled the suitcase across the carpet toward her, back around the corner of the couch, then lifted the lid carefully and searched inside. After sifting through her clothes, she spotted her purse, its contents dumped into the bottom of her suitcase. Beside the purse was Elena's phone. She reached in and retrieved it.

Gorev had knocked the phone from her hand and she wondered if it was still functional. There was no sign of damage, however. Placing her pistol on the carpet, she simultaneously pressed the power and down volume buttons. The cell phone vibrated and Christine froze, then shot her gaze upward. The man still had his arms on the back of the couch and the four men continued their discussion. She retrieved her pistol, and with the gun in one hand and cell phone in the other, prepared to slip from the living room.

She started crawling away when the man's arm dropped over the back of the couch, his hand coming to rest an inch from her head. Her eyes went to the ornate gold ring on his hand; the man on the couch was Gorev. The vision of him shoving his pistol into her mouth flashed in her mind, and emotions flooded her body.

Without considering the ramifications, she dropped the phone and sprang to her feet, grabbing a fistful of Gorev's hair, yanking his head back so he could see her face. She pressed the pistol barrel against his forehead. Christine looked at the other three men, their hands inserted inside their jackets, who had frozen when she'd placed the pistol against Gorev's head.

She had no idea if they understood English, but said, "Pull your guns out slowly and toss them onto the floor."

When none of the men followed her direction, she pressed the pistol hard into Gorev's forehead. "Tell your men to toss their guns unless you want your head to look like a Cheerio. You do have Cheerios in Russia, don't you?"

Gorev spoke to the three men in Russian, and they tossed their pistols onto the floor.

Then he looked up at her. "Hello, Christine."

"Hello, Simon." She deliberately mispronounced his name.

"Put the gun down," he said, "and no harm will come to you."

She almost laughed. When President Xiang offered his word in the Great Hall of the People, she believed him. Gorev, on the other hand, would kill her the instant he got the chance.

As if reading her mind, he said, "You have my word."

"I have a better idea," Christine said. "We're going to play a game tonight. It's called *Christine says*. Are you ready?"

Gorev didn't respond, but his eyes narrowed.

Christine smiled, then moved the pistol slowly down his forehead, between his eyes, and down the bridge of his nose. When she reached his mouth, she rested the barrel on his lips.

"Christine says, *Open your mouth*."

When Gorev didn't comply, she mashed the barrel against his lips. "Open your mouth or I'll blow a hole through your teeth."

Gorev slowly opened his mouth, and Christine slid the barrel inside.

"Simon, are you ready to die?"

Gorev didn't answer, not that he could talk with a pistol barrel in his mouth. Christine said, "It's a rhetorical question. No need to answer."

She pulled the gun out slightly, so he could see her finger wrapped around the trigger. She squeezed the trigger slowly, so he could watch the color of her index finger change from pink to white as she increased the pressure.

"You probably thought it was cute," Christine said, "terrorizing me with your game. How does it feel?"

Her thoughts returned to what he'd done to her in the

boathouse, and a dark mood settled over her. Gorev was a cruel, sadistic creature who enjoyed torturing others.

"We're going to play a new game," she said. "Want to know what it's called?"

She crouched down beside him, her eyes on the three agents as she whispered, "It's called *Seemon dies.*"

Christine stood and pulled the trigger.

Gorev's head recoiled as a hole was blown in the back of his skull, splattering the top of the couch with a red puff, followed by a rivulet of blood.

She pulled the pistol from Gorev's mouth. "It looks like I forgot to take the bullets out."

Christine pointed her pistol toward the three men. "I don't have a beef with you," she said as their eyes shifted between her gun and the former director of the SVR. She collected the three pistols on the floor, slipping her fingers through the trigger guards, then backed toward the living room entrance, her pistol still aimed at the three men.

"Stay exactly where you are for one hour, and no one will get hurt." She had no idea if the men understood her or if the extraction team would arrive within that time, but figured an hour would be enough.

After backing out of the living room, she sprinted down the hallway. She hadn't given much thought to her escape plan, which amounted to vacating the villa and heading toward the water. Maybe she could lose them in the dense vegetation along the brick walkway until assistance arrived.

Unfortunately, the three men either didn't understand her or chose not to follow her directions. There was a commotion behind her—men shouting and running feet. As she turned the corner, a bullet buried itself into the wall behind her, and Christine realized she wasn't going to make it to the brick path. After passing the indoor and outdoor pools on either side of her, she got an idea as she emerged onto the patio.

Maintaining a full sprint, she headed toward the balcony overlooking the Black Sea, dropping her pistols on the way. When she reached the railing, she leapt up, planted a foot on the edge of the stone balustrade, and launched herself into the air, plummeting down toward the dark water. She plunged into the Black Sea, arching her back to arrest her descent in case the water was shallow. As the brackish water stung her cheek and wrists, she kicked her legs and pulled with her arms, swimming underwater away from the villa.

Bullets zinged into the water around her, and Christine redoubled her efforts, trying to put as much distance between her and the shoreline as possible before coming up for air. Her lungs started burning and she angled upward, broaching the surface when she couldn't hold her breath any longer. She heard shouts from the villa balcony and a fresh barrage of bullets, some hitting so close she felt the water churning from their entry. To her left, the two SVR agents were sprinting down the pier toward Chernov's motorboat.

Taking a deep breath, she slipped beneath the water and continued away from the coast, hoping they'd lose her in the darkness as she swam farther away from the villa's lights. When she came up for air again, the two Russians were in the motorboat, headed toward her. Bullets pierced the water from the men in the boat and on the patio, and she ducked under the water again and changed direction, angling toward the left.

As the oxygen in her body depleted, a white light crisscrossed the water's surface above her, sometimes passing directly overhead. When she could hold her breath no longer, she rose to the surface for air, and before she slipped back under, the light blinded her as it swept by, then quickly returned, illuminating her face.

The boat turned in her direction, with the Russian at the bow bringing his weapon to bear on her.

She took a deep breath and was about to submerge again when heavy-caliber bullets riddled the side of the motorboat and tore into the agent on the bow and then the driver, knocking both men into the water. A second later, a red flame streaked above Christine, headed toward Chernov's villa, and the patio exploded in an orange fireball.

The light and rumble from the explosion faded, and an eerie silence fell on the water; no one was shooting at her. As Christine treaded water, she heard the faint sound of approaching outboard engines.

A voice reached out to her in the darkness. "Grab my hand."

Christine recognized the man's voice; he was never far from her thoughts.

A green glow stick activated, illuminating two Rigid Hull Inflatable Boats a few feet away, each carrying four men in combat gear wearing night-vision goggles. The man at the bow of the lead boat had his hand extended. She grabbed his hand, and Navy SEAL Jake Harrison hauled Christine into the boat.

"Are you hurt?" he asked.

Christine shook her head as the two boats turned and headed out to sea.

Even though it was fairly warm out, there was a brisk breeze on the water, and Christine was wearing only a thin, soaked nightgown. Whether from the temperature or because of what she'd just done, a chill came over her, and she started shivering. Harrison pulled her close to warm her, and Christine instinctively wrapped her arms around his waist, squeezing tightly as she buried her face into his chest.

"What happened?" he asked.

But Christine could only shake her head again.

97

BLACK SEA

The full moon's reflection wavered on the water as the two RHIBs headed farther out to sea, the glowing embers of Chernov's villa fading behind them as the shoreline retreated into the distance. Aside from the low rumble of the outboard engine on each boat, the journey was quiet; neither Christine nor the eight SEALs spoke. She kept her arms wrapped around Harrison, not caring where they were headed or how long it took to get there.

The SEALs idled the RHIB engines, then angled the two boats toward each other. They drifted together with a gentle bump, and a SEAL at the front of each RHIB fastened a line to both bows. Two green glow sticks were activated, one hung from each bow. The engines were revved a few seconds, and the boats coasted apart until they pulled the line between them taut. The engines were secured, and the two RHIBs floated on the dark water, bobbing in the waves.

As Christine wondered what they were waiting for, the SEAL at the front of her RHIB said, "Incoming at two hundred yards."

Christine looked ahead but saw nothing in the darkness. Then again, she wasn't wearing night-vision goggles like the SEALs. As she peered ahead, a submarine periscope materialized out of the darkness, approaching swiftly. The periscope snagged the line between the two RHIBs, and the boats were yanked around and pulled toward each other as the periscope towed them toward shore, then began a slow U-turn, hauling the RHIBs farther out to sea.

After reversing course, they picked up speed and waves occasionally broke over the bow of Christine's RHIB. When the Black Sea coast was no longer discernible under the full moon, the periscope slowed, then stopped.

Harrison released his arm from around Christine. "We have scuba gear for you," he said.

He helped Christine into her gear while the SEALs in both RHIBs donned theirs. As she finished wriggling into her equipment, the SEALs detached the engines and began deflating both boats. After verifying her face mask had sealed and her regulator was working, she and Harrison slipped into the water. With a firm grasp on Christine's arm, he pulled her downward.

It wasn't long before several green glow sticks appeared in the distance and the shadowy shape of a submarine formed in the murky water, along with two Dry Deck Shelters attached to the submarine's missile deck. The nine-foot-diameter door of the port Dry Deck Shelter was open, with two Navy divers waiting nearby. Harrison guided her inside, and a few minutes later, the two deflated RHIBs were hauled into the shelter, joined by the Navy divers and SEALs.

The hatch was shut, and after the water was drained from the shelter, Christine followed Harrison's example and removed her scuba gear. Harrison and Christine were the first to exit the hangar, dropping down through dual hatches into Missile Tube Two, then out through a hatch in the side of the tube, where a familiar face greeted her.

Commander Joe Aleo, the physician assigned to *Michigan*'s SEAL detachment, escorted her to Medical, where he conducted a preliminary assessment—pulse, blood pressure, and flashlight in her eyes. A concerned look formed on his face as she sat there listlessly, providing succinct answers to his questions and nothing more. At the end of his exam, his eyes went to her cheek.

"You've got a nasty cut, but I don't think it'll need stitches." After cleaning and disinfecting the wound, he carefully affixed Steri-Strips to her cheek, sealing the cut shut. "That should do it," he said. "If you end up with a scar, it'll be faint."

After cleaning the cuts on her wrists where the handcuffs had sliced through her skin, he applied an antibacterial salve and wrapped both wrists in white gauze.

Lieutenant Harrison stood outside Medical, waiting for Doc to complete his examination. After a reasonable wait, he knocked on the door, and after Aleo acknowledged, he stepped into his office. He eyed Christine carefully; she sat on the bed staring straight ahead, her eyes unreadable, her body unnaturally still. When she failed to respond to his entry, Harrison looked at Aleo.

"She's fine," Aleo said, answering Harrison's unasked question, "aside from a few cuts."

Physically, perhaps. Harrison wasn't a doctor, but he'd seen the symptoms before: acute stress reaction—Christine was in psychological shock. Aleo met Harrison's eyes and he nodded slightly, confirming Harrison's assessment. His eyes went to her bandaged wrists, realizing she'd been in handcuffs, and he wondered what the Russians had done to her.

Aleo turned back to Christine, touching her shoulder to get her attention. "The SUPPO will be here shortly with a change of clothes."

Christine didn't reply, but she looked down at her thin, soaked nightgown; it clung to her body and was practically see-through now that it was wet. On cue, *Michigan*'s Supply Officer, Lieutenant Commander Kelly Haas, entered Medical with a stack of clothes in her hand.

"I borrowed some of Lieutenant Stucker's underwear," Kelly said. "Pretty close to your size. Maybe we should stock some of yours for future deployments." Kelly smiled.

Christine accepted the clothing without a response, holding it as she sat on Doc's bed.

"Well, then," Doc said. "We'll let you change in private."

Doc ushered Harrison and the SUPPO from Medical, and as he closed the door, Christine was still sitting on the edge of the bed staring straight ahead, the stack of clothes in her hands.

98

WASHINGTON, D.C.

After descending to the ground floor of the executive residence and heading down the west colonnade, the president entered the Oval Office in the West Wing. Waiting outside his office and following him inside were McVeigh, Hardison, and DuBose, who settled into the three chairs opposite the president's desk. The president leaned back in his chair as McVeigh delivered an update.

"Russia's withdrawal from Lithuania and Ukraine is complete. They've also provided the locations where they attached explosives to oil and natural gas pipelines, and we've removed them. Regarding the Arabian Sea battle, every Russian surface combatant was either sunk or heavily damaged, while only six of our cruisers and destroyers were damaged. The more significant news is that we lost another eight submarines. Not bad considering we were outnumbered two to one, but the loss is significant considering our present force structure.

"We're taking a look at the water depth to determine whether the intact compartments would have imploded before they grounded, to see if we can raise the submarines like we did in the Taiwan Strait, but it doesn't look good. Fortunately, the submarines damaged in our war with China should begin exiting the repair yards in a few months.

"On a different topic," McVeigh said, "Christine is safely aboard *Michigan*. Her SEALs pulled her from the Black Sea after she killed Chernov."

"Thanks, Bob," the president said. "What's the plan forward?"

"Three carriers are heading to Hawaii and Washington State for repair. Of the two carrier strike groups remaining, we're leaving one in the Arabian Sea and routing one back toward China. Regarding the Russian facilities we've wired with explosives, we'll remove them whenever you give the word."

"Keep the explosives attached for now," the president said, "while we work the diplomatic front. I want to get a resolution through the Alliance, guaranteeing NATO will come to the aid of Ukraine or any other country Russia chooses to invade next."

The president surveyed the three men before him, then his features hardened as he said, "We have one last item to address. Give me a few options."

"Yes, Mr. President," McVeigh replied. "We're already working on it."

99

USS *MICHIGAN*

In the Wardroom of the guided missile submarine, Lieutenant Harrison stood behind his chair, as did the other nine officers and the one civilian present, waiting for Captain Wilson to enter and take his seat for dinner. On the Captain's end of the table stood Christine O'Connor, and across from her was Commander John McNeil, flanked by the submarine's Executive Officer. Due to being seated by seniority, with the higher-ranking officers toward the Captain's end of the table, Harrison was closer to the far end with the other junior officers.

Since he pulled her from the water the previous night, Christine had been withdrawn, barely speaking. The SUPPO had berthed Christine in the Executive Officer's stateroom, giving her the lower bunk while the XO moved to the top. With *Michigan* patrolling the Black Sea, the crew was focused and busy, but the SEALs had little to do at the moment and Harrison had found several reasons to cruise by the XO's stateroom. The door remained shut until just before lunch, when Christine emerged, wearing the blue coverall worn by the submarine's crew. He happened to be passing by as she stepped from her stateroom, and although she greeted him, there was no smile and her voice was monotone.

Captain Wilson entered the Wardroom and took his seat, and Christine and the officers settled into theirs. With Harrison at the opposite end, it was difficult to participate in conversations with the senior officers, but he glanced frequently in Christine's direction. She picked at her food, nodding and smiling politely on occasion, participating in the conversation only when engaged, her responses succinct. On more than one occasion, he caught her staring at her plate, her thoughts elsewhere until a mention of her name broke her reverie.

When the main course was finished, the culinary specialist serving dinner brought out the desserts, but Christine excused herself. Harrison stared at her empty chair for a moment, then obtained the Captain's permission to depart.

Guessing that Christine had returned to her stateroom, Harrison stopped by the XO's door and knocked. There was no answer, so he knocked harder. The door opened partway, revealing Christine inside the dimly lit stateroom, the only illumination coming from a small light above the XO's desk. Harrison didn't say anything, and after Christine searched his eyes, she opened the door fully, then retreated to her bed, where she sat on the edge, facing him.

"Request permission to close the door," he said.

Christine nodded and Harrison closed the door, then grabbed the chair by the XO's desk and sat across from her. There remained an unnatural stillness to her body as she sat there, her hands folded in her lap, staring at him.

"What happened?"

Christine didn't reply, and although there was no visible reaction on her face, her breathing quickened. Harrison reached toward her cheek and gently touched the Steri-Strips covering the cut. Christine leaned into his hand, and Harrison held her face before she pulled away suddenly, with an awareness in her eyes that she had lacked before.

"What happened?" Harrison repeated, this time glancing at the white gauze bandages on her wrists.

There was still no reply, but this time Christine stood. As he wondered why, she sat in his lap, her legs straddling his waist. She wrapped her arms around his chest, squeezing tight, and pressed the side of her face against his. It wasn't long before he felt wetness against his cheek; then she whispered in his ear, told him what she'd done.

Harrison wasn't surprised. He'd dated her for eight years and witnessed it many times—her tendency to turn vicious in the heat of the moment, remorseful for her actions the next morning. She'd gone too far in Beijing, and again on the shore of the Black Sea.

After Christine revealed what she'd done, emotion racked her body. He did his best to comfort her, caressing her back until the tears eased, then stopped. She remained in his lap, arms tight around him, and her breathing gradually slowed. Her muscles relaxed and a calm settled over her.

She pulled back, resting her forearms on his shoulders.

"How's home?" she asked softly.

It took a moment for Harrison to respond. In Christine's condition, she was emotionally vulnerable, and he knew the answer she was hoping for. After a moment of indecision, he replied truthfully.

"It's good," he said.

Christine nodded slowly, unable to conceal the disappointment in her eyes, then pushed herself to her feet.

"I appreciate you stopping by."

Harrison also stood, and there was a long silence until she spoke again.

"I'll be fine," she said, then forced a smile.

"If you need anything," Harrison said, "I'll be there for you."

"I know."

After another long moment, Harrison bade farewell and stepped from the stateroom, closing the door behind him.

WASHINGTON, D.C. • USS *MICHIGAN*

WASHINGTON, D.C.

A light rain was falling from a gray, overcast sky as Naveen Chandra's black limousine veered off Dupont Circle onto Connecticut Avenue for the short trip to the White House. As the American capital slid by rain-streaked windows, Chandra fidgeted with the brown leather satchel on his lap, pausing to straighten his tie unconsciously. It wasn't often that the American president met directly with a country's ambassador. The reason was obvious, although the outcome was unpredictable. The president had made a decision concerning India's involvement in the Arabian Sea last week, and as Chandra's thoughts churned through the various outcomes, a deepening uneasiness grew in his stomach. American-Indian relations were about to take a turn for the worse.

Relations between the two countries had come a long way since the Clinton administration tried to isolate India after its nuclear tests in 1998. Sanctions were eventually lifted, and the United States, searching for allies in the Pacific against the growing Chinese military, had adopted a policy of accommodation toward India. However, despite strengthening ties between the two countries over the last decade, the Indian government had sided with Russia during last week's conflict in the Arabian Sea. President Madan's administration had concluded Russia was reemerging as a global power, their influence in the region growing while America's waned. However, Madan's decision had proved shortsighted.

After turning onto West Executive Avenue, Chandra's limousine stopped in front of black steel bars guarding the White House grounds. Following a search of the vehicle for explosives, the gate opened and the sedan pulled forward, coasting to a stop under the West Wing portico. Waiting to greet him was a young woman barely out of college, flanked by two marines in dress blues.

Chandra stepped from the sedan and one of the marines saluted as the young woman stepped forward, introducing herself as they shook hands. She was Sheree Hinton, a White House intern. Instead of being greeted by the president's powerful chief of staff, as was customary, India's ambassador had been greeted by the lowest White House staffer on the food chain. It was an ill omen. The young woman led him into the Roosevelt Room, where she instructed him to wait until the president was ready, then departed.

USS *MICHIGAN*

"No close contacts!"

Lieutenant Jane Stucker made the call as the eighteen-thousand-ton submarine leveled off at periscope depth. After verifying there were no contacts close enough to pose a collision threat, Stucker slowed her revolutions on the periscope, and Christine watched from the corner of the Control Room as the junior officer conducted a low-power scan of the horizon, searching for distant ships or military aircraft.

Stucker completed the search and reported to Captain

Wilson, standing nearby on the Conn. "Sir, I have completed a low-power surface and air search. Hold no contacts."

Wilson acknowledged and took the scope, and as he conducted a detailed search of his own, Christine's thoughts turned to her pending departure. After Russia's capitulation and withdrawal from Lithuania and Ukraine, *Michigan* had begun her journey home to Bangor, Washington, for an overdue maintenance period, passing through the Suez Canal into the Pacific Ocean again. Christine's time aboard the guided missile submarine was drawing to a close; they'd soon be passing near Diego Garcia in the Indian Ocean, where she'd be transferred ashore.

In the week since *Michigan* departed the Black Sea, Christine had slowly begun to feel like herself again, emerging from her shell as the memories of what she'd done, and had been done to her, on the shore of the Black Sea faded. Harrison stopped by frequently to check on her, and while she found his attention comforting, their interactions left an ache in her heart each time. She began to slowly reconcile her feelings for him; despite his obvious concern for her, he would never be more than a close friend. She'd blown both chances, declining his offer to marry her after high school and college.

Wilson stepped back, turning the scope over to Lieutenant Stucker as an announcement came from the Conn speakers. "Conn, ESM. Hold no threat radars."

Stucker acknowledged ESM's report as Wilson stepped toward the communications panel on the Conn, pulling the 1-MC microphone to his mouth.

"Man Battle Stations Missile."

The Chief of the Watch, stationed at the Ballast Control Panel on the port side of Control, activated the General Alarm, and the loud *gong-gong-gong* reverberated throughout the ship. As the alarm faded, he picked up his 1-MC microphone, repeating the Captain's order.

Crew members streamed into Control, taking their seats at dormant consoles, bringing them to life as they donned their sound-powered phone headsets. When Lieutenant Eaton arrived, Wilson stepped off the Conn, leaving the safety of the ship in the Navigator's and Lieutenant Stucker's capable hands. Christine followed Wilson down the ladder to Operations Compartment Second Level and into Missile Control Center.

Like the Navigation Center behind the Control Room, Missile Control Center was also transformed during the submarine's conversion to SSGN. The refrigerator-sized computers were replaced with servers one-tenth their size, and a Tube Status Control Display was now mounted on the starboard bulkhead. The ballistic missile Launch Console on the aft bulkhead had been replaced with four consoles: the two workstations on the right were Mission Planning Consoles, the third was the Launch Control Console, and the fourth workstation displayed a map of *Michigan*'s operating area, which contained a small green hatched section.

Wilson stopped behind the Launch Control Console beside Lieutenant Mike Lawson, the submarine's Weapons Officer, with both men looking over the shoulders of a second class petty officer manning the workstation. Glancing at the fourth console, Wilson verified *Michigan* was within the green hatched area—the submarine's launch basket, where *Michigan*'s Tomahawk missiles were within target range.

Lieutenant Lawson reported to the Captain, "Five minutes to window. Request permission to launch salvo One."

Wilson replied, "Permission granted. Launch salvo One."

Following Wilson's order, there was no flurry of activity. Lawson simply turned back toward the Launch Control Console, his eyes focused on the time as it counted down the remaining five minutes. At ten seconds before the scheduled launch, the launch button on the Launch Control Console display, which had been grayed out until this point, turned a vivid green.

The Launch Operator announced, "In the window, salvo One."

Lieutenant Lawson replied, "Very well, Launch Operator. Continue."

When the digital clock on the Launch Operator's screen reached 00:00:00, the Launch Operator clicked the green button, and *Michigan*'s automatic Tomahawk Attack Weapon System took control.

"Opening tube Ten," the Launch Supervisor reported as the green indicating light for tube Ten turned yellow. Shortly thereafter, the indicating light turned red. "Hatch, tube Ten, open and locked."

A few seconds later, the Launch Operator reported, "Missile One, tube Ten, away."

The first of *Michigan*'s Tomahawks was ejected from the submarine, with the missile's engines igniting once it was above the ocean surface. In rapid succession, another missile followed every five seconds, with the Tomahawk Attack Weapon System automatically opening and closing the missile tube hatches as required. *Michigan*'s Tomahawks streaked east.

WASHINGTON, D.C.

Sheree Hinton returned to the Roosevelt Room, stopping by the door. "The president is ready to see you."

Ambassador Chandra rose without a word and followed Hinton into the hallway. But instead of entering the Oval Office, Hinton led the way to the basement of the West Wing. As they approached the Situation Room, an Indian idiom came to mind.

There is something black in the lentil soup.

The Americans were up to something.

Chandra entered the Situation Room, joining the American president, his chief of staff, SecDef McVeigh, and SecState Cabral, who were seated at the table. The Americans did not rise from their seats when he entered. Instead, Kevin Hardison pulled a chair back partway. Chandra took his seat while Hinton departed, closing the door behind her, sealing him inside the Situation Room with the four Americans.

The president said, "Thank you for taking time out of your busy schedule to join us, Ambassador."

There was a hint of sarcasm in the president's voice, for what reason Chandra was uncertain.

"For the last fifteen years," the president said, "the United States and India have worked diligently to improve relations between our countries, and we've made much progress. However, your recent actions have cast doubt upon our relationship."

Chandra had no viable response.

The president continued, "Your actions last week were tantamount to a declaration of war." There was a hard edge to his words, and his voice dropped a notch. "And now I must decide the proper response to your aggression and the future of our relationship."

Under different circumstances, Chandra would have avoided the president's incriminating gaze. A long silence ensued as Chandra chose his words carefully. As he began to respond, the president held up a placating hand.

"The United States values its relationship with India, and it would be a shame to discard so many years of progress. As China's influence in the Pacific grows, I cannot overstate the value of our friendship. What happened in the Arabian Sea was unfortunate. But accidents happen. I'm willing to consider the possibility that our ships and aircraft *accidentally* got in the way of missiles intended for the Russians."

Chandra was caught off guard. He couldn't possibly have heard the president correctly. Could India be this fortunate, the United States so desperate for allies in the Pacific? With Russia and China growing their military and economies at a faster pace than the United States, the writing on the wall was clear. But Chandra was surprised the Americans were willing to look the other way.

"I agree," Chandra replied. "Accidents do happen on occasion, and we will work to ensure they do not occur in the future."

"Excellent," the president said. "I'm glad we're in agreement." He offered a tight smile, then said, "I'd like to discuss this situation with President Madan. We've arranged a conference call."

Hardison punched the number into a conference phone on the table. The call was answered after the first ring.

"This is President Madan."

The American president conveyed his thoughts on the recent incident to Madan, following the outline of his discussion with Ambassador Chandra.

There was a long silence on the line before Madan replied, "I agree. We have forged a vital relationship over the last few years, and we will work to repair the damage done."

"As will we," the president said. "I look forward to setting aside what occurred, and is about to occur, so we can strengthen our relationship."

"About to occur?" President Madan asked.

The president checked the clock on the Situation Room wall. "You have five minutes to vacate the presidential palace. Anyone remaining inside will not live to see another day. Do I make myself clear?"

There was no response from President Madan. Instead, the line went dead.

Hardison grabbed a remote from the table and activated the video screen on the far wall. A satellite image of India's presidential palace appeared—the 340-room Rashtrapati Bhavan in New Delhi—and it wasn't long before men and women began streaming from the exits, dispersing into the 320-acre complex.

As the last few stragglers hurried down the front steps, the entire east facade of the building disintegrated as several dozen explosions rippled across the front of the palace, the black-tinged fireballs roiling upward.

Turning to Ambassador Chandra, the president said, "It looks like your presidential palace *accidentally* got in the way of a few Tomahawk missiles. As we learned all too well last week, accidents happen. Please convey my sincere apologies to President Madan."

MOSCOW

As sunlight streamed into his Kremlin office through tall Palladian windows behind him, President Kalinin sat at his desk, deep in thought. With two key positions temporarily vacant—Russia's minister of defense and director of the SVR—Kalinin had convened today's meeting in his office instead of the conference room. Seated across from him were General Andropov, Fleet Admiral Lipovsky, and Foreign Minister Lavrov. The three men waited while Kalinin sorted through the magnitude of their naval defeat.

Russia's Northern and Pacific Fleets had been ravaged, with every surface combatant sunk or heavily damaged. The submarine force had fared much better, still fielding over thirty attack submarines. The significant numerical advantage beneath the waves, with most of America's submarines still undergoing repair, weighed heavily on Kalinin's deliberation.

"What is the status of our Alexander class?" he asked.

"We have one operational submarine so far," General Andropov replied. "However, it was withheld from battle pending resolution of defects in its new capability. We are pushing the cutting edge of technology," Andropov offered as an excuse, "but we will test a solution next month. Additionally, two more Alexander class are nearing completion. With six Alexander class leading our submarine force, the American submarine fleet would be overwhelmed."

Kalinin replied, "As we experienced in the Arabian Sea, the Americans have more anti-submarine forces at their disposal besides submarines. Their surface combatants and aircraft are formidable assets."

General Andropov replied. "We still have the Zolotov option."

"That's a very dangerous plan," Minister Lavrov said. "A path from which we cannot turn back. We cannot predict how America would respond."

"There will be no response from the United States," Andropov replied. "That's the purpose of the Zolotov option: to eliminate their ability."

President Kalinin weighed his options in silence, moving slowly toward a decision. The United States had publicly humiliated both Kalinin and Russia. A response was required.

"You may proceed," Kalinin said. "Order both submarine shipyards to twenty-four-hour shiftwork to complete the next two Alexander class as soon as possible. Regarding the Zolotov option, we'll cross that bridge when we get there."

General Andropov acknowledged Kalinin's order. "It is a wise decision, Mr. President. We will make America pay for what they've done."

* * * THE END * * *

COMPLETE CAST OF CHARACTERS

AMERICAN CHARACTERS

UNITED STATES ADMINISTRATION
KEVIN HARDISON, chief of staff
BOB McVEIGH, secretary of defense
DAWN CABRAL, secretary of state
CHRISTINE O'CONNOR, national security advisor
BILL DUBOSE (Colonel), senior military aide
SHEREE HINTON, White House intern

MILITARY COMMANDERS
ANDY WHEELER (General), Supreme Allied Commander, Europe
BRIAN RETTMAN (Admiral), Chief of Naval Operations

USS *HARTFORD* (LOS ANGELES CLASS FAST ATTACK SUBMARINE)
DAVE THAMES (Commander), Commanding Officer
JOE WHITE (Lieutenant Commander), Executive Officer

USS *MICHIGAN* (OHIO CLASS GUIDED MISSILE SUBMARINE)-CREW
MURRAY WILSON (Captain), Commanding Officer

DAVE BEASLEY (Lieutenant Commander), Executive
    Officer
KELLY HAAS (Lieutenant Commander), Supply Officer
CHARLIE EATON (Lieutenant), Navigator
MIKE LAWSON (Lieutenant), Weapons Officer
JAYNE STUCKER (Lieutenant), Junior Officer
CHRIS SHROYER (Lieutenant), Junior Officer
PAT LEENSTRA (Electronics Technician Second Class),
    Quartermaster

USS *MICHIGAN*–SEAL DETACHMENT
JOHN MCNEIL (Commander), SEAL Team
    Commander
JAKE HARRISON (Lieutenant), SEAL Platoon Officer-in-
    Charge
ROB MAYDWELL (Special Warfare Operator First Class),
    breacher
WAYNE BROWN (Special Warfare Operator Second
    Class), communicator
RICHARD MENDELSON (Special Warfare Operator
    Second Class), sniper
JOE ALEO (Commander), Medical Officer

USS *MISSISSIPPI* [VIRGINIA CLASS FAST ATTACK SUBMARINE]
BRAD WALLER (Commander), Commanding Officer
GEORGE SKEENS (Lieutenant), Junior Officer

USS *HARRY S. TRUMAN* [NIMITZ CLASS AIRCRAFT CARRIER]
DAVID RANDLE (Captain), Commanding Officer
BRENT SITES (Captain), Combat Direction Center
    (CDC) Operations Officer
BILL HOUSTON / call sign Samurai (Lieutenant
    Commander), F/A-18E pilot
DAVE HERNANDEZ / call sign TexMex (Lieutenant),
    F/A-18E pilot

USS *THEODORE ROOSEVELT* (NIMITZ CLASS AIRCRAFT CARRIER)

RICH TILGHMAN (Captain), Commanding
Officer

DOLORES GONZALEZ (Captain), Combat Direction
Center (CDC) Operations Officer

OTHER MILITARY CHARACTERS

JOE MARTIN (Captain), Delta Force team leader

PATRICK TERRILL (Staff Sergeant), Delta Force team
member

MIKE PECK (Major), B-1B pilot

LEO FALARDEAU (Lieutenant), MH-60R pilot

JOHN MARTIN (Lieutenant Commander), P-8A Tactical
Coordinator

TIM JOHNS (Cryptologic Technician Networks Second
Class), U.S. Cyber Warfare Command

STU NELSON (Staff Sergeant), Army Explosive Ordnance
Disposal technician

JOHN BROWN (Captain), Army Explosive Ordnance
Disposal company commander

OTHER CIVILIAN CHARACTERS

JESSICA CHERRY, director of the Central Intelligence
Agency

JOHN KAUFMANN, Central Intelligence Agency
interrogator

KATRINA WETZEL, U.S. ambassador to the People's
Republic of China

NATASHA GRAHAM, U.S. ambassador to the Russian
Federation

BARRY GRAHAM, aide to the U.S. ambassador to the
Russian Federation

MARK JOHNSON, Russian translator (American
embassy)

ELENA KRAYEV, Russian translator (CIA agent)

RUSSIAN CHARACTERS

RUSSIAN FEDERATION ADMINISTRATION

YURI KALININ, president

BORIS CHERNOV, defense minister

ANDREI LAVROV, foreign minister

SERGEI IVANOV, national security advisor

MAKSIM POSNIAK, director of security and disarmament, Ministry of Foreign Affairs

SEMYON GOREV, director of the Foreign Intelligence Service (SVR)

ANDREI TUPOLEV, ambassador to the United States

DANIL SOKOLOV, ambassador to the People's Republic of China

MILITARY COMMANDERS

SERGEI ANDROPOV (General), chief of the general staff

ALEXEI VOLODIN (Colonel General), Commander-in-Chief, Aerospace Forces

VIKTOR GLUKOV (Colonel General), Commander-in-Chief, Ground Forces

OLEG LIPOVSKY (Admiral), Commander-in-Chief, Navy

LEONID SHIMKO (Admiral), Commander, Northern Fleet

PAVEL KLOKOV (Admiral), Commander, Pacific Fleet

VITALY VASILIEV (Major General), Commanding Officer, 448th Missile Brigade

K-456 *VILYUCHINSK* (OSCAR II CLASS GUIDED MISSILE SUBMARINE)

DMITRI PAVLOV (Captain First Rank), Commanding Officer

MIKHAIL EVANOFF (Captain Second Rank), First Officer

Ludvig Dolinski (Captain Lieutenant), Central
   Command Post Watch Officer

OTHER RUSSIAN CHARACTERS

Vadim Aleyev (Major), Sukhoi Su-35S pilot
Anton Belikov (Captain Lieutenant), Spetsnaz
   platoon leader
Roman Savvin (Sergeant First Class), VDV paratrooper
Anton Fedorov, detonator designer
Vagit Alekperov, president of LUKoil Oil Company
Bogdan Melikov, supervisor at Omsk Oil Refinery

OTHER CHARACTERS

BELARUSIAN

Alexander Lukashenko, president
Edward Aymar (Colonel), Commander, 11th Guards
   Mechanized Brigade

CHINESE

Xiang Chenglei, president of China and general
   secretary of the Party
Xie Hai, president's executive assistant

INDIAN

Deepak Madan, president
Ankur Kumar, minister of defense
Rahul Gupta, minister of external affairs
Naveen Chandra, ambassador to the United States

NATO

Johan Van der Bie, secretary-general
Susan Gates, United Kingdom prime minister
François Loubet, French president

EMMA SCHMIDT, German chancellor
DALIA GRYBAUSKAITĖ, Lithuanian president

UKRAINE
ALEX RUDENKO, Opposition Bloc politician
RANDY GUIMOND, Russian SVR agent

AUTHOR'S NOTE

I hope you enjoyed reading *Blackmail* as much as I enjoyed writing it.

This was the most enjoyable book for me to write thus far. My first book—*The Trident Deception*—was tortuous, as I was still learning how to write, and it went through many revisions before reaching the final version. (Over two hundred pages ended up on the cutting room floor, and the ending is quite different than the one my publisher bought. It's a long story, but the short version is that in the original novel, everyone died at the end—Wilson and Christine included. However, my publisher wanted a sequel, and that's hard to do if everyone dies. So I resurrected Christine and Wilson. If the scenes in *The Trident Deception* where it appears they die come across as convincing, that's because they originally died in those scenes.)

Each book continues to be a learning experience as I get feedback from readers, gaining a better understanding of what works and doesn't from a thriller reader's perspective. Due to how early my publisher requires my manuscripts (*Empire Rising* was turned in before *The Trident Deception* was published), *Ice Station Nautilus* was the first book where I had a chance to incorporate reader comments, and *Blackmail* incorporates additional feedback. I hope you like how it turned out.

I enjoyed writing the Russian paratrooper chapter in *Blackmail*, drawing on my personal experience. I'm a submariner who also happens to be a qualified paratrooper—I earned my wings at Fort Benning, Georgia. I was planning to go Marine Corps at the time, but for several reasons ended up going submarines. I wore my jump wings on my uniform for a few years, garnering quite a few odd looks and questions. A paratrooper aboard a submarine is obviously an odd lash-up.

Also, the usual disclaimer—some of the tactics described in *Blackmail* are generic and not accurate. For example, torpedo employment and evasion tactics are classified and cannot be accurately represented in this novel. The dialogue also isn't one hundred percent accurate. If it were, much of it would be unintelligible to the average reader. To help the story move along without getting bogged down in acronyms, technical details, and other military jargon, I simplified the dialogue and description of operations and weapon systems.

For all of the above, I apologize. I did my best to keep everything as close to real life as possible while developing a suspenseful (and unclassified), page-turning novel. Hopefully it all worked out, and you enjoyed reading *Blackmail*.

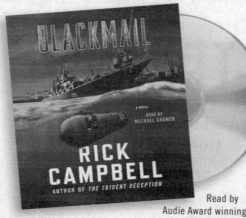
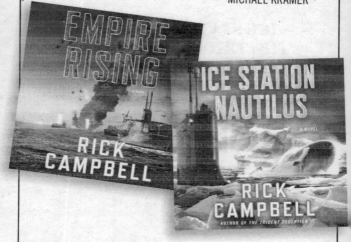

WILLOW

JULIA HOBAN

speak

An Imprint of Penguin Group (USA) Inc.

For Henry Grayson and Charles Grodin:
Two of the eighteen

Speak
Published by the Penguin Group
Penguin Group (USA) Inc., 345 Hudson Street, New York, New York 10014, U.S.A.
Penguin Group (Canada), 90 Eglinton Avenue East, Suite 700, Toronto, Ontario, Canada M4P 2Y3
(a division of Pearson Penguin Canada Inc.)
Penguin Books Ltd, 80 Strand, London WC2R 0RL, England
Penguin Ireland, 25 St Stephen's Green, Dublin 2, Ireland (a division of Penguin Books Ltd)
Penguin Group (Australia), 250 Camberwell Road, Camberwell, Victoria 3124, Australia
(a division of Pearson Australia Group Pty Ltd)
Penguin Books India Pvt Ltd, 11 Community Centre, Panchsheel Park, New Delhi - 110 017, India
Penguin Group (NZ), 67 Apollo Drive, Rosedale, North Shore 0632, New Zealand
(a division of Pearson New Zealand Ltd)
Penguin Books (South Africa) (Pty) Ltd, 24 Sturdee Avenue,
Rosebank, Johannesburg 2196, South Africa

Registered Offices: Penguin Books Ltd, 80 Strand, London WC2R 0RL, England

First published in the United States of America by Dial Books,
a member of Penguin Group (USA) Inc., 2009
Published by Speak, an imprint of Penguin Group (USA) Inc., 2010

10

THE LIBRARY OF CONGRESS HAS CATALOGED THE DIAL EDITION AS FOLLOWS:
Hoban, Julia.
Willow / by Julia Hoban.
p. cm.
Summary: Sixteen-year-old Willow, who was driving the car that killed both of
her parents, copes with the pain and guilt by cutting herself, until she meets
a smart and sensitive boy who is determined to help her stop.
ISBN: 978-0-8037-3356-5 (hc)
[1. Self-mutilation—Fiction. 2. Guilt—Fiction. 3. Grief—Fiction. 4. Orphans—Fiction.]
PZ7.H63487 Wi 2009
[Fic]—dc22

Speak ISBN 978-0-14-241666-2

Printed in the United States of America

CHAPTER ONE

Maybe it's just a scratch.

Willow Randall stares at the girl seated opposite her. Some might notice the girl because she is pretty. Others because of her flaming red hair. If the guys in the class were looking, they would see that the outline of her bra is clearly visible beneath her shirt. But Willow's eyes are riveted by something else: an angry red welt, about three inches long, that runs from the girl's elbow to her wrist. If Willow squints hard enough, she can just about make out a few flecks of dried blood.

How did she get it? She doesn't look the type.

Maybe she has a cat. A whole bunch of kittens.

Yeah, that's it. Playing with her kitty. That's probably how it happened.

Willow slumps down in her seat. But her scrutiny hasn't

1

gone unnoticed and the girl turns to one of her friends and starts whispering.

Sshshhsh . . .

What are they saying?

Willow looks at the other girls uncertainly. She has a bad feeling that they're talking about her, and she's pretty sure that she knows what they're saying, too.

She's the one without parents.

No. She's the one who killed her parents.

Their whispers remind her of the rustling of dried leaves. Willow has always hated the sound. She fights the urge to clap her hands over her ears, reluctant to call any more attention to herself. But she can't stop the river of noise that flows out of their mouths. *Shhhhsshhhsh . . .*

The sound engulfs her. Threatens to overwhelm her.

Only one thing can make it go away.

Willow stands up abruptly, but her shoelace gets tangled with the chair leg and she pitches forward. Her books fall to the floor with a crash. She grabs the desk with both hands, barely managing to stay upright.

Dead silence. *Everyone* is staring at her.

She can feel her face burning and glares at the two girls who were whispering.

"Willow?" Ms. Benson sounds alarmed. She's clearly concerned, and not just pretending. She's a good teacher.

She's nice to the fat kids, the pimply kids, so why not the orphan kids? Why not the killer kids?

"I just . . ." Willow straightens up slowly. "Just—the bathroom." Her blush deepens painfully. She's ashamed of her clumsiness. Ashamed at the way she looked at those girls . . . And couldn't she have come up with a *different* excuse?

Ms. Benson nods, but she looks doubtful, as if she might suspect.

Willow couldn't care less at this point. All she's thinking about is making a quick getaway and leaving those smirking faces behind. She picks up her books, grabs her bag, and as soon as she's out the door she starts running down the hall. Wait. No running in the halls. She slows down to a walk. That's the last thing she needs, to get busted for something as stupid as running in the halls.

The bathroom smells like smoke. There's no one around. Good. The door to one of the stalls swings free. Willow kicks it shut behind her and lowers the toilet seat before sitting down.

She rummages through her bag. Getting frantic because she can't find what she so desperately needs. Did she forget to get more supplies? Finally, just when she's given up hope, when she's about to start howling like a dog, her hand closes on smooth metal. Her fingers test the sharpness of the edge. Perfect. It's a fresh blade.

The girls' voices rustle in her head. Their clamoring pushes out all rational thought. She rolls up her sleeve.

The bite of the blade kills the noise. It wipes out the memory of those staring faces. Willow looks at her arm, at the life springing from her. Tiny pinpricks of red that blossom into giant peonies.

Peonies like the ones my mother used to plant.

Willow shuts her eyes, drinking in the quiet. Her breath

deepens with each dip of the razor. Silence reigns, not like when she tripped, but perfect and pure.

You couldn't really say that something that hurts so badly feels good exactly. It's more that it just feels right. And something that feels so right just couldn't be bad. It has to be good.

It is good. Better than good.

Better than anything with any guy ever.

Better than mother's milk.

CHAPTER TWO

"No, that's out till the twenty-sixth," Miss Hamilton says with a brisk professional smile. Willow stands next to her behind the circulation desk, stifling a yawn. She's tired. Thank God her shift at the library is almost over. She steals a glance at her watch. Well, not quite over; another forty-five minutes.

Willow knows she should be grateful for the job. After all, her brother had to pull enough strings to get it for her. Three afternoons a week she helps out in the university library. It brings in some cash. Not enough, but still, more than she would have made back home working in the local Häagen-Dazs scooping ice cream.

Of course, back home any money she made would have gone straight into her own pocket. Things are a little different now. Now she works to help her brother out with expenses. Now she has to worry about things like the electric bill. But that's not really so bad, at least not compared to the rest of her life.

"I think we can get that for you on interlibrary loan," Miss Hamilton continues. "Willow, will you set that up?"

Miss Hamilton looks at her sharply, ready to pounce if she makes a mistake. She's not a bad soul, not really. She's nice enough to everyone else, she just doesn't like Willow invading her library. Most of the other people who work there are graduate students, and those who aren't have chosen the library as their career. Suffice it to say, Willow is the only high school student there.

It's just like everything else these days. She simply does not belong.

Willow takes the card that the guy's filled out in his shaky, spidery handwriting. He's looking for some obscure work on twelfth-century philosophers. She glances up at him. An older man. Way older. Probably in his seventies. It's always interesting to see the different types that wander in.

"That should get here in a couple days," she says as she keys the call number into the computer. "You wrote your phone number down?" She looks at the card again. "Perfect, we'll let you know when it comes in."

"Wonderful," he says with real enthusiasm. Willow notices what a friendly smile he has. She bets that he's a retired professor who still likes to read. His eyes positively gleam at the prospect of getting his hands on the book. Her father would have been like that in another twenty years or so. Just the thought of some monograph about a little-known tribe in New Guinea would have been enough to make him drool.

Would have been.

She's blindsided by a wave of despair, it's hard to even stand. She grips the edge of the circulation desk so hard that her knuckles turn white. She simply cannot afford to lose it in here. Is there any way, any way at all, that she can excuse herself, go and do what she has to, without Miss Hamilton getting angry at her?

Willow can see her bag with all her supplies underneath one of the chairs. Just the sight of it calms her a little. She moves her hands away from the desk and rubs her arms, relishing the way the cotton irritates her fresh wounds. That will have to do for now.

"Willow!" Miss Hamilton's voice is sharp; clearly this isn't the first time that she's said her name.

"I'm sorry!" Willow is so startled that she practically jumps. She forces herself to look away from her bag and focus on Miss Hamilton's scowling face.

"I need you to go up to the stacks."

"Okay." She nods, even though she hates the stacks. They're filthy, positively caked in dust. They're scary too. Willow's heard rumors about ghosts. Not that she believes in ghosts, but still. . . .

"This young man forgot his ID, you need to go up with him."

Willow switches her attention to the guy leaning against the circulation desk behind Miss Hamilton. Now, *this* guy isn't any seventy years old. He's probably only a few years older than she is, if that. He flips the hair out of his eyes and flashes her a lazy smile.

Willow knows that she should smile back, but it's no good, she's lost the knack.

"I'll take him up in a second." She turns back to Miss Hamilton. "I just have to finish . . . " Willow makes a vague gesture toward the computer.

Miss Hamilton nods and turns away, but the guy doesn't. He keeps on looking. She can feel his eyes following her as she finishes taking care of the interlibrary loan.

Willow is sure that she's just being paranoid, but his scrutiny is terrifying. It reminds her of the girls back at school. She doesn't like the thought of going up to the stacks with him at all. Just to delay things, she takes more time than is strictly necessary to fill in all the information fields.

"So how about it?" he says after a minute or two. He's starting to get impatient. His fingers drum along the counter and his voice has a distinct edge. He doesn't seem so interested in her anymore.

Willow sighs in relief. *This* she can handle.

"Yeah, okay. Just a second." Her voice matches his.

"Why don't you let me do this for you?" Carlos says, taking the twelfth-century man's card from her. Carlos is one of the graduate students, he's almost as old as her brother. Willow likes him—well, as much as she can like anyone these days. He's nice to her, he's covered for her more than once.

"Thanks," she says under her breath. She wishes he would let her finish at the computer and take this guy up to the stacks instead.

"Well, c'mon then." Willow marches ahead of him toward the elevator.

"Do you know where this is?" she asks, looking at the card he's filled out. "Never mind, I got it." She steps into the elevator and punches the button for the eleventh-floor stacks. The doors close and they're alone. Willow stares straight ahead at the illuminated numbers.

"I'm Guy," he says after a moment. "What's your name?"

"Willow."

"Willow . . ." He trails off, obviously expecting her to respond. "Willow?" he prompts, after a second. "What's your last name?"

Willow can't think of any way, short of being downright rude, to avoid answering him. "Randall," she says.

"Are you related to David Randall?" He eyes her curiously. "I thought you looked kinda familiar. I took anthropology with him last year. He's great."

"He's my brother," Willow answers in a tone meant to discourage further conversation. His chatter is starting to make her nervous.

"You're not a student here, are you?" He frowns. "You look a little young. How did you get this job?"

Willow doesn't respond right away. The questions he's asking are making her a little uncomfortable. She starts counting the floors under her breath. She can't wait for the ride to be over.

"They usually only hire students," he continues. "Otherwise I'd try and get a job. I'd love to work in the library." His expression is pleasant and his voice is good-natured. If he notices that she's being slightly standoffish, it doesn't seem to bother him.

"If you're not a student, what are you doing here?" Willow is confused.

"My high school has this program where you can take college courses for credit," he says. "So what about you, how *did* you get the job?"

"I'm living with my brother right now," Willow says after a moment. "He worked it out." The elevator stops and they get off.

The stacks are dark; the lights are on a timer, which Willow quickly presses. She blinks rapidly as her eyes adjust to the dim lighting. Their gazes catch and for a moment she feels herself respond the way any normal girl would if she were standing next to a cute guy. She's a little flustered, a little embarrassed, and a little attracted too.

Willow steps away from him, as far as she possibly can. She can't deal with anything like this right now.

"Hey, watch it." Guy reaches out with his hand to steady her as she bangs against the metal stacks.

Willow jerks her arm away, stunned by how much his touch affects her. In a way his hand is as searing as the razor . . . only the effect is something quite different. The razor numbs her, makes her forget, but this . . . well . . . She shivers and rubs her arms convulsively.

"You cold?" He raises an eyebrow.

"I'm fine, thanks. I . . . C'mon, let's get your book, okay?" Willow checks the call number again, then turns and heads over to the shelves.

She finds the volume easily and is about to hand it to him, when she glances at the title and stops, transfixed.

"Everything okay?" Guy frowns as he watches her.

"Oh, sure, I just . . ." Willow trails off. She can't stop staring at the book. Well, she shouldn't be so surprised. He did say something about anthropology, and it is a classic.

"Do you know this book? I mean, have you read *Tristes Tropiques* before?" he asks as he takes it from her hands.

"Yes, a couple of times, actually," Willow says after a few seconds. She closes her eyes for a moment and pictures her parents' study with its wall of books. *Tristes Tropiques*, third shelf, second in from the left.

10

"I've never met anyone else who's read it!" Guy looks impressed. "It's amazing, isn't it?" he says as he flips through the pages. "I guess your brother must have told you about it, right? If it wasn't for this book I wouldn't have even taken his class."

"What do you mean?"

"Well, last year, right before I started classes here, I was wandering around downtown, trying to decide what I should take. I figured I'd end up doing something like chemistry or math, since those would look pretty good on my transcript and maybe help me get into a fancy school or something. Anyway, it started to rain and I ducked into this used bookstore. This literally fell off the shelf while I was looking for something else. I opened it up and four hours later I was still there reading. That's when I decided that I had to take anthropology."

"Really?" In spite of herself, Willow can't help being interested. She too has never met anyone else—anyone her own age, that is—who's read the book, let alone been so captivated by it.

"Really." Guy nods. "It's like an adventure story, isn't it?"

"That's it exactly!" Willow's face lights up. Just for a second she forgets that *Tristes Tropiques* was her father's favorite book. She forgets about sitting on the window seat in the living room on rainy Saturday afternoons working her way through *all* his favorite books. She forgets that she doesn't *have* a father anymore, and she even forgets to be unhappy. "It is like an adventure story," she says. "But you know what's funny? Remember how on the first page he goes on and on about how he doesn't even like adventure stories?"

"Right." Guy laughs. "And then he pretty much goes ahead and writes one."

The lights click off suddenly and they stand in the darkness for a moment before Guy reaches out and presses the timer. Then he sits down on the floor as if it were the most natural thing in the world, as if the only thing that he could possibly want to do with his time is talk to her.

Willow is a little unsure of what to do. She feels comfortable talking to him, but the way she felt when he touched her, that wasn't comfortable at all. She searches his face. He doesn't look as if there's anything on his mind besides books.

After a second Willow sits down next to him.

"Why do you need this?" She gestures toward *Tristes Tropiques*. "What happened to the copy that you bought at that used bookstore?" Of course she doesn't really care about what happened to his copy, and it's kind of a stupid question, stupid and boring, but she doesn't know what else to say, and she doesn't feel relaxed enough to sit there with him in silence.

"Lost it on the subway." Guy shrugs. "I should buy another, but I'm kind of low on cash right now. Do you know the place I'm talking about?" He puts the book down and turns to look at her. "I figure your brother's had to have dragged you down there about a thousand times. It's always packed with professors whenever I go."

Willow thinks for a minute. "Is it way downtown?" she asks. "And even though it's huge, it's really cramped, right?"

"Right." Guy nods. "There's hardly room to move. It's like the books have taken over. They've spilled off the shelves and there's so many piled all over the floor that it's almost impossible to walk."

"And it kind of smells," Willow says. "But not in a good,

old, bookish sort of way, but in a kind of . . ." She pauses for a second.

"A kind of unwashed and dirty way," Guy finishes.

"That's right." Willow laughs. "And the staff are really rude."

"If you ask them something, they act like you're bothering them."

"And it's almost impossible to find anything on your own, because they don't arrange things in any logical order."

"And the whole place is so far out of the way to begin with, you wonder why anyone even bothers to go there. But still, it's actually really . . ."

"Fabulous," Willow chimes in.

"So you do know it." Guy smiles. He stops talking and studies her face carefully. Willow shifts uncomfortably. She's suddenly acutely aware of how quiet the stacks are, how quiet and how empty.

"You don't really look that much like your brother," Guy continues after a few moments. "I mean, I don't think that's why I recognized you."

Willow isn't sure where this is leading, but she does know that she feels distinctly less relaxed than she did a few minutes ago.

"I'm such an idiot!" Guy exclaims. "I can't believe this. You go to my school, don't you? That's why I know you. I've seen you around the halls. You just transferred there this year, right?"

Willow is much too startled to answer this. They go to the same school? He knows her? Does he know *about* her?

She scrambles to her feet. "I have to go," she says in alarm. "I shouldn't have been up here this long anyway."

"Well, sure." Guy stands up and starts to follow her as she practically runs to the elevator.

Willow can't bring herself to look at him. She stares at the elevator floor, the ceiling, anything but his face. It's as if their pleasant little interlude had never even occurred. She feels used. Used and *stupid*. Had he known all along? Had that entire conversation been some act so he could report back to his friends at school that he'd actually managed to talk to the new girl? The *strange* girl, the girl who *killed her parents*?

The desire to cut is palpable, even stronger than it was back at the circulation desk. She has to get away from him. She has to be alone.

"So listen, do you think . . ."

"I have to *go*," Willow says. She bolts out of the elevator, leaving Guy behind, and rushes toward Miss Hamilton. For once her scowl is welcome.

"You certainly took a long time." Miss Hamilton seems suspicious.

"I . . . I had a hard time finding what he was looking for." Willow joins her behind the desk.

"You need to be more familiar with the call numbers," Miss Hamilton says. Excuses carry no weight with her.

"Hey, c'mon, it took me forever to figure out the stacks." Carlos flashes Willow a sympathetic smile.

"I suppose." Miss Hamilton looks back and forth between the two of them. "All right then, you're done, Willow. I'll see you in a few days."

Willow glances at the clock in surprise. She had no idea that her shift was over. Miss Hamilton was right, she had been gone for a while. She didn't realize that their conversation had lasted that long.

Well, that's one more day I don't have to live through again, she thinks as she grabs her bag and dashes out the door.

Willow pushes past the students clustered around the library entrance, filthying the air with cigarettes, and heads toward the rack where everybody stows their bikes. It takes her a second to remember that she doesn't have a bike anymore, that it's still back in her parents' house, leaning against the garage wall. Too bad, really—it would make the trip back and forth from work much easier.

But why should her life be any easier anyway?

She heads off campus and onto the street. Just two blocks and she'll be in the park. Somehow the trees make her feel better.

But not good enough, she thinks as she pats her bag. *Never good enough.*

Without a bike it takes about twenty minutes to walk to her brother's apartment. Her brother, his wife, Cathy, and their baby daughter's apartment. It's not such a bad place. David, Cathy, and Isabelle live downstairs and she has David's old office, the maid's room at the top. It's much better than it sounds, actually. Her room is very small, but kind of special, like something out of a fairy tale, or a movie about Paris. It's got a great view of the park, and Cathy made it pretty just for her, hanging lace curtains and painting the walls a pale apple green, not that Willow really cares about things like that anymore.

"Which way are you going?"

Willow whips around in alarm. She had no idea that Guy was behind her. Has he been following her? Hoping to hear more, maybe get her to tell him some juicy details?

"Are you headed toward the park?" he asks, his steps falling into place beside hers. "I always walk that way."

Willow wants to ask him what he knows about her, but she's not quite sure how. She wants to ask him if he was deliberately stringing her along before, or if he truly didn't recognize her at first. She supposes that it's possible—after all, she didn't recognize him. But she's been lost in her own world. Nothing makes any kind of impression on her these days. As the new girl in school, she's bound to be noticed, even if she didn't come with a scarlet letter *K* embroidered on her chest.

"Hey, Guy, hold up!" a tall dark-haired student calls to Guy from across the street. He hurries over, a pile of books under his arm.

"Adrian, what are you doing up here?" Guy stops for a second.

"Looking into some AP stuff." Adrian glances back and forth between Willow and Guy.

"Oh, sorry, Adrian this is Willow. She goes to our school."

"Oh yeah?" Adrian smiles at her. "Are you new? I haven't seen you around before."

"Yes. I'm new," Willow says. She looks at him carefully. He seems like he's being straight with her, and she feels a little better. Maybe she doesn't stand out quite as much as she thought she did.

"We should definitely talk if you're thinking of taking classes here. I've already picked out a couple of possibilities." Guy hands Adrian a piece of paper scribbled all over with course numbers and descriptions.

"Yeah, you know, I probably should take one of these."

16

Adrian glances at the paper. "But on the other hand, the idea of a really easy senior year is pretty appealing."

The spotlight's off of her. Willow breathes a sigh of relief. She should go now, while the going's good.

"Listen, I have to get out of here." She offers a glimpse of a smile.

"Oh, sure. Adrian, I'll call you later." To Willow's surprise, Guy says good-bye to his friend and continues walking with her. "So, where are you off to now?"

"I'm going home." Even as she says the words, Willow is struck by how misleading they are. Her brother's apartment may be her home now, but it doesn't feel like it. It doesn't feel like it at all.

"Want to stop on the way and get some coffee?" Guy asks.

No.

She does not want any coffee. She wants to be alone. Still, Willow can't help thinking that any of her friends from back home would be thrilled to have someone like Guy ask them out. She wonders how she would have felt if he made the offer, say a year ago. Would she have been flattered? Would she have liked the idea? Would she have liked *him*? Willow squints trying to see herself as she'd been the fall before. *Of course* she would have liked him. Why not? Cute and reads books too. Too bad last year's girl is dead.

"So how about it?" He shifts his backpack to his left shoulder and flashes her a smile. "There's a great place a few blocks from here. Best cappuccino you've ever had, and the pastries aren't bad either."

First coffee, then a movie. Then a few more walks in the park. Willow knows how this kind of thing works. Then *feelings.* Just the thought of it makes her flesh crawl. She's done with feelings. She doesn't ever want to feel anything again.

"No thank you." Even to her own ears her voice sounds cold and unfriendly. Perfect.

Guy shrugs. He looks a little disappointed.

Life's full of disappointments, Guy. Willow kicks a stone out of her path.

"Okay, sure, maybe another time." But he doesn't say good-bye, he just keeps walking alongside her.

Why doesn't he go away? Willow thinks fretfully. *Maybe he likes what he's been hearing. Maybe he just likes a challenge.*

She wonders briefly what he would think if he saw the blade marks on her arm. Would that be enough of a challenge for him? She's never shown anyone, and he certainly won't be the first. Still, how can she get rid of him?

"So how come you're living with your brother?" Guy asks. "Are your parents on sabbatical? Because I remember your brother saying that they were in the field too." He smiles again, completely unaware of the effect he's having on her.

Is he like Adrian? He really knows nothing about her? Or is it that he wants to hear her say the words?

In any case, he's given her an out. She knows how to get rid of him now.

"They're not on sabbatical." Willow's voice is hard. She stops walking and turns to face Guy head-on. She looks him straight in the eye. So closely, she can see the brown flecks in among the hazel. His eyes are beautiful, but that hardly matters to her. He returns her gaze. He's not smiling now, but looking at her just as deeply. Anyone passing by would take them for a romantic young couple. They must make a pretty picture as they stand facing each other under the leafy bower of trees.

"But your parents are profs, right?" He breaks the silence. "Your father's in anthro and your mother's an archaeologist? Because I once went—"

"They're dead." Willow says the words coolly, dispassionately. She enjoys seeing Guy's face turn pale. "They're dead," she repeats just to make sure he gets it. "And I'm the one who killed them."

CHAPTER THREE

How come you're living with your brother?

But your parents are profs, right? Because I once went . . .

Guy's questions ring in her ears. His pleasant voice is distorted by memory into something querulous and insistent.

But your parents are profs, right? Because I once went . . .

All right, all right, set it to music already!

Willow rolls onto her stomach, the book she's been trying to read for the past half hour tumbles to the floor as she buries her face in the pillow in a vain attempt to shut out the chattering in her head.

But it's useless. His questions keep repeating themselves and far, far worse than any question he could think to ask, is her own response:

I'm the one who killed them.

How many times throughout the coming years will she be called upon to say those words?

She can barely even remember it. It was raining, that's all

20

she knows. They'd been out to dinner and her parents had wanted to have a second bottle of wine, so they decided that Willow should be the one to drive. She remembers her father tossing her the keys, the slickness of the road, and the sound of the windshield wipers.

Sometimes in her dreams she hears the sound of the rain.

Willow turns her head listlessly to look out the window. There's a faint breeze stirring the lace curtains. The dying rays of the sun filter through them and make beautiful patterns on the floor.

The view outside her window is particularly nice, and if she could bring herself to be interested in anything, it would be that. In the morning and evening the park is filled with joggers. In the afternoon young mothers take over and there are always plenty of lovers winding their way down the leaf-strewn paths. It's like a living painting. Back before the accident, when she used to care about things, Willow used to spend a lot of time doing watercolors. Back then she would have liked nothing more than to sit by this window for hours and try to capture the changing scene outside.

Willow glances over at her desk, at the box of watercolors and assortment of brushes that Cathy bought for her. Like her bike, like most of her things, she'd left her painting supplies at home. It was incredibly thoughtful of Cathy to replace them for her, and she should repay that thoughtfulness, by at least attempting to use them, but somehow she can't summon the energy.

Of course Cathy has been kind in so many ways. She'd worked hard to make this room nice for Willow, and with its soft colors and pretty furniture, it is especially lovely. Far nicer than anything she had at home. At home she'd moved into David's old room because it was the biggest. The walls were black, a leftover from his heavy metal days, and Willow and her mother had always promised each other that they'd get around to changing them.

Who knew that four black walls could feel so safe?

Willow sits up abruptly, opens the window, and sticks her head out. The air is soft with just the slightest breeze that ruffles the hair around her face. This is her favorite time of day, just before the evening becomes the night.

If she were back home now, she'd probably be talking on the phone with one of her friends. That's the way things usually went: She used to hang out with her friends after school, come home and get her work done, gossip on the phone before dinner, or maybe, if she didn't have a lot of homework, go for a bike ride on the trails behind her house.

Now the pattern of her days is different. She sleepwalks through school, has no friends to speak of, goes to the library, tries and *fails* to do her homework, and eats whatever Cathy orders in—all to the accompaniment of the razor.

She's left her old friends behind as surely as she's left her old life. They all belong to another world, one she has no intention of visiting again. She never takes their calls, deletes their e-mails, and one by one they've all stopped trying to get in touch with her. The only person who still makes an effort to contact her is Markie, her best friend, and Willow knows that it will only take a few more unanswered messages before she too stops trying.

She shuts the window with a sigh. If she does nothing else, she should at least make an effort with her homework.

Willow picks up the book she'd been reading. *Bulfinch's Mythology*. She's supposed to get through fifty pages for tomorrow. After that she has to get started on a paper for the same class. It should be easy too. The book is one she's read a thousand times before. She flutters the pages of the cheap paperback as she recalls the first edition that used to rest on her father's desk, the flyleaf inscribed by him in his favorite deep blue ink.

Of course it's probably still there. The house stands just as it did, it hasn't even gone on the market yet.

At first Willow had thought that she would be staying there, that David, Cathy, and Isabelle would join her. In some ways it would make the most sense. After all, this cozy apartment, while just the right size for two adults and an infant, feels somewhat cramped now that she's moved in. But David had vetoed the idea from the start, claiming the commute would be too difficult. Willow's parents took the train in for over twenty years, but that was only twice a week, and while David's teaching schedule is similar, Cathy's job would require her to make the trip every day.

Still, as uncomfortable as things sometimes get, Willow has to agree with her brother. Although their house may be large and roomy, living there would be far from easy, and not because of the traveling involved. The house is simply too crowded with memories and reminders. It is too crowded with ghosts.

She's only been there a handful of times since the accident. The first occasion had been when David wanted to pack up their parents' books and move them to the apartment. That had proved to be a disastrous idea, which they abandoned before they even got halfway through. In fact, that excursion had affected David so badly that he refused to enter the house again. So the next time they went, he and Cathy waited outside in the car, while Willow, feeling like a refugee, a displaced person, fleeing her country for unknown territory, had run around grabbing whatever clothes would fit into her backpack. Now she wishes that she had taken the time to think about what she was packing. Her bag hadn't held much, and she's constantly borrowing things from Cathy anyway. Wouldn't she have been better off taking some of the books that she cared about instead of three pairs of jeans, a couple of shirts, and a skirt? She would love to be reading her father's copy of *Bulfinch* instead of this flimsy paperback that she bought at one of the chain bookstores around the city.

Willow doesn't know why her throat hurts. She can't understand the way her eyes are prickling all of a sudden.

It's just a book!

She throws the paperback across the room, where it hits the wall before landing on the floor with its pages all askew.

"Mouka touka hashatouka . . ."

Willow is stunned. Her face turns white and she grips the corner of the candlewick bedspread as her mother's voice floats up the stairs. It takes her a moment, then she realizes that it's Cathy singing to Isabelle. David must have taught her the song, an old Russian lullaby that their mother used to sing to them.

She gets up from the bed and walks into the bathroom to splash some cold water on her face. She stares in the mirror for a few seconds, looking at herself as if she were a stranger.

Who is this?

She supposes that to anyone else she looks exactly the same as she always did, except for her hair, that is. She doesn't have the energy or inclination to fuss with it like she once did, so she just wears it in a braid that hangs halfway down her back.

But *she* doesn't recognize herself. Maybe her face isn't any different, but the look in her eyes is. Worse than dead, their expression is simply blank. She reaches out a hand to cover them in the mirror. She remembers the reflection that used to stare back at her. Those eyes weren't dead.

Willow had never known that she used to be happy. It had simply never occurred to her that her life had all that she would ever need or want.

The one thing that can make Willow laugh these days is how much she used to take things for granted. In the past, little hurts, like doing badly in school, or getting dumped by a guy, really used to throw her. How was she to know what was lying in store for her? She shakes her head at how foolish she used to be, getting upset because her favorite dress got lost at the cleaners, or something equally stupid.

Stupid!

She has an urge suddenly to smash her head against the mirror. Wipe that silly expression off her face. She knows she can't, though. Not here, not now. Not with Cathy downstairs, and David just coming in the door.

Instead, she regards herself calmly, then screws up her mouth and spits at her reflection with as much venom as she can muster.

Willow knows she's being melodramatic, but so what? The

spit trails down the mirror and she's confronted, once again, by a pair of dead eyes.

Who are you?

This isn't the Willow that she's lived inside for the past seventeen years. This is someone else.

A killer.

A cutter.

Willow turns away from the mirror. Spitting at herself. That's juvenile, straight out of a B movie, and really, accomplishes nothing. But cutting, that's something else again.

She stares down at her arms for a moment. If someone were to look carefully, the angry red marks underneath the fine cotton of her blouse would be clearly visible. But nobody ever does look carefully.

She rolls up her sleeves and examines the most accessible cuts, then opens the medicine cabinet and takes out a tube of disinfectant. She's scrupulously careful not to let her wounds get infected. She doesn't need the complications. Already Cathy's been giving her strange looks. She keeps asking why Willow wants to borrow long-sleeved shirts when it's such a beautiful, mild Indian summer. She doesn't understand that Willow, who used to be so concerned with what she wore, now selects her outfits with one criterion only: Will her clothes cover her scars?

Taking care of her stuff isn't the easy task it once was either. She can't just toss her dirty things into the communal laundry hamper. The other day she had to bury one of her own bloodstained blouses in the park. She simply can't risk leaving things like that around. Losing the shirt didn't bother her, but she hated digging around in the dirt. Later on, when she was walking home, she was sure that she saw a Rottweiler playing with it.

Willow hears the phone ring. It's just about Markie's favorite time to call. Quickly, without thinking, she reaches behind her and turns on the shower.

"Willow?" Cathy calls. "Phone for you! Markie."

She leans out the bathroom door. "Yeah, sorry, I'm in the shower!"

That should take care of that. She leaves the shower running, takes off her jeans and shirt, and sitting down on the floor of the bathroom, she spreads some of the antiseptic cream on a particularly nasty-looking cut.

It takes a while, at least ten minutes, but finally she is done ministering to her wounds.

"Willow?" David calls. "Dinner!"

"Coming," Willow calls back as she turns off the shower. She puts her clothes on, wincing a little as her jeans stick to the cream. Of course it would make much more sense to bandage all of them, but the gauze would look too bulky under her clothes.

"Hey." She tries to look lively as she enters the kitchen.

"God, your hair dries fast." Cathy smiles at her.

"Oh, yeah, uhh ... Shower cap, didn't even bother to unbraid it." Willow smiles in return. It's something of an effort. Just the thought of sitting down and eating dinner is more than enough to wear her out completely, because it's the one time of day that she can be sure of coming face-to-face with the only other surviving member of her family.

It shouldn't be like this. Seeing her brother should be the lone bright spot in the otherwise bleak landscape that is her life, and yet it simply isn't so. Because somehow, that rainy night last March didn't just end her parents' lives. Somehow—as surely as if he had been in the car with them—she lost her brother that night too.

This feeling is with her always. Their relationship has been so fractured that for all intents and purposes she could be living with a stranger. In a way it is almost more difficult to bear than the loss of her parents, they are dead and gone forever. But to be in constant contact with her brother, to the person that she was once closest with, to the single person spared her—to see him, talk to him, and yet have no connection with him whatsoever is more painful than she could possibly have imagined.

Sometimes Willow tries to convince herself that things will return to normal between them. After all, there have been times in the past when they didn't get along. He is ten years older than she is, and that age difference hasn't always made for an easy relationship.

Willow thinks back to when she was five and he was fifteen. Back then David didn't like having a little sister. He wanted to be out doing his own thing instead of babysitting, and Willow hadn't liked him much either. But things had changed as they got older. Sometime around when she turned ten or eleven, things had evened out somehow, he'd become her confidant, her friend, her protector. Suddenly it had been fun to have a brother who was so much her senior.

If Willow tries hard enough, she can pretend, for moments at a time, that she isn't living with David, that she is merely visiting the way she might have last year, say whenever her parents' attention threatened to become suffocating, when their involvement in her life felt oppressive rather than comforting. At times like that she would stay with David and Cathy for the weekend, much to the envy of all her friends.

Willow spends a lot of time thinking about those weekends, about what things had been like then. David had just been finishing graduate school. He and Cathy had been about to become parents. Everything had seemed perfect.

But Willow has smashed her brother's picture-perfect life as surely as she smashed her parents' car. Cathy didn't want to go back to work. She *had* to go back instead of staying at home with Isabelle like she had planned to. Instead of preparing for his classes, David has to worry about money all the time. He has to worry about how he's going to make ends meet. He has to worry about Willow.

In many ways this is a burden that he appears to accept easily. He is so strong, so considerate, so capable, his treatment of her is so unfailingly correct that to the outside observer it must seem as if nothing is amiss. He is absurdly polite to her, it as if she is a stranger whose welfare has been entrusted to him, and he handles that responsibility with the utmost seriousness. But there is a wall of glass between them.

David never, *never* talks about the accident. His conversations with her are limited to the minutiae of her daily life. Even when they are forced to discuss logistical things, like how much of her library salary has to go toward household expenses, or when they should put their parents' house on the market, he manages to avoid any suggestion of how it is that they've found themselves in such an extraordinary situation.

At first Willow was sure that it was just a matter of time. That David would eventually confront her. She kept waiting for him to yell at her, scream, shake her, do anything but treat her with such aloof courtesy. But as the months wore on, it became increasingly clear to her that he had no intention of ever talking about what had happened.

She doesn't feel like she can broach the subject on her own either. If David doesn't want to talk about it, it can only be because of how painful the topic is, and Willow refuses, absolutely refuses, to hurt him more than she already has.

Still, his coldness toward her upsets her terribly; it is the worst condemnation that she could endure. And yet she is fully in accord with his assessment of her: She is no longer his little sister, she is their parents' murderer. Why should she expect any other treatment? Why should she even expect him to be as kind as he is?

"How was school today?" David asks as she sits down. Cathy passes her a cardboard container of cold sesame noodles. Obviously tonight is Chinese.

"Fine," Willow says. She dumps some of the noodles onto her plate with a sigh. She knows that that answer isn't good enough, that David expects a complete and full accounting of everything that she did, but she's so tired of lying to him, she just doesn't have the strength anymore. She stares down at her plate. The noodles look like worms.

"Uh-huh. Well, I don't really know what *fine* means. Why don't you tell me what's going on in your classes? Didn't you just have a quiz in French? How did that go?"

A quiz? The only thing Willow can remember about French class is seeing that other girl with the scratches on her arm—that, and the fact that she'd run out of class so that she could indulge in her extracurricular activities.

But she can hardly tell David about *that*.

Oh right, the quiz. . . . They did have one the other day, Willow realizes. She must have mentioned it to David at one of their nightly grilling sessions.

"We . . . I didn't get it back yet. I answered everything, at least." This happens to be true, but it was the merest stroke of good luck that she'd been able to finish the quiz, given that she'd barely even opened the textbook.

"All right." He nods thoughtfully. "What about your other classes? Is there anything special I should know about?"

Sigh.

Willow wishes that Cathy would interrupt him, change the subject somehow, but she's busy feeding the baby some noxious-looking concoction, so Willow has no choice but to answer.

"No—well, I do have this paper to do for that class I'm taking with the *Bulfinch.* . . . You know, the one about myths and heroes. . . ."

"Well, that should be easy enough for you," David says. "Do you have a topic picked out already? When is it due?"

"Uh . . . no. No topic, not yet. . . ." Willow avoids his eyes. She has a topic, all right, and not one of her own choosing. How can she tell her brother that the teacher has asked her to write about the themes of loss and redemption as shown in the relationship between Demeter and Persephone? She can't, she just can't look him in the eyes and talk to him about another motherless child. "It's not due for three weeks anyway, so I have some time to come up with one. . . ."

"What about the library? How was that today? Any better? Is Miss Hamilton being nicer to you? Do you want me to talk to her?"

"No! I mean, thank you, but no. She's fine, really. . . ."

An idea occurs to Willow. David wants to know how things went at the library? Maybe she should tell him about that guy she met, well, *Guy*, in fact. She wonders if possibly, just *possibly*, his reaction to this piece of news will be different from the way he responds to her daily recitations regarding school and homework. The responsibility of being in charge of her education may be new to him, but this kind of thing, well . . .

Willow remembers a time last year when she went to meet David at one of his classes. A fellow graduate student, not realizing that she was a sophomore in high school, had asked her out. Their father had not been at all amused, but David had thought it was hilarious.

"I . . . I met someone in the library who was in one of your classes last year." Willow says this tentatively. She's floating the idea out there, kind of like a test balloon. She wants to see how he'll take it. She wants to believe that somehow, some way, he's capable of unbending toward her, and that perhaps, talking about the kind of thing he used to tease her about might just be the key.

"Really?" Cathy says. She sounds interested and she glances at Willow as she continues unsuccessfully to try to get Isabelle to eat. "What was their name?"

"Male or female?" David says at the same time. He looks at her over the rim of his glass. His tone is anything but lighthearted.

Oh boy. . . .

"It's a guy. . . . Well, actually, his name *is* Guy. I thought that was kind of funny."

And nice too. It's a nice name.

"Guy?" David is thoughtful. "I think I remember Guy—he's still in high school, isn't he? I guess that's all right. . . ."

Oh for God's sake!

"He was taking my class to get some college credit," David continues. "He's very smart, and a lot more hardworking than most of the regular students I get. Believe me, I wish I had more like him. So what did he have to say for himself?"

Now that sounds a little bit like the brother she used to know. Maybe this was a good idea after all, except even as she thinks this, Willow realizes that she herself is no longer capable of lighthearted conversation. How can she even answer such an innocuous question? What can she possibly say?

He asked why I was living with you and I told him that I killed Mom and Dad.

Of course they did talk about other things, but those topics are also off limits. Maybe last year Willow would have felt free to tell David that Guy likes that bookstore downtown, but now she can't. She can't because any mention of that place—which David loves—would trigger too many memories of their father. He was the one who had first taken them there.

"Umm, I think he said that we looked alike. . . ." Willow looks at her brother in despair. It's impossible not to notice how tired he is, how worn, how empty his own eyes are.

She wishes so much that she could take that emptiness away.

But then she remembers something else Guy said. Something that it *won't* hurt her brother to hear, and she grasps at it like a lifeline.

"Oh, you know what, I almost forgot." She tries to sound enthusiastic. "He thought that you were a great professor, I mean, he kind of went on about that." It's not much, it won't bring their parents back, it won't make his life easier in any appreciable way, but it's the best she has to offer.

"Really?" David says slowly. Maybe he's not bowled over by the news, but he does seem a little interested, his eyes look a little less dead.

"Really." Willow is emphatic. She tries to think of something else to say. Some way that she can elaborate, expand the compliment. "I think he said that he was seriously thinking of going into anthropology, I mean, major in it when he gets to college. He said that your class had convinced him that's what he should be doing."

Of course he'd said nothing of the kind. Willow has no idea what he wants to do. And anyway, if anything had influenced him, it was *Tristes Tropiques*, not her brother. But still, she can't help feeling a glimmer of satisfaction as she watches David's expression change.

"Oh come on!" Cathy exclaims suddenly. She puts the spoon and the jar of baby food down in frustration. "I can't get her to eat anything."

"Well, what do you expect?" David asks as he picks up the jar and examines it closely. "Organic strained peas? Who *would* like that? She has good taste, that's all." He gets up and lifts Isabelle out of her high chair. "Wouldn't you rather have some spare ribs?" he asks the baby.

"Oh David, please!" Cathy gives him a look.

"Okay, I'm not being serious. But how about ice cream? She can eat that, can't she? There's nothing wrong with ice cream—we even have some too."

"There's a lot wrong with it," Cathy says, exasperated.

"But you'd like it, wouldn't you?" He holds Isabelle above his head as he talks to her. "I can tell that you're going to be a girl who likes her chocolate ice cream. Oh c'mon." David turns back to Cathy. "It would be kind of fun to see if she likes it."

Willow isn't jealous of her niece, not exactly, and she certainly has no desire for her brother to talk to her the way he does to an infant. But as she watches the way that David plays with Isabelle, as she sees his face finally light up, it is borne in on her, for perhaps the thousandth time, that she has *lost* her brother.

✳

Willow pushes the *Bulfinch* away listlessly. It's one in the morning and in spite of the fact that she's been sitting at her desk for the past four hours, she's managed to accomplish almost nothing. Not only has she gotten no work done, not only is she too restless to fall asleep, but she's starving, hardly surprising since she barely touched anything at dinner earlier.

Maybe she should go downstairs and get something to eat, maybe then she'll be able to focus on her work. She gets up from her chair, walks to the door and opens it a crack. The apartment is completely dark. Good. Willow steals down the stairs slowly, careful not to make a sound. But as she nears the bottom she is dismayed to see that she is not, after all, alone. David is in the kitchen, sitting at the table surrounded by dozens of papers. He's extinguished all of the lights but one.

Well, she has no desire to go into the kitchen now. She can only imagine how uncomfortable it would be for both of them, but as much as she wants to go back upstairs, she can't help staring at her brother. There's something not quite right about the way that he's sitting there.

David's head is in his hands. Is it because he's laughing? But what would he be laughing about? She's heard him complain about grading undergraduate papers enough to know that he doesn't consider it the most amusing task. Besides, he's hardly making any noise. And then Willow realizes why his shoulders are shaking that way, and the reason is so shocking, so disturbing that it literally takes her breath away. She barely has the strength to stand.

Her brother is crying, he is wretched and broken. Though his sobs are barely audible, he is weeping with absolute and total abandon. She's never seen him like this. She's never seen *anyone* like this. Such a naked display of emotion is both alarming and frightening.

Willow clutches the banister with an unsteady hand and lowers herself to sit down on the stairs. She knows what she's doing is wrong, that she should allow David his privacy. But she feels compelled to watch.

Willow stares at him in astonishment. She herself could never do such a thing, she could never give way to her grief like this. Willow wonders if she should go to him. But she knows she can't. Because she is the one who has put him in this position, it is her actions that have given him this pain.

As she's thinking this, Cathy comes up behind David. He doesn't see her, but Willow does. Her dark hair flows down her back, interrupted by the pink shawl that she's thrown on over her nightgown.

Cathy wraps her arms around David. Without turning, he grips her forearms, pulling her closer.

Willow is transfixed. The longing and need that are stamped across David's face are riveting. She watches as Cathy holds him tighter, as tightly as possible, then bends her head to kiss him.

Willow feels like a moth, inexorably drawn to the flame. How would it feel to cry like that? How would it feel to be comforted like that?

If she let herself, she'd drown in a world of pain. But she can't let that happen, she simply wouldn't be able to handle it, not *that* kind of pain. Thankfully she knows how to prevent such a thing.

Willow reaches into the pocket of her robe, feeling for what she knows is there.

She never takes her eyes off of them as she slices into her flesh. The blade bites so deeply that she almost swoons, but still, she never stops looking at David and Cathy.

Her blood spouts as voluptuously as David's tears. It drips unchecked, down her arm and onto the floor as Willow watches Cathy dry David's eyes with her long, long hair.

Willow knows that she should leave. At any moment they could look up. But she can't leave, she can't move. She can only slice deeper and deeper.

The razor doesn't hurt her. Not really.

Not like some things could, anyway. Willow savagely swipes at her wrist.

Not like some things could.

CHAPTER FOUR

Willow leans back against the linden tree in the school garden and closes her book with a deep sigh. She's been trying to read for the past half hour, but it's hopeless. She just can't focus. Instead of seeing the pages in front of her, she just keeps seeing her poor brother.

She's afraid of what will happen the next time they talk. Will her face give her away? She knows that he wouldn't have wanted her to witness that scene. There was something so profoundly . . . well, *intimate* is the only word she can think of—something so intimate, both about his misery and the way that Cathy comforted him.

For once it had been a relief to go to school in the morning. She'd left the house extra early just to avoid running into either of them, hoping that if she didn't have to confront David's red-eyed face over the breakfast table, then she'd be able to forget about what she saw.

Yeah, right!

Missing breakfast had accomplished nothing beyond an empty stomach. Because in spite of the fact that it's a beautiful day, in spite of the fact that she has a free period with nothing else to do but sit outside and read, she simply can't stop thinking about David. She'd known that he was in pain, *of course* she'd known, but to see him like that . . .

Even now she can hardly believe it happened. Since the accident, David has been so contained, so reserved, that to witness him in such a state, shattered and broken, well, it still doesn't seem credible.

Her stomach turns a little as she thinks of how she'd tried to cheer him up over the dinner table with some manufactured compliments. How could she have been so naive, so stupid? How could she think that anything she had to offer, anything that she could give, could help him after the horror that she's put him through?

She hates herself for what she's done to him. But even more than that, she hates herself for being so selfish. Because, after seeing his breakdown, she knows that her primary concern should be for him. But instead all she can think of is that if he can let go like that . . .

Then why is he always so cold and distant with me?

Willow looks up, momentarily distracted as a group of students come into the garden. She recognizes a few of them from some of her classes.

"Hey Willow, what's going on?" one of the girls calls over to her.

"Not much." Willow smiles a little at the other girl. Her

name is Claudia. Willow doesn't know much else about her, but she does know that this girl has been friendly to her once or twice before, and she is grateful for her kindness.

"You want to hang out with us?" Claudia sits down on the grass. She tilts her head to one side and gives Willow a pleasant smile.

No. Willow does not want to join them. She wants to stay under the linden tree and try to read. But she hasn't had much luck with that, and anyway, how can she say no? Claudia's being friendly, it would look odd to reject the overture, and she has a bad feeling that she looks *plenty* odd already.

Willow gets to her feet and slowly walks over to the group. She's a little unsure of what to do or say to these girls. If this had been a year ago, she wouldn't have even waited to be asked. It would have been the most natural thing in the world to go right over to Claudia and introduce herself to everyone else. But now . . . It's not that she's shy exactly, it's more that she doesn't know how to behave around people anymore.

There's something else too, she thinks, as Claudia shifts to make room for her. She wonders if this invitation is as innocent as it seems. Everyone knows that there's something different about her. Well, aside from everything else, she's new, and by itself that's enough to raise questions, even of the most innocent kind. But Willow is sure that the interest she's aroused is more sinister than that. There *must* be a million rumors floating around. There have to be some people who know what happened. There have to be some people who know she lost her parents. There have to be some people who know she *killed* her parents. So far nobody's asked her anything directly, but she can tell that they all want to know her story.

It's hard for Willow not to feel anxious as she sits there. By joining them she's opening the door. Any moment now and the questions she's been dreading could start. So instead of relaxing and enjoying the sunshine and the innocent chatter of the other girls, she waits, tense, to see what will happen.

"If I get into my first choice I'm coloring my hair red," the brunette sitting next to her says.

"Excuse me if I don't get the connection," another girl responds. Willow recognizes this one. This girl *is* already a redhead, she's the one that Willow had been staring at so intently the other day, right before her spectacular pratfall. She's the one with the scratch on her arm. The one that Willow thought might have been a kindred spirit. "And anyway," the redhead continues. "Why do you want to change your color?"

"Well . . ." The brunette lies back on the grass and shields her eyes with a baseball cap. "If I get into my first choice, my parents will be so happy that they won't care if I color my hair, and besides, I like red hair. You should be flattered."

"Yeah Kristen, it's so attention getting." This is from Claudia.

"Did you bring anything to eat?" the brunette under the baseball cap says. Willow can see her name written on one of the books that rests by her side: Laurie.

"I have a day-old Luna bar somewhere," Kristen says, and roots around in her bag.

"Thanks, but I'll pass." Laurie laughs.

"What about you. It's Willow, right?" Laurie lifts the

baseball cap off of one eye and looks at her. "I don't suppose you have anything more appetizing, do you?"

"No, I . . . Nothing . . ." Willow trails off.

"You want to cut out and go for croissants?" Claudia glances at her watch.

"I don't have enough time." Kristen shakes her head. She looks at Willow to see what she has to say about the matter.

Willow tries to smile, but it comes out sort of funny. More like a grimace. She avoids Kristen's gaze and stares at her shoes instead.

"So Willow," Claudia says, fanning herself with her notebook. "What classes are you in, besides history, I mean." She and Willow share fourth-period history.

"Oh, who cares?" Laurie complains from underneath the baseball cap. "I mean, no offense, Willow, but I've had it up to here with school." She makes a slashing motion with her hand at the base of her throat. "You're not a senior, are you? School is all I think about these days. Where will I go next year? What should I do for my last semester of extracurricular to look good on my transcript? I've had it. Can't we just gossip or something?"

"Just making conversation," Claudia says mildly. She nudges Laurie with her boot. "I was trying to be *polite*, you know, Laurie, find out about *Willow*."

"Oh sure." Laurie nods. "Don't think I'm not interested in you, Willow. I'm dying to know if you think I'd look better as a redhead."

But Willow is saved from answering this by the real redhead—Kristen.

"Oh, c'mon Laurie, you're *always* up for talking about this kind of stuff. You're just over it now because your first choice is already a missile lock. You've got the highest SATs of anyone I know." Kristen has found the Luna bar and bites into it. "You've got *nothing* to worry about."

"That's not all it's about," Laurie protests. "I'm not a legacy at any of my top choices. These days it's about a lot more than just grades and scores."

"Kristen's right, Laurie," Claudia says. "Your scores are so good that those other things don't matter. Besides, you've done so much other stuff it's like the Pope sprinkled holy water on your transcript. I'm the one in trouble here." She frowns for a second as she gathers her hair into a ponytail. "I mean, not only are my scores not that great, but what else have I done?"

"Maybe you should retake the SATs," Laurie suggests. "What about you, Willow? Are you taking any prep courses this year?"

"They're so worth it." Kristen nods.

Willow knows that she should say something. Anything. She feels more and more uncomfortable sitting there and not joining in, but what *can* she say? An SAT prep course? Nothing could seem less important.

Of course, if things hadn't changed so much for her she probably would be thinking about taking an SAT prep course. But things have changed. College? How about the moon? If she's thought about life after high school at all, it's only been to wonder whether David will have put the house on the market by the time she graduates—otherwise they won't be able to pay for college.

There's an enormous gulf that separates her from these girls. She knows, because she used to be on the other side along with them. She wishes—desperately—that she could connect with them, but she's simply forgotten how.

Willow casts about for something, *anything,* to say. Then Kristen crumples up the Luna bar wrapper and stretches out her arm to put it in her bag. For a second the red mark that Willow saw the other day is visible.

"Are you a cut—" Willow blurts out before she can stop herself. Her voice is much too loud, but even worse . . .

What am I saying??

"I mean, are you a cut—"

God almighty!!

Can she save this? They're all looking at her expectantly, she's got to do *something.*

Cut, cutters, cutting, what the hell can she spin out of *cut*?? Willow looks around at them, looks at Kristen and remembers. . . .

"I mean a *cat* . . . A cat person . . ."

Better than cutter, but just barely.

"What I mean is . . ." Willow pauses and closes her eyes for a second. If she stays like that, will they all just get up and go away? Forget it. She doesn't have that kind of luck, she'd better just finish this thing. "Do you . . . Do you . . ."

What?? Does she what??

"Do you have a kitten?" she finally manages after a few more seconds. The girls look at her in stupefaction.

Good God!

Willow can feel that her face is flaming. To think, she'd only sat down with them because she hadn't wanted to seem strange!

"No," Kristen says after a few moments. "I'm way too

allergic. Which reminds me." She turns to Laurie. "That lotion you told me to try gave me the worst rash." She rolls her sleeve up all the way and starts to rub her arm vigorously, and Willow can see that the mark she'd been so fascinated by is in fact *just a scratch*. Absolutely nothing more. Most probably brought on by the way Kristen is irritating her skin. Even as she watches, the other girl clearly raises a welt or two. Unlike the cuts that score Willow's arm, this girl's abrasions are perfectly innocent. She is no more a kindred spirit than anyone else in this little group. Than anyone else *anywhere*. "How come you want to know if I have a kitten?" Kristen fixes her shirt and looks at Willow. "Were you . . . Were you maybe thinking of getting one?" She says this slowly, as if she were talking to someone who doesn't speak the language very well. She's trying to be nice, but clearly, she thinks that Willow is an idiot.

Even worse, it's hard to miss the bemused glances that the other girls are sharing.

"Well," says Laurie. She removes the baseball cap and rolls over to rest her head on her hand. "My sister volunteers at a pet shelter if you need me to set you up with a kitten."

Willow nods. She can tell they all think she's weird. They'll try to be nice, offer to help with kittens, but behind her back they'll roll their eyes and thank God that they're not crazy like she is. Maybe they'll tell other people that they've hung out with the new girl. No, they don't know the whole story, but she is *strange*, all right. . . . Maybe they'll add a few rumors of their own.

"Excuse me." Willow scrambles to her feet. She can't sit there with them anymore. "I have to . . ." To what? She can't think of anything to say. But it doesn't really matter. Is it her imagination, or do they look relieved to see her go? The invitation had only been out of politeness anyway.

"See you in history," Willow manages.

"Right." Claudia nods.

Willow moves as fast as she can out of the garden and into the building.

She still has some time before her next class. But she doesn't know where she should go. Neither the library nor the cafeteria holds any appeal.

She doesn't know where she should go, but she knows what she wants to do, all right.

She's a little worried about the practicalities of it, though. Her arms have so many marks on them—you could almost play connect the dots. She's going to have to wait until some of the cuts heal before she can start working there again. What about her legs? She's wearing jeans—can she even get to her legs? If she does it on her stomach, will her sweater stick to it? Willow shakes her head. She should have planned for eventualities like this. Tomorrow she'll wear a button-down shirt.

Still, as desperate as she is, just thinking about the details helps to calm her down, makes her forget the embarrassment of what just happened, of how awful she sounded when she asked about the kitten. It almost makes her forget how sad it is that she *won't* be taking a stupid SAT prep course.

Willow heads for the bathroom with a sense of purpose, but she's in for a letdown, because the bathroom isn't empty. Two girls are smoking in there. Another illicit activity, only much more acceptable.

Willow isn't quite sure what to do. She could wait until they leave, but there's no knowing how long that will take. As

Willow considers this, the girl closest to her stubs out her cigarette in the sink and lights up another one.

"Want one?" she asks, offering the pack to Willow.

Willow shakes her head. She knows how ironic this is, she might as well smoke, why not? But cigarettes, while damaging, are pleasurable too, and besides . . .

Nicotine, that takes years before it hurts . . .

She backs out the door and it swings shut behind her. Willow looks up and down the hall, which is blessedly empty.

Willow starts walking. She doesn't know where she's headed, she's not even sure where this particular hall leads to, she just knows that she has to move, or she'll explode.

She's moving faster and faster, her legs hurt, she realizes suddenly that she's running, hurtling down the hall, rules be damned. Her ribs ache, both from the labored breaths that she just manages to draw and the way that her backpack is slapping against her shoulder.

But that's good. All of that is good. Not as good as a razor would be, but uncomfortable enough to distract her.

Unfortunately, the halls are only so long, and Willow only has so much stamina. She's furious, *furious* when she reaches a dead end and she finds herself staring at a brick wall. If it weren't such a cliché she'd start pounding the brick with her fists.

If it weren't such a cliché, and bruised hands weren't so hard to hide.

Instead she collapses against the wall, her lungs screaming, even if she herself is silent, and tries to focus on how badly her ribs hurt, on whether or not running that way opened up some of the cuts on her legs.

She moves one sneakered foot gingerly up and down her calf, rubbing, feeling if there are any open sores.

A hit! Willow looks down. A small bloodstain is creeping through the denim of her jeans. Not much, not something that anyone else would notice, but . . .

There's a hand on her shoulder. An inquiring voice. Willow looks up to see the face of her physics teacher, Mr. Moston.

He looks alarmed.

Willow doesn't want to talk to him. She wants to focus on the way that the wound on her leg feels. She wants to make it feel even worse by worrying it with her shoe. But unfortunately she can't. Somewhere in the back of her mind she knows that if she doesn't pull it together right now there'll be repercussions: a conference with a guidance counselor, a lecture. Maybe her brother will be called in. Most *probably* her brother will be called in. Just the thought of that is enough to shock her back into reality.

"Willow? Are you all right?" His manner is sympathetic, gentle, solicitous. Is it sincere? She can't tell anymore. There have been so many people over the past seven months asking her if she was all right in just that tone.

Willow has come to hate that tone.

"Are you all right?" He repeats the question, and Willow has to fight not to laugh at how absurd he sounds. Why is it that people only ask if somebody is all right when it's obvious that they *aren't*?

"Is there anything I can do to help?" he continues.

Willow is worried that his next move will be to offer to take her to the infirmary, or maybe worse, to get in touch with David. She'd better start talking, and fast.

"No. Thank you," she says finally. "I'm okay, really. I'm fine now. I was just a little . . ." She trails off uncertainly, hoping that Moston will be so relieved that she's actually responding that he won't demand more convincing answers.

"Do you want to come and help me set up in the physics lab?" Mr. Moston asks. He says this as if she were five years old and he was offering her an ice cream cone. It's clear he means well, but this is beyond him. He's young, probably younger than David. Willow's heard that this is his first teaching job. She's sure that he's never dealt with a student in her condition before.

Willow doesn't care that he's completely unable to offer anything in the way of real help, she's just glad that he doesn't really know what's going on with her. He probably just thinks she's fragile. Maybe he's already gotten the heads-up about her in the teachers' lounge: *Give her time, don't press her, she'll need a little breathing room. . . .*

"Okay," Willow manages to say after a few seconds. "I'll help you set up." After all, physics is the next class on her schedule, and there's nothing else for her to do. There's no place else for her to go.

Willow straightens up. She can feel a thin line of blood trickling its way down her right leg and she concentrates on that as she follows him to the physics lab.

Moston pushes the door open and Willow enters the musty room behind him. Class hasn't started yet, but there's already another girl puttering around in there.

"Hey, Vicki, how's the experiment going?" Moston asks.

The girl looks up with a start. "Um, well, not perfect yet," she stammers, clearly nervous, "but I think I can get it to work out this time."

"All right then." Mr. Moston nods. "I'll leave you to it in that case." He riffles through the papers he's carrying, a frown on his face. "Willow." He looks up. "I thought I had last week's corrected homeworks with me, but apparently I left them in my office. Do you want to come with me, or are you okay waiting here?"

"I'll be fine," Willow assures him, but she's embarrassed. He's made her sound like some kind of special case, which she guesses she is, but he doesn't have to advertise. She glances over at Vicki, but thankfully she's too busy with her own stuff to be paying them much attention. She probably didn't even hear.

Willow dumps her bag on the table. Mr. Moston leaves, and she sits down on one of the stools with a sigh. Now she can get back to exploring the cut on her leg.

She props her chin in her hands and watches idly as Vicki bustles around. It's important to keep her face clear, not to give anything away with her expression. She has to look like there's absolutely nothing going on underneath the table. She has to look like she's not trying to open the cut further, she has to look like she's not smearing the toe of her sneaker with blood.

She feels like a woman playing footsie with her lover at a fancy dinner party.

Her leg hurts. It's extraordinary that a two-inch cut could be so painful. It's easy to do, really, just open it up before it's healed, take something blunt like the toe of a sneaker and try to enlarge the cut up to three or four inches . . .

Now that she has her fix, now that the pain is flowing through her blood like a narcotic, Willow is free to think about other things. She tries to follow what Vicki is doing, but the experiment she's working on seems totally unfamiliar. She wonders if she should recognize what's going on. Maybe she's behind in this class too.

"What are you working on?" Willow asks. "That's not supposed to be part of this week's homework, is it?"

"Oh, no." Vicki scribbles something in her lab book without looking up. "I'm just doing this for extra credit. I . . . I barely passed last year, and I've really got to bring up my grades this semester." She flushes a little as she says this. "Moston said that doing some independent experiments was the way to go." Vicki snaps her notebook closed and narrowly misses knocking over some equipment.

"What's the experiment?" Willow asks. Her leg hurts enough that she can leave it alone now.

"Oh, I'm trying to figure out this thing about acceleration under gravity. I mean, who cares? I just want to— Hi, Guy," Vicki interrupts herself to say as the door swings open.

Willow knows before she turns around that it has to be the same Guy that she met in the library. Of course there *could* be others. He's not in her physics class, so there's no reason why it has to be him, but she knows it is. So what? She has nothing to be ashamed of with him. She didn't ask *him* about any kittens.

"Hey, Vicki, Willow." He smiles at them. "Is Moston around? I wanted to drop off this lab report."

"He should be back in a minute," Vicki says. She attaches a weight to a length of metal tubing and sets it to swinging back and forth.

Willow can't help thinking that it's no wonder Vicki has to do extra credit projects. The girl's completely clueless—anyone can see that the way she's set things up is extremely precarious. The little metal weight is swaying dangerously close to a group of glass beakers, some filled with fluid, clearly part of another experiment.

She's about to suggest that Vicki move the apparatus away from the glasses, when the weight smacks into one of them. Willow watches as several of them tumble to the floor with a loud crash, all shattering beyond repair. A nasty blue liquid starts to seep across the tiles.

"Oh, Christ!" Vicki exclaims.

"It's not that bad," Guy hastens to reassure her as he hurries over to inspect the damage.

"Not that bad?!" Vicki looks at him in disbelief. "Are you crazy? It's disastrous! I'm only doing this stupid experiment because I'm so far behind! The last thing I need is to wreck someone else's! He's going to kill me!"

"We should probably clean it up before he gets back," Willow says as she joins them, hobbling slightly. "Here." She grabs some sponges sitting near the sink and tosses one to Guy. "We need something to take care of the glass." She gets down on her hands and knees and starts wiping up the blue fluid.

"Oh, what's the use?" Vicki wails. She's practically wringing her hands.

Willow is shocked to see that she's on the verge of tears. Doesn't this girl know that a couple of broken beakers and a failed physics experiment are nothing to cry over? Willow sits back on her heels, the sponge dangling uselessly from her hand, and stares at Vicki. Doesn't this girl realize how *lucky* she is that the worst thing in her life is some broken glass?

Tears, actual tears, start to form in Vicki's eyes and roll down her cheeks.

Over some broken glass?

Willow is stunned. She can't help it, maybe she should be more charitable, but she simply can't bring herself to feel anything but contempt for someone so weak.

"What's going on?" Mr. Moston has come in. He stands behind Willow and looks at the mess on the floor.

None of them say anything for a few minutes. Vicki has managed to avert her face so that Moston can't see that she's crying.

Willow can see that Vicki is screwing up her courage to tell Mr. Moston what happened.

"My fault. Totally." Willow is surprised to hear her own voice.

She tosses the sponge on the floor and stands up to face Mr. Moston.

"I asked Vicki to show me the experiment," Willow continues, deliberately avoiding looking at Guy and Vicki. "I was trying to adjust the weight, and while I was doing it, well"—Willow waves her hand toward the mess on the floor— "everything just kind of smashed..."

Willow isn't quite sure why she came to Vicki's aid. Maybe it's because she knows that as the new girl she won't get in trouble. Maybe it's because she knows that Moston is already so worried about her that he wouldn't dare give her a hard time. Or maybe it's because if she's honest with herself, she knows that she *doesn't* really feel contempt for Vicki.

She feels jealous.

Because now that she thinks about it, *really* thinks about it, is it so awful that the worst thing in Vicki's world is some broken glass? Isn't that actually just the way things *should* be?

It wasn't that long ago when some smashed beakers would have been the worst thing that could have happened to her . . .

"All right." Moston nods slowly. "Don't bother cleaning this up, I don't want you getting hurt by the glass. It looks like you already have a cut on your leg, Willow."

Willow is startled. She must have opened it up even further than she thought. She hopes that he isn't going to suggest that she see the nurse. "Uh, it's nothing, honest, I got that before—shaving," she stammers, and immediately starts blushing.

Shaving???

"If you say so." Moston looks dubious. "Still, I don't want anyone else getting hurt. I'll find a maintenance man to take care of this. Guy, can you come with me?" He takes the lab report from him. "I don't want to keep you from your next class, but I need help carrying some equipment."

"No problem," Guy answers Moston, but Willow can feel that his eyes are on her. "I have a free period anyway."

The two of them leave, and Vicki and Willow are alone again.

"I can't believe that you did that," Vicki says. Her eyes light up with something like hero worship.

Willow didn't take the blame in order to win this girl's admiration. But the expression on Vicki's face, well, it's hard not to feel at least a little bit good about that. . . . It's been a long time since someone looked at her without pity.

"Forget it." Willow shrugs. "I knew that I wouldn't get in trouble." She smiles at Vicki as she walks back to her seat.

"Oh, sure, I know," Vicki says, following her. "I mean, forget the fact that you haven't been screwing up in here like I have, Moston would never give you a hard time. He's got to be feeling bad for you, I mean, you having no parents and all."

"Excuse me?" Willow is rifling through her bag for a Band-Aid since she doesn't want anyone else to notice her leg, but she stops and turns back to face Vicki.

"Well, I mean you're an orphan, aren't you? Your parents just died like last year or something? Right? You can probably play on that until you graduate."

Willow feels like she's been slapped. Vicki's casually delivered sentence crushes the little good feeling that was starting to bloom. She's as disenfranchised from this girl as she was from the other ones.

But she shouldn't be angry, not really. Vicki isn't speaking maliciously. She's simply too insensitive to know any better, as clumsy with words as she is with equipment.

Mr. Moston and Guy come back carrying a load of equipment. A group of students enter with them. It's time for class to start.

Willow watches Guy as he helps Moston set up. She thinks about the way he reacted to what she'd told him.

He'd turned pale. He didn't come out with some platitudes. He didn't say anything callous. There was nothing to say and he had the sense to know it.

Willow is so grateful as she remembers this that she almost wants to go up and thank him, to follow him as he leaves the classroom, and tell him how much his consideration meant to her.

For a moment their eyes meet. Willow can feel herself

blushing again, but she's not sure why. He can't possibly know what she's thinking, and anyway the moment's passed. She has no intention of thanking him, or even talking to him. She's learned her lesson. It's probably best to not talk to *anyone* at this point.

She can't talk to people anymore, and clearly, they have just as hard a time talking to her.

If she does speak to Guy again, maybe he won't be so nice. Maybe he'll have heard things about her that will make him change his mind, or maybe that's just the way he felt like acting on that particular day.

Whatever. She'll never know. Still, as she watches him leave, she can't help feeling a small pang. She thinks that he must be the only person she's met in the past seven months who didn't say something stupid or insensitive about the fact that her parents are dead.

And the only one she talked about *Tristes Tropiques* with too.

CHAPTER FIVE

Couldn't she talk just a little more quietly? Willow thinks as she rolls over onto her stomach and buries her head deeper in her book. She's still struggling with the *Bulfinch*; at least she has a couple of weeks before the paper is due. Ordinarily more than enough time, but things are far from ordinary these days, and the other girl's chattering is hardly making her job any easier.

"He *said* he'd call. . . ."

Willow tries to tune her out, but it's a losing battle. She'd cut out of school early and come up to the campus hoping to get some work done, but instead of concentrating on the *Bulfinch*, she keeps being distracted by everything that's going on around her. She'd had to move twice already to avoid being hit by a Frisbee, and then finally, just when she'd gotten herself settled, this girl had plopped down right next to her and started talking, *very loudly*, on her cell phone.

"It's been two days already! But you know what? He had

this really big test to study for, you *know* how stressful that is. I bet that's why ..."

Willow closes the book with a sigh. It's futile to even try to read. At least eavesdropping promises to be entertaining.

All of a sudden Willow is overcome by a wave of loneliness. She wishes that she could to talk to Markie, that she was *capable* of talking to Markie. Rewind seven months and it could have been the two of them gossiping this way. They wouldn't have sounded any different really. After examining the phone call problem from every possible angle, they'd move on to skin care, and then ...

"You should see how fried my hair is getting ..."

Oh, okay, split ends, not skin care, close enough. Willow smiles a little. Maybe she can still follow these things after all. Maybe every time she opens her mouth it doesn't have to be an unmitigated disaster.

"I tried doing my own highlights and it was a complete catastrophe."

Catastrophe? Willow sits up and stares at the other girl in disbelief. *That's her idea of a catastrophe?*

She'd like to show her some pictures of the accident.

Maybe she should have stayed at school, but really, was listening to this any worse than listening to Claudia and Laurie talk about SAT scores? At least up here no one expects her to join in; besides, she likes hanging out on the campus lawn. Back when her parents were alive she used to come into the city all the time and read on the grass while she waited for their classes to end. Then they'd pick up David and Cathy and go out to dinner.

Willow shakes her head. Ridiculous that she thought it would be the same now. After all, nothing else is.

She doesn't want to hear any more. She doesn't want to lie around on the lawn anymore. There's only one thing she wants to do. Odd really, because until this moment she hadn't even thought of doing any razor work.

Willow isn't stupid. She knows what's going on. Listening to this type of conversation is like a window onto her past. The actual crash, the angle of her mother's collarbone, the way her own hair was soaked in her father's blood, those things are too difficult to process. But trivial things, they get her *every* time.

She'd been foiled in her attempts at cutting the day before. Maybe she'll have more luck today. The campus is big, much bigger than school, and if she can't find a place on the grounds, there's always the park. . . .

But it's still daylight. She doesn't want to take the risk of someone seeing her in the park. Willow rummages through her bag in search of her library ID. Even though she hates going up to the stacks alone, they would be a good place, except it looks like she left her ID at home.

Of course she has everything else that she needs. She'd never think of leaving home without her supplies. But she has to be careful, exercise a little discipline. Do it too often and things could get tricky. Each time she indulges, the chance of someone finding out, the chance of infection, even the possibility of her losing too much blood increases. She's going to have to start rationing her sessions. Think about the razor the way other girls might think about ice cream.

Not only that, but concealment is getting more and more

difficult. It's just so hard to remember everything, all the little details that she has to keep on top of if she's going to keep her secret. Take a few nights ago, when she saw David crying. After Willow had finally fallen asleep, after the bite of the blade had soothed her like a lullaby, she'd awoken with a start, knowing something was wrong. Willow had tossed and turned for a good half hour racking her brain until she realized that she hadn't wiped up the blood that had dripped from her arm and onto the floor.

What if she'd forgotten to clean it up? What if Cathy had seen it in the morning?

The girl with the cell phone is getting ready to leave. Willow won't have to listen to her anymore. But she doesn't care, it's too late. If only she could find that stupid library pass. She digs a little deeper.

"Hey, how's it going?"

Willow is startled by the interruption. She jerks her hand out of her bag as if she's been caught stealing. Her heart is beating as fast as if she's just run a marathon.

It's Guy. Well of course. Who else would it be? He's the only person that she's talked to around here.

"Hi." She scrambles to her feet, wiping her palms, which are slightly sweaty, against her jeans.

"You headed over to the library?"

"No." Willow shakes her head. "I don't work today."

"Oh, are you meeting your brother then?"

"I . . . No." Willow almost laughs. She's gone out of her way to avoid David ever since she witnessed that little scene in the middle of the night.

"Okay." He considers this for a second. "Did you just come

up here to read then? 'Cause I do that all the time too. I find it a lot easier to get work done here than at school." Guy sits down next to her as he says this. He puts his backpack on the grass and, using it like a pillow, lies down with one arm across his face to shield his eyes from the sun.

Willow doesn't know how to answer. She's too busy trying to figure out how she can get away, so she can keep her date with the razor.

"*Bulfinch?*" Guy picks up the book. "You must be taking Myths and Heroes. I had it last year." He starts to flip through the pages. "I liked it, but it wasn't my favorite class or anything. I mean, the Greek myths are as good as it gets, but *Bulfinch?* Kind of dry, don't you think?" His smile is dazzling in the sunlight. "Who's teaching it this semester?"

He says all this easily, as if they've already had a million conversations. As if they were friends.

She should sit down and talk to him. There's no real reason not to. That conversation in the stacks, that had been good before it turned. Why not talk about the *Bulfinch,* talk about school, and maybe some other stuff too?

But Willow's already decided that it's too dangerous to speak to him. She thinks back to the other day—how does she know that when she's done talking, when she's laid herself bare before him, that he won't turn to her and say something as clumsy, as blunt, and as painful as that girl in the lab?

No. There will be no talking. Not about *Bulfinch* and not about anything else either.

She has other things to do.

"Sorry, I . . . I can't really talk. . . . I'm kind of in a hurry," Willow says as she reaches to pick up her bag.

"Oh, c'mon, stay. If you go I'll have to get to work, and I feel like wasting time. Look." Guy sits up, propping himself on one elbow. "If you stay and talk to me I'll buy you a cappuccino at that place I told you about." He grabs one of the straps on her backpack and tries to pull her down.

"I can't!" Willow says somewhat wildly. She pulls in the opposite direction, but Guy is stronger and she stumbles against him.

"Hey, watch it." Guy lets go of the bag and reaches out to steady her. His grip is stronger than he knows, and Willow can't stop herself from wincing as his wrists close around her fresh scars.

"Is something wrong?" Guy frowns.

"No." Willow pulls her arms away, but the damage is done. He's disturbed the cuts before they had time to scab over. She can see the blood seeping through her shirt. Willow doesn't look at him. She just starts moving as quickly as possible. She doesn't even care which direction.

"Hey." Guy stands up. This time his hand is on her shoulder as he turns her around to face him. "You're bleeding!"

Willow doesn't know what to say. She's frozen to the spot.

"That looks bad." Guy stares at the blood drenching her sleeve, staining her white blouse crimson.

He hasn't figured it out, Willow thinks, relieved. Is it possible that he doesn't make any connection between the blood that's dripping down her arm today, and the blood that was dripping down her leg in the lab yesterday?

If only she could think of some plausible story. If only the cuts weren't in such a telling place. It had been simple with her leg. Of course, she wishes that she had claimed some kind of fall, an accident, anything but shaving, but still . . . Legs were easy . . . but her *forearms?*

Guy seems more and more bewildered as he looks at the blood. He glances up at Willow, a question in his eyes.

Well, too bad, Willow thinks. She's not going to answer it. She yanks her hand away, mindless of the pain. Unfortunately, as she does so, her bag slips down her arm and the contents spill out onto the lawn.

"No!" Willow yells as Guy bends down to pick up her things. Why does he have to be so polite? She considers shoving him, pushing him, even doing something as outrageous, as crazy, as kicking him in the shins, *anything,* just so she can get him off her case, just so she can make sure that he stays away from her cargo.

Willow lunges for her stash, but it's too late. Guy is there first. His hand closes around her supplies. He stands up and starts to give them to her, along with a couple of pens, some gum, and the rest of her belongings.

Willow can't believe it. He's found her stuff and he *doesn't get it.* He doesn't make the connection between the blood spurting from her arm and the soiled razor that he's about to pass to her.

She's so relieved that she can't stop herself, she bursts into laughter. Guy looks confused for a moment—after all, there's nothing so funny about her dropping her bag. But he's a good sport. His face creases into a smile and he starts laughing with her. Willow thinks of how they must look: like a young couple in love. *That* makes her laugh even harder. Who watching them would know that she's laughing because he doesn't realize the meaning of what he's holding?

"Hey," Guy says suddenly. "I use this brand." He's looking at the blade, his laughter stops, and Willow realizes that she should have run, that she misjudged him, that he does, after all, *get it*.

"Hey!" His voice is panicked. Willow knows she should get out of there, but she's rooted to the spot. Her mind is racing furiously. But she can't think of anything to say, she can't think of any way to guarantee his silence.

"Hey!" Guy says once again. He rips up her sleeve and stares at her arm. Willow turns beet red. She couldn't feel more exposed if she were standing naked and he was staring at her breasts. She can feel his eyes as they drink in the terrible sight, the old scars and the fresh scabs, the bleeding flesh and the puckered ugly wounds.

He raises his head and looks her in the eye, his expression equal parts shock and revulsion. Willow stares back. Guy is as quiet as she is, and no wonder. There's simply nothing to say. Willow drops her arm. The worst is over. Maybe now she can just leave. After all, what can he really do? But as Willow watches him slowly back away from her, as she sees the look of horror on his face change to one of determination, she realizes that there is in fact something he can do, something that he is clearly intent on doing, something so awful that her knees nearly give way at the thought.

He can tell David.

Guy turns suddenly and begins running across the lawn. Willow doesn't hesitate, she takes off after him. But he's *fast*, faster then she'll ever be. He's crossing college walk, running up the stairs, in a second he'll be at the anthropology building, and she still hasn't caught up.

Willow wants to yell at him to stop, but she's afraid of attracting any more attention. Already people are turning to look at them. In any case, she is too breathless to get the words out, and what good would they do? Sweat is pouring down her back, her heart is pounding so hard, she's actually afraid it will burst, but that's nothing, *nothing* compared to the despair she feels at what is about to happen. She can't let Guy destroy her secret. She can't let him take away the only thing that gives her any comfort.

A group of students come out of the anthropology building just as he reaches the door. They're talking and laughing, blocking the entrance. Willow can't believe her luck. They stop him cold, there's nothing for him to do but stand there and wait until they move on.

She manages to catch up just as they finally clear out. Guy flings open the door, but she's on his heels now. He takes the stairs two at a time. Willow hurls herself after him, frantically reaching her arms out, determined to grab on to him, to halt his progress in some way, to prevent him from accomplishing his mission.

Willow catches hold of his shirt. She pulls on it, but he's stronger, and she lets go, afraid that if she doesn't she'll tear the fabric. He spins around then. Maybe he's surprised at how easily she's given up, or maybe he's surprised at the absurdity, the *insanity* of her unwillingness to destroy his shirt when she has no such hesitation destroying her own flesh. They stand there on the stairs, both of them with chests heaving, saying nothing, taking each other's measure. Then Guy turns again. This time as Willow lunges after him she is able to reach his hand, but even though she pulls on it with her full weight, he keeps on going. She grasps the banister with her other hand, drags her feet as if they're made of lead, but to no avail: He is relentless, and the only thing she can do is go along with him.

They arrive at the fourth floor, still holding hands. Guy pauses briefly in front of the door to David's office. He looks at Willow for a second but doesn't say anything.

"Please don't tell him," Willow begs, encouraged by his hesitation. "Please."

But she doesn't have time for any further entreaties. Because before Guy even has a chance to knock, the door opens and David appears, ushering the head of the department out.

"Well, hello there." David smiles widely as he looks at the two of them, both slightly flushed, both panting as they stand hand in hand.

It's clear from the expression on his face that he's completely misunderstood the situation. "I can't talk with you right now," he says after a moment. "I have to return a couple of phone calls, if you don't mind waiting. . . ." But he makes no move to go. He's practically beaming as he stares at their clasped hands.

Willow can hardly breathe; she feels as if she might collapse. She's not just frightened for herself either. The thought of having her fix taken away is bad enough. But the thought of Guy telling David, of seeing that smile disappear, is even worse. Her brother hasn't looked this happy in months.

And then it hits Willow. She knows how she can save herself; the relief that surges through her leaves her weak.

"I'll just be a second," David says finally. He shuts his office door, leaving Guy and Willow alone.

Guy sinks down onto the floor. His hand is still linked with Willow's and he pulls her down with him. Only now she's the one who's in control. Now she knows what to do.

"Did you see how happy he looked?" Willow hisses in Guy's ear. "He thinks that we were, you know, *together*."

"So?" Guy says roughly.

"Don't you get it?" Willow continues. "He thinks we're together. He thinks I'm getting better. I haven't seen him look that happy since, well, probably since the accident. Do you want to wipe that smile off his face?" She is relentless. "What do you think this will do to him? Do you think it will do him any good? This will *kill* him."

She wonders for a second if this is indeed accurate. Willow is sure that she has lost her brother's love, but that does not mean that he will not do everything in his power to take care of her. That does not mean that he isn't reassured by the sight of her and Guy, by the thought that she is getting on with her life. And that *most especially* does not mean that learning something new and dreadful about her could not still shatter his world even further. She simply will not allow Guy to do that to him.

But Guy looks less certain than he did a minute ago. He glances at Willow, then away.

"This will *kill* him," Willow repeats forcefully.

"But it might do you some good. You're going to . . ." Guy trails off. It's obvious that he can't bring himself to say the words.

"Kill myself?" Willow finishes the sentence for him. "That isn't my game at all."

"Fine." Guy looks at her in disgust. "You're just going to mutilate yourself. Hey, you're right, that's loads better."

"Better or not, what on earth makes you think that telling my brother will be the thing that gets me to stop?"

"Won't it?"

"Not even close." Willow's voice is like a whiplash. "Not even *close*," she says again. "The only thing you'll do is mess with his head so badly that . . . Well, I don't know what would happen, I just don't know, but something terrible, believe me. He's been through too much. How much more can he possibly take? And what good would it all do anyway? I mean it. Telling him *won't* get me to stop."

"What am I supposed to do then?" Guy looks at her angrily.

"I don't care what you do. But you can't tell him." Willow hears the door to David's office open. She leans back against the wall and attempts to compose herself.

"So what do you want to see me about?" David asks.

Guy gets to his feet. He's a little unsteady, and he holds Willow tighter than he realizes.

Willow stands absolutely still. She's done her best. Now it's up to Guy.

"I was . . ." Guy stops mid-sentence and looks back and forth between Willow and David. "I was just wondering if you already had your syllabus worked out for next semester," he finally mumbles.

Not bad.

Willow looks at Guy with some respect. Not that she really cares one way or the other what he tells David, as long as he doesn't give her up, but still, she's not sure that she could have come up with something that plausible on the spur of the moment.

Then the impact of his words hits her.

He hasn't given her up.

The relief is so overwhelming that she feels her knees give

way beneath her. If Guy weren't holding on to her so tightly, she'd fall down to the floor.

"Well, I've got to say, you have a pretty inaccurate impression of me if you think I have *next* semester together." David laughs. "I'm barely on top of this one. But c'mon in and I'll tell you what I'm thinking of, and maybe I can give you some ideas for a few other classes that you should take. My sister tells me that you want to major in anthropology next year."

Willow stares up at the ceiling and whistles a little tune under her breath.

But Guy doesn't seem to take in what David's saying. Clearly he's still quite rattled by everything that's just happened.

"I think that's great," David continues after a second. He sits down at his desk and gestures for them to take the couch. "But even if you do want that to be your major, maybe you should think about taking something in another department." He pauses and leafs through some of the papers on his desk.

Willow sits next to Guy on the couch. She's never been so uncomfortable in her life and she can't wait for their impromptu get-together to end.

"Oh, uh, yeah, I guess that's a point." Guy makes a visible effort to pull himself together. "But you know, last year I took two classes up here—yours, which I really liked, and then this really basic course in composition. I feel bad saying this, but it was a total waste of time. I only did it because my school sort of requires that most juniors taking classes here start with that . . ." He turns to Willow. "If you decide to take anything up here next semester, you'll probably have to—"

"Yes. Well, I don't think that kind of thing is appropriate for Willow right now," David interrupts, his tone abrupt.

Willow feels a little like she's been slapped. Not that she has any desire whatsoever to take any extra classes, but it's painful to hear her brother talk about her as if she's not even there. She's not sure that she likes the sound of *appropriate* either; clearly it's much easier for him to talk about Guy's prospects.

Maybe she's above letting herself be jealous of her six-month-old niece, but Guy is not exempt from her pettiness. She looks at him resentfully.

"You know what?" David goes on. "I thought I at least had some notes up here, but I must have left them at home. Why don't you give me your e-mail address, and as soon as I have my stuff together, I'll send you what I have."

"Great, thanks. I . . . um, well, I guess I'll see you next semester. . . ." Guy gets up from the couch, Willow follows him silently out of David's office and down the stairs.

"Fuck, Fuck, Fuck," Guy mutters under his breath. He gives the double doors to the building a savage kick.

The afternoon has turned into evening. There's a slight breeze that ruffles Willow's hair as they walk slowly across the campus. It's soothing after the turmoil that she's been through, and Willow is content to do nothing more than enjoy the sensation. She's too drained to talk, too drained to even think.

Guy, however, has no such problems.

"What am I doing?" he repeats over and over again. "I can't believe that whole charade just now! I must be as crazy as you are." Guy stops and looks at her, his expression a combination of disgust and disbelief.

"It was the right thing to do," Willow insists tiredly.

"At least let me take you to student health services," Guy says. "It's completely confidential. . . ."

"No."

"But I can't leave you like this! You can't put me in this position!"

"I haven't put you in any position," Willow says coldly. She quickens her steps. They've almost reached the park now.

"Yes you have," Guy says stubbornly. "I can't just forget about this. What if you—"

"I told you I'm not going to kill myself."

"Is that supposed to make it all right?" Guy sits them both down on a bench. "Slicing yourself up with a razor is cool as long as you don't die?"

"I guess what I mean is that you don't have to concern yourself, you don't have to—"

"Right!" Guy cuts her off mid-sentence. "I don't have to *concern* myself!

"I don't need this," he continues after a moment. "If I don't tell your brother, then what? Am I supposed to watch out for you? I can't do that! I'm taking some classes up here, I was going to start looking for a job. Goddammit! I have other things. Now I'm stuck with you!"

Willow stiffens at the thought. "No you're not! I just told you that!"

"I'm not?" He looks at her angrily. "Okay, let's get this straight. You don't want me telling your brother. . . ."

Willow nods fervently.

"So, fine, you make me promise that, and then you expect me to just walk away? Are you kidding me? I may have better things to do with my time, but that doesn't mean I need you on my conscience."

Willow has a sudden inspiration. "If I sleep with you," she says, "will you leave me alone then?"

Guy is silent for a few seconds, then he looks at her. He seems perfectly calm. Maybe the past hour has been so unsettling that he's immune to further shocks. He studies her carefully and Willow has the horrible feeling that he's deciding whether or not she's good enough for him to accept the offer.

And what will she do if he does?

Willow herself feels far from calm. Her heart is hammering as painfully as it did when she raced across the campus after him. She can't believe what she's just done. Would she actually be willing to sacrifice . . .

But after all, would doing that really be any different than the razor?

"Can I ask you something?" he says finally.

"Okay." Willow nods. She's sure that he's going to ask her if she's a virgin, or if she has any—

"Are you out of your mind?"

Yes.

"No. I mean it," he continues without waiting for an answer. "Are you out of your mind? Besides," he says as he kicks a stone out of the way. "Who says I feel that way about you?"

Willow is almost as humiliated as she is relieved. It never occurred to her that he would have to *feel* a certain way about her in order to sleep with her.

"Well, I just thought that, you know, you're a—"

"Stop talking," he interrupts her. "Now."

They are both silent for a while. He looks away from her and stares straight ahead. Willow isn't sure what to do next. Maybe she should just get up and go home, but even as she's considering this, Guy turns back to her with a question.

"Why do you do it?" he asks. "Can you at least explain that to me? Why you do it?"

"What makes you think I'd want to talk about that with you? What makes you think I feel that way about you?" Willow says, mimicking his words. She tries to inject as much venom into her voice as possible. She's smarting with embarrassment and shame, both by her crazy offer and his easy rejection.

"Right! You'd just be willing to have sex with me!" He shakes his head at the absurdity of the thing. For the first time Willow notices that he's still holding her hand. And, even though he's just humiliated her, even though he's just made her feel like an idiot, she's reluctant to relinquish the contact.

"What am I supposed to do with you?" Guy says the words out loud, but it's clear that he's not really talking to her. "I was going to have a great semester too. I can't spend my time . . . Jesus I don't *want* this!" he mutters angrily.

Willow can't help laughing. Does he think that she does?

"What's so funny?" He turns to her. "You think this is funny?"

Willow shrugs. "Oh sure, both of my parents dying, that was *hilarious*."

Guy looks embarrassed for a moment. "How . . . Do you mind telling me . . . How did it happen exactly? When did it happen?"

This isn't the first time that someone has asked. The answer never gets easier, but Willow appreciates the tentative way that Guy has framed the question.

"It was . . . I was . . . I was driving. And it was about seven months ago." She states the facts baldly.

"Did you even have your license yet?" Guy frowns.

"Huh?" Willow frowns in return. That was not the response she expected. "No. A permit. What does that matter?"

"Well, it—"

"Look," Willow interrupts. "I really don't want to talk about it, okay? It's hard for me." She shakes her head over how ridiculously inadequate that sounds, how mild.

"Yeah, I get that." He picks up her wrist and stares at the blood that's starting to dry. "I get that it's hard, but that doesn't mean that this is the way to go."

"When you're where I am, then you can tell me what to do." Willow jerks her arm away from him. She pulls so hard, the blood starts flowing again.

"Be careful, will you?" Guy snaps. He starts to rummage around in his backpack. "Here." He tosses some Band-Aids, a small bottle of hydrogen peroxide, and a box of sterile cotton into her lap.

Willow looks at him, a question in her eyes. It's one thing for *her* to carry stuff like this around . . .

"I'm on the crew team," Guy explains. "We're out on the river three mornings a week. Anyway, you get a lot of blisters rowing, and the last thing you want is polluted water getting into an open cut."

Willow nods. Should she clean herself up in front of him? Prolong this encounter, which has been nothing less than harrowing? The smartest thing to do would be to get up and run. Quit her job at the library, avoid him in the halls, *never see him again.*

"Well, go ahead," he says after a moment, gesturing toward the bandages.

Somehow the idea of taking care of herself in front of him seems embarrassing, as private, as intimate as cutting would be. *Right!* Unconsciously she echoes Guy's words. *You'd just be willing to have sex with him!*

With a sigh she unscrews the top of the hydrogen peroxide and pours some onto the sterile cotton. Willow should be a pro at this kind of thing by now, but she's having a little difficulty. For one thing, she's right-handed, and this particular slash is too inconveniently placed on that arm for her to be able to reach it easily with her left hand, and for another . . . The events of the afternoon have finally caught up with her. She's just completely worn out. She dabs ineffectually at the cut for a few moments before dropping the cotton in her lap, closing her eyes, and giving up. She is much too tired to care.

Willow is leaning back against the bench, thinking about whether she should just go to sleep there, trying hard to forget the last hour, when she feels Guy's hand on her arm.

What now?

She opens her eyes, wondering what he's up to. Is another confrontation in the offing? Maybe a lecture about her lack of hygiene? But it seems as if Guy has moved beyond arguments. He is completely focused on her arm as he examines the damage she has done to herself. She watches him through half-closed lids as he picks up the cotton and tenderly swabs the cut. His hands are beautiful, large and gentle. Willow can't remember the last time she was touched this way. He's actually much more careful than she herself ever is as he disinfects several of the more recent wounds, then deftly bandages her up and pulls down her shirtsleeve.

They have both been silent throughout. And now, although Willow feels she should thank him, not only for what he's just done, but also for keeping her secret, she can't find the words to speak. Guy too looks like he wants to say something, but doesn't quite know how or what. So they just sit there, regarding each other steadily, the dusk growing and deepening around them.

CHAPTER SIX

Willow glances at her brother as she eats her cereal. He has a cup of coffee in one hand and a scholarly journal in the other. He seems totally absorbed in what he's reading, but she can see he's almost at the end of the article, and she's dreading what will happen when he finishes.

She knows that he's going to bring up yesterday. He'll ask her all sorts of questions about Guy. He'll want to know if there's anything going on between them.

Willow hasn't seen her brother since she and Guy showed up at his office yesterday. David had some conference to go to and hadn't come home until after she was asleep. "Good morning" and "The coffee's hot" are about the only words they've exchanged, but she knows that sooner or later he's bound to bring up that little scene in his office yesterday.

Sure enough, David puts the journal down and turns to her with a serious expression on his face.

"So what's going on with you and Guy? Are you seeing a

lot of him? From what I remember he's very nice, very responsible too. . . ."

It's as if her life has become something out of a nineteenth-century English novel. She's an orphan. She's living in the maid's room in the attic. And now her brother's an inch away from asking her whether Guy's intentions are honorable. . . .

What's next, the workhouse?

Willow knows that he's waiting for an answer. Maybe she should just tell him what he wants to hear. After all, isn't this just the kind of thing she was searching for at the dinner table the other night, something that would make him happy? Why not go along with it? Spin some tale? She's done it before. After all, did Guy really say that he wanted to go into anthropology because of David? But this time it's too hard; the disconnect between why she and Guy were together and why David *thinks* they were together is too great. She can't lie about it, she just can't, not even for her brother.

"No. I haven't been seeing that much of Guy," she says after a few moments. "He hangs around campus a lot because of those courses that he's taking, and I've run into him once or twice up there. That's really all there is to it. I mean, don't get too excited, okay?"

"I see," David says slowly.

That came out more sharply than she intended. The last thing she wanted to do was upset him more than she already has. Her only intention was to stop him from prying. Willow avoids his gaze as she buries her face in her cereal bowl, but she can feel David's eyes on her before he too turns back to his breakfast.

Willow feels terrible, but what can she do? Thankfully there's a distraction at hand as Cathy comes in, dressed for work, carrying Isabelle, who is dressed for day care.

"We're off," she says, kissing David on the cheek.

"Oh hey, Cath." David looks up. "Have you seen my old issues of *American Anthropology*? I can't find them anywhere. Do you have any idea where I might have put them?"

"Well sure, didn't they used to be in your study?"

There is an uncomfortable silence while they all think about the fact that David doesn't have a study anymore.

"Yes, yes they did," David says after a moment.

"Well then, we packed them up when we were clearing the bookshelves for Willow. Remember, we shoved all the boxes under her bed?"

Cathy buries her head in Isabelle's hair and gives her a kiss. It's a natural gesture, but Willow wonders if she's doing it just to avoid looking at her.

"That's right, I forgot." David gets up, his journal tucked under his arm. "I guess I'll go look for them."

Cathy blows him a kiss as she heads for the door. "See you later, Willow," she calls over her shoulder.

"See you later," Willow calls back.

She can hear David rooting around upstairs, dragging boxes out from under the bed. She has nothing to worry about, not really. Under the bed is fair game.

But what if David doesn't confine his searching to that area?

Willow breaks out in a cold sweat. Maybe she hasn't hidden anything under the bed, but that doesn't mean that she hasn't hidden anything under the *mattress*. In time-honored fashion, she's done what countless other girls have done before her, only it isn't love letters that she's stuffed in there.

She imagines the look on David's face if he finds her stash. There's not much really. Some old blades, not very clean, along with some rags that she's used to staunch the blood, but their meaning would be horribly obvious to anyone.

Of course she should go up there after him, make sure that he doesn't find anything. But she doesn't seem to have the energy, the will, to get up from the table. For just a second she thinks about staying downstairs, letting fate decide the thing for her. Maybe it's better this way. After all, it's probably just a matter of time. Can she really trust Guy to keep her secret?

Willow considers life without the razors, thinks about her brother's reaction to the find. Those thoughts are more than enough to propel her out of her chair. She races up the stairs, two at a time, and pauses at the entrance to her borrowed bedroom, slightly out of breath. She watches her brother as he hauls carton after dirty carton out from under her bed.

So far things are okay. He's busy sorting through the various books and scholarly journals, totally absorbed in the boxes. He clearly has no interest in searching under the mattress.

Willow wanders over to the mirror and watches David in the reflection. She notices that he's placed the journal that he'd been reading earlier on top of the dresser, and starts idly leafing through it: some tome on the funerary rites of the ancient Greeks. Willow is about to put it down again, when she glimpses a piece of paper folded in between the pages. Her school's letterhead jumps out at her in bold black writing.

It can only mean one thing. It must be a summons. Someone must have found out about her. Her fingers tremble as with one eye on the mirror she unfolds the paper and starts to read.

But it's not that at all. It's nothing more than a generic letter addressed to the parents of students in the junior class. Each parent or guardian should make an appointment to come in and discuss PSATs, SAT prep courses that the school offers . . . Blah, blah, blah . . .

The same junk that Claudia and company were talking about. Nothing important.

Willow is so relieved that it takes her a second to realize all the implications of the letter. Sure it means nothing to *her*. She couldn't care less if David has to sit through some boring meet and greet with the teachers.

But what about *David?* This wasn't part of his game plan. He should be doing this kind of thing for Isabelle, for his *daughter*. He doesn't need a dress rehearsal. She's sure he resents her terribly for this added burden. If he didn't, wouldn't he simply have mentioned it? After all, school is the one thing that he seems able to talk to her about. Willow places the letter back in the journal, ashamed that her first thoughts had been for herself.

"David, I'm sorry." Willow turns away from the mirror.

"Sorry?" He frowns as he continues ferreting among the boxes. "What for?"

"Well, for . . ." Willow trails off. What can she say? Sorry for ruining his life? Sorry that she was driving that night? What can she say to him that would possibly express what she feels?

Maybe I should just go ahead and ask him if he has a kitten!

She could say that she's sorry for the fact that he has to

attend a parent-teacher conference fifteen years ahead of schedule. That *might* be something she could apologize for without sounding overly melodramatic, except clearly it's something she's not supposed to know about.

Talking to her brother has become like walking through a minefield. She has to step carefully to avoid setting foot in one of the traps.

"Hey, look at this," David exclaims as he reaches into one of the cartons and pulls out a small blue volume. "I forgot about this," he murmurs, blowing some dust off the spine. Willow can see that it's one of their father's. David puts it down on the floor, and shoves the cartons back under the bed. "So." He stands up. "You were saying?"

"Nothing," Willow says sadly. She grabs her sweater and her backpack from the chair. It's time to get going or she'll be late for school. She pauses in the doorway and looks back at David. "I have nothing to say."

And that, at least, is the truth.

※

Willow knows that to the outside observer she must look like a model student. Her hand races across the page as she takes down every word the teacher says. She's perfected the art of looking like she's listening when her mind is a million miles away. Not only that, but she knows when to nod along to show that she's really interested. . . .

The fact is she hasn't heard a thing. Not one thing all day. She might as well be on another planet.

Willow can't be bothered with irregular verbs or Greek mythology. Her mind is elsewhere. She keeps bouncing back and forth between relief that David didn't find her stash, and terror that Guy will out her anyway.

She hasn't seen him anywhere. Well, that's not so surprising since they don't have any classes together, but still . . . She needs to talk to him. She needs to figure out what the future holds. She still hasn't fully metabolized the fact that *someone else is in on her secret.*

If she had to pick someone to find out about her, she supposes that Guy is better than, say, Claudia, from history class. But that doesn't stop her stomach from turning over as the realization that he *knows* about her hits her once again.

Willow looks up as everyone around her stands and gathers their books. The bell must have rung.

Bonus points! Willow can't help smirking. She knows that she must look extra-conscientious, sitting there, scribbling away . . .

Fine. Enough of that. She slams her notebook shut and shoves it into her backpack. She's managed to get through a school day without embarrassing herself.

Well, that's something.

Willow heads toward the double doors along with everyone else. Time for her stint at the library. In her hurry to leave she collides with another girl, who's headed in the opposite direction.

"I'm sorry," Willow apologizes as they both attempt to untangle themselves.

"Yeah, don't worry about it. Listen, can I ask you something?"

Willow looks at her warily. What could this girl, this complete stranger, possibly want to ask her?

Maybe she just wants to know the easiest way to kill your parents, or else she's looking for the best price on kittens.

"I just need . . . If you could help me out . . ." the girl continues, somewhat impatiently. "I'm—"

"Excuse me?" Willow interrupts, completely startled by the request. The idea that anyone would look to her for help is so novel, so alluring, that it stops her cold.

"I'm kind of lost. I'm new here, and I'm supposed to meet . . . Look, you know your way around. Could you tell me where the library is?"

I know my way around?

Well, I do know where the library is. . . .

Should she just take her there? It might be uncomfortable, but wouldn't it be more uncomfortable to point her in the right direction and then walk five yards ahead of her the whole way?

Maybe going up together would be okay. After all, this girl doesn't know anything about her, not even that she's new too. And more than that, she has invested Willow with an aura of competence that is irresistible.

"Yeah, I'm actually headed that way myself. C'mon," Willow says after a few moments. She starts moving toward the exit again, the other girl in tow.

Maybe I should ask her what she's going up there for, we could—

"The library's in another *building*?"

"Huh?"

"How come we're outside? Where's the library?" The girl sounds highly irritated, and the expression on her face is distinctly less friendly than it was a minute ago.

"You looking for the library?" A really cute guy ambles over, clearly interested in Willow's companion. "It's back in there," he says, nodding at the building.

"Thanks. I didn't think it could be outside." The two of them stare at Willow.

Oh my God! Of course! She didn't mean that *library!*

Willow can't believe that she made such a stupid mistake. When she heard *library,* she just assumed . . .

"I . . . Look, I thought you meant the one . . . I work at the university library, and I just . . ."

"You're a *librarian?*" the guy asks. It's obvious that he doesn't mean this as a compliment, and the girl giggles a little. "C'mon, I'll show you," he says to her. Willow watches as the guy holds the door open.

So much for getting through the day without embarrassing myself!

"Hey, Willow!"

What now?

She turns and sees Guy standing near where the bikes are chained, Laurie by his side.

Willow nods cautiously. She's a little unsettled by what just happened, and she fervently hopes that Guy and Laurie didn't catch what was going on. She wonders if that's why he's calling her over. And what's he doing with Laurie? She shouldn't be so surprised that they know each other—they're both seniors and it's a small school. But it makes her nervous. Maybe the two of them are having a little talk about her kitten fetish, maybe they're talking about something worse. Is Laurie his girlfriend or something?

Not that Willow cares about *that.*

"Are you going to the library?" Guy calls out.

Is this some kind of joke?

"Which one?" Willow asks as she makes her way over to them.

"The university one," Guy says easily. "Walk you there? Laurie's headed that way too. You guys know each other, right?"

"Sure." Laurie nods.

Willow gives her a sideways glance. The other girl looks friendly, a little bored maybe, but nothing beyond that.

Still, are things as innocent as they seem? How does she know that the two of them haven't pooled information, shared stories maybe?

Willow feels terribly tense. She doesn't know why Guy wants to walk her to campus. Sure, she was hoping to talk to him again, but she's not going to do it now. Not with an audience.

"All right," she says after a few moments. She looks at the bike rack, once again wishing that she still had her own. If it were chained up there, it would give her the perfect excuse not to join them, but as it is, she can't see any way of getting out of going with them. Sweat trickles down her back.

"I didn't know you worked up at the library," Laurie says as they fall into step together. She fishes in her backpack for a pair of sunglasses. "That's a great gig, how did you get it? I thought you had to be in the college. I mean, you must have some pull or something to get special treatment like that...."

Pull? Not quite. After I killed my parents the school relaxed the rules a little. Kind of like a consolation prize.

"Oh hey, I almost forgot," Guy interrupts her—he's smooth,

but it's still a little jarring, and Laurie looks surprised. "I'm not going to be in history tomorrow," he continues. "Could you get the notes for me?"

"Yeah, no problem." Laurie shrugs.

"Thanks," Guy says. "I really appreciate it."

Willow isn't sure what just happened. Did she imagine it or did Guy just come to her rescue? Did he stop Laurie from asking painful questions?

"So." Willow clears her throat. "How come you guys are going uptown?" She's pleased at how that sounds. A little on the dull side, sure, but a real improvement over kittens.

"I'm trying to find out about an internship," Laurie says as they cross the street and head into the park. "I'd rather get a regular job or something, for the money. But an internship at a college? It's like the finishing touch that I need on my record."

"I have to do some research in the library," Guy says. "Plus I need to return *Tristes*."

"Oh, God, are you still hung up on that moldy old book?" Laurie shakes her head. "You're obsessed!"

"But it's a great book!" Willow exclaims. She's a little surprised by the intensity of her outburst, and judging by the look on her face, Laurie is too, but Guy smiles.

"Oh, you know it?" Laurie adjusts her sunglasses. "I didn't think it was that famous. I mean, Guy's into all these obscure books that no one else has ever heard of. Like, why? But I guess you're into all that stuff too, huh? What is it again, anthropology?"

"I . . . Yes," Willow says faintly. She's glad to see that there are only a few blocks left until they get to campus. Things aren't

87

going as badly as they did the other day, but trying to keep up without saying or doing anything stupid, well, it's a strain.

"Those are the kind of things that really make you stand out on your transcripts though," Laurie continues thoughtfully. "You know, reading all that stuff that isn't required."

Willow can't help finding this a little funny. She's sure that to Laurie, anthropology is nothing more than a way to spice up your resume.

"I mean classes in anthropology," Laurie goes on as if she can read Willow's mind. "That's pretty inventive."

Willow wonders what her father would have made of such a remark.

She wants to change the subject, but how? She can't think of anything that would be either appropriate or interesting. Maybe she should just say something nasty. Tell the other girl she finds her boring. Or better yet, frighten her with stories of people with perfect SATs who didn't even get into their *safety* schools. . . .

That would do the trick.

But Willow doesn't want to be mean. She only wants Laurie to talk about something different.

"What made you even think of taking it up?" Laurie asks, glancing over at Willow. "I mean, how did you even get interested in the subject?" If she notices that Willow is looking somewhat desperate, it fails to register. "Did someone tell—"

But Guy interrupts suddenly. Even more abruptly than the last time.

"Oh who cares?" He sounds bored. "Let's talk about something else. So what's this internship about anyway?" he asks as they leave the park.

Willow is impressed by how deftly Guy manages to change the subject. At how easily he saves her from saying something she would regret. It's the second time that he's come to her rescue just as things were starting to get uncomfortable.

He couldn't possibly be that considerate, could he? That kind? After all, she's nothing but a burden to him, she's just someone who's gotten in the way of his having a great semester.

Willow remembers the way that he bandaged her arm.

Without thinking she reaches out and touches his sleeve— just barely. He'd miss it he weren't looking directly at her. Guy seems confused for a moment. It's clear that he doesn't know what to make of the gesture, but after a second he gives her a small smile. Willow notices that Laurie is watching them and quickly drops her hand.

"Well, there are two different internships." If Laurie thinks it's strange that Willow touched Guy, she's not letting on. "One's helping out at the women's health center, which I'm sort of into, and the other is doing some pretty simple research for this comp lit professor. It's really basic stuff, he'd never give the job to someone in high school otherwise. He might be able to give me a good recommendation, though, and that's something, you know?"

"Well, sure." Willow tries to focus on what Laurie is saying. So maybe she asks a lot of awkward questions, but still, Willow is grateful to the other girl for not mentioning the episode in the garden the other day. The least she can do in return is to pay attention to what she's saying.

"That makes total sense," Willow continues. "Because I know that—"

"Hey!" This time Laurie is the one doing the interrupting. "Look at that!" She grabs Willow's arm, really *grabs* her—right where the bandage is—and drags her over to a drugstore window display.

"That's exactly what I'm talking about!" Laurie presses her face against the window. "That's the color I'm thinking of. Isn't it fabulous?" She takes off her sunglasses and waves them at a pyramid made out of boxes and boxes of hair color.

"Sure is," Willow murmurs. Her attention is riveted too. But not by the boxes of Auburn Flame. Willow is far more interested in the sign just off to the left. The one announcing a sale on stationery supplies.

That's a great price on razor blades.

Is it her imagination, or is Guy looking at her strangely?

Willow shifts her focus to the boxes of Auburn Flame. "I think you'd look amazing in that color," she says with perfect sincerity.

"Thanks." Laurie looks pleased by the compliment.

"Adrian wants you to be a redhead?" Guy asks.

"The only thing he really cares about is that we both get into the same school," Laurie says, putting her glasses back on. "I mean, he's so focused on other things right now, he probably won't even notice if I go red." She steps away from the window.

"Adrian?" Willow asks casually as they walk through the campus gates.

"My boyfriend." Laurie smiles.

"You met him, Willow," Guy interjects. "Remember, with me, up on campus?"

"Oh, that was your boyfriend?" Willow thinks about this

for a moment. "Well, this is where I get off," she says as they pass the marble steps leading to the library.

"Yeah, me too." Guy stops walking. "So Laurie, listen, thanks for covering me in history. I'll catch up with you after tomorrow, okay?"

"Great." Laurie nods to both of them and walks off, leaving them alone.

"Good luck with the internships," Willow calls after her. "I'd better hurry," she says, turning to face Guy. Her eyes don't quite meet his. She's feeling somewhat conflicted: The way Guy seemed to be looking out for her has confused her. She's grateful, but . . .

She'd have to be made of stone not to be touched by his concern, and yet—and yet—he has complete power over her. He could smash her world to smithereens if he chose, and that frightens her. "I'll be late for work." She starts up the steps.

"I called your brother."

Willow freezes. She turns back to Guy, a look of pure terror on her face.

"Relax," Guy says. He leans against the balustrade, his arms crossed in front of him. *He* certainly looks calm. "I kept my promise. I didn't tell him anything, I just asked when you'd be working. I wanted to make sure I saw you today. You and I, we have some things to talk over."

So *that's* why he wanted to walk with her. She should have figured that he would want to talk to her too. It can't be every day that he finds himself in a situation like this. Still, Willow can't help feeling nervous at the thought of what he might have to say to her. Her heart is beating nineteen to the dozen as she sinks down on the steps, oblivious to the students rushing past them.

"You okay?" Guy asks. He looks worried suddenly. He looks like he did when he saw her cuts, and now that she studies him more closely, Willow can see that his carefree demeanor is just an act. There are dark circles under his eyes, and his hair is disheveled. Odd that she didn't notice any of this on the walk. All in all he looks a lot less together than she realized.

"Stupid question." He laughs as he moves closer. "The last thing you are is okay."

Willow doesn't say anything, but she notices that in spite of his unkempt appearance his breath is sweet, like apples.

"Why . . . Well . . . I mean—why *didn't* you tell him?" she manages to stammer.

"Because I promised you that I wouldn't tell," Guy says simply. "But that doesn't mean that I still don't think I should. Or even that I won't. We have to talk, figure out some ground rules." He reaches out a hand and hauls her to her feet. "C'mon, tell the Hamilton witch I need help in the stacks. We can have privacy there." He propels her into the building, past the security guard.

Willow smiles a little at his description of Miss Hamilton, but, as it turns out, she isn't at the desk. Willow signs in and says hello to the clerk on duty before turning back to Guy.

"Now what?" She sighs. She knows what he wants to talk about, it's the last thing she feels like doing, but she doesn't see any way of getting out of it. After all, he holds all the cards.

"The stacks," Guy says decisively. "In fact, you can actually help me out." He shows her a piece of paper scrawled all over with call numbers. "I have some research I need to do."

Willow glances at the call numbers. Even if she hadn't been working in the library for the past few weeks she would have known which floor to go to. She hadn't spent all those hundreds of afternoons rooting through the stacks with her father for nothing. She knows that the books Guy wants are all going to be anthropology texts, and she knows what she's going to find when she goes up there.

"Okay," she says after a long moment. They head back toward the elevator. "This stuff is on the top floor."

"So," Guy says as they walk into the dimly lit stacks. "Why don't we get my stuff first, then we can talk about . . . well . . . you know . . ." He stops speaking for a second, and Willow can see that he's just as uncomfortable as she is. "We can talk about what's going on with you," he continues. "What we can do about it."

Oh, please.

Willow thinks that he sounds like one of those people you hear interviewed on afternoon television. The kind that come out with books promising self-esteem in ten easy steps.

"*We* don't have to do anything about it," she says.

"Oh yeah?" Guy raises his eyebrows as he follows her down the narrow aisles. "Sorry, but that wasn't the deal. If I'm not going to tell your brother, then you're going to have to promise me some things. You don't just get to waltz across my path, totally screw with my head, and have everything your way. It doesn't work like that."

"All right." She shrugs. She really doesn't have a choice. "Let's just get your books first, okay?" Willow stops in front of a dusty shelving unit, pulls some volumes out, and hands them to Guy.

She pauses for a second before reaching for the next one on his list. She feels dizzy. All of a sudden it's too warm. Her skin is starting to itch, but there's nothing she can do about that. Willow takes a few deep breaths, anything to calm herself, but it's useless, why is she even bothering? *Forget it*, she thinks as she holds on to the edge of the shelf to steady herself. *Just hand him the stupid thing already.*

"Here," she says in a brusque voice. She grabs the book, a monograph her father had written about five years ago. Willow remembers it well. The whole family had gone to Guatemala, where her father had done fieldwork. "Here," she repeats as she holds it out to Guy. But Guy is busy juggling the other books she's handed him and he doesn't accept it right away. "Will you just take it?" Willow is angry suddenly and she throws the slim volume at him, not caring whether she hits him or not.

"Hey, watch what you're doing." Guy tries to catch the book, but instead ends up dropping everything else. "What's up with you anyway?" he mutters as he bends down.

"Look, you practically broke the spine on this one." He's obviously upset. Willow watches him as he carefully turns the book over in his hands. Once again she thinks of the way his hands felt as they bandaged her the day before. He handles the book in the same gentle way. It's clear that he doesn't like destruction of any kind, flesh or paper.

"You shouldn't treat books that way," Guy lectures, but she can't hold it against him. She knows her father would have been appalled if he'd seen what she'd done. "I mean, this is a first edition," Guy continues. "Why would you want to . . . ." His voice trails off as he picks up her father's book. He doesn't say anything for a long moment.

"Are we done here?" Willow asks roughly.

"Well, done with the books anyway," Guy says. He sounds subdued. "Look, why don't we sit down for a while." He tucks the monograph under his arm. Willow notices that he deliberately turns her father's picture away from her. His thoughtfulness irritates her, it seems staged somehow.

"You didn't plan this little jaunt as some kind of test, did you?" she bursts out. "Just to see how far you could push me or something?" Maybe she's wrong about him. Maybe she misinterpreted his behavior on the walk. Maybe he kept changing the subject out of boredom, not consideration for her feelings. She crosses her arms over her chest defensively and glares at him.

"Of course not," Guy says. "I really needed this book. I honestly forgot for a moment what it was. I mean, who wrote it. I guess I should have found it on my own."

He looks stricken, and Willow knows, deep inside, that she hadn't been wrong about him. He *is* that considerate.

"I'm sorry," she says after a few moments, embarrassed that she could repay such kindness with hostility. She drops her arms and attempts a smile. "You'll like the book. It's good."

"How could it not be?" Guy is quick to agree. "You know . . ." He hesitates. "I heard your father give a lecture once."

"Really?" Willow is intrigued. "Where? When? Do you know if my mother was there too?" The questions tumble out of her. "What was it about?"

"It was about this," Guy says, gesturing with the book. "About the trip they took to Guatemala. And yes, your mother was there. It was at the museum, late last winter."

"Oh my God." Willow claps a hand over her mouth. She's

going to lose it, she's really going to lose it right here in the stacks. She is shocked by the sudden rush of bile that fills her mouth. But she supposes in a way that it makes sense. She has so conditioned herself to transmute emotional pain into the physical realm, that without the razor to blunt her feelings, her body is responding the best way it possibly can. She is literally making herself sick.

She knows exactly what lecture series Guy is talking about. She hadn't bothered to go, because why should she? She'd heard her parents speak a million times before, and she'd hear them a million times again. Except that late last winter was the last time they ever gave a lecture. Because it was only a few weeks after that that Willow decided to take them for a drive.

"Oh my God, oh my God! I'm going to throw up!"

The lights click off at just that moment. Guy hits the timer with his fist.

"Willow!" He places the books down on the floor and grabs her by the shoulders. "Do you need me to hold your hair back? Should I see if there's a garbage can around? Will you be okay if I leave you for a second and go and look for one?"

"No, no," Willow manages to gasp. "I'll be fine, really. I'm just a little . . ." She presses her hand against her stomach. "Give me a second."

"Of course. Here, let me . . ." Guy positions her so that she's resting with her back against the stacks. "Is that any better?"

"Uh-huh." Willow nods; she's grateful for the support. "Thank you," she says when she finally catches her breath. "Thank you. Really. I'm sorry about what just happened. I just . . . I was sort of overcome. I *can't* believe that you'd be willing to hold my hair back!" she exclaims as the absurdity of the situation hits her.

"No? Haven't you ever had someone do that for you before?"

"Well, sure. Who hasn't done Jell-O shots with their best friend? But c'mon, you've got to admit, it's kind of hard-core with someone you're just ... Well, someone you're just getting to know."

"Hey, I'm not saying I was going to enjoy the experience." Guy starts to laugh. "But at least getting sick is a reaction that I can understand." He stops talking and looks at her closely. "Willow, I'm sorry." He's no longer laughing. "I should never have brought any of that up." He lets go of her shoulders.

"No!" Willow is quick to reassure him. "I'm glad you did. Really! And I want to hear more. I was just thrown for a little bit, that's all."

"You want to hear more?" Guy asks dubiously.

"Yes." Willow is insistent. "Maybe that's hard for you to believe, but I do! David *never* talks about them with me. Cathy either. That's his wife. It's like my parents never even existed." Willow pauses and tries to think of how to make Guy understand. "You know, so much of what my parents were about was preserving other civilizations, keeping lost memories alive. It's just so ironic that David doesn't mention them. It only makes it so much worse."

"All right," Guy says slowly. "But if it gets to be too much, let me know—promise?"

"Promise." Willow nods.

"First of all, let's move. C'mon, this has to be the least comfortable part of the stacks." Guy picks up the books and leads them over to a far corner. He sits down cross-legged in a small patch of sunlight that filters down from the high mullioned windows and motions for her to do the same.

"We don't have to keep worrying about the lights here either," he explains.

Willow sits down next to him and picks her father's book up off the floor. It's a small volume, bound in light blue linen. She has always loved the feel of her parents' books—textured, rough almost, so different from the glossy hardcovers for sale in the bookstores. She turns each page by its top corner carefully, the way her parents taught her. Willow examines them slowly, looks without flinching, pausing to read certain descriptions. Guy is silent while she does so. After a moment she puts the book down and looks at him.

"Will you please tell me about the lecture?"

"What do you want to know?" Guy says. He picks up the book and begins leafing through it. Willow is struck by how he handles it, even more respectfully, if possible, than she herself did.

"Well, everything, really. What were your impressions of them?"

"Hmm." Guy puts his head on one side and considers this carefully. "About your father? Brilliant, of course."

"Okay." Willow nods encouragingly. "But don't just tell me what you think I want to hear."

"Umm . . . All right. Well then, he tells really bad jokes."

"The worst! I know. David and I always used to make fun of him. I mean, he had a good sense of humor, he'd laugh at funny stuff, but his jokes . . . forget it."

"Seriously, I mean he needed to get out of the ivory tower and into the real world once in a while. I distinctly got the feeling that he hadn't done too many Jell-O shots in his time."

"Absolutely right."

"But he was just so compelling." Guy sounds admiring. "He really got excited about what he was talking about. He *loved* his subject."

"And my mom? What did you think of her?"

"Not so exuberant about the topic maybe, but more in touch with the audience if you know what I mean."

"I know what you mean." Willow closes her eyes for a second.

"They talked a lot about the trip. The one to Guatemala. I have to say, they made fieldwork sound like the most amazing thing in the world."

"Right!" Willow snorts.

"It isn't?" Guy looks at her in disbelief.

"Maybe for some people." She shrugs. "But what always stood out the most to me were the mosquitoes. There were *always* mosquitoes, didn't matter where we went, and *really* bad showers."

"You're killing me!" Guy truly does look crushed. "I don't think I can handle that kind of thing."

"Oh, you'd love it," Willow reassures him. "You're the type who would be really good in that kind of situation. And I'm not just saying that either." She holds up her hands as if to ward off his protests. "David said that you were really smart. Hardworking too. Believe me, he doesn't say that about many people." Willow pauses for a second as she considers her own impressions of him. "You're careful about things, I can tell, and you're thoughtful. . . . That's the way you need to be if you're going to do this kind of stuff. . . . You probably think that I'm just spoiled," she concludes after a moment.

"Spoiled is about the last way I would describe you," Guy

says slowly. "And don't be so sure about me either. I have to say, I like my showers."

How would you describe me?

Willow has to bite her lip to keep from asking the question out loud. She's shocked that she even thought it, that she actually cares, quite a bit, what he thinks about her.

"But I have to say, I'm surprised," Guy continues. "I would have thought you'd want to go into the family business."

"Oh no, that's David's thing, not mine at all."

"You really didn't like fieldwork? I mean, all that traveling around and everything?"

"Traveling around can be fun, especially if you're just taking a vacation, but if you're asking me why I'm not interested in doing the kind of work my parents did, then I'll tell you something. I much prefer the kind of places that you can only visit in your imagination."

Willow shrugs her shoulders, a little embarrassed. She glances at Guy, half expecting him to be laughing at her or looking bored, but in fact, he seems anything but that. He looks . . . well, maybe *fascinated* is too strong a word, but . . .

"Tell me about an imaginary place," he says, leaning closer. "I don't know any."

"Okay," she says slowly. "I'll tell you about an actual place, but even though it existed, *I* think that you can only really know it in your mind."

"Go on."

"It's called Çatal Hüyük."

"Whosit whatsit?"

"Çatal Hüyük." Willow laughs. "It's in Turkey, or *was* in Turkey. I've never been there. Well, the whole culture was wiped out about seven thousand years ago. I mean, I've never been to the site, but my mother wrote her dissertation on it. You want to know what they had that makes it so interesting to me?"

"Yes."

"They were the first people to have mirrors. They were made out of polished black obsidian. That's what my mother wrote about. That's what a lot of people write about. They want to know *how* they made them, what tools they used to polish the stone, how long it took to make them. But don't they know that those aren't the interesting questions? I want to know *why* someone made the first mirror. Oh, I know that people must have seen themselves before, in water or whatever, but that's not really the same thing, is it? What did the first person who saw themselves in an actual mirror think? Were they embarrassed, or did they like what they saw? I want to know the things that you can never learn by carbon dating or digging around, I want to know the things you can only *imagine* the answers to."

"Those *are* amazing things to think about," Guy says thoughtfully. "And I'd really like to know what you think— sorry, what you *imagine* the answers might be."

"Oh, but I don't think about things like that anymore." Willow shakes her head. "Now I just think about the day in front of me, and if that's too much, I think about the hour."

And if that's too much, then I know just what to do.

She stops speaking. Guy too is silent; he appears to be mulling over what she told him. Willow is surprised at the turn the conversation has taken. She never thought when he told her that they had to talk, that she'd end up telling him about this kind of thing. She's never even talked to Markie about this stuff. She's surprised too by how peaceful she feels, and she realizes how frightened she'd been of having some big scene.

But Willow isn't prepared for what Guy does next.

"Don't you want to stop?!" he bursts out, shattering the calm. Willow doesn't need to ask him what he's referring to.

"I mean, how can you do it to yourself? Listen to you! You're so . . ."

"I'm so what?" she can't help asking. "I'm so what?"

"Never mind." He looks away from her, clearly making an effort to compose himself.

They're both quiet for a few minutes. So quiet that she can hear him breathing. Somehow the sound is reassuring. She wishes that she could just sit there with him and do nothing but listen to him breathe and watch the small particles of dust that float by highlighted by the sun streaming through the windows.

"Don't you want to stop?" he says once again, only this time he isn't shouting.

Willow doesn't want to talk about her cutting, not with him, not with anyone. But it's an interesting question, and one that not everybody would think to ask. Most people would assume that if she wanted to stop she would. But Willow knows it's not nearly that simple, and apparently Guy does too.

She decides that after all he's done for her—not telling her brother, offering to hold her hair back—she owes him an answer.

"If things were different, and I don't mean if my parents were alive, but if things were different, then yes, I would want to stop."

"What would have to be different?"

102

"I can't tell you that part."

Guy doesn't say anything to this. He just stares at her, his expression inscrutable, but Willow can tell that he feels uncomfortable, nervous even. This isn't what she was expecting. A lecture maybe, or even him yelling at her, but not this steady gaze, this unwavering focus directed straight at her.

He never takes his eyes off hers as he reaches for her hand. She's moved by how tender he is, and just for a moment she allows herself to imagine that things are different. That he doesn't know she's a cutter. That she *isn't* a cutter.

What if the reason he'd bandaged her hand was because she'd fallen Rollerblading? How innocent that would have been! What if they were up here now because they wanted to be alone together, and not because they couldn't risk anyone overhearing their unwholesome pact? What if they could just keep talking and laughing like they had been and not have to deal with the gruesome and gritty?

Guy rolls up her sleeve and she thinks he wants to check to make sure that his bandage is holding, but instead he peels back the Band-Aid and stares at the cut.

"It's so ugly." His tone is matter-of-fact.

Willow jerks her hand away. She can't believe that he said that and she can't believe that she cares. She knows the cuts are ugly, and she's not interested in his opinion, but still, she's horribly insulted. Hurt and insulted. It's almost as if he said that her *face* was ugly.

Guy tears his eyes away from her cuts and looks up at her. He must see from her stricken expression that his words have had an impact, but he doesn't apologize. "Getting back to what I said before," he continues. "I really did call your brother. And not just about when you would be working either."

Willow is stunned. Did he tell David after all? What happened? She's at a loss for words, but Guy goes on unperturbed.

"I called him last night. After I left you. I did." He starts drumming his fingers on the floor. "The thing is, though, I had no idea what to say. I just hung up after a few seconds of heavy breathing." He sighs deeply. "I wanted to tell him, but . . . I kept thinking about what you said. I mean, that it would kill him. What if you're right? Look, there's no way you can make me believe that he'd totally fall apart, but what if me telling him caused some kind of . . . I don't know what. Also, what if my telling him made *you* fall apart? What if it made you cut yourself so badly that . . . well, worse than you ever have before?" He chooses his words delicately. "Besides, I did promise you." Guy reaches for her arm again. This time he keeps his eyes on her face as he fixes the Band-Aid and rolls down her sleeve. "And I just figured, and maybe I figured wrong, that you would be okay, that between when I last saw you and now you wouldn't be able to, to well, do it. I mean, I kept wondering. *When* would you be able to do it? Not at home with your brother and his wife around, not at school either."

An image of the girls' bathroom flashes through Willow's head, but she doesn't say anything.

"Still," Guy continues. "I kept going back and forth between thinking I should tell him and deciding against it. I couldn't sleep all night, just wondering what to do."

Now Willow knows why he has those circles under his eyes. He does look completely wiped out, and she feels terribly guilty. She never meant to give anyone *else* pain.

"Will you tell me something?" Guy has a guarded expression on his face, as if he's afraid of her reaction.

"I might," Willow says thoughtfully. It occurs to her that she doesn't have to hide in front of Guy anymore. This isn't like hanging out in the garden with Laurie and the other girls. She doesn't have to worry about saying the wrong thing, she doesn't have to pretend *anything*.

"Why do you do it? I'm not asking why you're so unhappy, I think I got that. I mean why go this route?"

Willow nods thoughtfully. She should have seen that one coming. After all, it's the first thing *she* would ask. "It's not something that I can just explain so easily."

"When we were walking here ..." Guy starts, then trails off and looks away.

"Yes," Willow prods gently.

"I was worried that Laurie was going to say something that would set you off. Of course, it turned out that I was the one who set you off. I mean when I told you that I'd heard your parents' lecture. *I* was the one who said the wrong thing." He sounds unhappy with himself.

"There is no wrong thing," Willow says. She means it too, she can never tell what it is that will send her scrambling for the razor. "There is no right thing either."

Guy considers this for a moment. "Will you tell me something else? Can you tell me where you do it? I don't like thinking about it, but I can't stop, and I'm driving myself crazy."

"You mean where on my body, or where I am when I do it?"

"Well, both actually," Guy says. This time he's the one who looks as if he's going to throw up.

"Mostly on my arms," Willow says quickly, as if that makes it all right. "And you're wrong about school. I *do* do it there, at home too, if no one is around, but that's a little trickier."

"God," Guy whispers. "And I thought you were safe."

"I am," Willow assures him. "I told you that already. I'm very careful to keep the cuts clean. I never do too much at one time...." She stops speaking. Guy's mood must be contagious, because all of a sudden she can't bring herself to say the words.

"Oh Willow, the last thing you are is safe."

Willow doesn't know how to respond to this. She feels lost in a way that she can't describe. The stacks seem darker suddenly; their little patch of sunlight is fading. She moves closer to Guy.

"Can I see your bag?" Guy asks suddenly.

Willow doesn't get why he's asking, but she gives a little shrug and passes him her backpack.

Guy flips it open and takes out her stash: a used razor and a spare, still in its wrappings, along with the Band-Aids he gave her and some bacitracin.

"Of course it wouldn't do any good to throw these out," he mutters, turning the razors over in his hands.

"No," Willow agrees. "It wouldn't."

"Promise me something," Guy says suddenly. "Okay? Will you promise me something?"

"It depends." Willow is cautious. "What do you want?"

"You have to call me before you do it the next time. I mean it. Just call me before you do it."

"So you can talk me down?" Willow asks. She isn't sure why there's such an edge to her voice. "I mean, what for?"

"Talk you down?" He shakes his head. "I wouldn't even know how." He puts the razors back in her bag reluctantly. "Here's what for. You've got me spooked about calling your brother. I'm sure you're wrong about him, but I don't know really, and I'm afraid to take the chance. At least with you, things are fairly . . ."

"Cut and dried?" Willow can't resist saying.

"That's one way of putting it." Guy gives her a look. "I was going to say that things are out in the open between us. Listen, if you call me, at least I'll know that you're, well . . . obviously not okay, but at least . . ." He doesn't finish the sentence.

"At least?" Willow prompts.

"At least I'll know that you aren't fucking bleeding to death!"

Willow doesn't have a comeback for this. His vehemence has shocked her, it seems so out of character. She watches silently as Guy tears a piece of paper out of one of her notebooks and scribbles something down.

"Here, these are all my numbers, okay?"

"Why are you doing this?" Willow finally bursts out. "You don't have to help me. You don't have to talk to me. You don't have to come up with any answers. So why are you doing this? You didn't have to bandage me yesterday either, but you did anyway. Why? You could just walk away. I'm not asking you to do this. I don't *want* you to do this. I probably won't even call you."

"I can't just walk away. And you know what? You couldn't either."

"Oh yes I could," Willow is quick to correct him. "I'd never even look back, I'd—"

"Right," Guy interrupts her. "Just like you did with Vicki."

107

It takes a second for Willow to even get what he's talking about. "You mean that girl in the physics lab?" She is incredulous.

"That's the one." Guy nods.

"You've got me all wrong," Willow tries to explain herself. "You think I'm nice? That I'm kind? That's not the way it was at all. I thought she was *pathetic*, I thought she was a loser!"

"I know. That's why what you did was so special."

Willow is silent.

"You helped her." Guy's voice is quiet. "You didn't have to, but you did anyway. So don't go giving me some bullshit line about how you'd walk away, because it just isn't true."

"Look, I have to get going." He stands up. "Call me, or maybe don't. Maybe figure out another way to deal with your problems instead of slicing and dicing." He looks like he wants to say something else. But after a few moments he just gives her a sort of half smile and heads for the elevator.

The doors close and Willow is left alone. She crumples the paper with his numbers into a little ball and throws it as far away as she can.

She's not going to let him control her like this. How does he know how she'd behave anyway? She *would* walk away. And she *will* walk away from Guy's good intentions.

Willow grabs her bag and hurries down the side stairs—she doesn't have time to wait for the elevator—right into Miss Hamilton's welcoming scowl.

"Where have you been?" she asks. It's clear that she's upset. "You need to hurry and start shelving, we're backed up and Carlos isn't here. I don't want you taking your break today. Even if you had been on time I wouldn't have let you take it, we're simply understaffed. By the way, you made a mistake on the interlibrary loan you requested last time and I had to apologize to that nice old man. Do I have to tell you ..."

She yammers on relentlessly, her voice querulous and unpleasant. With her scraped-back hair and outmoded dress she's like a fugitive from a Dickens novel. Willow can hardly bear to listen to her. She doesn't know how she'll be able to make it through the next few hours under this woman's watchful eye. Unbidden an image of Guy flashes before her. His face. His hands. The way he held her father's book. The way he bandaged her.

"I'm sorry," she cuts off Miss Hamilton abruptly. "I'll do the shelving right away." Willow grabs a cart full of books and races with it into the elevator. She punches the button for the eleventh floor, not noticing or caring where the books belong.

C'mon, c'mon, hurry!

Willow flings the cart aside and runs over to where she and Guy had been sitting. The paper isn't there. For God's sake! She's only been gone a few minutes! Who else has been up here? Who would even take a crumpled-up piece of paper anyway? She drops to her knees and begins crawling around. How far could she have thrown it? Willow looks under the metal stacks. Nothing but dirt.

What's that?

She sees something small and white among the dust bunnies and scrabbles after it with her hand. Willow can barely reach it and she feels as if her shoulder is about to be dislocated as she stretches her arm as far as she can under the shelving unit.

Got it!

She uncrumples the paper and refolds it smoothly, but she's not sure what to do with it. She left her bag downstairs, and she's wearing a skirt today, so . . . no pockets. After a second Willow sticks the folded-up square in her bra.

She's not sure why she wants his numbers. She won't call. But really, what harm can it do to keep them? She likes the way the paper feels against her breasts. Scratchy, not painful like the razor, but not something she can just ignore either.

It stays there all day, until she gets undressed for bed.

She falls asleep easily. No problem, she's exhausted. But staying asleep—*that's* another matter.

Willow doesn't have nightmares, not exactly, at least not that she can remember, but something usually manages to wake her up at night, shivering and shaking. Maybe it's a car outside her window that reminds her of the accident, or maybe it's the sound of the rain pattering against the window.

She's not sure what it is tonight, some shadowy fragments of a dream come to her: the sound of broken glass, the *feel* of broken glass, is that what's making her tremble? It doesn't matter. Willow grabs her stash from under the mattress. She squeezes the blade convulsively.

She lies there, but she's not cutting, not yet. Suddenly she reaches out, knocking the phone off the bedside table. She roots around on the little nightstand until her hand closes over the piece of paper that she left there earlier. She never lets go of the razor, but she does take the paper and the phone back with her under the covers.

The phone's not a cordless, and the dial tone fractures the

silence. The noise is comforting, though, and so is the *idea* of calling Guy. She's not going to call him, she'd never do that. But her hand grasps the paper tightly, as if it were a lifeline, as she cradles the phone next to her chest, its insistent buzzing echoing the beating of her heart.

CHAPTER SEVEN

Willow hums a little tune as she roots around the various beauty products on offer at the drugstore. For once she's in a good mood. And why not? School had let out early today and she doesn't have to work at the library. She has almost a whole day to do whatever she wants.

She wants to buy more supplies.

So she'd gone back to the shop that she'd passed on her walk with Guy and Laurie. Buying razor blades wasn't always so easy. They were usually confined to art supply stores, but since she'd given up watercolors, she didn't like frequenting them, so finding a new source was particularly gratifying.

Of course any sharp edge could do in a pinch, and Willow has used them all: nail scissors, a steak knife, a man's razor—if he doesn't use safety blades—that's what she'd been carrying when Guy discovered her. But Willow is a purist. She likes to reserve her cutting implement for cutting herself alone. She just can't see hacking her flesh with the same razor she slices her dinner with.

Willow pauses near the boxes of Auburn Flame. Should she buy some? Not that she has any desire to color her hair, but she always gets a few things, just so she won't raise any eyebrows at the cash register.

She must have a dozen sketch pads at home. All with blank pages.

This time Willow grabs some shampoo—at least it's something she'll use—and hurries over to the cashier. Asking for the razors always makes her nervous. Why do they have to be behind the counter anyway? Her heart beats a little faster as she lays her things down. She tries to look as innocent as possible, but she can't help feeling like a criminal.

"Can I please have three boxes of the razor blades?"

"Three boxes? Why do you want *three* boxes?" The clerk gives her an odd look.

Twenty to a box, sixty razors! He has to know!

"I, well, I just . . ." Willow doesn't know what to say. Should she just get out of there? Make a run for it? Could he do anything anyway?

I mean, he's not going to call the police, is he?

"Because they're priced four for two dollars," he continues, unperturbed.

Oh.

"Right, I mean I knew that, I just . . . Sure. Four boxes, that would be great. Thanks." The worst is over. She feels almost light-headed with relief, she's back to humming to herself as she pays for her purchases and heads out the door.

Now what?

Willow stuffs her new provisions into her backpack as she starts walking down the street. She's not sure where she's headed yet. Maybe she should go up to campus to hang out on the lawn. Bad idea. She shakes her head as she recalls what happened the last time she did that. She could just go home and do some work, finish the *Bulfinch* and get started on that paper she's supposed to write for class.

That'll happen.

Of course she could always go to the park. That's a lot nicer than the campus lawn, and no bad associations either.

Funny how she thinks of Guy finding out as bad, but his bandaging her as . . . well, not something *bad,* anyway. Willow rubs the bandage absentmindedly. It's getting a little dirty, she should really change it. Somehow she hasn't had the time.

She heads in the direction of the park, but she's a little uncertain. Going to the park by herself . . . She's been so alone these last few months, and a lot of that by her own choice, but still. . . . Willow remembers the other day in the stacks with Guy. Even though much of their discussion was painful, there was a lot that was interesting. Certainly the pleasure of her own company is starting to wear thin.

That feeling is only intensified as she watches a group of girls from her school drift by and head their way into the park. Vicki is among them. Willow wonders what Vicki would do if she went up and tried to join them. Would she be nice, or would she just say something hurtful again?

Well, she has no desire to hang out with Vicki and her friends anyway.

Willow turns away from the park and walks back toward school. There are a lot of outdoor cafes scattered around the area, and maybe getting a drink at one of them wouldn't be such a bad idea.

She stops outside one with a pretty green and white striped awning and studies the menu. She doesn't have much money. She gives David and Cathy almost everything that she earns, but still, she has enough to get *something*.

"Willow!"

David?! What is he doing here?

Shouldn't her brother be teaching a class, or working at home? What is he doing sitting with an iced coffee at a sidewalk cafe in the middle of the day?

Willow's first thought, after she gets over the shock of seeing her brother at one of the tables, is that of course, *of course* she'd be likely to run into him. The reason that school had let out early was for those parent–guidance counselor conferences. The same ones that David had gotten a letter about.

Even as Willow thinks this, she notices other students walking by with their parents, stopping at other cafes.

"David," Willow says uncertainly as she goes over to where he's sitting.

How to play this? Should she let on that she knows why he's in the neighborhood? She's sure that he doesn't want her to know. If he did, he would have just told her about the whole thing. She would have been in the meeting with him.

"Don't you have a class or something like that now?" Willow asks. David removes his jacket and a stack of books from the other chair and she sits down next to him. "I mean, what are you doing over here?"

If he's not straight with her, then she'll know how to handle the conversation. She'll simply go on the way they have ever since the accident, speaking without saying anything.

"No, no class right now. . . ." David doesn't look at her as he says this. He fusses with his napkin, hands her a menu, does everything except meet her eyes. "I should be preparing a lecture, but I needed a break. So I just sort of wandered down here . . ." He trails off. Willow nods understandingly as if she totally buys into his explanation. Sighing deeply, she opens the menu.

"So, how are your classes going?" she says, after ordering an iced cappuccino.

Great, now you sound like you're trying to be the parent!

"Fine." David shrugs.

And a fabulously witty comeback from David in the right-hand corner!

"What are you teaching this year anyway?"

"Oh, you know, same old, same old."

How the hell would I know?! You never tell me anything anymore! And how same old *could it be? You haven't even been teaching that long!*

"Right." The waiter places her drink in front of her and Willow takes a long time adding sweetener, stirring it, trying to come up with something to say. But she doesn't have to worry, because David is ever ready with his topic of choice.

"How was school today?" he asks. "What happened with that French test? You must have gotten it back by now. Any problems, or did it go well? And what's going on with that paper you mentioned? The one on the *Bulfinch*?"

Why don't you tell me how school was today, seeing as how you were there too!

Willow has to bite her lip to keep from saying the words out loud. Why is he sitting there pretending to enjoy his drink, pretending that the only reason he came downtown was because he needed a break?

She knows why he doesn't want to talk about it. Maybe he's equipped to deal with all the stupid details of her education like papers and quizzes, but to have to sit through some parent-teacher conference, to have his face rubbed in the fact, that yes, he is the parent now . . .

Willow gets it. She gets it totally. But still . . .

Yell at me! Hit me! Do anything! But stop being like this!! Stop acting like nothing's happened! Stop acting like you're okay with it all!!

"So, did you get your test back?" David looks at her expectantly.

Willow doesn't even bother to answer. She's not going to sit there and continue this farce, and if she can't talk about what's really going on, then she'll at least talk about something more interesting. She casts about for something to say, she doesn't care what, as long as it isn't this meaningless chatter between two strangers.

She glances at the stack of books next to his elbow, hoping for some inspiration. "What are you reading these days?" Willow asks, and for the first time in the entire conversation her voice is natural. This is safe. Better than safe. This is *familiar*. This is the talk around the dinner table throughout her entire childhood. Why has she never thought of this before?

"Well, you know." David's face lights up for a second, looks, just for a moment, like it used to. "I've been doing some digging, going back and questioning some theories. Remember that journal I was looking for the other day? I wanted it because I'm fairly certain that some new finds completely contradict the accepted view regarding burial rites." He's more animated than she's seen him in ages, so interested in his subject that he doesn't even notice that she didn't answer his question.

Willow can't help laughing. She knows that if any of her old friends were with her, they'd be squirming in their seats, dying to get out of there. All of them used to beg to come into the city with her and do something with David. They all had a crush on him because he was so cute, and well, older. But once they got there they were inevitably bored by her eccentric, brilliant brother.

Willow isn't bored at all. Maybe burial rites aren't her first choice of topic, but who cares? He's talking, talking about something real to him, and she's happy about that.

"That's so funny." Willow leans forward. "Because you know what I've been thinking of reading again? *Tristes Tropiques*. I haven't looked at it since . . . in years." She carefully avoids any mention of their father. "But the other day I thought that I should read it again. It's such a beautiful book."

"Amazing," David agrees. "What's so extraordinary about it is that it reads as so much more than an anthropological text because . . . Wait a minute. . . ." His smiles fades as abruptly as a light being switched off. "Willow. I don't think you have that kind of time right now. Are you totally caught up in your classes? You're not falling behind, are you? And you didn't answer me about your paper. Do you have a rough draft already? Why are you even thinking of reading *Tristes Tropiques*?"

It's as if that brief, pleasant interlude never even happened.

"Right, you're right," Willow says, too dispirited to even argue. "I should be getting on with my school stuff. Here," she says, digging into her bag. "I cashed my paycheck yesterday and I forgot to give Cathy the housekeeping money before I left for school this morning."

She shoves a handful of bills across the table. David looks at them as if they were poisoned, then, reluctantly, puts them into his wallet.

"Thank you," he mumbles.

"You're welcome." Willow is just as stiff. She hates it when he thanks her for her pitiful contribution. Hates it.

"Hey." David is staring at her arm, his now familiar frown in place. "Did you cut yourself?"

Willow is startled for a moment. Then she glances down at her arm. She tries to see Guy's bandage the way that David might be seeing it. Dirty for sure, but not much more than that. A single bandage is a pretty innocent thing.

"Yes, David." She looks straight at him. "I cut myself."

The irony of this is overwhelming. The whole experience of sitting there with him is overwhelming. She can't stay there with him anymore, and talk without saying anything. She has to leave, but how? Willow is diverted suddenly by a group of people laughing and talking especially loudly on the other side of the street.

Guy.

Laurie's there too, and so is Adrian—at least Willow thinks she recognizes the guy whose arm is around Laurie's waist. Willow isn't familiar with any of the other people that are with them.

119

"I have to go." Willow looks back at her brother. "I'm meeting my friends." She barely winces at the lie. They're certainly not expecting her. And they're certainly not her friends. Well, Guy is something more than a *friend,* although just what he is exactly isn't clear. But they're a believable excuse, they're giving her a way out.

Willow hurries across the street. She's sure that her brother is watching her and she hopes that if she won't be greeted with open arms, she at least will be allowed to join their little group.

She's worried that Guy won't want to see her. Why should he, after all? She's nothing but trouble to him. Their pact didn't extend beyond cutting and calling.

Willow is a few steps behind them now. They haven't seen her, and in spite of the fact that she's feeling lonely, she knows that if her brother weren't looking she would walk away as fast as she could in the other direction.

Willow takes a deep breath.

Out of the frying pan ...

"Hi," she says, touching Guy's sleeve.

Guy turns around, as does everyone else. It takes all of her courage to stand there and hold her ground, but she's rewarded for it, because Guy smiles at her, and Laurie acts as if her joining them is the most natural thing in the world.

"Hey, Willow, wanna hang in the park with us? You can help me convince Adrian that I should color my hair."

Willow doesn't care that Laurie's range of interests is limited, to say the least. She's too relieved by her casual acceptance to be critical.

"Hi." Guy isn't quite as forthcoming, but he takes the time to introduce her around. "You remember Adrian? This is

Chloe, and Andy." He gestures toward the rest of the group. "You guys know Willow yet?"

"Oh yeah, I've seen you around school." Andy nods. Chloe doesn't really pay her any attention. She's too busy scrounging in her bag for something. "Can anyone lend me some money?"

"What for?" Andy reaches into his pocket.

"Ice cream." Chloe nods toward the small truck at the entrance to the park.

"Get me one too." Andy gives her a fistful of change.

"You want some?" Guy asks Willow.

"Oh, no. . . ." Willow shakes her head. She wonders if Guy thinks it's strange that she's joined them. She looks at him sideways. He seems to be taking her appearance in stride.

"Where to?" Andy asks as Chloe returns with the ice cream.

"I can't believe you eat that stuff." Laurie shakes her head at Chloe.

"Why not? No carbs." Chloe waves her fuchsia-colored Popsicle at Laurie.

"Try no *fat*. All carbs," Laurie says, but Chloe just shrugs.

"How about by the river." Andy looks at Guy. "I want to check out the boats."

"No river," Adrian says firmly. "I need to lie down. You know, *grass*."

"Haven't you guys had enough of the river anyway?" Chloe asks as she makes quick work of her Popsicle.

"You have a point." Guy looks at Willow. "Andy is on the crew team with me. I think I told you that we row three mornings a week."

"Yeah, this morning was pretty bad, though." Andy frowns. "I really want to shave, I don't know, about ten seconds off of our time."

"Then you're going to have to do some extra cardio," Guy says. "I'm telling you that's what's stopping us. But I've got news for you, I am *not* interested in spending more time at the gym."

"No rowing talk!" Chloe insists. "It's beyond boring."

"It's perfect right over here," Laurie says, gesturing to a clearing under some cherry trees. She flops down on the grass before anyone can object.

"Did you bring nail stuff?" She looks over at Chloe as she takes a file out of her bag and gets to work.

"I did." Chloe begins unloading her bag. "But I'm totally out of that color you like."

"Are you comfortable?" Guy asks Willow as she tries to arrange her backpack like a pillow.

"Not quite." She takes the *Bulfinch* out of her bag to see if that will make it any more yielding.

"My hands are all sticky now." Andy makes a face.

"Yeah, mine too." Chloe looks put out.

"Here, try this." Guy hands Willow a rolled-up sweatshirt out of his own bag.

"Thank you." Willow places it carefully on the ground, then turns toward Andy. "I have some of those wipey things," she offers. She carries them with her everywhere, they're perfect for cleanup after a little razor work.

"Great." Andy catches the little foil packets.

"Are you giving her your dirty old sweatshirt?" Adrian laughs.

"It hasn't been cold enough to wear it yet." Guy gives him a look.

Willow leans back on the rolled-up sweatshirt. It makes a perfect pillow, and it certainly doesn't smell bad either.

"Would you pass me the remover?" Laurie puts her nail file down and reaches out her hand.

"Here, give this to her." Chloe nudges Andy with her elbow. "How about you, Willow?" She makes a gesture with a bottle of nail polish.

"No, I'm good." Willow turns her hands palm side up to hide her nails, which are bitten to the quick.

"Aren't we going to a movie?" Adrian stretches out his legs and rests his booted feet on Laurie's lap.

"That's not until later." She gives him a shove. "Get off! You're way too heavy."

"Are you up for a movie?" Guy's voice is too quiet for anyone else to hear.

"Maybe," Willow is surprised to hear herself saying.

"Who's reading the *Bulfinch*?" Chloe asks. She waves her hands in the air to dry her nails.

"Myths and Heroes!" Laurie picks up the book and riffles through it. "I loved that class!"

"They should change the name to Gods and Goddesses," Chloe remarks.

"You're right," Guy agrees. "That's what the class is really about."

"You like Greek myths?" Willow looks at Laurie.

"Oh, you know, they're okay. It's more that it's such an easy class to do well in. I *love* easy A's. If only I had some classes like that this year." She puts the book down and reaches for the bottle of polish. "This semester is so key. It's like schools want to see that you're still really committed—"

"No! No!" Andy sits up and claps his hands over his ears. "Stop her, Adrian! I can't listen to her go on about this stuff one more time! She's obsessed! God, and you guys think *rowing* is boring!"

Laurie makes a face at him, but Adrian just laughs and turns toward Willow. "So what about you?" he asks. "Do you like the class?"

"I *should*," Willow says with a wry smile. "Because I do love the classics, but actually, I'm having a hard time with it."

"Really?" Guy seems surprised. "C'mon, you must have been raised on this stuff. I can't believe you'd find it difficult."

"Raised on it?" Chloe looks confused. "What do you mean?" She looks at Willow expectantly.

"Well, I . . ." Willow pauses. "My parents were both professors." It comes out in a rush. But there. She's done. They can all go back to talking about Myths and Heroes.

"What kind?" Adrian says.

"Were?" Andy says.

No. She's not done. There's no getting away from it. She will be pursued by this kind of question until the day that she herself dies. Out of the corner of her eye, Willow can see Guy getting ready to say something. She has a feeling that he's going to change the subject. Take the heat off, just the way he did with Laurie the other day.

But this time she won't let him. She deserves this question, this *punishment*.

"They're dead," she says flatly.

"That's pretty harsh, huh?" Andy shakes his head. "You know, I thought that I heard something like that."

Pretty harsh? Pretty harsh? You idiot! Harsh is Laurie not getting into the school she wants. Harsh is you not being able to shave some time off your rowing! This *is not harsh!*

"I'm so sorry. I had no idea." Laurie's voice is hardly above a whisper as she reaches out and gives Willow's arm a brief squeeze.

Willow just nods, but she's touched. She would never have looked for any kind of support from Laurie.

The rest of the group is silent. Willow is glad that she's not on the receiving end of the look that Guy is giving Andy.

"So." Adrian clears his throat. "Maybe we should check on the movie times now."

"Yeah, good idea." Chloe nods. She rifles through her bag for her cell phone and punches in a number. "I need a pen." She frowns.

"One sec." Andy looks in his backpack, but he doesn't find anything, and his gaze falls on Willow's, which is lying half-open, spilling her belongings onto the grass.

"You mind?" He reaches across for a pen.

"Excuse me?" Willow is startled. She had no idea that most of her things were on display.

"Here, let me get one for you . . ." She tries to head him off at the pass, give him the pen instead of having him root around in her stuff for it. In the process she manages to spill the boxes of razors out onto the lawn. The boxes themselves are plain brown, but the bright red lettering emblazoned on the sides looks like blood against the grass.

Andy raises an eyebrow, but it's Guy who says something. "Thanks for picking these up for me. What do I owe you?"

Willow is surprised, but she plays along. "Oh, don't worry about it, they hardly cost anything." She's sure that nothing too terrible would have happened if Guy hadn't copped to the blades. The brand-new boxes of razors are a lot less suspicious-looking than the single bloody razor that she'd spilled in front of him. Not only that, but she suspects that Andy isn't that perceptive. He'd *never* figure anything out.

But she's glad that she doesn't have to worry about the possibility. She's glad that Guy made sure that she wouldn't have to. For a second she feels like she and Guy are in a conspiracy against everyone else.

"What do you need with all those razor blades?" Laurie looks at Guy.

"Just something I'm working on." He brushes off the question.

"An extra credit project?" She looks interested.

"Okay." Chloe closes her cell phone with a snap. "There's a show in like twenty minutes. We can make it if we hurry." She jumps to her feet and starts gathering her things.

So does everyone else, except for Willow, who is silent, still thinking about the way Guy just covered for her, and Guy, who is watching her.

"You coming?" Adrian looks at Willow.

"You want to just stay in the park?" Guy puts the boxes of blades in his backpack.

Willow isn't sure if he's just continuing the charade, or if his goal really is to confiscate the razors. But would he do that? She did tell him, the other day in the library, that getting rid of her blades would be futile.

Well, now she has to stay with him. Just to get the blades back.

Is that why he did it? So that I would stay with him?

"Are you staying?" she asks.

"If you are."

"I'm staying," she says after a moment.

"I think we're going to forget the movie." Guy leans back on his elbows.

"Sure." Adrian doesn't seem to care one way or the other. Chloe is busy dusting the grass off of her jeans, and Andy and Laurie are already on their way out of the park.

"You didn't have to do that." Willow turns to Guy as soon as everyone is out of earshot. "I mean, about the razor blades. He would never have figured it out. I can tell." She blushes a little as she realizes how ungrateful she sounds. "Thank you though. For doing it anyway."

"I did have to do it." Guy shakes his head. "Oh, you're right, he would never have figured it out, but I was angry at myself. I put you in the position of having to tell everyone about your parents." He pauses for a second. "I can see how hard that is for you." His tone is particularly gentle as he says this.

But Willow is stung by the sympathy in his voice.

"Wouldn't it just be easier for you if he found out anyway?" She says this so loudly that a couple walking by turn and stare. She knows he's being kind, sensitive, unlike that clod Andy, but she *hates* being the object of anyone's pity. "Wouldn't that be better? Then you wouldn't have to worry about keeping my secret. Someone else could tell my brother."

"Yeah, well, maybe you're right," Guy snaps back. "It *would* be easier for me. But something tells me that Andy isn't exactly the best person to be in on this."

"I'm sorry," Willow says after a few moments.

"It's okay." Guy sits up abruptly. He picks up a twig and starts drawing in the dirt.

"You're the one who's right," Willow goes on. "He'd be the worst person. He's so crass, how do you two even know each other?"

"I don't know him that well—I mean, we row together and sometimes we hang out, but we never really talk. He makes fun of Laurie, but he's the same way. Only with him, instead of SATs and recommendations, it's all about rowing and what frat he's going to join."

"Laurie isn't so bad," Willow says thoughtfully, remembering the other girl's sympathetic gesture. She turns over on her stomach and props her chin on her fists; her elbows rest on the rolled up sweatshirt.

"Yeah, she's okay, a little obsessive maybe. . . ."

"You think?" Willow laughs. "How do you know her? *She's* not on the crew team, is she?"

"No. I really know her through Adrian." Guy tosses the twig away and lies back down. "We've been friends forever. I used to see Laurie around the halls, but I never really talked to her until they started going out, sophomore year. Same with Chloe, I know her through Laurie. I think Andy's kind of interested in her, and he figured that since we're on the same team, that was as good an excuse as any to hang out with us." He shrugs.

"Laurie didn't tell you anything about me, did she?" Willow asks as she fiddles with a dandelion.

"Like what? Does she know about your cutting?" Guy is taken aback.

"No! No. I just got to talking to her and some other girls in school a couple of days ago. And, well, as usual the whole thing fell apart. I said some really stupid stuff. I thought she might have repeated it."

"You know, Willow, I don't think people are really talking about you. At least not the way you mean. I certainly haven't heard anyone say anything." Guy takes the dandelion, which is now mangled, out of Willow's hands. "I think maybe it's all in your head."

"Andy seemed to know all about me," Willow mutters. She starts to bite her nails, then shifts her position so she can shove her hands into her pockets. "That girl in the physics lab, what's her name? Vicki? She said something too."

"Okay, I'll give you Andy, and Vicki too, and maybe there *are* some other people saying stuff, but really, I would think that's the least of what you have to deal with. I mean seriously, even though Andy was a complete idiot, was it so bad today? Wasn't it okay being with the rest of us?" Guy picks another dandelion. "Here, take this one." He tugs her hand out of her pocket and wraps it around the stem of the dandelion.

"Are you kidding?" Willow snorts. She starts shredding the flower. "Okay, so after I tell everyone *that my parents are dead,* and after Andy is so *sympathetic,* everyone runs out of here like I'm contagious! *Their* parents aren't going to die because they've talked to me!"

"I don't think that's what was going on," Guy says thoughtfully. "I *know* that wasn't what was going on with Adrian. He was trying to be helpful, change the subject, take the spotlight off of you."

"Oh." Willow thinks about this for a minute. She's not sure that she believes Guy, but she'd like to, and she has to admit that he has a point, with all the things that she has going on right now, suddenly whether or not people are gossiping about her doesn't seem to matter that much.

"So what did you say to Laurie anyway? Somehow I can't imagine you ever doing anything very stupid."

"Try me." Willow sighs deeply. "It's a long story, I just . . . Well, something I said about kittens."

"Kittens?" Guy starts to laugh. "That isn't at all what I was expecting. Is this because Laurie's sister works in some pet shelter or something?"

"I'm not going to go through it again!" Willow swats Guy with her hand, but she's laughing too.

"I'm just wondering because you don't look like the cat type to me."

"Yeah well, I'm not. But what do you mean anyway?" Willow says curiously.

"Well, you know . . . There's the kind of people who like cats . . ." Guy pauses and gives her a look. Willow shakes her head vehemently. "And then there are people like you. And me. People who like dogs."

"I got it." Willow nods. "You mean like there are the chocolate ice cream types, and the vanilla ice cream types . . . Of course, there are *some* people who like Day-Glo Popsicles." She studies him closely. "Coffee, right?"

130

"Good call." Guy laces his hands behind his head. "But too easy."

"Get out of here! How could I know?"

"Yeah, yeah, I gave you the heads-up when I invited you for cappuccino."

"Fine." Willow rolls her eyes. "But if you're going to divide the world into two types, can't you come up with some more interesting categories?"

"*Odyssey* or *Iliad*," he says promptly.

"Please! The *Iliad*!"

"Totally." Guy is approving.

"Okay, look, like you said, I was raised on this stuff, but what's *your* excuse?"

"You have a leaf in your hair." Guy reaches out and brushes it away. They are silent for a moment.

"C'mon." Willow pulls on his sleeve. "Tell me."

"All right." Guy drops his hand. He sits up and stretches his legs out in front of him. "My parents aren't profs. My dad's a banker and we traveled a lot when I was a kid. I mean to some really far-flung places." He pauses.

"Go on." Willow nods encouragement. She shifts around. Her leg has fallen asleep and she's uncomfortable. After a second she lies down again with her face pillowed on Guy's sweatshirt and looks at him sideways.

"Two things happened," Guy continues. "One, there wasn't any good television, but I could always order books. And two, just so I'd be ahead of the game, 'cause the schools weren't always fabulous, my parents set me up with this really old-world tutor. I mean, we're talking a waistcoat and a gold watch on a chain, right? He had to be about a hundred and fifty. He was from

England, I think he'd been a banker too, but he'd been retired for years. He'd been to Oxford and Cambridge . . ."

"People don't usually go to both!" Willow protests with a laugh.

"Yeah, trust me, he did. Or maybe he went to one and taught at the other. Who knows. Anyway, he got me into books."

"What did you read?" Willow is intrigued.

"Anything. Everything. He could just as easily give me science fiction as Milton."

"Science fiction?" Willow makes a face.

"What's wrong with science fiction?"

"Try everything. And Milton? Why not Shakespeare?"

"Read him too. Now *that's* a good category." Guy looks thoughtful. "People who like Shakespeare and people who like Milton."

"Except people who like Milton more than Shakespeare are crazy!" Willow is indignant.

"That's true—well, my tutor liked Milton better, actually."

"Yeah, and he also gave you science fiction! What's *your* favorite Shakespeare?" Willow wonders if it's the same as hers.

"Umm, probably *Macbeth*."

"Oh, please! That's just because you're a guy!"

"You don't like it?" Guy looks at her like she's crazy.

"Well, sure, but it's got nothing on something like *The Tempest*. Who needs some drafty old castle in Scotland when you could be stranded on an enchanted island?"

"Never read it."

"Oh, but it's the best one! It's got this great relationship between Ferdinand and Miranda! It's so much more romantic than *Romeo and Juliet*—"Willow stops abruptly. She can't help blushing a little.

"I'm guessing this enchanted island is one of those imaginary places that you like so much?"

"That's right." Willow nods. "So, anyway, talking about different places, where were you living when you were doing all this reading?"

"The Far East. Singapore. Kuala Lumpur."

"Do you speak any . . ." Willow searches for the right word. "Kuala Lumpurish?"

"Malay." Guy laughs. "No. I wish I did."

"Look good on your transcript, huh?" Willow nudges him.

"Exactly! I guess I speak it well enough to ask for coffee ice cream. But seriously, everyone there speaks English."

"Do you have any brothers and sisters?"

"What is this? Twenty questions? Yes, a sister. Rebecca, six years younger. Okay? C'mon, you come up with a category now."

"Ummm." Willow thinks for a minute. "Let's see. . . ." *How about people who'd rather live in the city, and people who'd rather live in the country. . . . Talk about boring. People who umm. . . . vote Republican and . . . Forget that one. . . . People who are like Andy and people who are like Guy. Yeah right, who else is like Guy? People who kill their parents and people who don't. . . . People who cut and people who cover for them. . . .*

But Willow doesn't want to dwell on that right now. She's having—can it possibly be—a good time, so she racks her brain to come up with an interesting category.

"I've got it." She looks at him triumphantly. "People who like Sherlock Holmes stories . . ."

"Yeah." Guy leans forward.

"With Watson—and people who like them without."

"Nobody likes the stories without Watson!" Guy is incredulous.

"How do you know?" Willow sits up on her knees.

"Okay, have you ever met anyone who did?" Guy asks.

"No, but that doesn't mean they don't exist! Besides, I don't even know that many people who've read them to begin with!"

"Yeah, well, anyone who likes the stories without Watson . . ." Guy makes a face. "Wait a second, you aren't one of—"

"No!" Willow exclaims. "Total Watson fan. I can't even read the other ones."

"Well, that's a relief." Guy collapses back on his elbows.

"Okay, now tell me more about Kuala Lumpur."

"Ummm, the weather's really bad."

"Is that the only thing you can come up with?" Willow laughs. "Okay, tell me more about your sister then. Are you guys close?"

"Well, we can be. We have been. But right now? She's twelve, so you know, we have different stuff going on."

"I get it completely." Willow nods. "David and I used to be like that, but when I got older things got better. Only now they're worse. Much worse."

"I'm sorry," Guy says, and he sounds it too.

"I . . . I was sitting at this cafe with him when I saw you and Laurie go by." Willow is talking very quickly and the words come out in a rush. "And, well, I just couldn't sit with him anymore, it was just too hard. So I told him I was meeting you.

I hope you don't mind. That I joined you, I mean." Willow looks away from him.

"Hmm. Well, let's think for a sec." Guy makes a show of considering the problem. "What's more fun to talk about? Rowing? Nail polish? Or Sherlock Holmes? Tough call, right?"

"Okay." Willow smiles a little.

"What was going on with you two anyway?"

"We weren't talking." Willow pauses. "We were sitting across from each other and saying things, but we weren't *talking*. It's just like everything else now." She lies back down on her side and faces Guy. "Things don't work."

"Like what exactly?"

"He was at school today. He had one of those guidance counselor meetings, you know where you discuss your whole life plan or something."

"Sure, I know the drill. My parents were there today too. I had to go with them." Guy stops suddenly. "Go on," he says quietly.

"He pretended like he never went." Willow is unable to keep the bitterness from her voice. "He couldn't talk to me about it. Why can't he just tell me what a pain in the ass it is for him to have to deal with stuff like that?"

"Maybe he didn't tell you for some other reason. Maybe he feels bad for you. If it were me with Rebecca ten years from now, I'd just feel sorry for her. I'd be sad that my parents were around to help me grow up, but not her."

"Maybe." Willow is unconvinced. "But that's not the only thing. What about this one? I give David, well, David and

Cathy, most of the money I make. It's not as if it's even that much, it probably only pays for the light bill and one package of diapers or something. I don't think Isabelle—my niece—was planned." She blushes once again. "And having me live with them for sure wasn't planned. I mean, it's just that there are all these extra expenses suddenly, and until my parents' life insurance comes through I really need to help out. But David is always so angry when he takes my money. Why can't he just tell me that it's not enough?"

"I think you're totally off base with that one." Guy shakes his head. "I bet it's something completely different, like that he feels guilty that he has to take your money."

"*He* feels guilty?" Willow is incredulous. "He's not the one who should be feeling guilty!"

"Is that what it's all about? I mean why you cut?" Guy looks at her. "Because you feel guilty?"

"That's not what it's about at all," Willow says. She doesn't like the direction the conversation has taken. She'd thought that they'd moved beyond his trying to analyze her.

"Is it—"

"Can I have my blades back?"

"Sure. Fine. Anything you say." Guy sits up abruptly. He reaches in his backpack for her things.

"I'm sorry, but it's not so easy to talk about. I can't just explain it to you, and I don't even—"

"Forget it," Guy interrupts. "I can't *believe* that I'm giving these back to you. Here!" He throws the boxes of razor blades at her.

Willow doesn't quite make the catch. She feels humiliated as she watches the boxes fall to the ground, breaking open as they hit, littering the grass with bright metal blades. But her desire for the razors is stronger than any embarrassment she could ever feel, so she scrabbles around in the dirt on her hands and knees until every last razor is safely in her hands.

"I shouldn't have done that," Guy says. "It's just—I don't get it, all right? I don't get it at all."

"I don't always get it either." Willow looks him straight in the face for a long moment. Then she turns away and busies herself with putting the blades into her bag, noting as she does so that she'll have to clean them off before she uses them.

"You didn't do it since I saw you in the library, did you? Well, what stopped you? Maybe you should try and figure out what sets you off. How did you manage to control yourself then?"

"How do you know what I have or haven't done?" Willow snaps. "And what makes you think that you can figure me out so easily?"

"Oh, I see." Guy's voice is even more biting. "I guess I was stupid. I just thought that since I gave you my word and didn't tell your brother, you'd keep your end of the bargain."

"I never promised you anything," Willow says angrily.

"Fine. You're right. No, really." Guy holds his hands up in front of him. "You think I was hanging out by the phone waiting to hear from you? Sorry, that isn't the way things are with me. I just figured that you were the type to keep *your* word, and I was really happy that you hadn't hurt yourself again." He pauses and takes a deep breath. "Look, this stuff is way beyond me. I can try and be your friend, but you're on your own with the rest of it."

"I haven't cut myself since I saw you." Willow is suddenly desperate to convince him of that fact, win his good opinion, have him smile at her again. She doesn't know how the conversation turned, but she knows that she doesn't like it at all.

"Good." But he sounds as if he really doesn't care. He stands up and starts gathering his things.

"Please don't go," Willow bursts out.

"Why?" He looks at her unflinchingly.

Why?

He has a point, doesn't he? Doesn't she want to be alone? Wasn't her first impulse on meeting him to push him away? Wasn't she bound and determined not to feel anything?

Except the only times that she's laughed in the past seven months have been in his company. When he's with her she's able to forget the lure of the razor for more than five minutes at a time. And when she talks to him, she actually feels like she's connecting, not just exchanging words like she does with everyone else.

But Willow isn't sure that she can tell him any of that.

She casts about for some reason she can give him. Something that might convince him to stay, but her mind's a blank. He's moving away from her, a few more seconds and it will be too late.

"Wait a sec!" She grabs on to his leg. "Don't go, okay? Because, because ..."

"Because what?" He still doesn't sound very friendly, but at least he's not going anywhere.

"Um, because, you know what? You never told me, um, well, which Sherlock Holmes story is your favorite," she stammers.

Willow closes her eyes. She cannot believe how *stupid* she sounds, how *inane*. God forbid that he thinks she's trying to be *cute* or something. Why did she have to drive her only ally away? She squeezes one of the blades that she picked up off the grass.

"Are you serious?" Guy says. Willow opens her eyes and looks up at him. She can see that he's starting to laugh.

"Kind of," she says in a small voice.

"You're just . . ."

Crazy, pathetic, strange.

"You're just so different from anyone else, aren't you?" He's really laughing now, but in a nice way.

"That was your first clue?!"

"Okay." Guy sits down again. "Since you ask, 'The Hound of the Baskervilles.'"

"What?"

"My favorite Sherlock."

"Oh! Oh, right!"

"Willow?"

"Hmm?"

"I meant what I said about . . ."

"About me not keeping my end of things? About this all being way beyond you? Don't worry, I know what a—"

"No," Guy interrupts her. He picks up her hand, the one that's gripping the razor. He doesn't try to take away her blade, he just closes his own hand over hers.

"Then what about?" Willow is confused. "Because I—"

"About being really happy that you hadn't hurt yourself."

"Oh," Willow says after a few seconds. She doesn't let go of the razor, she barely even loosens her grip on it, but she does place her other hand over his.

CHAPTER EIGHT

God that hurts!

Willow grimaces as she tears Guy's bandage off in one smooth motion. It never ceases to amaze her that even after all her sessions with the razor, little things still have the power to cause her pain.

Of course, the sting of the Band-Aid is nothing compared to the bite of the blade. It's only a minor irritation, not enough to give her what she really needs.

Willow examines the wound critically. She's impressed by how innocent this cut looks compared to some of her other lacerations. This one looks like something that anyone might pick up in the course of the day. The other marks that dot her arms aren't nearly so wholesome in appearance.

Obviously Guy knows a thing or two about bandages.

"Willow," Cathy calls from downstairs. "You'd better hurry, or you'll be late for school."

Yeah, yeah.

Willow picks up her backpack and starts down the stairs. She can hear David puttering around the kitchen and the sweet little noises that Isabelle makes as Cathy feeds her. She stops and sits down on the third stair in order to listen more carefully.

Everything sounds normal, everything sounds *good*. This is the way things are supposed to be—they're just a young family getting ready to meet the day.

Willow hates to join them, because she knows that as soon as she steps into the kitchen the illusion will instantly be destroyed. Her presence reminds everyone that there's something desperately wrong, that this isn't just an ordinary family going about its business. This family is different. This is a fractured family.

She sits on the stairs, delaying the moment as long as possible.

"Willow!" Now Cathy sounds irritated.

Willow jumps to her feet. She knows that Cathy has a thousand things to do—feed Isabelle, get ready for work—the last thing Willow wants is to make life more difficult for her.

"Good morning." David looks up as she walks into the kitchen.

"Morning," Willow mumbles. She busies herself with milk and cereal, her eyes on her brother as she does so. As usual he's surrounded by a mountain of books. She wonders what he's reading and briefly considers asking him, but yesterday's experience is still too raw. Clearly talking about books with David is no longer on the menu.

"How's this new thing you're working on going?" Cathy turns to ask him as she wipes Isabelle's face with a napkin.

Obviously Cathy has no such problems talking to David.

"Is it turning out the way you hoped?" she continues between sips of coffee.

"Hmm, hard to tell." David closes the book he's reading with a sigh. "I need to take a look at some other source material before I can go on. Unfortunately, finding some of the books I want is proving just about impossible, given how long they've been out of print."

"What about the library?" Cathy is once more focused on Isabelle. Willow can tell that she's only listening with half an ear, but Willow herself is all attention as she leans against the counter pretending to be totally focused on her cereal.

"They have most of the things I'm looking for, but not the one book that I really need immediately," David says unhappily. "I'm told that an interlibrary loan will take weeks."

"I bet you can find it online." Cathy is reassuring. She unties the little bib that Isabelle is wearing and picks her up.

"You'd think." David shakes his head. "But most of the sites that deal in out of print books don't handle this kind of thing at all."

Willow is sure that *she* can find whatever book he's looking for. Forget online, the easiest thing to do would be to go downtown to their favorite bookstore. The one she talked about with Guy. The one that their father introduced David to years ago, back when he was still in grade school. They have everything under the sun, out of print or not.

Could David possibly have forgotten about that place?

Of course he didn't forget about it!

Willow knows why he isn't going there. It's probably just too painful, it would stir up too many memories. Her actions haven't only deprived them of their parents. So much of the fabric of their daily lives has been changed because of her. Now a simple trip to the bookstore is impossible for David.

"I've got to get ready," Cathy says. "Excuse me, Willow." She puts her coffee cup and Isabelle's dishes in the sink, then starts to walk out of the kitchen with the baby in her arms. "Don't you have a class this morning?" She stops to give David a kiss. "Shouldn't you be getting a move on?"

"You're right." David pushes back his chair. "I'd better hurry."

"What about you, Willow?" Cathy turns toward her. "Are you working this afternoon? Or will you be home early?"

"I'm working," Willow says. She moves out of the way as David brings his own dishes to the sink. She's hoping that he'll leave his pile of books and notes on the table when he goes out of the room to shave or whatever it is that he has to do.

"We'll see you at dinner, then." Cathy smiles at her.

"See you later," David calls over his shoulder. He follows Cathy out of the kitchen.

Willow puts her cereal down and walks stealthily over to the table. If she's lucky, that legal pad that David's scribbled all over will give her some clue as to what he's looking for.

She glances over her shoulder. She definitely doesn't want David coming in and catching her going through his notes, but the coast is clear, and she picks up the pad.

There's a mass of things written down—not only that, but David's handwriting is barely legible. Still, Willow flips through the pages, hoping to be able to make some sense out of it all.

What's this?

It looks like a list of reference works. David's jotted down several different titles, along with notes as to their availability. One in particular is heavily underlined in red. Willow is sure that she's hit upon exactly what she's looking for.

A Study of the Social Origins of Greek Religion? Published in 1927? Sounds right up his alley.

If the bookstore is too painful for David to go to, then Willow will just have to do it for him. Of course, she's sure that it will be difficult for her too, but she doesn't care. She wants to do something for David so badly that she would brave almost anything. And at least this will have meaning for him. Unlike her other attempts to cheer him up, this is something that he truly needs and wants.

If she cuts her last class she'll have time to go down there before her stint at the library. Skipping school isn't the best idea, but school doesn't rank very high on her list of priorities these days.

Willow smiles a little as she rips off a page from the pad and writes the reference down. She's not sure exactly how she'll present the book to him, but she can't believe that he won't at least be somewhat pleased.

Finally, *something* she can do for her brother.

✳

"Oh, Willow?"

What now?

Willow stops dead in her tracks. She'd bolted out of French as soon as the bell had rung—unusual for her—but she simply can't wait to get downtown and scope out that book for David.

"Yes?" Willow turns around slowly. She studies Ms. Benson carefully, trying to figure out what it is that she wants. Does she suspect that Willow is going to cut her next class? Or that Willow cuts *herself*?

"You left the room so fast," Ms. Benson says. Her voice is pleasant, but the expression on her face is rather serious. "I didn't have a chance to give you this." She hands her the quiz she took the week before.

That's all?

Willow is relieved until she glances at it more closely. She can't believe it. She simply *can't* believe it. Just when she'd come up with this idea of how to help David too. . . .

"It's nothing to be too concerned about, it's early in the semester, and you have plenty of time to bring up your grade. However, the school policy is that when any student fails a test it has to be signed off on by a . . ." Ms. Benson doesn't finish, and it's obvious that she's even more uncomfortable than Willow is. "It has to be signed off on," she says after a moment. "I want to reassure you that this doesn't have to affect your final grade. There's plenty of extra credit assignments we can come up with to offset this. If you could bring it back signed tomorrow that would be great. Friday at the latest, okay?"

"Sure thing," Willow says, but she can barely meet her gaze. Her eyes are riveted by the piece of paper in her hand, by the red *F* slashed across the top of it.

It's not that she's failed a quiz—bad enough, since she's never failed anything before—it's more that she's failed her *brother*. The thought of giving this to David, of presenting him with further proof that she's screwing up is too much to

145

bear. She can't add to his worries, she can't give him one more thing that reminds him that he is the parent now. What's the point of even tracking down that book if she's going to hand him *this* at the same time?

She'll have to do a little forgery. Odd that she has qualms about doing something so minor.

After all, a little sleight of hand is nothing compared to murder.

"I'll get it back to you." She nods. "Tomorrow's no problem."

"Terrific," Ms. Benson says, and melts back into the press of students that are crowding the halls.

Willow hurries out of the school and onto the street. Walking is probably the quickest way to get to the bookstore, and she heads downtown as fast as her feet will take her.

She's so intent on getting there that she barely notices the other people on the pavement. Willow zigzags down the street, avoiding people when she can, but bumping into them more often than not. She doesn't care, though, as long as—

"Can you say excuse me?" An irate voice fractures her consciousness. "Oh, hey, Willow, right?" Chloe calms down as she recognizes Willow. "What are you in such a rush for?"

"I'm really sorry," Willow says somewhat breathlessly. "I just ... I have to get downtown, I wasn't really watching where I was going." She looks back and forth between Chloe and Laurie.

"We're headed that way too," Laurie says between sips of an iced coffee. "Shopping," she confides. "There's some serious shoe stores downtown."

"Shoes?" Willow gives Laurie a look. She never figured her for someone who would skip school to score the latest pair of shoes. "Don't you guys have class or something?"

"We have a study hall at the end of the day three days a week. Technically we're supposed to be in the library, but nobody cares if we just leave," Laurie explains.

"We spent our entire junior year trying to figure out how to schedule that," Chloe adds with a laugh.

"Seniors' privilege." Laurie shrugs. "So, you want to come with us?"

"Yes . . . I mean no." Willow shakes her head. "I mean, I'm headed downtown, but I don't have time to go shopping. Thanks, though."

"Well, walk with us anyway," Laurie urges.

"Okay," Willow says, somewhat reluctantly.

She feels more comfortable around them than she would have a week ago. She's no longer quite so worried about saying the wrong thing. Their time in the park has made her feel like she can be with people without making a complete fool of herself. But she wants to be alone. She needs to think about how she's going to forge her brother's signature. She needs to think about how she's going to find that book. Much as she wishes she could, she *can't* be thinking about shoes.

Won't it be obvious if she forges David's signature? Won't her writing look like a girl's?

Maybe I should just trace it. . . .

"So, Chloe and I want to know, what's going on with you and Guy?"

There's got to be some bill or paper with his signature on it lying around the house. I'll just—

"Excuse me?" It takes a second for Willow to realize that Laurie's asked her a question. It takes her even longer to process just what that question was.

147

"Sorry." It's clear that Laurie interprets Willow's confusion as embarrassment.

"Oh, don't pay Laurie any attention," Chloe says to Willow. "She has to know everything about everybody. Don't even answer. You'll only encourage her."

"I don't have to know *everything*," Laurie protests. "I was wondering, that's all. It just seems like there's something going on between the two of you." She pauses and looks at Willow.

You have no idea. . . .

"Fine, I'm more interested in shoes anyway," Laurie says. "They'd better still have that red pair that was on sale last week."

"The ones that were half off? With the kitten heels? You'll be lucky."

Chloe and Laurie start debating various heel heights and styles. Willow nods as if she's following the conversation, but she can't stop thinking about the failed quiz.

How can I trace his signature? The paper's so heavy. Will I even be able to see through it?

Without thinking she digs the quiz out of her bag and holds it up, trying to assess just how opaque it is.

"So you agree, Willow? Purple snakeskin stilettos are just too conservative for school?"

"Huh?" Willow doesn't even pretend that she knows what's going on.

"I knew that would get her!" Laurie grins at Chloe. "You're so totally in your own world!" She pries the paper out of Willow's hand. "C'mon, what could possibly be more interesting than shoes? Oh!" She looks at Willow with a stricken expression on her face, and for a moment Willow can't help smiling. Clearly, for Laurie, nothing could be worse than a bad grade.

"I'm sorry," Laurie says after a second. "And I shouldn't have grabbed it either." She hands the paper back to Willow.

"It's okay." Willow shrugs. Having Laurie and Chloe know that she failed hardly matters to her at this point.

"You know what?" Chloe says. "You'll be able to handle this really easily. Benson is totally open to extra credit projects and stuff like that. If you do better on the rest of the quizzes this semester, she'll probably even drop this one."

"Completely true," Laurie is quick to agree. "I did some extra work for her last year, just to lock in a really good grade."

"It's not that so much," Willow says. "It's more that my brother has to sign off on this." She is surprised to hear herself confiding in them.

"Okay." Laurie nods slowly; she's willing to listen, but she looks a little bit confused. And Willow knows that while Laurie is totally sympathetic about the bad grade, she's completely ignorant of the bigger issues at hand.

"I mean, that's something that a parent's supposed to do! Only now he's the one who has to deal with this kind of stuff!" Willow bursts out in frustration.

"Oh." Laurie pauses for a moment. "It's terrible about your parents," she says quietly. "But you know," she continues, "at least your brother's willing to do this kind of thing. I can't imagine mine would. I mean, it's sort of sweet, don't you think?"

Sweet.

Laurie's a nice girl. She's truly *nice*. She's willing to include Willow in whatever she's doing, she's willing to overlook stupid remarks about kittens, she's willing to commiserate about failed quizzes, and she's even, unlike some people, compassionate about Willow's situation.

But it's clear that kind as she is, caring as she is, she's utterly *clueless!*

"Yes," Willow says dully. She stops outside the bookstore. "It's sort of sweet.

"I have to go in here," she says after an uncomfortable pause. "I need a book," she adds unnecessarily.

"Sure," Chloe says agreeably. "If you feel like it, when you're done, you can catch up with us. We'll be across the street, down two blocks." She gestures toward some shops in the distance. "There's a whole row of shoe stores over that way."

"Okay." Willow manages a smile. "And good luck finding the red shoes, Laurie. They'll go with your hair, I mean when you get around to coloring it."

"Thanks." Laurie smiles back. "I'll wear whatever I get to school tomorrow."

Willow watches them walk away, then turns to head into the bookstore.

It's as if there's a plate glass wall standing between her and the entrance.

That's how hard it is for her to bridge the gap that lies between her and the door. Of course she'd known that coming here would be difficult, but she'd thought that she could handle it. As long as she was doing something for David, she figured that she could put up with just about anything.

Except she hadn't counted on the place itself being so overwhelming. Every time she's been here before, *every time,* has been in the company of one of her parents.

Willow stands still and watches as other people go in and out of the store. Suppose she went up to one of them, that cute guy going in right now for instance, and asked him to help her, to take her arm as if she were an old lady and walk her across the street. Would he look at her as if she were crazy? And if he did do as she asked, would it even be enough?

For a second Willow considers abandoning the whole project, running after Chloe and Laurie, seeing if she can help them find the red shoes with the kitten heels. But they're long gone, and besides, she so wants to do this. . . .

She'd better do it soon too, she doesn't have that much time left.

Okay, c'mon, deep breath now. . . .

She's sure that she must actually look like an old lady as she crosses the few feet of sidewalk. She's certainly never walked this slowly, this painfully, before. Someone holds the door open for her, not the way they would in the normal course of things, but more like they can tell that she's terribly sick, and they want to spare her any further pain.

"Thank you," Willow says. She sounds like an old lady too.

Willow looks around. The place hasn't changed since the last time she was here. Well, it probably hasn't changed much in the last fifty years, but still, the stability is unsettling. She can't help thinking that her parents' deaths should have changed everything in their world, not just the immediate world of their family.

She takes a few steps forward and is immediately assaulted by the smells, the crush of people, the sheer energy of the place. But it's okay, she can handle it now. The important thing is to get David's book, and then to head back uptown as fast as possible.

Willow walks over to the anthropology section—she could

find it blindfolded—and pulls out the scrap of paper that she scribbled the title on.

Harrison, J.E.

At least it won't be anywhere near her parents' books.

But after a few minutes of searching the shelves, she's forced to conclude that it doesn't look as if it's anywhere at all.

Fine, so I'll have to deal with the staff.

Willow goes over to the information desk and hands the slip of paper to the clerk. He's probably only about five or six years older than she is. Like the store itself, he's slightly unkempt. He doesn't look like someone who loves books. Willow can see that he's reading an alternative music magazine.

"Whas up?" True to form, he looks irritated at the interruption. Clearly, reading his magazine is much more important than helping a customer. She smiles as she remembers Guy's description of the employees.

"I couldn't find this anywhere," Willow says as sweetly as possible. "Do you think you might have it? Maybe upstairs in the rare book room?"

"Gimme a sec," the guy says between bites of his sandwich. "What is this, anthropology? Archaeology? Religion?" He squints at her handwriting.

"Most likely anthropology," Willow says. "But I guess technically it could fit into—"

"I'll find you, okay?" He interrupts her. "Just hang out in the anthro section and I'll let you know in a few minutes."

Willow wanders slowly back to the anthropology area, stopping at British imports on the way.

She leafs idly through a few books. It's strange, but except for school assignments, she really hasn't read anything in months, not since her parents died. Books used to be as vital to her as food, reading them, talking about them, but now . . .

Although of course, she and Guy did discuss—

"I said to hang out in the anthro section." The clerk startles her out of her reverie. "Anyway, we got it, I mean we *can* get it."

"Great!" Willow is beyond relieved. For a second there she thought that she'd have to leave empty-handed.

"Yeah." He picks his teeth as he looks her over from head to toe. "Special order, a hundred and eighty-six bucks, six weeks max, more like three probably. Oh, you have to pay in full now. You know, it being a special order and all that."

"I . . . Wha . . . It's . . . Huh?"

A hundred and eighty-six dollars? Three to six weeks?

She'd assumed it would be expensive, and figured that she'd pick up some extra shifts at the library, but . . .

A hundred and eighty-six dollars!

Willow is literally speechless.

"So how about it? You want it?"

Willow just stares at him. Her mind is a complete blank.

"You interested?" he persists. "Hey, is something wrong, because you look like you're going to . . ."

"Allergies." Willow swipes a hand across her eyes.

"Yeah? Me too. So you want to order it?"

"I . . . uh . . ."

"You live down here?" he interrupts. It's obvious that he couldn't care less about whether she gets the book or not. "I play in a band a couple doors down. After work. Wednesdays and Fridays. You could come down, listen to us, maybe hang out afterwards."

This isn't happening!

"Thank you, I . . . No. No, I'm sorry, I don't have the money for the book. And I live . . ."

Willow spins away, not sure where she's headed, but she has to be alone. And quickly too.

She pushes past people, desperate for a place that she can be by herself. She looks down each and every aisle, but they're never empty, there's always someone browsing through the dusty old volumes.

Willow is feeling more and more disoriented. She's hot, the dust is making her feel as if she really *does* have allergies. The place is too fraught with memories, and she's horribly, horribly disappointed.

Finally, as she nears the end of the store, she spies an aisle with only one customer who is slowly making his way out.

Willow shoves past him, with barely an excuse me, and collapses against the hard metal frame of the bookshelves. She's breathing heavily and doesn't even notice the way that the books jab into her. She sinks slowly to the floor and buries her head in her hands.

Well, what did you think? What did you think *would happen?*

She should have known better. Nothing else works out for her, so why should this have been the single exception? Why did she think she could succeed where David had failed? Her track record of late has hardly been impressive. Willow ticks off the mistakes that she's made on her fingers. One: She should have known the book would be that expensive. Two: She should have known that something that obscure wouldn't just be waiting for her on the shelf, for her to pick up and waltz off with. Three: She should have known that even if she had found the book, it would have made absolutely no difference.

But I was hoping . . .

Willow raises her head slowly. She hadn't realized just how much she was counting on giving David the stupid book. It had seemed like the perfect thing to do that morning, but really, now that she considers it more carefully, is it any less shallow than her attempts to cheer him up with some fatuous compliments? She's ashamed for thinking that something so simple would make her brother's life better. She's ashamed of herself for being so shallow.

And she's especially ashamed for thinking that buying David a book would be enough to make him love her again.

Willow opens her bag slowly, calmly. There's none of the frantic urgency that she usually associates with her need. Somehow it just seems inevitable now. She is someone who cuts. It's that simple. She's someone who killed her parents. She's someone who has lost her brother. And she is someone who has to cut.

She rolls up her sleeve, then shakes her head. She really will have to wait for some of those cuts to heal before she can work there again. Her legs are a much better bet, but getting to them is not so easy. Still, Willow leans forward and pushes up the leg of her jeans.

"Excuse me."

She jerks her head up as someone steps over her and reaches for a book.

Will nothing work out?

She squeezes the razor in frustration. It slices into her palm as she does so.

Good!

But that is all she can do. And anyway, it's time to go. She has to get to work.

Willow straightens her jeans, puts her things back into her bag, and starts to stand up. As she does so her eye is caught by an old and worn, but nevertheless beautiful, small leather volume jammed in helter-skelter amid all the other books.

She wonders what it's doing in this section and looks toward the end of the aisle, where a small card is posted.

Elizabethan and Restoration Drama.

Willow hadn't realized what part of the store she'd chosen for her little meltdown. She pulls out the book and looks at the blue leather binding, then leafs through the dog-eared copy of *The Tempest*, trying to read the faded purple ink where some earlier reader had annotated the margins.

"Hey, can I get by you already?"

She looks up into the face of an especially cute guy. An actor probably.

"Yes, sorry." Willow scrambles to her feet. She pauses for a moment in the act of putting *The Tempest* back on the shelf. Then she tucks it under her arm and walks toward the cash registers.

Willow isn't really sure why she wants to buy it. She's read the play a million times, she doesn't have time to read anything that isn't related to school right now, and if she did, there are several editions back in the apartment.

Besides . . .

Didn't he say his father was a banker? The last thing he needs is some old moth-eaten edition like this.

He'd probably think it was strange for her to be giving him a used book as a present, all written in and marked up. He'd probably think it was strange for her to be giving him any kind of present at all.

And why is she thinking of getting *Guy* something, anyway?

Unconsciously, Willow touches the cut that he had bandaged.

She doesn't have to give it to him. She doesn't have to do anything with it. She can even toss it out. It doesn't matter, it's just something to have.

Except he really should read *The Tempest*.

Maybe her visit wasn't a total waste, she thinks as she pays for the book and hurries to work.

✳

"Well, look at you." Carlos winks at her as she rushes into the library flushed and slightly breathless, nearly twenty minutes late. "I hope you've been having fun."

"Not exactly." Willow stows her bag underneath the circulation desk. "What kind of mood is she in?" she whispers as she pins her ID to her shirt.

"You're lucky, she isn't here. Emergency root canal."

"Ow." Willow winces in sympathy. She sits down on one of the high stools and tucks her feet underneath the rungs.

"Ask me if anything else interesting happened," Carlos says. He leans back in his chair and gives Willow an arch look.

"Anything else interesting happen?" Willow picks up her

cue, but she's not really listening. She's wondering if she can get some homework done—after all, Miss Hamilton isn't here. . . .

"Someone was asking for you."

"For me?" Willow is surprised. "You mean my brother?"

"Get out of here." Carlos rolls his eyes. "You think I don't know your brother? Younger. Your age. A guy," he adds, anticipating her next question. "I've seen him around before."

"Oh." Willow considers this for a minute. The only other person she can think of is Guy. "What did he want?"

"Wanted to know if you were working today. I told him yes."

"Huh." She shrugs and tries to look indifferent. "Well, maybe he'll come back."

"No maybe about it." Carlos brings his chair back down with a bang and stands up as Guy approaches the desk.

"Hey." Guy smiles at her. "I was working up here and I thought that maybe when you get a break we could—"

"She's got a break now," Carlos interjects.

"I just got here!" Willow protests.

"I'm in charge today," Carlos says. "Besides, things are pretty quiet here. Go on, see you in thirty."

"Well, thanks," Willow says slowly. Of course she's happy to have a break, but she feels a little shy all of a sudden. She takes her ID off and stuffs it into her bag, then pauses for a second.

It's totally safe to leave her bag here. She always does when she takes her break, just takes her wallet and puts it in her pocket.

But Willow can't help thinking about the copy of *The Tempest* that's lying at the bottom of her backpack.

Not that she knows what she's going to do with it or anything, but she might as well take her bag with her for once.

"See you in a bit," she says to Carlos as she slings her backpack over her shoulder.

"That was nice of him," Guy says. They walk down the marble stairs and out of the building.

"Uh-huh." Willow nods. She's sure that she can feel the book weighing down her already heavy bag. It must be her imagination, though. After all, it could hardly be more than a few ounces at most.

"So." Guy gives her a smile. "I was working in the library, and I needed to take a break. I thought maybe I could drag you to that place I told you about."

"That place with the cappuccinos? Sure." Willow pauses. "So what were you working on?"

Willow *is* interested to hear what he's been working on, but there are a million things that she'd rather know first—like *why* he wants to take his break with her in the first place.

Is it because he feels he has to keep tabs on her illicit activities since he hasn't told David?

Is it because he might just kind of want to be with me?

Maybe she should give him the book after all.

"Oh, I'm just doing some reading for the class that I'm taking up here. Hey, watch out." He pulls her back on the curb as a bike messenger whizzes past.

"Thanks." Willow is startled. Not so much by the bike, although it did almost knock her down, but by the feel of his arm on hers. She should be used to his touch, though. After all, he's bandaged her, pulled her up the stairs, held her hand. . . .

Perhaps she's so affected because she's still off balance from her experience in the bookstore. Or perhaps it's because this is the first time that he's touched her for a reason wholly unrelated to cutting.

"This is the place." Guy opens the door.

Willow sits down across from him at one of the green marble tables and picks up a menu, then puts it down and starts biting her nails.

Lovely.

She picks up the menu again, but makes no attempt to open it, then busies herself with the napkin dispenser.

"Are you okay?"

"Oh sure, just a little . . ."

Nervous and uncomfortable.

But that doesn't make any sense. After all, he *knows* about her, she has nothing to fear from him.

Then why is she so edgy?

She thinks back to the other day in the park, when she persuaded him to stay with her. She should have let him go then. She's broken her post-accident resolution. She's starting to feel things. Feel a *lot* of things.

Willow can't allow herself to do that. She should never have let him get to her this way. She has no business talking to him about what he likes to read or where he grew up or anything like that at all.

And what is she doing buying him presents? As soon as she gets back to work, she's throwing it out. First thing. . . .

"Do you know what you want?" Guy asks.

"Huh?" Willow hadn't even noticed that a waiter had shown up. She opens the menu, but it's upside-down.

"Never mind, I'll take care of it." Guy laughs at her, but in a nice way. "Umm, two iced cappuccinos, and two, God, what would you like? Umm, let's see, she'll have . . . a strawberry tart." He looks at her. "That work?"

"Well, sure." Willow nods. "But I really don't have that much time, I have to be back in . . ."

"I know, but something tells me that Carlos will cut you a little slack." Guy looks back at the waiter. "So that's two iced cappuccinos, a strawberry tart, and a—"

"Wait." She manages to turn the menu around. "Umm, he'll have the mocha napoleon."

"Got it in one." Guy hands the menus back to the waiter. "So you know, I was wondering. . . . Wait a sec . . ." He stops talking suddenly and reaches across the table to take hold of Willow's hand. This time his touch is rough, harsh almost, and Willow gives a little gasp.

He opens her hand palm side upward, and stares at the line of dried blood that runs from one end to the other.

"It's not what you think."

"Isn't it?"

"No." Willow squirms a little in her chair. His gaze is too intense, and she looks away. "All right, you want to know the truth? It's not what you think it is, but not for lack of trying, okay?" She pulls her hand away.

"What do you mean?"

"I mean, I wanted to but I couldn't. I wasn't alone. Look, you want to help me?"

"Yes."

"Then talk about something else."

"Okay," Guy says. "What?"

"Well . . ." Willow rests her chin on her hands and thinks for a moment. "I don't know, anything. The weather."

"The weather?"

"Okay. How about the weather in Kuala Lumpur?"

"We already did that." Guy crosses his arms over his chest and gives her a look.

"So tell me about the rest of it. What was it like over there?"

"You're really fixated on that place, aren't you?"

"I like the name." Willow shrugs.

"Whatever." Guy pauses for a second while the waiter sets their order down. "Okay, you want to know what it was like? Everything was really different. I mean *everything*. The people, the buildings, the food, the whole culture. It might as well have been on a whole other planet. But I really couldn't appreciate it, because, well, it was just sort of difficult for me there."

"Difficult? But it sounds like it would be fun," Willow protests. "You were living in this whole other society, you got to read all the time . . ." She trails off as she realizes how shallow she sounds. She might as well be telling him that it sounds *sweet*. "I'm sorry, how was it difficult?"

She can't believe what she's asking. She should get up and walk away instead of getting in deeper and deeper. The last thing she needs is to hear things that make him matter *more* to her.

So much for resolutions. She's like an ex-smoker in a cigarette factory.

"Don't get me wrong." Guy shakes his head. "It wasn't bad exactly. There was a lot about it that was great. We got to do some really incredible stuff, like travel all over the place, go to Thailand ... Also, it is incredibly interesting getting to see this whole other world up close. But I just never fit in. I mean, I expected Kuala Lumpur to be different. What was weird, though, was that the kids I hung around with and the school I went to were different than anything else I'd ever experienced too. They were all British, all very, very wealthy. They were as strange to me as everything else over there, only the thing is, I was supposed to be just like them. I wasn't. And that was . . ."

"Difficult," Willow says slowly. "That does sound like it would be hard. I'm sorry you didn't have such a great time, but you know what I think?"

"Uh-uh. Tell me."

"Well, being an outsider like that, I think maybe *that's* what made you interested in anthropology. I mean way before you ever read any books or took my brother's class. Observing another culture from the outside, that's sort of what anthropology is about, right?"

"I never thought about it like that." Guy takes a sip of his coffee. "I just complained that I didn't belong, but you're probably right." He stops talking and looks at her for a minute. "You know what? I'm doing a lousy job of distracting you."

"Oh no, listening to someone else's problems ... believe me, total distraction."

"But it's your problem too. Being an outsider. Well, at least you *think* it is. One of them anyway, and the last thing I want to do is remind you of stuff like that."

"Oh." Willow looks down at her plate. He has a point, of course, but oddly enough, listening to him hasn't made her think of her own situation at all. Still, it would be nice if they could talk about simple things for once.

"All right then," she says. "I don't suppose the weather in Thailand was any better? Wait a sec." Her eye is caught by a flash of red outside the window. "We're in luck, something much more interesting." Willow leans sideways, almost out of her chair, and cranes her neck to look out the glass. "Sorry, false alarm."

"What were you staring at?" Guy looks out the window too.

"I thought I saw Laurie go by, correction, Laurie's new red shoes." Willow relaxes back in her chair. "She went shoe shopping this afternoon, she's going to wear them tomorrow."

"That's more interesting?"

"About a million times. But it wasn't her, so forget it."

"Yeah, I'm totally lost—you went shopping with her?"

"No," Willow sighs. "I should have, but I didn't. She and Chloe were walking downtown to go shopping, and I was going to that bookstore we . . . you like. So we just sort of walked together."

"The one where I told you I bought *Tristes*?" Guy perks up. "Did you get anything?"

"No," Willow says after a moment. "Nothing really."

"I wish I'd known you were going there, I would have gone with you. Were you looking for anything special?"

Willow doesn't answer for a minute. She's too busy thinking about her botched errand. She's too busy thinking about the fact that she has nothing to give David when she sees him later, nothing except a failed quiz, and she *won't* give her brother that.

"Willow?"

"Sorry, I was just . . . Look." Willow grabs her backpack and digs the quiz out. She's careful to keep the bag with *The Tempest* in it hidden from view. "I'm supposed to give David this." She hands Guy the paper. "He has to sign it. I *can't* give it to him, though. I'm going to have to forge his signature or something." She toys with her strawberry tart for a second, then pushes her plate away.

"This must be a new experience for you," Guy says as he takes in the red *F*.

"You're not kidding."

"It will look like a girl's handwriting unless you trace it." Guy holds the paper up to the light. "And the paper's too thick for that." He hands her back the quiz. "I know what you told me in the park, but I think you may be wrong about the whole situation. I mean, are you sure that you just can't give it to him? Okay, it's a really bad grade, but he'll be able to handle it. Signing this isn't that big a deal, is it?"

"It's what signing it *means*, it's what it represents. He could barely handle that parent-teacher conference. How am I going to . . . It's just . . . It's too much. And it's not the grade either, it's more that . . ." Willow shakes her head, at a loss for what to say. Nobody understands, nobody *gets* it. "I bet you think it's sweet, don't you?" Willow says after a moment, a distinct edge to her voice.

"Sweet?" Guy is baffled.

"I mean that he would do stuff like this for me, you know, sign off on a quiz, be the parent."

"Sweet?" he repeats incredulously. "Are you *kidding*? It sounds really, really hard, but I still think that you—"

"I bought you something," Willow blurts out.

"You bought . . . What?"

Willow closes her eyes for a second. She's a little surprised that she's going to give it to him after all, but there's no going back. Now she has to.

"At the bookstore." She reaches into her bag again and pushes the package across the table toward him.

Guy takes the book out of the bag slowly. Willow waits for him to look disappointed, to look confused that she would buy him such a battered, old—

"I love it when used books have notes in the margins, it's the best," Guy says as he flips through the pages. "I always imagine who read it before me." He pauses and looks at one of Prospero's speeches. "I have way too much homework to read this now, but you know what? Screw it, I want to know why it's your favorite Shakespeare. Thank you, that was really nice of you. I mean, you really didn't have to do that."

"But I did anyway," Willow says, so quietly that she's not sure he even hears her.

"Hey." Guy frowns for a second. "*You* didn't write anything in it."

"Oh, I didn't even think . . . I, well, I wouldn't even know what to write," Willow says shyly.

"Well, maybe you'll think of something later," he says.

Willow watches Guy read the opening. There's no mistaking it, his smile is genuine, and she can't help thinking that if she can't make David look like this, at least she can do it for someone.

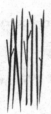

CHAPTER NINE

"You can only take this out overnight," Willow says as she checks the girl's ID to make sure that she has borrowing privileges.

"That's all I need, because this paper's due tomorrow," the girl responds somewhat breathlessly. She grabs the book. "Thanks."

"Good luck with the paper," Willow says as she watches her dash down the stairs.

She settles back on her stool, careful not to check the clock again. Her shift isn't over for another hour, but she's so bored that she doesn't think that she'll be able to make it.

"So how'd it go?" Carlos comes up behind her.

"Hmm, no big deal," Willow says innocently. "Just a simple checkout, she didn't need an interlibrary loan or anything."

"You idiot!" Carlos swats her arm. "You know exactly what I'm talking about." He sits down and pulls his chair close to Willow's. "Liven up my day, honey. C'mon. Tell me stuff."

"Don't you have anyone else you can bother?" Willow says.

"No."

"All right," she sighs. "Umm ... it was good. Great strawberry tarts at that place a few blocks from here."

"I want a restaurant review, I'll read the paper."

"Why are you so interested in what happened?" Willow turns to look at him.

"'Cause I've never seen you smile like this before." Carlos tips his chair back and regards her solemnly.

Oh.

"Never mind." He laughs at her. "You're just fun to tease. Why don't you get out of here now?"

"I have almost an hour left!" Willow objects.

"Like I told you before, this place is dead today. Really, I can handle it by myself," Carlos assures her. "Besides, you work too hard."

"A lot you know." Willow thinks of the giant red *F* splashed across her quiz, which is nestled in among all the overdue homework assignments languishing in her bag. "But thanks, Carlos, you're really kind." If he's willing to let her go, then she's not about to argue. Willow slides off of the stool and grabs her things from underneath the circulation desk.

"Don't worry, I intend to collect on this one," Carlos says dryly. "You can cover one of my shifts later on, maybe next week."

"Absolutely," Willow calls over her shoulder as she runs down the stairs two at a time. It must be all the caffeine she had earlier, there's no other reason for her to feel so buoyant.

It can hardly be that she's that thrilled to get off forty minutes early. And it certainly can't be that she has a hundred and fifty pages of the *Bulfinch* to read before tomorrow, as well as finally getting started on that stupid paper.

And it definitely isn't the fact that she has to figure out some way of faking David's signature on that quiz.

Willow slows down, her good mood plummeting as she thinks about the task ahead of her. Tracing seems like the best way to go, in spite of the thickness of the paper. If she rifles through his desk she should be able to find some cancelled checks fairly easily. She'll just have to hold the paper up to a really strong light. . . .

She hates what her life has become.

Willow stops dead in her tracks. There up ahead is David. He sees her too, and gives a brief wave as he heads over toward her. There's nothing strange about bumping into him on campus, after all, it is where he works. . . .

But his sudden appearance affects Willow in uncomfortable ways, and not only because she's planning to forge his signature. It's more that seeing him like this reminds her of all the other times she's met up with him on campus.

She thinks back to the beginning of March, just a few days before the accident. It had been very cold and gray, flurries too, if she remembers correctly. She and Cathy had been shivering because they had expected it to be warmer. Wasn't spring supposed to be around the corner? David had been mad at Cathy for not dressing more warmly. Not really mad, more protective— she was, after all, seven and a half months pregnant.

They'd all gone out to dinner, where David and Cathy had bored her to tears by spending the evening picking out names for the baby. Well, she really hadn't been that bored, she was actually pretty excited about becoming an aunt. At sixteen, none of Willow's friends had any nieces or nephews. Still, acting bored and demanding to talk about other topics had seemed like the thing to do.

Helen. That had been the name they had finally decided upon. Not so surprising; her brother's always been an *Iliad* fan too. David was sure that their parents would approve.

They may have liked the name. Willow never asked them. But they never lived to see their first grandchild.

Isabelle was her mother's middle name. Born six weeks premature, nothing to worry about these days, but nothing that would have happened either, Willow is sure, if Cathy hadn't been under so much stress.

Sometimes she's amazed that Cathy can even look her in the face.

"Hey," David says, walking up to her. "I'm on my way home, but I wasn't expecting to see you. You're out early, aren't you?" He shifts the pile of books under his arm. "Is something wrong? Do you feel sick, or did you get into trouble?"

"Nothing like that," Willow hastens to assure him. "It was just really quiet today, so they let me out early."

"Good." David nods. "We can walk home together. I wanted to—Stephen, what are you doing here?" He greets the tall, slightly disheveled man who's wandered over their way.

"David, how are you?" Stephen shakes his hand. "You know, I had no idea I was going to be here. If I had, I would have e-mailed you ahead of time and let you know."

Willow has no clue who this Stephen is. She's never seen him before, and she waits patiently for David to introduce her.

"So what's going on with you?" David asks.

"I'm interviewing at some local colleges, and I thought I'd stop by here and take a look around the department." Stephen makes a rueful face. "I heard they might be needing someone next fall."

"Yeah, you know, I think there is something opening up." David looks thoughtful. "But it's a little junior for you."

"Get out of here, I'll take anything. Hey! I heard that you were married. Is that possibly true?"

"Married with a *kid*." David nods. "Can you believe it? Remember Cathy? We got married. We have a daughter. Isabelle."

"Good God! It's only been about a year and a half since I last saw you! It's incredible how things can change in such a short time! What else has happened since then?"

Willow looks at her brother anxiously. She knows how uncomfortable this question must make him, how much pain it will give him to answer.

"Yes, it's amazing what can change in such a short time," David says after an appreciable pause.

"Like what else could possibly happen besides getting married and becoming a father?" Stephen laughs. "Please don't tell me that you've got tenure already—even you're not that much of a prodigy."

"God no, I wish." David laughs along with him.

Willow is the one who is amazed. It's true that she was not looking forward to David reciting the litany of woe that has been heaped upon him since he last saw this guy, that she was worried about how it would affect him . . . but for him to say *nothing*?

"And who's this?" Stephen looks at her. "A student?"

171

"Oh sorry, I'm not thinking clearly today. Stephen, this is my sister, Willow."

"Your sister!" Stephen extends his hand. "Do you go to school here?"

"No, I—"

"Willow's living with me and Cathy now," David interrupts. But that's all he says. He offers no explanation as to why this is so.

"That must be fun for you." Stephen smiles at her. "God, when I was a teenager I would have given anything to get out from under my parents. Speaking of which, I didn't even think to ask, how are your parents? You know it's been ages since I spoke with them, but I'll never forget that recommendation your father wrote for me. It was years ago, but I still think about it, and him too."

Willow closes her eyes for a second. Stephen's careless good cheer is just awful under the circumstances. She steps closer to her brother. She wants to take his hand, reassure him by some gesture if possible, do *something* to support him through this ordeal. Unlike a few moments ago, there is no way he can avoid answering this with anything less than the full and brutal truth. The silence stretches out, Stephen looks at David expectantly.

"He . . . He thought very highly of you," David says finally. That is *all* that he says.

Willow is stunned. She can't believe it. She honestly can't believe it! Why didn't David tell him what happened? Why didn't he let Stephen know that the man he admired so much is gone? Gone! His wife with him. That Willow was there at the end. That she was driving. That the reason she lives with

David and Cathy is *not to get out from under their parents*, but because their parents are *dead*?

What is wrong with him? Why is he in such God-awful denial?

For once, Willow is angry with her brother. Furious, in fact. What is he hiding from? Why is he always, always acting as if *nothing ever happened*?

Something inside her snaps. Gone is the girl who's desperate to make his life better. She is not the same person who left the house that morning. She no longer has the desire to flatter him on the off chance of seeing him smile, she couldn't care less about finding him a book in the vain hopes of making him feel better. She has no wish to comfort him—or worse, collude with him in his rejection of the facts. At that moment she almost hates him. Almost as much as he must hate her.

She's desperate to set the record straight. To say . . . No, to *yell* the truth in her loudest voice. She'll do it too.

Sorry, Stephen, David's not letting you in on all the details! Our parents are dead. I killed them. That's why I'm living with him and his wife, because I killed our parents! Okay? That's what's happened in the past year!

Unfortunately it's not so simple to break the training of seventeen years. Willow can't, she simply can't just stand in the middle of campus and start shouting at the top of her lungs.

If only there was someone she knew walking around. Laurie, say. Or Andy, even better. Someone she could grab and introduce to David. Someone to whom she could tell her version of events while David and his friend stood there and listened.

Willow looks around wildly, but of course, nobody she

knows is around. She's simmering with rage, completely powerless to do what she wants. She just stands there and listens to David's stupid friend carry on about his stupid job search.

"So, I'm hoping that I can get something around here, I mean I'm from this area originally and . . ."

Suddenly Willow has an idea. She knows just what to do to shock David out of his complacency, to force him to tell Stephen the truth about their situation. Forget about not wanting to remind him that he is the parent now, forget about trying to spare him! She rummages frantically in her bag. "Here," she says loudly, as loudly as she dares, interrupting Stephen mid-sentence. "Here!" she repeats, thrusting the quiz under David's nose. "You need to sign this!"

Both men look startled.

Good!!

"Go on, David," Willow insists, shoving a pen into David's hand. "You have to sign this for me. I need a *parent or legal guardian* to sign it." She looks triumphantly back and forth between her brother and his friend, expecting Stephen to ask what she means by legal guardian, expecting David to look stricken with horror.

But the moment has fallen flat. Stephen does not seem to have picked up on the key words, and David is too busy studying the quiz to pay her much attention. It's true that as the meaning of the paper sinks in, he looks concerned, but it's also clear that unlike Willow, he has no intention of making a scene in front of his friend. She realizes that the only thing she has accomplished is looking crazy, or at the very least, extremely rude.

"I should get going," Stephen says after an uncomfortable pause.

"Best of luck with the job search," David says as he scribbles his signature on the quiz and hands it back to Willow.

Willow watches Stephen walk off with a twisted little smile on her face. Maybe her actions didn't have quite the effect that she wanted, but still, she's sure that there will have to be some reckoning now. She has to believe that David will finally give her hell. Not just for failing a quiz, but also for being so incredibly ill-mannered. And once he does, she'll have her opportunity. At last they'll be able to get things out in the open.

"Let's go home," David says after a moment. It's abundantly clear from the expression on his face and the tone of his voice that he's livid. But it's also clear that he has no intention of calling Willow on either her behavior, or her grades. He doesn't even look her way as he heads out of the campus gates and toward the park.

And Willow really has no other choice but to follow silently after him.

✳

"Well, you two are home early," Cathy calls out from the kitchen as they walk into the apartment. "Good, I'm starving—in fact, I already ordered."

"Hi, Cath," David says, coming into the kitchen. He puts his books down on the table, then goes to Isabelle's high chair to gives her a kiss before turning to his wife and wrapping his arms around her.

"I hope you're up for Japanese." Cathy smiles over David's

shoulder at Willow, who has followed him into the kitchen. "It should be here any minute."

"Great," Willow says as unenthusiastically as possible. She wishes she could get away from them, go up to her room and be alone for a while. But clearly that's not on. There simply isn't time before they all sit down to eat. She'll just have to try to act like everything's fine, just like she always does, except she doesn't think that she'll be able to tonight, not after what just happened.

"Oh, you know what else?" Cathy continues, handing Willow place mats and cutlery. "Markie called again. I got the feeling that she'd really like to hear from you."

"Huh." Willow could hardly give less of a response. She starts laying the place mats and silverware around the table, dumping David's books unceremoniously on the floor as she does so.

"There's the food," Cathy says as the doorbell rings. She hurries to answer it.

"It would probably be good for you to see Markie," David remarks as he gets some plates from the cupboard and joins Willow in setting the table. "Why haven't you been returning her calls?" He almost trips over the pile of books, but manages to grab the table just in time. David picks them up with a frown and puts them on one of the empty chairs, then sits down and puts his napkin on his lap.

Is that all he's going to say to her? He's *still* not going to mention what just happened? She finds it incredible that he's not even bringing up the quiz. After all, her schoolwork is the one thing he has been able to talk to her about. Maybe the scene rattled him more than she thought.

Good.

"Because she doesn't get what it's like to be an orphan," Willow replies after a moment. She bites each word off succinctly. She sits down on the opposite side of the table from David, crosses her arms over her chest, and looks at him evenly.

Now, this isn't the whole reason that Willow has lost touch with her old friends, but she wants to state their situation as baldly as possible. She wants to rub David's face in it, get a reaction out of him. Somehow, some way, she's going to force him to respond.

David doesn't reply to this, but she does have the satisfaction of seeing him flinch.

He leans back in his chair and regards Willow thoughtfully. He looks confused, and maybe even slightly angry. One thing is for sure, though—her antics are finally starting to get to him.

"I got California rolls for us," Cathy says, coming back into the kitchen. "And tempura for you, Willow. Is that okay?" Neither David nor Willow answers her.

"I'll take that as a yes," she mutters, opening the food and placing it on the table.

Except for the sounds that Isabelle makes as she fusses in her high chair, there is total silence.

"So how was work today?" Cathy asks David. Clearly, she senses the tension around the table, and is hoping to dispel it with small talk.

"It was fine," David replies after a moment. He looks away from Willow. "Nothing really special."

Willow wonders if she should mention the incident with Stephen. Would Cathy be surprised that David didn't say anything to him about their parents dying? Would that finally bring things to a crisis?

"Wasn't seeing your old friend—"

"I thought that we could—"

Willow and Cathy speak at the same time.

"Sorry," Willow says after a second. "You go first."

"I was just going to say that *I* had a really hard day at work, and I'd really love to do something tonight." Cathy sounds a little on edge.

Willow gives Cathy a sideways glance. She does look like she's had a hard day, there are circles under her eyes, and her hair is somewhat disheveled. Not so surprising, she has a job working in a law firm and a six-month-old. She looks like she needs a break, maybe a movie or something. Willow knows that she should offer to babysit.

Odd that they've never asked her to before.

In fact, it's *extremely* odd that a young couple with a six-month-old wouldn't ask the *seventeen-year-old* to babysit at least once in a while. Wouldn't having a live-in babysitter make more of a material difference to their lives than the few measly dollars she gives them each week?

Although, now that she thinks about it, hasn't *Cathy* suggested that she take care of Isabelle a few times? But somehow, they've always coordinated their outings with other couples who have infants, either bringing Isabelle along with them, or leaving her with the other couple's babysitter.

But that's okay, Willow doesn't care that she's never taken care of her niece before—in fact, she's glad, because now she has the ammunition she needs.

"You do look kind of stressed, Cathy," Willow says. "You

should take a break, why don't you guys go out to the movies or something?" She looks over her deep-fried shrimp at David, all big eyes and innocence.

"I'd *love* to go to a movie." Cathy brightens up. "Wouldn't that be great?" She smiles at David.

"Well, I guess so. . . ." He trails off uncertainly.

"What time would work for you?" Cathy asks as she reaches behind her for the paper. "I think there's a show in about half an hour."

"Tonight?" David puts down his fork and looks at Cathy as if she were crazy. "We can't go to a movie *tonight*." He makes the idea sound ludicrous, as if Cathy had suggested going skydiving or something equally outrageous.

"Why not tonight," Cathy answers distractedly as she leafs through the paper. "Too much work?"

"Why not tonight?" Willow echoes her.

Willow knows goddamn well why David won't go out of the house, but she wants to hear him say it. She'll *make* him say it if it's the last thing she does.

"No, not too much work." He shrugs. "I just don't feel like it."

"Why not?" Willow asks again.

"I'm really not in the mood for the movies," David says, but he's never been a good liar and his voice sounds hollow.

"Why not?" Cathy sounds annoyed. "It would be so great to do something spur of the moment."

"*Why not?*" Willow spits out the words. Her chair makes a hideous scraping sound as she pushes it back and stands up.

"What's gotten into you?" David looks at her in confusion. "Why do you want us out of the house so badly?"

"Willow," Cathy says, "maybe you should—"

"Why don't you tell Cathy why you're so desperate to *stay in,*" Willow cuts Cathy off with a savage gesture.

"I'm not so desperate to stay in. . . ."

"Fine." Willow's hands are shaking. She places them on the back of the chair to steady them. "I'll tell her." She turns to look at her sister-in-law. "You see, Cathy, David is afraid to let me be alone with Isabelle. He's too scared. I guess he thinks that I want to finish off the rest of the family. Mom and Dad weren't enough."

For a second there is total silence. Even Isabelle stops fussing in her high chair. Willow can't believe that she had the guts to say it, but judging from David's ashen face, she's *finally* hit a nerve.

"Willow!" Cathy exclaims in horror. "How could you possibly think something like that?!" She looks back and forth between the two of them. It's clear that she expects David to make some kind of denial, but he isn't saying anything.

"I'm right, aren't I?" Willow says. She stares at David, but he's focused on his plate and refuses to meet her eyes.

"Well?" she persists. "Why don't you just say it? Why don't you just tell Cathy that you—"

"It was a hideous accident," David interrupts her, his face even whiter than a few moments ago. It's clear that he's having a hard time controlling his voice.

"Really? Then why are you afraid to leave me alone with—"

"*It was a hideous accident,*" he repeats. "But staying with a six-month-old . . . Well, you have to be on top of things, it's—"

"Oh, c'mon David," Willow interrupts him. "You've got to do better than that! It's not like I haven't babysat for years.

Admit it. You're scared to leave her alone with me. You're *scared* because you think I'm a—"

"I think that you're still raw," David cuts her off. "You have a lot going on right now, it's unfair to expect you to . . ."

"Stop it!" Willow is breathing heavily. "Just stop it!" She can't bear to hear him lie like this. "Tell the truth! Just say it already! Admit that you blame me for killing them! Admit that you hate me now!"

Willow claps a hand over her mouth. She's close, *dangerously* close to completely falling apart. If anything could make her feel the absolute horror, the pain of her situation, it's this— knowing for sure that she's lost her brother's love. If she weren't grasping the chair so tightly, she'd collapse on the ground in a flood of tears, and that is something that she simply cannot allow to happen. She's not equipped to process that kind of grief.

She shuts her eyes tightly, desperate for some kind of control. She pushes herself away from the chair, which falls to the floor with a loud crash, and heads for the stairs.

Willow knows that David and Cathy are calling after her, but she doesn't listen. She's too intent on reaching her sanctuary. She gets to her room and shuts the door behind her, grateful for the lock that a previous owner had put there.

She can still hear them shouting her name as she sinks down to the floor, covering her ears with her hands. Anything to shut out the noise. Because the noise is threatening to overwhelm her. Not just Cathy's and David's voices, but the squeal of the brakes. The crack of her mother's head hitting the dashboard. The silvery sound of the windshield breaking into a thousand pieces.

Willow can't take it anymore. She has to make it stop, she has to block the tidal wave of feelings that are starting to engulf her. Unfortunately she's left her bag downstairs, but thankfully her room has everything she needs. She crawls across the floor toward the bed and fumbles under the mattress for her equipment, knocking the phone off the bedside table as she does so.

Some part of her registers the sound of the dial tone piercing the air. But it's not enough, nowhere near enough to drown out the sounds that are filling her head. She grabs the razor convulsively, ready to do what she has to.

Willow pauses for the briefest instant. She doesn't know what she's thinking, she doesn't know what she's doing, but suddenly she's dialing the phone, punching in the numbers that she's already committed to memory.

"Hello?" His voice sounds like it's coming from incredibly far away.

"Hello?" Guy repeats.

Willow can't speak. She leans against the bed and unbuttons her shirt with trembling fingers. She looks down at her stomach, searching to find a likely place, and makes the first cut, waiting for the moment when the pain of the razor erases everything else. It's not happening as fast as it usually does, and her breath comes in little gasps as the razor sinks deeper and deeper into her flesh.

"Willow?" Guy asks. His voice is louder.

Willow closes her eyes, trying to let the sound reach her. It's a struggle. She can't stop hearing the windshield splintering, and it's getting worse. Now the pictures are starting. She sees her father's face crushed beyond recognition, a bloody pulp.

She sees her mother, intact, but with her eyes glazed over. She sinks the blade deeper, as if her blood could wash away theirs.

"Willow?" Guy repeats.

Willow doesn't talk, she's breathing shallowly. She watches as the blood springs from the cut she's making, but it doesn't change anything. Not this time. She swipes again, deeper. Now she feels pain, but will it be enough?

"Willow," Guy says a third time. Only this time it's not a question. This time it's clear that he's just making his presence known.

Willow tries to focus on his voice, on the lifeline he's throwing her. The pictures aren't fading, but as she listens to Guy's breathing, the sounds of the accident grow dim.

She stops cutting. The razor dangles uselessly from her hand; it has finally done its work. Willow watches the blood trickle over her skin through half-closed eyes.

Her breath deepens, becomes more regular, in concert with Guy's. The sound of their breathing in tandem is shockingly intimate, and soon, the only noise that filters through Willow's pain is the gentle swoosh of their shared inhalations as she drifts off to sleep grasping the phone as if it were a living being, as if it were her lover.

CHAPTER TEN

The first thing that Willow thinks when she wakes up is that the light fixture isn't where it's supposed to be. It takes her a second before she realizes that it is she herself who is in the wrong place. Instead of being in bed, she's lying on the floor, still dressed in all her clothes, grasping a dead phone. She hasn't felt this dazed, this bewildered since she woke up in the hospital after the accident.

But that momentary disorientation over the light is the only confusion that she feels. Everything else is crystal clear. She knows why she's on the floor, she knows why she's still in her clothes, she knows why those clothes are sticking to her, and she knows why there's the faint metallic smell of blood in the air.

Willow remembers everything from the night before. The look on her brother's face, the look on Cathy's face . . .

And Guy's voice on the other end of the phone, the sound of his breathing as she cut.

She rolls over onto her stomach, dropping the receiver

and wincing as the hard floor makes contact with her fresh cuts. She rests her chin on her hands and thinks about the fact that she called him. It never occurred to her, when she took his number, that she would actually phone him, but then again she never expected to sit in the park with him, or buy him a book, or do any of the things that they've done together.

But none of that means that Willow feels good about actually having called him. Shame washes over her as she remembers the inarticulate noises that she makes when she hacks at herself. Why *did* she decide to make him privy to that? Why did she give him a day pass into her world of pain? He deserves much better.

Willow knows that Guy was the one who told her to call in the first place, but she has to believe that he couldn't have known what he was letting himself in for. Maybe Guy knew that she was a cutter, but knowing and witnessing—even through the filter of a phone line—are two vastly different things.

She wonders how he'll act when she runs into him at school. Will he bring up the phone call? More to the point, how will *she* act? Of course, it's possible that she won't even see him at school.

In any case, she has more pressing things to think about. Forget *Guy's* reaction. How is she going to face David and Cathy?

Willow glances at the clock. She's overslept, so there's a chance that they've already left. On any other day either Cathy or David would have made sure to wake her up, but surely they must be as anxious to avoid her as she is them.

She hauls herself to her feet, not an easy task given how worn and tired she feels, hangs up the phone, then tiptoes to the door. She unlocks it as quietly as possible and sticks her head out.

Silence greets her.

They must have left already. Good. She has a little breathing space. Maybe, with enough time, she'll be able to figure out what to say when she sees them. Should she apologize for the night before? Maybe David will be the one to apologize. Maybe she should just act like it never happened.

Yeah! That'll be easy!

Willow shuts the door quietly, even though she knows there's no one to hear, and heads toward the bathroom. It's time to get on with the day. She stops for a second to pull some clean clothes out of her dresser.

The first thing that comes to hand is a short-sleeved T-shirt—not at all the kind of thing she can wear these days, given how much it reveals of her arms. Willow pauses in the act of stuffing it back into the drawer.

Of course, if she doesn't go to school, she can wear anything she wants. . . .

Maybe she should stay home, actually open her French book, or see if she can finally get some work done on the *Bulfinch,* like finish the reading or get started on the paper. Wouldn't that make more sense than going to school, where she'll only sleepwalk through her classes, still dazed from the events of the night before? Not only that, but if she does skip school, that would solve the problem, at least for today, of how to act when she sees Guy.

Fine, one problem solved. Too bad she just can't skip the

rest of her life. She slings the clothes over her shoulder, walks into the bathroom, and turns on the shower.

She leans against the wet tiles as the water cascades over her and watches in sick fascination as the dried, scabbed blood swirls down the drain. Unlike the act of cutting, which never fails to soothe her, this sight offers no comfort. In fact, it makes her more than slightly ill. Willow knows that there's a terrible disconnect between what she does and what she feels when she sees the fruits of her labor, but it is not so easy to be rational when the urge to cut is upon her.

Willow turns off the shower with a sigh, gets dressed, and walks down the stairs into the kitchen.

There's not much to eat, beyond a half-empty bag of pretzels and a few jars of baby food. Cathy never has time to shop, that's part of why they order in so much. Maybe she should go shopping later, that could be like a peace offering, of sorts.

Right. As if that'll make everything better!

Willow takes a handful of stale pretzels and wanders over to the table. There, propped up against the sugar bowl, is a note with her name on it in Cathy's handwriting.

She stares at it for a moment, too frightened to open it up. But really, there's nothing Cathy could say that could possibly make things any worse. Willow wonders if the letter is a reprimand, or an attempt to smooth things over.

Only one way to find out.

She grabs the paper before she can change her mind.

Dear Willow,
I decided to let you sleep in today. . . .

You must know how much David and I both love you. Don't ever think that he blames you for what happened or that he doesn't trust you! Nothing could be further from the truth.

David said that he thought you were so overwrought because you've had some trouble in school. You mustn't worry about that! You have plenty of time to bring up your grades. In any case, we both think you're doing incredibly well in the given circumstances. Take the day off if you want. Maybe you should go to the park and do some watercolors.

Try and feel better.

Love, Cathy

Willow folds the note carefully and puts it into her pocket. She knows that she should be relieved, and she's touched by Cathy's concern, but still, in many ways the letter only depresses her. Cathy's assurances prove that she just doesn't get what's going on. In a way, her protestations of love are no different from David's unwillingness to discuss what's happened. In both cases, there is simply a huge failure to connect.

She's turning away from the window, about to go back upstairs and get to work, when something outside catches her attention. There's always a lot to look at—young mothers with strollers, harried-looking businessmen rushing to work, joggers in colorful outfits, but this morning there's something more. Because this morning, Guy is part of the commotion taking place on the other side of the street.

At first Willow is sure that she's imagining things. But no, he's really there, standing just outside the park, watching her building. The obvious, the *only* explanation she can think of is that he's waiting for her.

So much for skipping school. . . .

Willow isn't sure what her move should be. She could always stay in the apartment and avoid him that way, but who's to say he won't cross the street and ring the bell?

And besides, she's not really sure that she wants to avoid him.

Yes I do. . . . I mean . . . Well, don't I?

Willow is ashamed that she called him, no doubt about that, and ashamed that he's heard her in the throes of an . . . episode. Still, along with the shame is another feeling. She's connected to him—maybe by a thread of blood, maybe by the bond of the razor, or maybe by something else again— but whatever has caused it, it's something that she cannot deny.

And it would be kind of rude to ignore him. . . .

Willow doesn't stop to analyze the situation further, but grabs her keys and heads out the door.

She pauses in front of the building and stares at him, a thousand questions forming in her mind. She wants to know why he's there, she wants to know what he thought about her calling him, but somehow, the only thing that she manages to say as she stands there shivering in her shirtsleeves is:

"How did you know where I lived?"

"There's this thing called the phone book," Guy says as he crosses the street. "And your brother put his address on the website for his class."

"Oh. Right." Willow nods as she rubs her arms.

"What are you doing barefoot?" Guy says as he looks her over.

Willow glances down at her feet on the pavement. She hadn't even realized that she wasn't wearing shoes.

"I . . . I just ran out of the house when I saw you. I didn't stop . . ." Willow trails off. She wonders why they're discussing such trivial things. Is it because he's also reluctant to bring up the phone call?

"Well, don't you think you should put some shoes on?"

"Yeah, well, I guess so." Willow shifts back and forth uncomfortably. "Come on, let's go inside," she says after a second, and leads him back into the building.

Guy is staring at her intently as she unlocks the door to the apartment. His scrutiny makes her very nervous. He must be thinking about the phone call, about what the phone call meant, but he's not saying anything, he appears to be—

"Your arms," Guy interrupts her thoughts.

"Yes?" Willow stops at the entrance to the living room and turns to face him. "What about them?" She looks down at her arms and tries to see them as he might. There are plenty of marks, but so what? Guy's seen her cuts before, surely he's the one person in the world that she can wear a T-shirt in front of.

"There's nothing new," he says after a moment. He gestures at the thin red lines that score her flesh. "Those aren't recent."

Willow knows exactly what he's getting at, but she has no intention of answering his unspoken question. "In here," she says as she walks over to the couch and collapses against it. After a moment, Guy sits down too.

"Well, where did you do it then?" Clearly now that he's brought the subject up, he has no intention of letting it drop.

"On my stomach," she says, having decided that in the long run, it would just be easier to tell him.

"But that's ... I thought ... I mean, you said that you only did it on your arms!" Guy objects.

Willow stares at him, confused by his protests. Is he saying that it would be *better* if she had cut her arms? Is it that he doesn't *believe* that she cut her stomach? Does he—God forbid—think she made the whole thing up? That she was pretending when she called him in order to get his attention or something? Willow is horrified at the thought.

"I said that I *mostly* do it on my arms." Her voice is rough. "Here, you don't believe me, you want to see?"

She pulls her T-shirt up over her bra, unzips her jeans, and pulls them down to just above her underwear. "Here!" she says angrily, practically shouting. "Take a look if you don't believe me!"

Willow is surprised by her own actions. She can't help thinking how different the scene would be if she were taking off her clothes for the normal reasons. If that were the case, her concerns would be about whether her underwear looked good enough, whether she looked good enough, not whether her scars looked recent enough for him to believe her.

Guy, however, is determinedly not looking at her stomach. His face averted, he stares at the faded Persian carpet, the bookshelves, anywhere but at her naked skin.

"Go on!" she admonishes him once again.

Guy turns his head slowly, careful to keep his eyes on her face. "I never said that I didn't believe you, I just was wondering ..." He trails off miserably.

Willow looks steadily back at him. She doesn't think that

she's ever seen anyone look as unhappy, as uncomfortable, as he does at that moment.

Finally, his eyes drop down and he looks at her stomach, *really* looks at it, takes in each and every cut.

Willow leans back and watches him through half-closed eyes. He appears transfixed. She knows that there is something perverse about this scene. The reason that he's staring at her, completely speechless, is not because he's captivated by her beauty, but because of the horror of what he sees.

Guy slowly reaches out a hand and places it on her abdomen. His hand is large and it covers every slash that she's made. Placed like that, with her scars concealed, it's easy to pretend that there is nothing out of the ordinary about the skin that he's touching. It's easy to pretend that his hand isn't there to hide her cuts but for another reason entirely.

But Willow *can't* pretend. It's true that Guy's hand, as it rests on her stomach, is affecting her in ways that are completely new. But those wondrous sensations are mixed with the pain that he is causing as he irritates the freshly broken skin.

And as for Guy, he does not look as if he is enjoying or even grasping the romantic possibilities of their circumstances. If anything he looks more than slightly sick. His face is white as a sheet.

He whips his hand away suddenly and claps it over his mouth.

"Do you want me to hold your head?" Willow asks, a distinct edge to her voice. She remembers the time in the stacks when Guy offered to hold her hair back, how struck she had been by his incredible kindness, how struck she is by it now. She wishes that she could be as considerate in return, but she is too traumatized by recent events to behave with such grace.

"No, no." Guy shakes his head. "I . . . No."

"Good." Willow yanks down her shirt and zips up her pants.

Guy doesn't speak for a moment. He's sitting the same way that she is, slumped against the couch, his expression dazed.

"What . . . Could you tell me *what* made you do it?" he says haltingly.

"I had an argument with my brother," Willow responds. She doesn't quite know how else to describe what happened.

"What . . . About what? The fight. I mean . . . what was it about?" Guy asks. His normal facility with speech seems to have deserted him. Willow realizes that she's never heard him sound so inarticulate before.

"About whose turn it was to do the dishes," Willow says. She's much too tired to go into it all.

"Fine," Guy says. "That's just fine." He struggles to an upright position. "Don't worry about being honest with me, I couldn't care less. I mean, I just came over here this morning for fun, right? This stuff doesn't matter to me. It's no big deal. Don't knock yourself out trying to give me a straight answer or anything."

Willow nods. His anger doesn't faze her; she certainly didn't expect him to buy what she was saying.

"Look, I'm sorry," he says after a second. "I shouldn't have gotten so angry—"

"No," Willow interrupts him. "You *should* be angry. I'm not being very nice to you, and you're being . . ."

Kinder than I ever had a right to expect from anyone ever.

193

She's more moved than she can say by the fact that he showed up at her door. Ambivalence has turned into gratitude. She wants to ask him why he's there, but is a little afraid to hear the answer. Would he tell her that it's because she frightened him? Willow knows that she has forfeited the right to be called normal, but still, she hates to think that he might consider her . . . *crazy* or something.

Is he there because he promised he wouldn't tell her brother, and that makes him feel responsible?

Is he there because he *cares* about her?

Willow sighs deeply. She feels unable to talk to him about any of this. She feels unable to tell him what his actions mean to her, and she realizes, given all that, that the least she can do is tell him the truth about the night before.

"The fight was about the fact that David hates me now." Willow says this simply, without drama. "He hates me because I killed our parents."

Willow waits to hear the inevitable. To hear Guy say, like everyone else does, that it was just an accident, that she didn't set out to kill their parents. That her brother loves her more than ever now that she's an orphan. She's heard the empty words countless times before.

But Guy is silent. He just looks at her.

"I can't imagine how hard it must be for you," he says finally. He looks stricken. "For both of you, actually," he adds after a moment.

"You're right, you can't," Willow says in a small voice. She should have known that he wouldn't fob her off with some pabulum answer, that he wouldn't try to talk her out of her feelings, or tell her that she was imagining things. "But . . .

thank you for, well, at least for not telling me that it's all in my head."

"Well, you're welcome, I guess." Guy pauses for a second. "Look, maybe I shouldn't say this after what you just said. I know I can't really get what you're going through, and I believe that *you* believe that your brother hates you. I mean, I totally don't think that it's all in your head. I'm sure that things are really . . . well, hard between the two of you." He shifts around on the couch and turns to look her in the face. "But are you sure that maybe you're not, well, maybe, I don't know, misinterpreting things somehow? I'm just thinking about the David Randall that I took a class with last year. There's no way he would hate his sister. I mean, who would, right? But him especially, I just don't see it."

"I think I know him better than you do," Willow says stiffly.

"I'm not trying to tell you what you feel or don't feel. I guess I just wished that I could make you feel *better*, and maybe looking at things in a different way . . ." He doesn't finish the sentence.

"It's not that simple," Willow says. Now she is the one having a hard time looking at him. It's painful for her to see just how miserable he looks, because she knows that she's responsible. "Look, don't go thinking that talking to you doesn't make me feel . . ." She fumbles for the words. "Well, you don't talk to me like anyone else does," she finishes lamely, but that isn't what she really wanted to say, not by a long shot.

"Yeah well, you don't talk to me the way that anyone else does either," Guy says.

"I don't?" Willow is surprised.

"Oh sure, discussions about *Tristes Tropiques*, sandwiched in between talking about where on your body you cut yourself, because you think that you're a murderer. Totally standard, every other girl I know is *just* the same. What is it with you people? I mean really, if I have to sit through one more conversation like that, pretending not to be bored . . ." He shakes his head.

Willow cannot believe, she really cannot believe that she's laughing, Guy is too, and for a moment they are both literally convulsed with laughter. "That isn't why I cut myself," she says after she calms down.

"Then why don't you just—" Guy begins, but Willow interrupts him.

"Look, what I was trying to say a minute ago is that, well, you're the only person who listens to me, who doesn't have to pretend that everything is okay." She stops, not sure if she should go on, but really, it's the least that she can do for him, considering how much he's done for her.

"You know, I realized something after my parents died." Willow's voice is a little shaky. "I realized that what people say, the way they react, tells you more about *them* than it does anything else. People may think that they're offering you condolences or whatever you want to call it, but really, they're letting you see what *they're* all about."

"I'm not getting you, exactly." Guy frowns.

"Well, okay, here's what I mean." Willow takes a deep breath. "After the funeral, this one old lady came up to me to tell me how sorry she was. I barely knew her, but my parents did a little bit. Anyway, she said that she was sorry, and then she said *at least they didn't die alone.*" Willow closes her eyes as the sights and sounds of that day come rushing back to her. It's not easy, but she collects herself after a moment and goes on.

"Now, that's a bizarre thing to say when you think about it. I mean, *my parents were dead,* they'd died in a car crash, that's a horrible way to go, and she was saying that at least they didn't die alone, she was saying that it was good that they died together." Willow stops talking for a second and looks at Guy. She can see how intently he's listening.

"When I say she was old," Willow continues, "I mean she was *old,* mid-eighties, I'm guessing, and I knew, everyone knew, that her husband had died thirty years before, and that her only son had died in Vietnam right before that. And I realized that all she had in front of her was the knowledge that she was going to die alone. She wasn't being insensitive—for her, my parents really did have it easy.

"And here's another example, the other day I told Laurie about my brother, how he has to do all these parent things, and you know what she said? That he was being *sweet.* She wasn't being insensitive either. It's just that she doesn't get it." Willow pauses and shifts her gaze away from Guy. "But with you, well, the things you say . . . You *do* get it, and that does make me feel . . . better." Willow can feel herself starting to blush.

"You blush a lot," Guy says after a moment.

"I can't help it."

"Well, don't help it. I mean, blushing. I think *that's* sweet."

"Oh."

"And I'm really happy if anything I do makes you feel any better."

"Oh." Now Willow is really red, but she doesn't turn her

197

head away from him, she just lets him look at her, flushed face and all.

"We're going to be so late for school," Guy says. "We definitely missed first period."

"I'm not going to school today," Willow tells him. "I just can't, not after last night, and anyway, I'm so behind in my work that I should really just stay home and try to catch up."

"Maybe I won't go either." Guy stretches out his legs and crosses his hands behind his head. "It might be nice to take the day off."

"You don't have to do that because of me," Willow says hastily. "I mean, you don't have to worry that I'm going to do something. . . ."

"Maybe I'm doing it because I feel like it," he says. "But now that I am, is there anything you want to do? I mean before you get started on all this homework?"

Willow thinks of all the things that she would like to do: go to sleep for about three days straight, get her work done—finally. Maybe even do something for Cathy and David, like clean up the house or go shopping, but all those things pale in comparison to the one overriding need she has right now.

"You know what I'd really love to do, more than anything?" Willow leans forward. "I'd *love* to have breakfast. I'm completely starving."

"That sounds really good," Guy says. "I'm starving too. Let's get out of here." He stands up and pulls her to her feet.

"What are you in the mood for?" Willow asks, grabbing a sweater from the hall closet. "Do you even know anyplace near here that we can get breakfast?" She locks the door and walks down the stairs in front of him.

"I know the *best* place," he assures her. "And it's only a couple of minutes away."

"There's no place a couple of minutes from here," Willow objects as they walk along the pavement.

"Shows what you know," Guy says as they turn the corner and stop in front of an old-fashioned diner. He pushes the door open with his shoulder. "Two bacon, egg, and cheese sandwiches to go," he gives their order to the guy behind the counter. "We'll take them to the park, okay? Sit on a bench or something."

"This is pretty good," Willow says as she bites into her sandwich a few minutes later.

"You've never had a bacon, egg, and cheese before?" Guy is incredulous. "They're like a classic hangover remedy."

"Yeah well, I've never been hungover before."

"What was all that stuff about Jell-O shots with your best friend?" Guy looks at her suspiciously as they enter the park. "No benches, c'mon, I know a nicer spot anyway."

"If you remember, I told you that I threw up when we did Jell-O shots, no hangover," Willow says as she follows him through the park. "And if you really want to know, that was pretty much the only time I did anything like that."

"This is perfect," Guy says. They sit down at the top of a small hill, underneath a Japanese maple with their backs against the tree. It's a particularly pretty place, shady, surrounded by flowers and with a view of a small man-made pond. "So, do you still see any of your old friends, anyway? I mean, what happened to this Jell-O shots girl?"

He shifts around, trying to get comfortable. Willow is sensitive to every move that he makes. He stretches his legs out, jostling hers, and for an instant they are joined at the hip.

Willow's first reaction is to move away, give him more room. But after a second, she edges back and lets her leg fall into place against his. He doesn't appear to notice. Why should he? It's very tame, especially after what happened on the couch, but Willow is acutely aware of the way her body feels against his.

"No, I don't really talk to my old friends anymore," she says after a while. "Markie, that's who I did the Jell-O shots with, I haven't spoken to her in months." Willow finishes her sandwich and wads up the wrapper.

"Don't you kind of miss them?"

"Well, yes, but . . ." Willow thinks about the phone calls she and Markie used to have. She wonders what Markie would think of Guy, and imagines the kind of conversations the two of them would have about him. Too bad she won't be talking to her any time soon. "You know why I don't talk to my old friends anymore?" Willow turns to look at Guy. "I can't because it just hurts too much. At first I thought it was because they just didn't get my situation, but then I realized it's because they remind me too much of the life I used to have. Seeing them with their parents, doing the kinds of things we used to do, whatever, it's all too hard. Things seem the same, and then at the end of the day, they go back to their same old lives, their same old world that they've always known, and I'm stuck on my own, in this new world that I've woken up in. I'm just a tourist in theirs." She starts shredding the wadded-up sandwich wrapper nervously.

Guy takes the paper from her gently and throws it along with his own in a nearby garbage can.

"You say that I'm wrong about my brother," Willow goes on. "But that's part of how I know that I'm right. I'm a constant reminder to him of what his life used to be like. He can never get away from it, not even for five minutes at a time. I've invaded his world. Every time he sees me, he knows that something has changed forever." She pauses. "I'm sorry. You ask me a simple question and I . . . Look, even I don't want to talk about this stuff anymore. Do me a favor, okay?"

"The weather in Kuala Lumpur?" Guy raises his eyebrows.

"Well, something, anyway."

"Okay . . . You know what I was doing when you called?"

"Uh . . ." Willow thinks for a minute. "Watching the game?"

"What game?" Guy looks confused.

"I don't know, isn't there some game?"

"You mean the World Series?"

"That'll work."

"You're about ten days ahead of schedule."

"Okay, so what were you doing?"

"Reading *The Tempest*."

"Oh." Willow thinks about this. "And . . ." she prompts.

"You may have a point," Guy concedes. "It is better than *Macbeth*."

"I told you!"

"I said you *may* have a point. You can't really compare because they're so different. I mean, *The Tempest* really is this magical, romantic—Hey look at that," he interrupts himself. "Look, over by the pond."

"What?" Willow follows his gaze but can't see what he's interested in, unless it's the man getting out of the rowboat.

"He's just leaving it there," Guy says. He sounds excited. "You're supposed to return them, I know because I've rented here a couple of times. It's really expensive, but that guy's just leaving it! C'mon." He grabs her hand, jerks her to her feet, and starts running down the hill.

"Do you know what you're doing?" Willow says as she watches him get into the boat.

"Excuse me." Guy looks at her. "I row on the *river* three mornings a week, you think I can't handle a pond?"

"Whatever." Willow shrugs, then climbs gingerly into the boat and sits down as he grabs the oars and steers them toward the center of the pond. "So did you and Andy ever, I don't remember, shave three minutes off your time or something?"

"Try ten seconds." Guy pulls on the oars. "We do the 2500 in eight minutes and twelve seconds right now. If we took three minutes off of that, we'd be beating the world record by a pretty wide margin. Anyway, I'm not expecting to beat eight twelve. Andy doesn't work hard enough, and I don't care enough. I really just row because I love being out on the river early in the morning."

Willow watches the deft action of his arms as he rows. There's something incredibly soothing, almost hypnotic, about his movements. She can't take her eyes away from the smooth motion that his strong, lightly tanned forearms make as they manipulate the oars.

She reaches her hand down into the water and lets it trail behind her in the little wake that they're making. Maybe it's the fact that she's worn out from the night before, or maybe it's the gentle sound that the oars make as they dip into the water, Willow doesn't know and she doesn't care. The only thing she's certain of is how peaceful she feels, better than she's felt in days, weeks even. She watches Guy through half-closed lids, and the last thing she sees before she drifts off to sleep is his smile.

CHAPTER ELEVEN

"Now, that one looks like a rabbit."

"Are you out of your mind?" Willow turns her head to look at Guy as they lay side by side on the grass staring up at the clouds. "If anything it's a swan."

"You're the crazy one, look." He points toward the sky. "See the ears?"

"No, that's the *neck*."

"Ears."

"Listen." Willow rolls over onto her stomach and props her head on her hands. "I don't know how to break this to you, but you might be in serious trouble."

"Oh yeah? How's that?"

"You know those inkblot tests? You must have read about them somewhere, the ones where a shrink makes you look at all these pictures of, well, of *inkblots*?"

"Yeah, sure." Guy turns on his side to face her.

"Okay, so the way they work is that most people will look

at some splotch of ink and think that it looks like a house or something, but then you get someone else who thinks that it looks like a . . . I don't know, a spider . . ."

"Or a rabbit."

"Exactly! And *those* people are certifiable."

"Your point?"

"Well, thinking that cloud looks like a rabbit . . . that's a bad sign."

"Maybe thinking it's a swan is more worrisome," he says with a yawn and flops down on his back again. "So what's this homework you're supposed to be doing now?"

"Please, don't remind me," Willow groans. When she decided to skip school that morning, she really *had* intended to spend the day looking over her French quiz, or getting to work on her paper. She never expected that she would spend it hanging out in the park with Guy. But in the three hours since they had breakfast, they've done nothing more demanding than rowing, taking a long walk, and then finally, just sitting around and talking.

Willow knows that she shouldn't be doing this, and yet, it would be impossible to tear herself away. Because in spite of the fact that she still hasn't really processed what happened the night before, in spite of the fact that she's so far behind in her work, she doesn't feel the need to do anything beyond sitting and talking to him. The girl who killed her parents, the girl who cuts, that girl's a million miles away. Right here, right now, Willow is simply and only a girl spending a day in the park with a guy.

"Well." Guy gives her a nudge. "C'mon, tell me."

"I'm way behind in that class all of you like so much, Myths and Idiots, or whatever it's called," Willow says as she pulls a couple of blades of grass from the lawn. "I have tons of reading, and I've got to get started on this paper already." She tries to use the grass as a whistle. "How come this isn't working? I thought you could use grass as a kind of whistle or something."

"Myths and Idiots?" he laughs. "That's good. Andy would appreciate that one. And yeah, you can whistle with a blade of grass, but I haven't done it since I was about five, so don't ask me to show you how."

"Some help you are." Willow lets the grass scatter in the wind. "You know what this paper is supposed to be about? About Demeter and Persephone, loss and redemption, how after Persephone is abducted to the underworld they're dead to each other. I mean, this should be pretty easy for me. I'm probably the only one in the class with personal experience, right?" Willow pauses for a second. "Except you know what? It's not about loss, it's about rebirth, how they get to be reunited . . ."

"Did you pick the topic?" Guy seems surprised.

"No, what's his name . . . Adams? He gave it to me."

"Yeah, well, that was really sensitive of him."

"Oh you know, he probably wasn't even thinking about what he was doing."

"Obviously not." Guy turns his head and looks at her carefully. "Well, listen, if you're really having a hard time, maybe I can help. I'm sure that I still have my old papers hanging around somewhere, maybe looking at them would make it easier for you to get started." He turns back and stares at the clouds again.

"Thanks," Willow says. "What . . . What are you doing?" She looks at him suspiciously. He's flat on his back staring up at the clouds, but his arms are outstretched and he's moving them as if he's . . .

"What does it look like?"

"Uh, if I had to guess, I'd say you were trying to direct traffic or conduct a symphony."

"Sort of. Actually, I'm trying to move the clouds closer together," he says. He looks serious too. "See? That one that looks like a rabbit, *okay*, swan, and that one that looks like a layer cake. I'm pushing them closer together."

"All right." Willow sits up abruptly. "I told you seeing a rabbit was a bad sign, you've obviously completely lost it, this is just the . . ."

"Did you see that?" Guy interrupts her. "It moved, you can't deny it! And relax, I'm not crazy, this is a very old and respected technique that I'm using."

"Huh?"

"It's from the *Boys' Book of Magic*, out of print since 1878, I bought it downtown. Trick number nineteen. How to control the weather and astonish friends at outdoor tea parties."

"Tea parties?"

"I told you, it went out of print in 1878. Besides, it was English. It was full of references to things like garden parties and playing cricket, and how to behave when doing tricks for your betters."

"Uh-huh, and you umm, bought this recently?"

"I bought it when I was twelve," Guy says. "And, okay, this is really embarrassing, but I actually believed that stuff like spells for controlling the weather would work. There! Did you see that! I'm telling you, I'm moving these clouds!" He looks at her with a triumphant expression on his face.

"Please." Willow doesn't even bother to glance up at the sky. "It's the wind. It's been getting windier and colder for about the past hour." She lies back down on the grass. "*Boys' Book of Magic?* It sounds like something that tutor of yours would have liked."

"I'm sure a long-lost relative of his wrote it," Guy answers her, but he's totally focused on the sky. "Actually, I think it was the last book I bought before we moved to Kuala Lumpur."

"I would have thought that it would have helped you fit in with all those British kids," Willow says as she watches him. He's infinitely more interesting than the clouds. She wonders what he must have been like when he was twelve.

"Maybe if we'd all been living a hundred years ago, and maybe if I ever learned any good tricks. But the only magic I ever figured out how to do was really stupid card tricks that would irritate your friends and make you look like an idiot at outdoor tea parties." Guy makes a face. "I haven't actually even thought about the book since then. I got bored with it pretty fast, but reading *The Tempest* reminded me of it. Remember the way that Prospero conjures up that storm? See! You're not watching." He gives her braid a little pull. "C'mon, give me some credit here. Obviously the book had something going on, and I was just too young to really grasp how hard it is to control the weather. I'm telling you, those clouds are moving, we are definitely on the way to having a storm here." He stops and turns to face her. "You see? Just like Prospero."

"You're not at all like Prospero!" Willow objects. "If anything, you're ..."

Well, he's exactly like Ferdinand.

Willow is struck by just how true that is. Of course he's like Ferdinand: He's a *perfect* romantic hero. She's reminded too of Miranda's words when she first sets eyes on Ferdinand:

Oh brave new world that has such people in it ...

Unlike Miranda, Willow *is* in a new world, and though she would never have chosen to be there, it is amazing to her that it has such an incredible person in it.

"Look," Guy says, interrupting her thoughts. "It *really* is going to rain. We should get out of the park. Unless you want to stay. It is pretty fun to be outside during a storm. You should see the way the lightning looks over the river."

"No," Willow says shortly. "I hate the rain."

"No! Don't say that!" Guy looks genuinely distressed. "I mean, that's a really serious category, people who get how great the rain is and people who just get mad because it screws up traffic. Please don't say that you hate the rain."

"I used to love it." She thinks back to all the times at home, when she would spend hour after hour curled up on the window seat with a book, while the rain beat against the glass.

"Then why don't you—"

"It was raining that night," Willow says suddenly. "It wasn't supposed to rain, but it did. And it wasn't *beautiful* rain, the kind you're talking about. It was torrential. I've always wondered what would have happened if the weather had been just a little bit better." She doesn't elaborate further. She's sure that he'll understand which night she is referring to.

"Why were you driving anyway?" Guy clearly picks up on

the reference. He moves closer and takes her hand. "I don't get it. You told me that you didn't even have your license yet, and the weather was so awful. What was going on?"

"Nothing. There was nothing going on. What do you mean? We were out. My parents felt like drinking." Willow shrugs. "It's just so awful, what I did. There's just no way to ever . . . Last night, I had this . . . scene with my brother. This argument. You know what started it? We ran into some friend of his and he asked David about our parents, and David didn't tell him. He *couldn't* tell him. He can't face what I did. He can't face what I am."

"Maybe he just didn't want to get into all of it. Maybe he was trying to protect *you*. Spare you from this guy asking any more questions," Guy says.

Willow stares at him without speaking, considering this for a moment before rejecting it as implausible.

"We should probably leave the park," Guy says as the rain starts falling. He stands up, pulling her with him. "Do you want to go back to your house, or maybe get some lunch? I'd say go to my house, except my mom will be there, and she'll wonder what I'm doing home in the middle of the day. She's a painter," he adds. "So she works from home."

"I'm not ready for lunch," Willow says. "And my house is too far away." They start walking faster to avoid the rain, but it's a losing battle.

"You know where we could go?" Guy says suddenly. "We could . . ." But he doesn't finish the sentence, and he has a hard time meeting her eyes as they exit the park and cross the street.

Willow is sure that she knows what he's thinking. It's the obvious place, barely a block away, free if you're a student, fascinating, and, unfortunately for her, full of memories.

They could go to the museum. The one where Guy heard her parents lecture, the one where she herself has been countless times.

"You were going to say the museum, weren't you? C'mon, that's a good idea. Let's go." She tugs on his sleeve.

"Are you sure?" He looks worried.

"No, but let's go there anyway," Willow says over a peal of thunder. The rain is coming down in driving sheets, it's madness to stay on the streets, and it's by far the most sensible option.

"Okay."

They run as fast as they can down the block and up the stairs into the museum.

"I'm soaked!" She shakes her head and droplets of water fly all over. Guy is also dripping water over the polished marble floor.

"I have that sweatshirt that I lent you the other day in my backpack," he says. "We could use that as a towel."

"Please." No sooner is the word out of her mouth than she finds herself swathed in his sweatshirt and being given a vigorous rubbing. "Ow! Stop!" Willow laughs. "Not so rough!"

"Don't you want to get dry?"

"Yeah, but I'm not a puppy!"

"I wouldn't be so—"

"Ssh!" A security guard admonishes them.

Willow stops laughing—not so much because of the guard's reproof, but more because she's suddenly become aware of her surroundings. She looks around slowly, testing out how she feels. Will this be like the bookstore?

But as she gazes around the great marble entrance hall, she experiences none of the feelings that she did in the store. Maybe it's because, unlike the bookstore, the museum seems completely different than she remembers. Willow has never visited on a weekday afternoon before. It's practically empty. She's never seen it be anything but crowded, but now it seems as if they have the whole place to themselves. Maybe it's because she has memories of this place that are separate from her parents, having been many times without them.

Or maybe it's just because she isn't alone.

"So what do you want to do?" Guy says as he finishes drying himself off. "What do you feel like seeing?"

"Forget what I want to see," Willow responds as they head toward the stairs. "I know exactly what *you* want to see. The dinosaurs, right?"

"Got it in one."

They walk through the vast corridors, past rooms filled with jade ornaments and tribal masks, past the lecture hall where her parents spoke, until finally they reach the dinosaur exhibit.

"These are my favorite," Guy says as he leads her over to a pair of ornithomimids. He leans over the velvet rope, and for a second Willow thinks that he's going to pet one.

"No touching," a bored guard cautions.

"As if I would," Guy mutters under his breath. "I guess I can understand it from his perspective, though." He stands up straight and turns to Willow. "I've been here on the weekends and the place is packed with little kids. You should see them, they practically climb all over these things. Especially the T. rex. They go crazy for that one." He walks across the room to examine another skeleton.

Willow can't help smiling a little. As far as she can tell, he's no different from the five-year-olds, at least when it comes to dinosaurs, anyway.

"So."Guy tears his eyes away from a model of a reconstructed jawbone and looks at Willow. "Where to now? What's your favorite exhibit? Wait, don't tell me. I know I'm going to get it, just gimme a sec. Okay, you probably like the gems and minerals, right? I'm not talking about that room with all the really fancy stuff, the crown jewels or whatever, those are too formal for you, I mean the semiprecious stuff, those great hunks of amethyst and topaz."

"You're right,"Willow says. In fact, the massive purple and golden crystals with their peculiar luster are among the things that she likes best in the museum. She's not surprised that he's guessed that, not after everything that they've shared. But still, the fact that he can so easily pinpoint her wants and desires makes her slightly uncomfortable. The ambivalence she felt earlier that morning comes rushing back.

She steps away from him a little, twists her hands together, and thinks. It's not like she feels ashamed the way she did before. His knowledge of her isn't necessarily bad, far from it. The bond that they've forged is the only positive thing in her life. It's more that he knows *everything*. He knows the most awful thing about her, and, as she stands there in front of him, it is impossible for her not to feel horribly vulnerable.

"So, how about it, do you want to go downstairs?"

"You know everything about me,"Willow bursts out. Guy looks startled and she realizes that she's not making any sense, that as far as he's concerned what she's just said came out of nowhere. "I mean, it's not just that you knew that I'd want to

213

see the amethyst . . ." She trails off, unsure of how to go on.

"Well, you knew that I'd want to see the dinosaurs, I don't get—"

"That's different," Willow interrupts. "You're a guy, you're hardwired to like dinosaurs."

"You know, if I said that because you're a girl you're hardwired to like jewels, you'd be telling me that was some sexist—"

"You're not getting it," Willow says somewhat wildly. "I mean that you know the worst thing about me, and I . . . don't know the same about you. I know all the good things, but I don't know what you're ashamed of, I don't know something about you that you'd want to hide from everyone else."

"Oh." Guy still looks a little surprised at the turn the conversation has taken.

"Never mind," she mutters after a second. "Look, let's just go look at the gems, okay? C'mon." She tugs his hand. "Forget I said anything."

But Willow is having a hard time forgetting. Unfortunately, holding his hand isn't making things any easier. With anyone else, holding hands would be so innocent, but that isn't the case with Guy. His hands, his big and beautiful hands that have bandaged her arm and felt her scars, only remind her that he knows her deepest secret.

"This is it," she says as they enter the hall of gems and minerals. As with the dinosaur exhibit, they're alone, without even a security guard, most probably because everything here is behind shatterproof glass.

The room is underground, without windows. But the whole place is illuminated both by artificial lighting and the luminosity that the jewels give off. The strange ghostly radiance and the uneven crystal formations have always made Willow feel as if she were walking on the surface of the moon.

"You know, there's a huge oyster here somewhere. You might not like it, but I think it's fascinating. It had the biggest natural pearl ever. I forget how much it weighed, but . . . Wait a sec, it's right over here, if I remember . . ." Willow feels like she's babbling, but she doesn't know what else to do. The things that she said upstairs are still hanging in the air, and she's desperate to get back to the carefree banter that they shared in the park.

"What do you think?" she asks with artificial brightness as they stop in front of the oyster.

"I don't think that I'm, well . . . I don't think that I'm *ashamed* of anything," Guy says, completely ignoring the oyster and turning to look at her. "There's nothing I've *done* that I have to hide from other people. Or nothing that's not completely trivial anyway. I'm sure I cheated on some algebra test back in eighth grade or something else like that."

"Oh," Willow says faintly.

"What I mean is, it's not like there's some particular act that I'm afraid people will find out about," Guy continues. "That isn't the way things are for me. I'd say that it's more like I'd hate for people, my friends, Adrian even, to know what's going on inside me most of the time." He pauses and looks into Willow's eyes, and she can see that even with all his strength, he's just as vulnerable as she is.

"You see, I'm . . . well, I guess the best way to describe the way I feel is that I'm scared, *completely* scared. And I know that deep down a lot of people are, but still . . . I mean, I know Laurie would tell you that *she's* scared. She's afraid that she won't get into the right school, or that she and Adrian will have to go to different schools. And I'm not saying that those fears aren't real for her, but with me it's something different. I'm more afraid that maybe I'll get into the right school, and maybe after that I'll get the right job, and that from the outside everything will look great, but I'll never really do anything or think anything special. And even if it all looks good on the surface, *I'll* know I've failed, and not at something unimportant like school, but at *life*." He stops talking for a second.

"Keep going," Willow says. She squeezes his hand.

"Okay, remember when we were in the stacks that day and you were telling me about what fieldwork is like?"

"Yes." Willow nods.

"Well, we were joking, and I know that this sounds like a meaningless example, but I said maybe I wouldn't like fieldwork either, because I like my showers. Well, sometimes I worry that my whole life will be based around what's comfortable and easy. I'll care too much about what makes me feel good to ever really reach for anything. And then I worry that even if I do, I won't succeed."

Willow doesn't say anything. She's too busy mulling over everything that he's told her and she can't figure out why, when he's exposed himself so completely, made himself so vulnerable, he only seems stronger.

"But these days, I haven't been worrying about those things so much," Guy says. "I guess what scares me the most now is the thought that I won't be able to protect you."

Willow stares at him. She doesn't know how to respond to this extraordinary thing that he's told her. She squeezes his

216

hand more tightly and she's aware that he's slowly moving closer to her, very slowly. She feels as if they're both underwater, and she knows that he's going to kiss her.

"Ahem." They jump apart as a security guard comes into the room and clears his throat.

Guy gives her a lopsided grin. Willow can tell that to him, the interruption is unwelcome but amusing.

But Willow feels differently. As much as she would love to have kissed him, she is also somewhat relieved that the guard prevented it from happening. Her heart is beating wildly, both from anticipation of how that kiss would have felt, and from fear.

Because now she's the one who's scared, *very* scared. Not of him, but of herself, or rather, of her feelings for him.

Didn't you know? Well, didn't you know that this is the way things would go?

She should have known better. Couldn't she tell from the first time she talked with him in the library—talked to him the way she's almost never talked to anyone else—couldn't she tell *then* that this would happen? And she tried to prevent it too. That first day when he wanted to walk home with her, she tried to send him away then.

What happened to her resolve? She should never have called him last night. She can't believe that she's spent so much time talking to him and finding out about him, that she practically begged him to show her the deepest recesses of his soul.

And most of all, she can't believe that she let him get under her skin and mean so goddamn much to her.

Willow knows that a year ago, if she found herself in such

a situation, with such a guy, she would be happy beyond belief, but her life is not as it was a year ago.

It is nothing less than astonishing that her new world—so far from brave—has such a person in it. But most unfortunately for Willow, she cannot let herself feel for him the way she would have if she were still living in her old world.

The silence between them is starting to become awkward. Willow knows Guy is expecting her to say something first. That he's waiting to hear her response to the things that he told her, and maybe even more, her response to his attempt to kiss her. She should say *something* to him, she should respond to this gift that he's offering her. But she can't. She can't tell him that she's moved, because she won't let herself be moved. She can't tell him that she cares, because she's trying very hard not to care.

Willow doesn't know what to do. She needs to get away from him, get away before things get any more complicated, but she doesn't know how to make a graceful exit. She doesn't know how she can ignore the appeal that's written so clearly on his face.

"I bet it's stopped raining by now. I should head on home and see if I can get anything done on that paper," is what Willow finally does choose to say. She can tell from the change in his expression—he looks like he's been slapped—that it's possibly the worst thing she could have come out with.

"Your paper?" he says incredulously. "Are you kidding me? *That's* your response? Fine." He backs away from her, *pushes* her away. Unlike before, his movements are quick; clearly he can't wait to get away from her either. "Fine, you do that. I guess I'll head up to the library, see if I can get some work done too." His

218

voice is cold, and Willow can tell that he's hurt and confused.

"I'll walk you there," she says in a rush. Now he looks more confused than ever. And why not? She knows how crazy she must sound given the rejection that she's just handed him. But Willow's not quite capable of walking away from him yet.

And she can't bear to leave him with that look on his face.

"If you like," he says diffidently. "C'mon, let's get out of here."

It has indeed stopped raining. Once again the sun is shining and there is a light breeze, but they are both oblivious to the beauty of the day. Neither one of them speaks a word during the entire walk to the library.

"Well, I'm headed for the stacks as usual, you want to come?" Guy doesn't look at her as he says this, and Willow wonders why he's even bothering to ask. If their situations were reversed, she doesn't know if she would bother to talk to him. Maybe, like her, he feels that there's something unfinished in the air.

"All right." She nods.

They walk silently through the campus and into the library. After flashing their ID cards for Carlos, they take the elevator and get off on the eleventh floor. As usual they're alone. Guy presses the button for the lights and Willow blinks in the sudden glare.

"It's not that I wasn't moved by what you said," she says suddenly, grabbing his wrist and pulling him close. "It's not that I didn't want you to kiss me. It's that I can't let myself be kissed. You don't understand, I can't *let* myself."

Guy gently disentangles his arm and places both hands on her shoulders. "You're right," he says. "I don't understand." But the coldness is gone from his voice.

"I want to tell you something. I'm *going* to tell you something," she amends. Willow has made a decision. He's done so much for her, given her so much, that she simply has to give him something in return. She reaches up and covers his hands with hers. "C'mon, let's be comfortable at least." She walks him over to the place where they sat and talked about her parents' lecture.

"I'm going to tell you something," Willow repeats. She sits down cross-legged on the floor, and pulls him down alongside her, close, so close that it is as if they are joined from shoulder to hip.

"I'm listening." Guy seems reserved, but attentive.

"All right." Willow takes a deep breath. "After the accident, I was in the hospital for a week. There wasn't anything wrong with me, but, you know they keep you in there for *observation* or something. Anyway, the one good thing about it was that I was so drugged that I didn't really get what had happened. Oh, I knew, all right, but I didn't *get* it. I was conscious maybe two, three hours a day, I just slept all the time." She pauses for a moment to gather her thoughts.

"Then David and Cathy came to pick me up. Of course they'd visited me all the time, I mean that they came to take me home, well, to *their* house. Obviously I had to move in with them, I couldn't go back home and live by myself, and David didn't want to leave the city. He worked out how I could finish the school year by sending in some extra papers and things. I was always ahead in my classes, and anyway, my old school got out mid-May, so there were only about eight weeks left." Willow stops talking. She knows what she's going to say, it's just hard to come out with things that she has never before spoken of to anyone.

"It was terrible after the hospital. The hospital was, I don't know, oblivion. But being with David and Cathy, not having sleeping pills or pain pills, was just awful. I was dazed all the time, not from drugs anymore, but because now I really knew what I'd done. I mean, I got it in my head, I understood what had happened, but I didn't feel any pain, not then anyway. I guess I was still in shock.

"Well, after about another week of just hanging around in my bathrobe and sleeping all day, David decided that he wanted to go home and pack up our parents' books to take to his apartment. You can imagine that our house has a lot of books—I'm talking thousands upon thousands. Anyway, when we got home, David gave me a screwdriver. He wanted me to take apart this old bookcase down in the basement, while he got to work on some of the ones upstairs. Now that I think about it, what he did doesn't make any sense. I mean, there's no place in his apartment for all of those books, and why would I have to dismantle this crappy old bookcase anyway? Why not just pack up all the books? You know what I think was going on? I think for David, destroying the bookcases that way was like when the ancient Greeks would rend their clothes and tear their hair as a way of mourning. I think that's what it was all about, even though, in the end, we didn't get very far with it.

"So I was downstairs in the basement, with this screwdriver. Now, me and a screwdriver is not a good mix, it's like high heels on Everest, something you never want to see together, and I'm trying to take this stupid bookcase apart and it's just not happening. And all of a sudden, maybe it's being back home, I don't know, maybe it's what books meant to my parents, and the fact that I'm trying to dismantle their collection, but all of a sudden, I start to *get* it. I don't mean *think* it, I mean *get* it. It was like there was this extraordinary pain just knocking at the door of my consciousness—this overwhelming, extreme sensation, and I knew that if I let it in, I would go under.

"And then, just when I thought that I had no control over what was about to happen, I realized two things. The first is that the emotional pain was going away, it was leaving, it *wasn't* going to consume me, and the second was that I was stabbing myself, really *attacking* myself with the screwdriver, and that the physical pain that I was causing was better than the best drug the hospital had. It was just forcing everything else out. This pain, this *physical* pain, was flowing through my veins like heroin, and I was numb, immune to the rest of it, I couldn't feel anything but the pain, and I knew that I had found a way to save myself.

"When you found me out, you thought that I wanted to kill myself, that all this slashing was like target practice until I got up enough courage for the real thing. You don't understand at all. You just don't get it. I'm *saving* myself.

"I've taught myself, I've trained myself, not to feel anything *except* physical pain. I'm completely in control of that. Do you understand? Do you get what that means?"

Guy doesn't say anything. He is ashen-faced. Willow is also silent, spent from having revealed so much, but something else is happening too. As she sits there next to him she is acutely aware of the way his body feels, of the way his arms look with his sleeves rolled up, of the texture of his bare skin as it brushes against hers, and of the sensations all of those things evoke deep inside of her. And she realizes that try as she might to prevent it, try as she might to only feel pain, now there is something else she feels as well, and there is nothing she would rather do than kiss him.

She's shocked that her mood has swung so wildly. How did anguish suddenly morph into desire?

Maybe it's because she has never revealed so much of herself to another person. Maybe it's because she wants to test if her hypothesis is true. Is it really so dangerous for her to feel anything? Will kissing him, feeling for him, *falling in love with him*, really be so disastrous?

This time she is the one who leans forward. She is on her knees in front of him, grasping his shirt collar, pulling him close to her. He is clearly as startled by this as she herself is, but he allows himself to be drawn in. Their mouths meet, she moves even closer still until she is sitting on his lap, takes his hands from her waist and puts them on her breasts, does everything but devour him, desperate to see if she can have something beyond her bondage with the razor.

Willow doesn't know the exact moment that the extraordinary pleasure she's feeling turns into the pain of her worst fears. Pictures of the accident start writhing beneath her closed lids, competing for attention with the image she holds of his face. A tidal wave of emotion threatens to engulf her. She is suddenly back in the basement with the bookcases.

"I can't." Willow pushes him away. "I can't!"

She's breathing heavily. She barely even registers that Guy is on his knees in front of her. The bloody dashboard, her mother's crushed limbs, these are the things that she sees.

Willow claps her hands over her ears in a vain attempt to drown out the dreadful sounds of the accident.

She jumps up, wheels away from him, fumbles in her pocket for the razor that she always keeps there.

But just as she's preparing to slice, to save herself, to end the nightmare visions, Guy's hand clamps down on hers. He pulls her down on the floor again roughly.

"No." He's shaking his head. "Not here. Not now. Not with me around."

"I have to." Willow is gasping. "Just let me be. Let me do it!"

Guy sits back on his heels and regards her solemnly. "All right then," he says finally. "You can cut yourself, but not like this, not like some cornered animal. You have to do it in front of me."

"You . . . You want . . ." She stares at him openmouthed. She can't imagine cutting herself in front of him. It is something so intimate that it makes their kiss seem like nothing more than shaking hands. She can't do it. She just can't. She just sits on the floor in front of him, the razor dangling uselessly from her hand.

But the pictures in her head won't stop, and there is only one way she knows of ending them.

Willow doesn't flinch as she presses the blade into her flesh. She stares at Guy, aware that although she is fully clothed, she is completely bare before him. It hurts. It hurts badly, and within seconds the pain is swirling through her like an opiate, completely crowding out everything else.

"Oh my God. Oh my God!" Now Guy is the one who is clapping a hand over his mouth. "Stop it! I can't watch!" He grabs the razor and flings it across the room, grabs her arm and stares at the blood, grabs *her* and crushes her close.

Willow is so close that once again she's sitting in his lap. She's so close that they might as well be sharing the same breath.

"You won't let yourself feel anything but pain?" He holds her more tightly than she would have thought possible.

Willow leans back against his chest. Now that the razor has done its work, it's not so overwhelming to be there with him. She watches through half-closed lids as he wipes the blood on her arm with his shirttail. Now that she's numbed herself, she'd like nothing more than to stay there with him, like this, forever.

Instead she does the next best thing. She stays there, like that, long after the lights flicker out and leave them in the darkness. She stays there long past the time that she should go home. She just stays there, like that, for as long as she possibly can.

CHAPTER TWELVE

Willow was sure that she had perfected the technique of pretending to pay attention in class when her thoughts were completely elsewhere. She knew how to make it look like she was industriously taking notes when she was doing nothing more than scribbling, she knew how to make it look like she was following along in the text even when her book was open to the wrong page, and she knew how to nod along at key moments to make it look like she was listening.

But somehow those dubious skills seem to have deserted her. Because today, Willow knows that it's all too obvious to anyone who cares to look, that although she may physically be in French class, her mind is far from present.

She can't stop thinking about what happened in the stacks. She can't stop thinking about what happened with David the night before that, and she can't stop wondering how she will behave, how she *should* behave the next time that she sees either Guy or her brother.

At least she'd been given a small reprieve with David. When she'd finally gone home the night before, dreading the confrontation that she was sure would take place, Cathy had reminded her that David had gone to yet another conference, and wasn't due back until much later today. As for Cathy, she hadn't said much of anything to her about the whole mess. She'd already expressed her feelings in her note, and Willow was grateful that she clearly didn't see the need to discuss it any further.

Willow is sure that when she sees David again, things will be very uncomfortable, but she's nowhere near as sure of what seeing Guy will be like. There's no reason that things shouldn't be fine, better than fine, actually . . . except for the fact that she herself is far from fine.

Willow closes her eyes as unbidden images of their afternoon wash over her. It is impossible to think of their day together with unmixed emotions: It was wonderful to talk to him. She should *never* have talked to him about how she became a cutter. It was wonderful to kiss him. It was *terrifying* to kiss him. It was incredibly moving to hear about his hopes and fears. She's not strong enough to take on someone else's pain.

Things were simple before she met him. There was the accident, and there was the razor. Life revolved around both of them. Now things are far from simple.

She sighs deeply, miserably aware that the girl next to her is looking at her strangely.

Maybe she just needs a little time to sort things out. Who's to say that she's going to see him today anyway? This is her last period, he may or may not be outside afterward, he's never called her or anything, she's the one . . .

Willow starts to laugh. Not really loudly, but enough for the same girl to give her another look.

This time it doesn't bother her, though. It is absurd to her that after everything that's happened, all she can think about is *Will he call or should I call him first?* It's the sort of thing that she and Markie used to spend hours obsessing over. For a second she feels just like a regular girl again.

Class ends and she leaves the room with everyone else. She looks over her shoulder as she walks down the hall, both relieved and disappointed that he doesn't seem to be around.

Well, you wanted some time alone to think about things, didn't you?

There are plenty of students milling around on the pavement outside school, but again, no Guy. Willow does see Laurie and Chloe, however, and she walks over to them.

"So, whaddya think?" Laurie smiles at Willow as she pivots on one heel. Willow is confused for a moment until she realizes that Laurie is asking about her new shoes.

"Oh, they're absolutely fabulous!" Willow says in admiration. "And I really love the color."

"Aren't they amazing? I couldn't believe that they had a pair left in my size. They're comfortable too."

"You should have come with us," Chloe joins in. "They had a lot of great things on sale. I got two pairs, but I'm not wearing either of them today," she adds as Willow glances over at her feet.

"What did you get?"

"The same ones as Laurie, only I promised not to wear mine until next year when we're at different schools." Chloe makes a rueful face. "And then a pair that are way too fancy to wear to school, but they're really great. Black. *Super* high. *Super* strappy."

"We're headed to the park right now," Laurie says. "No money left to do anything else. You want to hang out with us today?"

"Sure," Willow responds after a few seconds. This is probably exactly what she needs. No scenes with her brother, no rehearsing those scenes beforehand, no wondering about Guy and how things are going to proceed with him, just hanging out in the park and talking about nothing more emotionally demanding than shoes. Perfect.

"So, did you ever get that internship you were interviewing for?" Willow asks Laurie as they cross the street and start walking toward the park.

"Haven't you figured out by now that it's dangerous to ask her questions about stuff like that?" Chloe says, kicking a stone out of her path.

Willow looks at Chloe with a question in her eyes, which quickly turns to a shared grin as Laurie launches into a diatribe regarding the pros and cons of working for a recommendation versus working for cash.

"I mean, it would look so good if I had that kind of experience." Laurie chews on her lower lip fretfully. "But I'd love to have some money right now. Especially now, since I spent practically everything I had the other day. The thing is, though, I don't even know if I've gotten the internship. I'm supposed to hear this week—"

"What do you think of Andy?" Chloe interrupts suddenly.

"Who, me?" Willow asks.

"Yeah, well, I already know what Laurie thinks."

"How is Willow is supposed to know?" Laurie protests. "She's barely exchanged two words with him!"

"True," Chloe concedes. "Great arms, though, huh? Rowing is the best for arms, it really develops them."

"It sure does." Willow doesn't remember *Andy's* arms at all, but she has to agree with Chloe. Rowing really does give people amazing arms. She turns her head away, aware that not everyone finds blushing sweet. "Are you . . . interested in him?" Willow asks after a moment.

"Let's put it this way." Chloe sighs. "He's the only one who's interested in me right now."

"Maybe you should give him more of a chance," Laurie interjects. "After all, we hardly know him any better than Willow does."

"He's not new, is he?" Willow frowns. "I mean, how come you guys don't know him that well?"

"No, he's not new or anything like that," Chloe says as they enter the park. "We just never really spent any time with him before."

"He used to go out with the most horrible girl," Laurie adds as they all sit down on the grass. "Elizabeth something or other. She left last year, though." She takes off her new shoes and starts rubbing her feet. "I shouldn't have worn these two days in a row."

"Yeah, it's sort of like a worrisome sign that he's interested in me after her." Chloe represses a shudder. "I mean, am I like *Elizabeth* in any way?" She looks at Laurie.

"Yeah, just like her, that's why we've been best friends for three years now. God, these blisters are killing me."

"Weren't you just saying how comfortable they were?" Chloe raises an eyebrow.

"Comfortable for *heels*."

"I have some Band-Aids," Willow offers. She starts rooting around in her bag for the box that Guy bought her.

"You're so well prepared," Chloe observes.

"What do you mean?" Willow asks warily. She tosses the Band-Aids over to Laurie.

"I don't know." Chloe shrugs. "You just seem to have stuff that people need, like when we were here with Andy and you had those handy wipey things."

"Oh." Willow nods. She wonders if Chloe notices that it's a rather odd assortment of things that she carries around with her, far more unusual than the nail polish and other paraphernalia that Chloe obviously packs. She feels exposed, guilty even, like a heroin addict who's been caught with her works.

"Anyway, getting back to Andy—Ouch!" Laurie exclaims as she pops a particularly nasty-looking blister. "Don't make up your mind about him yet, who knows, he may turn out to be okay. I'm sure that when Adrian shows up, he'll be tagging along and—"

"Adrian is showing up?" Willow blurts out. She doesn't know why that surprises her. It makes total sense, obviously he and Laurie are together but . . .

"Yeah, he had to do some stuff after school, so he said he'd meet us here." Laurie tosses the Band-Aids back to Willow.

"Oh." Willow wonders if Guy will be along for the ride too.

"I'm pretty sure that Guy will be coming with them," Laurie says, as if she can read Willow's mind. "Because I know that he was going with Adrian on whatever errand it was he had to do."

"Whoever shows up, I hope that they brings some Diet Cokes." Chloe yawns.

"That should be good though, right?" Laurie looks at Willow. "I mean, and don't give me a hard time, Chloe," she says as the other girl starts to speak. "You do like him, right? I didn't mean to bother you the other day, but, c'mon, tell us."

"Yes," Willow says. "I like him." Privately she thinks how bland and pallid the word *like* is as a way to describe her feelings. But as much as she might feel for him, she hopes that he won't show up. She was expecting some time alone to sort things out, she wasn't counting on their first meeting after the stacks being in mixed company.

"Now *he's* someone to have interested in you." Chloe leans forward, her eyes sparkling. "Oh, don't worry." She touches Willow's arm. "I've known him for three years and nothing . . ." She shrugs eloquently.

"Well, it's not really like what you're thinking," Willow says. "I mean, it's just—"

"Speak of the devil," Laurie interrupts, looking over Willow's shoulder.

"And no Diet Cokes." Chloe groans. "Maybe I can get Andy to go find one of those hot dog carts. There's usually a couple in the park, somewhere. It shouldn't take him too long."

Willow turns to watch the three of them approach.

Her hands tremble a little and she drops the box of Band-Aids in the grass. She curses under her breath, annoyed at herself for being so flustered. Well, at least now she doesn't have to wonder how she'll feel when she sees Guy.

"Ah, that brief blissful time when you can get them to do your bidding." Laurie laughs.

"Right, like finding me a Diet Coke compares to the stuff that Adrian does for you."

"Sssh!" Laurie elbows Chloe in the ribs. "He thinks everyone is that way. *Please,* it took me *months* to train him, don't go giving him any ideas." She stops talking as they come within hearing distance.

"Do something for me," Chloe says as Andy drops his backpack down next to her.

"Sure," he says easily.

Willow watches Adrian give Laurie a kiss. She feels rather than sees Guy sit down across from her. She shoves the Band-Aids back into her bag. There should be nothing awkward about this. He's someone she really likes, and unless she's completely mistaken, he likes her too, so what's the big deal? There's nothing so unusual about that.

Except everything about their time together has been unusual.

"Get me a Diet Coke," Chloe begs. "No, *two* Diet Cokes, please?"

"Hi," Guy says to Willow. He smiles at her. Not the same way that he's smiled at her when they've been alone. There's nothing particularly intimate about it, but it is genuine.

Willow looks at him. Okay, so *he* doesn't feel uncomfortable. *She* won't feel uncomfortable either.

"Hey, get me a Sprite while you're at it." Laurie fishes in her pocket for some change.

"Hell—" Willow starts to say.

"Anyone else want anything?" Andy interrupts as he moves

between her and Guy. He not only cuts her off verbally, but physically as well. "What about you, Willow?"

"Huh? Oh, nothing for me." Willow knows that he's just trying to be nice, but still, she finds him irritating. Did he have to get in the way like that?

"Okay, be back in a second."

Now Willow has her chance to smile at Guy, but he's too busy looking in his backpack for something to even notice. As he shifts things around, Willow can see the blue leather corner of *The Tempest* stuck in there among his other books. The sight of it makes her feel better. He wouldn't really be carrying it around unless it meant something to him, would he? Unless *she* meant something to him?

He looks up suddenly, their eyes meet, and she can't help it, she starts to blush. Willow glances away for a second, embarrassed, but then turns to him, determined to get over her awkwardness and to finally say hello. Only, as she looks at him, it is impossible not to think about everything that happened. The memory of what it was like to kiss him washes over her, blotting out the here and now. His features become fragmented, images of their time in the stacks are suddenly superimposed over his face.

Willow's blush deepens as she remembers grabbing his hands, forcefully *grabbing* them and placing them on her breasts. And then, as if that weren't bad enough, she remembers starting to cut in front of him. She can't think about these things right now—it would be one thing if they were alone together, but surrounded by everyone else? Willow drops her head in her hands for a second, as if by covering her eyes, she can blot out the pictures.

"Willow!" Laurie sounds alarmed. "Are you okay?"

"Oh." She jerks her head up.

This just isn't working.

"I have a headache, I get the most terrible migraines," she stammers. She avoids looking at Guy, avoids looking at any of them.

"And you don't have any aspirin in that bag of yours?" Chloe asks.

"No, well, the thing is, it's more that I just have so much work . . . I should get going." Willow shakes her head regretfully. "I'll see you all later, okay?" She gets her things together and stands up. Slowly, calmly, as if she really does wish that she could stay there with them.

Willow turns and walks out of the park, resisting the urge to run.

Well, that went well, huh?

If she was embarrassed and uncomfortable before, there simply aren't words to describe how she feels now. She briefly considers ramming her head into the stone wall that borders the park. It would make a novel change from cutting anyway.

The thing to do now is go home, forget the last twenty minutes, erase it. Get home and . . .

She wonders if Guy will follow her, or if he's had more than enough already.

Well, it's not like he hasn't already picked up on the fact that I'm a little different. . . .

If he does follow her, what will *she* do? Maybe her first instincts were right, maybe she has room for only one relationship.

Too bad that relationship just happens to be with a sharp piece of metal.

Don't think about it! Figure it out later! Get home! Open your French book! Get to work on your paper!

Willow can't stop herself from reliving the incident throughout the entire walk home. She goes back and forth between convincing herself that nothing so very dreadful happened and being sure that she's completely ruined everything.

Ruined what anyway?

Do I even have anything to ruin?

She's looking forward to sitting at her desk. Maybe getting to work will prove to be the distraction that she needs. But unfortunately, as she unlocks the door she's confronted by the sounds of Isabelle, screaming as if her lungs are fit to burst. Cathy is holding her while she paces back and forth on the phone. She looks completely overwhelmed. Willow drops her keys on the hall table and goes into the kitchen.

"Cathy?"

"I'm glad you're here," Cathy says above the screaming. "What?" she speaks into the phone. "Okay, thank you, yes, call it in to the pharmacy." She hangs up and looks at Willow.

"What's going on? What are you doing home? Is Isabelle sick or something?"

"She's burning up, poor little thing." Cathy presses a kiss against Isabelle's forehead. "They called me at work to come and pick her up. It's just an ear infection, the doctor said that there's nothing to worry about, that super high fevers are really common . . ." Clearly she's trying to reassure herself as much as Willow. "I have to go to the pharmacy and pick up her prescription. Will you be okay with her until I get back?"

"Of course," Willow says, taking Isabelle from Cathy. Now

is not the time to remind Cathy that David wouldn't approve of her staying with the baby. "I'll be fine," she says calmly. "Go to the pharmacy."

"Thank you," Cathy says, pulling on her sweater and grabbing her purse. "I don't know how long this will take, sometimes they make you wait while they make up the prescription. I'll be back as soon as I can." She dashes out the door.

Willow walks over to the window, Isabelle in her arms, and watches as Cathy runs down the street. "I'm sorry you feel so sick," she says, bouncing the baby up and down on her hip. But Isabelle seems a little calmer than she did a few minutes ago, she's no longer crying quite so forcefully. Her tears are subsiding, punctuated by little snuffles. Willow thinks how wonderful it would be, and not just for poor Isabelle's sake either, if when Cathy came home, everything was under perfect control, Isabelle calm, sleeping even, the kitchen clean. . . .

"Wouldn't that be nice, sweetie? Wouldn't you feel better?"

Willow wants rather desperately to repay Cathy's faith in her. Not only that, but she's sure that taking care of Isabelle, taking care of her *perfectly* that is, might go a little way toward smoothing things over with David when he finally comes home.

And if she's totally focused on Isabelle, then she won't even have time to think about what just happened in the park.

Of course, she's not exactly sure what taking care of Isabelle perfectly might entail. There's only so much she can do with a sick baby, after all, but maybe feeding her, and changing her, would be a good start. She does feel wet.

"So, let's get you changed, and then make you something to eat. You'll like that, won't you?"

Willow walks into Isabelle's bedroom and lays her down on the changing table. Now, she may have changed many diapers in her time—she's been babysitting since she was thirteen—but she's never changed Isabelle. Although it's not the most challenging activity, it is a little more difficult than she would have thought, since Isabelle, alone among all the babies that Willow has ever met, wears cloth diapers.

David gives Cathy a hard time about this, since they're incalculably more expensive than disposable diapers, difficult to even find, and more inconvenient in every way possible, but Cathy, who studied environmental law, always insists.

"Okay, so this shouldn't be so difficult. . . ." Willow grabs a cloth diaper and two diaper pins.

But Isabelle is not as cooperative as she might be. Clearly the poor little girl doesn't feel well. Instead of lying still she fusses and kicks, and Willow, unused to diaper pins, manages to stab her. Rather sharply too, if the baby's screams are anything to go by.

"Oh, no!" Willow is horrified. How could she do such a thing? She stares transfixed at the minute pinprick blossoming red that mars her niece's perfect, tender flesh. There's something absolutely obscene about damaging something so flawless.

Willow slowly reaches out her hand and touches the spot where she pricked Isabelle. Just as when Guy touched her, Willow's hand completely obliterates the mark that she made. Well, that's not very surprising. What she has inflicted on Isabelle greatly differs from the gashes that score her own stomach. But what if that tiny little mark were to grow? For a second she imagines Isabelle's skin scored all over, savaged by a razor, the way that her own is. How would she feel if, say, ten or fifteen years from now she found out that *Isabelle* was a cutter?

Willow jerks her hand back.

And what if she killed David and Cathy, then what? Would you still think her being a cutter was so bad?

She finishes diapering Isabelle without incident, although her hands are trembling, and carries her into the kitchen.

"Well, we're off to a great start here, don't you think?" she says in a shaky voice. So much for taking care of her niece perfectly. At least Isabelle has stopped crying. Willow can't help feeling that the baby has recovered from the episode far better than she herself has.

"How about something to eat?" She opens the cupboards and rummages around. Today even the pretzels and baby food are gone. "Yeah, so much for that." Willow slams the doors shut and moves to the refrigerator.

At least the refrigerator is more promising. There are half a dozen eggs, and some butter among other things. Willow puts Isabelle in her high chair and grabs a couple of the eggs and a bowl. She sets a pan on the stove and throws some butter in. As she beats the eggs she thinks about what just happened. She absentmindedly pours the eggs in the pan, then dumps the bowl in the sink.

Willow stares out the widow, but she barely even registers the park outside. The only thing she sees is Isabelle's perfect skin. She's so lost in thought that she forgets about the eggs for a second.

Willow turns back from the window and gasps in horror. The eggs are on fire. The pan is on fire. The kitchen is on fire.

Not again!

This is her first thought. *She has done it again.* David was right, she really will finish the rest of the family off. As her eyes start to tear from the acrid smoke, she has another thought as well. What if this time around she managed to save Isabelle? What if this time things are *different*?

The vision of herself as a heroine is delicious.

But the smoke starts to dissipate, and Willow can see that really, of course there is no fire. How likely would it be that some burned scrambled eggs could turn into a three-alarm fire anyway?

There is no fire, she will neither kill nor save Isabelle in some dramatic gesture. She is simply a girl who has made a filthy mess, a girl who is incapable of taking care of her niece, as incapable of that as she is of everything else these days.

Willow takes the smoking pan and tosses it into the sink, where it hisses and splutters angrily. As she stares at the smoke that drifts toward the ceiling, it occurs to her that maybe for once, David was being completely honest when he said that his reservations about leaving her alone were simply because she is too overwrought to take care of a six-month-old. Based on the evidence she'd have to agree with him.

The doorbell rings. Willow can only hope that it isn't Cathy, so weighed down by packages that she can't manage her keys, or even worse, David, home from his conference.

At least give me time to clean up, for God's sake.

But when she opens the door, it is Guy who is standing there.

This time Willow doesn't blush, and she doesn't feel flustered either. She's much too relieved that it's him as opposed to David or Cathy.

"Migraines?" He leans against the door jamb.

"Yeah, well, I thought the plague might sound suspicious. C'mon in." She steps back and opens the door wider.

"Something smells like it's burning."

"Tell me about it," Willow says. She walks in front of him toward the kitchen.

"What are you doing?"

"Umm . . ." Willow surveys the smoky kitchen. Her plan, to take care of Isabelle perfectly, could not have backfired more spectacularly. "I guess I'm continuing to screw up my life and anyone else's who comes into contact with me." She goes over to the sink and picks up a sponge, intending to scrub the burned pan. "That sounds about right, what do you think?"

"Just 'cause you burned some . . ." He joins her at the sink and glances into the pan. "Hmm, I'm guessing these were eggs at one point?"

"No, that's not the only reason." Willow attacks the pan with the sponge. It's tough going. She should have soaked it first.

The whole process of washing the pot seems futile suddenly. She wonders what would happen if she just threw it out the window. Instead she settles for the trash can under the sink. Maybe if she covers it with enough garbage David and Cathy won't even notice.

"You're just throwing it out?" Guy seems to find this funny.

Willow shrugs. "Oh, by the way, this is Isabelle."

"About those migraines in the park—" Guy starts to say, but they are interrupted by the sound of a key in the lock, and David's voice calling out.

"Hey, I'm back. Who's here?"

Willow is glad that the smoke has cleared somewhat, and that she has managed to get rid of the pan, but she'd prefer it if he didn't enter the kitchen just yet. She picks up Isabelle and walks into the foyer.

"Hi," she says warily. This is, after all, the first time that she has seen David since her fit a couple of nights ago. She has no idea how to act toward him. Given how close-mouthed David's been lately, she can hardly expect him to start something in front of Guy. Still, she imagines that he will make reference to the other night *somehow*, if only because her being left alone with Isabelle would have to reactivate the argument.

"Hello." David nods to Guy, but it's clear that he's preoccupied. "What's going on?" He looks confused. "Where's Cathy?" David reaches out to take the baby from Willow.

"She went to the pharmacy," Willow says. "Isabelle's sick, an ear infection, I think she said."

"You didn't try and put her down for a nap?" he asks mildly.

Willow can't believe how stupid she's been. Of course it would have made much more sense to do that than anything else. She braces herself for David's condemnation.

But David doesn't seem as if he cares very much about reprimanding her. He's far more interested in Isabelle's welfare. Willow knows that this is only natural and correct. Furthermore, she has no interest in having any kind of replay of the other night. Yet as she watches David kiss his daughter, she is struck by a pain so sharp, so brutal, that she nearly doubles over.

She clutches her stomach. For a second she is sure that she is going to faint. The ache is so intense that she is surprised, when she looks down at herself, to see that there is no blood springing through her clothes, that this pain is not self-inflicted. This is the pain that she has been fighting for so long.

Of course David's first concern would be for his daughter. Willow is not hurt by the fact that she is not first with *him*. It is that she will *never* be first with anyone again. She will never be anyone's child again. This happens to everyone, it will happen to Isabelle too, but surely not as soon as it has happened to her.

"Willow?" David grabs her arm, no easy feat since he is still holding Isabelle. "What's wrong?"

"I'm okay, just . . ." Willow straightens up. The pain is gone. She has no idea how, she can only be thankful that it is so. "I'm just a little . . ." She searches for the right thing to say. Migraines won't fly with David. "I'm really tired, that's all. We're . . . I'm going to go upstairs and lie down." She winces at her choice of words, and wonders if David or Guy has picked up on them, but David has already turned back to Isabelle.

"C'mon," she says to Guy. "Let's go."

Willow walks up the stairs to her room. The episode has left her feeling completely drained. She feels like she could sleep for a thousand years. She opens the door and eyes her bed longingly. She wonders what Guy would do if she just got under the covers and closed her eyes.

Instead of doing that she sits at her desk and Guy is the one who gets the bed. He doesn't get under the covers, but he does sit down and lean against the pillows. The sight of him on her bed is anything but comfortable and she has to look away for a few moments to compose herself.

But even though she is uncomfortable, even though she is

still reeling from what happened downstairs, seeing him like this, without the complications of other people, she knows, suddenly, what her feelings are. She can't rationally say that being with him is too complicated, that her fidelity is only to the razor. She is powerless to make such a decision. She cannot do otherwise but be with him.

"So about the park," Guy says. "I was wondering if your getting these migraines was a way of—"

"Oh," Willow interrupts him. "I . . . was . . ." She wishes she could tell him that she ran out of the park because she was so overcome by the memory of the way that they kissed, but saying those words is nearly as overwhelming as the act itself. "It was just that I was . . . Well, I wasn't going to *do* anything." She hopes that he will get her oblique reference. Surely this must be why he is asking, because he's worried that she had a date with her blades?

"Yeah, that isn't what I was thinking. I was just wondering if you really get migraines or if you were just trying to avoid me. Either way, you were kind of rude." There is a definite edge to his normally calm voice, and Willow is sure that she can hear something else beneath the words.

"I was . . . Huh?" She blinks as the meaning of what he's said sinks in. But she has to admit that while she wouldn't necessarily brand her behavior as rude, she knew, even as she was doing it, that it was at least very odd.

"I asked if you were trying to avoid me."

Now Willow *knows* that he has something going on. She wants to reassure him, she wants to tell him that she can't stop thinking about the day that they spent together, that right now, she wants nothing more than to crawl underneath the covers with him. But the words die in her throat, so instead she says:

"It's just sort of complicated . . . I mean *you're* complicated and . . . difficult . . ."

"*I'm* complicated? *I'm* difficult?" he asks incredulously. "Are you out of your mind?"

"Apparently," Willow says unhappily.

"You think you're not *complicated* and *difficult?*" Guy goes on as if he hadn't heard her. "You think you're easy to deal with? You think what happened after we kissed is the way things normally go?"

"No, I never thought that." Willow shakes her head vehemently. She knows that he's right, she'd be the first to say so, but she can't help feeling hurt. Was the only thing that he took away from the other day the *strangeness* of it all? Didn't he feel any of the things that she felt? "But I did think that maybe . . . maybe you had some fun. . . ."

Fun? Fun! Okay, guess it's back to asking about kittens!

Willow cannot believe that she has said something so profoundly stupid, and judging from the look on Guy's face, he can't either.

"Fun? Fun! Oh yeah! It's been really *FUN*! You think that this isn't playing hell with my *mind*? Fuck that!" Guy practically spits the words out. Willow blinks. She's not used to hearing him talk that way. "You think that this isn't playing hell with my *life*? I've barely slept since the first time I saw your arm, let alone gotten any work done. You think I like this? That this is all fun? Fuck all of it, and *fuck you too!*"

Willow feels as if he's slapped her. She didn't realize that calm, easygoing Guy could get so angry. She didn't realize that

245

their day together didn't hold any magic for him. She didn't realize that he had the power to wound her quite so deeply.

"I don't think that this is all fun," she says after a few moments. Her voice is cold and hard. She is no longer interested in reassuring him. "But guess what, Guy, I never asked you to hang around either. Nobody invited you here today. You can just walk away. You can just leave."

"Right, I can leave," Guy says sarcastically. "You think I could just walk away after what happened in the library?"

Willow is dying to ask him which part of their time in the library he's referring to. Does he feel that he can't walk away because of their kiss, or because of her cutting? But she doesn't say anything.

"Yeah, okay," Guy continues. "Maybe I would like to be around somebody who doesn't need talking down all the time, but then what? I don't need you on my conscience."

Willow has her answer. She doesn't like being his community service for the semester, and, if that's all that's keeping him, then she wants no part of it.

"Don't make me your project, Guy. That's what this is about? You don't want to feel guilty? You don't want me on your conscience? You look a little too old to be a Boy Scout." Willow tries to make her voice as harsh as possible, but she is no more successful at this than she was at taking care of Isabelle. In fact, she sounds nothing so much as scared and vulnerable. "Go back to the other things you said you had going on this semester. The things you said I was going to complicate. All those classes you take up at the university, your rowing. Go ahead. Go somewhere else. Knock ten seconds off your time, but don't worry about me anymore."

246

"Don't worry about you?" Guy shakes his head. "So you'll be okay, no slicing and dicing? You're all together now?"

Willow has no answer to this. Instead she thinks about all the things that she's told him, all the things that he's told her, and all the things that they've done together. How did it all get to be such a mess right now? She wishes that she could press the rewind button and simply erase the last ten minutes, but unfortunately that's not possible, and she realizes that, difficult as it may be, it is up to her to salvage the situation.

"I'll be all right," she says after a moment. "If you're staying here because you think you're going to stop me from cutting, then leave. If you're afraid that if you do leave I'll *always* be a cutter, then that's another reason for you to get out of here as quickly as possible. I don't want you to stick around because of that. I don't even know how that part of the story ends, but I do know if you go . . ." She trails off, puts her elbows on the desk, and rests her head in her hands. It is far easier to cut herself, to *mutilate* herself than to tell him how she feels.

"Then what? If I go, then what?" Guy's voice is angry, angry enough so that Willow almost backs down from what she is going to say.

"Go on. Tell me, if I go, *then what?*" Guy says once again.

There are many answers that Willow can give to this question. She can tell him that if he goes she might be better off. She won't be afraid of experiencing the things that so overwhelmed her in the stacks, that are starting to overwhelm her even as she sits there with him now. She won't worry that there is someone who is intent on weaning her off of her extracurricular activities. She won't have to worry about protecting someone else's feelings. But she will have no one to talk to, no one who knows her, no one who understands. Willow looks at him, and the only answer that she can give, the truest answer is simply:

"If you go, then I'll miss you . . . *terribly.*"

"Oh," Guy says. He gets up from the bed, crosses over to where she is, and lowers himself until he is sitting on his heels in front of her. Willow wonders if he is aware of how closely he is mimicking her posture from yesterday. "You're not my project," he says finally. "You're not my project," he says again more forcefully. "And I don't want to go anywhere else."

Willow is speechless. She had no idea, she really had no idea that anybody would ever look at her in that way.

She leans forward, until her forehead is brushing his. The most natural thing right now would be for them to kiss each other once again, but Willow knows that she can't do that, she simply can't risk it. She wonders why he wants to stay. He can get so much more somewhere, *anywhere* else, without all of her added complications.

"I . . . I don't want you to go anywhere else either," she says finally.

"Then what do you want?" Guy asks.

Willow isn't sure if she has the energy to answer this. She's bone weary. Exhausted. Trying to take care of Isabelle wore her out. The scene they just had wore her out. Just telling him the truth wore her out. Her *life* is wearing her out. But all of that fades away as she looks at Guy. She thinks that he's beautiful. And as she remembers the way that he looked on the bed, so calm, so strong, so *right,* there is only one thing she wants to do. It may not be the answer that he was looking for, but it is the only one that she can give him.

"I want to go to sleep," she says finally. "Just to sleep, for a long time, and not wake up until I'm ready."

Guy doesn't say anything. He just nods as if this is not only the most natural response she could give, but the only one.

"Okay." He gets to his feet, pulls her up off the chair, and walks her to the bed. Guy lies back down in his former position, but Willow just sits on the edge and looks at him. She wonders if he can possibly feel her secret stash hidden under the mattress. She offers him a shy smile, because as much as she wants this, it is still difficult for her. *He* doesn't appear to be having any difficulties, however. He just smiles back at her and holds out a hand.

Willow kicks off her shoes and, grasping his hand, crawls across the bed toward him. She has moved far beyond exhaustion and his chest is the best pillow she could ever imagine. But for all that, she's trembling. What she has told him has left her naked; she feels as if she has ripped off a layer of her skin. Willow feels things, good things, to be sure, even wonderful things, but she is used to being deadened, anesthetized, and she knows of only one way to process this.

Guy is asleep within moments. But it is not so easy for Willow. She stares up at the ceiling. She tries to mimic his calm easy breathing. But she can't quite do it, her breath remains a little panicky. She tries to focus instead on how wonderful his arms feel. She even laughs a little as she remembers Chloe's comments about rowers. But still, she can't stop trembling. Her hand strays to the edge of the mattress, goes underneath, feels for her supplies.

You can handle this, can't you? It's not so difficult.

It occurs to Willow that she has handled far worse. Whatever it was that happened downstairs with David just now, however savage, was *survivable*. The realization makes her bolt upright. How is that she managed to endure that pain without any recourse to her trusty equipment?

Willow knows that she should find this comforting, but in fact it scares her more than almost anything. She breaks into a cold sweat. The idea, however fleeting, that she could possibly survive without her constant companion of the past seven months is simply too unsettling. She searches under the mattress more frantically. When her hand finally closes around the razor she squeezes it tightly. She has no need of more right now, but she does need to know that more is possible.

Guy shifts in his sleep, moving both of them, and somehow manages to dislodge her grip. The razor falls to the floor with a faint metallic ping.

Willow gets out of bed to retrieve it, and as she does so her gaze falls upon Guy's backpack. An idea occurs to her. She checks to make certain that he really is asleep and when she is sure that he is, walks over to her desk and gets a pen. She pauses for a moment, looking at the box of still unused watercolors. It would be wonderful to do some kind of illustration, something that would go along with what she's about to write, but it would take too long to dry, and besides, she's in too much of a hurry to get back in bed with him. She goes over to his bag, unzips it as quietly as possible, and takes out the copy of *The Tempest*.

She doesn't even have to think twice:

For Guy,
Oh brave new world that has such a person in it . . .

She smiles a little as she imagines his reaction when he finds it, and she wonders when that will be—tonight, tomorrow?

Willow gets back into bed, still clutching her razor, but it doesn't matter, because she finds that this time her breathing does match Guy's, and she too sleeps.

CHAPTER THIRTEEN

At first Willow thinks that it is a nightmare that has woken her up so suddenly. Then she is sure it must be the sounds of the late-night traffic that filter through the window. But as she looks out onto the moonlit street, she sees that there are no cars, that the road is completely empty.

Willow is used to waking up in the middle of the night with a start, but this time seems different. There is no reason that she should be sitting bolt upright in bed at three in the morning. There are no hideous images that permeate her dreams, no sounds that recall the accident.

Is it just that she is overwrought by the events of the past few days? The stacks, her nap with Guy, the pain she felt as she watched David with Isabelle. *Especially* the pain she felt watching the two of them. These are disturbing things, but are they enough to startle her awake in the middle of the night?

Willow hugs her legs to her chest, rests her chin on her knees and thinks. Should she—

What's that?

She raises her head at a noise, faint but unmistakable.

Oh.

Now Willow knows exactly what it is that has woken her up so abruptly. It is nothing that would rouse anyone else, being barely audible, but the sound goes straight to her heart. Once again her brother is weeping.

She swings her legs over the edge of the bed and reaches for her bathrobe. She has no conscious plan, no thought that she is going to help her brother, and indeed, not only would she not know how to do such a thing, but she knows that her appearance would be a profound invasion. Still, though, she cannot stay in bed when her brother is crying, and when she herself has caused his tears.

She creeps down the stairs, pausing on every step, determined not to make any noise that will alert him to her presence.

The sound of his crying is even more painful than the sounds she remembers from the accident.

Willow sinks down on the steps, careful to position herself so that David cannot see her if he were to look up. Although it seems unlikely that he would do such a thing. His head is buried on his arms, which are folded on the table, and his glasses lie off to one side.

Willow doesn't think that she has ever seen anyone weep with such total abandon. It is a punishment to watch, and she knows that she cannot witness his grief, she cannot see such naked emotion, without succumbing to her crutch, her remedy, her razor.

She reaches in her bathrobe pocket for the blade she keeps

there, but stops just before she sinks the razor into her flesh.

It occurs to her that finally, there is something that she can do for her brother. She cannot bring their parents back, her attempts to help him in even the most superficial ways have failed completely, but here, *now,* there is something that she can do.

She can sit and watch him, bear witness to his pain. She can *force* herself to sit through this, live through every sob with him, without resorting to the one thing that has protected her from feeling such pain herself.

He will never know what this will cost her, the entire act will go unacknowledged, but Willow will feel as if she has finally done something for David.

Willow remembers the last time that she saw him cry, how shocked she had been, frightened almost, to see him reduced to such a state. She is not so much scared now as awed. Impressed, as she had not been that other time, by how strong he must be in order to withstand such misery. She knows better than anyone what kind of inner fortitude it must take to let oneself be so overcome.

It is something that she will never be able to do. Even to watch it without allowing herself the luxury of cutting is almost more that she can bear.

His sobs wound her far more than anything she can inflict on herself, but it is not only pain that she feels as she watches him. She takes a bittersweet comfort in the fact that her brother is capable of feeling such grief. That he will never have to resort to the kind of remedy that she does, that he has an endless reservoir of strength that allows him to weep in such a fashion.

No, she herself is far from being that strong. But she will sit there and watch him, watch every tear, until he is spent.

It takes a long time, a very long time, but finally, David stops crying. He sits at the table resting his chin in his hands and stares at the wall for a few moments before he gets up and walks out of the room.

Willow gets up too. She walks back up the stairs as silently as she came down them, crawls into her bed, and stares at the ceiling. She is still awake when the sky starts to lighten outside her window. She is still awake when the sun comes up. She never falls back asleep. She just lies in bed and stares at the ceiling, until the rest of the household wakens and Cathy calls her for breakfast.

✳

The image of David crying stays with Willow throughout the day. She is so tired that she can barely keep her eyes open, but every time that sleep threatens to overtake her, she manages to jerk herself awake by remembering the way he looked seated at the kitchen table. Willow is able to make it through her classes by doing this, but she is absolutely exhausted by the time she gets to the library.

"Hey, Carlos." Willow can barely get the words out, she's yawning so hard. "I'm sorry!" She covers her mouth. "I barely got any sleep last night."

"Well, this is your lucky day then," Carlos says as he takes in the dark circles under her eyes. "Because I'm in charge this afternoon. Maybe you should just stick with shelving today, okay? It's probably easiest."

"Whatever you think," Willow says, stowing her bag underneath the circulation desk. She knows that Carlos is trying to be kind, and shelving *is* often easier than dealing with people and their questions, but she would rather not be up alone in the stacks right now with nothing but her thoughts to keep her company.

"You've got more than enough to last your whole shift." Carlos waves his hand at the pile of battered metal carts overflowing with books that are blocking the entrance to the elevator.

"What did you do, save them all for me?" Willow grumbles as she grabs the first cart and wheels it into the elevator.

But to Willow's relief, shelving so many books proves to be more than distraction enough to blot out all thoughts of the previous night. Certainly it is more pleasant than torturing herself with memories of her brother's misery. The time passes quickly and uneventfully, and Willow is grateful that Carlos gave her the job, until she sees the last batch of books, destined for the eleventh floor.

As she gets off the elevator she can't help but think of all the things that have happened there between her and Guy. From the first conversation that she had with him to their kiss the other day, she feels as if these walls have witnessed the most important events in her life since her parents died.

Willow leaves the cart and walks over to the area near the windows. She kneels down and touches the floor where they sat. She knows she's being fanciful, but it seems strange to her that the concrete is so cold and raw, when the heat they generated was so intense.

She closes her eyes and allows the memory of their embrace to wash over her, but jumps up with a start as she hears the whirr of the elevator. Having other people up in the stacks while she's working makes her uncomfortable enough, but she would die of shame if anyone were to walk in on her communing with the floor.

She races back to the cart, grabs it, and is in position in front of one of the bookcases with a volume in her hand, when the elevator doors open. Willow glances over her shoulder, mildly curious to see who it is.

"Oh!" She is startled to see that it is *Guy* who is getting off the elevator, and for a brief moment she thinks that he is just a vision conjured up by her intense longing.

"Hello," she says after a second. "I didn't know that you'd be up here today."

"Hi." He walks over to her. "That guy downstairs at the circulation desk said you'd be on eleven."

"Carlos?"

"Yeah, sorry, I forgot his name. Anyway, I brought you something."

"Really?" Willow puts the book she's holding back on the cart and looks at Guy. "That was nice of you. What?"

"Contraband." Guy takes his hands out from behind his back. He's holding a brown paper bag, from which he removes a container of iced coffee.

"Oh my God!" Willow laughs. "That is the sweetest thing! It's just what I needed too! How did you know? And how did you manage to sneak it up here?" She pushes the cart out of the way and moves closer to him.

"Umm, Carlos said you were really tired, and I got the feeling that he wouldn't care if I brought you this."

"Oh, it's perfect." Willow takes the coffee from him and sits down with her back against the wall. She closes her eyes and takes a sip. "You even put the right amount of sweetener in."

"I'm observant." Guy sits down next to her.

"You're not kidding." Willow shifts so that their legs are touching. "Want some?"

"No thanks." Guy shakes his head. "Too sweet for me. So how come you're so tired? I thought maybe we could do something together after work, but if you're not up for it . . ." He trails off.

"Oh no, I'm not too tired. I mean, I am." Willow yawns between sips. "But I'd really like to do something, and besides"—she gestures with the coffee—"this is helping."

"Were you up all night working on your paper or something?"

"Not exactly." Willow sighs. "I haven't even started on that. I just . . ." She pauses for a moment. "Well, I couldn't sleep, that's all." She wonders why, when she's told him so many important things, she is hesitant about letting him know the real reason she stayed up all night. "That was amazing," Willow says as she drinks the last of the coffee. "Thank you so much." She smiles at Guy for a second, then stands up reluctantly.

"Hey, you know what?" Guy gets up too. "I finally finished reading *The Tempest*."

"Really?" This perks Willow up even more than the coffee. "What did you think? Did you love it? Admit it, it's his best play, isn't it?" She takes a handful of books and starts sorting through them.

"Yeah, I really did like it. *Okay*," he amends quickly as he sees her smile fade. "I loved it, no seriously, I did. Is it his best play? I don't know 'cause I haven't read them all, but I'll tell you what, I like imaginary places too. And I'll tell you something else."

"What?"

"I'll tell you what my favorite part of the whole thing was."

"Don't tell me, let me guess." Willow stops shelving and leans against the stacks as she considers this. "Umm, one of Prospero's really great speeches because—"

"Nope." Guy shakes his head. "Not even close."

"No?" Willow is surprised. "Okay, you're not going to tell me you liked Caliban better? You like categories so much, *that* would be a really weird one. I mean, people who think he's a better character than Prospero?!"

"Forget Caliban," Guy says. "You're still about a million miles away." He folds his arms, rests them on the edge of the metal cart, leans forward, and smiles. "Want to try third time lucky, or should I just tell you?"

"Just tell me."

"Okay. My favorite part was the dedication."

"The *dedication*?" Willow frowns. "Shakespeare didn't write a dedication for *The Tempest*. I don't think he did for any play, did he?"

"I'm not talking about any dedication that *Shakespeare* wrote."

"Oh." Willow bites her lower lip as the meaning of his words sinks in. "Okay." She smiles and starts shelving again.

"You know what?" Guy says slowly. "You're—"

"I am not!" she protests.

"How do you know what I was going to say?"

"You're going to say that I'm blushing, and I'm *not*."

"Yeah, you are." Guy leans even closer.

Willow is dismally aware of how perfectly romantic the

moment is, and of where the moment should lead. She wishes more than anything that she could lean in toward him, let things develop the way they ought to, but she can't, she knows what the consequences would be.

"Well, anyway, I'm glad you liked what I wrote," Willow says awkwardly. She moves a few feet away and stares at the bookcases as if they hold the secret of life. Her hands tremble as she shoves the volumes in any which way, and she manages to drop several on the floor.

"Did you ever look at any of these titles?" Guy says as he picks up the fallen books and hands them to her. "*The Research Activities of the South Manchurian Railway 1907–1945.* Someone actually *wrote* this? Someone actually *took this out*? And I thought I liked weird stuff!"

"That's nothing." Willow manages to laugh. "If you were here an hour ago you could have helped me with *The Proceedings of the Fourth International Congress of Lithuanian Entomologists.*"

"Okay, you had to have made *that* one up."

"I didn't, I swear! Fifth floor if you don't believe me!"

"I believe you." Guy smiles. "So when do you get out of here, anyway?"

"Oh." Willow looks at her watch. "In about . . . Well, *now* actually."

"You want to go to the park? It's really gorgeous out. Or I don't know, maybe you want to go back to that place and have another coffee?"

"I'd much rather go to the park. Who'd want to be inside if it's so beautiful outside?" Willow says as they walk to the elevator. "But if you'd like to get something, then I'm happy to go there." The doors open and they get on.

"No, don't worry, I'm good," Guy reassures her as they exit the elevator on the main floor.

"Hey Carlos." Willow gets her things from under the circulation desk. "I guess I'll see you in a couple days."

"Have fun," he says, giving her a wink, which Willow pointedly ignores.

"Have you ever been out on the river?" Guy asks as they leave the building and start walking across campus. Willow is relieved that he doesn't seem to have noticed Carlos's gesture, or that if he did, he's not about to mention it.

"You mean like in a boat?" She's a little confused.

"Umm, okay, so tell me, how else would you go out on the river?"

"Don't ask me." Willow shrugs.

"You should try it," Guy says as they enter the park. "I'll take you sometime. Anyway, let's at least walk by the water now, okay? This way." He leads her down a narrow path, underneath an arcade of chestnut trees, to the river.

"It's beautiful here," Willow says. "I've never even walked this way before." She leans her elbows on the stone wall that separates them from the water and stares out at the sailboats.

"You should see it when we go out rowing in the morning. It's perfect. It's like there's no one else in the world." Guy jumps up on the wall.

"You're going to fall in!" Willow exclaims in alarm.

"Right, this thing's got to be like two feet wide at least."

"Try half of that, *maybe*," Willow looks dubiously at the narrow expanse of stone. "Really, unless you're going to tell me that along with that *Boys' Book of Magic* you bought the *Boys' Book of High Wire* or something, you should get off."

"You think I haven't fallen in the water a million times since I stared rowing? C'mere." He extends his hand. "No." Willow shakes her head. "Have you really? Fallen in, I mean? I thought it was so polluted?"

"Of course I've fallen in, and it is polluted. I told you, that's why I had that peroxide and stuff with me, everybody carries it, so you can disinfect any . . ." He stops talking for a moment. "Anyway, you wouldn't believe how cold the water gets by the end of October."

"Yeah, I would believe it! That's why I'm staying where I am!"

"Get up here," Guy says. He ignores her protests, grabs her hands and hauls Willow onto the stone parapet. "It's not so bad, is it?" he says above her outraged shrieks as he pulls her close to him. "You're not going to fall, and even if you did, I'd catch you."

"I know," Willow says slowly. "You would." They stand face-to-face. Willow is sure that they must look like a postcard, silhouetted against the dying rays of the sun, but she knows too that there is something wrong with this picture, and that something happens to be her.

"Hey, Guy! Over here!"

Willow turns to see Andy waving at them. Chloe, Laurie, and Adrian are walking a few feet behind him.

"Do you see that boat?" He hurries over to them and scrambles up on the wall, nearly knocking Willow over as he does so.

"Watch it, will you?" Guy says, tightening his grip on Willow.

"Yeah, sorry." He barely glances her way. "Come on, look at that!" He points at a racing sloop in the distance. "Could you imagine what it would be like to sail something that big?

That's got to be about seventy, eighty feet. You'd need a crew of, like, twenty."

"I thought you were interested in *rowing*," Willow says.

"Yeah, you know, I do it for school." Andy shrugs. "But I love to sail. That's how I spent the summer."

"It's all he ever talks about too," Chloe says, coming over to join them. She shields her eyes from the sun and looks up at Willow on the parapet.

"I'd kill to crew on a boat like that." Andy shakes his head. "It would be so amazing."

"Well, first you'd have to—" Guy begins.

"Hey, you guys want to come with us and get something to eat?" Andy changes the subject abruptly. "I'm tired of hanging in the park, I'd much rather be inside somewhere."

Of course you would, Willow thinks as she disengages herself from Guy and jumps down from the wall.

"Willow." Chloe tugs on her sleeve. "Come with us." She says under her breath, "C'mon. I need a second opinion."

"About what?" Willow is confused.

"Him." Chloe nods toward Andy, who's still standing on the wall with his back to them. "Laurie's no good. She's too desperate for things to work out between us. She won't rest until everyone is a couple like her and Adrian." She looks over to where the two of them are kissing. Willow's eyes follow hers and she feels a pang as she watches Laurie break away and smile. Obviously she's thrilled by her boyfriend's attention.

"You want to go?" Guy jumps down beside her.

"I . . . well . . . Sure," Willow says. She wishes that they hadn't run into everybody else, but she *is* flattered that Chloe wants her along.

"We can go to that place right next to the boat basin," Andy announces as he gets down from the wall and stands near Chloe.

"It's so expensive," Laurie says as she walks over.

"Who cares?" Andy responds with a shrug. "It's near here, and it's good."

"He has a point," Adrian says. "We might as well just go there." He takes Laurie's hand and starts walking in the direction of the boat basin. Andy and Guy fall into step behind them.

"So are you that interested in sailing?" Willow asks Chloe. They hang back a few feet behind the others.

"Depends. Do you mean would I like it if he took me out on a boat like that? Sure. Do you mean would I like it if he talked about something else occasionally? Sure."

"Got it."

"*We* should talk about something else." Chloe sighs. "I have so much homework, I shouldn't even be here now. It's just, I don't know, I'm like the opposite of Laurie. Now that I'm a senior I'm less and less focused."

"I know the feeling." Willow chews on her nails fretfully, then shoves her hands into her pockets.

"You could really use a manicure," Chloe says as they approach the cafe. "Don't take that the wrong way or anything! It's just that I usually do Laurie's nails for her, and if you wanted I could do yours sometime. . . ."

"Oh . . . thanks. I'm not offended at all. I know they look terrible, but to be honest they always have. My best friend from home used to give me a hard time about them too," Willow admits with a rueful smile.

"It's way too crowded, we're never going to get a table,"

Laurie calls over from where she and Adrian are standing at the entrance to the restaurant.

"So we'll wait a couple minutes," Andy says, clearly unconcerned.

Guy walks back to Willow. "We don't have to stay if you don't want to."

"Oh, that's okay. Thank you, though," she says, too softly for anyone else to hear.

"Hey, they have a table if we're willing to sit out back," Adrian says after conferring with the waitress.

"Then we won't be able to see the water," Andy complains.

"You're the one who's insisting on eating here," Chloe points out.

"Fine, forget the water." Andy follows Adrian and Laurie as they walk into the cafe.

"This is actually really nice back here," Laurie says as they crowd around a small table set underneath a striped umbrella.

"Who wants what?" Andy looks around for a menu.

"I just want dessert," Chloe says.

"Me too," Laurie agrees. "No, sorry. A salad."

"Then I'll have to get one too! C'mon, stick with dessert. What are you having, Willow?"

"Umm. Maybe a . . ."

Willow sees her before any of the others. A walking skeleton, the victim of some terrible wasting disease, like something out of the history books, a death camp survivor. It takes Willow a moment to realize that the girl is none of those things. She's just a girl, a girl like Willow, who's chosen to inflict terrible pain on herself. Only this girl's weapon isn't a razor, it's starvation.

Willow can hardly bear to look at her, but she's transfixed, spellbound. Every lineament of the girl's wasted body is a testament to her inner turmoil. Willow can only imagine what kind of pain she must be in to destroy herself that way. She knows there's something ironic in her compassion for the other girl, but she can't help feeling that this utter mortification of the flesh is far worse than anything that she herself has done.

"Oh my God, that poor girl," Laurie whispers. Clearly she has noticed the apparition as well.

"Who?" Adrian asks, his voice unnaturally loud in contrast with Laurie's.

"Ssh!" Laurie elbows him.

Guy twists his head to see what they're talking about, and Willow can see that he too is affected by her appearance, as anyone would be, really.

Willow turns away from the spectacle and her gaze falls on Andy. He is also riveted by the girl, but his reaction is very different from Willow's and the others'. It's clear that he looks at this walking skeleton and sees only that she is breastless, sexless, *ugly*.

"Yeah, I wouldn't go feeling too sorry for her," he says to Laurie with a smirk.

"Excuse me?" Chloe gives him a look.

"C'mon, she's in someplace like this, she obviously has the money to eat. It's not like she's some poor starving kid from Africa, you know?"

"No." Chloe shakes her head. "I *don't* know. What are you talking about?"

"I mean it's something she's doing to herself . . ."

"Yeah, it's called an *eating disorder*," Laurie says angrily.

"Right, I know, okay? Don't talk to me like I'm an idiot."

"Why not? You're acting like one," Chloe snaps.

"Oh, sorry if I don't *genuflect* because some girl who can't handle whatever problems life is throwing at her hides behind the disease of the week."

"What the hell could you possibly know about what *life is throwing at her*? What the hell could *you* possibly know about why she's doing that to herself?" Chloe demands.

The rest of the table is silent. Willow is sure that she's not the only one who wishes she was someplace else. She doesn't look at Adrian or Laurie, she can barely bring herself to look at Guy.

"Look, I know the type," Andy continues, not even bothering to lower his voice. "Society, the media, everybody else is responsible for her problems. It's like it's become this hip thing to starve yourself and complain that the rest of the world is driving you to do it. Trust me, it's just that she can't deal with things, so she manufactures this problem—"

"Stop it!" Willow bursts out. She can't help herself. She can't listen to another word. Willow rests her forehead on her palm. Maybe she really is getting a migraine. She feels Guy's hand on her shoulder and raises her head to look at Andy.

"Thank you, Willow," Chloe says.

Willow knows that Chloe is upset because of how insensitive Andy is being. But she herself is bothered for more selfish reasons. It's as if Andy is addressing every word straight to her. What would he say if she were to lift up her shirt and show him her cuts the way she did for Guy? Would he say that she has manufactured her problem?

Would he be right?

"Yeah, okay. Look, I'm outta here," Andy says after a few moments.

267

"Me too, but guess what, I'm headed in the *opposite* direction." Chloe throws her napkin on the table. "See you guys tomorrow."

"Can we leave too?" Willow says to Guy. "I'm sorry." She looks over at Laurie and Adrian.

"*You* don't have anything to be sorry about." Laurie gives Andy a dirty look. "I thought you were leaving?" she says pointedly.

"Yeah, let's get out of here." Guy stands up. "Hey Andy, just so you know? I totally agree with Chloe on this one."

"So I guess Chloe won't be needing a second opinion," Willow says as they walk out of the cafe. The sun has set completely now, and it's a beautiful, mild night.

"Huh?" Guy looks confused. "What are you talking about?"

"Chloe wanted to know what I thought of Andy," Willow explains. "You know, if she should go out with him or something."

"You guys talk about stuff like that?" Guy looks at her incredulously. "I mean, she can't just make up her own mind?"

"I don't know." Willow shrugs. "I guess not." She doesn't really have the energy to make small talk. She's too upset, the scene in the cafe is too fresh. She's angry, and not just about what Andy said regarding that poor girl, but because of what his words imply about *her*.

"I don't feel like walking right now," Guy says. "Do you mind?" He sits down on the grass and pulls her down next to him. "Is this okay? We can see the water from here."

"I don't just make my own problems," Willow says suddenly. "I don't just do what I do because it's hip, because it's the *fashion.*" She pauses for a moment. "I do it because I have to," she says finally. "There's no other way."

"No." Guy shakes his head. "You won't let yourself have any other way. There's a difference."

"I *can't* let myself have any other way! You know that! You *saw* that!" Willow insists. Guy doesn't say anything and the two of them sit in silence for a few minutes and stare at the water shimmering in the moonlight.

"Maybe Andy was right," Willow continues. "Me and that girl, we just can't face what life is throwing us, so we hide behind our sickness. Maybe everything he said about *her* is true about *me*."

"Why would you even listen to anything that he has to—"

"My brother cries at night." Willow interrupts suddenly. "Don't laugh," she says hurriedly. "I know that you're not like Andy, you would never say anything insensitive or stupid, but well, some people think a guy crying is . . . I don't know."

"I'm not laughing."

"That's why I didn't sleep last night. He cries. And I watch him."

"Why are you telling me this now?" Guy asks.

"I have no idea." Willow is surprised herself. "I have no idea," she repeats. "I just . . . He's so strong, if you think his crying like that is anything else, you're wrong. I don't even know how he manages to do it, to get through it, I mean." Willow pauses. "Do you think I'm like that girl?" She searches his face, barely visible in the faint light from the stars.

"I don't know," he says slowly. "But I do know this. The way her body affected you, that's the way your scars affect me."

"Oh." Willow doesn't know how to respond to this. How

wonderful that she should affect him so strongly, how awful that it should be in that way. She can't help thinking that almost any other reaction would be preferable, and that it is her own fault that when he looks at her he doesn't just see a girl, he sees a *cutter*.

She rolls up her left sleeve and examines her cuts, really looks at them the way she might if she were alone, tries to see them the way that she imagines he does.

There's no denying that they're hideous. It's very clear why he told her they were ugly that day in the stacks.

That shouldn't matter. Her cuts serve a purpose and that purpose is independent of such trivial considerations. She knows this as deeply as she has ever known anything. But still, for a moment she wishes that they looked different, that they *did* look like the kind of scratches a cat might make.

She starts to roll down her sleeve, but Guy stops her. He holds her arm, looks at her cuts, traces the pattern of her razor marks with his hand.

"Don't, it's . . ."

Willow stops speaking as he bends his head and kisses the scars.

She knows she should tell him to stop, but she can't because she wants him to go on forever. She knows too that she will probably pay for this feeling with other less pleasurable ones, but still she can't bring herself to pull her arm away.

And then Willow does something that surprises herself more than anything she has ever done. She moves her other arm, and, very tentatively, holding the side of his face with her hand, raises his mouth to hers and kisses him. She can't believe that she is willing to risk this, not after what happened in the stacks. Given that, this act is even more shocking to her than when all those months ago, she found herself stabbing her arm with the screwdriver and knew that she had found her calling.

She waits for the cataclysm to happen, to be overwhelmed the way she was in the library, but, at least for that moment, feels only how wonderful it is to kiss someone, to kiss *him*, underneath the stars, and how odd it is, how *refreshing*, that after all she has been through she can at last respond to something the way anyone else would.

"Will you do something for me?" she whispers against his mouth. She is trembling slightly, both from excitement and fear, and she cannot yet bring herself to believe that her act will not have consequences.

"Yes," he whispers back. "Just tell me what."

"Take me home."

Willow has no idea why she has requested this, where this desire has come from, if it has been building for a long time or if it is a sudden need. But she is sure that it is genuine, she is sure that it is what she wants.

"Now?" Guy pulls away from her. "You mean you want me to walk you back to your brother's apartment?"

"No." Willow shakes her head. "I want to go home. Back to my parents' house, where I grew up. *Home*."

"Oh." Guy nods. He looks confused, but thoughtful. "It's not far, is it? I mean, you could borrow your brother's car and drive out there, couldn't you?" He stops for a second. "Sorry. Have you driven since . . . I wasn't thinking."

"No, I haven't. I can't go there by myself and I can't borrow my brother's car. He'll want to know what for and I can't tell him. I need *you* to take me, Guy. Please."

"Why do you want to go home? Is it, is it because maybe you're afraid that now your home has become a place you can only visit in your imagination?"

"No, I don't think that's it . . ." She trails off.

Willow wishes that she could answer him. That she herself knew the answer. She thinks about the two times she's been home since the accident, the time with David and the bookcases, and the time that she gathered her clothes. There is no reason to think that going home now will be any different. Willow has no idea what she is looking for, what she hopes to get out of such an excursion. And why does she think that if her brother, her *unbelievably* strong brother, has been unable to withstand the emotional impact of being in their parents' house, that *she* will be able to?

Maybe she just needs to drive along the road where it all happened again. Maybe she needs to bury her head in her mother's closet and see if she can still smell her. Maybe she needs to look at those bookcases again.

"I want a book," Willow blurts out finally. She supposes that this answer makes as much sense as any other. "*Bulfinch's Mythology.* I want my father's copy."

Guy nods slowly, as if this makes perfect sense. He doesn't say, as someone else might, that she can walk into almost any bookstore and buy a copy, he doesn't say that he knows that she already owns a copy, that he's seen her with it any number of times, or that he can lend her his own. Instead he just turns to her and says: "Okay then, looks like I'm the one who's going to have to find a car to borrow."

CHAPTER FOURTEEN

Of course it would be raining.

Willow stares listlessly out of the window, but there's really nothing to see. Nothing, that is, except the driving sheets of rain, the futile back and forth of the windshield wipers, and the occasional flash of lightning.

Even though the weather report had promised nothing but blue skies, even though the past few days have been perfect fall weather, Willow had known that the second she got in the car with Guy it would start to pour.

She wonders if Guy's nervous, if he's worried about driving in such nasty weather—the only time the rain had let up was when it had started to hail. Or maybe he's worried that *she's* worried, worried that she'll be in an accident. *Another* accident.

Willow isn't concerned about anything like *that*, but she feels distinctly uncomfortable. There's just something unsettling about so much rain.

"We turn here, right?"

Willow doesn't respond. She's staring out the window, straining to see beyond the rain-streaked glass. It's useless, of course—she can barely make out the road—but it's also unnecessary. She doesn't need to see. She would know where she was even if she were blindfolded.

"Hey, aren't I supposed to make a turn here?"

"Stop."

"What?"

"Stop the car."

Guy pulls the car over to the side of the road, next to a wide-open field. "Are you okay? Are you going to be—"

Willow doesn't wait for him to finish, she opens the door and hesitates for only an instant before plunging into the driving rain.

She isn't dressed for this kind of weather—within seconds she's soaked through to the bone, but she hardly notices as she stumbles across the field. There, maybe five or six yards from the road, is an enormous old oak.

"What are you doing?" Guy calls after her. He gets out of the car and walks through the rain to where Willow is standing in front of the tree.

"Willow," he has to shout to be heard over the thunder. "Come on, get back in the car." He takes her arm.

Willow looks at him without seeing. She reaches out her hand and touches the side of the tree, touches a huge section that has its bark sheared clean off, leaving in its stead a smear of midnight blue paint.

Odd that after all these months, after all this rain, the paint would still be there.

She sinks on her knees before the tree. The crackle of cellophane makes her look down and it takes her a second to realize that she is kneeling on the remnants of dozens of floral offerings, now turned into compost, unrecognizable except for their soiled ribbons and plastic wrappings.

The scene should be affecting, disturbing, *shattering* even, and yet Willow feels nothing so much as uncomfortable as the rain sinks through her clothes and drenches her skin. She is unmoved, the drama of the weather, the import of the place, they have no power over her. She doesn't know what she was expecting, what she was looking for, but it certainly wasn't this, this emptiness, this meaninglessness.

Guy appears to be much more affected than she is. His face is white as the meaning of the sheared bark, the traces of paint, and the rotten floral tributes sinks in.

"Let's go." She stands up. "C'mon." Willow takes his arm. His clothes are soaked too. "Let's get out of here." She pulls him back to the car.

Guy gets in and slams the door, gives her a searching look, but doesn't say anything beyond: "About a mile and a half, right?"

"That's right. Take the next left and then it's just straight on from there."

Neither of them says anything else for the rest of the trip. Willow hopes that Guy doesn't feel as cold and uncomfortable as she does.

"Is this it?"

"Um-hum. That's right. It's that mailbox up ahead."

Guy turns into the driveway and turns off the engine. She's home. After all these months, she's home.

Willow gets out of the car, slowly, gingerly, as if she's suddenly become old and infirm. She's transfixed, staring at the house, no longer noticing the rain as it drips unchecked down her face and plasters her already sodden clothes against her skin.

"Maybe we should go inside?" Guy suggests tentatively.

"Oh, yes." Willow stares at him without really seeing him. "We should go inside."

She starts forward, but trips on the gravel. "You sure this is okay?" Guy catches her arm. "You sure you want to do this?"

"Maybe . . . Maybe . . . I don't know." Willow shakes her head—she's *not* sure all of a sudden. "Maybe we could go somewhere and . . . um, I don't know . . . have lunch first?" she says finally. Willow knows the suggestion is idiotic. It's just past ten in the morning, they're both soaking wet, the house, while daunting, at least offers the *possibility* of comfort. They would certainly be able to dry off and change inside. Almost all of her clothes are still there, and she's sure that she could find something for Guy as well.

"Whatever you say. It's completely up to you."

"You're so . . . You're too . . ." Willow trails off.

Perfect, wonderful, heavenly. . . .

"I'm too what?"

"Nice," Willow says finally. The word is completely inadequate. "You're too nice."

"Well, I'm not exactly going to drag you in there. Look, whatever you want to do, it's your call. Totally. But maybe you could decide soon. This rain is really starting to get to me."

"Let's get back in the car." She walks to the passenger side.

"Now what?" Guy turns to look at her as he gets in and turns the key in the ignition. "You really want to go and get *lunch*?"

"At least it's dry in here." Willow doesn't answer him directly. "Whose car is this anyway?"

"Adrian's brother's."

"Did you tell him what it was for?'

"Nope. And he didn't ask."

"Oh." Willow nods. "Listen, what I said out there . . ." She drums her fingers on the dashboard. "It's true. . . ."

"What?"

"That you're too . . . You're so . . ." To Willow's astonishment her voice breaks. She is shocked that Guy's kindness has the power to move her so much. How strange that he can affect her like this when the scene of the accident left her cold.

"Willow?"

"Yes?" Her voice is steadier and she is once again in control.

"You are too."

"Oh." She puts her elbows on the dashboard and rests her forehead against her palms. "If you say so."

"Are you crying?" Guy touches her shoulder.

"No." Willow lifts her head up. "You should know by now, I don't cry. Look, let's go and get lunch, okay? I know it's really early, but let's just go. There's this place everyone at my school used to hang out at. It's only about two miles from here." She glances at the clock. "It will be completely empty now."

"Okay." Guy backs the car out of the driveway. "I guess I could use something hot. Do they have good coffee?"

"Hot chocolate."

"Huh?"

"Hot chocolate. It's this little place run by this couple from France, and that's what they do best. Or at least it's what everyone from school used to order. But you can get the half espresso, half chocolate. You'll like it, I promise."

"Keep going straight?"

"No, make a right, and then another right. You'll see it after that."

"Is this it?" Guy pulls up outside the cafe. It's nestled among a row of shops that form one side of a semicircle set around a statue of a Revolutionary War hero. "My clothes are sticking to me," he says as he gets out of the car.

"I'm sorry." Willow can't help feeling guilty. "Mine are too. Maybe we'll dry off a little inside."

The cafe is as empty as she had hoped. They have the whole place to themselves, and Willow picks her old favorite spot, a booth near the window.

"Is it too early to get dessert?" Guy asks, looking at the menu.

"Go ahead." Willow shifts uncomfortably against the banquette. Her wet jeans are making her miserable. "I know what you want, that mocha cream thing, I can't even pronounce it. You should definitely get it."

"Is there a waitress around here?"

"You have to go to the counter to order."

"And you just want hot chocolate?"

"Umm, yeah, because—"

"Willow?!"

"Markie?!" Willow is so stunned that she can hardly speak. She half stands up as she stares at what must surely be a ghost, because she can't quite believe that what she's seeing is real. After all these months, after all the phone calls she's avoided, she's finally face-to-face with her best friend.

"What are you doing here?" she asks as Markie walks over to the table. "I mean, why aren't you in class?"

"What am *I* doing here? *I* live here. How about what are *you* doing here?" She looks at Willow in disbelief as if she too can't believe that what she's seeing is real.

"You cut your hair," Willow says stupidly.

"Yeah, about a foot. . . ." Markie pauses; she looks back and forth between Willow and Guy.

"Oh, uh, sorry, this is Guy, and I guess that you've figured out by now that this is Markie."

"I've heard about you," Guy says, clearly more comfortable with the situation than they are.

Willow is surprised by the remark. It's such a cocktail party kind of comment, but she is grateful to Guy for saying it. She can see now, as she looks at Markie, that she has hurt her old friend. Willow hopes that Guy's words will at least show Markie that she has not forgotten her, that she has thought about her and talked about her over the past eight months, that all the things that they have done together over the years still matter to her.

"Hi." Markie nods at him. "So what *are* you doing here?" She shifts her attention back to Willow.

"I . . . had to pick up something at the house," Willow answers after a second. It's the only thing she can think to say, and in fact, picking up the *Bulfinch* is really the only concrete reason she has for being back home. "So what are you doing here in the middle of the day?" She turns the question back to Markie.

"Oh, I'm getting some stuff for my mom." Markie shrugs. "She's having a dinner party. There was a water main break in school. The whole place flooded. We have the next two days off while they clean up." She speaks in short staccato bursts.

"That makes sense, I guess. . . ." Willow tries to smile, but it comes out all wrong.

"I'll go give them our order." Guy stands up and looks at Willow. Clearly he is waiting to see if she will ask Markie to join them.

"I have to hurry back," Markie says. The words come out in a rush—it's obvious that she doesn't want to give Willow the chance to reject her yet again. But as soon as Guy leaves, she slides into the banquette. She stares at Willow, but neither of them speaks, and the silence between them is not the comfortable silence of two friends.

"I like your hair that way," Willow finally says.

"Thanks." Markie doesn't seem particularly flattered. She looks at Willow closely. "I haven't seen you with your hair in a braid since you were about six years old. I remember your mom used to do it for you."

Is that true?

Willow had completely forgotten about that, but now an image comes back to her. She remembers squirming on a footstool, desperate to go out and play with Markie, while her mother sat behind her with a brush.

She blinks to clear away the vision, bringing her focus back to the present. "So is your hair easier to deal with now it's so much shorter? I mean, it used to take you forever to blow it dry. . . ." Willow can't believe that this is all she can say to her friend after so many months, that their relationship has been reduced to this kind of small talk, and she knows that it's all her fault.

But Markie's having none of it. Now that the two of them

are alone, she gets right to the point. "My mom said that the reason you never called back or e-mailed me or anything, is just that things are so hard for you right now. . . ."

"She's right," Willow begins eagerly, glad to have the chance to explain. She leans across the table. "You see—"

"But I said that was impossible," Markie cuts her off. "Because I told her if that were the case, then you would just say something to me, like 'Hey Markie, I can't deal with you right now, the second I'm ready, you're first . . .' I told her that you wouldn't just *ignore* me, that you weren't like that. You wouldn't be so . . . dishonest. *Emotionally* dishonest, I mean."

Willow pulls back in shock. "I'm . . . I'm *really* sorry," she stammers. She feels as if she's been slapped, but she can't be mad at Markie, because she knows that her friend is right. "I should never have . . ."

"I hate saying stuff like this to you!" Markie bursts out. "I don't want to be talking to you like this! I feel like you're my ex or something and I'm begging you to call me! And I feel so selfish too! I should be asking you how you've been holding up, not getting mad at you." She pauses. "So, how have you been holding up?" she says after a moment.

"Not always so great."

Talk about an understatement!

Willow wonders what would happen if she showed Markie her arms. Would she forgive her for not calling? Would she understand what her life has become?

Would she tell her mother? *Of course* she would. She wouldn't even think twice. She wouldn't be like Guy. Markie has known her whole family since they were both five. She wouldn't listen to Willow's protests. She would tell her mother. Her mother would tell David. Her razors would be taken away. *Something* would be done. That part of her life would be over.

Willow is not yet ready for that to happen, but for the briefest instant she is overcome by an urge so powerful that she literally has to restrain herself from flinging her arms out at Markie. All she would have to do is roll up her sleeves and the thing would be set in motion. . . .

Instead she jerks her hands off the table. Puts them in her lap. Starts twisting her napkin, does anything to keep them occupied.

"I . . . I miss you," she finally says, her eyes firmly fixed on her napkin. "I miss you and I miss the way things used to be between us. And even though your mother was right . . . you were too." Willow looks up at Markie. "I should have just let you know that I couldn't talk to you." Once again, to her amazement, she feels her voice start to break. But as before, the moment passes quickly.

"What about now?" Markie asks.

"I'll . . . I *will* call you," Willow says. "I'd like to see you."

"Really?" Markie looks skeptical.

"Really," Willow assures her. "But listen . . ." She blushes as she thinks of Markie's earlier reprimand. This time she's determined to be straight with her. "I don't think that it's going to be anytime soon."

"Oh," Markie says slowly. "Well, I guess I'll just have to wait then. I . . . Well, I really hope that it's not going to be another seven months or anything. And Willow . . ." She gives her a funny little half smile. "I did kind of buy what my mom

282

was saying. If I hadn't, I wouldn't have kept calling you all these months."

They look at each other across the table without saying anything, but this time the silence isn't nearly as uncomfortable.

"So." Markie leans forward and looks at Willow with a little of her old sparkle. "Is he part of the reason you haven't called?" She gestures at Guy, who is standing near the counter, with his back to them. "Because I might forgive you for *that*."

"No, but I *have* wondered what you would think of him," Willow confides as she too leans across the table. Their elbows touch and for a moment it is as if they have never been apart.

"He's incredibly cute." Markie glances over at him again. "Is he your . . . boyfriend or something, or just a friend? I mean, who is he?"

"Well . . ." Willow follows Markie's eyes. How can she possibly explain what Guy means to her? He's something far more than a friend. Something other than a boyfriend, a lover maybe, in everything but the technical sense. . . .

And then she looks back at Markie and says the truest, most honest words that she has ever said to anyone: "He's someone that *knows* me, and someone that I *know*."

"Oh." Markie nods thoughtfully as she takes this in. "Umm, maybe we should talk about something else," she murmurs. "'Cause he's headed back this way. You know what?" she continues in her normal voice as Guy approaches the table. "I have to get going, I mean I really don't want to. I wish I could stay, but my mom's expecting me, and I'm guessing that you would rather not have her know that I saw you . . ."

"Definitely, don't mention it. Please."

"Okay, so, I mean, I can't use running into you as an excuse for why I'm late." Markie stands up. "Well, I guess that I'll just have to save everything I wanted to talk about until I hear from you . . ." She says this awkwardly, but her earlier hostility is gone.

Willow stands up too. "I hope that . . ." she begins, but words fail her. She reaches out to her friend, tentatively, afraid of embracing her when she is so wet. But Markie is not hesitant at all. She grabs Willow in a fierce hug.

"See you." Markie lets go after a moment. She looks at Guy, smiles a little, and walks off.

"Good-bye." Guy smiles back at her. He sits down in the spot she has just vacated. "Our stuff will be ready in a couple minutes," he says to Willow.

"Oh . . . good." Willow stares at him vacantly. She's too focused on what happened with Markie to really take in what he's saying.

"Everything okay?" he asks. "I mean, was it good to see her?"

"Well, I'm glad I did, anyway. . . . Listen, do you mind getting the stuff to go?"

Guy just looks at her.

"I know, I'm complicated and difficult, but look, you said it was all up to me. I just feel like getting home now. Sorry."

"No, no, I mean it's not that hard to get our stuff to go, and I don't exactly need to sit in some girly place, but are you sure that this time, you're ready?"

"You think this is a *girl's* place? All the guys in my school used to love it!"

"Uh-huh. What kind of guys went to your school? Anyway, are you sure this time?"

"I'm sure."

"Hey, could you wrap that stuff up?" Guy calls over to the woman behind the counter.

"Well, wait a sec." Willow tugs on his sleeve. "What's so girlish about it here?"

"Describe your napkin."

"Pink linen with violets embroidered on it." Willow shrugs.

"Right. Okay, let's go." Guy gets up and pays at the counter.

The drive back to the house is uneventful, except for the fact that the rain is coming down as heavily as ever, and that their clothes got even more drenched as they ran to and from the car.

"Can you hurry up and open the door?" Guy says, his teeth chattering.

"Sorry." Willow fumbles in her pocket for the key. "Got it."

She opens the door and they both step inside. The house smells musty, it seems obvious somehow that it's unlived in, empty. "Well," Willow says as they stand in the entryway shivering in their wet clothes. "We're here." She puts down her bag and the cup of hot chocolate, still untouched, on the floor.

"Okay," Guy says slowly. He steps closer to her. "What do you want to do now?"

Willow has no idea what she wants to do. She still hasn't figured out why she needed to come home in the first place. She'd expected that the moment she entered the house she'd know, that she'd open the door and everything would become clear.

But nothing is clear. There is no great epiphany. The moment seems as flat and meaningless as before when she stood by the side of the road staring at the place where her parents' lives ended.

Willow's at a loss. Guy seems anxious on her behalf, curious as to what her next move will be.

"Do you want to see my room?" she asks suddenly.

Guy looks surprised. It's clear that this isn't what he was expecting.

"Sorry." Willow shakes her head at how stupid that must have sounded. She isn't in first grade and she doesn't want to show him her doll collection. "That didn't come out right. I meant I have some stuff up there, and we can change into something dry."

"Oh great." Guy nods. "Only, I'm not sure that we're the same size."

"Stop it." She laughs. "My brother has some things here too. C'mon." She takes his hand and leads him upstairs.

"You do have a lot of books," he says as they enter her room. "I've got to say, though, I never pictured you as having black walls." He wanders over to the bookcases, still holding her hand, and looks at the different titles.

"Oh, this used to be David's room, he painted it black," Willow explains. "When he went to college I inherited it. Now he uses my old room when he visits." She pauses, aware that she has just used the present tense.

"Let's go to my *old* room," she says, pulling him down the hall. "My brother keeps his things there. In here." She opens a door on the right. "Some of this should fit." Willow frowns as she rummages through the chest of drawers in the corner. "I mean, you are the same *height*. . . . Here." She tosses him a sweatshirt and a faded pair of jeans. "I'll see you in a few

minutes. . . . Umm, I'm going to uh, change in my room."
Willow closes the door hurriedly as Guy starts unbuttoning
his shirt.

Willow undoes her braid and runs her fingers through her
hair. Markie's comment had made her feel self-conscious
somehow. In any case, it should dry much faster now that it's
loose. She goes through her closet searching for something to
wear. She is amazed at all the things she owns, clothes that she
has forgotten about, and she wonders if David or Cathy would
notice and question her if she brought some of them back
with her.

Maybe I should put a dress on.

She runs her hands through the folds of the many skirts
hanging in her closet. Guy has never seen her in anything like
that. . . .

Willow shakes her head at how frivolous she's being. The
purpose of this visit is not to stage a fashion show. . . .

Except she really doesn't know *what* the purpose is. . . .

"Hey, are you ready in there?" Guy knocks on the door.

"Uh . . . Just a sec." Willow steps into a dry pair of jeans and
buttons up a shirt. "Come on in," she calls out.

"What should I do with these things?" he asks, walking
into the room with his wet clothes in his arms. "Hey, your hair
is different."

"Easier to dry this way." Willow shrugs.

"I've never seen it like that. It looks beautiful."

"Thank you." Willow blushes, then she looks at him and
starts to laugh. "I guess you and David are the same height,
but that's about it."

"What's wrong with what I'm wearing?"

"Nothing, absolutely nothing, it's just, well, that sweatshirt is a little small."

"Hey, you're the one who gave me this stuff. . . ."

"No, no, it's great." Willow can't stop laughing. "Listen, promise me that you'll never stop rowing, I mean really. Even if you end up doing fieldwork, pack a pair of oars or something."

"Whatever." Guy shrugs, but Willow can tell that he's flattered.

"Umm, you know what?" She looks at the bundle of wet clothes in his arms. "I guess we should do a load of laundry." She gathers up her own assortment of dripping things. "C'mon, it's in the basement."

As they walk through the empty rooms, Willow can't help thinking how strange, how lifeless the house is. No one coming in for the first time would mistake it for the home of a family that has gone on vacation. There is a quality in the air that absolutely forbids such a notion. It is as if the house senses that its occupants are gone, dead, scattered, and has reacted in sympathy.

Willow stops dead in her tracks halfway down the stairs to the basement. How could she have forgotten what was here? She sinks down onto the steps and stares at the half-dismantled bookcases. The screwdriver, her first accomplice, lies off to one side.

"What is it?" Guy sits next to her.

Willow shakes her head. Once again, she feels that she should be overcome, that the sight of this, like the site of the accident, should be her undoing. She wonders why she isn't in desperate need of her razor, why everything is leaving her cold. She turns to look at Guy and is shocked to see how strongly the sight is affecting him. He is pale, ghostly almost, as he stares at the screwdriver. He is the one who needs to be talked through this.

"Are you okay?" she asks, concerned. "Guy, are you all right?"

"I don't know." He turns away from the screwdriver and looks at her. "I just know that that has to be the ugliest thing I've ever seen in my life."

"I'm sorry. I don't know why I dragged you here." Willow brushes the hair out of his eyes. "I mean, why I made *you* drag *me* here. I thought . . . I don't know what I thought." She shakes her head. "I think I made some connection with David and the way he was that time we came here and the way he cries. . . . But I don't know, and that doesn't make any sense anyway. And even if it did, I've spent so long *not* crying, *not* feeling, making sure that I *can't* cry, so . . . why would I be courting it now?" She buries her head in her hands.

Guy puts his arm around her shoulders, but doesn't say anything.

"Maybe I was just supposed to run into Markie," Willow says. She lifts her head up and looks at him. "Maybe that's why we came out here." She shrugs. "I mean, it's not like I even knew that was going to happen, but . . . Whatever. . . . Look, I guess I'll just run the wash, and then I might as well get the *Bulfinch*, and then I don't know, do you want to wait here until the rain stops before we head back?"

"Okay, well, at least until the laundry's done anyway. But are you so sure that you're finished here?"

"I don't even know what it is I came to do," Willow says as she gets up from the stairs and dumps their clothes into the washing machine. "That'll take a while." She puts the detergent in and presses the on button. "So, let's go back upstairs, and I don't know, I'll just get the book. . . ."

She climbs up the steps dispiritedly. "You want to wait in here?" She gestures toward the living room. "I'm just going to go and get the *Bulfinch* . . ." Willow doesn't want Guy to go with her, because there is something she wants to give him, something from her parents' study, where the *Bulfinch* is, and she wants it to be a surprise.

"Are you sure that you want to be alone now?"

"I'm fine. . . . I just . . . look." Willow walks him into the living room. "This used to be my favorite place in the whole world to read." She climbs up on the window seat. "C'mere." She smiles a little as Guy sits down next to her. "I'll just be a second, okay?"

"Take your time."

Willow walks down the hall to the study, wondering if the room where her parents spent most of their time, where they did all of their work, will leave her as numb as everything else has. But as she opens the door and surveys the floor-to-ceiling bookcases and huge partners desk with the burgundy leather blotter, she realizes that once again she feels nothing.

She crosses to the bookcase and pulls out the *Bulfinch*. Then she looks for a few seconds until she finds *Tristes Tropiques*. She knows that if David ever finds out that she's given their father's copy away, a first edition in perfect condition, he'll kill her. But she can't imagine that will be anytime soon, and anyway, she's sure that it will have meaning for Guy. She desperately wants to give him something special.

Willow walks around the study for a few moments desultorily picking up random books. There is a fine layer of dust that covers everything like sand. She supposes that there's something fitting about the way the house now seems like an archaeological site. She sits at the partners desk and leafs through the papers on the blotter, morbidly curious to see what her parents had been occupied with on the last day of their lives.

There is nothing special, some notes in her father's barely legible handwriting, a few bills, and a letter to the housekeeper in her mother's bold script:

Hannah,
Thank you so much for staying late and helping with the party, I couldn't have gotten everything together without you. Don't worry about the vacuuming today, but when you go to the store could you make sure to get the calcium-enriched orange juice?

Calcium v. v. imp for Willow!

Willow takes the note—she thinks maybe that she would like to have it on her desk back at David's house. She has no other keepsake of any kind. She can't take a picture, David would certainly notice something like that. There doesn't seem to be another piece of writing to hand that might be more interesting, anything like that would be on the computer anyway. It's just a little thing, quite meaningless really, but she would like the small scrap of paper with her mother's handwriting on it.

She takes the books and the paper and leaves the study,

stopping on the way back to the living room to tuck the copy of *Tristes Tropiques* in her bag.

"Hey, what are you reading?" she asks Guy, who is flipping through a book as he sits on the window seat.

"You weren't kidding when you said that your parents had thousands and thousands of books," he says, gesturing at the shelves in the living room.

"Oscar Wilde." Willow sits down next to him and looks at the title he's holding. "He's pretty fun. I bet that tutor of yours must have given you a lot of his stuff to read."

"What are you holding on to, I mean besides the *Bulfinch*?" Guy asks, looking at the piece of paper in her hand.

"Oh just some note my mother wrote. . . . Nothing really." Willow shrugs. "I'm sorry that I made you drive me here. I mean, it was a lot to ask, and I don't know how much you minded missing school and . . . Well, it didn't accomplish anything. Thank you for doing it though."

"You don't have to thank me," Guy takes the paper from her hand. *"Calcium v. v. imp for Willow,"* he reads.

Willow doesn't realize that she's crying until Guy takes his hand and reaches over to wipe away her tears. And she knows then that she was right about her brother, that it takes unbelievable strength to feel this kind of grief, and she doesn't know if she can handle it, because it really hurts, hurts her more than the razor ever could. And she doesn't know why, after visiting the place where her parents lost their lives, after looking at the spot where she forged her unholy alliance with the screwdriver, that something so simple, so trivial should finally affect her so much.

Maybe it's because, as she listened to Guy read the note,

she realized as she did when she saw David with Isabelle, that she will never be anyone's child again. No one will ever worry about her the way that her parents did, or care about her the way they did. The only other time that Willow will ever experience a bond like that is when she herself becomes a mother. And even then she will still need her own mother, and she won't be there, she won't be there because she is *dead*. Dead. Decades too early.

And she is amazed, really amazed, that the razor managed to numb her so well and for so long, because the way she's feeling now is so overwhelming, so *overpowering*, that it would take a lot more than a few slashes with a blade to transmute her anguish.

She holds her stomach, afraid that if she doesn't she will double over from the pain. Guy doesn't say anything to her, he just holds her hair back from her face and occasionally blots her tears with his hand.

"I'm ... I'm ... not ..." She chokes on the words. "I'm not anyone's *daughter* anymore!" Willow says this as if it is something that she has just figured out. "And I know ... I know that I should be sorry for my brother, that ... that ..." She stops for a second; she's gasping for air so violently that she thinks she might hyperventilate.

"Can you breathe?" Guy asks.

"Yes, I mean no. Just give me a second." Willow wipes her nose with the back of her hand. "That was polite, I'm sorry." She laughs, a little hysterically. "I can't breathe when I cry really hard. ... And I can't remember ... the last time I cried like this. ..."

She stops talking for a second and tries to dry her eyes. But it's useless, like trying to stem a tidal wave. Her hands get entangled with his and she grips his wrists and turns to face him as they sit side by side on the window seat.

"I should . . . feel sorry for David because he doesn't have parents either. And I know . . . I know that . . . that I should be sorry for my *parents* because they didn't wake up that morning knowing that they were never going to see another day. . . ." She squeezes his hands so tightly that she wonders why he doesn't cry out in pain. "But all I can think about is that I'm not anyone's *daughter* anymore. . . ."

She stops, once more overcome with tears, and gasps for breath.

"Do you need a paper bag or something?" Guy looks alarmed.

"No, no, I just . . . I never *will* be anyone's daughter again," Willow continues after a few minutes. "And I was right to be . . . to become a . . . cutter, because maybe you think this doesn't look so bad, that girls cry, people cry, but you'd be wrong, you'd be so wrong, anything . . . anything at all . . . would feel better than this does. I'm . . . sorry." She tries to catch her breath. "I'm sorry to be putting you through this. . . ." Willow wipes her eyes once more. Their hands are still clasped, and she feels the backs of his brush across her forehead. "This isn't what I had in mind when I said to take me here. . . . This isn't what I was expecting. . . . Or maybe it was. . . . I just . . . I don't even know."

"Willow, you haven't put me through anything."

"I need a Kleenex." She sniffs.

Guy disengages his hands from hers, takes the hem of his sweatshirt, and wipes her nose with it.

"That's romantic," she says, embarrassed.

"Well, it is sort of, because I wouldn't do it for anybody else in the world."

"I . . . I . . . well that's . . . That's the . . . the nicest . . . I . . ." Willow hiccups. "Excuse me. I also get the hiccups really badly when I cry." She takes his sweatshirt and wipes her nose again. "I'm a mess." She laughs shakily. "But guess what? There's no one else in the world whose sweatshirt I would want to wipe my nose on." She hiccups again.

"Do you want some water for those hiccups?"

"No." Willow shakes her head. "No, thank you. But you know what I would like? Could you get me my hot chocolate? I left it near the door."

"Okay." Guy shrugs. He gets up and is back within seconds. "Here you go." He looks dubious as he watches her take a sip of the now stone-cold drink. "Is that really good?"

"Well." Willow makes a face. "It depends on what you call good. It kind of tastes like river mud at this point."

"Is that something you've had a lot of?" Guy asks as he sits back down alongside her.

"I'm guessing." Willow puts the cup down on the floor. She leans back against the cushions with a deep sigh. "Thank you," she says suddenly.

"For what?"

"Thank you for bringing me out here. Thank you for not telling my brother about me. Thank you for being such a . . ."

"You're crying again." He shifts so he can take her in his arms.

"Yeah, I know. Gimme your sweatshirt."

"Okay, hang on." He wipes her tears away. "You going to start hiccupping again?"

"No." Willow shakes her head.

"Do you want to stay here and, I don't know, maybe take a nap or something? Or do you want to go back to your brother's house now?" Guy says after a few minutes.

But Willow wants neither of those things. And she's shocked by just what it is that she does want. The past half hour has hardly been conducive to passion. And yet, as she sits there with him on the window seat, with his strong arms around her, she knows that if she can survive crying, then there are other things that she can survive too. And that if some things are lost to her forever, there are others that she has not yet begun to experience. She knows too that what she wants is not because passion is the natural antidote to grief, but because it is the most natural, most perfect, most complete expression of what she feels for him.

"Do you remember when you first . . . when you first found out that I was a cutter?"

"I'll never forget it."

"But do you remember . . . Well, do you remember how I tried to bribe you?"

"I'll never forget that either."

"Well." She swallows. "I . . . well, I hope that now, maybe you would . . . I mean, I want to . . . If we could . . ." She stumbles over the words but looks at him expectantly, hoping that since he is so often able to know her better than she does herself, that he will understand what she is trying to say.

To her dismay he looks completely baffled.

"Oh, this isn't coming out right!" Willow exclaims, wonders if perhaps this isn't a good idea after all, if it will shock him, following as it does so closely on her breakdown, except she can think of nothing that she has ever wanted more. "Never mind!" she says dispiritedly. "This isn't how I imagined it would be anyway, not with my nose all runny."

"Imagined what?" Guy asks slowly.

Willow moves closer to him. "What do you think," she says finally.

"I . . . Well . . . I'm not sure *what* to think." Guy pulls back from her a little until she is at arm's length and studies her face. "And I'd really hate to make a mistake right now. Because, well . . . It sounds like you're saying that you want . . . Well, you want . . ."

"I've never heard *you* sound so flustered before." Willow laughs. She wipes the last vestiges of her tears away. She can't believe that he doesn't get what she's saying, and she can't believe that she can laugh about it either.

"Willow, are you . . . I mean are you referring to when . . ."

She decides to make things easy for him. "C'mere." She pulls him forward again. She has kissed him twice before. Once with disastrous results, once not nearly so catastrophic, but never with all that she feels inside. She hopes and believes that now, finally, she can show him how much she cares for him, but still, she is trembling slightly as she moves to close the gap between them.

"You're sure this is okay?" Guy whispers against her mouth.

"It's okay," Willow whispers back as she helps him find the buttons on her shirt. "It really is okay," she repeats, amazed and thrilled that it should be so. She pulls the tearstained sweatshirt off over his head.

"But you're so shy." Guy's breath is soft against her throat as he slides her bra off her shoulders. "And you're so vulnerable. Please tell me that you're sure."

"I'm sure." Willow reaches for the buttons on his jeans. "I'm sure, but . . ."

"But what? What's the *but*? What's the *but*? Why . . . Why are you saying *but* all of a sudden?" Guy stammers a little as he helps her shed the rest of her clothes.

"But . . . Well, have you ever done this with anyone else?"

"Never." He pulls her down so that she is lying on the window seat.

"Good." Willow is surprised that shy as she indeed is, she isn't embarrassed to be naked in front of him. Maybe this is because in every other important way she already has been.

"Have you?" Guy lies down on his side next to her.

"No!"

"Good." He kisses her hair, her face, her neck.

"Wait, wait a second." Willow pushes her hand against his chest. "I have to ask you something else. Do you . . . Do you . . . Umm. Do you have . . . *anything*?"

"What?" Guy frowns. "Oh! Umm-hum, I have . . . uh, I have something in my wallet."

"Good."

"Can I . . . Can I . . ."

"You can do anything." She shivers as his hands move over her body, but this time it is wholly unmixed with fear and she cannot believe how wonderful it feels.

"Wait a sec . . ." Willow sits up suddenly. "You do? Have something, I mean?"

"Well, aren't you glad that I do?" Guy sits up too and looks at her.

"Wait a sec . . ."

"*Again* wait a sec?"

"If I had something in my bag you'd want to know why . . . I mean, how *long* have you had *something* in your wallet?"

"Since I was twelve."

"No!" She hits him with the flat of her hand.

"Of course I haven't." He moves in to kiss her again.

"Well, tell me."

"Don't you want to stop talking now?" he says against her mouth as he pushes her gently back down on the window seat cushions.

"No."

"But if you keep talking, then I can't kiss you, and then we can't do what follows after that. . . ."

"But I like to talk to you. Because I can ask you *anything*, tell you *anything*, and no matter what I say to you, I know it will be all right."

"That wasn't fair." Guy sighs against the side of her face. "Now I have to answer." He props himself up on one elbow. "I've . . . had *something* in my wallet ever since I knew . . . Well, ever since I *hoped* that there would be a time when I would need to . . . protect you like this."

"And when was that?"

"If I answer that, *then* will you stop talking?"

"Yes." Willow bites her lower lip and runs her hands over his shoulders. "I will, because your answers are so perfect."

"Oh." He looks down at her and smiles. "Then would you believe me if I told you that I put it there after the first time I met you?"

"No."

"Okay." He pauses and Willow can tell that he is going to

tell her the truth. "I . . . Well . . ." He runs his hands through her hair and watches as it drifts back to her shoulders. "After I saw you in the physics lab."

"I don't . . . I don't get it."

"We'd already talked in the stacks, and I knew you were different from any other girl I'd ever met. And then you told me that your parents were dead, and I thought that you were so . . . lost and vulnerable. So when I saw you in the physics lab . . . and I saw you try and take care of someone that you thought was weaker than yourself, I couldn't believe that someone who had been through what you'd been through could be that . . . well, generous, and thoughtful . . ."

"But you hardly knew me."

"I know. And I don't want you to think that I rushed right out to a drugstore or anything. I didn't know that we'd even talk again, or that if we did, if we'd get along, or maybe you were seeing someone else. . . . I just knew that the way you tried to protect someone like that, especially given your situation. . . . I just . . . I thought that you had to be the most special girl I would ever meet. . . ."

"I'll stop talking now." Willow twines her arms about his neck.

"Isn't that interesting."

"Hmmm?"

"When you blush, it doesn't stop at your collarbone."

"Oh."

"I'll tell you something else."

"What?"

"I just figured out why someone would want to make the first mirror."

Willow blinks in surprise. That is not what she was expecting to hear.

"Why?"

"I think some lover wanted his beloved to see how she appeared to him. He wanted her to be able to see herself the way that he did."

Willow has nothing more to say. She watches him as he kisses her cuts and she hopes that her inexpert exploration of his body has the power to affect him the way that he's affecting her.

"Ouch." She winces as he inadvertently pulls her hair.

"Sorry, I . . ." Guy can't help crushing her as he leans over and reaches down to the floor. "I . . . um . . . I just um . . . need my wallet and it's in this pocket. . . ." He searches for the borrowed jeans.

"Are you nervous?" he asks as he finds the pants and fishes his wallet out of the pocket.

"Uh-huh." Willow nods. "What about you?"

"Very."

"Oh. Well, don't be, because I'm nervous enough for both of us." Willow wonders if what is about to happen will hurt, and she thinks how ironic it is that she of all people should have this concern.

It *is* painful, she flinches involuntarily, but it is Guy who cries out. "I'm sorry! Did I hurt you?! I didn't mean to, but . . ."

Willow covers his mouth with her hand. "Only for a second," she assures him. "Only for a second." And she realizes that this is true. Pain has somehow transformed into pleasure, and that pleasure is better than any pain could ever be.

CHAPTER FIFTEEN

*Persephone dwells among the shadows in Hades, among
them but not of them, she is . . .*

   *Maybe talk about how her mother as a goddess
of the harvest represents fertility, so that when she
(Persephone) eats the pomegranate, it's kind of like an
act of solidarity, since pomegranates are a symbol of
fertility, even though it means that she'll have to stay in
the underworld. . . .*

Oh, who cares?

Willow looks at the notes she made in the library a few
days earlier and sighs in frustration. They're absolutely
useless. Still, trying to make some sense out of them is better
than staring at a blank screen. She can't even bring herself
to turn her computer on. But if she doesn't get something
done soon, she'll be in trouble. The *Bulfinch* paper is due first

thing in the morning, and she hasn't even written a sentence.

She'd thought that she'd had trouble concentrating on the subject before. But now that it's two in the morning of what has been, excepting the day of the accident, the most eventful twenty-four hours of her life, it's proving to be absolutely impossible.

Willow pushes her notebook away and reaches for her bag. She takes out the note, the innocent piece of paper that her mother had written to the housekeeper, and lays it flat on her desk. She finds it extraordinary that such a little thing has the power to move her so greatly.

Perhaps she had known all along that something of the kind was waiting for her at home, that to be confronted by such a thing would be to let loose with all that she had been suppressing for so many months. And perhaps even if she hadn't found the note, there would have been something else, something equally innocuous that would have set her off just the same.

Willow thinks back to the way she cried earlier in the day, the pain that she allowed herself to finally feel. She is staggered that she was able to process such overwhelming emotions, and wonders if she will be able to do so again.

Is she ready to part company with her constant companion?

Willow opens her desk drawer, takes out one of her many razor blades, and places it beside her mother's note.

Well, what's it going to be, then?

She looks at the dull metal blade, then shifts her eyes to the faded ink, wondering if the message will once again move her to tears, and if it does, if she will once again be able to withstand the onslaught.

Oh God I hope so!

But maybe her earlier tears have no implications beyond their immediate and obvious meaning. She was affected by her mother's letter to the housekeeper, by the small reminder that once her welfare was paramount in someone else's world, and for whatever reason, she was able to process that feeling without the alchemy of cutting.

Or maybe the reason is obvious after all. Maybe by allowing herself to care about somebody, to *love* somebody, she herself set the entire chain in motion, and maybe it is his love that enabled her to endure the grief that issued forth.

Willow pushes herself away from the desk and wanders over to the dresser, then looks at herself in the mirror that hangs above it.

She doesn't think that she looks any different. Shouldn't something so profound, so life-changing, mark her as visibly, as decidedly as her razors do?

Willow pulls up her shirt and examines the scars on her stomach. They are slowly fading, and in the dim light from her desk lamp, their shadowy outline is less vivid to her than the memory of the way that he kissed them.

Look at that. I guess when I blush it doesn't stop at my collarbone.

She drops her shirt and stares at her face again. Her hair is still down, she never bothered to braid it again. She wonders now if she had really been wearing it that way all these months because it was so convenient. Perhaps it had simply been an unconscious attempt to return to an earlier time. She pushes it back and focuses on her eyes. Maybe there is a change, albeit one that is invisible to her. Maybe there is something that would be immediately obvious to anyone else.

Would Markie notice? If she were to meet her tomorrow, would she see a difference? Will Laurie be able to tell?

Willow wonders if her mother would have noticed. And more, if her mother hadn't noticed, would she herself have told her?

Willow has no answer to that, but she knows this much is true: The rest of her life will be filled with moments just like this, moments when she will want more than anything to tell her mother something, ask her father a question, and simply not be able to. All the tears that she lets fall will never change that. And neither will the razor.

She walks back to the desk. She has to get some work done on her wretched paper, but as she sits down she hears a faint silvery sound, and this time she understands immediately just what she is hearing.

She should be accustomed to the sound of her brother weeping by now, but listening to his tears is even more painful than it was for her to cry herself.

Willow puts on her bathrobe, moves to the door, and walks out to the landing. She grips the banister, kneels down, and looks through the bars. If she cranes her head she can just see him seated at the kitchen table.

It is unbearable to watch.

She has a sudden urge, different from before, to go to him, confront him, *comfort* him if such a thing is possible. Now that she knows how weeping that way feels, she can't bear the thought of him there alone. But how can she possibly comfort him, when she knows that she herself is the cause of his tears?

Without thinking, Willow reaches into her pocket for her razor. She grips it tightly, but she doesn't cut. She can watch him without cutting. She has proven so to herself, but watching is no longer good enough. Can she go to him, can she face his pain, is she strong enough for that?

She takes a tentative step down the stairs, but this time she doesn't hide in the shadows. If David were to look up, there would be no way that he could miss her.

Willow reaches the bottom. She never takes her eyes off David as she grips the razor tightly. Without any choice on her part, the edge of the blade is already cutting into her skin.

Is this what she wants? To continue the same way that she has? Is this in fact the answer to her earlier question?

She sinks down on the stairs, unable to go to him yet unable to look away. She can feel the blood as it starts to spring from her palm. Willow knows that she should put her razor down. She should get up and walk the remaining few feet that separate them. But she is incapable.

And so Willow sits there, just sits there, waiting for David to notice her. Will he ever look up? Will he ever let her into *his* world of pain, even if only to lacerate her himself? And then David does look up. He does see her.

Willow slips the razor back into her pocket, and walks slowly toward him. Today has been a day of firsts, and she is desperate to connect, in some way, with her brother. She needs to let him know that she still loves him, even if she has forfeited his love, that she is made miserable by his anguish.

She watches his face as he watches her. She doesn't shy away from his tears. She doesn't turn away from his pain.

Willow stands in front of her brother. She sees him open his mouth, barely hears him whisper her name.

She leans closer, so she can hear what he has to tell her. Suddenly he grips her hand with surprising force, grips her so tightly that she can barely move.

"Oh Willow," he says. "Oh, Willow, what if you had died that night too?"

CHAPTER SIXTEEN

"Okay, I guess that's it. You need to do the footnotes, though, because I'm just not up for that right now."

"Are you sure?" Willow looks anxiously at the computer screen. "I still think we should put that stuff in about how ironic it is that the pomegranate, the thing that keeps her stuck in the underworld, is a symbol of—"

"Look, you don't want this to be too good, do you?" David gives her a look. "I mean, you don't want everyone to know that your brother did most of the work, right?"

"But you didn't come up with that, I did!" Willow protests.

"How about this, then." He pushes the chair back from the desk and stretches his arms over his head, then looks down at where she's sitting on the floor. "I'm done. I haven't stayed up all night working on a paper since I was in college, and I could really live without the experience. I'm not kidding, Willow.

You told me this thing was assigned three weeks ago, if you wanted help with it, couldn't you have come to me before two a.m. on the morning that it's due?"

"Okay, I guess. I mean, yes," Willow says between yawns. She still can't believe that she even asked him *this* time.

After she had come upon him crying, after his extraordinary statement, which moved her more than she would have thought possible, they had sat at the kitchen table and talked. Not, however, as she would have hoped, about anything of significance.

Certainly, after such a naked display of emotion, it had proven impossible for David to continue to act with his cold reserve, and his manner toward her had softened considerably. And yet the content of their conversation, to her intense disappointment, had remained on the most superficial level. And so, Willow found herself *not* speaking about how much she missed their parents, about how strange their new circumstances were, but talking to him instead, finally, about the French quiz, and also about the trouble she was having with her paper. David had suggested writing it with her, *for* her, really, as it turned out. Surely this is something that would not have occurred a few weeks ago, at least not as easily or as comfortably, and yet, as she leans back against the desk and watches him make the last few corrections, she feels empty inside. There is still something, *everything*, unresolved between them, and although talking to him like this is better than not talking to him at all, she still wishes for more.

"Anyway," she continues as she shifts her legs, which have fallen asleep from sitting still for so long. It is almost six thirty in the morning, they have been up in her room for the past four hours. "Thank you, I would never have gotten this done on my own."

"Yeah, sure, of course," David responds, but Willow can see that he's not really paying her any attention, he's looking at their father's copy of *Bulfinch,* which is lying on the desk, and which unbelievably enough, she has forgotten about. "Did you . . ." He trails off, picks the book up with a frown and flips through it. "This is . . . this is . . . from the . . . from the . . . *house,* isn't it?"

"Uh-huh." Willow nods. She can see how hard it is for him to even say the words. "I um, I uh . . . I took it that time I . . . that we went back for me to get some clothes. I knew I would need it. . . ."

"You did?" He glances down at her backpack lying on the floor.

"Uh-huh." Willow nods. "Sure."

"Really?" He looks at her in confusion. "But I keep seeing you dragging around some cheap paperback. Besides, I remember that day. Cathy gave you a huge lecture about the fact that your bag wasn't nearly big enough to fit anything. . . ." He frowns for a moment, then reaches down to the floor to pick up her backpack.

"Don't!" Willow says. But it's too late. She thanks God that her stash is inside a zippered pocket, she's sure that he won't open that, but for once she's carrying other contraband that is almost as worrisome.

David looks inside the bag. Maybe he's just trying to see how much room there really is, but that doesn't stop him from pulling out the copy of *Tristes Tropiques.*

"I . . . I hope you don't mind," Willow stammers. "But I want to . . . I'm going to give that to Guy."

Stupid! That was a stupid thing to say!

Okay, so maybe she hasn't been able to stop thinking about Guy all night, maybe she was trying to get David's mind off of whether she really did bring the *Bulfinch* back with her that time . . .

But it was still a stupid thing to say!

"There's no way that you've had both of these books with you the whole time you've been living here," he says slowly. "You've been back to the house."

"No, I . . ."

"Willow." David looks at her in alarm. "Please tell me, and please be honest, you didn't *drive* out there by yourself, did you?"

Willow knows that any attempts she makes at concealment are useless, that the truth is written all over her face for anyone to see. Not only that, but it is obvious to her that his main concern is not that she went out there, but how she got there. Clearly the thought of her driving by herself terrifies him, and she wants to spare him that anxiety.

"No, I didn't go out there by myself, and I wasn't the one doing the driving anyway."

"Pretty nice of someone to drive you all that way just so you could pick up a book. Sorry." He looks at the copy of *Tristes Tropiques*. "So you could pick up *two* books. Pretty nice of you to want to give him this too. I have an idea of what it must mean to you." He pauses and looks at her for a moment, deep in thought. "Willow, you can't tell me that's why you really went out there."

Willow stares at her brother in amazement. How could he

possibly know what she herself didn't. That her odyssey had a deeper purpose, that her desire to go out there for the *Bulfinch* had been nothing more than . . . And then she realizes that David's mind is elsewhere, he thinks she went out to the house with Guy—he *knows* that she went with Guy—just so they could have some privacy so that they could . . .

"Willow," David says suddenly. "You're bright red. *Bright* red. Go look in the mirror."

But Willow doesn't need a mirror to know that her face is flaming.

"Oh my God. Oh my God." He starts to laugh. "I am not equipped to deal with this, I'm just not equipped to deal with this kind of thing at all."

Maybe it's the lateness of the hour, or maybe it's just that he'd been crying the way he was, but for whatever reason, David seems to be thawing. He is looking at her, really looking at her the way he hasn't in months. He is finally connecting with her, teasing her the way he once would have. . . .

Okay, she wanted her brother to unbend toward her, to talk to her the way he used to . . .

But did it have to be about this?

"You would *not* be turning that color over a simple road trip."

"Fine. Just shut up already, okay?!"

"Sure. Look, I guess it had to happen sometime, and I think you picked the right person, because—"

"Gimme my stuff back!!" Willow snatches both the books and her bag from him.

"No problem. Just . . . look . . . Is there anything that you need to tell me?"

"No."

"Okay, is there anything that *I* need to tell you, or rather, explain to you about how—"

"NO!" Willow cuts him off.

"Well then, is there anything that maybe *Cathy* has to talk to you about? I want to make sure that you—"

"NO!" Willow cannot believe that she is having a conversation, or rather, trying very hard *not* to have a conversation like this with her brother.

"What's so funny anyway?" she asks belligerently after a few moments. She's sure that his laughter is not directed at the situation, but at *her*.

"Oh, I'm just thinking that when Isabelle is seventeen I'm locking her up."

"Will you stop it!" She hits his arm.

"All right." He is serious once again. "But Willow, I'm not joking about this. If you need me to explain anything, if you need me to talk to you . . ."

"I *do* need you to talk to me! I do need you to talk to me! I do need you to talk to me!" Willow startles both of them with her outburst. Unlike the day before with Guy, she is immediately aware that she is crying. "I do need you to talk to me," she repeats once more, burying her head in her hands.

"Willow!" David gets up off the chair, sits down next to her, cups her chin in his hand, and lifts her face to his. "What is it? What's happened? Did you . . . Did he . . ."

"I do need you to talk to me, and not about that kind of stuff. . . . I've known about things like *that* since I was in fifth grade. . . . You need . . . You need . . . You . . ." She can barely get the words out, she is hyperventilating so badly.

"All right, take a deep breath." David moves so that he is sitting next to her on the floor with his arm around her. He's trying to sound calm, but Willow can tell that he is, in fact, very worried by this sudden fit of tears and has no idea what it might signify. She is hardly less astonished than he is, and she can't help wondering if this is the way things will be from now on. That perhaps her grieving apparatus, frozen for so long, will now erupt at any moment, and, if that is indeed the case, if that is something she can tolerate.

"Give yourself a second," David continues. "Just take a second and then try and tell me what's going on."

"You . . . You . . . *We* need to talk about the way things were," Willow finally says. "We need to talk about *them*. Maybe they're dead, but they shouldn't be dead to *us*. They shouldn't be dead *between* us. You need . . . You need to talk to me too. You need to tell me how . . . how angry, how *furious*, you are with me about, about what happened. You need to talk to me too!"

"I . . . I do. I know that. . . ."

Willow wipes her face and turns to look at David in surprise. "You do?"

"Yes. And maybe I've done something very wrong these past months. I've wanted to talk to you, it just doesn't seem fair, I mean to make you relive . . . I never know how to talk about what happened. Or when. And I worry that if I do talk about things, then you won't be able to keep going the way you have, or that I won't. And I think that maybe it's just best to keep things contained. But obviously I don't know what I'm talking about." He pauses for a second, reaches up to the desk where she keeps a box of tissues, and hands her some.

"Thank you." Willow blows her nose very loudly.

"I . . . I'm even less equipped to deal with this kind of thing than I am the other. . . ." David sighs deeply and for a second he looks like someone twice, three times his age. "It's so hard for me to think about what happened and even harder to see what it's done to you. So I just try and focus on getting on with things, on taking care of you, which I don't know the first thing about. But I try and do one thing, I try and make sure that I don't constantly remind you, so that *you* can get on with things. And you *do* seem to get on with things. I'm so amazed at how well you've been dealing with all this, that I thought that bringing up the past would be cruel."

Willow doesn't know how to respond to this. He's said so many things that it's hard to focus and let them all in. She's dimly aware that he has alluded to what he considers her ability to deal with things well, and she is sure that she should disabuse him of this notion. But other thoughts are fighting for prominence, and she needs to reassure him that he has not been wrong. That even if she has wanted to talk to him, at times wanted that more than anything, that does not mean that he has failed her like she has failed him.

"But you do, you do handle things well," she stutters after a moment. "I know how hard it is, how hard it must be for you and Cathy to have me here and how hard it is financially, and how I barely contribute. It's all my fault. And I—"

"Oh Willow," David cuts her off harshly. "None of this is your fault. Did you ever think that maybe it was irresponsible for them to drink enough so that a sixteen-year-old with a learner's permit was forced to drive in what was one of the worst storms of the year? Did you ever stop to consider that if

315

I was on top of things I would sell the house, that it wouldn't matter how long the insurance was taking, and that if I did, we wouldn't have any money worries *at all*, for *years*? That the only reason you have to contribute *anything* is because I can't face doing that? That it's my fault that you have to give me all your money instead of spending it on yourself?" He looks angry, angrier than she can ever remember seeing him, and she can only be thankful that it seems to be directed at himself, because she doesn't think that she could handle him looking at her like that.

"I'm mad at myself for that, because with everything else that's going on, that should be one area where things are easy. And I know I'd better deal with it soon too. I need to sell our house before you have to start thinking about college."

"Okay, I guess I never did think about that exactly—I mean, make that connection about me having to work at the library and you selling the house." Willow puts her hand on his arm. "But still I think that—"

"And I get mad at other things too," David interrupts her once again. But Willow doesn't care because she can see he is about to say something very important. "I get mad at other things too," he continues. "I get mad that I'm forced to think about things like you going to college and putting the house on the market to pay for that college. I get mad that I can't have sex with my wife whenever I want because this apartment is so small and I don't want my little sister to hear us. I get mad that I can't walk around the house in my underwear and that I have to behave as if I am the parent of a seventeen-year-old and not just an infant." He pauses for an instant and takes a deep breath. "I don't ever get mad or hold you responsible for our parents dying. That would be worse than crazy. I meant what I said at dinner. It was a hideous accident, it was just an inexplicable event, and my first thought about it is *always, always, always* how hard it is for you. How hard the next ten years will be for you, ten years that I had parents to help me with, but that you won't. But you're right. I do get mad at you. I'm mad at you for the fact that almost every aspect of my daily life, every *stupid* aspect, has been irrevocably changed. And I'm mad that our relationship has changed too, that even though I still adore you and always will, it is not the same easy feeling that I had before." He holds on to her hand where it rests on his arm. "I have always been responsible for you. Just by virtue of loving you, I've had a responsibility to you and for you. You have that responsibility to me too, to anyone that you will ever love. But it's different now. Now on a daily basis, my responsibility for you has been put onto a practical plane, now I have to deal with French quizzes and teacher conferences, and there are times when it drives me crazy, when I know I'm not *old* enough to have these additional worries. And then, then I *hate* myself for thinking that, because I know how petty, how irrational, how unfair I'm being. And I look at you and I see how strong you are, and I'm amazed that you can be that way, and then I get even angrier at myself that I can't handle these little everyday problems, when you're able to handle so much more."

"But I'm not strong! I'm not strong," Willow cries. She takes her hand away and once more covers her face. She is so moved by what her brother has told her, she is so relieved by his emotional honesty, by his admission that he still loves her—an amazing thing!—even though he has been angry and frustrated and confused and conflicted, that she can't bear to sit there with him under false pretenses.

She should show him her scars, show him the razor marks, let him know that his image of her is fraudulent. Only his praise is like balm in Gilead, and she is terrified of forfeiting that. Neither does she want to add to the burden of his responsibility. She knows now, really knows that what she told Guy was true. It would *kill* him to learn this about her.

And she has not yet decided to give up her razors either. She realizes now that she is not quite ready to let them go. Yet she sits there next to him, takes her hands away from her face, holds her arms out in supplication, almost wishing that he somehow would take it upon himself to roll up her sleeves and discover the truth. And she thinks as she did before with Markie that it would be so easy. All it would take is for her sleeves to be pushed back, and the thing would be over, done, finished! She would be separated from her instruments, taken to a doctor, watched over, protected.

But she will not be the one who makes this happen. She will not put herself in a position of having this happen to her. She thinks that she still needs her blades, and she is sure that she can never tell her brother. That although he may love her, and although they now will be able to talk, they are still separated. His image of her is on one side, and the reality of what she has done, of what she chooses to do, is on the other.

"I'm not strong." She continues to weep. *"I'm not strong."*

"Willow." David grabs both her hands above the wrists, grabs them and holds them tight. He does not roll up her sleeves. Why should he? "You're trembling! You're just shaking all over! Was I wrong to tell you? Should I—"

"No! No! You were right, and don't stop talking to me, because—don't stop. . . ." She cannot talk anymore. She is too tired, she is crying too hard, and anyway, her brother is hugging her much too closely for anything she says to make much sense, because all her words are muffled in his shirtfront, and in any case, she has started to hiccup.

"Ssh." David tries to hush her much the way he would Isabelle if she were weeping so disconsolately. "Ssh, try and calm down. Willow, just try and . . . Goddammit, I hear the baby." He pulls away for a second. "Cathy needs to sleep, she's been up every night with Isabelle over this ear infection. . . . I . . . I should go downstairs. Are you going to be okay for now?" He holds her at arm's length and studies her face carefully. "Can we keep talking about this later?"

"Uh-huh." Willow swipes at her eyes with the back of her hand. And as she watches him go, go to his *daughter,* she is once again struck by the fact that she will never again be anybody's child, and that although some things in her life will improve, her relationship with David most certainly among them, that fact will never change.

✳

Willow walks out of the school building surrounded by dozens of other students. The day is over, and she could not be more thankful, not just because she is exhausted emotionally and physically, but because she is longing to see Guy. And since they don't have any classes together, the only time that she can be sure to find him is right after school.

She looks around a little worriedly. He's nowhere to be seen. But then she catches sight of him over near the gates.

And as she walks toward Guy, she can't stop thinking about the fact that she, alone among all the girls there, knows him, really knows him, in every possible way.

Willow wants to run up and grab him, run up and hold him, see if he feels as wonderful as he did the day before, but she's too shy, so she just walks over to where he's standing, and waits to see what he will do.

He grabs *her*, he holds *her*, and she realizes that he feels even better than he did the day before.

"Hey, you know what?" He holds her as closely as possible and looks deep into her eyes. "I really want to talk to you."

"Well, of course." Willow frowns. "I mean, what else? I don't get—"

"No, I mean, I need to talk to you about—"

"Hey Guy," Laurie calls from across the courtyard. "Take Adrian with you wherever you're going. You guys do something together, Willow can come with us." She starts walking over to them, Adrian and Chloe in tow.

Willow steps back from Guy reluctantly and stands at his side as she watches their approach.

"Seriously," Laurie continues. "Don't you and Adrian need to talk about rowing or something?"

"Adrian isn't on the team." Guy looks at Laurie in confusion.

"Yeah, I know," Adrian says in a wry voice. "And Laurie does too, she just wants to get rid of me," he explains needlessly.

"That's right." Laurie nods. "Chloe and I are going to a cafe. You too, Willow, if you want—we need to make a list of all the eligible—"

"Shut up, Laurie," Chloe interrupts her good-naturedly.

"Uh, sorry, Laurie," Guy says. "I wanted to be with—"

"You look different, Willow," Laurie says suddenly.

"Whaaa?" Willow jumps about four feet in the air. Out of the corner of her eye she can see that Guy is trying very hard not to laugh, and she knows that he knows exactly what she's thinking.

"What . . . What do you mean *different*?" Willow reaches for Laurie's hand and pulls her away from the rest of the group. "How different? What do you mean exactly?"

"Oh, I just . . . Well." Laurie lowers her voice a little. "You look like maybe you've been crying. I'm sorry, I shouldn't have said anything when everyone else was around, I just . . . Are you okay?" She squeezes her hand.

"Oh! Oh, sure!" Willow laughs. She gives Laurie's hand a return squeeze before letting go and moving back to Guy's side. "I'm fine. I was just up all night doing a paper for that class you liked so much. You know, the *Bulfinch* thing, but thanks for asking."

"Okay, so listen." Laurie turns her attention back to Guy. "Could you—"

"Forget it, Laurie." Guy shakes his head. "You'll have to drag him along with you. I feel like being alone with Willow, we're going down to the river. Besides, he probably has much better ideas than you do about who to fix Chloe up with."

"Yeah, I have no interest in this at all," Adrian protests.

"Deal with it." Laurie loops an arm around him. "C'mon. Maybe it's better this way anyway. Now you can pay."

"Did you really get your paper done?" Guy asks her as the others walk away. "I know I said I'd help you and I never did. . . ."

321

"Well, don't repeat this, because it's embarrassing and probably illegal, but my brother really did most of it."

"Really?" Guy looks at her in surprise as they walk out of the gates and down the street. "Does that mean that you, well, that you *talked* to him?"

"I did actually." Willow nods.

"So you're . . . I don't know, I mean you kind of worked things out? That sounds really stupid, but you know what I mean. You were so convinced that there was no way things could be okay between you. But you think that you can talk to him again, for real?"

"Umm-hmm." Willow feels that she owes Guy a fuller explanation of what exactly did transpire between her and David, but she can't give it to him, because she is laughing too hard.

"What's so funny?" He looks at her suspiciously.

"Oh, I don't know." Willow walks backward in front of him. "I just think that, maybe even though *I'm* more comfortable talking to him right now, *you* might not be."

"What, what do you mean, exactly?"

"I just have this feeling that you wouldn't be so comfortable around him right now, that's all." She falls back into step beside him as they cross the street and head into the park.

"Willow." Guy stops in his tracks. "You didn't . . . You didn't *tell* him that we slept together or anything like that, did you?"

"Oh, no!" Willow shakes her head vehemently. "I would *never* have told him that."

"Good." Guy looks vastly relieved.

"That's not to say he didn't figure it out on his own, though."

"Oh no!"

"What's the matter?"

"Oh, my God!"

"What do you care? Guy, I was joking about you not wanting to run into him, he doesn't have any problem with us doing—I mean, are you embarrassed about what we did? Or ashamed or something?" She looks stricken.

"You don't get it at all." Guy pulls her close to him. "It's not that, it's just . . . I do not want to know about this kind of thing with Rebecca, okay?"

"She's twelve!"

"Yeah, well, whenever it happens, I don't want to know about it. Oh, my God." He shakes his head. "How am I ever going to take another class with him?"

"I don't know." Willow starts laughing again. "But you know what? *You're* blushing!"

"Yeah, okay, I don't blush, all right?"

"You are!"

"Look, I'm not a girl."

"Oh, you don't have to tell *me* that! I mean if I ever had any doubts about that, they're gone after yesterday!"

"Thanks," Guy says dryly. "Listen, can we just sit here and talk."

"I don't like that wall." Willow bites her lip as they approach the water. "I really don't feel like falling in."

"You're not going to fall in," Guy says patiently. "I mean, unless you keep talking the way you have been, in which case I'll push you. C'mon." He gets up on the wall and helps her up beside him. "See, totally safe." They both sit down and swing their legs out over the water.

"So, what did you want to talk about so urgently?" Willow smiles at him.

Guy regards her steadily for a moment without saying anything. He leans in closer, and Willow thinks that he's going to kiss her, and she is disappointed when he reaches for her bag instead.

He opens it up and rifles through it until he finds the box of blades. "I was hoping that these would be gone." He looks back up at her. "I was really hoping, and you know what? I was halfway to being sure that they would be."

"Is that what you wanted to talk about?" She stares at him in surprise, but he is no longer looking at her, he is gazing out at the water instead. "You wanted to talk about me cutting?"

"That's right."

"But why?" Willow shakes her head at how stupid that sounds. "I mean, why *now*, this is nothing new, you've known about this, you've—"

"I thought things had changed."

"I see," Willow says slowly. "You thought it was just going to be that simple. That all it would take is me crying a little . . . and maybe us having . . ." She bites her lip. She can't, she absolutely can't bring herself to say anything that will cheapen what happened between them. "I guess, I guess you like happy endings, don't you?" she says after a moment.

"Everybody does." He puts the box of razors down between them on the parapet and turns back to look at her. "I don't believe that there are two categories for that—people who like sad endings and people who like happy ones. *Everybody* likes a happy ending."

"Well then, let me tell you something about happy endings," Willow says angrily. "I told you I talked to my brother. That's true. We did talk. We talked like we haven't since my parents died. Is *that* what you mean by a happy ending? 'Cause guess what? He still doesn't know about these." She gestures toward the small package of blades. "Even though we talked about everything else, I couldn't tell him about this. I can't tell him yet. It would just be too much for him. But maybe one day I will tell him. I'll tell him because I won't be able to keep having this secret between us, this wall. I'll tell him because enough time will have passed since the accident that maybe he'll be able to handle something like this. Does that sound happy to you? Does that sound good? Because, you know what? No matter *when* I tell him, it will hurt him so much. . . . It will be so painful for him. It might make me feel a little better, but it will make him feel so much worse. And you know what else? Maybe I haven't lost my brother like I thought I did, but my parents are dead. Gone. No matter how much I talk with my brother, no matter how much I tell him, from now until the end of time, nothing will change that. Is *that* what you mean by a happy ending?"

"No. Of course not. But you know what? You can't change that." He rolls up her right sleeve. "You can change this."

Willow looks down at her arm. The cuts on this side have faded considerably. More white than red, they look some-what . . . innocent, like she might well have gotten them from scratching herself too hard, or coming into contact with an enthusiastic kitten. She starts to cover herself up again, but Guy stops her. She feels terribly exposed, but something else too: She has forgotten the sensation of sunlight against bare skin, and she makes no move to resist him.

"You said, that day in the library," Guy continues after a moment. "You said that if things were different, you would want to give them, it, the whole thing, up. Well, things *are* different now. Don't you *want* to stop?"

"I don't know!" she cries in genuine anguish, appalled to find herself bursting into tears once more. "I thought that I would, but it's not that simple. It's just not that simple!"

"Oh Willow, the last thing I wanted to do was make you cry again." Guy is genuinely upset. He moves closer to her and tries to put his arms around her. "I didn't—"

"You *should* want me to cry!" Willow pushes him away so that she can look him in the face. "You *should*! Because every time that I do, it's like ... it's like ..."

How can she explain to him that every tear takes her further and further away from the box of razors that lies between them. How can she explain that she is terrified of such a thing happening. That although she thought she wanted freedom from her implements, she doesn't know if she can handle what she's experiencing now. That she wants to know that she is still in charge of her grief. That her blades have always done her bidding.

"It's like what?" Guy says. He grasps her upper arms. "Every time you cry it's like what?"

"I ... I don't know if I can take this," she says between tears. "You think cutting hurts? You don't know anything!" Willow picks up the packet of razor blades and presses it against her breasts. "These have saved me from *this*. From feeling like this! Yes! I thought ... I did think that if I could cry like this, *feel* like this, I could let them go. But I'm not so sure now...."

"Willow." Guy bites his lip. "I'm your lover now." Even in the depths of her misery the words give her a thrill, but he's not done talking. "That box of blades can't be your lover anymore, no matter how much they've been there for you in the past."

"You knew about this from the beginning," Willow says. "You've seen me do it. Heard me do it. What's so different now?"

"You have to ask me that after yesterday?" Guy looks at her incredulously. "All right, then. I'll tell you. Everything's different. Just everything."

Willow knows what he's talking about. They are no longer the two people they were yesterday. Her cutting and its consequences no longer affect her alone, if indeed they ever really did.

Her brother's words about responsibility come back to her, about what it must necessarily mean to love someone. And she knows that that responsibility must start with her, and that if in the past, cutting was the best way she knew of to take care of herself, there is a different way open to her now. And then, after that, she must extend that responsibility to Guy as well, because she cannot do everything to shield herself from pain while she forces the person she loves to endure even worse.

Willow looks down at the box and thinks about her other lovers nestled inside, about the pain that she exacts from them, so different from the pleasure that her flesh-and-blood lover gives her, and she knows that their lure is a pitiful thing against all that Guy has to offer. And that not only would renouncing that box of blades be the most responsible action, but it would also be the most beautiful, the most gratifying, the most rewarding thing that she could do.

And she knows these things, stronger than she has ever known anything, but still . . .

"I know I should get rid of them," she says finally when her tears have subsided just enough for her to talk more coherently. "I know I should, but I just can't do it. I can't. I thought I would. I thought I could. I thought about it when I was with Markie. I thought about it last night. I thought about it when I was talking with my brother . . . but I can't!"

"That's it, then?" Guy grabs the box from her. "That's it, then, you've chosen? You're going to be faithful to *them*?"

"I . . . I don't *want* to be!"

"Then get rid of them! Do it! Here, throw them in the water! I'll help you. Full fathom five, like it says in *The Tempest*!"

"You think that's all it would take?" Willow starts to cry again. "You think I couldn't go out and buy some more tomorrow, go to one of those all-night stores if I had to, improvise with a screwdriver if that's all there was around?"

"I know that," Guy says. He takes her hand and closes it over his as he clutches the box. "I know all about it, okay? Maybe you will get some more tomorrow, or maybe even tonight, but at least for right now, for right now, you would be free of them."

"All right!" Willow presses her face into his chest. She cannot stop weeping and she knows that her words are practically incoherent. "All right! I'll do it," she says against his shirtfront.

"What did you say?" Guy disengages himself and holds her at arm's length. He looks at her in amazement as if he cannot quite believe what he has heard. "Willow, what did you say? It's very hard to understand you when—"

"I'll do it, I will! You just . . . Give me a second. . . ."

An hour, a month, a year. . . .

"Look," Guy says. "I'm going to help you, okay? It's going to be easy. C'mon. I'll just hold our hands out over the water and count to three, and . . ."

But Willow doesn't even wait until three. She knows as she watches the box drift down to its watery grave, that although she can indeed go out and buy more anytime, that that part of her life is most probably over. The curtain is drawing closed over the past seven months, and her brave new world with Guy beside her is beckoning. And that if this is not a happy ending, it is perhaps a happy beginning.

A c k n o w l e d g m e n t s

I am very happy to thank the following people, who helped so much and in so many ways:

Andrea Haring, for her unfailing support and faith. David Damrosch, for his time, energy, and suggestions, each one of which made the book better; and Jenny Davidson, who answered many eleventh-hour queries with grace and enthusiasm.

At Dial Lauri Hornik not only bought *Willow* but teamed me up with the extraordinary Kate Harrison. Kristin Smith provided a beautiful and inspired cover, and Regina Castillo caught countless embarrassing inconsistencies.

And finally to the wonderful Erin Malone, of the William Morris agency, to whom no thanks could ever be great enough.